Gift of
Imogene Bercaw
Estate

FOX
AT THE
FRONT

Forge Books by Douglas Niles and Michael Dobson

Fox on the Rhine

Fox at the Front

FOX
AT THE
FRONT

DOUGLAS NILES

and

MICHAEL DOBSON

A TOM DOHERTY ASSOCIATES BOOK
NEW YORK

FOX AT THE FRONT

Copyright © 2003 by Douglas Niles and Michael Dobson

This book is printed on acid-free paper.

Cartography by William W. Connors

A Forge Book
Published by Tom Doherty Associates, LLC
175 Fifth Avenue
New York, NY 10010

www.tor.com

Forge® is a registered trademark of Tom Doherty Associates, LLC.

Library of Congress Cataloging-in-Publication Data

Niles, Douglas.
    Fox at the front / Douglas Niles and Michael Dobson.— 1st ed.
      p. cm.
    Sequel to: Fox on the Rhine.
    "A Forge book"—T.p. verso.
    ISBN 0-765-30479-1
    1. World War, 1939–1945—Fiction. I. Dobson, Michael Singer. II. Title.

  PS3564.I375F68 2003
  813'.54—dc21

                                                                  2003049141

First Edition: November 2003

Printed in the United States of America

0 9 8 7 6 5 4 3 2 1

This book is respectfully dedicated to Allison Niles, serving in the U.S. Army National Guard, and John Patrick Dobson, who served in the U.S. Army Special Forces and the U.S. Army in Germany.

THE NEXT GENERATION

AUTHORS' NOTE

Fox at the Front is a sequel to *Fox on the Rhine*. They are novels of alternate history, in which an historical event—and the consequences of that event—are changed. The point of historical divergence in this story was the failed assassination attempt on Adolf Hitler—the "Bomb Plot"—on July 20, 1944. In *Fox on the Rhine*, the attempt succeeded, and the Führer was killed in the explosion. As a result, the course of the Second World War during the last half of 1944 was altered. In *Fox at the Front*, this alternate history continues.

Historical characters are portrayed in a fictional way; their actions, thoughts, words, and behavior after the point of divergence are solely the authors' invention. Other characters in this book (with one exception) are fictitious. Any resemblance to actual persons, living or dead, is purely coincidental.

Additional information may be found at our Web site at http://www.dobsonbooks.com.

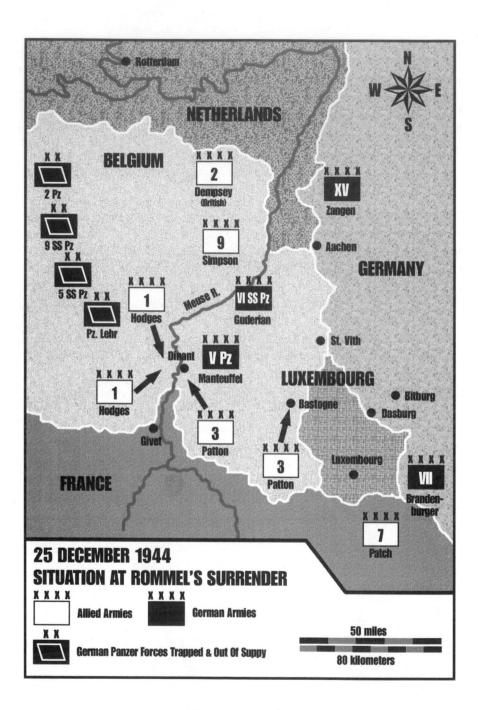

N
W E
S

● Rotterdam

NETHERLANDS

BELGIUM

XX
2 Pz

XX
9 SS Pz

XXXX
2
Dempsey
(British)

XXXX
9
Simpson

XXXX
XV
Zangen

● Aachen

GERMANY

XX
5 SS Pz

XX
Pz. Lehr

XXXX
1
Hodges

Meuse R.

XXXX
VI SS Pz
Guderian

● St. Vith

XXXX
1
Hodges

● Dinant

XXXX
V Pz
Manteuffel

LUXEMBOURG

● Bitburg

● Bastogne

● Dasburg

XXXX
3
Patton

● Givet

XXXX
3
Patton

Luxembourg ●

XXXX
VII
Branden-
burger

FRANCE

XXXX
7
Patch

25 DECEMBER 1944
SITUATION AT ROMMEL'S SURRENDER

XXXX
☐ Allied Armies

XXXX
■ German Armies

XX
◇ German Panzer Forces Trapped & Out Of Suppy

50 miles

80 kilometers

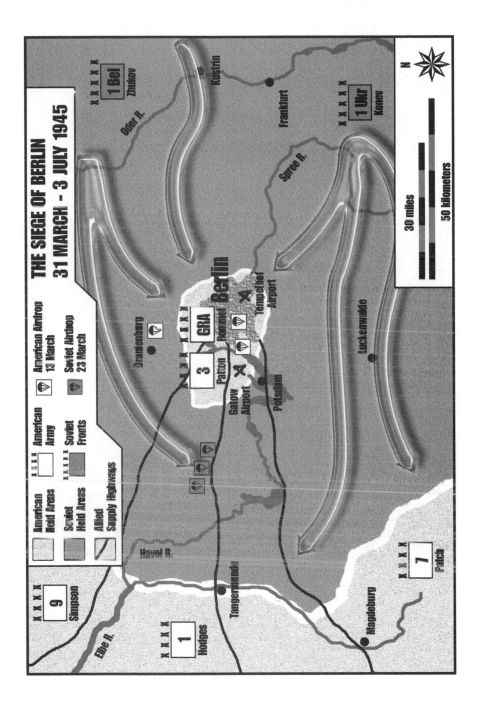

THE SIEGE OF BERLIN
31 MARCH - 3 JULY 1945

American Held Areas
Soviet Held Areas
Allied Supply Highways

American Army
Soviet Fronts

American Airdrop 13 March
Soviet Airdrop 23 March

XXXX 9 Simpson
XXXX 1 Hodges
XXXX 7 Patch
XXXX 3 Patton
XXXX GRA Rommel
XXXX 1 Bel Zhukov
XXXX 1 Ukr Konev

Elbe R.
Havel R.
Oder R.
Spree R.

Tangermunde
Magdeburg
Oranienburg
Berlin
Tempelhof Airport
Gatow Airport
Potsdam
Luckenwalde
Kustrin
Frankfurt

N

30 miles
50 kilometers

FOX

AT THE

FRONT

PROLOGUE

OPERATION FUCHS

AM RHEIN

I have seen war. I have seen war on land and sea. I have seen blood running from the wounded. I have seen men coughing out their gassed lungs. I have seen the dead in the mud. I have seen cities destroyed. I have seen two hundred limping, exhausted men come out of line—the survivors of a regiment of one thousand that went forward forty-eight hours before. I have seen children starving. I have seen the agony of mothers and wives. I hate war.

I have passed unnumbered hours, I shall pass unnumbered hours thinking and planning how war may be kept from this nation.

I wish I could keep war from all nations, but that is beyond my power. I can at least make certain that no act of the United States helps to produce or to promote war. I can at least make clear that the conscience of America revolts against war and that any nation which provokes war forfeits the sympathy of the people of the United States. . . .

—Franklin Delano Roosevelt
Chautauqua, New York, 1936

25 DECEMBER 1944

BATTLE FOR THE BRIDGES OF DINANT

NARRATOR

With the Sixth Panzer Army trapped along the banks of the Meuse River, Rommel's Fifth Panzer Army is the major remaining threat to Antwerp and Allied supplies in Europe. Using the remaining bridges at the Belgian city of Dinant, Nazi troops continue to advance. Patton's Third Army continues its northward move, and the U.S. Nineteenth Armored Division is poised for an attack into Dinant to try to cut the German supply line. Until the weather clears, Allied air superiority can't be brought to bear on the city.

. . .

As Nazi troops shelled the historic battlefield of Waterloo in Belgium, on their way to Antwerp, British Field Marshal Bernard Montgomery is reported dead. Montgomery, who led the Twenty-first Army Group, was a noted military strategist whose role in North Africa . . .

26 DECEMBER 1944

DINANT, BELGIUM, 1202 HOURS GMT

Lieutenant Colonel Frank Ballard's command Sherman rumbled out of the narrow alley, long barrel extended toward the cross street. He shouted the order over his intercom. "There's a Tiger right in front of us! Fire!"

The tank lurched as the M4 spat its armor-piercing load at point-blank range. As the round slammed home, the Tiger's ammunition cooked off in a chaotic eruption of smoke and fire. That tank was gone, but there seemed no limit to the numbers of the advancing German armor.

. Ballard's role—the role of the Thirty-eighth Tank Battalion, Combat Command A, Nineteenth Armored Division, United States Third Army—was to delay the advance enough to allow Combat Command A's engineers to destroy the bridges across the Meuse, and sever the German spearheads from their bases in the Westwall. He would either succeed or die in the attempt.

The latter option looked increasingly likely. Ballard stuck his head up. The street was thick with smoke and rubble, and the sky grew darker by the minute. Filtered by clouds and the fires smoldering throughout the small Belgian city, every bit of color had been drained from the landscape. Only a pervasive gray remained.

More gray: German soldiers—infantry—moving from another narrow alley. Ballard saw one man kneel down, looking in his direction. *Panzerfaust!* The reaction registered in his mind in an instant. He shouted a warning down into the tank, the sound moving terribly slowly in contrast to the fire that flashed from the weapon's mouth, the missile that sputtered toward him like a meteor.

The impact came with a deafening explosion. Ears ringing, he felt a blast of heat below him. By reflex action he scrambled up, rolling over and down into the street as an ugly blossom of black smoke shot through with hungry yellow fangs surrounded him. Time seemed to slow as he rose to his feet, struggling to comprehend the effect of the tank-killing missile.

Shards of turret sprayed the air where his body had been only moments before. In the smoke, he could not tell whether any of his crew had escaped. Vaguely, he tried to take inventory of his own injuries. His body had thudded against the hard, jagged concrete fragments that covered the narrow streets and sidewalks. His left arm had taken the brunt of the fall, the skin tearing as fragments tore through his jacket. It was painful, but the limb didn't seem to be broken.

Ballard's right hand unsnapped the leather holster containing his .45 sidearm, and he moved forward in a crouch. Briefly sticking his head around the front of the tank, he saw the other soldiers of the panzerfaust squad readying potato-masher grenades, studying his crippled Sherman. They looked like menacing shadows, dark black silhouettes against the flames still coming up from the Tiger he'd destroyed seconds before. Ballard fired his automatic once, twice, again, and a German fell.

The first grenade splattered against the tank's front armor, but its explosion merely darkened the metal plates. The driver, Sergeant Tim Brown, his face black and dripping blood, pushed open the forward hatch and began to crawl up from the body of the ruined tank. Ballard spared him a brief look, eyes questioning if anyone else had survived, and Brown shook his head.

Ballard fired again and the large German carrying the panzerfaust toppled forward. Two more shots from his pistol forced the remaining Germans to drop and take cover. He reached out with his good arm to help Brown scramble down the tank's hull. The sergeant was a mass of small cuts and soot, stunned but able to walk.

"No one else, Colonel," he mumbled, confirming what Ballard already knew. With his good arm, he patted the sergeant's shoulder and the two men backtracked into the alley, using the burning Sherman to screen them from the German panzergrenadiere.

There was a flash of pink in the corner of his eye and he whirled, his automatic at the ready, only to see a female mannequin, armless like the Venus de Milo but headless as well, standing in the rubble of what once had probably been a clothing store. This was the first sight of a female form Ballard had seen in weeks, and he found the image jarring.

There were more of his tanks nearby, and as he moved steadily in their direction he waved his right arm at them.

"You okay, Colonel?" came a shout from the nearest M4 as Ballard and Brown approached. Lieutenant McCullough's head poked up through the turret hatch.

"Just ducky," Ballard snarled. "There was a bastard with a panzerfaust in the next block. Brown and I are it from the command tank."

"Shit." McCullough shook his head. "Colonel, we're holding, but those fucking Tigers keep coming."

"We've just got to keep hitting 'em until the sappers blow the goddamn bridges," replied the colonel.

McCullough nodded in response. They all understood that the opportunity to bug out would probably come too late for most of Combat Command A.

"I need communication, and I need it now," ordered Ballard.

The tactical situation was grim. Ballard's Thirty-eighth Battalion consisted of a hundred tanks when at full strength—eighty medium and twenty light, all the tanks of Combat Command A organized into three companies. Ballard's flank attack against the advancing German armor of the Panzer Lehr division had used A and B companies, a bit more than half his strength, including all the upgunned Shermans, those with the 76mm guns. These were the only American tanks that had a decent chance to take out the German armor. The third element, C Company, was in the lower city with Colonel Jimmy Pulaski, the commander of CCA, shooting up the wharf and opening the way for CCA's other assets to do their job.

Those other assets included an armored infantry battalion of an authorized strength of about a thousand men, and the engineers and sappers whose job it would be to wire the remaining bridges with satchel charges and blow them to pieces. The artillery battalion, under Major Diaz, had set up in a park on the south side of Dinant where it was in easy support range of the entire combat command.

The problem was that Combat Command A had injected itself right into the path of the entire German Fifth Panzer Army. Ballard had no idea how his boss Pulaski was faring in the lower city, and he needed to know now. His flank attack had slammed into a substantially stronger force. His forces were suffering steady attrition; how much longer was it necessary for him to hold out? Did he need to husband his steadily decreasing force, or advance with cannons blazing for a final blow? There were two unknown variables: whether or when the bridge would be destroyed and when Colonel Bob Jackson's Combat Command B would reach Dinant. Last he'd heard, they were a couple of hours away.

Mindful of his torn-up arm, Ballard scrambled up onto the tank. McCullough handed him the radio handset. "Popcorn Ten—this is Popcorn Eight," he announced, giving the code for Colonel Pulaski. There was a pause. "Popcorn Ten, this is Popcorn Eight. Come in." Still nothing. "Popcorn Eight to all Popcorns."

That led to some replies. Two of his three company commanders responded—the third was with Pulaski in the lower city, and no reply. The infantry commanders also checked in, and then came real news. "Ducky Six to Popcorn Eight." It was Diaz with the artillery battalion.

"Go ahead, Ducky Six," responded Ballard.

"Okra Ten has met up with our position," crackled the radio.

That was very good news indeed. Okra Ten was Bob Jackson of Combat Command B, the other armored fist in Nineteenth Armored's one-two punch. Jackson, an unregenerate Southerner, actually claimed to like the slimy vegetable. "Put him on, Ducky Six."

"Hold on" was the response, and about a minute later, "Popcorn Eight, this is Okra Ten. What's the situation?"

Quickly, Ballard briefed Pulaski's CCB counterpart, concluding with "No word from Popcorn Ten or anyone in the lower city. And no sign that the bridge has blown yet."

"Roger," came the reply.

Ballard pushed down the Send button again. "Okra Ten, if you can reinforce into my position, I can move in the direction of the bridges to handle any unfinished business."

"Roger that, too," came back the drawling reply from Jackson. "Start your move; we'll come in behind you and keep those Tigers in their cage where they belong."

"Thanks, Okra Ten, will comply," replied Ballard. "Popcorn Eight and remaining Popcorns heading downhill."

"Say hello to Popcorn Ten when you see him, and tell him to get his radio fixed," came the reply.

"Roger. Popcorn Eight out." Ballard knew it was more likely that his commander was a casualty, but the reassurance and calm confidence of the lanky Southerner was just what he needed to hear.

"Good hunting, Popcorn Eight. Okra Ten out."

Changing frequencies from the command channel, Ballard began issuing orders to his remaining forces, starting the slow move down from the upper city toward the riverbanks, the lower city and harbor still occupied by German troops.

Then Ballard heard a new noise, a thunderous boom that overwhelmed the normal cacophony of battle, the explosions and whines of bullets and shrapnel, the rumblings of powerful tank engines, the crashes of falling masonry from ancient and historic structures collapsing under the rude violation of modern weapons of warfare. The new explosion shook the entire valley, even rocked the massive iron vehicles themselves. It was the sound of powerful demolition, which meant that the engineers had finished their dangerous job on the bridges. A huge smoke bloom billowed above the town—but what Ballard couldn't tell for sure was whether the explosion had done its job.

Lieutenant McCullough's Sherman, now serving as Ballard's mobile command post, rumbled down narrow medieval streets. Parts of heavily damaged buildings collapsed as the leading tank passed; as the long 76mm gun swept around street corners it barely missed obstructions ranging from window boxes to streetlamps. Lumbering over wreckage and other obstacles, the tank growled through the narrow pathways that moved it down the bluff and into the lower city.

It was getting too dark to see, even though it was not yet 1600 hours local time. The tank's headlights and the fires that raged unchecked through the swaths of military destruction were the only illumination, and it was difficult for Ballard to pick out the correct route through the destroyed town.

In the irregular illumination, he was surprised to see a square open up, an unusually wide space for this narrow city. He saw burned-out Shermans and soldiers sprawled in the rubble, recognized the grotesque postures of death. And then he saw a half-track, its armored door shredded like confetti. It was the command half-track of Colonel Pulaski, almost certainly his tomb. Frank Ballard was the remaining senior commander near the bridge. If that span was not already destroyed, it was his job to eliminate it once and for all. He decided to make his command post in the square, and issued orders for his tanks to take up positions blocking all the routes converging here.

As his tanks moved into position, a growing trickle of CCA troops from the lower city began to arrive. He stopped one young man, who looked hypnotized by the bright headlights of the tank, wearing the poleaxed look so common among the men—the boys—who had stared death in the face for hours. "Corporal! Report!"

"The bridge is blown, sir."

"Thank God. Are you sure?"

"Yes, sir." The corporal's voice was thin, distracted, numb. "Saw it collapse. About four panzers went down with it. One had been spraying us pretty good."

"How many of you are left?" Ballard asked. There was an increase in small-arms fire off to his left. One tank responded.

"Just me, sir," said the corporal.

Ballard pointed in the direction of what seemed to be a tavern except that its front wall had mostly disintegrated. "Get checked out by the medics over there."

"I'm not wounded, sir," replied the corporal.

"Go," Ballard ordered. The corporal moved off.

Ballard regretted that he couldn't send the corporal into the tavern for a beer or two. He didn't even know if his highly improvisational hospital had water for patients to drink. The aid station had been put together by several of the company-level medics as the remaining lower-city CCA soldiers began to center around the new field headquarters. Realizing those men, all of them, were now his responsibility, Ballard felt the full weight of command come to rest upon his shoulders.

Over the next hour, as ragged fire continued in isolated parts of the dark and freezing town, Ballard improvised a headquarters. The medics shortly had a growing collection of wounded awaiting safe transport out. Many could wait, even though in pain. Many could not, but had to anyway.

Making contact with General Henry Wakefield, commanding general of Nineteenth Armored, was luckily straightforward, and he was able to coordinate more closely with Bob Jackson of CCB. The situation was defend and wait, wait to discover what the enemy would choose to do, and only then to know the final fate and disposition of his dwindling force. Ballard listened as the occasional bursts of firefight steadied, became regular, and then . . . faded away to silence.

"King Popcorn to Popcorn Eight!" barked the radio peremptorily. It was General Wakefield.

"Popcorn Eight," acknowledged Ballard.

"Frank?"

"Yes, sir?"

"Are you sitting down?"

"Sir?"

"Never mind. We've had a situation."

"What's that, sir?"

"The Germans have surrendered!"

"Say again, sir, the message was unclear. Sounded like 'The Germans have surrendered.' "

"Damn right!" roared the voice on the radio. "The goddamn Krauts cried uncle! Rommel himself called. General Patton and I are heading for Dinant; be there in a few hours. In the meantime, immediate cease-fire dependent on good behavior. They don't shoot, you don't shoot. Get some forces along the river road; that's supposed to be ours now for our approach. Put lots of scouts out and watch like hell. Radio if a mouse sneezes too loud. Got it? See you in a couple of hours. King Popcorn out."

"Popcorn Eight out," replied Ballard, dazed.

German surrender? It made no immediate sense. Where he was, he was outnumbered and outgunned and waiting to be overrun. True, the enemy didn't have the bridge anymore, and though the situation for the Germans overall was fairly bleak, generals didn't surrender like a chess player tipping over his king with mate a good ten moves away. It had to be a real checkmate when anybody decided to surrender, and it didn't feel like an Allied checkmate right now. But maybe there was plenty Ballard didn't know about, and just maybe it was some kind of trap.

Play nice if they play nice, those were the orders, he recalled. But keep a real good eye on them, too. He decided not to shout out the news just now; he didn't know what might happen and decided it was best if his men didn't have a distraction just then.

He began calling over his officers and issuing carefully worded orders, checking each time to make sure he was fully understood. This was no time for mistakes.

Next, he moved his forces along the river road, and settled down to wait.

27 DECEMBER 1944

ARMEEGRUPPE B HEADQUARTERS, DINANT, BELGIUM, 0529 HOURS GMT

Field Marshal Erwin Rommel had never thought that surrendering would prove to be so complicated. He had personally forced the capitulation of thousands of enemy soldiers in two wars and numerous campaigns, and it had always seemed like a straightforward procedure. He would call upon them to lay down their arms, they would do so, and he would detail sufficient guards to escort them to the nearest POW holding facility. Very quickly they would become the responsibility of some rear-echelon formation, and he would maintain his focus on the continuing battle.

But now there was no continuing battle, neither for him nor for his great army group. His head ached and his eye, the one that had been wounded in an Allied strafing attack the previous summer, watered constantly. This was annoying, but not unprecedented. Sometimes he thought he'd fought more of his battles sick than well. Of course, there was not only the pain and stress of this surrender, but the price for several sleepless nights finally catching up with him.

He took a sip of cold and somewhat stale coffee, and glanced out the window for a moment. It was still dark, new clouds coming in, harbinger of yet more dreary December weather in Belgium. The dark was penetrated by the headlamps of motor vehicles and guardpost lights, a monocolored illumination that gave everything it touched an eerie, unearthly look, as if he were looking at the surface of the moon. With all the fighting this poor city had taken, the resemblance to the lunar surface was even greater. Heaps of rubble were strewn everywhere. At the very limit of his vision, a single tree stood bare and unadorned, facing the elements.

Rommel turned back to the details of the order of battle. Armeegruppe B, consisting of the vast majority of German forces in the West, included three complete armies: the Fifth Panzer Army, under von Manteuffel, the Sixth Panzer Army, under Guderian, and the Seventh Army, under Brandenberger. Two more panzer armies had been relocated from the Eastern Front after the Soviet treaty had been signed; they were in reserve behind the Westwall and the Rhine River. While the Sixth Panzer Army was stopped at the Meuse, elements of the Fifth Panzer Army had already crossed the river at Dinant before the remaining bridges had been destroyed, and were trapped without hope of resupply or relief deep behind enemy lines.

His job was to arrange the surrender of all those forces, and looking at some of the individual divisions and their commanders, he knew that not all of them would surrender. What would happen then, he did not know.

He had another concern, for his wife Lucie and son Manfred. As soon as he realized that surrender was a necessity, he had telephoned Lucie at their home in Herrlingen. Quickly, using agreed-upon code words, he'd told her to grab Manfred and leave. There were people in Bitburg he trusted, and he had arranged a rendezvous there. He worried, but there was nothing more he could do.

The Desert Fox turned back from the window. He was not alone. Sitting at the conference table was his opposite number, General George S. Patton, who had driven in a jeep with a small escort to accept his surrender. Rommel had studied Patton for years, had been aware of Patton even before the war started, but of course they had never met. And while he would no doubt have appreciated a meeting with Patton after the war was over, two victorious generals comparing observations, this was not the meeting he had in mind. Rommel was determined to be gracious, but it was hard not to feel some bitterness as well. Patton and the Americans had such a matériel advantage that the campaign had been lopsided from the start.

Patton, though by all accounts a rather brusque and insensitive man, was obviously aware of the essential awkwardness of the situation. His first words to him had been "I thought *Infanterie Greift An* was a masterpiece. I've read it fourteen times."

Infanterie Greift An was Rommel's first book, a study of infantry tactical operations based on analysis of Rommel's own World War I campaigns. The book had first catapulted him to public recognition, and had set the stage for much of his later advancement. "Thank you," he had replied. In an effort to return the compliment, he added, "I thought your advance to the Westwall was rather a masterpiece as well."

Patton had laughed as soon as the remark was translated. His laugh was irresistible and hearty, much like the man himself. Rommel felt himself almost unwillingly put at ease. He rather liked the American general, even under the difficult and painful circumstances.

While the official surrender had first taken place at the more-or-less neutral setting of the Church of Notre Dame in the lower city of Dinant, the business end of the process had quickly led to the parties relocating to Armeegruppe B headquarters, just outside the city. Accompanying Patton was General Henry Wakefield of the U.S. Nineteenth Armored Division, which had successfully attacked Rommel's flank and blown the final bridge at Dinant, and Lieutenant Colonel Reid Sanger, the Nineteenth Armored's intelligence officer, who was acting as Patton's translator. Initially, Rommel had used the translation services of Chuck Porter, a captured Associated Press reporter, but

Porter's German was not up to the challenge of complex technical negotiations, so Sanger was shouldering the load for both sides.

"I believe the biggest immediate challenge is to arrange the surrender of Sixth Panzer Army. Their headquarters is here—" Rommel pointed to the map. "—near Namur. I have sent a radio message to Generaloberst Guderian. He sees the rationale in the same way I do, and has agreed."

"Good," said Patton, his incongruously high voice standing in contrast to his imposing physical demeanor. "I read his book, too. Our military people did translations of both his and yours. Brilliant. Used it a lot."

Guderian's *Achtung Panzer* was one of the seminal works on the use of armor. "I wonder if this means Guderian and I are both guilty as authors of the crime of giving aid and comfort to the enemy," Rommel mused, only partly in jest. What he or Guderian could have accomplished, if only he had the resources of the Americans!

Sanger, the translator, laughed before he repeated the sentence in English. Patton grinned when he heard the statement. "Hell, Field Marshal, amateurs borrow, but professionals steal. I thought you knew that. I stole from the best. Haven't you gotten an idea or two from our side?"

"A few," Rommel admitted.

"So, we're even. Right?"

Rommel smiled in agreement. Patton was rather like a tank himself, barreling through obstacles as if they were not there. He was what Rommel thought of as typically American, so cheerfully ignorant of the manners of the European gentry that it was almost charming—almost. "I shall take that under advisement."

Patton was already onto the next item. His finger was pointing to the large operational map. "So, Sixth Panzer Army HQ is here. That's good. I can ask Hodges to send the Ninety-ninth Infantry Division from First Army down to meet them. How about the two panzer divisions across the Meuse?"

"Now that they're cut off from resupply, I don't think there will be any problems. I note that you have the British XXX Corps near Waterloo that can make contact with those units." Rommel placed his finger on the map. "I've radioed the necessary orders from this end." He smiled internally. His intelligence about the Allied order of battle and location was good, and he hoped Patton would notice.

Patton did, and immediately riposted with evidence of his own intelligence. "Now, about half of Panzer Lehr managed to cross, and its leading elements are here." He pointed to another spot on the map, grinning broadly. Patton's boyish pleasure made it difficult for Rommel to resent the bragging.

"Closer to three-quarters of Panzer Lehr is actually across, but yes, the leading elements are here. I've spoken with General Bayerlein, and they are withdrawing back in the direction of Dinant."

"They'll hit Nineteenth Armored first, right, Henry?" asked Patton, turning to his subordinate general.

Henry Wakefield nodded. "Combat Command B is in the upper city. That's Bob Jackson. I'll let him know to expect contact shortly. By the way, General, I'd like to get my engineers up here. We need a pontoon bridge across the Meuse pronto. Plus, I've got some wounded I'd like to evac."

"Good idea, Henry. And see if you can get your kitchens to ship up a hot meal for the boys."

After the exchange was translated, Rommel interjected. "If my hospitals are more convenient, your wounded are more than welcome. I would offer my own engineers in support of the bridging, but I am in the position of a surrendered foe, so cannot. Officially, at least, we are still enemies."

"I understand, and I appreciate the offer, Field Marshal. I'll check with Ballard in Combat Command A—they got the brunt of the fighting down in the lower city."

"Combat Command A. That was Colonel James Pulaski, correct?" Rommel asked. He had stopped Pulaski once at the Somme, heard him accused of barbaric war crimes in the massacre of Metz, and now was in his current position because of the daring and aggressiveness of that same Pulaski.

"Yes it was. He bought it in the attack. Lieutenant Colonel Ballard ran the tank battalion; he's acting CO right now."

Rommel nodded gravely. This was not an uncommon experience, hearing about brave men who were now dead. "Please convey my personal respects to Lieutenant Colonel Ballard. He and his men fought courageously and well."

"I appreciate that as well, Field Marshal. I'll pass it along. General Patton, if you'll excuse me, I've got some work to do."

"Go ahead, Henry. Holler if you need me."

"Yes, sir." Wakefield left the conference room, pulling out a stogie as he went.

The two old adversaries looked across the table at one another. "General Patton, you understand my motives in this," Rommel stated. "In fact, you have expressed similar thoughts."

The American general grunted in response. "The Soviet Union. That's right. I guess I'm about the only one who wasn't shocked down to his boots when the separate peace deal broke. Those Red bastards won't be satisfied with crushing Nazi Germany; they've got designs on all of Europe—hell, all the world!"

"I believe this to be true. Our führer was always surprised that the West didn't understand that our attack on the Soviet Union was of benefit to them as well as to us."

"The choice we had was either Commies or Nazis. And pardon me for saying so, but that wasn't a hell of a choice."

Rommel nodded. "I understand. But the Nazi threat is over. Kaput. So the choice is easier now, don't you think?"

"And we pull your fat out of the fire at the same time?"

"We can help you."

"You've surrendered. That means you're out of the game."

"I understand. But at least the way is clear for you. This surrender not only eliminates much of the forces that would oppose your advance, but also can deliver a safe crossing of the Rhine far ahead of any schedule you could have set for yourself."

Rommel sat back. He needed to show Patton that, surrendered or not, he still had cards to play.

As Patton chewed on the idea, Rommel reinforced. "Armeegruppe B controls a significant section of the Westwall and numerous bridges across the Rhine. I suggest that the Waffen-SS and Wehrmacht troops still under Berlin's control will want to retake and reinforce the areas I have left unguarded, but it will take some time to do this. General, I am not any longer a supporter of the Nazi government, but I am still a German. Work with me, and I can deliver Germany safely into the hands of the West, and save us all from Soviet domination."

"It sounds like a good idea," Patton said slowly. Rommel watched his body language, listened to the sound of his voice while the translator did his work. He was swaying the American armor general, just as he planned, just as he must.

"There's only one question," added Patton.

"And what is that?" replied Rommel.

"Will all of your forces surrender?"

"I wish I could be sure."

SHAEF HEADQUARTERS, PARIS, FRANCE,
0720 HOURS GMT

"Can *anybody* tell me what the *hell* is going on?" demanded the Supreme Allied Commander. "I've had to make two calls to Washington and I've got to answer half their questions with 'How in hell should I know?'"

"Ike, all I know is we got some crazy call from Nineteenth Armored Division HQ in Givet saying that Rommel has surrendered, and that George Patton and Henry Wakefield were driving into Dinant to accept the surrender," replied General Omar Bradley. The mild-mannered man with the schoolteacher demeanor commanded an army of nearly 1,300,000 men, the largest field command in American history. And his failure to keep track of the whereabouts of one single man among them, General George S. Patton of Third Army, was giving his boss the Supreme Commander a king-sized pain in the butt.

"I know you've said this already, but *surrender?* Why would he surrender? Rommel's breakout attack has failed, but he's got plenty of troops left. He can go back where he came from not too much the worse." General Eisenhower shook his head, perplexed.

"Hell, who knows what the crazy Germans are thinking? Or what George has been drinking?" Bradley was irritated with his subordinate. It was too easy for him to become overshadowed by his onetime boss, George Patton, and he wanted to remind his CO that he worked hard to keep Patton from running amok and hurting himself and the mission.

"God damn it, he should at least have called one of us before driving God knows where in the middle of the goddamn night," Eisenhower growled. "I suppose it never occurred to him it could be some sort of ambush? What the hell am I going to say? 'George Patton ran off on a midnight wild-goose chase and got himself shot'? How will that look on the front page of the *New York Times?*"

"Ike—I've got people looking for George right now. Nineteenth Armored says they're in contact with their combat commands in Dinant, and they've got a cease-fire in place right now. Evidently they still believe there's going to be a surrender, and word is that Wakefield and Patton drove in through their lines in a jeep around midnight."

Eisenhower looked out the window at the Paris skyline. A predawn fog turned all the famous landmarks into shadows in the haze. "You don't suppose Rommel really is surrendering to George, do you?"

Bradley thought about it. That would be the ultimate headline, and he and Ike would be lucky to get a mention on page 4. But knowing Patton's luck . . . "I guess stranger things have happened in this man's war. But not many."

"Mmm," Eisenhower replied noncommittally. "It'd sure make my life easier."

"Now that you mention it, mine, too," replied Bradley.

It was then that the telephone rang in the outer office. Kay Summersby came in, her eyes wide. "General Patton is on the phone, General," she told her boss, the Supreme Commander. "He says he's got Field Marshal Rommel with him, and he sounds . . . well, he sounds pretty happy."

28 DECEMBER 1944

R O M M E L S U R R E N D E R S !

NARRATOR

With the destruction of the remaining bridges in Dinant, Rommel stuns the world by offering to surrender unconditionally to the Allies! The motive behind this amazing event is still unclear, because even with the bridges of Dinant destroyed, Rommel is still in command of two panzer armies with substantial reserve forces ready to move forward. Early news suggests that Rommel's growing distrust of the Nazi regime is a key to the event, and there are rumors of an attempted assassination aimed at the Desert Fox.

. . .

Combat Command A of the Nineteenth Armored Division, the leading force into Dinant, is reported to have taken heavy casualties, including the loss of commanding officer Colonel James Pulaski, Silver Star winner in North Africa. Pulaski, who was in command at the time of Rommel's Somme counteroffensive and who was accused of brutality in the Metz Massacre, is . . .

OPERATION
VENGEANCE
27 – 31 DECEMBER 1944

*The leaders of the American economy and the American General
Staff have achieved miracles. The organization, training and
equipment of the U.S. Army all bear witness to great imagination
and foresight, and, above all, to the positive determination of the
American people to act in unison and create a war machine with
real striking power . . .*

*Technically and strategically the landing in Normandy was a
brilliant achievement of the first magnitude. It showed that the
Americans had the courage, at any rate in the technical field, to
employ a multitude of devices hitherto untried in action. European generals of the old school could certainly have executed the
invasion with the forces available, but they could never have prepared it—neither technically, organizationally, nor in the field of
training. The functioning of the Allied fighting machine, with all
its complexity, surprised even me, and I already had a fairly high
opinion of their powers.*

—Field Marshal Erwin Rommel
Early August 1944

27 DECEMBER 1944

NEAR NAMUR, BELGIUM, SOUTH SIDE OF THE MEUSE
RIVER, 0700 HOURS GMT

"Es gibt keine verzweifelten Lagen, es gibt nur verzweifelte Menschen." There are no desperate situations, there are only desperate people. Generaloberst Heinz Guderian, *Der Schnelle Heinz* (Hurrying Heinz) or sometimes *Heinz Brausewetter* (Hurricane Heinz), currently commanding officer of the Sixth Panzer Army, was fond of aphorisms and used them frequently.

Guderian was the sort of man referred to as a "natural leader." Handsome, with a warm, inviting smile and eyes that saw everything around him, he was popular with his men and always confident of himself and his mission. His weakness was his hot temper and his frequent and flagrant disregard of orders. It was the latter weakness that had ultimately led to his removal from command and appointment as *Generalinspekteur der Panzertruppen*. Rommel, with whom he had an ongoing rivalry of sorts—for Guderian, not Rommel, was the supreme theoretician of panzer operations—had pulled him back into the game with control of Sixth Panzers. And to his utter and complete frustration, he'd been stopped cold at the Meuse, unable to force an opposed river crossing.

It was that bastard Montgomery, who used British and U.S. troops to establish a solid line on the north side of the Meuse from Namur through Liège. With a force superior in numbers (but not, Guderian reflected with some satisfaction, superior generalship) and time to destroy the bridges and build a strong defensive position, Monty had been able to block every thrust Guderian had made along a fifty-mile front. But Guderian was still thrusting, still probing, and was confident of an eventual breakthrough . . . as long as Manteuffel could hold up his end with Fifth Panzer Army. Manteuffel was lucky enough to find undestroyed bridges at Dinant, and so had leading elements across the river already. Eventually, Manteuffel's advance would force Montgomery to respond, and then Guderian would show everyone what a real panzer offensive looked like.

Finally, however, it had all come down to this: the bridges of Dinant destroyed, his forces blocked . . . and a transcribed message from Rommel himself at Armeegruppe B headquarters. Surrender. *Scheisse!* he thought as he clenched his fist in helpless rage. *Scheisse!* The mere thought of surrender made him want to vomit. Even when it was a necessary act, it was shameful, disgusting—not to be borne.

At least he could take some small satisfaction that Montgomery was dead, according to intelligence. That smirking little English bastard could rot in hell. And as for Rommel—arrogant Hitler's boy, the shameless self-promoter, the jumped-up corps commander acting the role of baby field marshal, the comfortable bastard who'd only faced a clean (and warm) enemy in North Africa and never seen a Russian winter . . . or muddy springtime—well, Guderian knew that if their positions had been reversed he would have done better.

There was only one problem. He agreed with Rommel that surrendering was the right thing to do. Better the Allies than the Soviet bastards. Now that the real führer was dead, the imitation führer didn't have what it took to win the war anymore. That *arschloch* Himmler strutting around in his SS uniform couldn't survive as a junior lieutenant in any real army.

Because of all this, though the battle was not yet lost the war was over. Guderian well knew that the Soviet "peace" would last not a second longer than the moment either side found itself with an advantage. Besides, he knew that the Soviets advanced in a wave, then stopped for resupply. Certainly Stalin would have made "peace" only during the period his forces needed rest and refurbishment, then start rolling forward. And no one knew better than Heinz Guderian that the Soviets were now unstoppable. Western Allies or Soviets. The only choice was which side—and that decision was easy.

His forces were in cease-fire status for the moment. In a few minutes he would start his command meeting to handle the business of surrender. He looked at the sheaf of papers on his desk, started to pick them up, then dropped them again. He could do this job off the top of his head.

Straightening his cap and drawing in a deep breath, Guderian walked out of his office, closing the door behind him.

Obersturmbannführer Jochen Peiper was awakened by his orderly. It was still dark on the cold and dreary late December morning. For a moment he was disoriented, back in the depths of the Russian campaign, before he realized where and when he was. Then he was fully awake. "Time to start the day again already?" he had asked his orderly in a pleasant, if sleepy, voice.

"No, Herr Obersturmbannführer. It's Berlin. They're on the radio for you."

"On my way." Peiper was instantly out of bed, pulling on his pants and grabbing a jacket. He had his personal headquarters in a commandeered farmhouse, and the radio room was in the dining room, just downstairs from the bedroom where he had been sleeping on a thin and worn mattress.

"Here he is, Berlin," the radio operator said into the microphone, then pulled off his headset and handed it to Peiper.

The crackling and hiss of the radio blared into his ears, a sudden attack of sound that made him wince slightly. "This is Obersturmbannführer Peiper. Go ahead."

"One moment, Obersturmbannführer," he heard, and then the next voice was one he recognized.

"Peiper?"

"Ja, mein Führer!" Peiper came to attention as he heard the instantly recognizable voice of Heinrich Himmler. The SS colonel was every bit as loyal to the second Führer of the Third Reich as he had been to the first.

Peiper knew him well. He had been a member of Himmler's personal staff before the war, rising to be Himmler's first adjutant. He had even married one of Himmler's staff secretaries. Few people knew Himmler well on a personal level, but Jochen Peiper was one of those few. Although like most Germans of his generation he had admired and even revered Adolf Hitler, and was devastated by his assassination, his opinion of Heinrich Himmler was nearly as high, and he had instantly transferred his total loyalty to the new führer.

"I have had extremely disturbing news from Armeegruppe B headquarters," announced the Führer of the Third Reich. "It seems that our Desert Fox has lost his taste for war."

"I beg your pardon, *mein Führer?*" Peiper answered, puzzled.

"SS-Brigadeführer Bücher told me that Rommel has decided to surrender his army group." Bücher was an SS general placed on Rommel's staff by Himmler's direct order. Peiper understood that Bücher's responsibility included watching Rommel for political unreliability, and that if necessary Bücher's role would be to stop him by any means necessary.

"*What?* Surrender? Rommel? Not possible. There must have been a mistake." Only in the depth of shock could Peiper argue with his führer for even a moment.

"Peiper, it is true. Absolutely true and confirmed. Another radio message has informed me that Bücher is now dead."

"But *why?*" Peiper said, his voice revealing his anguish at this betrayal. Bücher's death was the proof, for Bücher would have fought such a move with every breath in his body.

"Rommel has gone weak in the heart, I'm afraid. He was never the same after his wounds." Rommel had spent most of the previous summer hospitalized after being strafed by Allied *Jabos.* "Right now, it makes no difference. What is important is that Rommel's weakness must not infect the rest of Armeegruppe B. I know I can depend on you to ensure that your own officers are reliable . . . or at least in a position to do no harm. Do you understand me, Peiper?"

"*Jawohl, mein Führer!*" Peiper understood completely. He was a ruthless man, one that others looked toward when difficult jobs had to be done.

"Report as soon as you have any new information. Make sure that you keep in touch with my headquarters at all times. And take decisive and final action when it is necessary."

"Jawohl, mein Führer," Peiper said again. "I am heading to the command staff meeting shortly. I will report instantly as soon as I have additional information."

"Berlin out" was the radio answer.

Peiper put down the microphone and pulled the earphones off his head. "Lay out my uniform," he told his orderly, who had followed him downstairs. The orderly nodded as he handed Peiper a cup of much needed, if ersatz, coffee.

Shortly, he was on his way. His driver paid close attention to the unlit road in the dark, his headlights carving a path through the early morning fog as he drove along with reckless speed. The unrelieved blackness was beginning to lighten into a deep gray as the car arrived at Guderian's command post in an abandoned school building near Namur.

Emerging, Peiper stretched and looked around. Other cars were pulling up, and he spotted several other officers emerging. Those from the Wehrmacht marched straight into the building, but a number of the SS men stood around quietly, looking to each other with narrowed eyes and unspoken questions.

Peiper went over to a small knot of these, several Sturmbannführers who saluted him grimly. "I have spoken to the führer," he began bluntly. "The reports of treason are accurate. He needs our loyalty, and our courage, now."

"We are ready, Herr Obersturmbannführer!" replied one. Peiper nodded, watching as the men straightened, visibly donned a sense of purpose and pride. Among them were other, higher-ranking SS men in the group, he realized, but all of them seemed to be looking to him for leadership.

"Spread the word, quietly," he commanded. "Station yourselves where you will be able to act."

Seeing that his commands were understood, Peiper set his mouth in a thin line, lips tightly pressed together as he marched across the frozen yard to the command staff meeting. His clear blue eyes were also tight and focused, his dark, pencil-thin brows forming a single straight line across his brow.

He was a handsome and stylish man, freshly dressed and washed, wearing a ribbed white mock turtleneck under his trim and neat SS uniform. His Knight's Cross of the Iron Cross with Oakleaves and Swords, awarded for achieving the bridgehead across the Mscha River on the Eastern Front in the recapture of Kharkov, was fastened tightly across the collar of the turtleneck on a black band. His brown hair was crisply parted and slicked down on his head.

How had it come to this? Victory had seemed so close, and then first stalemate at the Meuse, the loss of the final bridges of Dinant . . . and now news so stunning, so disturbing, he could hardly credit its truth.

Scant days ago, his own Kampfgruppe Peiper was unstoppable. Tearing through the Belgian countryside, he had one of the places of honor in the great Fuchs am Rhein offensive, as befitted the Leibstandarte Adolf Hitler, the First

SS Panzer Division, which he had proudly served throughout the war, in battles both east and west. It was he and his kampfgruppe who had stumbled upon the fuel supplies at Malmédy, then again upon the great Allied fuel dump at Stavelot. His contempt for the Allies had increased as he saw the flagrant display of wealth that Stavelot represented. Anyone could win a war with unlimited supplies. It took military genius to win without them—and that was a quantity with which the Germans were well supplied.

Peiper hardly remembered the incident at Malmédy, when he forced Allied POWs to fuel the tanks of his kampfgruppe. He had had no time for prisoners, so after they had finished the job, he'd ordered them shot. It was a necessity of war—time was short and resources were short. War was not a business for the sentimental.

There was a loud buzz in the conference hall as Peiper entered to take his seat in the first row of the large, crowded room. He was sure a thousand rumors were making the rounds, each wilder than the next, many so amazingly incorrect that he wondered sometimes what on earth could have inspired them. He glanced over his shoulder, saw that the men he had spoken to were taking positions in the back corners of the room.

As Guderian entered the room, everyone stood at attention with a Nazi salute. The panzer general's face was stern. His face was lined and leathery, his mustache trim and gray.

Guderian returned the salute casually. Peiper could see in his face that Guderian also knew about the surrender. He confidently sat down and leaned back, knowing that Guderian would have the correct response.

"I have received word from Field Marshal Rommel at Armeegruppe B headquarters," he began without prelude. "The bridges of Dinant have been destroyed. The divisions that have crossed the Meuse are almost certainly lost to us. We are blocked at the Meuse, and Antwerp appears out of the question now."

He paused and looked over the assembled senior commanders, generals and colonels all. "Feeling that the war in the West is now over, and convinced that our old friends the Soviets will shortly resume their offensive, Generalfeldmarschall Rommel believes the best hope for Germany lies in immediate surrender to the Allies."

"What? No—you can't be . . . Ridiculous! We aren't beaten yet!" Military discipline temporarily evaporated at the stunning announcement, many officers voicing their gut-level objections. Peiper held his tongue, for he had already experienced his moment of surprise. He looked at the face of each person in the front of the room, searching for signs of weakness, futility, or betrayal. He saw some expressions worth noting for the future, but he was satisfied that most of the faces reflected the same sort of shock and anger that he had felt. Confidently, he turned back to face Guderian, still standing, facing his officers.

" 'Surrender' is the most distasteful word in any military, and I regard that option with the same disgust I am sure each of you feel." He paused again. "But as officers, we must see clearly and act strongly in the way that most benefits the Fatherland. I believe, with Generalfeldmarschall Rommel, that the most important thing is to save Germany from the Soviet Union. And though it goes against every feeling I have as a general officer, I must reluctantly conclude that Generalfeldmarschall Rommel's analysis is the correct one. I therefore am ordering that Armeegruppe B's directives be implemented for Sixth Panzer Army. We are . . ." His voice caught for a moment, then cleared. ". . . surrendering."

Chaos broke out in the room, with generals and colonels yelling and shouting their arguments, both for and against. Guderian tried to speak above the noise, and when he could not, finally roared out "Attention!" with all the power his command voice could muster.

"You are still officers of the Wehrmacht!" Guderian raged. "You will follow military discipline and you will behave like officers in this as in every situation. This is not a matter for discussion or vote. As commanding general of Sixth Panzer Army, and in accordance with orders from higher headquarters, this is my decision in line with the lawful and correct orders I have received."

Peiper was disgusted, especially at the last claim, for Guderian's disregard of orders he thought were stupid or incorrect or contrary to his own ideas was legendary, and had nearly brought down his career numerous times. His inability to follow the orders of Field Marshal von Kluge had led to his dismissal from service only a year ago, to be recalled only after Stalingrad and then to an inspector role rather than line command. To give the excuse of following orders at this time and on this order was beneath contempt. He could at least have the decency to declare this as his own judgment, not Rommel's.

Although numerous people in the room outranked him, it was Peiper who stood up. Immediately, Guderian's temper turned to him as a visible target. "Sit *down*. I am not finished."

"Yes, sir, you *are* finished," said Peiper coldly. His grossly insubordinate tone and manner temporarily surprised everyone in the room, including Guderian, who was taken aback momentarily. Exploiting the moment, Peiper continued. "I am now acting under the personal orders of the führer, who radioed me earlier this morning."

As it was well known that Peiper had been Himmler's adjutant, eyes turned to him. "Führer Himmler is aware of the alleged surrender, which is a flagrant violation of the military oath each of us has taken to the State and the Party. He rejects the surrender and orders us to take action. He states that anyone obeying the surrender order is guilty of the crime of desertion under fire."

Guderian's rage was now full-blown. "Shut up and sit down, Peiper. You and that *arschloch* Himmler may be willing to turn Germany over to the *schweinische* Russian *hurensohnnen,* but I'm not."

Peiper went white in the face. "The führer is in charge of the army and the nation, not you! You will speak of our führer with respect, not in that filthy manner!"

"Sit down right now before I have you arrested and shot!" screamed Guderian. "I am commander of Sixth Panzer Army. Don't you *dare* talk back to me in that tone of voice!"

"You have forfeited your rights as a commander by this cowardly and traitorous act!" shouted Peiper in return, his own temper exploding.

Caught up in the drama, everyone else around the table waited in silence for the conflict to resolve.

"*Cowardly?*" yelled Guderian in rage. He started striding toward Peiper, his fists clenching, ready to enforce his dominance of the room.

But Peiper's gun was already in his hand.

ARMEEGRUPPE B HEADQUARTERS, DINANT, BELGIUM, 0709 HOURS GMT

Generaloberst Doktor Hans Speidel, Rommel's chief of staff, had been leading a double life for more than a year now. When he first was recruited into the conspiracy to assassinate Adolf Hitler and replace the Nazi regime with a new German government, he quickly became a power in the organization. Regardless of how morally upright, how idealistic, or how determined the many conspirators were, they tended not to be outstanding leaders. After all, to be a conspirator meant that one was dissatisfied with the regular order of things, not a part of the power structure, not in charge of that which one wished to overthrow. Such people were generally not found at the top of the organizations of which they were a part.

Speidel was a pragmatist above all else. There were many high-ranking German officers who were aware that their nation was heading toward certain and complete destruction, many who could see that Adolf Hitler and his most intimate associates were responsible for that destruction, and even many who understood at least some of the crimes against humanity being committed by the Nazis. But for many, the path of least resistance meant to follow their soldier's oath, to continue in their hopeless jobs, to comply with or at least to avoid knowing too much about such things as the ongoing liquidation of the Jews.

Speidel was different.

As was often the case, Rommel's genius had astonished his chief of staff. Surrender reconceived as an offensive move! How brilliant and how obvious, especially in retrospect. Now it was up to Speidel to perform the detailed maneuvering within Rommel's broad strategy. He would get Patton alone and give him the story of the conspiracy, and then he would somehow find an opportunity to tell the story to Eisenhower. For Rommel's surrender was only the opening move—Speidel was still committed to a new Germany, a free Germany, with the right leadership at the helm.

And Speidel fully intended to be one of Germany's new leaders, alongside the Desert Fox once again.

Now he had a perfect chance to prove his value. He had seen orders dispatched to the various components of the army group; he had marked the latest positions on a map of Belgium; he had seen to the functioning of the entire staff. Rommel had been out already this morning, supervising the conduct of the surrender, while Speidel remained here, behind the scenes, making sure that everything functioned. Who knew how long the field marshal would be making his rounds?

But that was all right, as it should be. The great man would make his presence felt, that powerful force of personality that caused things to happen just by being there. And Speidel would see that Rommel's orders were carried out.

THE WHITE HOUSE, WASHINGTON, DC, 0753 HOURS GMT

A hand shook Hartnell Stone's shoulder. "Mr. Stone?" A muffled sound resulted. A second shake. "Mr. Stone!"

"Mmmph?"

A third shake. "Mr. Stone, the president is awake."

"What time is it?"

"Almost three o'clock in the morning."

"All right," he replied, voice thick. "Let me throw some water on my face and I'll be right down." He sat up slowly on the office sofa and bent down to fumble with his wing tips, moving, but still mostly asleep. His eyes scrunched tightly shut when the aide turned on the light, then opened very slightly, sticky with sleep. The aide stood patiently by as Stone tied his shoes, stood up, and crossed the hall to the men's room.

The cold water splashing on his face woke him more fully. He combed his jet black hair, pulled up his Windsor-knotted tie, and retucked his white shirt. He smoothed his shirt and trousers as much as he could, but he was still rather rumpled. Well, it couldn't be helped. He was on call, and the president was awake and in his study, an oval room—variously called the Oval Room or the Oval Study—on the second floor of the White House next to the president's bedroom.

This room, distinct from the president's formal Oval Office on the ground floor of the West Wing, was the actual nerve center of the Roosevelt presidency, a chaotic, messy room filled with cast-off furniture from other federal agencies, sofas, card tables, ship models, bookcases, and anything else that had caught FDR's fancy during three—and now a fourth—terms in office.

Franklin Delano Roosevelt, thirty-second President of the United States of America, looked old, tired, frail. His skin was white, nearly translucent, like crumpled parchment. Only the inner circles of the White House knew just how perilous the president's health had become, but anyone with eyes who saw the president in candid moments could tell that he had aged terribly. His hands shook, his memory faltered on numerous occasions. He had an increasingly hard time sleeping in the cold and damp Washington winter—indeed, anywhere except for his Warm Springs retreat.

The study looked out onto the south lawn of the White House in the direction of the Washington Monument. The skies were clear and the gibbous moon was bright. The white marble obelisk shined silver in its light. In the room, a single lamp cast a thick yellow light onto the old man in the wheelchair.

"Good morning, Hartnell," the president said. His voice was thin and dry. "I see they sent you in to keep an old man company." He gestured at the table with the lamp. His cigarette holder sat next to an ashtray, with a pack of cigarettes beside it. Stone fitted a cigarette into the holder, gave it to the president, and picked up the heavy silver table lighter so the president didn't have to bend forward. Roosevelt's hand trembled as he lit his cigarette.

Stone stood as Roosevelt smoked and looked out the window across the broad expanse of the Ellipse and Mall. He still felt a sense of awe in the presence of the president, even though he had known him since childhood as "Uncle Franklin." The president was not actually a relative of his, but Stone's father had been a longtime friend. Hartnell had grown up knowing the aristocratic governor of New York even before he had been stricken with polio. The personal connection was critical. It was, after all, how a man in his early twenties with no experience beyond a Harvard degree gained a presidential appointment. He felt no guilt about that; it was the way the world worked, the way it had always worked. After all, personal connections were the only ones on which you could truly depend.

"There are times I almost think I can see the artillery fire," Roosevelt said. His voice was weak and distant, not the mellifluous tone with which all Americans had become familiar. "The war is that way, you know." He pointed his cigarette holder out the window in the direction of the monument. "While you and I sit in peace and quiet, there is a battle raging over the horizon. Boys are dying in the mud right now. Boys I sent."

There was a long pause, and Stone waited patiently. He knew there were boys dying in the mud, and not infrequently he felt guilt because he was not one of them. He had been in ROTC at Harvard, and held a current Army commission as a major, but he hardly ever wore a uniform. He had served on the SHAEF staff in England for a year, as one of hundreds of officers preparing for

Operation Overlord, and had even set foot on the beaches of Normandy a few weeks after D-Day. That was as close as he'd come to combat. Soon thereafter, he had been transferred to Washington, to the White House staff, as one of the many aides surrounding the president.

"Hartnell, pick up that folder on my desk. No, the other one. That's right." The folder was labeled TOP SECRET, as were others on the president's private desk. Although Stone had as much curiosity as any man, he accepted the need for secrecy. He handed the folder to the president, but the president waved his hand. "No, open it. Read it."

There was a long telegram in the folder, from the current SHAEF head-quarters in France. Stone scanned it quickly. His eyes widened. "Surrender?"

"That's what it says," Roosevelt replied.

Stone kept reading. "But nothing has been confirmed."

FDR chuckled. His voice warmed as he spoke. "That, my boy, is the bane of my existence. No one wants to go out on a limb even so much as predicting that the sun will rise in the east in a few hours. No, it's not confirmed. Even so, it opens a host of possibilities. It could cut months off this terrible war. I might yet live to see its end."

"Of course you will, sir," Stone interjected.

"Ah, my boy, the certainty of youth. No, I'm an old man and just about used up. At least Uncle Joe did me a favor by dropping out of the war when he did."

"Sir?" It was well known in the White House that FDR had been furious about the Soviet double cross, the separate peace Himmler had negotiated after the assassination of Adolf Hitler.

"We would be having another conference about now—Stalin, Churchill, and I—and I don't think I could survive another long trip. Now I can stay home and husband my strength just a little longer. A little longer . . ." His voice grew bleak and thin again. "If only I could sleep. . . ."

Roosevelt's eyes were focused far away, past the monument. "Do you know what I most wanted, Hartnell, my boy?"

"No, sir."

"I wanted to make this war the end. The last one. And for that I needed Stalin at the peace table. Without him, all we will get is a temporary respite. Germany defeated, of course, and Japan not far behind. Then, as soon as everyone recovers a bit, on to World War Three. Democracy versus Communism." He shook his head. "I would have given Stalin almost anything to avoid a third global war. I'm not sure humanity can withstand another such conflict as the one we are about to conclude. The progress in weapons has been terrible . . . terrible. . . ." His voice trailed away, and he was lost in thought. Stone continued to stand, watching, listening.

Roosevelt's next words came as a whisper. Stone strained to catch them.

"Terrible weapons. And shortly we will have the most terrible of all." Another pause, lasting more than a minute. Stone grew more and more uncomfortable in the silent room, illuminated only by the single lamp.

"Communists believe in historical inevitability, you know," Roosevelt said, his voice returning to a slightly more normal volume again. "I had hoped that would be enough to gain Stalin as a partner in peace. After all, he believes time is on the side of the Communists. Give them the shattered nations of eastern Europe to digest, and that would keep them busy for decades. It would let them draw comfort from 'historical inevitability' while we rebuild the West. We could let our two systems compete in how well they serve their people, and the conflict would resolve itself without a need for another war."

"Will we win?" Stone asked.

Roosevelt's eyes focused on him, and his famous jaunty grin briefly illuminated his face. "Who cares, my dear boy? Who cares? If it becomes clear that one system benefits humanity better than the other, whichever it may be, then let that one triumph. We Americans are pragmatists, you know. The proof of the pudding is in the eating." His chuckle was dry, and drifted away. His expression became distant again. "A peaceful conflict is infinitely preferable to war, to more death and destruction. But Stalin couldn't see it that way. He thinks I will reward him after he deserted us, or be willing to simply turn back the clock and behave as if nothing has happened. But I cannot. As much as I despise war, I do know how to wage it. . . ." His voice trailed off again. "So much death. So much death. And now I must order more.

"What I would have given Stalin freely as a partner I cannot give him as a reward for his betrayal," Roosevelt kept on. "I thought we might have to go directly from this war into the next war, but if this surrender is real, there is hope. We can reach Berlin before Stalin's armies, and we order him back to his own lands without a new war." His voice was a whisper again.

"And if he won't go?" asked Stone, his own voice now a whisper. He had a good idea how strong the Soviets were, and a detailed understanding of how strong the Western Allies were. The Western Allies would not have the necessary might to enforce Roosevelt's order, not without the horrible new war Roosevelt hoped to avoid.

The President of the United States looked grim as he turned to look directly at Stone. "He will go. Believe me, he will go."

ARMEEGRUPPE B FIELD HOSPITAL, NEAR DINANT, 1442 HOURS GMT

The short, pudgy man had been pacing back and forth in the waiting area for the past hour, periodically removing his round, wire-rimmed glasses to polish them, then slipping them back on over his watery blue eyes. He could overhear the occasional whispers. *"That's* the man who saved the field marshal's life?" He knew he didn't look the part of the hero, and he didn't feel the part either. But he had indeed managed to chase a trained SS assassin through dark, battle-strewn streets, then kill the killer before he could end the career of the Desert Fox.

Colonel Wolfgang Müller was in charge of supply operations for Armeegruppe B, and until the previous night had never fired a gun in anger or at a living target. Nervous around superior officers, not particularly assertive, Müller survived because he was good and careful with his work.

"Herr Oberst?" asked a doctor just coming out of the operating room, pulling off spattered gloves as he walked.

"Is there news?" Müller responded, a combination of desperation and concern in his voice.

The doctor's face was stern, his words carefully chosen. "I'm Dr. Schlüter. Yes, Herr Oberst. Your friend is in very serious condition, but he's past the worst of it. The prognosis is only satisfactory, but I have good hopes for this one."

Müller let out a deep breath he had not been aware he'd held. Relief flooding his body, he suddenly remembered to ask, "And the feldwebel—the field marshal's driver? How is he?"

"You mean Mutti?" Schlüter smiled. Everyone knew Mutti, Carl-Heinz Clausen, Rommel's driver, orderly, and mother hen. "The wound was less serious than it first appeared. His condition is good. He'll be up trying to help his wardmates before too long. We'll probably have to tie him down to the bed to give him time to recover."

Müller smiled broadly. Hearing the news took a huge burden off his shoulders. This was good news all around in a time when good news seemed increasingly scarce. "Is it possible to see either of them?"

"Briefly," replied the doctor. "Follow me, please."

Müller followed the doctor through double swinging doors into a long hall. Doctors, nurses, and aides of all sorts were bustling around, but it was only ordinarily busy rather than utterly chaotic—the worst of the battlefield wounded had been dealt with, and now the hospital's business had returned to a more normal state.

Carl-Heinz was in a large, brightly lit ward filled with heavily bandaged soldiers. Some were sitting up; others were even ambulatory. Hospital machinery surrounded the feldwebel's bed, an IV drip fed into his arm. Müller was shocked at how pale and drained his face had become. Carl-Heinz was normally filled with life and confident energy, and to see him like this was unsettling.

As Müller approached, Carl-Heinz smiled, and something of the old energy showed through in his face. *"Guten Tag,* Herr Oberst," he said. "Pardon me for not saluting. My salute hand is temporarily occupied."

"How are you, Feldwebel?" Müller asked. "The field marshal asked me to make sure you were all right, and to tell you that he would be here to visit you shortly, as soon as he can. He depends on you utterly, you know."

Carl-Heinz smiled. "I know he does. And now the rest of you will have to take care of him until I get back. You tell the field marshal that he is to get a good night's sleep and a real meal into him before he comes traipsing over here. I won't have him straining himself, you know."

"I'll relay your orders to the field marshal as soon as I see him." Müller smiled in return.

"I can get back to work soon. It will be in a couple of days, all right? Definitely no more."

Müller nodded. He knew it would likely take more than a few days before the brave feldwebel was back at his post.

"Herr Oberst—that was a heroic act you did, killing Brigadeführer Bücher before he could assassinate the field marshal," said Mutti. "Thank you."

Müller waved off the thanks with an embarrassed shrug. He still could hardly believe he'd done the act, and the thought brought back the sheer terror of the event. "I—er, well—it was . . ." He stammered for a minute, then simply replied, "Er—thanks. Is there anything I can do for you, anything you need? Something to eat, perhaps?" Müller remembered that there was still some cake his mother had sent, one made with real flour and real eggs.

"No, Herr Oberst, nothing at all. They're taking wonderful care of me and granting my every whim," Carl-Heinz said with a grin, his expression seeming more robust. But the fatigue and pain were also still clear.

The doctor lightly touched Müller's arm. "I must leave you alone now, I think," the pudgy supply officer said. "If there's anything I can do, send word immediately." He moved on.

The intensive-care ward was only dimly lit, and smelled of carbolic acid and other odors he didn't want to dwell upon. Numerous tubes dripped into one patient; a nurse sat beside him, monitoring his vital signs as the pudgy colonel hesitantly approached. The patient's face reflected in the highly polished metal surfaces of the equipment.

"Günter? It's me—Wolfgang," he said in a voice only slightly above a whisper.

The eyes of the patient remained closed, but his lips moved slightly. "Did you do it?" Oberst Günter von Reinhardt, Rommel's senior intelligence officer, had been the first to try to stop Bücher and was shot in the process. Müller had found him near to death, and had taken over the mission simply because no one else was there.

"Yes, Günter. Bücher is dead. It's over."

"And our field marshal lives?"

"Yes, he lives. I'm glad you live, too. I thought you were dead."

"So did I. The surrender—did it go all right?"

"Yes, yes, Günter. It's all over now."

"Not quite, I think," said the gravely wounded intelligence officer. "But this is good news. Wolfgang, you did well." He seemed to drift into unconsciousness at that point, surrounded by reflections of his own face. Müller reached down and touched his hand lightly, then followed the doctor out of the room.

"He's in bad shape, isn't he, Doctor?"

The doctor nodded. "Yes. He's young and strong and there's a good chance he'll escape death, but he'll never be quite the same. The bullet punctured one of his lungs, which collapsed. We were lucky that he didn't die before we got him here."

"When will he be out of here?"

"Within a few weeks, assuming no serious complications. But that means out of the hospital, not a return to duty. For that—well, it's too early to tell."

"Thank you, Herr Doktor," Müller said, shaking his hand with both of his own. "Thank you very much."

"It's mostly God's work," the doctor said, waving off the compliment with a smile, "but I'm happy to take the credit."

28 DECEMBER 1944

Private Billy Cooper was marching along with his fellow infantrymen. The day was cold and somewhat dreary, but spirits were high. Rommel had surrendered and it looked as if the war would soon be over.

The infantrymen sang as they marched.

"There's the highland Dutch
And the lowland Dutch
The Rotterdam Dutch
And the goddamn Dutch

Singing glorious
Glorious
There's one keg of beer
For the four of us

Praise be to God
That there are no more of us
For the four of us
Can drink it all alone
Damn neur!"

Billy stayed quiet on the "goddamn" and "damn." He had first tried to substitute of "gosh darn" and "darn" but he was tired of being kidded about his reluctance to use bad language. He knew he was one of the more innocent and naïve members of his company, but he still was not convinced that it was a failing on his part. His Iowa upbringing had stuck with him, at least mostly. Once or twice he'd caught himself using some words he didn't even know before he went into the army.

Billy hadn't ever had a particular desire to see the world, though he always liked reading copies of *National Geographic,* which his parents received in the mail each month. Some of his friends liked to look at *National Geographic* because you could occasionally see some woman from Africa or Asia or one of those places where girls didn't wear anything on their tops, but the pictures mostly just embarrassed Billy. His fellow soldiers seemed real interested in that stuff. Sometimes it seemed that they weren't interested in anything else, except maybe getting that "million-dollar wound" that would let them go home.

Billy wanted to go home, too. And it was looking like a good day for it. They were marching to accept the surrender of a German general, a pretty famous one too, except for the fact that Billy had never heard of him before. The scuttlebutt was that this surrender pretty much meant the end of it all, like there was nothing else remaining between here and Berlin. Billy hoped that was true, but if there was one thing he'd learned from all this, it was not to get your hopes too far up and to keep your head way down.

He looked up at the gray, cloud-filled sky above for a minute. No airplanes flying in this soup. That was a shame. He liked airplanes and wished he'd gotten to fly them in the war. Especially because pretty much every plane he saw was on his side. The Krauts, when they looked up, never wanted to see an airplane, because it was almost always bad news as far as they were concerned.

An engineer battalion, working feverishly for a few hours during the cease-fire, had thrown together a pontoon bridge across a small stream just ahead, and Cooper's company began their march across the bobbing platform.

"You know, there's enough dynamite wired underneath this thing to blow the battalion all to hell," joked Private Sam Wood, a city boy with a particular fondness for kidding the yokels, as he called anyone not from New York. "Better watch where you step. . . . Hey, look out!"

Billy jumped in surprise, breaking the rhythm of the march for a moment. "Hey, Wood, cut it out, okay?" Wood merely snickered.

Sergeant Wykowski swiveled his head around without breaking step for an instant. "Knock it off, you guys. The goddamn bridge isn't going to blow up."

Embarrassed, Billy shut up. Wood continued to snicker.

Once across the bridge, the troops continued their march as the day brightened a little. Although the air was still frigid and Billy's face and lips were chapped, body heat warmed his torso while his face and hands were still chilled. His toes were cold, too, which always concerned him because of the ever-present danger of trench foot. Getting trench foot was considered a "self-inflicted wound" and was a court-martial offense. Billy religiously changed and dried his socks to the best of his ability, even though it was difficult to do out in the field, with no laundry or anything. Everything he wore was dirty, and his body itched.

The troops continued their march for another half hour or so, and then the order came to halt. Billy saw a German waving a white flag, just ahead. The captain went forward to talk with the man, who obviously spoke little English. The captain spoke no German, but after lots of hand-waving and gesturing it slowly became clear that the Kraut would lead the captain and the rest of the company to the German headquarters to accept the surrender. At least that's what Billy thought was going on.

Wood had much the same opinion. "We're either finding out where the German general's HQ is, or the captain is getting directions to the nearest toilet."

Billy couldn't help thinking that was kind of funny, so he stifled a little laugh, which drew a quick withering gaze from the sergeant. He straightened up to attention. Wood didn't move from his slouch.

Finally the order came to march. The file of infantry turned down the side road indicated by the German, a narrow lane with pine trees pressing close to either side. As they neared the German HQ, they began to see more and more enemy soldiers standing around on both sides of the road. There were panzers and staff cars and trucks, all the hardware and transport required by a large military organization. Most of the Germans were armed, and Billy had a queasy feeling marching right into an enemy headquarters.

As they neared a large redbrick building with French writing on a white-marble slab forming an arch over the door, Billy knew they had reached their destination. There was an unmistakable look to any military command post, regardless of nationality. The staff cars, the jury-rigged telephone wires, the bustling traffic, all gave a sense of improvised organization, of confusion and control. A higher-ranking German officer came out of the building and saluted the captain with a normal salute rather than the Nazi "Heil Hitler." The captain returned the salute.

In heavily accented but understandable English, the German officer said, "General Guderian is waiting inside. If you will come with me, the general is ready to make a formal surrender."

"Very well," replied the captain. "First platoon, follow me."

Sergeant Wykowski snapped to attention. "Yes, sir! Platoon, right shoulder arms. Forward, march!"

Billy did as he was told, falling in behind the captain just like it was a parade drill back in basic training. This was about the first time since then he'd been ordered to do a formal parade march, but he still remembered how. Up four white marble stairs, then single-file through the open wooden doors, the platoon marched into a narrow hallway. There was a staircase in front of them, and a hall going to the stair's right. Doors on either side were open, and Billy could see numerous German soldiers standing, armed, as they marched forward. The hall ended in a door with a frosted glass window with some French lettering on it; Billy had no idea what it meant. The German officer opened the door and the men started after the captain into the room.

Billy's eyes widened. The room was large, a conference table dominating the space. At the head of the table, dangling on a noose from the ceiling, was a German general in Wehrmacht gray. There was extensive bleeding on his uniform front from a chest wound; his face was blue-black and swollen, tongue protruding, eyes open and lifeless.

"God damn it, it's a trap!" shouted the captain, but Billy had already figured that out. He aimed his rifle at the German officer, who dodged around a corner toward another door. He got off one shot, missed, and then he was scrambling for cover in the conference room. There was a scream behind him—somebody was hit, but he couldn't tell who.

An overturned chair was hardly any cover, but it was all he had. He aimed over the chair and fired again, then he felt a sudden stab in his abdomen—a bullet had passed right through the chair and into him. He was surprised at first that it didn't hurt very much. Then he looked down. For a minor wound, it was bleeding pretty heavily.

He was scared, more scared than he'd ever been, but in a way it didn't matter, because he just had to keep firing, keep crouching, move to get away, to get out of the trap. He fired again and this time he thought he might have hit something or someone, because a flash of gray pulled back around a door.

He looked wildly around. Several of his platoon were already down. Next to him was Wood, eyes wide open in panic, blood bubbling out of his mouth and spreading quickly over his chest.

Sergeant Wykowski had smashed open a window and was shouting, "Out! Out! Everybody out!"

A few members of the platoon were able to dive through the window. The captain fired his pistol and picked off another German as he covered the retreat. Billy, grabbing his wounded side, struggled toward the window, which suddenly seemed a million miles away. "Move! Move!" Wykowski was still shouting. The sergeant was bleeding from his leg. As Billy started through the window, the sergeant gave him a big push and he went flying through the window to land with a thud on the ground below. He still held his rifle in his hand.

Outside there was a lot more fighting, as the rest of the company came under fire from the German ambush. There were more screams, both German and American. As Billy crouched and ran for the cover of a German half-track, still cupping his abdomen, he could see lots of soldiers down and others fighting back. There seemed to be a lot more Germans now.

Then he felt another pain and he toppled forward clutching his leg. The bullet had smashed the bone; he could see the jagged white edges along with the spurting blood.

"Jesus, oh Jesus!" Now it was Billy who was screaming. "Oh, Jesus!" He crawled forward, pulling himself by his arms and his remaining good leg, trying to prop himself up behind the half-track to continue firing. "Oh, Jesus, I don't want to die!" he screamed again, and he propped his weapon up and fired wildly, no longer aiming at anything in particular, but just firing.

A shadow fell across his position, and he swiveled his head around and upward to see a German soldier, odd-shaped helmet and all, a big man, strong and grinning with cruel anticipation as he jabbed his bayonet through Billy's throat.

Billy continued to scream, this time for his mother, but there was no longer any sound. He felt himself choking on the taste of his own blood, as he gasped for a breath of air that would never reach his lungs.

NEUE REICHSKANZLEI, BERLIN, 1000 HOURS GMT

The new, monumental Reichs Chancellery was an expression of Albert Speer's architectural genius. It symbolized the majesty and power of the Thousand-Year Reich. Now it stood in a bombed city, a city in the grips of winter, the frigid destruction symbolizing what the Reich had become.

The führer's office complex was now occupied by Adolf Hitler's successor: Heinrich Himmler, formerly Reichsführer of the SS. He had not been Hitler's personal choice to take over the reins of the state, but the others were either dead or outmaneuvered. Himmler had been elected to his role by the only voters who mattered: the massed troops of the Waffen-SS and the Gestapo.

The führer sat in his darkened office, blackout curtains draped over the large windows. A single desk lamp illuminated his round, nearly chinless face, a face more suited to a bookkeeper than the absolute ruler of Germany. His eyes watered behind his round, wire-frame glasses.

Verdammte Amerikaner! he thought. He had planned so well, first by buying a temporary peace from Stalin, and second by conceiving of a massive, jet-supported breakthrough in the West. Had the second plan succeeded, he would have had time— precious time—to rebuild Fortress Europa and secure a Germanic empire that could, in time, become a pivotal world power once again. But his time was getting short. Stalin would hold off only until he was ready to resume his offensive, and with that traitor Rommel's surrender, the Americans and British were preparing to roll right through the Westwall into the industrial heart of Germany itself.

Well, he was not devoid of options quite yet, and if nothing else, he could inflict extra damage. It would take a lot more than the Americans had to defang the führer! he thought. He smiled as he regarded the next document that had been prepared for his signature—a new law branding those guilty of terror attacks against civilians as ordinary criminals, exempt from the Geneva Convention. The Americans prated on about their exemplary moral standards, so superior to the rest of the world. Yet they had unleashed the *Terrorfliegers,* the strategic bombers, against the civilian population. They claimed they sought only military and industrial targets, but in practice they incinerated cities full of civilians, then had the audacity to claim protection as ordinary prisoners of war. From now on, that would change. Now they would be treated as the criminals they were, sent to concentration camps, not POW camps. Himmler initialed a note that the Buchenwald camp should prepare a barracks for these new criminals. Let them work in factories and cities to repair what they had destroyed. Let them work until they died. He smiled. At least one good thing would happen this day, he thought.

The large, ornately inscribed double doors opened, letting a slice of light from the anteroom into his office. "*Mein Führer, SS-Obergruppenführer Diet-rich ist hier*" his secretary announced.

"Send him in," the führer responded. He stood up to greet his visitor. "Sepp—it's good to see you. What do you make of this situation?"

Sepp Dietrich gave the German military salute, then accepted Himmler's outstretched hand. "It's good to see you too, *mein Führer*. This is a bad situa-tion. Very bad." Dietrich had a pleasant, open face with the look of a boxer who'd taken one too many punches.

Himmler pursed his lips slightly, but did not respond. Much of this disas-ter, he thought, had been brought on by that idiot Dietrich's own stupidity, in allowing himself to be maneuvered out of command of Sixth Panzer Army right before the launch of the Fuchs am Rhein offensive. Rommel had prom-ised Dietrich the role of military governor of Antwerp at the successful con-clusion of the operation, and sent him back to Berlin to provide liaison for the operation. Since it would be Himmler, not Rommel, who would have made any such appointment, it was doubly stupid of Dietrich to believe him.

Of course, Rommel's real goal was to remove a potential SS thorn in Rommel's side, for he and Dietrich had locked horns more than once in north-ern Italy. It was also done to put the panzer genius Heinz Guderian in com-mand, a maneuver Himmler couldn't fault.

Sepp Dietrich was generally regarded by his peers and superiors as decent, loyal, and stupid. Barely literate, unable even to read a map, he owed his high rank to having been one of Hitler's intimates in the Beer Hall days. A World War I sergeant-major who worked after the war as a gas-pump attendant and butcher, he'd been a Party member from the beginning, and had organized Hitler's first bodyguard, a group of bullyboys and toughs that formed the ori-gin of Leibstandarte Adolf Hitler. He'd played an active role in the Night of the Long Knives, and had been willing to take on any challenge for his führer. He and Himmler had been at odds frequently over the years, but now he was one of the dwindling number of senior officers Himmler could trust.

"I can't believe it. I just can't believe it." Dietrich had continued talking, an endless chain of the same remarks. "This is very bad. Very bad."

Himmler took control of the conversation. "Yes, it's bad, and yes, it's unbelievable. But it happened. Your friend Rommel has surrendered Armeegruppe B to the Allies. Fortunately, not all units in Armeegruppe B are in agreement. I've already heard from your old friend Peiper in the Leibstandarte. He's going to make sure that Sixth Panzer Army, at least, doesn't surrender."

"But what about Guderian? Surely he won't surrender."

"That's right. He may try, but if he does, he won't live long enough to pull out a white flag."

Dietrich was shocked. "But—Guderian? How can you even doubt him?"

"Because that snake Rommel has his hooks into him. Those two may be rivals, but they think alike in lots of ways. Rommel's surrender isn't a surrender of a defeated and destroyed force, it's a strategic move to undermine my government. We know quite well that he was in league with the murderers of Adolf Hitler. In fact, he was their choice to become chancellor, if you can believe it! Chancellor! After all that the Third Reich did for that man, after all the kindness and personal attention showered upon him by our late führer, he was willing to be part of the conspiracy of assassins!"

Dietrich was silent, not only because of the shocking accusations, but also because he was aware personally that they were not altogether false. He had also been swayed by Rommel's charisma and intelligence, and had told Rommel that he was willing to place himself under the Desert Fox's orders, before Rommel had been wounded the previous summer. With a potential military coup averted, the conspirators resorted to assassination. A cowardly act, the assassination. Even Dietrich realized that something drastic had to be done in response to Germany's grave situation, but an act of assassination was not the right thing. Even now, he could hardly believe that Adolf Hitler was really dead.

Himmler continued, his passion rising as he talked. "I gave personal orders to Peiper to ensure that command of Sixth Panzer Army remained utterly loyal. Sepp, I want you to take back command and at once, not only of Sixth Panzer Army but also whatever elements of Fifth you can reach. I'm appointing Mödel as Commander-in-Chief West."

"*Jawohl, mein Führer!*" Dietrich was overwhelmed by the assignment, but he had been feeling overwhelmed by his assignments for a good many years now. He would do his best, as he always did, and hoped it would be good enough.

Himmler opened a folder on his desk. "Here is the order of battle for all forces in Operation Fuchs am Rhein. I want to review them to determine which we'll be able to keep and which we must assume will surrender."

Dietrich looked at the long list. Fortunately, he knew many of the officers personally, and could make recommendations based on that knowledge. He looked at Himmler, a man he used to refer to as "the *Reichsheini*," and thought: *He is all we have left.*

He bent to the study of the list, moving his lips as he sounded out the words. "If Sixth Panzer Army command does not itself surrender, I am confident that the subordinate units will not surrender unless their military position appears hopeless. Right now, they are not threatened, and have a clear route back toward the Fatherland. I think we need to fortify the Rhine crossings, especially those held only by the Volkssturm currently."

"Good thinking. Now, how about Fifth Panzer Army? Can any of those units be saved?"

He squinted at the list, mumbled to himself, and ran a finger down the column. "Hmm—Fifth Panzer Army has almost no SS units in it," he observed.

"Indeed. Quite suspicious of our Desert Fox, don't you think? Perhaps this is evidence that he knew all along of his own intent to surrender." Himmler scowled at the treachery. "What about Seventh Army?"

"Brandenberger?" General der Panzertruppen Erich Brandenberger commanded Seventh Army, which had been responsible merely for protecting the left flank of the advance. "He's a reliable man, but his army is between Fifth Panzer Army and the Americans to the south—Patton's men, I think. That doesn't look too good."

Himmler glowered at the news. The new führer, Dietrich observed, didn't have the military skills or vision of Adolf Hitler, but he did have a sense of political intrigue and loyalty games, appropriate to the head of the secret police. "We'll call him at once to see what can be arranged. There is one more thing, Sepp."

"*Jawohl, mein Führer?*"

"I want to see if we can neutralize more of this threat. How about a counterattack on Armeegruppe B headquarters?"

"You mean, attack Rommel?"

"Certainly. He's proven himself a traitor, the penalty for treason is death, and if his command is terminated, perhaps more of Fifth Panzer Army will see the light of reason and return to their sworn duties."

That thought made Dietrich pause. An attack against Rommel himself was nearly inconceivable. Dietrich regarded the Desert Fox's military genius as nearly magical and certainly incomprehensible. To attack him . . . "I will, of course, follow the führer's orders."

"Very good," replied Himmler. "Kampfgruppe Peiper's original mission, if I recall the battle plans, was to be first across the Meuse in the Sixth Army area of operations, correct?"

Dietrich had to concentrate for a moment before replying, "Yes, that's correct."

"And he is a ferocious fighter, yes?"

"That he is." Dietrich nodded in agreement. "Ferocious" was a good word to describe Jochen Peiper. When there was a difficult objective to be reduced, Peiper had been his first choice on several occasions. He was a fury when unleashed. "If anyone can face up to Rommel, it would be Kampfgruppe Peiper."

"And it's your old division that will get the honor," Himmler said with an insinuating grin.

The old soldier straightened up. "If the honor goes to anyone, it should go to Leibstandarte Adolf Hitler. It's only appropriate."

"And I agree fully," replied the führer. "I've given the order already. I don't mean to tread on your prerogatives, but you've just now been given the command. And so, Sepp, I want you to get to Sixth Panzer Army as soon as you possibly can to straighten out at least part of this unholy mess. I have a meeting shortly with OKW, and I intend to find out which other potential traitors I have in my ranks." The cold look in Himmler's eye made the battle-hardened veteran feel a slight chill. What he felt, the Wehrmacht high command would shortly feel also.

"Very well, mein Führer. I will keep in contact with you and report as soon as I have any news."

"The hopes of the Third Reich travel with you," Himmler said in final dismissal. Dietrich saluted and left the room.

KREMLIN, MOSCOW, USSR, 1955 HOURS GMT

Major Alexis Petrovich Krigoff felt a tingling of nervousness in his belly—not quite fear, but instead a clear understanding of the stakes involved in this imminent meeting with the most powerful man in the Soviet Union. He had been summoned back to the Kremlin a few hours ago, with no indication of why he was to be here, and he knew that this could be either very good or very bad.

Only yesterday Krigoff had been a young lieutenant laboring anonymously in the bureaucracy of Red Army headquarters. A chance to carry a message to Chairman Stalin, combined with Krigoff's quick-thinking interpretation and the audacious spin he had placed on that message, had resulted in a promotion, jumping over two grades. Then, today, after he had already returned to his plain room in the officers' barracks near the Kremlin, had come the messenger with the invitation: Stalin wanted to see him again, tonight. Krigoff understood all too well that a single misstep could have placed him in the bowels of Lubyanka Square—as the headquarters of the NKVD, the Soviet security agency, was commonly referred to. But that was life at the apex of the Soviet Union—and a small price to pay for being at the glorious center of power.

The square-faced woman, a captain who had lost a foot at Stalingrad and now served as Stalin's appointment secretary, studied him dispassionately as he handed her the handwritten note.

"You may go into the anteroom, Comrade Major," she said briskly. "The chairman will see you shortly."

He entered the large chamber, with two bright hammer-and-sickle banners hanging from opposite walls, but he was too nervous to take a seat on any of the cushioned chairs placed around the fringes of the room. The tall windows were screened with blackout curtains, so he could not take the view—which in any event would have been minimal in this city darkened by war and winter's night—so he merely strolled around, forcing his steps to slow. Pausing before a bust of the chairman, he admired the manly mustache, could even imagine the genial twinkle in those stony eyes.

The door behind him opened and he twitched nervously, then drew a breath and turned slowly. Emerging from the inner office was not the sturdy, masculine figure he had expected to see, but rather a woman in trousers and a plain jacket. Her raven hair was cut short, and the most dramatic feature about her appearance was the patch that covered her left eye. The visible eye was a very deep blue. Her face was free of cosmetics, but her skin was milky and soft. Her lips were full. The trousers and military-cut jacket made it difficult to tell what her figure was like, but she was tall and slim.

"Comrade Major," she said politely. "I am to tell you that the chairman will summon you within a few minutes."

"Thank you, Comrade," he said, with a discreet nod of his head. He smiled his most charming smile.

She took a step toward the outer door, then stopped and turned to approach the marble bust. "It is a good likeness," she suggested. "Though mere stone cannot capture his vitality, his spirit."

Krigoff nodded again. "I was thinking much the same thing," he said, but his eyes were on the woman. He was intrigued by this person, who wore civilian clothes but spoke with fond familiarity about their great national leader. "Have you met the chairman often?" he asked.

She shook her head, a shy smile curving her full lips. "Just today," she said. She hesitated a moment, then held out her hand to show him the small silver medal. "I am honored to say that he awarded me with the People's Medallion."

Krigoff was impressed; the award was one of the highest nonmilitary medals in the Soviet hierarchy. "Congratulations," he said sincerely. "You must have performed valiant service in the name of Mother Russia." He took her open hand in his and lifted the medal up to get a better look at it. "What was the nature of your heroism, if I may ask?"

She shook her head dismissively, another gesture that he found appealing, but she didn't pull her hand away. "It was a small thing, only—nothing compared to the sacrifices made by the men and women who wear the uniform of the Red Army."

Krigoff, who had never been within twenty miles of a front line, waved away the compliment even as he felt a flush of pride. "No, please, I would like to know," he said encouragingly.

Her hand went to the patch over her eye, a self-conscious motion, as she drew a breath. "I was merely a camera operator—assigned to a documentary project. We were filming a movie called *One Day of War*. Many of my colleagues were killed as we tried to capture the heroism of the soldiers. I was wounded, but survived. . . . I accepted this medal on behalf of those who lost their lives."

"The work of the film industry has been a great comfort and encouragement to our people during the Great Patriotic War," Krigoff said in a sincere voice. "I have been privileged to see many of these great works. I am sorry to admit, though I have heard of *One Day of War* I have yet to see it. But I shall make it a point of doing so, especially because I will think of its camera operator."

"You are too kind, Major," she said with that shy smile.

Krigoff smiled in a self-deprecating manner. "There is a place in Gorky Park," he noted. "A bluff above the River Moskva, from where one can see the towers of the Kremlin and so much of this great city. I go there often, to reflect upon the greatness of our people, and the immensity of the task before us. The next time I am there, I shall share a moment of reflection for those of you who have risked your lives to uplift the spirits of our great people."

"Comrade Major, I would be honored if you did." She straightened as if a soldier coming to attention.

"Please," he said. "My name is Krigoff, Alexis Petrovich. Alyosha to friends, Comrade . . . ?"

"Mine is Koninin," she replied. "Paulina Arkadyevna."

Krigoff was eager to say something else, to continue this conversation, when the inner door of the waiting room was pulled open and he looked up to see the genial, avuncular face of the chairman himself. Immediately the woman was forgotten.

"Ah, Alexis Petrovich," said Stalin, ignoring Paulina. "Please, come in!"

Krigoff hastened to obey, and moments later he was shaking the chairman's strong hand, then stammering his acceptance to the glass of vodka that Stalin offered him, having poured two as soon as he had led his visitor into the spacious inner office.

"To the confusion of our enemies!" toasted the leader of the Soviet Union, his voice underlain by an easy chuckle.

Krigoff drank, and as the clear liquid ignited its fire over his tongue and down his throat he found that he was breathing a little easier. Stalin extended the bottle and the major reflexively held up his glass for a refill, noting that the chairman had not yet touched his own glass.

"That was good insight you showed yesterday, when you perceived how Rommel's surrender would play into the hands of my own policies," remarked the chairman, idly waving his hand toward a seat. Alyosha sat across from the great desk, and watched as Stalin took a sip from his vodka and then took his own chair, setting the bottle on the wooden surface between them. Another sip of the vodka sent tongues of fire through Krigoff's belly, and he allowed the compliment to warm him further.

"I have a question for you," said Stalin, reaching across with the bottle to refill the glass that was, again, nearly empty. "Please, take your time—finish your drink!—and then give me your best reply."

Alarms were going off in Krigoff's subconscious, and he nervously quaffed the clear liquid, which barely even burned his throat anymore. An important question from Stalin would most certainly require a careful answer. The warmth was spreading through his belly, and into the fringes of his mind, and he squinted, focusing on what the great man was saying to him.

"What do you think the Nazi government will do now, in reaction to Rommel's treachery?" asked Stalin.

Krigoff had no idea, but he knew he couldn't admit this. Frantically he grasped at thoughts, whatever he knew of Nazis, and fascism, and Himmler. Somehow these threads wove themselves together, until there seemed to be only one logical answer.

"They will keep fighting, Comrade Chairman—at least, those Nazis in the SS and the other fanatical elements. Their strength will be weakened by the defection of Rommel's troops, but not broken entirely."

Stalin looked at him, his eyes twinkling merrily. Mutely he accepted another drink, as the chairman at last topped off his own glass, which was only half empty.

"I believe you are correct, Comrade Major. You display the kind of quick-thinking courage that I like to see in my officers, and most especially in my commissars. I commend you."

"Th-Thank you, Comrade Chairman!" stammered Krigoff, flushing with pleasure.

"You will hear from me, or perhaps from Comrade Bulganin, regarding an assignment," said Stalin, who was now walking the major to the door—though Krigoff couldn't exactly remember standing up. "A man of your talents has clear uses to Mother Russia, and those uses will not be put to waste." A strong hand came down on his shoulder, and the officer felt a squeezing pressure that seemed genuinely affectionate. "Good night, Alexis Petrovich—and thank you."

"Thank *you,* Comrade Chairman!" declared the major. As he made his way out of the anteroom, and through the wide halls of the Kremlin, it seemed as though his feet were some distance off the floor, and his head might be in danger of rising to the lofty ceilings.

ARMEEGRUPPE B HEADQUARTERS, DINANT, 1959 HOURS GMT

Chuck Porter, Paris Bureau Chief for the Associated Press, ex-prisoner of war, and currently finishing a special role as Rommel's personal translator, was an Underwood-typewriter man, and the German-made Olympia *Schreibmaschine* he'd been able to scrounge felt different, awkward. The umlaut key didn't have a space advance, for instance. And while it was nice to type a real umlaut rather than backspace and put quote marks over the vowel, it wasn't as if he could teletype an umlaut when sending the story over the wire.

He was just superstitious enough to want the very best typewriter to help him write what he knew was a sure Pulitzer story, the most important story of the war, the story of Rommel's surrender—a story in which he'd actually played a part.

He had just finished reopening the AP Paris bureau, closed upon the German occupation of Paris, when he had driven north into Belgium to cover U.S. forces there. He'd started to staff up the office but didn't have everyone he needed in place, so he used that as an excuse to get out of the office and do some reporting himself.

Captured during the opening days of the Fuchs am Rhein offensive, Porter was singled out by Oberst von Reinhardt for his reporter status and knowledge of the German language and transferred to Armeegruppe B headquarters. Upon the collapse of the final bridge at Dinant, he was a witness to Rommel's portentous decision to surrender his army group to the Allies. In fact, he personally had made the telephone call to Nineteenth Armored Division HQ to put Rommel in touch with General Henry Wakefield, and shortly thereafter, with Patton himself. Reporters were supposed to cover news, not make it, but in this case it just worked out differently.

Porter rolled a fresh sheet of paper into the typewriter and began pecking away, marshaling his thoughts as he strove to turn them into the right words for this incredible story. A neat sheaf of pages sat beside the typewriter— several different story pieces all ready for transmission, just as soon as he could arrange to get to a teletype.

The surrender conference at the Church of Notre Dame in Dinant, with Rommel on one side and Patton on the other, had lasted for several hours. The immediate act of surrender was easy enough, but it turned out that the mechanics of arranging the cease-fire, surrender, and turnover of forces and control were surprisingly complex—especially since Rommel was unable to guarantee that all the forces under his command would accept his order to surrender.

After all, Rommel's surrender was not so much the act of a man who was completely defeated and without options, but rather a careful calculation of threats to his fatherland. One remark of Rommel's had stuck in Porter's mind. "The mark of command is not one's ability to make good decisions, but rather one's ability to make a decision in cases where all alternatives are unpleasant and dangerous."

Porter was struggling with the comment when Patton's translator, an American intelligence lieutenant colonel named Reid Sanger, injected his own translation. Patton had laughed heartily and knowingly at the remark. "Hell, that's the truth," he'd said. "Any jackass can make a good decision. Making the right bad decision—now, that's an art!"

Seeing Patton and Rommel in their first face-to-face meeting was an interesting experience. Although sharing no common language and serving enemy governments, the two instantly seemed to relate on a deeper, personal level, one born of shared experience and shared passion. Patton did not treat Rommel as a defeated enemy, but rather as a business colleague engaged in a necessarily adversarial, but mutually respectful, transaction.

Yet the two could hardly have been more different in personal style and demeanor. The tall, loud Patton, very American in his personal style, was oddly matched against the stocky, somewhat reserved and analytical Rommel, scion of a long German military heritage.

One thing the two had in common was rapidity in their thinking. Not being a student of the military arts, Porter was quickly overmatched in trying to translate complex military terminology. Fortunately, Lieutenant Colonel Sanger was quick to interject when necessary, and the two commanding generals themselves had a rapport that seemed almost telepathic at moments. After a while, Porter found himself dismissed from the meeting, and had used his time to scrounge up a typewriter and get to work.

How to describe it all? Porter worked to find the perfect words to capture the moment and all its import: adversaries united in mutual respect, knights of the battlefield meeting on the field of honor, the culmination of the Second World War in a single meeting on the hallowed soil of a church.

Porter had no doubt that this meeting spelled the effective end of World War II. While Rommel's army wasn't the entire German army, it was a large enough section, especially as it had been heavily reinforced with troops from the Eastern Front, that its surrender effectively eliminated German ability to mass sufficient forces at the critical point.

And with Patton, whose concerns about the Soviets had been so loudly expressed, the idea of "unconditional surrender" had slipped into abeyance. Patton seemed to be forging a peace of his own design, not that of his government, as if he were channeling the ghost of Ulysses S. Grant to Rommel's Robert E. Lee.

Porter stopped, typed a few lines. That would make a very interesting sidebar—how this surrender would stack up against the Allied declaration of intent, and whether Patton would find himself in trouble yet again for exceeding his mandate as a negotiator. He'd have to make a few calls as soon as he could get near a working civilian telephone.

Another sidebar that needed telling was the story of the near assassination of Rommel only hours before the surrender was to take place, and how it was narrowly foiled by a German supply officer, of all people—Müller, his name was. It was a narrow escape from disaster for everyone concerned; if it had gone just a hair differently, there was a good chance that Patton would be dead by the same hand right now. The German intelligence officer who had first taken Porter to his own headquarters instead of a POW camp had been shot by the same SS officer, as had Rommel's personal driver. Porter made himself a note to find out whether those two had lived or not.

Porter continued to type, then paused as he realized that he probably would have been dead as well, shot at the hands of some Waffen SS bastard just on general principles. The Nazis weren't big on freedom of the press. At the start of the war, quite a few foreign correspondents had been rounded up, and some of AP's German stringers had been arrested on loyalty charges. One American AP reporter, Joe Morton, was still in Nazi hands, in some kind of concentration camp. Porter hoped he was okay.

He looked down at what he'd written so far. Not bad, even for a long day's work. The wastebasket next to the desk he'd commandeered had thirty or so wadded-up sheets of typing paper in it, but that was par for the course. The classic advice for new reporters was "Don't try to put more fire in your work; put more of your work into the fire." The ratio of trashed pages to finished pages was fairly reasonable.

Porter stood up, stretched, and decided to go in search of some coffee—or what passed for coffee around Rommel's headquarters. He'd put in a long shift of work after a sleepless night; he deserved a break.

Porter pushed a hand through his thinning hair and patted his comfortably thick belly. He was wearing American military fatigues without any insignia, and thick, heavy boots fit for an infantryman but not for a primarily deskbound reporter and editor.

Rommel's headquarters looked more or less the same as American headquarters he'd seen—it must be a function of how a military organization was run. Aside from the fact that most of the people wore Wehrmacht gray instead of American olive drab, it was pretty close. Clerks typed, officers scurried into and out of meetings, cigarettes were stubbed out into already overflowing ashtrays.

Which reminded him, so he lit up a Lucky Strike and took a big drag from it. He saw another flash of olive drab, and there was General Wakefield, CO of the Nineteenth Armored Division. Wakefield was a short, squat man, built a little like the tanks he commanded. He took his ever-present cigar out of his mouth. "Porter—just the man I'm looking for."

"I was just getting ready to scrounge a cup of coffee, General. What can I do for you?"

"I need a little translation support. You available?"

"Sure thing, General."

"Good. Patton stole my translator, my G-2, Sanger."

"I met him in the surrender talks. His German's a lot better than mine," Porter said.

"Parents are German. He was there before the war. Speaks like a native."

"I spent a couple of years there before the war myself, but my German's weak at best."

Another grunt. "Best I've got right now. I need to talk to some of the Krauts as well as my own men. I could use your help."

"Sure, General. I'm at your service."

Porter followed Wakefield out of the headquarters, grabbing his field jacket from the back of his chair on the way. At the door, two German guards snapped to attention. Seeing two Americans, one with stars on his shoulders, confused them.

"Halt! Excuse me, sirs, you can't leave this building without proper permission," the guard said in German.

"This is an American general," Porter replied, also in German. "He can go wherever he likes."

The guards looked warily at each other. "We must have a pass before you can exit."

Porter thought for a moment, then smiled. "One minute." He pulled out his reporter's notebook and scrawled a few words on it. "General, please sign here."

"What's this?" Wakefield growled.

"The Germans need a pass so they can let us through."

"Hrrumph!" Wakefield snorted, but he signed the form.

The German guards looked carefully at the pass, then back at Porter and Wakefield. Porter said, in German, "He is the American general. He is able to issue any required pass or order."

Finally, the guards decided that the pass was satisfactory, snapped back to attention, and opened the door.

The outdoor air cut through Porter's jacket at once, making him shiver. Wakefield, no more warmly dressed, seemed not to notice. The smoke cloud from his cigar grew larger as he puffed; Porter's cigarette made its own smoke cloud.

There were several jeeps parked outside Armeegruppe B headquarters, one flying Patton's three-star flag, another flying a single star. Wakefield got into the one-star jeep and started the engine; Porter climbed in beside him.

It seemed strange wending their way through German armor in an unarmed American jeep, but then nothing much seemed normal right now. Porter didn't know if he should initiate a conversation, but Wakefield did it for him.

"Reporter, eh?" said Wakefield in his gruff voice.

"Bureau chief, actually," Porter replied.

"German bureau?"

"No, sir. Paris."

"Paris." Wakefield put the cigar back in his mouth, puffed a cloud of blue smoke as he thought about it. "This ain't Paris," he observed.

"No, sir. But the Paris bureau covers a lot of territory, especially right now. It's not like we can set up shop in Berlin, at least not yet."

Wakefield grunted in response. "How'd you get here?"

Porter decided that short and quick was the best communication style for this man. "Captured."

"Yeah? Where?"

"Trying to get out of Stavelot when the Germans captured the fuel dump. I was there looking for a story."

"Story's simple. Hell of a lot of good men died, and it looks like it's about over. That's the story," the general replied.

"Well, General, some of us get paid by the word, and I think I'd better find a few more to write down."

Another grunt, and a nod, then silence.

They passed through the German cease-fire line into the part of Dinant that lay hard against the waterfront of the Meuse, quickly reaching the wreckage of the final bridge. Across the ruined span he could see tanks from Wakefield's own division, CCA of the Nineteenth, lined up along the shore and covering approaches from the left and right. The onion-shaped tower of the Church of Notre Dame dominated the ruined town. Directly behind the church was a cliff face, and at the top of the cliff face was a huge medieval citadel dominating the view. Both the citadel and the church seemed oddly out of scale for the tiny city.

Wakefield stared across the frigid Meuse for a moment. "Find me a German officer," he ordered.

Several curious Germans had followed the strange solitary Americans, and Porter picked out one with officer's insignia, a major. *"Entschuldigen Sie mich, bitte!"* he called out.

The officer responded. *"Jawohl, Herr . . ."* he replied, letting the sentence trail off.

"Ich bin Herr Porter. Dies hier ist Generalmajor Wakefield." A one-star

was a brigadier general in the U.S. Army, but a major general in the German Wehrmacht.

The German saluted and clicked his heels together. *"Herr Generalmajor!"*

Wakefield returned the salute. "Tell him I need this area cleared. My engineers are going to be setting up a pontoon bridge across the Meuse. While he's at it, I want to get some scouts out. My people will take the other side of the river, but we'll need Germans to cover this side. Got it?"

"Yes, sir," Porter replied, and immediately began to translate.

The German major looked puzzled, then embarrassed. He shrugged, then began speaking rapidly.

"He's very sorry, General," Porter translated. "He says he understands that his forces have surrendered to you, but that he cannot take the actions you request without permission from his own superior officers."

"Yeah, I kinda figured that," Wakefield growled. He chewed his cigar for a minute.

"Tell him I'll get an okay from his superiors. But I don't want to waste any time. Tell him to get a work detail here and ready to coordinate with my engineers, and tell him that if the German army has got the sense God gave green apples, he's already got scouts out."

Porter tried to translate both the words and the forcefulness of the delivery. Something of Wakefield's intent must have gotten across, because suddenly the major was stammering his agreement. "Yes, yes, of course we have scouts out. And a work detail can be arranged—but you must get approval from my superior as soon as possible!"

When the agreement was translated, Wakefield nodded with satisfaction. "Good. Have the scouts report as they normally do, but I want a runner to inform me about anything out of the ordinary. And tell the major he has half an hour or so before the work detail needs to be here. It'll take my engineers a few hours to get their work done." He looked at the major. "Dismissed," he said firmly. Some orders seemed to be the same in any language, because the major immediately saluted. First he started with the Nazi salute; then he changed course to give an imitation of an American salute. Wakefield returned the salute with gravity. The major clicked his heels, said, *"Herr Generalmajor!,"* and left.

"I understand the bridging, but not the scouts. Why, General?" Porter asked.

"Rommel has surrendered two armies that have God knows how many SS divisions in them. He's already said he can't guarantee that everyone will stand down. I want scouts out on both sides just in case. I've already radioed to my combat commands and their scouts are out already. Maybe nothing is going to happen, but I'd hate like hell to be caught with my pants down."

Wakefield stood silently at the water's edge for a minute or so. "Something doesn't feel right," he growled. Striding back to his jeep, Wakefield picked up a large walkie-talkie. Giving his radio call sign, he made contact with Colonel Bob Jackson, commanding CCB. "Bob? This is General Wakefield. I've got the wind up my shorts, and it's probably nothing, but I want a line of field artillery covering the river valley. Set it around the fortress I see on the cliff. Make sure you've got scouts out in all directions. Armor covering the roads into town, good cover. Dig in like you were preparing for a siege. Got it?"

The crackling voice over the radio responded, "Got it, General. No specific threat indication, this is a just-in-case. Artillery at the citadel and along the cliff, scouts out and active, roads into town fortified. Call you if anything happens."

"Right, Bob. That's exactly what I want. Thanks for humoring an old man."

"Any time, General. Jackson out."

"Good man," growled Wakefield. Then he was on the phone to Frank Ballard, commanding what was left of Combat Command A in the lower city.

"Good evening, General. My scouts can see you down there by the river," came the voice over the walkie-talkie.

"Got a damage assessment put together yet?"

"Yes, sir, and it's not real pretty. In a nutshell, we're running about half strength with damn little ammunition left. We've gotten some ambulances in and the worst of the wounded are out. The first company of engineers has arrived, and they'll be bridging the river pretty soon."

The general shook his head in concern. "Frank, get some scouts out around your perimeter and get someone into the highest building that's still standing. I guess it'll be that big church. Try to shape what you've got into a defensive line."

"Yes, sir. Any specific threat indication?"

"No, Frank," replied Wakefield. "Just an old man's rheumatism acting up."

"Well, better safe than sorry."

"You've got it, Frank. Listen, I'll get this typed up as an order of the day, but in the meantime, you should pass this along. Met with the Desert Fox himself, and he sends his 'personal respects' to you and your men for fighting 'courageously and well.' I concur."

"Thanks, General. I'll pass the word. And you can give him my 'personal respects' as well. Those were some tough Krauts."

Wakefield cracked a small smile at the remark. "I'll tell him. And Frank—"

"Yes, sir?"

"There's a hot meal on the way."

"That beats a compliment any old day, General. Ballard out."

Porter was scribbling rapidly in his reporter's notebook when Wakefield put down the walkie-talkie. When Wakefield looked up, he stopped writing. "What now, General?" he asked.

"I'm going to get that formal okay I promised the major, and see what else I can do."

"Do you really expect trouble?" Porter asked.

"I always expect trouble," growled Wakefield. "Only sometimes it doesn't happen."

29 DECEMBER 1944

THE WHITE HOUSE, WASHINGTON, DC, 1226 HOURS GMT

It was still early morning in Washington, DC, and the day was surprisingly bright for late December, the golden sunlight glinting along the reflecting pool that lay between the Lincoln Memorial and the Washington Monument. Hartnell Stone had chosen to walk the relatively short distance from his apartment in Foggy Bottom to the White House to get a little bit of that sun. Working a regular day, not to mention a long day, in the Washington winter could mean not getting a glimpse of sun for days on end. It had been nice to get out of the White House for a bit; sometimes several days would pass between visits to his apartment. He was freshly showered, freshly dressed, with two cups of coffee in his stomach and his third cigarette of the day in his mouth. The world was his.

It was cold, but not too cold. Stone wore a long navy wool coat over his gray suit. Although he held military rank as an Army major, his regular duties let him wear civilian dress for the most part. His fedora was tilted just slightly to keep the glare out of his eyes; his jet black hair underneath was slicked back in the best style. Freshly polished wing tips clicked along the pavement as he walked briskly along Constitution Avenue.

He turned left toward 17th Street beside the Ellipse. A line of government cars, mostly dull green Fords and Chevrolets with the occasional Studebaker for contrast, filled every available parking space—another reason for him to walk. Although he was a White House staffer, that wasn't enough to always rate a parking space in Washington, DC. The ability to park wherever and whenever you wanted won the mark of real power in the nation's capital.

He showed his pass to the Marine guards at the entrance to the Executive Office Building, a huge and ornate building in the French Second Empire style, with columns everywhere. Stone privately thought it was the ugliest building in Washington, especially when set next door to the classically elegant White House. He knew his way around the building, so once past the guards he made his way to the lower level and the passageway that connected to the White House itself.

The morning meeting was to be held in the Cabinet Room on the ground floor. Stone hung his coat and hat on a peg outside the room, quickly checked his hair in the mirror, straightened the knot in his tie just so, and opened the door.

He was neither the first nor the last to arrive at the meeting. The president was already there, of course, sitting in a cushioned chair with a blanket spread over his legs. His famous cigarette holder was in his mouth. "Good morning, Hartnell," FDR boomed in his cheerfully mellifluous voice. He still looked old and tired, but being surrounded by company brought him to life again. Those who had not seen him late at night, or at the end of a long working day, couldn't tell how sick the great man was.

"Good morning, Mr. President," replied Stone. He would be one of the lowest-ranking people at the meeting, it seemed clear. General George C. Marshall, army chief of staff, was already in the room, along with Cordell Hull, secretary of state. He nodded a good-morning to each; they acknowledged him only in passing. Henry Stimson, secretary of war, accompanied by an aide, was the next to enter. Several other Cabinet-rank officials and senior war advisers were also present, each with aides appropriate to their status.

"Good morning, Mr. President," Stimson intoned in a formal voice.

"Good morning, Henry," FDR replied. "Glad you could make it this morning. Gentlemen, it seems to have been an interesting few days. It looks as if we have an opportunity to cut short the war in Europe by a matter of months, if everything goes according to plan. You've all received a briefing by now, I'm sure?" Nods came from all the participants. "Good. Here is the question I've been pondering: Is it time for us to plan for a postwar German government?"

"Mr. President . . ." Marshall was the first one to comment.

"Yes, General?" Marshall was one of the only people that FDR, a habitual first-namer, always addressed by title.

"Even with the surrender of Rommel's army, the Germans have substantial strength, especially with all the forces that had been fighting in Russia. We don't yet occupy a single inch of the German homeland. While it's never too early to plan, of course, I wonder if a thorough discussion at this point might be somewhat premature."

"Thank you, General Marshall. Cordell, how about you? Premature, or worth discussing?"

Hull paused to think for a moment. "We do have the doctrine of unconditional surrender to deal with, although at least part of the heritage of that declaration was our supposed friendship with the Soviets. And, of course, there's the reality that the Berlin government hasn't attempted to open up any diplomatic channels recently. We were ready last summer in case Stauffenberg and his friends had been able to take over the government, but we all know how that turned out." Most of the figures in the Bomb Plot to assassinate Hitler were themselves dead following Heinrich Himmler's successful countercoup.

"So, if there happened to be a German government more amenable to negotiation, you might feel differently?" asked the president. He smiled in a slightly annoying way, one that signified he had an ace up his sleeve and was just about ready to play it. Roosevelt was well known for having his own mind made up and then asking others for their advice.

"Well, of course, Mr. President. But unless Bill Donovan has brought you evidence of a new Bomb Plot, there is only one German government around right now." "Wild Bill" Donovan was head of the Office of Strategic Services, the major American intelligence agency.

"No new bomb plot that I know about right now," injected Donovan, a large, muscular man who looked the part of the star college football player he'd been. "But who knows? We could always get lucky."

"Or," added FDR, "we could make our own."

"I beg your pardon?" asked Hull.

"We could make our own," repeated the president.

The president's idea was breathtaking in its simplicity. The Allies included several "governments in exile." Some, such as the French, Belgians, and Polish, were able to field a fighting unit or two, normally incorporated into the larger army groups commanded by the Americans or the British. Others simply maintained an office in London and worked toward the day their homelands would be finally liberated. Why not, proposed Roosevelt, use this opportunity to create a German "government in exile" with Rommel's forces as their military arm? It could simplify many elements of postwar German administration.

Hartnell Stone was quite impressed with Uncle Franklin. This was creative politics at its best. Some of the other attendees weren't so sure.

General Marshall spoke up: "Pardon me, Mr. President."

"Yes, General?" FDR's full attention focused on the army chief of staff.

"Sir, this assumes that Rommel has not merely surrendered, but has had such a total change of heart that he will be willing not only to serve the Allied cause, but actually to fight Germans in that cause. And not merely fight the Nazi leadership, but also fight against German soldiers on the field of battle. I can tell you, sir, that regardless of one's feelings for the leadership of one's country, this would be an extremely difficult undertaking for any honorable soldier, and Rommel is nothing if not an honorable soldier."

Wild Bill Donovan was the one who replied to that. "We have reason to believe that Rommel's change of heart is actually that strong. For one thing, his chief of staff, General Speidel, was deeply involved in the Stauffenberg group, and tells us that Rommel actually agreed last summer to accept the position of Chancellor of Germany in a military coup. It's a crying shame that one of our planes managed to shoot Rommel up just before the assassination—if we'd missed, he might have already taken over the German government."

"I'm sorry our airmen did such a good job," said Marshall with heavy irony.

"No, no, that's not what I mean. We didn't know it in time, and these things just happen. I'm just saying that Rommel was sick and tired of Hitler and felt it was time for him to go. In fact, Rommel was evidently opposed to the assassination—felt it was dishonorable, that a military takeover was more appropriate." He shook his head at the strange idea.

"Really?" interjected Hull. "He was ready to overthrow his own government?"

Donovan nodded. "That's what we're told. I mean, don't get me wrong, he's a German and a patriot and all. Frankly, I think his objection to Hitler was not so much that he was a tyrant than that he was losing. And one thing is perfectly clear to any German who thinks about it—if they are going to lose, they're a sight better off losing to us than to Stalin's gang. Because one thing I'm certain of is that the Russians are going to double-cross Himmler the way the Nazis double-crossed them."

Hull nodded. "Well, that's clear enough. I agree. I figured that the Soviet-German deal was a temporary convenience, and now it's in Stalin's interest to attack again. Rommel must see that as clearly as we do. So his real motive is to stave off a Soviet takeover of Germany. All right. That ought to be one of our motives, too. All we need is a government of Reds replacing the Nazis. We'd be back where we started. Maybe even worse."

"If we create our own German government and recognize it," the president said, "especially if it's got people in it that the Germans themselves recognize as legitimate, I think there's a decent chance that the German resistance will pretty much collapse and we can just waltz into Berlin and take it over. Once we've got it, the Soviets will have to stand down or go to war with us, and I'm pretty sure that Stalin doesn't have the stomach for *that* fight." Stone noticed that the president didn't mention "terrible weapons" or his certainty that Stalin would in fact back down.

Henry Stimson nodded. "You're right about that, Mr. President. Stalin is nothing but an opportunist. He did the separate peace because he got Norway and Greece out of it. I can just see Stalin and Himmler shaking hands, each with fingers crossed behind his back. Himmler bought himself a few extra months, and Rommel decided to give it the old college try one last time. When we stopped his Hail Mary pass, he figured the clock had run out and so he blew the whistle. Interesting man, this Rommel. I think we can probably trust him, because his interests lie with us."

"Exactly," interrupted Donovan again. He leaned forward, his excitement at the complex intrigue obvious. "I know he'll hate fighting his fellow Germans, but I'd bet my shirt that a lot of Germans will hate fighting him even more. Every division the Nazis throw at him will have about half of them desert to the other side. Basically, he'll parade across Germany and straight into Berlin with his army growing bigger every day, especially when it's clear who's going to be the winner."

"So, do we make Rommel the chancellor?" asked Hull.

"I imagine so," said Roosevelt. "But we need to surround him with the right people. Bill, you've pulled together a list of German dissidents and exiled politicians for me, right?"

"Yes, sir, Mr. President," replied Donovan.

"So, we pick out a cabinet for him and write his constitution for him. As soon as he declares the new government, they execute an unconditional surrender, and then we implement the plan," said Roosevelt with satisfaction.

"Yes, sir, Mr. President," came a chorus of the senior staff. Pens took rapid notes. This would take some time to implement.

"Of course, we'll need a new ambassador to the government," interjected the president. "And he'll need a staff."

"I'll have recommendations for you shortly," replied Cordell Hull.

"Thank you, gentlemen," said the President of the United States in dismissal.

KAMPFGRUPPE PEIPER, NEARING DINANT,
1231 HOURS GMT

High in the turret of his command tank, Obersturmbannführer Jochen Peiper scanned the area around him with his binoculars. The skies were still gray, which kept enemy aircraft, the hated jabos, away from his forces: nearly one hundred panzers, currently roaring along the snow-shrouded forest roads.

Once again, Kampfgruppe Peiper had the role of greatest glory to play, and the honor of Leibstandarte Adolf Hitler was preserved. While Sixth Panzer Army began its pullback to the Westwall, he would launch a surprise attack on Armeegruppe B headquarters. With luck, he would kill the traitor Erwin Rommel and rescue some of the units of Fifth Panzer Army from their ignominious surrender to the Allies.

The hilly and forested terrain limited the kampfgruppe to a narrow front, but if Peiper moved fast enough, he could gain the element of surprise. This area was a backwater of the earlier battle, known to be free of Americans or British. The German targets would sit, unsuspecting in their sublime treachery.

The air was damp and cold; it cut through his uniform coat and penetrated his bones. His lips were chapped and his face began to burn with the continual wind whipping at it. Still he did not go inside the turret. He needed his eyes and ears, wanted them unencumbered by the metal shell.

He heard shots, the rapid firing of a .50-caliber machine gun from one of the armored cars at the head of his column. Peiper strained to see through the binoculars in the gray light, to get a sense of what was going on. The machine gun uttered several short bursts, then silence. Moments later, a motorcycle approached, engine whining high-pitched over the rumbling tank. "Herr Obersturmbannführer!"

"What is it?"

"Our forward scout contacted a Wehrmacht picket, dispatched him with such speed it is virtually impossible that he got off a radio message."

"Virtually impossible, you say?" said Peiper with a hard edge in his voice. "I appreciate the speed of the action, but I don't wish to gamble any lives in support of that proposition."

The scout motorcyclist immediately responded, "Sorry, Herr Obersturmbannführer. In any event, the scout is terminated."

"German or Allied?"

"German, sir."

Peiper thought about this for a minute. Were the scouts in response to an actual perceived threat, or were they simply there as part of normal military discipline? Did they know of his planned attack, or did he still possess the element of surprise? There was no way to be sure, but a single scout was not sufficient evidence of an active defense.

"I want you to go to the scout car and get the *Soldbuch* for each soldier. Perform radio check-in using standard codes for Armeegruppe B. Those shouldn't have changed yet. Break off part of the antenna so you will have poor reception. If you get a question you can't answer, the static will mean you didn't hear it or they didn't hear your answer. If they get too suspicious, let me know. Otherwise, check in with them every half hour. Got it?"

"*Jawohl, Herr Obersturmbannführer,*" replied the motorcycle scout. He snapped off a salute, swung his motorcycle around, and headed off.

Peiper decided to continue the advance. He waved his arm and the long column started up again. A regular automobile could travel the thirty kilometers between Namur and Dinant in half an hour or so. Moving at full speed, the kampfgruppe took nearly three hours to come within a few kilometers. The river was on the right of the advance. On the other side of the river, cliffs began to rise. At this point, Peiper called a halt.

Calling together his senior commanders, he issued his orders. "We will attack toward the center of the city, along two axes. Task Force Potschke takes position on the waterfront," He pointed to a relatively unpopulated area a kilometer or so north of the main city, then continued. "With Seventh Panzer Company supported by Eleventh and Twelfth Panzergrenadiere, Potschke makes his way south along Chaussée D'Yvior to attack the American and German forces around this cathedral, Rommel's headquarters."

Sturmbannführer Werner Potschke nodded. *"Jawohl, Herr Obersturm-bannführer,"* he acknowledged.

"In the meantime, Hauptsturmführer Diefenthal will concentrate the artillery in support of our advance. I will take the panzer column into the city along the Rue Leopold." Task Force Peiper would consist of three companies of Panzer IV and Vs, along with three companies of motorized infantry; it would pack the kampfgruppe's hardest punch.

"When we break off combat, we will also move toward the east. The rest of the Leibstandarte is currently moving to occupy Saint-Vith and ensure that it does not fall into the hands of the traitors; this is critical to move all of Sixth Panzer Armies and whatever other units we can rescue back to the Westwall and the Fatherland.

"Good luck. In the tradition of Leibstandarte Adolf Hitler, we advance to defend the purity of the Fatherland." Peiper looked at his subordinates one after another. "Heil Himmler," he said, and all saluted.

Peiper climbed back onto his tank. "Let's go," he ordered.

ARMEEGRUPPE B HEADQUARTERS, DINANT, 1312 HOURS GMT

The first indication of trouble came in the form of a radio call to Patton from Lieutenant General Courtney Hodges, commander of the U.S. First Army, who had felt the brunt of Operation Fuchs am Rhein. The normally mild-mannered voice was trembling with rage.

"Georgie, I sent the Ninety-ninth Infantry to take the surrender of the Sixth Panzer Army yesterday, but they've been double-crossed. Those Nazi bastards have massacred my men. I'm treating this as a cease-fire violation and am passing back to the attack. Somebody who holds up a white flag and starts shooting again is a no-account bastard in my book. I don't know what you and your Nazi pal are up to, but I hope you've got some firepower, because your head sure as hell is in the lion's mouth."

"Goddamn!" snapped Patton. "Court, are you sure?"

"Goddamn right I'm sure. George, you better find out what the hell is going on and you better find out right now."

"Hell, Court, I'm sorry. Do what you have to do. I'll do the same here, and I'll call you as soon as I've got some real information."

"It better be real this time," growled the general on the other end of the line. "Hodges out."

Reid Sanger, standing behind Patton, listened carefully to the entire conversation—he could hear Hodges' roar quite clearly on the other end of the field telephone—before deciding whether to translate for the benefit of Rommel, who was standing right behind him. "Herr Generalfeldmarschall, it looks as if all your forces did not surrender, or that they did not stay surrendered."

"*Verdammt!*" replied the Desert Fox. "Who?"

"It seems that Sixth Panzer Army headquarters has ambushed American infantry in a massacre committed after the white flag was shown."

Rommel shook his head. "That can't be right. That's Guderian. Such an action would be impossible for any officer with honor."

"Then it must not be Guderian," suggested Sanger quietly.

The Desert Fox looked at him. His right eye seemed to penetrate into Sanger's innermost soul; the left seemed watery and weak. A scar from that eye moved upward along the edge of his cheek from his wounding the previous summer. Finally, Rommel nodded. "You are correct, I'm afraid. He's a prisoner, or he's dead."

"Sixth Panzer Army has more Waffen-SS divisions than the others in this operation, correct?"

Rommel nodded agreement. "I had just replaced Sepp Dietrich as their head. And Dietrich—"

"—founded the Leibstandarte Adolf Hitler," finished Sanger.

Patton turned around angrily. "What the hell are you jabbering about?" he demanded. "Speak English."

"Yes, sir," Sanger instantly responded. "We believe that Guderian has been involuntarily removed from the command of Sixth Panzer Army. Directly under him are multiple Waffen-SS divisions, including Leibstandarte Adolf Hitler."

"Jesus Christ!" growled Patton. "So it's a bunch of SS bastards—"

"That's a guess, sir, but probably," Sanger replied.

Patton looked directly at Rommel. "So, what now, Field Marshal?" he growled.

"I would imagine they would most likely withdraw to the Westwall and fortify the Rhine—I can't see Himmler issuing a 'stand and die' order in this situation." Rommel seemed to be thinking out loud, Sanger observed. A man after his own heart. "This means that all of Sixth Panzer Army, the reserves not yet committed, and the other forces supporting the Western Front are all available to refortify the Westwall and also to move to block that portion of the Westwall and access to the Rhine normally occupied and controlled by Fifth Panzer Army and Seventh Army," the Desert Fox continued.

The two generals began to work this new strategic problem, but Sanger interrupted.

"Pardon me, sirs," he interjected in between translations. "There is one additional possibility to consider." He said it in both languages, drawing the stares of both generals, who were unused to having subordinates interrupt with their own thoughts. He took advantage of the pause to continue. "An attack on Armeegruppe B headquarters, especially if it should kill the

Desert Fox as well as Old Blood and Guts—excuse me for putting it that way, sir . . ."

"Go ahead," growled Patton, who was looking at him with a somewhat jaundiced expression.

". . . would be a significant propaganda and morale achievement, especially at the hands of a division that already had a good deal of fame."

Rommel at first shook his head. "I'm not that important . . ." he began.

It was Patton who interrupted first. "Hell, Rommel, I'd have called it a propaganda and morale achievement myself—especially if you could kill Old Blood and Guts at the same time. . . ." He gave Sanger a hard look, softened by a slight twinkle in his eye. "Yes, I think the kid here has a point."

Sanger felt he deserved the "kid" reference after calling Patton by his famous nickname to his face. He felt himself blushing slightly under the attention of the two senior generals.

"Perhaps you're right," replied Rommel. "General Patton, I am a surrendered enemy officer, but the forces available are primarily under my command. A surrendered soldier cannot take aggressive action, but can defend himself under these circumstances, if you agree."

"Absolutely," said Patton. "Let's shake on it." He reached out his hand to grasp that of the Desert Fox. "Now let's make sure we have one hell of a surprise waiting for any son of a bitch that decides to take on the two best goddamn tank generals in the world!"

At that, even Rommel had to smile. "Very well, General Patton," he said. "It's time for us to earn our pay."

NORTHWEST EDGE OF DINANT, 1319 HOURS GMT

A small group of warehouses right at the city's edge afforded some cover. "We'll stop here," announced Hauptsturmführer Diefenthal. His two companies of mobile artillery began to set up, trucks pulling the wheeled guns into a wide lot screened by a brick wall and a line of evergreens. Diefenthal climbed to the roof of one of the warehouses to look around.

He could see through his binoculars the humpbacked shapes of several American tanks nestled at the outer base of the citadel wall. There was undoubtedly an enemy scout at the top of the onion-shaped bulge of the large church. Looking downward, he noted tanks near the shore. Engineers had nearly finished a pontoon bridge near the twisted wreckage of the destroyed span.

Farther ahead, along the main road, he could see concentrations of armor and half-tracks, mostly German. The bustle of activity indicated that enemy headquarters—it was still odd to think of Rommel in that way—was somewhere in that area.

Sliding back down the roof to the waiting ladder, he descended to his men and ordered the artillery to test the range.

CITY OF DINANT, 1320 HOURS GMT

"Panzers in the city, moving south! No white flags seen!" came the call from the church tower scout Frank Ballard had put in place.

"Yes, sir, General Wakefield," he said into his radio. "We've just seen them ourselves. No immediate hostile indications, but they aren't waving white flags, so we'll regard them as hostile. We're getting their range now and are ready to open fire."

"Hold on for another few minutes, Frank. Not quite till you see the whites of their eyes, but let's give them a chance to smarten up."

"Yes, sir," replied Ballard.

He hoped he looked less haggard than he felt. The last few days hadn't given him much chance for a good night's sleep, and it had been longer than that since he'd washed. He itched and he stank. The only good news was that it didn't bother the soldiers around him; they stank too.

Thrust into a larger command role, he had suddenly become responsible for the remnants of a large and battered force holed up in the ruins of a city. He had set up liaison with the elements of the Panzer Lehr division that had been his enemy only hours earlier, and worked with their commander to exchange prisoners, help the wounded, and ensure that the cease-fire didn't accidentally come unraveled.

Even after the surrender, there was still the need for caution, the worry that something would come unraveled. He and his men were completely outnumbered by the forces ostensibly their prisoners. These few short days felt like weeks to him, and now with the dim, clouded December sun past midday, it was looking like he was going to have to engage in combat with exhausted troops and damn little remaining ammunition.

He took a deep breath, consciously straightened up, and began issuing orders.

"I want you, you, and you to move down to the corner of Rue Saint-Pierre and Saint-Jacques." He pronounced the street names in American English with no attempt to mimic the French pronunciation. "The top of the church will provide fire direction, but nobody fires until my say-so. Infantry—dig in facing north to fire up the river, again on my order, then firing at will. If you're providing food or medical services, move to the south side of the church; I don't want anybody blocking us if we have to pull back. Anybody who's fit but can't get back into the line, you're ammo runners. We don't have much, but we'll use what we can get."

He paused and looked behind him, where the engineers were continuing work on the pontoon bridge. He picked up the telephone again. "General Wakefield?"

"Yes, Frank?"

"I'd like to get the Germans to cover the engineers if that's possible. I don't think it's a good idea to put them in the front lines."

"You're right. I'll get the okay from this end, but send a runner to your Panzer Lehr guys and tell them what's up."

"Got it. We're getting pretty good at sign language and drawing stick figures. Ballard out."

"Enemy at eight hundred meters and closing," came the call from the church tower.

TASK FORCE PEIPER, ENTERING DINANT, 1323 HOURS GMT

Peiper could see the church clearly in the city center, the citadel high above him. "Now!" he shouted, and the roar of all his guns firing at once echoed in the valley.

The attack was on. Waving his arm, the task-force commander urged his panzer forward, relished the fire and fury of the assault. There were panzers to both sides, adding their ordnance to the barrage, rolling over barrels, crushing sheds, smashing fences in this shoddy industrial neighborhood.

Peiper was elated as he went into battle. This time he would be fighting Germans, rather than Russians or Americans or British. But these Germans were traitors. And killing traitors was joy of the highest order.

The panzer lurched as it fired again. The high explosive shell exploded against the stone wall of a tall building, bringing down a cascade of debris. More plumes of smoke and flames were visible in the town ahead of him, as Diefenthal's guns joined in. The artillery battery rained shells upon the citadel and the church, both places that had been identified as possible headquarters for Rommel and his staff.

A machine gun opened up, tracers ripping toward the lead panzer. Two more tanks concentrated fire, machine guns and tank cannons joining to blast the outpost to smoky shards. Peiper's tank, a modern Panther, rolled over the pile of rubble, and he saw that the gunners were German—he sneered at these "prisoners," allowed to man a weapon by the Americans. If he had needed any further convincing of the worth of his cause, this was it.

Another gun opened up, a light antitank gun that cracked a shot off the armor of a Panzer IV. Peiper's own gunner had seen this target, and the colonel grinned fiercely as the turret purred around, the gun barrel parallel to the ground as it blasted out another deadly shell.

And still more of the city began to burn.

ARMEEGRUPPE B HEADQUARTERS, DINANT, 1323 HOURS GMT

The roar of cannon fire surprised Rommel as he exited the headquarters building. It was sooner than he had anticipated. Part of him was gratified—his Germans had organized, reacted, and moved well ahead of schedule. That was professionalism of the highest order, and he was proud to see them—at least, part of him was. It would be difficult, he realized, to separate his new position from the loyalties that had so far dominated his entire life.

But at the sound of the guns, his reflexes took over, and he was running into the street, his long greatcoat flapping behind him like a cape. There was the expected chaos as shells burst in the compound, but at the same time there was more order than he expected. Then he noticed the American division commander, Wakefield, sitting in the jeep parked in the compound, one hand clutching a cigar, the other his radio, seemingly heedless of the enemy fire landing all around him. Standing next to him was the reporter Porter, desperately trying to keep up a stream of translation and cringing every time a shell exploded nearby.

Rommel was impressed that Wakefield had been able to exercise command over German forces so easily. His original impression of the overweight and unkempt man had not been an inspiring one.

As Rommel approached, he heard Wakefield issuing orders, the German translations coming close behind from both Porter and Sanger. "Bob, have you got the range on the enemy artillery yet?"

"Working on it," came the crackling voice of the CCB commander. "We'll have counterbattery fire going in less than two minutes."

"Porter, I want a fire lit under those Germans. We need that pontoon bridge operational *now,* got it? That means more engineers on the job." Another shell exploded close to his jeep and the resultant spray of dirt showered everyone around, including all three generals.

"I'll take care of that, General Wakefield," interjected Rommel, shrugging the dirt off his shoulders. His wounded eye was giving him fits again, making him blink rapidly in the dust and dirt that filled the air around him.

The American general acknowledged the German field marshal. "Thank you, Field Marshal. We need to get some ammunition down to the river for my boys and some of your Panzer Lehr troops to repel this attack. My boy Bob Jackson is up in the citadel; he's directing counterbattery fire and spotting troops. You need to get your boys into their tanks and into the fight, and, if you'll pardon me, sir, you need to get yourself the hell off the field. I think they're gunning for you personally."

Rommel could figure out most of what the American general was saying even before the translation was finished, both because of his hand gestures and because of Rommel's own *fingerspitzengefühl,* or battlefield intuition.

"General, I've never commanded from the rear and never will. I'll get my troops moving, but I'm not planning to go anywhere."

"If that's your decision, sir," responded Wakefield, giving the distinct impression he thought it was the wrong choice. Then he turned his attention back to his own responsibilities. He put the cigar back in his mouth and picked up his radio to issue new orders.

CITY OF DINANT, 1331 HOURS GMT

"Frank? This is Bob," crackled the radio. In the chaos of the last day, the division had failed to announce a new code for wireless communications. The two colonels solved that problem by the simple expedient of first names.

"Go ahead. It's getting a little noisy here," replied Ballard, the acting CCA commander.

"Frank, I can't aim my tank guns downward enough to hit those damn panzers that are heading toward you. I can place some fire along their path as they move in, but once they're past Rue des Orlevres, they're invisible to me."

"Got it, Bob. How many are getting through?"

"I've counted about ten of the large panzers so far."

"Damn," replied Ballard. "I don't have that many more Shermans left."

"I'm sending you a company of CCB tanks. Throw them into the line wherever you need them," said Bob Jackson.

"How long before I get them?"

"Those damn streets are filled with curves. Probably fifteen minutes. How are you doing with the friendly Germans?"

"They're sending down some panzers, but we're all running low on ammo."

"Good luck. See you shortly," replied Jackson.

"CCA out."

Frank Ballard began to run forward from his CP to where his tanks and infantry were dug in, accompanied by his driver and orderly Sergeant Brown. As soon as the enemy had opened fire, his own armor roared back its response. His infantry were taking opportunity shots at German infantry on the advance.

Bullets winged by as he approached his own front line; a shell burst nearby. He put his head up cautiously over a pile of rubble and used his binoculars to scout out the situation. The intelligence assessment he'd gotten from Bob Jackson wasn't able to reveal just how much depth the Germans had in their attack force; he could see units only as they rounded the crest in range of his citadel post.

Defense being the stronger position, he could handle a large attack, especially as it could advance only on such a narrow front: Dinant at this point was only a few blocks wide before it began to climb the mountainous hillside leading away from the river. His big problem was ammunition and supply. He could hold out only so long. He'd tried to raid Panzer Lehr for supplies, but they didn't have much to spare, and their ammunition wouldn't fit his guns anyway.

Suddenly a shell burst in among his forces from a new direction—it was artillery coming from the waterfront, just a mile or so up the Meuse!

"What the hell was that?" he called on the radio.

"Enemy has set up an artillery position," reported Jackson calmly—after all, it wasn't his ass on the firing line. "They're firing at the pontoon bridge and at Rommel's HQ. Looks like a stray shell landed over in your position. We're getting their range now and we'll get 'em knocked out of action shortly."

Frank Ballard looked around at his tactical situation once more. The narrow battlefront meant that he, too, was limited in the number of tanks and guns he could position for defense. And because he couldn't yet tell how large the opposing force would turn out to be, he quickly decided that he had better start building secondary lines of defense so he could fall back if necessary. "Back to the church," he told Sergeant Brown. "We'll start moving tanks into position as a second line, and I also want you to receive CCB tanks and ammo."

"Yes, sir," acknowledged Brown. The two got up and prepared to run.

The ground shuddered underfoot, the effect of a huge explosion. A fireball bloomed from the narrow streets wending their way down from the citadel. "Goddamn!" groaned Ballard. "That's got to be the ammo truck. Shit!"

The force of the explosion triggered a rockslide on the cliff front. He watched with amazement as several Shermans were swept off the narrow streets and began to tumble side-over-side down the hill. More tank shells were coming inbound from the enemy attack, and seeing the damage done, the enemy artillery fire was now redirected right into his formation.

Ballard was standing, looking, figuring which way to go next, when suddenly a shell exploded near him, the blast knocking him to the ground. As he stood up shakily, he noticed a mass of blood and torn uniform scraps where moments before his sergeant had stood.

He retched as he saw a torn-off arm pouring its remaining blood into the shattered street; then he straightened himself and began moving back toward the church to direct reinforcements to his secondary line.

ARMEEGRUPPE B HEADQUARTERS, DINANT,
1334 HOURS GMT

Erwin Rommel was in his element as shells from the enemy bombardment landed in the headquarters compound. Blooms of huge explosions shot up showers of dirt and rock. The haze of battle smoke was already forming. The noise of shelling mixed with increasing numbers of panzer motors revving up made the ground shake; it was a noise that penetrated the body, became part of the new reality of his existence.

He could see his own troops running for cover, running for their panzers and half-tracks. He jumped up on the hood of a half-track so he could see more clearly, and began to direct traffic.

"You—get five panzers up here on the double! I want a defensive line established over here, behind these barrels. Infantry—move up past the pontoon construction area. Opportunity-fire at approaching enemy."

His eye fell on the major whose area of responsibility included headquarters support. "Why weren't scouts out?"

"They were, Herr Generalfeldmarschall," said the major, trying hard not to cringe under the bombardment. "We were in regular contact with them and had no reports of this force coming toward us."

Rommel glowered. This was not professional. "And why aren't our troops already in position like the Americans?"

"The American general asked, but as he did not have the authority—"

"What? How could you be so idiotic?" Here was a specific failure he could reprimand, and he laid into the major with relish. "Number one, we have surrendered. The American generals are now in your chain of command. Number two, being ready for this kind of trouble is your fundamental responsibility. Number three, we will not be caught in any way doing a less competent job than our American captors. Is that fully understood, Major?"

The hapless major quailed at Rommel's tongue-lashing, undoubtedly realizing that any additional protest or argument would be the end of his career. "I apologize, Herr Generalfeldmarschall. I will get things moving immediately."

Rommel's glower followed the major as he ran to do his duty. The Desert Fox hated stupidity and lack of imagination and vision above all else. He had been trying to beat those skills into his officers for years, with marginal success.

He looked up, saw the Americans occupying the citadel targeting the enemy and returning fire. Now, those, he thought, were professional troops. He was furious that any force under his command could be any less competent. This was an embarrassment he could not stand.

At last some panzers moved forward, though still far too slowly to suit him. He waved furiously, shouting, trying to move his force into position by sheer act of will. "Do you want the Americans to think you're soldiers, or just civilians in uniform?" he screamed. Finally, he was pleased to see his own troops firing back. The first of his panzer shells were blasting the advancing enemy. "Schnell machen!" he roared. "Move quickly!"

PONTOON BRIDGE, RIVER MEUSE, DINANT,
1341 HOURS GMT
Shells splattered into the river uncomfortably close to the bridge. Spumes of water shot up, drenching the engineers in frigid wetness. Two men had slipped

and fallen into the water; now one was shivering of hypothermia and the other was slowly slipping into shock. No one was available to remove him to an aid station.

Everyone on the bridge knew that one lucky hit would spell the end for them. They continued working quickly, laying long metal sheets over the strung-together floats.

A German officer in a flapping greatcoat appeared at the west end of the bridge. He waved his hands to direct a force of German engineers who began bridging from the west, moving toward the sections the Americans had completed.

One of the American engineers looked up. "You know who that is?" he said to the soldier working next to him.

"Naw. Who is he?"

"That's the goddamn Desert Fox himself! Field Marshal Rommel."

The soldier looked up with mild interest. "No shit?" he said with a complete lack of emotion, then returned to his work.

"I can't believe you."

"Yeah? Is he planning to do some work on this bridge? If not, who gives a fuck?"

The first engineer was about to answer when an artillery shell crashed down on their section. The explosion tore a huge hole in the bridge, and sent shards of shrapnel to rip smaller, but even more lethal, holes through his body.

TASK FORCE PEIPER, DINANT, 1344 HOURS GMT

Jochen Peiper was very satisfied with the progress of the battle, but realized that resistance was substantially heavier than he had initially thought as enemy shells began slamming into his advancing panzers. Diefenthal's battery had been smothered by fast and accurate counterbattery fire. He had no idea whether his mission to kill the Desert Fox had been successful, but he knew he had inflicted additional damage on the Americans and successfully delayed their ability to pursue. That looked to be the best he was likely to achieve, and it seemed a reasonable success. It was time to withdraw.

"Potschke, Diefenthal—all task forces begin withdrawal, passing to the west of the agreed-upon position." The acknowledgments came in from Potschke, who had farthest to go. But he reported progress along the road to Saint-Vith. There was no reply at all from Task Force Diefenthal, and Peiper assumed the worst. He would have to provide cover, to allow a successful withdrawal from the field.

A calculated risk had been taken and been achieved, he thought with pride. Kampfgruppe Peiper and the Leibstandarte Adolf Hitler continued to serve the führer and the Reich with distinction.

As Peiper gave the order to fall back, an enemy shell burst in front of his command tank. A shard from the shell tore across the left side of his face, shredding his cheek, removing his ear, and sending gouts of blood spurting into his eye. He screamed with pain and shock, and a member of his tank crew, a feldwebel, quickly pulled him down and began applying dressings to the wound. It looked horrific but not fatal.

"Hang on, mein Obersturmbannführer. You're all right. We'll get medical treatment shortly." The feldwebel turned to the driver. "Get us out of here, like the obersturmbannführer said."

Peiper was able to whisper one more command. "For the time being Potschke is in command. Radio him."

"Jawohl, mein Obersturmbannführer," said the feldwebel.

Peiper closed his one good eye and tried to conquer the pain.

OUTSIDE ARMEEGRUPPE B HEADQUARTERS, DINANT, 1351 HOURS GMT

"General, they're withdrawing," came Bob Jackson's voice over the walkie-talkie.

"Hell, they did most of what they came for," growled Wakefield in response. "But good riddance anyway. Kick them in the ass as they're going, will you?"

"You got it, General. CCB continues to fire on retreating forces. Jackson out."

The fire into the headquarters compound was diminishing but had not yet stopped. It became more scattered and more random as it came from moving enemy units firing backward to cover their retreat.

Wakefield looked around. The road down from the citadel was demolished, the pontoon bridge had buckled near the far shore, and parts of Armeegruppe B headquarters had been shelled into rubble. The German equivalent of "Medic!" could be heard from wounded soldiers in the compound. Infantry moved forward, and the panzers were finally turning into a fighting force. But Rommel and Patton were alive, his forces were slapped around a bit but largely intact, and it looked as if they were going to be able to put together a pursuit. "I guess that about does it for right now," he said.

Patton, who had been watching Wakefield run the battle, interjected. "Henry, when did you first figure out what was going to happen?"

"I didn't, General. I figured I was paid to think about trouble before it found me, and so I moved some stuff around just in case."

"Well, hell, Henry—you've only done one thing wrong that I can see," growled Patton.

"What's that?" asked Wakefield, his eyes narrowing slightly. He and Patton went way back before the war, and their relationship had been characterized mostly by a series of fights. Patton's enmity had kept Wakefield in a training command and out of the real war until after D-Day.

Patton grinned. "You didn't leave me anything to do. I feel like tits on a bull right now."

Wakefield grinned back. That was okay. "The rest of Third Army should keep you busy enough."

"All right. I think I'll get back to the office and start moving some tanks around. And Henry, this is the damnedest order I've ever given, but I'm going to attach you to Rommel for a while. Technically he's still surrendered, but it looks like he's going to do some fighting on our side. I'll straighten everything out with Ike . . . as soon as I can get in touch with him." He smiled at that, and Wakefield knew that he intended to delay telling Eisenhower as long as possible.

"You need anything from me, you holler. Got it?"

"Got it, General."

"Hell, call me George. See you later, Henry. Good hunting." He turned to leave.

"Hey, George," Wakefield called. Patton turned around.

Wakefield held out one of his stogies, "Have a cigar."

Patton took the cigar and sniffed it. "Jeezus, Henry, what the hell do you pay for these things? Fifty cents a dozen?"

Wakefield snorted. "Hell, no. Too rich for my blood." He let out a cloud of blue smoke.

Patton laughed and lit the cigar. "I oughta put you on report for trying to assassinate a superior officer, Henry." He punched Wakefield on the arm, got into his jeep with the three-star flag, and waved at his sergeant to move out.

Chuck Porter, who had discreetly moved back but stayed within eaves-dropping distance, thought about writing the exchange down, but realized he'd never get anybody to believe it.

Patton waved for his driver, and his jeep with the three stars began to move out.

ARMEEGRUPPE B FIELD HOSPITAL, NEAR DINANT, 1623 HOURS GMT

"Make way! Make way! Wounded man coming through!" The panzer crew carried the officer into the makeshift field hospital. Quickly, hospital orderlies provided a stretcher onto which the wounded man was placed, and he was wheeled into the triage area. Because the fighting had died down, there were few other injuries waiting for medical attention.

"And what do we have here," said the doctor in charge, who appeared at the stretcher side almost at once. He wore Wehrmacht major insignia along-side his caduceus. "Hmm." Carefully, he peeled away the bandages to look at the raw and seeping flesh beneath. "Painful, but not life-threatening. Looks like the shell fragment missed the eye, but bleeding and surrounding damage to the muscle are not so good. We should be able to restore sight, however. For the rest—I'm sorry to inform you, Herr Obersturmbannführer, that our field hospital is virtually out of anesthetics. Only the most serious cases get any at all, and those not enough. We have had to revert to more barbaric practices here. I apologize to you in advance. This is likely to be rather painful."

He turned to the panzer crewmen. "I am Major Doktor Hans Schlüter. I will be working on your officer personally. This will not be an easy experience. He must be strapped to the operating table, because otherwise he will jerk free and harm himself. I will have a nurse clean the wound area, and then I will suture the damage. You have all seen blood before, no doubt."

The soldiers nodded their agreement. "We have all been on the Russian front."

"Then you have seen such things before. You may find the atmosphere of an operating room somewhat different. I will not have fainting or vomiting. If you cannot refrain from these behaviors, you are to leave at once and get me a replacement. Do you understand?"

"*Jawohl, Herr Major Doktor,*" the soldiers said in unison.

"Very well. We will begin shortly."

The shrieks of human agony echoed down the hospital corridors and into the wards. Feldwebel Carl-Heinz Clausen looked up. "It looks as though someone else is enjoying the finest medical care available," he said mildly.

The soldiers around him laughed meaningfully. Most of them had enjoyed the same experience within the last few days. The fact that they were here in the open ward meant they had come through the operation in good shape, or that they had not been severely wounded.

Carl-Heinz looked at the long, skinny man in the next bed. He had a leg wound and had evidently also taken a piece of flak between his eyes. He'd worn an American jacket when he was brought in, but now he wore only a hospital robe, like the other patients. Most of the American wounded had been transferred to American field hospitals earlier in the day; because this patient was a downed aviator, he'd simply been overlooked, because he was no one's direct responsibility. Probably the Americans would come for him in the morning. Another night made little difference, especially now with the war nearly over.

"American—yes, you. How are you doing?" he asked.

The American pointed to himself. "Staff Sergeant Franklin O'Dell, Three Hundred and Ninety-second Bomb Group. Serial number T-zero-zero-one-nine-two-one-six-five."

Clausen knew he was receiving the obligatory "name, rank, serial number." He knew that "sergeant" meant *Feldwebel*. He pointed to himself. *"Feldwebel— 'Saarjint.' Carl-Heinz Clausen. Verstehen Sie?"*

The American replied, "Carl-Heinz," and pointed at the German. Then "Digger. American. Feldwaybul," and pointed back at himself.

"Dig-ger," replied Clausen. *"Sehr gut. Willkommen in Deutschland."*

The American thought about it for a second, then replied, "Danke shone." His accent was terrible, but at least he was trying.

Another scream. The wounded in the ward took up other activities or started loud conversations to drown out the noise. It was about all they could do. Anything beat sitting still and listening to the sounds of agony.

Clausen kept up his conversation with the American aviator, in part to keep himself distracted, in part because he was genuinely curious. This was the first American he'd actually met in person. And even though he was a *terrorflieger*, he seemed like a nice enough fellow.

Finally the screaming ceased. The poor bastard in the operating room was done. Slowly the room returned to normal. Conversations that had been started only to drown out the sound ceased.

But suddenly there was a new type of noise: the noise of marching boots.

"Danke schön, Herr Major Doktor," Obersturmbannführer Peiper said. His face was now stitched together, and although the agony was still intense, nothing would ever equal the sensation of being held still while a needle and thread was stuck through the skin of his face over and over again. With fresh hospital bandages covering the wounds, he could only imagine what his ruined face now looked like. Peiper had been a handsome man, but would be considered handsome no more.

"Bitte schön, Herr Obersturmbannführer," replied Schlüter. "I recommend you rest here a day or two, but technically, you're all right. Have your bandages changed regularly and keep clean. Within a few weeks those stitches will be able to come out. I'm pretty sure I saved your eye, though you may have some difficulties with it. Too early to tell."

"I would take you up on your kind hospitality," said Peiper, "but as this field hospital is about to move, I don't think there will be much rest for anyone."

"Move? I've heard nothing about a move. In fact, with Armeegruppe B's surrender, I can't see us doing anything other than remaining here."

At the word "surrender," Peiper's eyes narrowed. "There has not been a surrender. I spoke to the führer personally early this morning. It is true that some traitors have ceased their struggle for the Third Reich, but I am under direct orders of the führer to bring all units of Armeegruppe B back to the safety of the Westwall and the Fatherland. Please prepare your hospital for immediate movement. You will be escorted east by Kampfgruppe Peiper of the Leibstandarte Adolf Hitler."

The doctor was obviously shocked, and equally obviously had embraced Rommel's surrender. "But Obersturmbannführer—that's impossible! We are a simple medical facility and we have wounded, both German and American." Peiper's cold glare shut him up.

"Americans? You will point out all American patients to me. The Third Reich does not have any medical supplies to spare. Horst!" he called to one of his soldiers. "Take one of the nurses to each ward. If there are any American patients, kill them. All patients who are able to move will get ready to move. Those who can be transported will be moved onto trucks and ambulances. We will leave only those who would die if moved. And Doctor—" His glare was piercing. "—I expect your best medical judgment in these matters."

Peiper was pleased that Dr. Schlüter was too cowed to do anything but stammer his obedience. That was as it should be. More of Peiper's troops moved into the building and began ordering medical staff around.

The tramping footsteps of soldiers was not lost on Clausen, and when shots rang out in another ward, his suspicions were confirmed. The ward's male nurse entered with an armed Waffen-SS Sturmmann. "Are there any American patients here?"

The nurse looked around. "N-No, no, Sturmmann," he stuttered, pointedly not looking at Digger.

"You will ready yourselves for immediate departure," ordered the sturmmann in a harsh voice. "If you can walk, get dressed. The rest of you will be transported. Any shirkers will be disciplined."

All hope ripped away, the patients sullenly began to slide out of bed if they were able. Digger looked questioningly at Clausen. The feldwebel put a finger to his lips and pointed meaningfully at the door where the SS soldier had gone. Digger nodded his head as if he understood. Clausen hoped he was getting the message across. His own clothes were under the bed. When he moved, the agony in his stomach made him stop. He could not walk. He pulled his jacket out and wrapped it around his shoulders, then threw his uniform shirt over to Digger and motioned that he should put it on.

Within about twenty minutes, he, Digger, and other non-ambulatory patients were being loaded onto a truck, one of many vehicles waiting with idling engines outside the hospital. When the truck was full, a Waffen-SS trooper banged hard on its side twice, the signal to pull away into the dark, cold night.

The unwilling passengers huddled in miserable silence, knowing only that they were being carried toward the Westwall, Germany, and the east.

EXCERPT FROM *WAR'S FINAL FURY*, BY PROFESSOR JARED
GRUENWALD (ZURICH: UNIVERSITY OF ZURICH PRESS, 1955)

[NOTE: War's Final Fury *is well known to scholars as the definitive
analysis of the final chapters of the Second World War following the assassi-
nation of Adolph Hitler. Dr. Jared Gruenwald is Distinguished Professor of
History at the University of Zurich, Switzerland. His other books include*
Rommel: A Study in Leadership and Transformation, Himmler's Reich, *and*
Stalin's Time. *We are grateful to Professor Gruenwald and the University of
Zurich Press for permission to reprint these excerpts concerning the overall
strategic situation in Europe during this critical time. The Authors.]*

The days following Rommel's dramatic surrender of Army Group B
to the Americans set the stage for following events. While the final defeat
of Nazism was certain, there was a question as to who would deliver the
coup de grâce: the Western Allies or the Soviet Union. Stalin's essential
perfidy in accepting a separate peace with Germany is well understood,
and certainly his motives were no more dishonest than those of the Nazis
in turn. Stalin had to stop his advances until January 1945 in any event
because of supply difficulties, and the "separate peace" gave him control
of two additional nations, Norway and Greece.

Himmler's government, on the other hand, bought one last chance to
defeat the West and recover in time to make it a one-front war against the
Soviet Union. The failure of Operation Fuchs am Rhein meant the chance
had been squandered, and that in turn would mean a renewed Soviet
offensive beginning soon.

The German-Soviet armistice was, as we have shown, an exercise in
mutual cynicism on the part of both parties. In one famous observation,
Führer Heinrich Himmler compared the pact to throwing babies off the
back of the sled to distract the pursuing wolves. The babies were, of
course, the countries of Norway and Greece. Neither morsel was large
enough to slow down the Soviet wolf for very long, but Himmler's hope
was that it would be long enough.

Poland, that oft-contested plain, was labeled as a neutral zone in the
armistice treaty, a mostly demilitarized buffer between the two great powers. The Nazis were able to keep control of the western part of the country, including the majority of the operating death camps; the machinery of
the Holocaust required slight adjustment to cope with the change. The
Balkan countries, meanwhile, had been subjected to heavy Soviet political
pressure. By the end of 1944, Bulgaria and Rumania were prepared to
change sides. The Gestapo had wind of these developments, however, so
the Wehrmacht had been quietly evacuating their garrison units, as well

as the significant counterinsurgency forces they had maintained in Yugoslavia. These troops were deployed to the north, in Hungary, Poland, and East Prussia; they would form the first line of defense when hostilities were rejoined.

For Germany then, this Army Group Vistula fortified the area between the Oder and the Vistula, though was hampered by the demilitarized zone. Behind this formation, Army Group Center had been recreated from the ashes of the previous summer. These troops had spent the last four months of 1944 creating defensive positions behind the Oder River.

This left only a few Volksgrenadier divisions available as reinforcements in the West. Their mobility was severely hampered by the overwhelming Allied air superiority. Field Marshal Erwin Rommel had often observed that commanders whose experience was primarily in the East had no conception of the meaning of such air superiority. Unless the weather was too bad for the Allies to fly (which created operational problems in its own right), troops were able to move only under cover of darkness, with significant logistical difficulties involved in concealing vehicles and supplies before daylight. German rail was mostly wrecked and unusable; those bridges that remained had been wired by the Germans themselves for demolition ahead of advancing Allied troops. It was for this reason that the Germans were not able to mass even a greater army in support of Operation Fuchs am Rhein. The forces were there, but the mobility was not.

In the bitter days of December and early January of 1944–1945, weather allowed the German forces greater mobility of operation, and a large force was available inside Germany itself. If those troops could be deployed along the difficult barrier of the Rhine River, they could make the allied crossing a dangerous and costly operation. But whose orders would these soldiers obey?

There were two competing German commands. One was Field Marshal Rommel's Army Group B, renamed the German Republican Army on January 1. It claimed not only Rommel's original command, but all German forces in the West. As a practical matter, it claimed only volunteers. The second command was the newly appointed Field Marshal Mödel's Heeresgruppe West. It consisted of all German forces in the West, primarily the original Operation Fuchs am Rhein reserves as well as Westwall defensive units. Each of the two commands had all the codes, passwords, and command protocols for all German units in the West. Each issued orders to all units it could reach, not merely those that had acceded to its authority, with the result that commanders of individual companies were receiving conflicting orders on a daily basis. Choosing one's loyalties had to be done immediately—no one was able to remain neutral.

While the majority of Fifth Panzer Army and Seventh Army followed Rommel first into surrender and second into the newly created German Republican Army, the majority of Sixth Panzer Army (which was shortly thereafter renamed Sixth SS Panzer Army) remained under control of the Nazi government in Berlin. General Sepp Dietrich, whom Rommel had earlier replaced as head of Sixth Panzer Army with General Heinz Guderian, returned to his previous command and oversaw the extraction of Sixth Panzers.

The initial plan was to return to positions in the Westwall and defend, but the loss of two armies had torn such a hole in that line of fortifications that it became quickly clear that the barrier could no longer be held successfully. That meant the next defensive line was the Rhine itself. Field Marshal Mödel took command of two army groups that were stationed in western Germany, both for defensive purposes and for potential exploitation had Operation Fuchs am Rhein been successful. These were Army Groups G (Upper Rhine) and H (Ruhr). As both were understrength (like most German commands at that stage of the war), Mödel simply planned to incorporate all salvaged parts of Army Group B into one of the two remaining army groups. From there, he planned to fortify the Rhine against the imminent Allied advance. This was made difficult because the same cause that had torn such a large hole in the Westwall also meant that a portion of the Rhine defenses was now nonexistent, and renewed Allied strategic bombing made it daily more difficult to move troops and guns into position.

Of the Army Group B forces, reserves and slow-moving troops, ironically, were the easiest to recover, because they were already far behind the front at the time of the surrender and had the shortest distances to go in their withdrawal. The elite panzer forces at the leading edge of the Fuchs offensive were either trapped and cut off by the surrender or forced to fight their way through increasingly hostile and uncertain territory in which even other German units had to be considered suspect. In fact, German vs. German battles were some of the most savage and bloody of those terrible winter days, as neither side had any intention of taking prisoners.

Western Allied troops, especially Third Army units situated along the flanks of the surrendered Fifth Panzer Army and Seventh Army areas, suddenly had their opposition vanish, and were able to move ahead with astounding speed, rushing through what had been enemy-held areas with the cooperation of the enemy themselves! (A few regrettable incidents on both sides were only to be expected, but by and large, the surrendered Germans seemed relieved and even proud in their new role supporting the newly created German provisional government.)

Because of this, it began to seem as though even the Rhine itself was no longer secure as a line of defense. . . .

OPERATION
CAN OPENER
30 DECEMBER 1944 –
20 JANUARY 1945

There is one great thing that you men will all be able to say after this war is over and you are home once again. You may be thankful that twenty years from now, when you are sitting by the fireplace with your grandson on your knee, and he asks you what you did in the great World War II, you won't have to cough, shift him to the other knee and say, "Well, your granddaddy shoveled shit in Louisiana." No, sir! You can look him straight in the eye and say, "Son, your granddaddy rode with the great Third Army and a son-of-a-goddamned-bitch named Georgie Patton!"
                    —George Patton's speech to the Third Army, 5 June 1944

30 DECEMBER 1944

NORTH OF BASTOGNE, BELGIUM, 0130 HOURS GMT

The name Volksgrenadier was a poor joke, one that was not lost on the men of the 218th Volksgrenadier Division. Although grenadiers were historically elite soldiers, modern Volksgrenadier units were a mix of boys, ancients, walking wounded, and those previously unfit for military service.

"I say we thank God Almighty for this surrender and consider ourselves the luckiest men alive. We're alive, and that makes us lucky. Why screw it up?" Obergefreiter Felix Durr, corporal of his platoon, was old enough to wear his cynicism proudly. His previous experience had been in World War I, and he had thought himself too old for any sort of service in the new war. But he'd turned out to be wrong.

The soldiers around him listened avidly. One of the few in their unit to have seen actual military service, he was the unofficial man to whom everyone turned, including the twenty-two-year-old feldwebel who officially was in charge.

Lukas Vogel was only fifteen, but he disagreed violently. "Defeatism is evil! We owe our lives to the Party and the Fatherland. Our führer has ordered us to go on fighting, and we must obey!

"Ah, so young to be so certain," the obergefreiter said in a patronizing tone that put Vogel's teeth on edge. Vogel was a newly promoted oberschütze, or PFC.

"Nah, that's the KLV talking," laughed another soldier. All German youth had been shipped to KLV camps wherever there was little bombing going on. With a shortage of adults to supervise, the camps quickly turned into a hierarchy of children preying on children. What official activities there were involved Nazi indoctrination and military training. Vogel had been in a KLV camp since 1941. He could scarcely remember living at home, or visualize his mother's face if he tried.

He jumped to his feet, fists clenched. "Piss on you, Manfred. I bet you never amounted to shit in Hitler Youth." He was thin and wiry, with a shock of blond hair falling across his forehead into his eyes. His eyes were hard.

Manfred Bauer was on his feet as well. Bauer was nearly twice the size of the small, wiry youth. "Yeah, tough guy? What were you, some big-shit stabsführer?"

Vogel had only made it as high as bannführer, but that was good for his age. Damned if he was going to admit it, though. "I ranked a lot higher than you did, I bet. And I'm the same rank as you in the army even though you're a lot older. I guess they didn't draft you earlier because they don't take pansies, right?"

"You goddamn little shit!" roared Bauer as he came for the young boy, his fists raised and ready for action.

But Vogel had been dealing with bullies for years. At KLV camp, if you didn't learn to take care of yourself, you were in deep shit. He had his knife out so quickly that none of the other soldiers spotted him, and as Bauer closed, Vogel slashed him across the face.

Bauer screamed and his hands flew up to his nose, and Vogel kicked him in the balls with all his might. The huge soldier folded up and lay groaning on the ground. "My face, my face, that little bastard cut my face," he moaned. "I'll kill him!"

Vogel wiped his knife on his pants leg. "It's just a little cheek cut. If I'd wanted to do damage, you'd be missing an eye now." He turned around quickly. "Anybody else want to try me?" He made no directly threatening move, but his cold eyes fastened on each soldier in the tent. "No? Smart of you."

Obergefreiter Durr felt that as senior enlisted man in the tent, it was his duty to negotiate peace. "Now, now," he said in his most soothing voice. "Vogel, put your knife away. Bauer, you started it. Let me look at your face. Hmm. Just a long scratch. You could go see the medic, or you could just wash up and put some gauze over it. Tomorrow, you'll barely know you have a cut. Let's everybody calm down. Remember, the war is over for us. Let's try to get along like civilized Germans."

"The war is *not* over and I will *not* stand here and listen to some old fart without the backbone to stand up for the führer and the Reich. I tell you that we can take over this unit from any cowardly officers who don't have the stomach for a fight anymore and get back in the war. Who's with me?"

There was silence. A few soldiers were actively uninterested, and a few looked away with sheepish expressions. Even considering his youth, Vogel's fanaticism and passion made him a force to reckon with. "So." He looked at his fellow Volksgrenadiers with disgust. "No one. Not a single real German. Very well. Then I will tell each one of you: This war is not over. It will not be over while I have a single breath to draw. It will not be over until every true German is dead. And we will prevail."

"Vogel, wait a minute," Durr interjected. "Calm down. Wait until morning. Ask around camp. Decide what you're going to do."

"There is no decision to make. I am a German soldier, and I am going to fight. Good-bye." Vogel turned to leave.

"Wait—that's desertion! You can be shot!" pleaded Durr, "Come on,

Lukas—I've got grandchildren your age. Listen to me. Calm down. Wait. You'll see things differently. You're young. You have a life to lead, children to sire." His persuasion fell on deaf ears.

"It's not desertion to leave a nest of traitors, and make no mistake, this surrender is treason. I'm going. Your grandchildren will stand with me, Herr Obergefreiter. You're old, and perhaps yon don't have what it takes anymore. But I do. Good-bye."

And this time he did leave, grabbing his coat and his duffel and slipping out of the tent into darkness. There was silence in the tent, except for the groaning of the man on the floor.

RED SQUARE, MOSCOW, USSR, 0352 HOURS GMT

The air was cold enough to freeze the tiny hairs in Krigoff's nostrils with each harsh, dry inhalation. He loved the challenge and discomfort inherent in this wintry bite, for it was proof of the primacy of his people, the anointed leaders of World Communism. How foolish the foe who felt that he could defeat not just Mother Russia, but Father Winter as well!

It was fitting that the major had been invited to meet Nikolai Bulganin here, outside, under the pure, cold sky that had been such anathema to his country's enemies. The invitation had been waiting for him when he had returned to his barracks the previous night, following his meeting with Stalin. Krigoff had been impressed—and a little frightened—at how quickly the Soviet bureaucracy seemed to be noting his presence, and giving him attention. Bulganin was a powerful man in his own right, and it was no doubt significant that he had ordered Alyosha to meet him here in the chilly pre-dawn hour, away from the eyes and the ears of the Kremlin's staff.

Krigoff stopped at the low stone wall above the river and looked out at the River Moskva, now a ribbon of ice that curled its way through this great city. A great statue of Chairman Stalin, the landmark for this meeting, towered behind him. He was early, he knew, but that was only appropriate as he awaited yet another great man in the Soviet hierarchy.

There were few people about, and, like Krigoff, they were muffled into anonymous shapes of fur and wool against the cold. The major relished a few minutes of silence and solitude as he breathed the frigid early-morning air— the day at its very coldest!—and wondered about the purpose of this newest summons.

Political Marshal Bulganin was one of the most powerful men in the country, a member of an elite handful ranking just below the chairman himself. An esteemed member of the state defense committee, Bulganin had been established by reputation as one of the few political appointees with the power to keep even the highest-ranking military officers under observation, and control. His agents were seeded throughout the Red Army, charged with supervising even the army commanders in the state's relentless search for any act of sedition or disloyalty.

"Comrade Colonel Krigoff?"

The question startled him and he spun about to salute the marshal, who strode around the statue to soundlessly approach Alyosha from the rear.

"Comrade Marshal! It is an honor—though I beg to explain that I am but a humble major."

The political officer, a short man with dark hair and thick glasses, chuckled at a private joke. He wore a heavy woolen overcoat, but that did not conceal the wiry, athletic nature of his compact frame. "I must remind you not to correct your superiors, Alexis Petrovich, on matters about which you lack the necessary knowledge. I have your promotion orders in my pocket."

Krigoff was very startled by the news—he had been a mere lieutenant only three days ago—but he recovered quickly. He bowed with sincere respect and gratitude. "Thank you, Comrade Marshal. I will strive to prove myself worthy of this great honor."

"I assume you will. More to the point, the chairman believes that you will do so; this promotion is a direct order from him. I trust that you will not disappoint him."

Again Krigoff felt those butterflies, the mingled senses of danger and opportunity. Of course, no man in his right mind would want to disappoint Josef Stalin, but in this case the opportunity side of the equation seemed to beckon with clear advantage.

"Your trust is not misplaced, Comrade Marshal," he replied. He was desperately curious to know why they were here—a political marshal did not take strolls in frigid winter mornings merely to dispense promotions to young officers—but he forced himself to bide his time while Bulganin lit a cigarette and drew deeply, exhaling a cloud of aromatic smoke.

"Smells good, eh?" said the older man, looking sideways at Krigoff. "American 'Camels.' Lend Lease was a wonderful thing, while it lasted."

Krigoff smiled narrowly, longing for a cigarette himself. "The capitalists are useful for making such luxuries," he allowed. "Though it is Soviet tanks, and Soviet blood, that will win this war."

Now it was the marshal's turn to smile. "Comrade Stalin told me that you were an astute officer, and I see that his judgment—as always, of course—is correct. You know, then, that we will be attacking the Nazi devils once more?"

"It is a guess, Comrade," Krigoff allowed. He decided to be daring. "I can only hope that I will have a role to play in this great campaign."

"You will, Comrade Krigoff, you will," said Bulganin. He scrutinized the young colonel, making Krigoff very nervous as the inspection dragged on for the better part of a minute. There was only the puffy fog of their breathing, vapors wafting through the night air between them, as he waited for the marshal to speak.

"We have decided to send you to the front, in the role of political commissar. You will be assigned to the Second Guards Tank Army, one of Konev's units. The chairman and I would like you to observe the activities of the army commander, one General . . . ?" Bulganin's voice trailed off, as if he was searching his memory for a name, though Krigoff instantly recognized the test for what it was.

"General Petrovsky, I believe, is in command of that army, Comrade Marshal," he said quickly.

"Indeed, Petrovsky," Bulganin acknowledged quietly. "An effective, veteran commander. His division was triumphant at Moscow and Stalingrad. He led a corps against the Nazis at Kursk, and his army contributed much to the annihilation of Army Group Center last summer."

"A great victory," Krigoff noted sincerely.

"One of the greatest in all the history of war," Bulganin declared, as if correcting the younger man's lack of hyperbole.

Alyosha flushed in embarrassment. "Of course, Comrade Marshal. We broke the back of the Nazi war machine—now it is a matter merely to dispose of the broken corpse."

"I hope you still think so, Comrade, after you have observed our crossing of the Vistula. We have reports of a half-million Nazis standing against us, and they have been fortifying their position since the end of summer. I daresay, the Wehrmacht and the SS are more than a broken corpse."

Krigoff clenched his teeth. He did not want to wage a no-win war of words with his new superior, so he simply nodded and waited for Bulganin to continue.

"Your orders will be delivered within a day. I assume you can be packed and ready to leave for the West quickly?"

"I would go at this minute, if so ordered, Comrade Marshal."

"You will have your opportunity soon enough, Comrade Krigoff. For now, I bring a personal message from the chairman: He would like to see you again, today. He expects you before noon."

Krigoff was thrilled. "I shall go to the Kremlin at once, Comrade Marshal!" he declared, snapping off a salute.

"Good." Bulganin seemed pleased by the direction the conversation was going, and the freshly minted colonel allowed his own delight to grow, though he tried his best to keep his expression serious as his new superior continued. "My expectation is that you will be sent westward very soon; things are beginning to move, now. I advise you to take a day, make your farewells in Moscow. Your orders will include a train ticket, and instructions on when to report to Kiev Station."

"Thank you, Comrade Marshal. I am ready!"

Bulganin scrutinized him again, and Krigoff felt like a bug under a microscope. "Our chairman has taken a special interest in you, Comrade Krigoff. That can be good for you, and good for the commissar service. Do you understand?"

Krigoff understood that if he did *not* make it good, then these developments would prove to be very, very bad, at least for him, personally. He enthusiastically proclaimed his understanding, and his gratitude.

A moment later, he watched Bulganin walk off into the night, which remained bitter cold. How odd, Krigoff thought, that he himself was sweating profusely.

NINETEENTH ARMORED DIVISION FORWARD
HEADQUARTERS, DINANT, BELGIUM, 0227 HOURS GMT

"General? General Wakefield?"

"Harrr?" came a querulous growl in return.

"General Wakefield, wake up, please sir."

"This had goddamn better be important, son," Wakefield muttered, still mostly asleep.

"The Nazis who attacked last night have taken a field hospital prisoner and massacred all American patients there."

Eyes opened. "Oh, it's you, Sanger. All the bad news in one lump, eh? Like to give an old man a heart attack before you give him a cup of goddamned coffee, do you? What time is it?"

"About oh-two-thirty, sir," replied Lieutenant Colonel Reid Sanger.

"All right, I'm up, I'm up." Wakefield did not move. "Hospital gone, American POWs killed. Right?"

"Yes, sir."

"Sanger, I want you to know I'm as goddamn sympathetic as any man in this fucking army."

"Yes, sir?"

"I've just got one question. What in the Sam Hill do you expect me to do about it?"

"General, I've coordinated with Panzer Lehr's recce battalion commander and we've assembled a fast task force to scout out Kampfgruppe Peiper. I've talked to Captain Smiggs and arranged to take him and half his jeeps and add them to the Panzer Lehr recce group. The Germans will supply a captain in command of their forces but they'll listen to us. If the opportunity presents itself, we'll snip off the trailing edge where the hospital staff and patients are most likely to be. If not, we'll have them spotted and maybe be able to call in airstrikes, or if we get up into First Army's area of operations, maybe they can run an attack. And if none of these options pan out, we'll at least know where they are and we can pay the bastards back some other time."

Wakefield paused so long that Sanger wondered if he'd gone back to sleep. "So whaddya need me for?"

"I figured if I ran off with the Germans and half of CCA's recce company without telling you about it first, it'd look like hell on my efficiency report."

Wakefield snorted. "Fine. You want permission? You got it. Now let an old man get back to sleep."

"Yes, sir." Sanger turned to leave.

"One more thing," came the general's growl.

"Yes, sir?"

"Good hunting."

"Thank you, sir."

Hitting a hidden moving target in the dark without revealing your own position and strength had too many similarities to finding needles in haystacks to suit Reid Sanger. There was no direct road route to Saint-Vith; as he approached Pessoux, Peiper would have to decide whether to turn southeast toward Bastogne or northeast toward Liège. The woods were heavy here; it was about the only potential place for an ambush.

Captain Smiggs, the recon commander, drove like a maniac in the dark; Sanger thought for sure they were going to crack up five or six times, but somehow, miraculously, the nimble little jeep seemed to avoid all obstacles—except for potholes. He bounced around like a rubber ball. At least that took his mind off his other major discomfort. He brushed old snow off his coat front. His fingers were numb in the gloves. "Christ, it's cold out here."

Smiggy laughed. "Yep. You G-2 types tend to hang out in heated headquarters. This is what it's like out here in the real war."

"Come summer, I'll swap with you," retorted Sanger. "You can be in a stuffy building and I'll be outside under the stars."

"Come summer, this will be all over, and we'll both be heading home." Smiggy had a quick comeback for most occasions.

"Don't we wish. You probably will, but I'll be part of the occupation force. I won't see home for a long time," said Sanger over the sound of the engine.

"Yeah? Where's home, Colonel?"

"New Jersey. You?"

"Sunny California, where we don't have any of this white shit except on mountaintops where we ski. Paradise on earth. You ever surfed, sir?" The jeep hit a mudhole and lurched, then continued on at breakneck speed through the darkness, headlights off. Sanger had no idea how Smiggy could drive like that without getting instantly killed.

"Surfed? What's that?"

"Surfing. Just the greatest sport ever invented. You go where the ocean waves are really big, and you take this board, paddle out, and when the wave comes in, you stand on the board and ride the wave toward shore. If you're good, you can ride the crest right as it comes over and end up shooting right through the curl."

"Sorry, can't visualize it. But anything that you can do in a place where they wear bathing suits sounds like a good idea."

"Come to California after the war and I'll show you. Of course, first time on a California beach, most guys can't keep their eyes off the California girls."

"Now, that I can visualize," grinned Sanger. "As I said, anything in a place where they wear bathing suits sounds like a good idea."

The jeep continued its bumpy ride for another couple of minutes; then Smiggy braked suddenly. "Here we are. That'll be two bucks for the cab ride, not including tip."

"Catch me on payday," retorted Sanger as he jumped out of the jeep. The Panzer Lehr forces were nearly in position on the hilltop. Sanger peered through his binoculars again, "Well, Hauptmann Schmidt, it looks like it's showtime," he said, switching gears effortlessly from English into German.

Now that battle was imminent, Sanger suddenly felt slightly queasy. In every other battle, his position had been in headquarters, processing raw data into some sort of picture, describing the picture to others, and retranslating the big picture into operational details. Now he was one of the operational details, and it occurred to him that he didn't have the slightest idea of how it worked at this level. As the ranking officer present, he was technically in over-all command, but he had less of this sort of experience than anyone else.

Up until now, the excitement of the chase had kept him going, but now he suddenly felt his stomach lurch. He had time only for a brief "Excuse me" before he had to turn his head, drop to his knees, and vomit several times. There wasn't much in his stomach except some acid that burned his esophagus on the way up. He wiped his mouth on his coat sleeve and looked up.

The German captain looked down at him with concern. "Are you all right?" he asked.

"Sorry—just a bad case of nerves," he replied, embarrassed.

Hauptmann Schmidt took his hand and pulled him up. "I feel the same way myself sometimes," he said quietly. "I usually throw up afterward, that's the only difference."

ARMEEGRUPPE B HEADQUARTERS, DINANT, BELGIUM, 0421 HOURS GMT

"Entschuldigen Sie mich bitte, mein Generalfeldmarschall," came the soft voice of Rommel's batman, Lance Corporal Herbert Günther. Rommel stirred,

but did not wake. The aide paused, then repeated his request. "Excuse me please, Field Marshal. There is an important situation."

Again, no answer. Rommel rolled over on his side. This was unusual behavior; Rommel normally woke up quickly and completely when called, and this was especially late for him to remain in bed. A third time Günther called out, and reached over to touch the field marshal gently on his shoulder.

At the first touch, the field marshal's eyes flew open and his hand grabbed his batman's wrist. Günther responded in a quiet but firm voice, "I'm sorry, Field Marshal. I am afraid this is very important."

Rommel closed his eyes again for a moment, then opened them, fully awake. He released Günther's hand. "Yes, very well." He sat up, and shook his head very slowly side to side. "Hand me my coat, please, Günther." The batman noticed that Rommel still moved stiffly, evidently still suffering from his terrible wounds. He was well familiar with the numerous scars over the field marshal's body. Rommel had seen hard action for years, and Günther had taken care of him for many of those years, including throughout the Afrika Korps days.

Rommel grabbed his pants and drew them on, then pulled on the coat. Günther noticed that Rommel's injured eye was tearing. "What is the important news—or did they tell you?"

He knew, but did not want to be the one to tell. "General Speidel is waiting for you in your office. I think you'd better speak to him."

Rommel looked at him. "Mmm," he replied. "That bad, eh?" As usual, Günther felt as if the field marshal had looked right through him, knew exactly what he was thinking, but had the courtesy not to pressure him about it. Rommel slipped on his shoes, gave a quick glance in the mirror as he ran a comb through his hair, and daubed at the corner of his damaged eye with a handkerchief. The batman opened the door for him as Rommel strode from his sleeping chamber.

Speidel stood as Rommel entered his office. "What is it, Hans?" Rommel asked in a firm voice.

The chief of staff looked stricken. "The hospital—it was raided last night by men of the First SS Panzers. They have taken the staff and all the wounded who could be moved—including your driver."

"Carl-Heinz?" asked Rommel, in shock. He was quite fond of his personal driver, who had been shot during the attempted killing of Rommel.

"American prisoners in the hospital were all shot. A few of the seriously wounded were left behind, those for whom being moved would have meant death. Two hospital orderlies were left behind to tend to those patients. All the rest are gone." Speidel's expression was dark as he quickly briefed his commander.

Rommel sat down heavily in his chair. "My god, it's all my fault, isn't it," he said, the burden of the last few days rushing back into his mind.

"No, I don't see how—"

"I should have thought of the hospital as a potential target. But guarding Germans against Germans—"

"You can't blame yourself for this, Erwin," interrupted Speidel quietly, talking man-to-man instead of officer-to-superior. "This is unprecedented territory for all of us. It would never even have occurred to me—"

"But they were Waffen-SS. I know them; I know how they behave," said Rommel with finality. When he was commander in chief for Italy, he had ordered SS troops out of his area because of their brutality; he had protested to Hitler personally when the Das Reich SS division had massacred civilians in Oradour-sur-Glade the previous summer.

Speidel did not pursue the argument. Rommel would always construe events in such a way as to load the primary responsibility onto his own shoulders. "Some of the officers volunteered to lead a rescue mission—they went tearing off in armored cars and some American jeeps—to follow the trail and see if recovery of the hospital staff and patients is possible. The Americans were notified, and Lieutenant Colonel Sanger, the translator, has gone with them. Since the movement is into the Sixth Panzer Army area of operations, and the SS raiders had nearly an hour's head start, I don't hold out a lot of hope for recovery."

"No, it doesn't seem likely to me, either," said Rommel with sadness. "But I'm glad they tried. Sanger, you say? Interesting. I must talk with General Wakefield as soon as possible. He will be concerned particularly about the American dead, but he should be aware of any military operations we undertake, since we are all technically American prisoners of war right now."

"There is a meeting set up on the hour; we'll provide a briefing then," said Speidel, looking over his glasses onto a clipboard.

Leaning back in his chair, Rommel laced his fingers together in front of him. "Hans, I'm tired."

"So are we all," replied Speidel. "This has been an exhausting few days."

"No, I mean a different tired. Tired in my soul. Tired of work. Tired of problems. Funny, I thought surrendering would relieve me of some of these responsibilities, but so far that does not seem to be the case. Right now, for example, I can think of a hundred things that must be done, but for once in my life I don't seem to have the drive to accomplish any of them. Thank you for organizing the task force, Hans. I apologize for leaning on you so heavily."

"You're not leaning heavily, not at all," replied Speidel. "For a man with no drive, you're accomplishing quite a lot." He smiled. "It's not really a surrender in the classic sense, after all. It's a way to save our homeland. I think General Patton understood that about you, and that's critical to the plan."

Rommel nodded acknowledgment. "Patton, of course, is not the final decision maker. I look forward to meeting General Eisenhower in person sometime soon. It's very interesting to meet these people after studying them for so long. Eisenhower is more politically aware than Patton, which poses both opportunities and risks for us."

Speidel nodded. Left unstated was Speidel's well-justified sense that Rommel's own political awareness was not terribly well developed. Speidel had been the one with connections to the conspirators, the one who had persuaded Rommel to lend his name and reputation to the cause, the one who had carefully steered a course through a minefield of political obstacles. "Yes, by all means, we must meet Eisenhower soon. The endgame is upon us, and every move must be precisely calculated and arranged to achieve the results we need."

"How is the surrender going for our remaining forces? While Sixth Panzer Army is lost to us for the most part, has there been more trouble?" asked Rommel. He reached his hand up to massage his temple, the place where his headache was worst. His sight in his wounded eye was continuing to deteriorate as well. He supposed he should see a doctor, but later.

"There seems to be some desertion going in both ways. Hard to quantify, but in balance I think it favors us. Not only those who agree that this is best for the Fatherland, but also those who are looking simply for a way out. A few reports of gunfire within units; nothing serious of note yet, but I have no information at all from some of the commands." Abruptly, Speidel changed the subject. "There is good news this morning as well."

"Yes? I could use some good news," replied the Desert Fox. "Has someone managed to smuggle a bomb into Himmler's conference room?"

Speidel laughed. "Alas, not yet. His time is coming soon, though. No, much better news. We've received word from Lucie and Manfred."

"Thank god," breathed Rommel. The safety of his wife and son had preyed upon his mind ever since the surrender. "Have they reached Bitburg?"

"Yes, and are safely hidden by people in whom I have the utmost trust. You'll see them within a few days, I am sure."

"As long as we're certain that the roads are free from leftover remnants of units joining Sixth Panzer Army," Rommel said with a firm voice. "I can wait longer, if necessary. Safety is paramount."

"Of course, of course," said Speidel in a soothing voice. "No one plans to take any risk. We can easily wait for Patton's troops if desirable. Then you can go and meet them personally."

"I'll probably be on my way to a prisoner-of-war stockade by then, as no doubt will you."

"I don't think so. The Allies, if they are smart, will figure out that there is far more profit to be had by leaving you free to help them. I'm afraid that surrender will not relieve you of any of your responsibilities."

Rommel nodded tiredly. "There is one thing that is good about all this."

"I think there are quite a few good things. Which one did you have in mind?"

"At least this time I am sharing the fate of my surrendered army, not returning home and leaving them behind." At Hitler's insistence, Rommel had not been allowed to try to extract the rest of his Armeegruppe Afrika, but had been forced to stay in Berlin while over 200,000 of his soldiers surrendered to the Allies.

"You had no choice then, Erwin," said Speidel.

"I have no choice now, Hans," replied Rommel.

NEARING PESSOUX, BELGIUM, 0508 HOURS GMT

Carl-Heinz Clausen felt every jolt of the truck as it drove through the night. He was not normally one to feel a lot of pain, but then he'd never been shot in the belly before. The truck was filled with the moans of other wounded. The American aviator, Digger O'Dell, lay next to him, wearing the German's uniform jacket. Digger had a large bandage on his forehead covering one eye, and one leg stretched out straight in a cast. Clausen wanted to help; if he could just get around and get at his tools, he would be able to put together some decent slings and cushions to protect the men. It was the sort of thing he did, the reason for the nickname "Mutti." He didn't mind the nickname, really. It gave him joy to help others. It was frustrating when he couldn't.

"Strange, being taken prisoner by our own side," he said aloud.

"It's that fucking Rommel's fault," one of the patients said angrily. "First he abandons the Afrika Korps, then he sells us down the river."

The returns came quickly. *"Arschloch!"* "This isn't Rommel's doing, it's those Waffen-SS *arschlöcher."* "All those goddamn generals are alike. Not a one of them gives a shit whether we live or die, as long as they get their Iron Crosses."

"Shut up. Let's get some sleep while we can."

"You shut up!" "No, you!" *"Leckmich am Arsch!" "Du Kanst* mich *am Arsch lecken!"* "When I can walk again, I'll take my crutch and beat your head in!"

The noise level in the truck rose until pounding on the rear of the driver's cab warned everyone into quiet.

Clausen looked over at the American, who gave him a thumbs-up gesture. He grinned in return, then lay back on his stretcher and tried to go to sleep.

ARMEEGRUPPE B FIELD HOSPITAL, NEAR DINANT, BELGIUM, 0823 HOURS GMT

The American jeep followed the German staff car into the hospital driveway. Several squads of German infantry were on the scene, at full alert, rifles ready and aimed in all directions. A number of American trucks sporting the red cross of the medical corps were parked in the compound; a steady parade of soldiers marched supplies into the building with antlike precision.

Rommel's batman opened the door of the staff car to let the field marshal out; Henry Wakefield opened his own door. Bob Jackson and Frank Ballard climbed over the sides of the backseat. Chuck Porter, who had been uncomfortably wedged in between the two, took somewhat longer to clamber out in an awkward fashion. Their driver sat in the car and waited.

Guards snapped to attention as the brass trooped into the nearly empty field hospital. The emergency room sported a growing pile of boxes, some being unloaded by enlisted men under the supervision of officers wearing the caduceus. Except for a few damaged stretchers and broken bottles the wards were stripped of almost everything German, from tables to bedding to stretchers. It was well known that the German medical corps was in a state of perpetual shortage; the raiders from Kampfgruppe Peiper had not only taken the patients, but as much of the supplies and equipment as could be loaded onto trucks quickly.

Only one ward still had patients—the intensive care wing filled with men for whom movement meant certain death. Two enlisted orderlies had been left behind to care for those patients, and they now had been pushed aside by Allied doctors busily *tsk*ing at the perceived deficiencies of their German counterparts. All the drugs and IV units except for those actually hooked up to patients had been taken from that room as well. Doctors called to their assistants to get the goddamn boxes unpacked.

There was a German supply officer hard at work, clipboard in hand, compiling a list of what was needed most urgently, making a list of what had been taken, stumbling through translators who themselves struggled with the technical terms of the medical trade. He saluted as the commanders entered.

"Ah, Müller," said Rommel as he spotted the officer. "I'm glad you're here. You've taken charge of the supply situation?"

"In a way—I mean—well, yes, sir," replied Müller. "There wasn't anybody else, and I thought—"

Rommel smiled at the pudgy colonel who had saved his life. He knew Müller was frequently tongue tied around senior officers. "Good work. Carry on. Tell me, did they take von Reinhardt?" Rommel's intelligence chief, who was Müller's best friend, had been shot in the chest in the same incident.

"No, sir," replied Müller. "I think—well, he couldn't be moved safely. He's all right, though. Well, sort of—I mean, he's still wounded and . . ."

"Good. I will speak to him. Are the Americans providing the help you need?"

Müller glanced over at the Americans and nodded in their direction. "Yes, yes, sir. They've been most helpful and courteous. As soon as I contacted the American headquarters, General Wakefield himself made sure I got everything

I requested . . . and then some! Field Marshal . . ." His voice dropped to a conspiratorial register. "They don't seem to have any supply shortages at all! Everything I asked for, they delivered, and more besides!"

Rommel smiled. "That's very good to hear," he said, bowing slightly in the Americans' direction. He dropped his own voice to match his supply officer's. "And yes, they do seem to have nearly inexhaustible supplies. I'm glad for once their supplies are working in our favor, rather than against us." Raising his voice once again, he turned to the American general. *"Danke schön, Herr Generalmajor,"* he said with a deeper bow and heel click.

Gravely, Wakefield returned with his own bow, a halfhearted head-duck. "Bitty shine, Herr Field Marshal," he said, his gruff voice mangling his attempt at the German language.

Rommel turned back to Müller. "I'd like to talk to Oberst von Reinhardt if he's well enough."

"Yes, sir. Of course, sir. Right this way, sir." Müller tucked his clipboard under his arm and led the field marshal toward the intensive-care unit.

Chuck Porter wondered if he'd died and gone to reporter heaven. Not only did he have a ringside seat at Rommel's surrender, but this hospital-capture story had all the earmarks of front-page news around the world. And he, once again, was the only reporter on the spot. Of course, he was here as a backup translator more than as a reporter, but nothing stopped him from doing both jobs at once.

In a day or two at most, correspondents from every major news gatherer would be accredited here, and the days of exclusives would be over. He'd be sitting in press briefings along with everybody else, asking questions, filing stories, serving as a conduit between his editor's questions and the information the armed services felt it appropriate to share. Of course, as soon as that happened he'd be heading back to the office anyway and delegating that kind of work to his staff. He wasn't in any great hurry for that to happen.

"So, General Wakefield—what do you think about wounded American prisoners being murdered by the Nazi SS?" he asked. For now, his notebook was safely buttoned in his pocket. He'd use it later to gather all the details; right now he just needed to get up to date on this story.

Wakefield looked at him like a not-too-pleasant bug under a microscope. "What do you mean what do I think? I think it stinks." He grunted with disgust.

Porter realized he'd put his foot in it. "No, I didn't mean that—I mean, what did you think could or should be done about it?"

"Sanger woke me up around oh-dark-thirty with some cockamamie rescue plan. I didn't have any better ideas, so I told him to go ahead."

"And then—?"

"I went back to sleep."

It's a good thing I'm not looking for a way to ruin you, Porter thought to himself. *I could even hang Eisenhower with a statement like that. Went back to sleep? Christ!* He was amazed that officers who knew so much about heavy weapons knew so little about the weapons of the press. He understood what Wakefield meant, that it wasn't the evidence of dereliction of duty and lack of caring that the blunt words suggested, but what Wakefield really meant wouldn't count once the words were in black-and-white on the newspaper page. If he kept on working with Wakefield, he'd have to try to educate him about the press—but he suspected an education wouldn't take. Wakefield just didn't care about such things.

"So, what's Sanger's plan?" he asked, moving along to the next subject.

"Take some armored half-tracks and jeeps, chase after the enemy, and try to recapture the hospital."

"Pardon me for saying so, General, but that really doesn't sound like a really well-thought-out plan."

Wakefield took a puff on his cigar. "It ain't."

"Sir?" Porter responded, somewhat confused.

"Sometimes all the options are shit, but you still gotta do something," Wakefield replied. "Sanger was willing to try. Said he had a German captain, Schmidt, who was cooperating, also wanted to catch these Nazi pricks. So I turned them loose, and hope for the best. Can't let some bastard hit you without hitting back. Shows him there's a price to pay."

"I see," mused Porter, finally pulling out his notebook and scribbling down a few thoughts. He pictured the heavy German tanks growling through the night, with a few jeeps racing after them, and he was awed by the courage of the would-be rescuers.

Oberst Günter von Reinhardt was normally a thin man, but he looked much thinner in his hospital bed. His sharp-featured face seemed stretched so thin that it was nearly translucent. An IV tube protruded from his arm, and his sheet was flecked with blood where it lay over his chest. Two doctors stood over him, examining the wound and shaking their heads sadly as they commented on the primitive medical work of their German colleagues.

"Forgive me for failing to salute, Herr Generalfeldmarschall," he said in a weak voice.

Rommel sat down beside the bed. "How are you doing, von Reinhardt?"

"Surprisingly well, all considered. As Marcus Aurelius observes, 'A little flesh, a little breath, and a Reason to rule all—that is myself.' I have time to contemplate, and that is good, for it seems I am not a man of action." He smiled. "I would not have thought my friend Müller was, either, but it seems there I am incorrect."

The pudgy supply officer reddened slightly at the compliment. "You stood up to him too, Günter. That's why you got shot."

"That's right, you know," added Rommel. "If we only considered manliness to accompany victory or immediate success, I would hardly qualify myself, especially at the moment." He smiled ruefully. "I am grateful to you both."

"Thank you, sir," Reinhardt replied. "Mein Generalfeldmarschall, I was given a private message for you during the capture of the hospital."

"A message? From whom? From Peiper?" asked Rommel.

"No, sir. From the führer."

"Himmler?" Rommel was confused. "How can that be?"

"It is private, sir," hinted von Reinhardt.

"Ah, yes," acknowledged the field marshal. He turned to the doctors. *"Sprechen Sie Deutsch?"* he asked.

One of the doctors held up two fingers with about an inch between them. *"Sehr wenig,"* he said. A very little.

Rommel nodded in acknowledgment. "Please leave us alone for a minute," he said in German. With the aid of hand gestures, the doctors agreed to leave—but only for a minute; the patient needed them. When the doctors had left, he turned back to von Reinhardt. "And the message?"

"Yes, sir. It seems that our beloved führer, learning of the surrender of Armeegruppe B, telephoned our friend the obersturmbannführer and asked him to take action where Brigadeführer Bücher had failed. Peiper personally killed Generaloberst Guderian at the staff meeting when Guderian announced he was supporting the surrender. He told me that with some pleasure."

Rommel shook his head. "Poor Heinz. An ignominious way to go. But why give me this as a message from the führer?"

"That was only background. Himmler wishes to offer you the opportunity to return to the honorable service of the Third Reich, he says. Although he believes you to be terribly misguided in your current path, he knows you love the Fatherland as much as he does, and so he suggests that it would be beneficial to all concerned for you and he to have a channel of private communication and negotiation."

Rommel was quiet as he considered this. "And your judgment, intelligence officer?"

Reinhardt thought for a moment. " 'Learning carries within itself certain dangers because out of necessity one has to learn from one's enemies,' " he stated.

"And who said this?" Rommel had learned to recognize when von Reinhardt was quoting someone.

"Leon Trotsky."

"The communist?"

"Yes."

"Mmm." Rommel considered the phrase. "So you recommend that we open this diplomatic channel privately, and use it as an opportunity to learn?"

"Yes, sir. I think that's only prudent."

Rommel laughed. "You see, I am starting to figure you out! Ah, what an education I receive from you every time we speak."

Reinhardt grinned weakly in return. "Thank you. As do I from you, mein Generalfeldmarschall. I will be out of this bed soon, and I will manage this channel for you, if the field marshal wishes."

"Yes, by all means. There's no one I would trust more, and I also look forward to your return to duty. But that will not be for a little bit yet. Now it's time to rest. You'll be under the care of your American doctors shortly. Try to let that brain of yours relax for a while. The war will keep until you are with us again." Rommel patted his shoulder and then stood up. "I'll see you soon."

"I look forward to it, mein Generalfeldmarschall."

Commotion arose outside the hospital, and both the American and German officers went to investigate. They witnessed the return of Task Force Sanger, accompanied by one truck liberated from Kampfgruppe Peiper.

Hauptmann Schmidt climbed out of his armored half-track, followed by Reid Sanger, who had chosen to ride in enclosed comfort rather than share Captain Smiggs' open-to-the-air reconnaissance jeep. Smiggy pulled in right next to the half-track and jumped out. Doctors and orderlies swarmed out of the hospital to start the process of bringing the wounded back into the hospital.

Rommel pushed his way through the growing crowd to shake the hands of all the victors. "That was a brave attempt," he repeated, moving from officers through all the enlisted. Wakefield reached Sanger first, while Frank Ballard went first to congratulate his reconnaissance officer and the men of his own command.

"I only got one out of ten trucks," Sanger said before Wakefield could open his mouth. "And that one broke down. The Krauts—I mean, the Nazis—were all ready to abandon it when we came up to them. But the rest of the column was screened by a couple of big tanks. We couldn't even get close."

Wakefield mangled his cigar with his teeth as he growled, "Hell, I'd have laid odds you wouldn't have even caught up to them, much less get any of the trucks back. That was good soldiering, son, good soldiering. Aggressive and fast."

Sanger took a deep breath. "Damn it, I hate that I couldn't get more of the men out of there."

"Welcome to the world of officers, Sanger," Wakefield said with gruff sympathy. "If the choice is a half-assed job on the one hand, and doing jack shit on the other, then you have to do a half-assed job. People get hurt and get killed no matter what you do."

"It still hurts, General."

"Damn right. Doesn't stop, either." Wakefield shrewdly changed the subject. "Reminds me. What were you doing last night over at Rommel's shop?"

"Couldn't sleep, so I decided to look around the enemy HQ. It's not every day a G-2 gets to do that without risking being shot as a spy," replied Sanger. "When the news arrived, I happened to be there along with Schmidt over there—who's damn competent, by the way—and so we worked out a plan. Sorry to have to wake you, but I figured it was best to get permission. I talked to you, he talked to General Bayerlein, and you pretty much know the rest."

Wakefield grunted in acknowledgment. "What do you know about a man named von Reinhardt?"

"He's Rommel's G-2. Evidently he was on the mission that negotiated the Soviet peace treaty and is supposed to have done all the heavy lifting after von Ribbentrop, their foreign minister, had a stroke. A very smart man, by all indications."

"What's he doing in the hospital?"

"Took a bullet trying to gun down Rommel's would-be assassin, an agent Himmler had planted on him."

"Looks like he's definitely on Rommel's side, then." Sanger nodded agreement, and Wakefield asked, "Did he get him?"

"No. The kill went to Colonel Müller. The man over there." Sanger pointed to the plump balding man in the round glasses.

"The supply officer?" Wakefield asked in surprise.

"Yes, sir."

Wakefield shook his head. "Doesn't look the type, but I guess you never know."

"No, sir, you don't. The way the story goes, the supply colonel chased this SS officer into the Notre Dame church in Dinant, the one where we first met Rommel, and shot him dead right before he could get the field marshal."

Wakefield shook his head in disbelief. "Hell, we must have been this far away from walking right into an ambush." He puffed on his cigar as he contemplated the thought.

"If it weren't for Müller, probably so, sir. We'd be dead, or at least prisoners, right now."

"We're all living on borrowed time, son. You did good, Sanger. Real good." Wakefield abruptly changed subjects. "Okay being our translator?"

"Certainly, sir. Good place for an intelligence officer, wouldn't you say? Right next to the enemy commander."

That drew a snort that resembled laughter. "All right. Keep it up. Think I'll make it official. You're the American liaison officer for this arrangement, at least until some seat warmer from SHAEF decides to pull rank on you. Okay?"

"Yes, sir. Thank you, sir. It's an interesting assignment. You know, I worked for Rommel before."

"Yeah? How?"

"Hitler Youth. I was over here in '37, staying with relatives. Rommel was their military adviser for a while."

"Big fan?"

"I guess, sir. Back then, most Germans were fans of Hitler and the Nazis. I was, myself, before I got a good close look. I've paid attention to Rommel for a long time. It's interesting to be up close and personal."

"Keep it up, then."

"Yes, sir."

Rommel had worked his way over to the two men. "If I may intrude," he said in German. "I would like to offer my deepest thanks. These were not your men, but you risked your life to save them."

"Thank you, Generalfeldmarschall," Sanger said. "I deeply regret that your driver was not in the truck we were able to rescue."

"It's little short of miraculous that you brought away this many. I am happy for those who have been returned. And the book is not yet closed on the others."

"Thank you again, sir."

"Will you ask your general what medal he plans to award you? Under other circumstances, I would ask him how to award you one of ours, but it would be rather awkward, I'm sure."

Embarrassed, Sanger translated Rommel's question, and added, "I don't need or expect anything, sir."

"Don't look a gift horse in the mouth, son," Wakefield said. "I had already decided on a Silver Star if you brought anybody back."

Even more embarrassed, Sanger stuttered through the reverse translation.

Rommel nodded. "I think that's quite appropriate. While I'm at it, please ask your general if he would be amenable to having you continue to provide liaison between our two forces. That is, if you don't mind—it may be a comedown from the intelligence work you usually do."

"My general had just finished offering me the same assignment," Sanger said, after quickly translating the exchange. "I had accepted with pleasure once already, so let me do so again. Thank you. It is an assignment of great honor."

"The honor is mine," replied Rommel. "A brave man is always welcome."

Sanger saluted, then bowed and heel-clicked in the German fashion. Rommel returned the bow.

Wakefield grinned as Sanger quickly brought him up to date. "Always like to make a POW happy," he said, then quickly added, "Don't translate that."

"Yes, sir," replied Sanger, smiling.

THIRD ARMY ADVANCE HEADQUARTERS,
NEUFCHÂTEAU, BELGIUM, 0854 HOURS GMT

General George S. Patton was proud to tell anyone who'd stand still that he personally owned the world's toughest, meanest, fastest, and best military force, the United States Third Army. Put up against anyone, anytime, and anywhere in the whole history of the world, Patton guaranteed he could beat anything that moved, walked, slithered, or crawled. And once again he was going to take command of the immense fists of Third Army, this time to beat the hell out of the Nazis in the final round.

When the massive United States Third Army moved, it changed the very earth it crossed. That mighty force consisted of three entire corps, each with two armored divisions and two or three infantry divisions, with battalions of engineers, antiaircraft guns, field artillery, mechanized cavalry, along with headquarters companies, hospitals, mess facilities, officers' and enlisted clubs, supply depots, repair shops, and everything else needed to operate. The associated XIX Tactical Air Command, though not an organic part of Patton's army, carried out thousands of sorties, an entire air force dedicated to smoothing the Third's path across the ground. In full movement, the army consumed an average of 350,000 gallons of gasoline a day. Combined with the other supplies needed to keep a hundred thousand men and thousands of pieces of equipment operating, an immense trucking apparatus known as the Red Ball Express operated over six thousand trucks running a nonstop convoy operation just to keep the rest of the army on the move.

Taking advantage of every opportunity, the army had exploited captured enemy supplies. During one period, eighty percent of the artillery ammunition used by XX Corps had been captured from German units. Working with French civilians, the Third Army had even taken over a large part of the extensive French rail system, operating it as their own. French factories provided repair shops, antifreeze, coal, and even dry-cleaning for Patton's men. Even the French rubber manufacturing plants became part of the Third Army supply apparatus, producing fan belts and tires.

Third Army engineers had built and were still building thousands of bridges and entire road networks. The army's Signals Corps operated a telephone system that handled over 13,000 calls per day. A chaplain corps, a finance corps, a complete legal system, a network of hospitals—there was no service and no function that men needed that was not provided. Third Army was in effect its own city, but a mobile city, capable of rapid movement, often against heavy resistance.

A force of this size could hardly be manhandled around like a platoon. Yet, at the outbreak of Rommel's Fuchs am Rhein offensive, General George S. Patton's Third Army had stopped a full-scale attack then in progress, pulled back the entire force, swung it around ninety degrees to the north, moved one hundred miles, and launched a full-scale attack on the southern flank of the German forces, all in only three days. Nothing like it had ever been done before in the history of warfare.

And now, only days later, it was time to do the impossible again: disengage from a wide front, swing ninety degrees around to the east, and move forward to cross the mighty Rhine River and establish itself in the German heartland, all before the remaining German forces could seal off the hole made by the surrender of Rommel's Armeegruppe B. It was a chance for nearly instant victory, but the effort required was once again nearly superhuman.

Patton's driver, Sergeant Mims, had said on the way north, "General, the army is wasting a lot of money on your staff officers. You and I can run the whole war from your jeep."

Patton had laughed at that, but the truth was that his intelligence officers had sent warnings about German troop buildup and maneuvering to SHAEF headquarters well in advance of the attack. When Eisenhower and Bradley had dismissed the indicators, claiming that the German POL situation was so bad that no major attack was possible, Patton had gone ahead and had his team develop plans just in case. When the word came down, he simply called his headquarters and gave one code word: "Nickel."

This wasn't going to be nearly as easy, because this time he didn't have plans prepared in advance. Of all the things George S. Patton had anticipated, dealing with a friendly Field Marshal Erwin Rommel after a sudden surrender was not one of them.

Third Army headquarters was already bustling when his jeep pulled into the compound. They had left Paris and SHAEF headquarters after 0300 hours and had driven through the night. Patton had caught a few winks in the back of the jeep as it jounced along the roads. He was enough of an old soldier that he could sleep anywhere, even in the back of a jeep in below-freezing temperatures. "Stick around, John," Patton said as he stepped out of the jeep. "I may need you on very short notice."

"Yes, sir, General," replied the sergeant. "I'll be gassed up and ready to go whenever you are." Patton knew that Mims would get the jeep ready and then sack out himself, but that he would be awake and alert at a moment's notice.

Two sentries at the door to his commandeered headquarters snapped to attention and saluted as he approached; he returned the salute absently, his mind already racing as he roughed out his new campaign.

His senior staff was already hard at work as he strode into the large planning room. Wall-size maps dominated the open space; more maps covered table after table, each with numerous men standing around working. The room was brass-heavy: majors and colonels and generals doing the active strategic planning, and sergeants and corporals turning decisions into orders. Every officer wore a tie, and each uniform—if somewhat unkempt and wrinkled—was complete per U.S. Army regulations. A line of Gestetener mimeograph machines ran off stacks of paper that were then carefully collated and placed into cubbyholes. The room was thick with stale cigarette haze. One table had a large metal percolator and numerous old, crusty coffee cups. The buzz of conversation was constant; occasional words and phrases cut through the general din.

"Ten-HUT!" called out a sergeant as Patton strode into the room. Discussion ceased suddenly.

"As you were," replied Patton as he returned his men's salute. "You got my phone call, and I'm glad to see you're all at work already. This has been the goddamndest few weeks I think I've ever seen. Thanks to your outstanding work, we responded to a German breakout that could have knocked us flat on our ass, and now the Desert Fox has surrendered to Third Army."

The men in the room cheered and applauded. Patton let it go on for a minute before he raised his hand.

"Field Marshal Rommel told me that the biggest reason for surrendering was that he wanted to make sure it was us Americans, not the fucking goddamn backstabbing Rooskies, that finally beat the Nazis and took over Germany. When we started this, I told you that I wanted the goddamned Germans to piss themselves and howl, 'Jesus Christ, it's the goddamned Third Army again and that son-of-a-fucking-bitch Patton.' And that's just exactly what they said."

There were more cheers. Patton grinned. He knew his men. He raised his hand again for silence.

"We showed the Germans, and now we're going to show the cocksucking Russians what the United States Third Army is all about. The Desert Fox has given us a free shot at getting across the Rhine, but some of those Nazi bastards that haven't had the good sense to surrender yet may want to knock out a bridge or two before we get there. But when they show up—if they aren't too piss-soaked and addled to show up—they are going to find themselves staring down the barrel of one of Georgie-fucking-Patton's tanks!"

This time he didn't stop the cheers.

ARMEEGRUPPE B HEADQUARTERS, DINANT, 1059 HOURS GMT

"Very well, gentlemen," said the Desert Fox. "Let me summarize. General Bayerlein and Panzer Lehr will move southwest on the Rue de Philippeville, accept the surrender of units it encounters, and clear the road of any obstacles. General Wakefield and the U.S. Nineteenth Armored Division will share our headquarters and provide defense for us, as we are officially surrendered."

He could see it was still difficult for his senior staff to accept the new reality.

"Patton will be moving his Third Army elements north and east. We will give way and assist him in taking control of our portion of the Westwall. His objective, and ours, will be to reach the Rhine bridges between here and here." Rommel pointed to the map, indicating Remagen on the north and Koblenz on the south. "We will provide Patton's forces with the opportunity to secure a bridgehead across the Rhine, and defend ourselves against potential attacks from Sixth Panzer Army or other Wehrmacht or Waffen-SS forces that may not respect the surrender. Whether the Amis accept that opportunity is, of course, up to them. But we will make it possible."

He stopped his formal briefing for a moment. "Gentlemen, this is no less painful to me than it must be to you. However, I firmly believe that this is the only way for us to protect the Fatherland from being devoured by the Soviet Union. If we receive dishonor for this, that is a price we must pay for the sake of our nation and our people. If you would prefer to revert to the status of an ordinary American prisoner of war, however, you may do so. It is your right."

He paused for a full minute. His officers looked guiltily—and wearily—at each other, then back at him. No one spoke up, a fact that did not surprise the Desert Fox. Several of these men, notably his chief of staff, Generaloberst Doktor Hans Speidel, had been strongly in agreement from the first. Speidel had been one of the original conspirators in the Bomb Plot and was Rommel's personal link to the conspirators. He had been one of the first to recognize the inevitability of Nazi Germany's fall, and the consequent choice between East and West, the choice that would frame the postwar future of Germany.

"I thank you for your service, your skill, your honor, and your devotion to duty and to the Fatherland. Questions? No? Dismissed."

Rommel felt weak, sick to his stomach. The strain of the last few days was beginning to catch up with him. His bowels were in an uproar—the legacy of his African campaign dysentery—such that he could tolerate no food other than thin soup, and the taut skin around the edges of his recent wounds pulled and tugged and threatened to split. It took all of his concentration and strength to move at even a reduced pace; he was afraid that his intelligence had completely deserted him.

He looked over at the American general, Wakefield, who had attended the meeting accompanied by his translator and intelligence officer Sanger. Wakefield had been awake nearly as long as Rommel, and he was showing signs of strain as well. No wonder. He might not have been recovering from wounds, but he was significantly older than Rommel, which should balance the scales somewhat.

Interesting man, this Wakefield, Rommel thought as the meeting broke up. It was obvious that he and Patton had some history of tension. Not unprecedented, especially noting that Wakefield was comparatively old for his rank, older than both he and Patton, for example.

Rommel could understand the slowness of his own forces to respond given the unprecedented circumstances with which they were faced, but it annoyed him all out of proportion to be less than perfect before his American audience. It was not so much his own ego at stake as his sense of the honor of the professional German military. He massaged his throbbing temple once again—it gave little relief—and spoke to Wakefield.

"I don't know whether you are acting as a general under my temporary command or as my official captor," he said.

"A little of each, Field Marshal," replied the gruff American. "I've posted scouts and am maintaining a watch. Otherwise, let me know what you need me to do."

"Thank you, General," answered the Desert Fox. "You and your men fought very well over these last days—as, indeed, you have done since Normandy."

"Thanks, Field Marshal. Don't mind my saying so, you're not so bad yourself."

"Thank you. There is no compliment so welcome as that from a fellow professional," Rommel replied with a smile and a slight bow. He liked a man with no fear and no pretenses. "If there is any way I can help your General Patton reach the Rhine, I intend to do so."

SHAEF HEADQUARTERS, REIMS, FRANCE,
1640 HOURS GMT

It was nearly dark when George S. Patton arrived at SHAEF headquarters near the Reims train station.

"Georgie! Come in!" ordered the Supreme Commander with a growl. "Where the hell have you been?"

"Ending the war, General," replied Patton with a broad grin. "Here's Rommel's document of surrender, and he's going to open the roads into Germany. I'll have forces across the border within forty-eight hours. The Desert Fox has offered us a clear path all the way to the Rhine, and I should be across that little creek in a matter of a week or two."

Eisenhower was too stunned at first to reply. Then he said, "A week?"

"Or two." Patton grinned; he loved to shock people like this. "I've given the orders to set things in motion—and the Germans have opened the roads all the way to Trier. Third Army can be on its way at first light. And once we're in Trier, we're through the Westwall. The Rhineland country would be a hellish battlefield, you know—hills, ridges, caves, dense forests—and Rommel is *giving* it to us!"

Omar Bradley stood up from the sofa where he'd been stretched out, try-ing to catch forty winks as he waited for his errant subordinate to arrive. "You've given the orders? How about checking with me—or the Supreme Commander—first?"

"Brad, when I give you victory wrapped up and tied with a bow, how can you question my methods?" asked Patton genially.

Bradley looked ready to argue about matters of protocol, but Eisenhower raised his hand. "Hang on. Let's get the details first, okay?" He ran his hand over his bald head. It had been a long day, one of many through this cold December.

"Okay," replied Patton heartily. "First, Rommel's surrender. He's turned against the Nazi government and wants us to take over Germany before the goddam Rooskies can get there. As a result, he's holding a line for me all the way from the Ardennes through the Westwall and over the Rhine in the entire arc from Koblenz down to Mannheim." He walked over to Eisenhower's large wall map to indicate the area of operations. "He tried to get us the entire Army Group B front, but turns out that Sixth Panzer Army up here—" Patton pointed. "—has had some SS elements mutiny. Rommel has delivered Fifth Panzer Army and Seventh Army and their entire area of operations. Ike, Brad: I have an open road all the way to Berlin!"

It was well known that Patton ached to be the first one to Berlin, an honor that was originally intended for the Soviet Army. After Stalin's treacherous armistice, the plan had tentatively called for the British to take the northern path. With Montgomery's death, however, and the continued resistance of the Germans in the north, the British looked to have some serious obstacles in their path. Naturally, there would be significant negotiation involved if Eisenhower took charge, so Patton hoped to present him with fait accompli.

"George," Ike said sternly. "I want you to remember that Berlin is not that important. We have military targets to deal with—hell, you know that liberating cities can be more trouble than it's worth! We have Nazis to kill, and that is our top priority."

"Goddammit, Ike—let me go for it! We can get there before the Rooskies—it's an historic opportunity! We have the tool in the right place for the job—for Christ's sake, let's use it! Hell, it's like I've got my own personal can opener—and Germany is the can!"

"Damn it, George, you will follow orders, or so help me God I will give your job to someone else who will!"

Patton immediately backed down. "Sorry, Ike . . . I know, you're the boss. But the Rhine—surely you can see how big it is to get across the river! Jeezus Christ, how often does somebody come in here with a prize like this?"

"First, explain this all to me," said Eisenhower, fixing Patton with a stern look. "You've promised Rommel that we'll take over his country, and save it from the Soviets, eh?"

"You've got to admit it's a hell of an opportunity," urged Patton as he sat down. "It's the least we can do."

"I don't know if we can do it at all. This doesn't look too much like an unconditional surrender to me, and that's still policy, Soviet dropout or not."

"Oh, the surrender was unconditional enough. Everything else was a request, not a condition."

"What about POW status? Those Germans are officially POWs, and you say they're out there screening for you? Is Army Group B still performing military operations?"

"Yeah, sure they are, but they're working on our side now. They helped us shoot up an attacking column of SS panzers, trying to hit Dinant from the north. Rommel and I had an excellent meeting of the minds. He's a class act, the Desert Fox. You'll enjoy meeting him, Ike. You too, Brad," he said, indicating his direct superior officer with a casual wave of the hand.

"So let me get this straight. Instead of turning Rommel and his men into POWs the way it's supposed to be, you've turned them into units of Third Army and sent them out unsupervised to perform military actions on behalf of the Allies?"

"Yeah, well, sort of. But not unsupervised. The Nineteenth Armored is with them. Henry's got things under control. Hell, they've already worked together to break up an SS attack."

Eisenhower blinked again. Patton enjoyed seeing the man nonplussed like this. Patton's grin continued to widen, Cheshire-cat-style. "Look, Ike," Patton said in a calmer tone of voice. "I really didn't mean to go this far out on a limb without talking to you. But this was the sort of opportunity that comes only once. I *had* to act. Rommel decided to surrender when we blew the bridges and his attacking spearheads were cut off from supply. He called the Nineteenth Armored HQ in Givet, who were the closest unit to him. CCA of the Nineteenth cut the final bridge in Dinant, you know."

"Yeah, I know," said Eisenhower. "Pulaski, right?"

"Yep," replied Patton. "He bought it in the attack."

"Too bad. The boy had promise," said Eisenhower quietly.

There was another brief pause, and then Patton continued. "I just happened to be at Nineteenth Armored HQ when the call came in. Otherwise, Henry Wakefield would have taken Rommel's surrender all by his lonesome, because there just wouldn't have been anyone else to do it."

"You'd have hated that, Georgie," interjected Bradley, back on the sofa.

Patton turned and regarded Bradley for a moment, then turned his attention back to Eisenhower. "So the call came in, and there I was. I didn't have any choice."

"Did you consider that it might be a bluff? That I might be looking at two dead generals, including the head of Third Army, with no clue as to what was really going on?"

"Well, I assumed you'd miss me most days, but some days you wouldn't," Patton observed.

"You're damned right some days I wouldn't miss you," growled Eisenhower. "But it would have been one hell of a mess."

Patton nodded in acknowledgment. "It might have been a trap, but I talked on the phone to Rommel and I was convinced it was real. So I hotfooted it into Dinant and we started palavering." Patton decided that the story of Rommel's near assassination would wait for a better time. "Like I said, we got into a little rough-and-tumble with some of our old friends in First SS Panzers, but between Henry Wakefield's boys and Panzer Lehr, we saved the day."

"Henry Wakefield and Panzer Lehr fighting the Leibstandarte Adolf Hitler." Eisenhower shook his head. Then, unable to help himself, he cracked a smile, and then began to guffaw. "And now you want to pop open Germany like it's a big can of beer? Operation Can Opener, huh? God damn, George," he said, laughing helplessly, "what the *hell* have you done?"

"I won the war, Ike. Third Army has goddamn won the fucking war." Patton found himself joining in the laughter, and even Bradley was swept up to the extent of cracking a smile on his schoolteacher's face.

NORTH OF BASTOGNE, BELGIUM, 1914 HOURS GMT

"I'm tired," whined the thirteen-year-old soldier. "I can't keep marching like this." He stopped dead in the middle of the road and dropped his backpack.

"All right. Let's stop for a minute," Lukas Vogel announced. It was cold, too cold to stand around for long, but he himself could hardly walk another step along the snow-crusted road leading (he hoped) back toward the Westwall, back toward the Fatherland. He couldn't expect his men to do any more.

The others nodded or grunted their acknowledgment. They were tired, too. Lukas surveyed the faces of his small group of followers, mostly young like him. After he had left his tent, he circulated around the rest of the compound, listening to the arguments and discussions that raged back and forth. The surrender was on everybody's mind. Most welcomed it, but some were like Lukas, prepared to continue the fight. Quietly, he recruited them into his own private Freikorps, committed to move north and east, to rejoin the German army and save the Fatherland. He had about twenty men with him now. The youngest was, he judged, about twelve years old; the oldest perhaps twenty. They all seemed willing to acknowledge him as leader, and he was proud of that.

He knew he was a leader; he'd always been a leader from his first Hitler-jugend days on into the beginnings of the war. When he was twelve years old he'd been in charge of an antiaircraft gun outside Hannover, firing at the great waves of bombers that filled the skies, their evil drone sounding like a wave of horrible insects. Air-raid sirens wailed throughout the city, but they could not overpower the droning of the planes. Then the roar of his own big gun had answered the challenge, the sound blotting out all other noises at least for a moment, making him deaf for a time afterward so he couldn't hear the bomber.

He had cheered when he saw one of the bombers burst into flame, spiraling downward trailing smoke, but there were always more, far more, dropping strings of bombs like endless rain over the city. The explosions made the ground shake and replaced the droning engine noises with other, even more evil sounds, followed by smoke and fire that blotted out the sky itself.

He had done what he could, but it was not enough. Finally he, along with most other children, were shipped off to the *Kinderlandverschickung*, the KLV camps, to protect them from the strategic bombing campaign. His camp, one of an uncounted number, had about three thousand boys in it. He protested—he was a soldier and he wanted to be in the war—but to no avail. Oh, they pretended to drill and practice, and there were classes in National Socialism to attend, but it was just a way to keep the kids out of the way, and he hated it. He hated the boredom and he hated the uselessness and he hated the bullies and the sexual predators and the hypocrisy he saw everywhere.

And so he had escaped, run away, returned home to Hannover only to find that his family home was a crater. He assumed his mother was dead from the bombing; his father had gone east into Russia long before and Lukas had no idea whether he lived or not.

He tried to enlist in the Waffen-SS but his records were still at the KLV camp, so he joined the *Volksgrenadierien* because all they cared about was that he was a warm body. But he was a soldier, a good soldier and a leader of men. And this band of men and boys following him here, tonight, proved it.

The moon was nearly full, but hidden behind clouds so that only a dim glow illuminated the forested landscape. There were no stars visible. He shifted the position of his heavy duffel from one shoulder to another to relieve the pressure a little bit, and wriggled his numb toes in his boots to try to ward off frostbite. His nose was runny from the cold, and he wiped it on his coat sleeve.

"It's freezing here, and there's no place to camp," he said. "If we stand around too long we'll freeze."

"I can't, Lukas, I just can't," sniffed the boy who had dropped his pack. His name was Friedrich Gross, and he was a Grenadier, the lowest rank.

Lukas walked over to him and put his hand on his shoulder. "There isn't a choice, Friedrich. We've got to keep going until we find someplace warm. As soon as we do, we'll all rest. That's a promise." He looked over the boy with a critical eye. "Give me your pack." Lukas hefted it, then slung it over his shoulder while picking up his own duffel.

"Everybody ready?" he asked. "We can't stop too long in this weather." When he heard enough acknowledgment, he ordered, "Move out." Then he trudged forward, his boots crunching in the leftover snow. More boots crunched behind him.

He thought about his last encounter with his old unit. It made him angry that there were Germans who weren't devoted to the cause. He wished he'd killed Bauer back in the tent, put a knife through his throat and shut him up once and for all. He was a better soldier than that ignorant dummkopf any day, even if he was technically still a kid. He should have put his knife through Obergefreiter Durr, too. The old fart might have meant well, but age had made him soft and weak. If he couldn't help bring his fatherland to victory, then he was useless and ought to be dead so he didn't consume any more precious supplies. The future belonged to the young, didn't it? Not to patronizing old shits who mooned over their grandchildren and laughed and were happy about surrender.

Lukas marched along under the weight of double packs for a while, but they slowed him down tremendously. He ached under the strain, but he knew that he couldn't show weakness before his men. They looked up to him as their leader. And that thought made him fret. He wasn't sure how much longer they would have to march, or what would happen if they were caught outdoors too long. He wanted to ask someone else what to do, but that also would be a sign of weakness. He shifted his duffel yet again. His toes were completely numb and so were his fingertips. There were the tingles that he knew were the first signs of frostbite. He had to do something, and soon.

Then came a rumbling sound—it was an engine, a large one. "Everyone off the road," he snapped, and his soldiers obeyed. Lukas stayed out in the open, looking carefully down the road they had traveled as the engine sound increased. Then there was a glimmer along the line of a hill, which grew brighter and suddenly turned into the blaze of headlights. It was a truck.

"Men, cover me. We need this truck. If the driver doesn't cooperate, be ready to attack on my signal," he ordered. He heard the sounds of packs dropping, rounds clicking into the chambers of several carbines.

Lukas stepped out into the road, leaving his packs behind him. He unslung his rifle and rested the butt on his boot so it wouldn't end up in the snow and mud, and began waving his hand back and forth at the oncoming vehicle. As it drove closer, he heard the grinding sound of gears downshifting and the squeal of badly maintained brakes as the truck stopped. The headlights had completely blinded him; he blinked in the painful light.

A head leaned out the window. "Who the hell are you, and what do you want?"

"I'm Obergefreiter Vogel. I'm heading for Sixth Panzer Army."

"Yeah? So what?"

"I need a ride. It's freezing out here."

"I'm heading in a different direction, kid. There's no room."

"Are you heading for Sixth Panzer Army?"

"No."

"How about the Westwall?

"No."

"Are you going back to the Fatherland?"

"Kid, what's the matter with you? The war has ended. We lost and we've surrendered. Now get the hell out of my way."

Lukas made a hand signal, and his men rushed forward, pulled open the driver's door, and pulled the driver out into the snow. His eyes now adjusting to the glare of the headlights, he walked over to the man. "I'm afraid we're commandeering your truck."

"Wait, dammit, you can't do that. Hey, you're just a bunch of kids! What the hell do you mean—"

Lukas gestured and two rifles were shoved into the driver's face. "Shut up," he said in a calm voice. Looking wildly around at his captors, the driver obeyed. Lukas looked up into the truck, seeing a second man there. He thought about his rifle, but instead pulled out his knife and leaned closer. The soldier's eyes widened at the sight of the menacing steel blade. "Out," ordered the young soldier.

"No problems, kid," the man in the truck said. "I'm coming, okay? I'm just along for the ride, you know?" He slid out of the truck and stood shivering in his uniform shirt and unbuttoned tunic. His coat was still in the truck. Lukas noticed that the man kept his hands clearly in view at all times.

"What's in the truck?" he asked.

"Just some supplies, some food, some miscellaneous shit—nothing important," the passenger said. "Hey, can I get my coat?"

"Stay where you are," Lukas ordered, then turned to another of his men, Hans Braun, another oberschütze. "Check in the back."

It was a flatbed truck with a rounded cloth cover, just the size for his unit. In a moment, Braun leaned out of the back of the truck. "Lukas, just supplies. Not enough room for the group. But there are a big stack of blankets."

"Good. What kind of supplies? Necessary, or can they be abandoned?" Braun ducked back into the truck. Lukas shifted from foot to foot to try to get sensation back into his toes as he waited.

"Lukas, there's something funny here," Braun announced, sticking his head out. "It's a lot of electronics, some tools, and a bag of money."

"Money? Are you sure?"

"Sure, I'm sure. I haven't ever seen so much money."

Lukas looked at the two men. The shivering passenger spoke first. "Hey, it was him, not me. He figured if we were going to surrender, we might as well take some of the good stuff ourselves instead of let it get into American hands, right? At least it would stay German."

Lukas nodded. "I see. You took the money and tools and equipment you could sell to keep it out of American hands and were heading home."

"Yeah, sure. You understand, don't you?"

"I do understand," he said calmly. "And so I think I'll follow in your footsteps. We'll take the equipment you rescued from the Americans and put it back into the military when we reach Sixth Panzer Army. Hans," he called out. "Let's throw out anything we can so we've got enough room to get the boys in the truck, and then get everyone loaded up. I'll drive." He hoped that wasn't a mistake. He had never driven a truck, but he could drive a car and he supposed the two weren't that different.

"Listen, we'll go along with you, okay?" said the passenger. "We won't make any trouble at all. And we'll give everything to the first officer we find, just like you want."

Lukas ignored them and issued the orders necessary to get his men on board, blankets wrapped over them. "Hans, you ride up front with me."

"Okay, Lukas," replied Braun. "How about these two?"

Lukas looked at them. "They want to get some stuff back to Germany and sell it for money, and that's all right. Everything we dumped in the snow is theirs. So all they have to do is carry it to the nearest division. It shouldn't be much more than about ten kilometers away."

"You can't do that, kid!" pleaded the passenger. "We'll freeze to death!"

Lukas smiled. "That's a definite possibility," he said, and stepped up into the driver's seat, passing his rifle over to Hans, who kept his own rifle trained on the two coatless men.

The passenger continued to plead for help. "Hey, how about my coat, at least? Please, kid?"

Finally, Lukas took the man's coat and threw it out into the snow. "There you go," he said.

"But that's just one coat, and there are two of us!" the passenger said.

"That's what you asked for," said Lukas as he started the engine. With a tremendous sound of grinding gears, the truck lurched forward into the darkness. He could hear the loud sounds of argument fading out behind him.

THE PENTAGON, WASHINGTON, D.C., 2030 HOURS GMT

Brigadier General Leslie Richard Groves, U. S. Army Corps of Engineers, built the Pentagon in 1942. After that, they gave him a really big job. It wasn't the job he wanted—he wanted to go overseas and get in the war—but he was a soldier. When they said frog, he jumped, just like the book said.

Groves was a big man, nearly six feet tall, tipping the scales at just over three hundred pounds. He had curly dark brown hair and blue eyes. He was a tough son of a bitch they could trust to get the job done. He was loud, he had little tact, and his people mostly hated his guts. Not that he gave a rat's ass. He wasn't running a personality contest. And besides, the flakes and nuts that made up the brain trust of the Manhattan Project needed a firm hand to keep focused on the goal: the construction of a fission bomb—if such a thing was even possible, which nobody seemed to know for sure. He wasn't the first man to compare his job to herding cats, but the comparison was apt, anyway.

He was an engineer, not a physicist; he was a construction project manager, not an ordnance specialist; he was a practical man, not an academic. That made him just about the opposite of most of the professionals he now managed. They were smart, even geniuses when it came to things like atoms and elements, but that didn't make it any easier to keep them on schedule.

His intercom buzzed, and he slapped down the switch. "Yes?"

Static. A second buzz. "Yes?" More static.

Groves raised his voice. "Damn thing is on the blink again. Get it fixed this time! I mean it!"

His secretary, a sergeant, opened the door. "The secretary would like to see you in his office," he said.

"Now?"

"Yes, sir."

"Tell him I'm on my way. And get this fixed before I get back!" The big man grabbed his hat and headed down the long Pentagon corridors to the E-Ring, where the secretary of war and the most senior officers kept their offices. He was waved through the layers of assistants, secretaries, and aides that surrounded Henry Stimson. "Mr. Secretary," he said in greeting when he entered the innermost office. Stimson had a great view of the Potomac through the window, the Fourteenth Street Bridge crossing the river, flowing into the federal buildings and monuments on the other side.

Stimson got to the point immediately. "The president wants to see us."

"All right," Groves replied. "Do we know what about?"

"Project status. What's the word from the Hanford?"

Groves reviewed. "They've solved the problem of the piles fizzling out— turns out they needed more uranium rods in there. There was enough space in the core to drill the extra holes. D pile went critical, nearly two weeks ago. B pile got started up just two days ago. But they're working now."

"Making . . . what is that stuff, again?"

"Plutonium." Groves limited his reply to the one word. He knew that the massive Hanford industrial complex, built along the Columbia River in the northwest and screened by mountains and military security from the rest of the country, was dedicated to the creation of this potent substance, the most valuable material—gram for gram—on the planet. Plutonium was, for all intents and purposes, a new element, something that had been previously unknown in nature. And Leslie Groves had seen a massive factory made just so it could be produced.

"Good," replied Stimson. "How soon till we have a working gadget?"

"Maybe July," replied Groves. "That's still our best-case scenario. Of course, that's the plutonium device—the Fat Man. Our Little Boy is a simpler design, but it's complicated, separating out the uranium for that one. I don't see how it could be ready before summer, either."

"That may not be good enough," Stimson said, shaking his head.

The look on Groves' face made his thoughts clear, but all he said was "Yes, sir." The Corps of Engineers had a World War II slogan: "The difficult we do at once. The impossible takes a little longer." His problems were of the "takes a little longer" variety, but he'd be damned if the war took one extra day because he couldn't get the job done. He started thinking of ways he could squeeze a little bit more out of his schedule.

KREMLIN, MOSCOW, USSR, 2200 HOURS GMT

Alexis Krigoff had accomplished a feat achieved by few men in the history of warfare—three promotions in a matter of as many days! Even more unusual, he had achieved this without his superior officers being killed in battle. Within hours after his previous meeting with Comrade Stalin, he had received an envelope containing not only his promotion to *podpolkovnik*, or lieutenant colonel, but assignment to the First Ukranian Front as a political officer, a commissar.

The First Ukranian Front, commanded by Marshal Ivan Stepanovich Konev, was a mammoth force of over 500,000 men and 1,400 tanks, and was one of two main Soviet fronts advancing into Germany. The other, the First Belorussian Front, under the command of Marshal Georgi Konstantinovich Zhukov, had 750,000 men and 1,800 tanks. Although the First Ukranian and First Belorussian fronts were the most important in this stage of the Great Patriotic War, they were not the only ones. The Soviet military was right now the strongest on earth. Mere years before, it had been unable to resist the great tank advances of Operation Barbarossa; now it was the Germans who crumbled before the unstoppable onslaught of Soviet might.

It was interesting that Krigoff was assigned to Konev rather than to Zhukov, because Stalin distrusted Zhukov, whose fame and competence threatened to overshadow the chairman. Stalin could brook no threat, not even an implicit one, to his own status, and as a result had removed Zhukov from command several times, only to restore him later on when the need proved greatest.

Being assigned to the front commanded by Marshal Ivan Stepanovich Konev was no disgrace, however. Stalin must have surrounded Zhukov with numerous agents to watch for any signs of danger, but Konev, a highly competent and effective commander, needed watching as well. As the Soviet Union continued on the road to true World Communism, the bourgeois tendencies were always something with which to be concerned. Everyone must be watched.

His uniform now carrying the shoulder boards of a *podpolkovnik,* two red stripes each with a star, he returned to the Kremlin, flushed with the anticipation of another meeting with the great man. His transition from an anonymous staff lieutenant to his new rank had come in such a dizzying swirl of events that he had not begun to adjust. He almost saluted the captain of the gatehouse guards; a last-second impulse held his hand until the man made the first gesture, which Krigoff crisply returned.

A lesser man, Krigoff reflected behind his tight smile, would have been frightened, even overwhelmed, by the rarefied atmosphere surrounding his new assignment. Even yesterday he had been a little awed. But he understood now that he had been destined for this place and this time. It remained only for him to see how he could turn that destiny toward his further advancement.

The means, he could see already, would come through the resumption of the campaign against the Nazis. Implicit in his appointment, of course, was Krigoff's duty to report everything he saw, heard, and otherwise perceived to the ever-suspicious chairman. This was the way in which he had first attracted Stalin's attention, and he was certain that it was the means by which he would secure his own place in the history of this great movement that was inevitably leading toward World Communism.

"*Tovarich Podpolkovnik Krigoff?*"

Alyosha looked up to see a major hastening out of an office. The man's face was pale, as if he was terrified that Krigoff would move on without speaking to him.

"Yes, Major?" He made his response as curt as possible, knowing that this was the way a busy lieutenant colonel was expected to act.

"I have been asked to show you a document—it was requested that you read it, before your meeting with the chairman. If you will come this way?"

"Could you not bring it to me? I am here on a matter of some urgency."

"Begging the colonel's pardon, but no—it is a top-secret communiqué and is not to be removed from the decoding section."

Krigoff nodded; this might prove to be interesting. "Take me there," he ordered.

For the next hour he perused the memorandum, which had been authored by none other than Marshal Zhukov himself. Zhukov had composed the document from his headquarters in eastern Poland; it was dated but two days ago. Krigoff was fascinated by what he read, though he maintained a critical detachment, for he knew that this was what the chairman expected of him.

In the paper the renowned hero of the Great Patriotic War outlined the dispositions of his military fronts. Operationally equivalent to the army groups of the Western Allies and Germany, though significantly larger, these fronts consisted of from three to seven armies, and they were poised for imminent attack. Against that mass of military might, it was difficult to imagine how anything the Fascists did could stand in the way of the great Soviet advance. But generals always found reasons for worry, and so long as they did, and Lieutenant Colonel Alexis Petrovich Krigoff was near, he would always have something to report to his mustachioed master.

After he completed the reading, he returned the document to the still sweating major, who carried it back to a massive safe as if it were nothing less than one of the treasured Fabergé eggs of the tsars. Krigoff continued on, climbing the stairs until he arrived at the anteroom of the chairman's office.

"He is ready for you, Comrade Colonel; you may go right in," declared the female captain, Stalin's appointments secretary. She was older than Krigoff, and he remembered that she had seen terrible action at Stalingrad while he, a lieutenant colonel, had never yet heard a shot fired in anger. No doubt she resented his quick ascension. At the same time, she was experienced enough in the ways of the Kremlin that no trace of her true feelings was revealed in her neutral expression.

Vaguely irritated in spite of her lack of affect, Krigoff stalked past without acknowledging the captain or her words.

The armed Red Army sergeant who opened the door also avoided revealing any emotion. This impassivity, or fear such as the major had displayed, were the two most common behaviors exhibited in the Kremlin. Krigoff had avoided both, a strategy not devoid of risk but one with a potential payoff, as his new shoulder boards signified. When Krigoff entered the great office, he was greeted like an old friend, and that distinction made his heart swell with pride.

"Ah, Alexis Petrovich, it is good to see you," declared Stalin, who was alone in the large Kremlin office. He rose from behind his massive desk and ambled to an open liquor cabinet. "Vodka?"

"Indeed, Comrade Chairman, a drink would be most welcome. Thank you." Assertiveness was clearly pleasing to Stalin, Krigoff noted. He offered a toast—"To the heroic armies of the Soviet Union!"—and swallowed the potent beverage, feeling the burn through his esophagus, the pleasant heat warming his belly. But only for a moment—he sensed that Stalin was ready for him to speak. Of course, the chairman already had far more extensive reports and briefings and analyses than Krigoff had read in the single, albeit detailed, memo. Indeed, Stalin no doubt had access to far more documentary information than any person in the world. But a factual recitation was not the kind of report he expected from his newly minted lieutenant colonel.

"Do you think my army is ready for this campaign?" Stalin asked, a genial chuckle concealing the gravity of the real question.

"Undoubtedly, Comrade Chairman. Spirits among the generals are high, and the staff work has apparently been meticulous. I believe that all of them are eager to go to work."

"Nice thing about enemies, that. They bring a wonderful focus."

Especially when the enemy has raped and blackened an entire country, Krigoff reflected privately. There were plenty of Russians who hated Stalin with an abiding passion—though he was not one of them—but even the most rebellious Russian hated the Nazis even more than they did the chairman. This hatred did in fact bring a unity to this endeavor that was being called the Great Patriotic War.

"Do you detect any indications of hesitancy, or fear?" pressed the chairman.

"There are . . . concerns," Krigoff said. "Marshal Konev seems to be very worried about the crossing of the Oder, after we clean up the rest of Poland. He claims that the Germans have used the interval of the armistice to dramatically fortify that line. His front will be secondary, of course, to Marshal Zhukov's, but it is still crucial to the campaign. Also, there is the matter of Konigsberg . . . even Zhukov acknowledged that great improvements had been made to the defenses there."

"Konigsberg!" Stalin spat the word, his eyes flashing. "That place will be worse than Leningrad, even than Stalingrad before we are done. Hah—it was once the capital of Prussia! By the time we are done, Prussia will be but a bad memory—I think it would be a fine joke to give half of it to Poland! We will take the rest, of course. And let the fucking Nazis see what it is like to have their beautiful cities blasted into rubble, their people dragged into slavery."

"The generals seem to feel that all of these obstacles can be crushed, though they are unwilling to predict an accurate time frame. And there was the one general noted, Petrovsky of the Second Guards Tank Army, who was still asking for more men and matériel."

"Bah!" Stalin was impatient and grouchy now, his earlier cheerful spirits having vanished as quickly as the Moscow twilight of a few hours earlier. "We stand on the brink of greatness, of historic opportunity! Even as we speak, Rumania and Bulgaria are being cleansed, not just of fascist influence, but of capitalists as well. The Second and Fourth Ukranian Fronts stand ready to bring about the same result in Hungary. I have the two Belorussian Fronts and the First Ukrainian Front ready to move into Poland. I want them to understand that, once they advance, they are not to stop—not for the Oder, not for Berlin, not until they reach the Rhine!"

Krigoff remained silent, sensing that a response was not necessary, might even be dangerous. A wise Communist always said nothing when there was any chance of saying the *wrong* thing.

"There is another weapon that will come to bear," Stalin continued. "And I would especially like your impressions of its efficacy. It is a new technology, something that we have obtained from the Germans—through diplomacy, believe it or not!" The chairman had a hearty chuckle at that statement, and of course Krigoff joined in the laughter, though he did not understand what his leader was talking about.

"Rockets!" Stalin said, still laughing. "And not the little Babushkas that we launch by the hundreds from our trucks! No, these are the size of airplanes, and we can send them a hundred miles. I intend to rain them down upon Warsaw as we open the attacks, and I would like a firsthand report as to their effectiveness. You will communicate directly to me, Alexis Petrovich—do you understand?"

"Of course, Comrade Chairman! I am ready to go at once!"

"Soon, soon. The generals, the *world,* must understand that this is a race— the timetable cannot be fixed in advance, because we do not know what our adversaries in the West will plan. Though I do expect them to be aggressive, as well as fast. Perhaps they have the audacity to desire Berlin for themselves— *this is why we must reach the Rhine!*

"It is any inclination toward hesitancy or caution that I wish to guard against," Stalin continued, speaking conversationally, as if his burst of words had exhausted his temper. "I am assigning you to the mobile general staff; you will be assistant commissar in a tank army. Your official superior will be General Yevgeny Yeremko—a loyal old communist, though I wonder if in fact he is getting *too* old." Krigoff made a mental note of that analysis; a superior's weakness was something that could almost always be exploited.

Krigoff considered his assignment. He was best qualified for the role as a commissar, or *zampolit,* that he had been assigned. This was a particularly important role in the Soviet military organization, the role of political officer— the instrument of Party control. At every military level from battalion on up, a deputy political commander provided an appropriate Marxist-Leninist oversight of the commander and conducted training and indoctrination activities for the troops.

This was a role of the highest Party importance, and there were special schools for zampolits just as study at Frunze Military Academy prepared military officers for their role. Krigoff's Party credentials and performance were beyond reproach, a critical qualification for such a position. But there was a problem: The commissar was consumed by internal duties involving the development of Marxist-Leninist thought among the soldiers, and was known as an instrument of Party control. This meant less opportunity to participate in the serious business of military operations, and also made people less willing to speak openly.

The chairman was still speaking. "You will further serve as liaison between the First Ukrainian and the First Belorussian fronts. You, Alexis Petrovich, are to be my eyes and ears on this campaign. You will report to me everything that you observe, no matter how trivial—you will let me decide if it is important."

"Yes, Comrade Chairman. It is my honor to obey." Krigoff's mind whirled over the task, and he ventured to speak further. "May I make a small suggestion that will help me better perform my mission?"

Stalin gestured curtly with one hand, indicating that the lieutenant colonel should speak.

"May I suggest that my assignment be recorded as a military rather than a political role. I only say this because it is my impression that soldiers are more free with their opinions among their own; an appointment as commissar might make me less open to their opinions, and especially their fears." He waited with some trepidation for Stalin's reply; making suggestions to the great man was a risky business. But he had started with audacity and would follow that course no matter what.

Once again, Krigoff's instincts proved right, because that blocky face brightened with a dazzling smile. Stalin might have been a proud grandfather, ready to pat his young grandson on the head for an impressive school report. "That is the kind of thinking I admire, Alexis Petrovich. . . . Yes, a good suggestion. An intelligence officer, of course . . . yes, you shall be the . . . let me think . . . ah, yes. How does Special Intelligence Adjutant to the General Staff sound?"

"Very good, Comrade Stalin, and thank you."

The vodka's warmth had dissipated by the time Alyosha Krigoff left the chairman's office, but the pleasant glow of satisfaction more than made up for it. He could pack in less than an hour—and at last, he would be off to the war.

The opportunities before him suddenly seemed even more limitless than before.

31 DECEMBER 1944

LONDON, ENGLAND, 0849 HOURS GMT

The fictional 221B Baker Street was much better known than its real-life analogue at 64 Baker Street: the headquarters of the British Secret Intelligence
Service, popularly known as MI-6. Going east on Marylebone Road, you
turned left to reach Sherlock Holmes' flat. If you turned right instead, you
would see a nondescript row of buildings, the center of Great Britain's far-
flung intelligence operations.

Section 5 of MI-6 was responsible for all European counterintelligence,
and one of its missions was liaison with the various anti-Nazi conspiracies in
Germany, including the von Stauffenberg group that had successfully assassinated Adolf Hitler. It was therefore to Section 5 of MI-6 that the government
turned when it was asked by the President of the United States to put together
a list of candidates for a provisional post-Nazi German government. And the
Chief of Section 5, Major Felix Cowgill, turned to his deputy chief, the person
responsible for day-to-day operations, for his advice and counsel.

The Deputy Chief of Section 5 liked his morning walk to work. It cleared
his head and helped him to establish priorities for the working day. London
was foggy and damp in late December, but it was not bitterly cold. The pervasive grayness emphasized the stonework in much of the city's construction.
When there was rubble from bombs and reconstruction, it all seemed part of a
seamless whole, a concrete blandness that pulled every drop of nature, of life,
of color, from the souls of the poor benighted masses who trudged to their
daily work, obtained money for rationed food, and ate it for the energy that
allowed them to work another day. This was capitalism at its finest.

Inside some of the stone buildings the privileged went to their private
clubs, where the dominant color was brown instead of gray, and servants wore
black-and-white. The only hint of a wider spectrum could be found in old
school ties, patterns of colored stripes that set the upper classes apart from the
lower and kept the machinery of the world humming smoothly.

Umbrella properly furled, trench coat buttoned, the Deputy Chief of
Section 5 was himself a model British gentleman, firmly rooted in his world, a
man of power and means. His father, a noted Arabist, had been best man at
the wedding of the late Field Marshal Bernard Montgomery. Accordingly, the
son attended Cambridge University, entered the Foreign Service, and progressed rapidly in his career. He knew full well that much of his advancement

was the product of the circumstances of his birth. Although his intelligence and ability were unquestioned, he knew equally well that in the absence of proper birth, he would never have been permitted the career he currently enjoyed.

It was a subject of ironic amusement that this was true for two entirely separate reasons. The first reason led inexorably to the second. It was because of the opportunities provided by his birth that he had first been recruited as a deep-cover Soviet agent. The class system that oppressed the masses was the same class system that allowed him to be positioned for maximum results.

He was a shy man with a stammer, though comfortable with large groups. Although he was very successful with women, he preferred men. He was a brilliant man, able to play a complex role to perfection, to convince others of his absolute loyalty, and to see the innermost twists and turns in the most elaborate of puzzles. His name was Harold Adrian Russell Philby, but he was nicknamed "Kim," after the character in Kipling.

Intelligence offices tended to be open around the clock. The door guards recognized him, but nevertheless he showed them his identification pass. They said, "Good morning, Mr. Philby," as if they did not know his name until they saw it on his pass, and he acknowledged them with a class-appropriate nod as he passed into the building. Others said "Good morning, Mr. Philby" to him without demanding his identification in advance, and he nodded or replied to each depending on their position in the organizational hierarchy.

His secretary stood as he entered—a product of military training rather than merely class roles in this instance—and Philby said, "Good morning. P-Please inform M-Major Cowgill that I'll see him in about an hour. J-Just have a few more files to r-review." As his secretary turned to the telephone, he entered his office, hung his rumpled trench coat and hat on the rack, and slid his furled umbrella into its holder. His secretary brought him tea on a silver tray and made a space for it on his crowded desk. The desk was heaped with files on all the characters in the conspiracy, those who had brought the situation to its current crisis point.

For most of the war, his primary mission had been to sabotage any hint of a pro-West and anti-Communist dialogue between the Germans and the British. Stalin rightly feared that this would quickly reduce Germany to a single-front war, and that would be extremely bad for the Soviet Union. Although von Stauffenberg's success was Philby's failure, at least the result had been an SS takeover of Germany. Nothing fundamental had changed.

That is, until the shock of the new Soviet-German armistice pact. Philby had only a few days' notice that it was coming, and it took him that amount of time to get himself under control. The earlier Soviet-German pact was, he understood perfectly, a matter of convenience, and so, he came to understand, was this also. Norway and Greece were great prizes: a year-round Atlantic port and a warm-water Mediterranean port. He could understand their value. Still, his own job was made far more complicated now that the Soviet Union was again an enemy, not an ally, of Great Britain.

But it was all forward movement for the cause. That is, until the second shock, that of Rommel's surrender. A brilliant move, Philby realized at once. It reminded him of a chess master sacrificing a queen to uncover a hidden checkmate. And Roosevelt, that master manipulator, now planned to build a new German government around Rommel's army.

Philby and his Soviet colleagues were determined to undermine the new German government, but he would have to proceed delicately indeed. It was not worth risking his position for a goal that small. And there would be many other opportunities to hamper his enemies. This day, therefore, his work would be what his MI-6 superiors wished it to be. As a double agent, he always found it interesting when he had to choose the work of his official job over the secret role he played. Mirror after mirror, chess move after chess move, each day required a thousand new calculations.

He loved his life.

Rustling through the file folders, he began to classify them. Politicians: Dr. Carl Goerdeler, ex-mayor of Leipzig. If Rommel was not to be the acting chancellor, Goerdeler was the likely choice. He went underground in the aftermath of the assassination and nearly was captured several times, but made it to safety in France. The folder went in the first pile.

Dr. Julius Leber. The conspirators' choice for vice-chancellor. He'd been imprisoned at the time of the assassination, killed in Himmler's replay of the Night of the Long Knives last September. Leber's file went into the next stack. Wilhelm Leuchner, labor leader. Also dead. Too bad. He was associated with the proletariat, and might have proved useful. Count Ewald von Kleist-Schmenzin. Conservative anti-Nazi, pro-Brit. Alive, worse luck. First stack.

On to the foreign ministry. Ernst von Weizsaecker. Currently ambassador to the Vatican and very much alive. Ambassador Ulrich von Hassel. Arrested and killed. Second stack.

Hans-Bernd von Haeften. His brother had been von Stauffenberg's aide and had died with the old soldier. Went out fighting, too, Philby mused. The older brother was a raging firebrand, wanted to go back on the attack immediately. He had been smuggled into France and to safety. A hothead. Philby might be able to do something with him. First stack.

Von Trott. Dead. Dr. Theodor Kordt. Ambassador to Switzerland, alive. Philby knew him because he had been the German ambassador to Great Britain just before he war. First stack. Count Helmuth von Moltke. Dead. Count Peter von Wartenburg, Stauffenberg's cousin. Dead. Dr. Eugen

Gerstenmaier, a clergyman. Arrested, tortured, still alive. This started a third stack. Some of these people might be liberated later.

Dr. Hans Gisevius. Alive and in Switzerland. Admiral Canaris. Philby shook his head. He had done everything in his power to have Special Operations assassinate Canaris, who was the mole inside Hitler's own secret police. Canaris was Hitler's Philby, he thought with a slight smile. Except not nearly so successful. Currently in Berlin under house arrest. Perhaps able to be rescued, but probably as good as dead. Second stack. General Oster. Dead. Colonel Alexander Hansen. Current Abwehr chief. Alive, but vulnerable.

Philby knew that Himmler had a long-range goal of dismantling the Abwehr altogether as soon as he could get enough evidence. The only thing that had stopped him thus far was his agreement with the Wehrmacht to let them run the military part of the war without interference. That agreement, Philby was sure, would last up until the moment Himmler had the power to do away with it, and not a moment longer.

Dr. Hans von Dohnanyi, brother-in-law of the famous theologian Dietrich Bonhoeffer. Currently in Sachsenhausen concentration camp for his role in Operation U-7 to get the Abwehr in the business of saving Jews from the death camps. Philby shook his head. Awful business, the matter of the Jews, and Philby was no sentimentalist. When that story came out, it would be enough to finish off any would-be German government. That would give the Soviet Union more room to claim for itself the role of liberator. Philby paused, glanced out the window to collect his thoughts. That was an idea worth exploring for its propaganda aspects. He would have to suggest this to his NKVD handler.

There was the man known as "X," who was really Dr. Joseph Mueller. Agent "X" had tried mightily to get British intelligence to agree to a temporary cease-fire in case of a coup. Philby smiled. Frustrating "X" had been fun. The good doctor was currently in prison, and could stay there for all Philby cared.

Popitz. Dead. Hjalmar Schact, Reichsbank president. Probably finance minister in the new government. Unimportant for now. First pile. Von Helldorf and his Berlin police allies. All dead. Lots of military leaders, from Beck on down. Most of them dead. Besides, Rommel will almost certainly push his own military candidates, like his chief of staff, Speidel.

As for Rommel himself . . . Philby thought about the man. He didn't know him well, but other German military leaders thought he was a show-off, a commander who owed his success to kissing Hitler's ass. The man normally went around with his own motion-picture team filming him, for God's sake! Although he hadn't done so lately, since his wounding. Vanity, Philby assumed.

Well, many of the more dangerous candidates were safely dead or prisoners of the Nazis. The Germans could easily form a government out of the remainder, but this late in the war they would have a hard time reversing their military losses and mounting a successful single-front offensive back into the Soviet Union. At best, they would be able to stalemate further Soviet gains, and that only with active support from the Western Allies. And the Western Allies had little stomach for continued fighting. Wrap it up and go home—that was the goal of most of them right now. The Americans, no doubt, were looking forward to wrapping themselves in their little fantasy world inside their own borders, convinced the rest of the planet could successfully be ignored. Soon enough, their day would come, and the Communist movement would take that nation, too.

Philby thought briefly about putting together notes to brief Major Cowgill, but he knew the players well enough through years of work. He slid the files he needed into his briefcase and called his secretary in to refile the rest, then headed off to the briefing.

NEAR PESSOUX, BELGIUM, 0927 HOURS GMT

"I *will* check on my patients," snapped Dr. Schlüter, "and you *will* get the hell out of my way. *Now!*"

The SS hauptscharführer was nonplussed at the doctor's rage. "But sir, I can't let you in the trucks without proper authorization."

"Am I a German officer, or am I a prisoner of war? If I'm a German officer, get the hell out of my way and say 'sir' while you're doing it. If I'm a prisoner of war, then I demand official notification and I demand to see my patients under the Geneva goddamn Convention. Either way, you will get the *hell* out of my way. *Now!*" His volume steadily rose alongside his temper. Fists clenched, face turning red, he stepped toward the towering SS sergeant, a man nearly twice his size. Such was the force of his rage that the man stepped backward without realizing what he was doing.

"You are a German officer, of course, and entitled to all the respect due to your rank and profession," interjected a smooth voice. "As are our other guests whom we have rescued from becoming prisoners of war of the Americans. When we reach the safety of Saint-Vith, you all will return to normal service for our fatherland."

Schlüter swiveled around, still furious. It was Peiper himself, his uniform still surprisingly neat and crisp, though he had worn it for nearly twenty-four hours straight, his hair properly slicked on one side, but covered on the other by the bandages that still swathed nearly half his face. Schlüter's medical eye surveyed his work. "Then I will attend to my patients. Afterward, I'll see you. Those bandages need changing. And it doesn't help if you keep picking at them. It likely itches now, and will itch even more as the healing gets under way. You will simply have to control yourself. Is that clear?"

Peiper was a man clearly unused to being ordered about in such a way, especially by a mere major. He stiffened reflexively, then forced his body to relax. Calmly, he replied. "Of course, Herr Doktor Major. We must continue moving at once, however. Please take a quick look in each of the trucks for any medical emergencies. Then you can work on those as we continue to move. As soon as we reach Saint-Vith, I will be quite pleased to have you change my bandages. In the meantime, I will attempt not to scratch. Is that satisfactory?"

Peiper's reasonableness took the wind out of Schlüter's sails. "Yes. Quite satisfactory. Thank you." He glared at the hauptscharführer, who stepped back again, now fully intimidated by the ferocious doctor, and headed for the first truck.

In spite of the savagery of the brief raid, the patients were unharmed. Here one had torn loose a bandage, here another had moved in a way that tore a suture, but these were minor indeed and could be fixed as the column moved forward. With some annoyance, he noticed that one of the trucks had contained hospital supplies and some of his own staff. If they were going to rescue people, it would have been a lot better to rescue patients rather than steal supplies that he could put to good use, he groused to himself. Of course, they could hardly be expected to check truck contents in the middle of the night. Still, that didn't help him.

In the fourth truck, he found Carl-Heinz Clausen, Rommel's driver. Clausen had the constitution of an ox, and it was clear he would return to good health quickly in spite of a belly wound. Next to Clausen, his eyes widened slightly as he recognized one of the American patients, wrapped in a Wehrmacht jacket that didn't fit—Clausen's, he presumed.

"And you look in good shape," he said to Clausen in a slightly louder voice, for the benefit of any listeners. "And you," he looked at the American. "Your voice is still damaged, so no talking. Not a word! Only sign language, Understand?" He grabbed his throat with his hand, hoping the American would figure out the gesture.

Clausen turned toward the American and winked broadly, then nodded his head slowly. The American got the idea, and touched his own throat in reply. The doctor nodded again. "Ill get you some more lozenges, if I can find some. Rest your voice for a few more days at least."

He withdrew from the truck rapidly, shaking his head in surprise at Clausen's temerity. *He could get us all killed* was his immediate thought.

Peiper strode down the long column until he reached the Tiger tanks bringing up the rear. "I expect the utmost alertness, the utmost focus, and the utmost drive, from all of you. We are the Fatherland's elite, and in every way and at every moment, each of us must do his duty to the fullest degree. If you cannot, then may God have mercy on you because I will have none. Is that clear?"

A ragged chorus of subdued "Yes, sir"s made him angrier. "What was that?" he demanded.

"Yes, sir," came a chant of more satisfying strength.

"Let's get moving," Peiper ordered. As he turned, he reached up to scratch his face through his bandages, but arrested his hand just in time.

1 JANUARY 1945

APPROACHING DINANT, BELGIUM, 0739 HOURS GMT
The long procession of American vehicles bumped and rattled across the snow-crusted roads as the first light of day strained through the heavy cloud layer, presaging another gray day in Belgium. Motorcycle riders formed the advance scout, frost threatening to overwhelm their goggles at any moment. Behind them rolled jeeps sporting .50-caliber machine guns at the ready, then a line of several official Army-green Packards bearing VIPs, and then two trucks of infantry and another filled with communications equipment. The flags on the lead Packard showed five stars in a pentagon—the insignia of the Supreme Commander of SHAEF.

"The sign says only three more klicks to Dinant, General," said his driver, Kay Summersby, over her shoulder. "We should be there in about ten minutes. There's an escort from Nineteenth Armored Division that will lead us straight to Field Marshal Rommel's headquarters."

"Okay, Irish," Eisenhower replied. "As long as they've got coffee perking when we get there." As the attractive young driver turned her attention back to the road, Eisenhower turned to his companions: Omar Bradley, next to him in the backseat, and George Patton, sitting across from Kay Summersby in the front seat but swiveled around so he didn't miss a moment. Eisenhower sighed internally, hoping his two generals would eventually find a way to make peace. And now another esteemed field commander entered the mix—but in what role?

"You'll like Rommel," said Patton with great assurance, his high-pitched voice grating this early in the morning. "He's a class act all the way."

"So you've been telling us," replied Eisenhower. "Actually, I'm looking forward to it."

He looked over at Bradley, who had leaned back against the seat and gone to sleep. Eisenhower hadn't had a lot of sleep himself, and wished he could join the Twelfth Army Group CO in a quick forty winks. Patton, on the other hand, was as alert and energetic as if he'd slept for a week—even though Ike knew he'd had no more rest than anybody else.

The car began to decelerate. "Here's the escort," observed Summersby. She followed her own lead vehicles into the line. The entire column slowed somewhat as they accommodated the new vehicles. Ike peered out the window, rubbing the condensation off the inside so he could get a look. Dinant probably used to be an attractive town, he guessed, but it had the same look as most other towns after they'd hosted a war—heaps of rubble, dust everywhere else, an unrelieved absence of color.

It took only a few more minutes before the convoy arrived at Rommel's Army Group B headquarters. Military police, both German and American, waved vehicles around. The VIP cars got directed right in front, and Ike saw an honor guard drawn up to meet him, all proper and official. It was time for him to put on his "company face" and go to work. First, however, he had to punch his seatmate. "Brad! Wake up."

"I'm awake," yawned Bradley. He twisted his neck around in a stretch and then shook his head. "Ready when you are."

The ritual of one commander paying a call on another was carefully prescribed; for the hosting general it was a source of great embarrassment if anything happened to be less than absolutely perfect. Eisenhower was appropriately impressed at Rommel's attention to detail, but then he expected nothing less. He had seen Rommel's work before in the long North African campaign, and knew that if it were not for the unquestioned Allied superiority in resources, that campaign might have had a different outcome.

The only problem with the ritual was that it extended the time until Ike could get a cup of coffee, and this morning it took all his self discipline to keep smiling and keep looking as the ceremony dragged on. Kay had slipped away almost immediately, and was almost certainly in the canteen or mess tent by now enjoying her own cup.

Rommel looked older and more worn than Eisenhower had anticipated. He walked carefully, like an old man whose bones were brittle. Of course, he had been severely wounded the previous summer—Ike had read all the intelligence reports as they had come in. It was clear to Ike that Rommel's healing was not yet complete. Rommel's left eyelid drooped next to where the scar tissue had formed and his eye watered constantly. Eisenhower made a mental note to himself to have his own doctors check out the Desert Fox. His health right now was a prime Allied consideration.

Finally the ritual drew to a close, and the senior generals retired to Rommel's conference room. On the American side, there were the three senior generals, Eisenhower, Bradley, and Patton. On the German side there were Rommel, Speidel, and his two remaining army commanders—von Manteuffel of Fifth Panzer Army and Brandenberg of Seventh Army. And at long last there was a big pot of perking hot coffee and uniformed aides to pour.

There was small talk, difficult when passed through translators. Introductions were made and expressions of mutual admiration were exchanged. The whole "after you, Alphonse" diplomatic dance was one of Eisenhower's talents—he knew that it was—but still, part of him itched to get down to real business. Patton was also at home in this environment. For all his vulgarity and outrageousness, he was upper-class born and bred, and did well when with senior officers. He had everyone laughing with an off-color joke, even the somewhat prim Rommel.

And it was time. "Field Marshal, I would also like to convey to you the respects of the President of the United States," Eisenhower said, as the other generals fell silent.

"I'm delighted," replied Rommel, bowing slightly while still sitting down. "But what does your president want with a simple prisoner of war?"

"You're anything but a simple prisoner," replied Eisenhower. "In fact, what to do with you has commanded the attention of the very highest levels of my government."

"Has there been a decision?" inquired Rommel in a deceptively light tone of voice.

"Perhaps the word 'proposal' would be more appropriate," returned Eisenhower.

"Interesting. I would very much like to hear what your president has in mind."

"How does Chancellor of Germany sound to you?"

SAINT-VITH, BELGIUM, 0807 HOURS GMT

There was noise and near chaos everywhere as the remaining units of Sixth Panzer Army moved back along the wide front on which they had originally advanced. Saint-Vith, a town far too small to accommodate the forces passing through it, rumbled and seethed with the sounds of engines and marching men. It was there that Kampfgruppe Peiper reunited with the rest of its division to re-form the Leibstandarte Adolf Hitler. The orders were urgent: Keep moving east, into the Westwall positions north of the ancient German city of Trier.

Jochen Peiper still felt as if half his face were still on fire. The pain was excruciating, yet in a way it was a clean pain, a transforming pain. Bandages still covered the flesh that had been so terribly shredded only two days before. He was uncertain whether his injured eye would be able to see again, but his unbandaged eye remained a clear, penetrating blue. He could stand and give orders and conduct a battle, and that was all an SS officer was expected to do. Peiper did not like retreating and regrouping, but the treason of the Desert Fox made it necessary, at least for now. As the convoy pulled into the center of town on the narrow old streets, Peiper got some good news as Sepp Dietrich came out to welcome him. Dietrich shook his hand and congratulated him on his amazing victories, his lightning raid on Rommel, his skill in extracting himself and his men from a dangerous situation. He said nothing about how Peiper had removed Guderian from command, though Dietrich's friendly face, his obvious solicitous reaction to Peiper's wounds, spoke volumes to the SS-Obersturmbannführer.

"The führer has restored me to command," said the old general. "Sixth Panzer Army is now Sixth SS Panzer Army."

"A welcome development, General! Kampfgruppe Peiper stands ready to avenge the treason to the Fatherland!" Peiper announced, saluting proudly.

Dietrich returned the salute. "You're injured, Jochen. Badly?"

"Mostly cosmetic, and it should heal," Peiper replied. "It won't slow me down."

"Well, just remember, women love a good scar. They know a man with a scar is a real man, proven in battle. And the way the fräuleins flock over a little dueling scar, how much better to have a real mark of battle. Jochen, you've always been too pretty. Now you're much more manly looking." Dietrich, whose own homely face was battered like a boxer's, grinned as he punched his subordinate lightly on the arm.

Peiper could not help but smile in return, even though the smile pulled at his stitches and turned it into somewhat of a grimace. "I brought the doctor and those among the patients who could expect to return to duty along with us."

Dietrich nodded. "Good thinking, good thinking. Absolutely. We need all the doctors we can get. And the wounded? Yes, well, most of them will recover quickly and return to the fight. The severely wounded?"

"I left them behind with two orderlies. They will be an extra burden on the Allies, and they could not return to the battle quickly, if ever in some cases."

"Good, good, good," nodded Dietrich, rubbing his hands together. "Yes, yes. And we have a good, strong army left, and reinforcements coming in. Field Marshal Mödel has told us that we must close off the portion of the Westwall and the Rhine approaches that are left exposed by the . . . by the unfortunate situation." Dietrich could hardly bring himself to say the name "Rommel" or the word "surrender" in an actual sentence. It was obvious that he felt Rommel's treason as a personal blow. After all, the men had once been friends, of a sort.

"We are ready, mein Obergruppenführer!" said Peiper. "We can turn around and attack as soon as you give the order."

"Good, good. Good man. Knew I could depend on you. Always can depend on the Leibstandarte Adolf Hitler, right?" As the founder of the division, Dietrich glowed with patriotic pride whenever his unit went into action. The Leibstandarte had originally been a personal bodyguard for Hitler, way back in the early days of the Nazi party when Sepp Dietrich was still a member of the Freikorps.

"Yes, sir," replied Peiper with enthusiasm.

"Well, we'll get to it very shortly, I'm sure. My job right now is to get us all back safely into the Westwall, with as much haste as possible—after all, we cannot afford to allow our enemies, German or American, to take those fortifications, or they will have a free road into the Rhineland. You will need to move out at once. Once we have taken that line, our new Commander-in-Chief West will outline the strategy for blocking the hole. So take care of yourself and your men, and I'm certain we'll see some action very soon. Very soon. All right? Good man. Good man."

ARMEEGRUPPE B HEADQUARTERS, DINANT, BELGIUM, 0922 HOURS GMT

Generaloberst Doktor Hans Speidel, Rommel's chief of staff, had been leading a double life for more than a year now. He understood that assassinating Adolf Hitler was all well and good, a necessary starting point but just that: a beginning. There needed to be a military plan in place, a charismatic and popular figure ready to become head of state, something positive rather than solely the elimination of something negative. Now it seemed as though all his planning and all his striving reached an apex as General Eisenhower himself offered Rommel the chancellorship of Germany.

Rommel's outright refusal, however, shocked Speidel to his core.

"Chancellor? I'm afraid I could never accept such a role. No, I will do whatever I can to free Germany from its Nazi yoke, but I cannot possibly consider being its head," the field marshal had replied, after a moment's surprised reflection.

Speidel could tell that Eisenhower was surprised as well. "May I ask why, Field Marshal?" the American inquired.

"I have surrendered, General Eisenhower. I fought and I lost. Worse, I have violated my soldier's oath, even to the point of consorting with the enemies of my nation—no offense intended, of course."

Eisenhower nodded. "I guess I can understand that. I suppose it wouldn't help to remind you that you truly are acting in the best interests of your nation and your people—because you are, I know."

"Would that make you think differently if our positions were reversed?" replied Rommel.

The American general thought for a moment. "I'd like to say it would, but I suspect it wouldn't. The problem is that your nation needs you in this role, whether you want it or not."

It was Rommel's turn to think for a moment. Speidel wanted to interject, to say, "Eisenhower's right. You must take it for the good of Germany," but he knew that a direct approach was not always good strategy where Rommel was concerned. Months and years of trying to influence the man had taught him that, if nothing else.

Rommel spoke slowly and carefully. "If it were for the good of my countrymen, I could refuse nothing. But you assume that I am the only viable leader fit for such a role, and I do not agree. There are any number of people free of the Nazi taint—freer than I am, in fact—who have the credentials and the ability to serve as the leader of a government-in-exile. That is what you are proposing, is it not? After all, none of us are actually in Germany at the moment."

Eisenhower was not so easily dissuaded from his mission. "Yes, there are others. But not with your fame, your military record, and your stature."

Rommel looked at his folded hands on the conference table. "All three, I submit, are of questionable value right now. In any event, if President Roosevelt is planning to build a new German government, there must be others he considers worthy of leadership. There cannot very well be a government of a single person, after all. As you know, this kind of discussion has taken place among many members of the Wehrmacht officer corps over the past years. The brave men who assassinated Adolf Hitler were Wehrmacht officers. Others in the political establishment, the foreign ministry, and elsewhere supported them in their efforts from the earliest time onward. I am somewhat of a latecomer to this effort. Those whose roles are of longer duration are the right men to create a provisional and transitional government. As for me, I am willing to remain in my role as a soldier, and to put my armies—such as are willing—in the service of such a government. But I can do no more."

Speidel watched Eisenhower's face carefully as the American translator Sanger rendered Rommel's words into English. He was disappointed but not surprised at Rommel's refusal to lead the government. Rommel was right; there were others, but without his stature in the eyes of the ordinary people of Germany. But what were Eisenhower's orders from Roosevelt? Would Rommel's rejection of the chancellorship cause the Americans to react the wrong way? He discovered that he was holding his breath.

Eisenhower looked as if he was choosing his own next words with care. "Field Marshal, I actually understand quite well what you're saying and what you must be feeling. Moving from the military sphere to civilian leadership is not easy, and I suppose there's even a question whether it's really an increase or a decrease in rank." He grinned boyishly at his own joke, then his expression turned more serious again. "Maybe we could compromise. Maybe we could say that because of the military exigencies, you think it's best to remain as field marshal and maybe war minister for right now, but that you may be willing to stand for the chancellorship in an election after Germany is liberated." Eisenhower's voice got lower, as if he were passing along a secret. "Personally, I think you shouldn't just outright refuse—keep your options open and keep the politicians guessing. It helps when you're trying to make sure important decisions go your way."

Rommel could not help but smile at Eisenhower's friendly advice. He turned his hands palms upward as if in surrender. "Very well, General Eisenhower. I agree exactly as you suggest; I will 'keep my options open.' Except perhaps for one small suggestion: the position of war minister. I think my chief of staff would be an excellent choice for that role. *Nicht wahr, Hans?*" With that aside, Rommel's smile turned into an actual grin.

Speidel was stunned. He could only stammer, "Y-Yes, mein Generalfeldmarschall. I am always at your service."

SAINT-VITH, BELGIUM, 1037 HOURS GMT

Shifting into low as he entered the city limits of Saint-Vith, Lukas Vogel once again produced a terrible racket of grinding gears as the truck lurched. Hans Braun, sitting in the next seat, grabbed the dashboard to keep from slamming into it.

"Damn it," Lukas groaned with frustration.

"Don't sweat it," replied Braun. "Hell, if it wasn't for you, we'd be walking right now."

The transmission finally engaged, and Lukas twisted the heavy, awkward steering wheel to the right. Driving the truck down unfamiliar and twisty Belgian roads through the long night had taken all the rest of his strength. Braun had catnapped a little bit, but his sleep had been interrupted numerous times by Lukas needing him to jump out and decipher a road sign or check around for other vehicles. At least the boys in the back of the truck were able to get a little sleep around the jostling, the noise, and the pervasive cold. The truck heater worked well, but the warmth kept making him dangerously sleepy, so he'd ended up driving most of the night with the window open. He thought about stopping someplace for some rest, but it seemed too dangerous.

With the first gray hints of dawn, he felt himself getting his second wind, and he was finally able to risk rolling up his window most of the way and letting a little heat thaw his numb fingers and toes.

"What now, boss?" asked Braun.

Lukas thought about it a minute. Although he liked being boss, he was increasingly getting a sense of its challenges. "I guess the best course is to find an officer and see about getting assigned to a unit still fighting."

"Yeah, but there are officers and then there are officers, if you know what I mean," replied Braun.

Lukas nodded. "That's all we need, one more *blödes Arschloch* of a Wehrmacht coward too chickenshit to lead us to victory."

"Well, how do we know which officer?"

Lukas braked hard at an intersection. A Panzer Mark IV rumbled by on the cross street. "Looks like we've reached a place with a lot of officers. Let's look around until we find someone who looks like he doesn't have his head up his ass."

Braun snorted a laugh in response, then turned around to pound on the back of the truck. "You back there! Time to rise and shine! We're in Saint-Vith, so we'll be stopping soon," he shouted.

When he rolled down the window, he could hear the replies through the canvas covering the truck body. "Hey, how about finding us something to eat and drink? We're dying back here!" came one voice, followed by another yelling, "How about some place to take a piss?"

Lukas shook his head. "Not a very soldierly bunch, these boys."

"Oh, I don't know," replied Braun. "Even the old farts spend most of their days pissing and moaning about something. That must be what soldiers do."

"Not German soldiers," replied Lukas with utter confidence. "At least not *real* German soldiers." Absently, he ran his hand over his still-smooth chin. "Hey—look over there! There's a skeleton key painted on that panzer. That must be part of Leibstandarte SS Adolf Hitler!" Lukas could name every SS division and recognize their insignia instantly. "Damn! Wouldn't it be great if we could join up with the LSSAH?" He pounded the steering wheel with the flat of his hand in his excitement.

"Yeah? Don't get your hopes up."

Lukas looked at Braun. "I know what I'm going to do. I'm going to ask them "

"Ask them what? If we can join the most elite panzer division? Fat chance."

"Hey—you wanted an officer who wasn't a chickenshit with his head up his ass. You think that guy qualifies?" He pointed to the sidewalk, where a tall SS officer with his face swathed in bandages and the skeleton key insignia on his unit patch stood, apparently waiting for somebody. There was a panzer nearby with command markings. Lukas braked the truck to a stop.

"Wait—Lukas, are you sure this is a good idea?"

Lukas turned, the door half open. "Braun, what's the worst that can happen? He tells me to go fuck myself, then we look for someone else."

Braun shook his head. "You're braver than I am."

Lukas smiled. "That's why I'm the boss." He opened the door the rest of the way and jumped lightly to the ground. His legs were a little wobbly from the long ride. He looked down at his sadly wrinkled and dirty uniform coat and brushed at it futilely for a minute, then walked up to the officer. His nervousness increased as he got closer. He looked back at Braun in the truck, then kept going. He couldn't turn back with Braun watching. The officer turned to look his way, and Lukas snapped to attention, his arm shooting out in the proper salute. *"Sieg heil!"* he said, and then "Excuse me please, sir—"

The officer looked at him with ill-concealed amusement, and returned the salute in a more casual manner. "Yeah, kid, what is it?"

"Excuse me please, sir, we come from the Eighteenth Volksgrenadier Division in Fifth Panzer Army—"

"Yeah? And what are you, their advance guard?"

"No, sir. You see, the Eighteenth surrendered, and we decided not to surrender with it."

"Oh," said the officer, this time with a bit more interest. "You deserted, then?"

Lukas was indignant. "No, sir! The first duty of any prisoner of war is to escape and return to his own side!" he snapped out in a formal parade-ground voice.

The officer laughed. "At ease, son. You said 'we.' Those your buddies in the truck?"

"Yes, sir," replied Lukas, still carefully formal. "About twenty of us."

"And you're the leader?" inquired the officer.

"Yes, sir," replied Lukas. "Oberschütze Lukas Vogel, at your service, sir!" He heil-Hitlered again, to which the officer replied with a wave of his hand.

"Well, Oberschütze Lukas Vogel, I'm SS-Obersturmbannführer Jochen Peiper."

Lukas' eyes grew wide. "Th-This is a great honor, sir! To-to meet the hero of the Mscha, I-I mean, sir." He couldn't think of anything else to do, so he heil-Hitlered yet again.

Peiper's response was a wave even more casual, but the officer was smiling. "Relax, son. I don't bite—fellow Germans, anyway."

Lukas was still tongue-tied. Trying to work up the nerve to ask if he could join the LSSAH, he was even more discomfited to see a man in a gray SS uniform sporting the insignia of an SS-Obergruppenführer, accompanied by another officer who appeared to be his aide-de-camp. He'd never even seen a general officer in the flesh, much less had one standing next to him.

Peiper smiled as he said, "Obergruppenführer Dietrich, may I present Oberschütze . . . Vogel, was it?"

Lukas nodded dumbly. He put out his hand once again in a Hitlerian salute, but no words issued from his mouth. He was in the presence of Sepp Dietrich, a personal friend of the führer's himself, a hero with roots in the earliest days of the Nazi movement. He felt woozy, as if he were going to faint.

Amused by Lukas' obvious discomfort, Peiper went on. "He was with the Eighteenth Volksgrenadiers when they decided to join Rommel's treason. He recruited some other soldiers and led them here."

"Well, good work, good work," said Dietrich heartily. "Glad you made it out safely. Bring some men with you, did you?"

Finally Lukas managed to squeak out a reply. "Y-Yes, sir. They're in the truck, sir."

"He—ah—liberated the truck as well. Kept it out of the enemy's hands."

"Not exactly, sir—some other men stole the truck, but they were using it to sneak stolen goods and money back into Germany."

Dietrich looked at Peiper. "Stolen goods and money?" he asked.

"First I've heard of it," replied Peiper. "This boy gets more interesting by the minute."

Dietrich's rank was more intimidating than Peiper's, but Dietrich was a friendlier and more approachable man. He obviously liked talking to enlisted ranks. Lukas remembered vaguely that Dietrich had been a feldwebel in the First World War. Under Dietrich's gentle prodding, Lukas told the story of how he and his men had taken the truck.

"You pulled a knife on him, eh? Instead of using your gun?"

"I wanted to frighten him, sir. It seemed to work—at least, he got right out of the truck."

"Very resourceful young lad," Dietrich said to Peiper.

"Evidently so," Peiper replied, his amusement growing with every new revelation.

"All right, son, let's see about all this and get it put right," said Dietrich.

Lukas could scarcely believe his problems were drawing the personal attention of a senior general, but at Dietrich's order he called his men out of the truck, lined them up in a rough approximation of a formation, and got them to attention. Dietrich inspected the line with the same gravity and formality as if it were a real command; Peiper went along with it but in a more joking manner. Dietrich kept mumbling, "Good, good, very good. Good boys, good boys," as he looked over each of Lukas' charges.

Then Lukas had his soldiers bring out what was left in the truck. There were typewriters and other office items, several field telephones, an adding machine—all items easily sold into the black market, he could see—and a satchel filled with deutsche marks.

"Hmm, Peiper, look at this," Dietrich said.

Peiper looked at the money with a bit more than casual interest, and then at Lukas. "You could have easily kept this," he said.

Lukas was indignant at the implication. "Sir!" he snapped back. "This money is the property of the German government!"

Again, Peiper laughed. "At ease. I wasn't questioning your ethics—after all, you told us you had the money. I was just observing that other men might not have been so honest." This mollified the young soldier somewhat, but his ears were burning red.

Dietrich hefted the satchel. "I guess they stole the contents of the paymaster's safe," he mused.

"That's very probable," replied Peiper. "I'd feel sorry for the soldiers, but they're all POWs now, so paying them is someone else's problem. Besides, if the Allies had gotten hold of this, the soldiers wouldn't have seen a pfennig of it anyway."

"Well, what are we going to do, Jochen?" Dietrich asked.

"Office equipment is always in short supply; it'll be easy to put it back in service. As a matter of fact, we could probably use it ourselves."

"Okay. You've got it. Have your men carry it away," Dietrich said.

"Then there's the truck. Anybody can use the truck, but why not let the boys take it wherever they end up going, and then they can give it up."

"Good idea. Much too cold for these boys to walk. Much too cold."

Peiper nodded, then turned to Lukas. "Any ideas about what you want to do? It's almost as if you're reenlisting, in a way."

Lukas' hopes and dreams burst out of him before he could stop himself. "It would be the greatest of honors to serve in the Leibstandarte Adolf Hitler under your leadership, sir!" he said, and his face burned red as he said it.

Peiper thought for a long minute, then shook his head sadly. "Sorry, Oberschütze Vogel. I can use men, but you're not even . . . what, fifteen years old yet?"

"I will be sixteen next month, sir!" he responded with passion.

"Went through panzer training?"

"Er—no, sir . . ."

"I can't. But you could check back in a few years."

Dietrich shook his head sadly. "Peiper, I'm disappointed in you. These boys are the cream of German youth, and our nation's hope for tomorrow."

Taken aback at his general's criticism, Peiper quickly backpedaled. "Well, if it would please you, I would—"

"No, no. Can't make a man take someone he doesn't want. It's not right. Doesn't work. No, no. But there's the Hitlerjugend division, if he wants panzers."

"That's a wonderful suggestion, sir," said Peiper obsequiously. "The Twelfth SS Panzer Division would be a great place for these boys. They're obviously the sort of people who belong in the Waffen-SS rather than the Wehrmacht." Peiper's one good eye ran lazily down the line of unwashed, sleepy, rumpled teenage boys.

"How about it, Vogel?" Dietrich asked. "How would you like to be part of the Hitlerjugend division?"

Lukas didn't need to think about it. It wasn't the LSSAH, but it was a Waffen-SS panzer division and a home. "My men and I would be honored, sir!" He saluted again. Dietrich returned the salute with grave solemnity.

"All right, then. All right. Good, good. I think that's a fine decision." He motioned to his ADC. "Write up an order of transfer and sign my name to it. All these boys are joining the Waffen-SS and going into the Hitlerjugend division. And this fine young man here—" Dietrich clapped his hand on Lukas' shoulder. "He's a natural leader. I'm making him an SS-Untersturmführer as of this date."

Lukas was stunned—a move from private first class to second lieutenant in one jump!—and could barely stammer out his thanks. Dietrich dismissed his stammers with a friendly wave, and asked, "Which of these boys is your second-in-command?" Lukas indicated Hans Braun. "And make this boy a sturmscharführer while you're at it," he said to his ADC. Braun, as astonished at making sergeant as Lukas was in making second lieutenant, stammered out his thanks as well.

In a generous mood, Dietrich then made the grenadiers into SS-Oberschützen, effectively bumping up all the privates to PFC, and the remaining oberschützen into the SS corporal grade of sturmmann.

Lukas had completely forgotten about the satchel of cash, but Dietrich pulled him aside for a confidential chat on the other side of the truck. "It's a tough time, a real tough time," he said, shaking his head sadly. "You're a brave lad, and I hope you do well. You and your friends are Germany's future, no matter what happens. So I'm going to give you a private order, son. Understand?"

"Yes, sir!" Lukas snapped back, and nearly went into another heil-Hitler until a slight shake of Dietrich's head made him stop. "Officers are like fathers, and so you're the father of those boys of yours now. Understand? Some of them will get other fathers as they get assigned, but your first job is to take care of them. Here . . ." To Lukas' utter shock, Dietrich unsnapped the satchel, and took several wads of bills and threw them up into the driver's seat through the open truck window.

"Sir, you don't need to—"

"Never argue with a general, son," smiled Dietrich. "It'll take you a few days to get in with the HJ panzers, and I'm not that sure how your truck will hold up. I used to work in a garage, you know, and I understand these things." He patted the truck side as if it were a horse. "You'll need some money if you need to get it fixed. You need new insignia and the boys need some new warm clothes. And all of you need to eat. Eat well and eat often. You're an officer now, and that's your payroll. Take care of these boys for me, and take care of them well. I want you all to report for duty well fed, well rested, and warm. Do you understand me, Untersturmführer Vogel?"

This time Lukas did snap to attention and salute, *"Jawohl, mein Obergruppenführer!,"* Dietrich returned it with equal gravity.

OKW HEADQUARTERS, BERLIN, 1830 HOURS GMT

The innocuous little one-story house with a gabled roof, surrounded by woods, had thus far escaped the fury of the Allied bombing campaigns. More and more of the German industrial and military capabilities had been moved underground, and the military command structure was no exception. The house was known as Maybach I, and beneath it could be found an extensive bunker network that served as the German Armed Forces High Command, known as OKW.

Deep beneath the ground, the boots of Field Marshal Walther Mödel echoed in the halls of OKW headquarters as he walked to his next meeting.

Even after dark, the Oberkommando der Wehrmacht, Germany's supreme military command, was active. The planning and operations teams worked around the clock.

Mödel opened an office door, and a male secretary looked up. "Heil Himmler, Generalfeldmarschall. The Generalfeldmarschall is in his office; please go right in. He's expecting you."

Mödel nodded to the secretary and opened the door to the inner office.

"Walther, come in. Have a seat. How is the planning going?" said Field Marshal Wilhelm Keitel, chief of OKW. Keitel was a gray-haired, mustached man of distinguished features. His prominent eyes gave him an appearance of depth, though in fact he was known primarily as a tireless desk worker whose lack of imagination and personal drive had shackled him to a thankless job that no one else wanted. His nickname, "Laikaitel," was testament to his role as a lackey, to the well-known fact that it was Jodl who did all the real work.

Generaloberst Alfred Jodl was technically Keitel's subordinate, but it was he who had given concrete military shape to many of Adolf Hitler's strategic decisions. A balding man with a long, sharp nose, Jodl was the one most deeply and personally affected by Hitler's assassination. He had not been able to develop quite the same rapport with Himmler that he had enjoyed with the first führer, but he still possessed significant power and influence.

Restoring broken fronts was the military specialty of Walther Mödel, a little man with a pleasantly ugly face who had become known as the "Führer's Fireman" after stabilizing the Belorussian and Polish sectors during the destruction of Army Group Center. Mödel had been one of the German Reich's wartime discoveries, a creative and skilled man who climbed the ladder of advancement rapidly as a result of his accomplishments.

More and more, however, Mödel's work seemed futile, plugging gaps, restoring disaster into some semblance of order, moving hither and yon in support of the varied missions he was assigned. And now he had to make sense of out of one the most surprising situations he had yet encountered: Rommel's sudden surrender.

He looked at Keitel and at Jodl. Old Laikaitel was reliable for the paperwork and administrative functions, but had no vision. Jodl had vision and skill, but was pulled in multiple directions by the needs of the west and the east.

"I've got a first roundup of the situation," he announced. "Most of Sixth Panzer Army has been recovered. Some minor desertions appear to balance out by people who've left the surrendered units to join ones still loyal to the Fatherland. There has been an armed struggle for control in at least two divisions, one in Sixth Panzer Army, one in Fifth. We kept control of Sixth Panzer Army by the narrowest of margins. Guderian was about to surrender along with Rommel, but Jochen Peiper executed him on the führer's orders."

The entire subject of surrender was anathema to Keitel's conservative

Prussian heart. "If he was a coward, then it is right that he died as one, at the hands of a true warrior," Keitel pronounced.

Jodl let a small giggle escape. "I heard about that. Seems that Peiper wasn't content to kill him. He hanged him in his own conference room as a warning to others." A stern look from Keitel put an end to this indecorous line of conversation.

Mödel continued with his briefing. "The success to date of the Soviet armistice means that we have substantial reserves within Germany, though most of these have been deployed in the east against the expected Soviet treachery. We have a limited ability to move some of these divisions to the Rhine, but you both know the difficulties in such movements: the state of our railroads, the presence of Allied air power. In sum, it will be difficult to put a force on our great river barrier in less than ten days or two weeks. We will have to hope that enough of our loyal forces remain to establish resistance in the Westwall, and throughout the Rhineland. If the American advance to the Rhine can be delayed to more than ten days, we will be able to form a defensive line at the river. If not, I can make no promises."

He paused. "I think we all know the difficulty here: how long before Stalin recommences offensive operations in the East. He would have paused at this time anyway to permit resupply; in addition, we threw the dog two juicy bones to distract him. But before long, the dog will grow hungry again, and when that is the case we will return to our former dilemma: a two-front war and gradual destruction of our resupply capabilities."

Any hint of defeatism, no matter how realistic or how justified, tended to draw disapproving looks from Keitel. "The original goal we sought in the armistice was to buy us enough time to quiet one front so we could turn all our attention to the other. Stalin is not on the march again yet. With the failure of Fuchs am Rhein, the question becomes, can we slow down the advance in the West before the forces must be rushed East again? In other words, how much time do I have?"

That was a real question. It was the key question, on which all else needed to be built. The two OKW chiefs looked at each other. Mödel kept his attention on Jodl, for the opinion of the operations chief was the one that would inevitably become the opinion of Keitel as well.

The pause stretched for several seconds. Finally, Jodl punctured the silence. "Walther, I think your analysis is basically on target. I don't expect our friends in the East to stay quiet much longer, and although I will hate to do it, when they begin to march once again, I will need to transfer forces back to the Eastern Front as quickly as possible. For you, speed is of the essence. I can't tell you if you have weeks or months, but I would base my plan on days, if possible. The Westwall must be stabilized, the hole created by Rommel's treason plugged, and the Allies delivered a sharp counterblow that will return them to the slow campaign of the fall. Patton is no good when slowness and caution is called for. He's somewhat like Rommel in that way. Give him the opportunity for speed and dash and he is dangerous; without that opportunity he is far less effective. Afterward, you need to plan how you can hold the line with an absolute minimum of forces. I imagine that we'll be pulling away everything we can."

"That's about what I thought," nodded Mödel. "We need an excellent defense, with enough teeth to make the hungry dogs to the West think twice about a push forward. Then the dogs of the East, *nicht wahr?*" Both generals laughed. "But I must bring up a very delicate point. In this room, being realistic about the enemy's relative supply situation is not to be construed as pessimism, and we must be realistic to make the right decisions for the Fatherland. Correct?"

Keitel once again began to put on his disapproving face, but Jodl interjected. "It's not pessimism if there's a constructive and positive answer following."

"Depending on Stalin's speed, there must be a secondary plan in place. If you must take away too much of my force, what next?"

Jodl thought seriously for a moment. "I suppose then it will become time for Operation Werewolf."

"I agree," replied Mödel. Keitel also nodded after a moment.

"And while we're on the subject of Werewolf, I think an excellent lesson would be learned by all if our old friend the baby field marshal received an appropriate punishment for his treason," said Jodl, his face turning ugly. "The führer sent Gestapo to arrest his wife and son, but it seems they have already fled."

"I'm sure the long arm of the Gestapo can reach even outside the borders of the Fatherland," replied Mödel. "I agree. Rommel must be made an example to all. One surrender of this sort is one too many. There must not be a repeat. And this is disgraceful, completely disgraceful behavior on his part. Doesn't he know that a field marshal above all else must never be captured alive?"

On that point all three men agreed.

GORKY PARK, MOSCOW, USSR, 2044 HOURS GMT
Alyosha Krigoff came to the park in the evening, climbed to the overlook over the River Moskva, and admired the domed towers of the Kremlin rising from the city on the opposite side of the valley, three or four kilometers downstream. This was the place he came for reflection, for privacy, for contemplation. He would miss it, more than any other location, or person, in this great city.

His train ticket was in his pocket, and he would cross the bridge shortly, making the short walk so that he arrived at Kiev Station in the early hours of the morning. The train would depart for the west before dawn. But for now, he was happy to take Marshal Bulganin's advice, and relish one last look around the capital of his mighty nation.

Even in the darkness, with but a sliver of a moon, the view was spectacular. Though the city was still under a war-induced blackout, the Kremlin stood out in clear relief, and the white band of the river was a smooth, winding S through the heart of the city. He wondered about the illumination—how could it be so bright?

He was startled to hear a hushed sound nearby, a mechanical click emerging from beyond a nearby pine. His feet crunched on the snow as he stepped around the tree, drawing a startled gasp from a photographer who was bent over a tripod, camera pointed not at the city but at the northern skies.

"Comrade Officer! You startled me!" said the photographer, in a woman's voice surprisingly devoid of fear. She lifted her head and he saw the patch over her eye. Immediately he felt a surge of unnatural delight.

"Comrade Koninin? Paulina Arkadyevna? It is I, Colonel Krigoff."

"Comrade Major—er, Colonel?," Paulina said, coming forward to shake his outstretched hand, noting the new insignia on his high-brimmed cap. "It would seem that your meeting with the chairman went well."

He loved that slight smile that once again tightened across her full lips, and he shrugged modestly in reply, letting his new rank speak for itself. His masculine ego was quite gratified that she had come to this place, to seek him out again. "I see that you found this place. The view is splendid, is it not?"

"Indeed," she replied. "Though I was not expecting such a treat."

Her words seemed a bit too forward, and he must have looked puzzled, for she pointed past his shoulder, upward to the north. "The aurora is spectacular tonight."

He spun about to see what she meant, and saw the green curtain of the northern lights sprawling and pulsing in the night sky. How could he have missed it? The brilliance faded and then surged back, tendrils of sparkling illumination spreading like a spiderweb from the far horizon into the cosmos directly overhead. That was why the city had been so brightly visible on this winter night, he realized. For a moment he stared in wonder, rapt at the fluorescent display of nature's majesty. It was an omen, a splendid omen, as if Father Winter were displaying his pride over Mother Russia. *Ah,* he thought, *it was the photographer's eye that brought her here.* She was not here for him. At least, he thought, not yet. He was a patient man where the chase was concerned; he felt no need to rush.

"A rare treat, indeed," he agreed. "You are capturing it on pictures?"

"I have a roll of color film," she said. "Only my second since the war began. It seemed like a good opportunity. And I remembered what you told me of the view from this place, and thought that I would come here. I have some pictures that should show the Kremlin, as well as the brightness of the aurora borealis. Furthermore, the park is close to the train station, and I must be there in a few hours."

"You, too?" Krigoff asked, delighted. "That is, I am departing from there, traveling to the west, before dawn." *This is quite convenient,* he thought.

"Congratulations, Comrade Colonel," she said with apparent sincerity. "I am going west, as well. Perhaps both of us will get to witness the end of this war."

Krigoff smiled in the glow from the northern lights.

2 JANUARY 1945

ARMEEGRUPPE B HEADQUARTERS, DINANT, BELGIUM, 0903 HOURS GMT

Omar Bradley came into the small anteroom, shaking his head. Rommel couldn't tell if it was a reaction of amazement or pleasure—perhaps a little of both. The Desert Fox had been waiting here with General Patton and the translator, Sanger. Bradley had been in the private office beyond the anteroom, to take a phone call from the Supreme Commander; through the other door was the large conference room, where the top staff officers of the American Third Army and the German Armeegruppe B were gathered, waiting expectantly.

"Well, Brad?" asked Patton, bouncing out of his chair, his full height looming over the other men in the room. "What's the good word?"

"I can't quite believe it," Omar Bradley said. This time, Rommel could sense the scowl behind that benign visage. "But it's a go. Ike says to run for the Rhine and try to get across!"

"Goddamn! I knew it!" Patton crowed, his voice all but squeaking in his excitement. "I've gotta give Ike credit—now that he doesn't have Monty whispering in his ear every step of the way, he's showing some real balls!"

"George," snapped Bradley, clearly appalled. "That's *enough!*"

Patton settled back onto the edge of his chair, his grin a mile wide. He looked at Rommel, and the German field marshal couldn't help but share in his former adversary's delight—though he was far too circumspect to make a reference to the gonads of the Supreme Allied Commander.

General Bradley drew a deep breath, looking from Patton to Rommel and back again. "It's the plan as you outlined it—Third Army runs for the river, cutting through the Westwall at the gap held open by Fifth Panzer Army. For the time being, Field Marshal Rommel's men will be responsible for holding open that gap against SS pressure, which seems mostly to have developed in the north, in the Sixth Panzer Army area; First Army will move into that role over the course of the next week. Mobile German formations, notably Panzer Lehr, will commence the pursuit of the withdrawing forces of the Sixth Panzer Army, with Hodges' First Army advancing behind them as quickly as they can get over to the offensive."

"And the Brits?" Rommel could tell that Patton was trying hard not to grin.

"They'll keep the pressure on in the north, together with our Ninth Army. But for now, it looks like the broad front strategy is out the window—we're authorized to make a single, strong punch. It'll be called Operation Can Opener: We pry up the lid, and the rest of the Allied Expeditionary Forces let the beans spill out."

Bradley fixed a glare upon Patton, his eyes icy behind his wire-rimmed spectacles. "That was a cheap shot about Monty, George. Surely you know that, if Ike hadn't insisted on the broad front advance, it would have been Monty, not you, who would have gotten the resources, the chance to make the single punch that you've wanted to do for so long. After all, his forces were approaching the plains in the north, the fastest route to Berlin—at least, until the gate swung open for us down here in the south."

"Aw, Brad, I know. Truth is, Monty was a good soldier, in a McClellan sort of way. He built up a hell of an army, just hated to see it dirtied in the field. We both know he never could have moved fast enough to make that dash."

"Be that as it may—" Rommel noted with interest that Bradley didn't exactly disagree with his underling's assessment, which in fact echoed the Desert Fox's own opinion of his old British adversary. "—this has more to do with the Russians than the Brits. They stabbed us in the back with this armistice last summer, and we're not inclined to forget about that. Any thinking man has to see that they're ready to start attacking again, and who's to say they'll stop with Berlin? The president seems to think Stalin will make a grab for all of Germany, and wants us to do what we can, as fast as we can, to see that doesn't happen.

"And Georgie, you are the man with the right tool, in the right place, for the job."

"Brad—a chance to keep attacking. That's all I've ever wanted!" Patton replied. Rommel could tell that the American general was speaking the utter and complete truth.

ARMEEGRUPPE B HEADQUARTERS CAFETERIA, DINANT, BELGIUM, 1231 HOURS GMT

Reid Sanger felt a little schizophrenic when he translated. It was as if he put part of his brain in neutral and put it in the service of someone else, taking in words in one language and delivering them in another, without any conscious sense of the process. The rest of his mind, aloof from the process, operated as a free-floating observer, commenting on people and reactions. He took an odd pride in being able to disconnect himself in that way.

By now, he was almost used to having all the senior brass around him. Eisenhower, Rommel, Patton—these were figures destined for the history books, people who were real in one sense and unreal in another. When he thought about being in the presence of living history too much he became nervous and tongue-tied, but he was slowly developing an immunity, learning to see these men as mortal while still being aware of their special roles and impact.

Fortunately, there were other translators from SHAEF who could shoulder some of the load. After the initial meeting, the group fissioned into smaller breakout units of specialists. There was an enormous amount of coordination and planning to be accomplished in a very short period of time, and it would take everyone's focus to get it done.

The staff meeting had lasted past the noon hour, as the dazzling plan code-named Operation Can Opener was revealed to the officers of two armies. They understood the unspoken potential of this operation: the crossing of the Rhine had gone from a goal to a preliminary step, and the true objective was nothing less than the liberation of Germany. Roles were outlined, assignments made, and preparations were already under way. Finally Patton had given a truly inspiring speech centering on the historic opportunity awaiting them.

This led to a break, and Sanger was able to slip away for a quick cup of coffee—Rommel's headquarters had some of the worst ersatz coffee he'd ever tasted—and a cigarette.

Sanger thought about the major groups and their assignments. Eisenhower, Bradley, Rommel, and Speidel—with Sanger as translator—would work on the high-level issues involved in turning Rommel's force into an Allied army. Policy, rank, status, chain of command, all of these highly sticky and political matters required extreme delicacy even in the approach.

Patton, von Manteuffel, Bayerlein, and Wakefield, along with their senior aides, would develop the revised military plans. Since Rommel's army group was located in what had been the Third Army area of operation, this involved modifying large amounts of previously settled strategy. Sanger wondered if Patton was frustrated that his military target had now become his ally, but then realized that Patton had already claimed credit for the entire situation—Old Blood and Guts would be fine as long as there was at least one more battle to be fought.

Other working groups included intelligence coordination—Sanger would normally have killed to be part of that group, but he was otherwise occupied—supply and logistics, and even finance. Those maintenance issues were incredibly tricky. Army Group B had drawn its supplies from Germany, and that was obviously no longer possible. The Allies could resupply them, but there were differences in ammunition, spare parts, even standard ration issues. The Germans would certainly appreciate getting American cigarettes, though, Sanger thought, taking a puff on his Lucky Strike.

And finance: that was going to be what the British called a sticky wicket indeed. Soldiers needed to be paid, and obviously Army Group B could no longer draw on the Reichsbank to meet its payroll. The new government was not in a position to issue money, and there was not even a legal structure that would allow the provisional government to borrow money! They would be able to finesse their way around this situation, no doubt, but only at the cost of breaking regulation after regulation. Some senior officer would have to sign a lot of incriminating documents, but there was little choice in the matter. Situations got ahead of themselves sometimes, and one simply had to cope.

Sanger's train of thought was interrupted by a familiar voice barking, "Sanger?"

Sanger looked up to see his old boss at SHAEF intelligence in London. "Colonel Cook!" he said, standing up. Cook stood out in any crowd, since he weighed over three hundred pounds. He was nearly bald, a thin ribbon of hair surrounding his crown somewhat like a monk's tonsure. There was one thing different about Cook since Sanger had seen him last: a star on each shoulder replacing the eagles that had lived there previously. "I mean, General Cook," he amended quickly. "Congratulations, sir. How are you doing?"

"Fine, Sanger, fine. See you made light bird. Congratulations to you, too. Still prefer the front lines to the home office?" The general reached out a beefy hand and Sanger shook it.

"Yes, sir. Nothing like it. Thanks for giving me a shot at it."

"You're welcome, Sanger. You remember Keegan, don't you?"

Of course Sanger did. The two men had worked together as captains in SHAEF headquarters in London. Keegan, now a newly minted major, had been the bane of Sanger's life back in London. He was a product of the American upper class, complete with an aristocratic nasal drawl through teeth that did not move. He had attended the right prep school followed by Yale, and jumped into a career liberally lubricated with Daddy's money. When the war was over he would slip right back into a Wall Street life. He stood elegant in a crisply tailored uniform, and everything from his expression to his sneering tone showed that he was completely convinced of the inferiority of the working classes—of, in short, Sanger himself. "So, Sanger," came his annoying nasal drawl. Keegan looked around the busy, somewhat dirty headquarters. "Slumming again?"

Sanger as usual wanted to reply with a fist sunk into his fine aristocratic features, but he restrained himself. "Hi, Keegan," he replied, then couldn't resist a slight dig. "I see it's *Major* Keegan now. Congratulations." It was petty of him to call attention to his own superior rank that way, but he couldn't help it. He could see by the brief flash of anger across Keegan's face that the dig had worked.

"Congratulations on your own promotion. I hear you've swapped intelligence work for the translation business. More opportunities in that department?" drawled Keegan in return, with the edge of a smile flashing across his lips.

Sanger felt his own anger rising in return. He could never score a clean hit on Keegan; the man always had a comeback. He decided not to go another round. "Yep. Lots more opportunities," he said neutralizing the attack. Then he turned back to Cook. "You'll be working with Rommel's G-2 people on intelligence sharing?"

"Yep, that's what we're here for. This is an absolute gold mine of information. Of course, it's nearly cheating when you sit down with the enemy commanders and they hand you their top-secret documents."

Sanger laughed. "I had much the same feeling last night. I kept thinking someone was going to shoot me as a spy. So, what's the plan?"

"Since Rommel's army is going to be part of SHAEF, we're setting up the intel liaison office. We'll be running the G-2 coordination function," said Cook in his gruff voice.

Sanger felt a real pang at this news. He had thought of himself as the sole person in charge of intelligence coordination between SHAEF and Army Group B. Of course, on reflection he knew that there was no way anyone would permit a mere lieutenant colonel to be in charge of something like that. Wakefield had given him the assignment, but it had been with the warning that it would only be true until some SHAEF chair-warmer shoved him out of the way. And here was the shove. Keegan's dig about him merely being a translator now rankled even more because it was turning out to be true. That was about the only role left for him—if he wasn't shoved out of that as well.

He fought to keep his feelings off his face; the thought that Keegan would witness his despondency was the only thing that could make his humiliation worse. The only good news was that it was time to get back to work. "Good luck, General. You too, Keegan," he said. "I guess I'll see you around the campus." He stood up to make his leave.

When he got back to Rommel's office, he found that there was another translator—this one only a major—allowing Rommel and Eisenhower to converse. That was all he needed; he was too low in rank to be in charge of intelligence or liaison, and too high to be a mere translator. He was going to be shoved right out of the action, and the thought was killing him. There was nobody around in whom he could confide, either. He resolved to be stoic, to continue to do his job. After all, everyone was aimed at the same goal. What did it matter who led? In his heart, he knew it mattered very, very much.

Eisenhower interrupted his reverie. "Sanger, I want you to know that

Rommel has been telling me what an outstanding job you've done under tough circumstances over these last few days."

Dully, Sanger replied, "Thank you very much, sir." He stole a brief glance at Rommel, who was sitting back comfortably in his office chair.

"You've been filling in as SHAEF liaison, and I want you to know I appreciate that as well. You've done fine work."

"Thank you very much, sir."

"Unfortunately," and here Eisenhower paused, "the role of military liaison at this level requires an officer of appropriate rank. I'm afraid that there's no possible way I can permit the role to be filled by a lieutenant colonel. You understand, of course."

Sanger nodded. This was even faster than he expected. "I understand perfectly, sir. I expected that to be the case. It's been an honor to serve in that capacity, even on a temporary basis."

Eisenhower nodded. "It's good you feel that way, because Rommel has asked for you to continue in the role. And since I can't put a lieutenant colonel in that slot, you're a colonel, effective today."

Sanger took a moment to process the words. "Sir? I mean—thank you very much, sir—it is a great honor and I will do my very best—" He realized he was beginning to babble a little bit, and decided that shutting up was the best course of action.

"Congratulations, Oberst Sanger," Rommel said in German. "I hope you will be willing to remain in this assignment."

"It is a very great honor, Generalfeldmarschall," said Sanger, getting himself back under control. He switched to English and said, "Thank you very much, General Eisenhower." He saluted.

Eisenhower leaned forward and said, "Now you get to earn your pay. Back to work."

"Yes, *sir!*" replied Sanger.

ARMEEGRUPPE B FIELD HOSPITAL, NEAR DINANT, 1323 HOURS GMT

The hospital door opened on the other side of the patient cot, but the patient saw his visitor reflected in a mirror.

"Ah, Müller! How nice of you to visit," von Reinhardt said to Müller's image. His voice was louder and fuller than the previous day, and he was smiling, even while an American military nurse, a lieutenant, administered a shot. His chest was uncovered and Müller could see the bandages strapping him together like packing material. There was a brownish red stain near the wound site; some oozing was still taking place.

Müller smiled. "You seem to be a lot better today," he said, sitting down on a wooden folding chair beside the metal-framed hospital cot. "I brought a little something to eat." He produced a box containing nearly half a cake he'd purloined from the American mess.

The American nurse interrupted. "No—*nein*. No food." Müller looked imploringly at her and she repeated the order. With a regretful look, he put it back in the box. The nurse finished the shot, adjusted the IV that hung on what looked like a hat rack on wheels, and made notes on the clipboard that hung at the foot of the bed. Her expression was serious, more serious than Müller liked, but who could interpret what such an expression meant? It could mean something truly terrible, or merely that a temperature was elevated a single degree above normal. The nurse said in English, "I'll check back in two hours. Two—" She held up two fingers. "—hours." She pointed to a clock on the wall.

"*Zwei Stunden,*" repeated von Reinhardt in German, holding up two fingers and pointing to the clock in response. The nurse patted his hand and left; von Reinhardt turned his attention to Müller and said, "Yes, I am a lot better. The incident is over, the outcome was favorable, even if not by my personal doing, and I am alive. Now it is history, and as the English author of *Tristram Shandy* would have it, 'The history of a soldier's wound beguiles the pain of it.' It is, to be sure, only a partial palliative, but as the alternative is still more pain, I am happy to take comfort in history."

Müller shook his head. "Günter, I don't know how you keep all those quotes in your head, I really don't."

"It's a mental quirk, nothing more. I can remember entire pages from books I read as a child, but can hardly keep three practical items together in my mind long enough for a trip to the bakery without writing them down."

Müller wanted more. "But do you plan for them in advance, all ready for delivery, or do they just come to you?"

Von Reinhardt laughed. "A fine and insightful question! Of course, the desired answer is that each quote springs naturally from the font of my intellect as did Athena from Zeus' brow, but between you and me " His voice dropped to a lower tone. "—some quotes I prepare in advance, when I believe certain matters are likely to arise in conversation."

"I thought so!" said Müller triumphantly. "You have a talent for *le mot juste*—" He paused in pride at his own cleverness in injecting a French phrase into the conversation. "—but sometimes your quotes are just *too* perfect."

Von Reinhardt laughed, but his laugh turned into a choking cough. Alarmed, Müller reached over for a tissue and handed it to his friend. It took nearly a full minute for the cough to get under control, and when Müller took back the tissue it had flecks of blood on it. "Shall I get the nurse?" Müller asked in concern.

Weakly, von Reinhardt waved the hand not tied down with an IV. "No, no," he said, his voice hardly more than a whisper. His face was drawn tight with pain. "The cough comes and goes, but it tears at the wound, you know. I'm all right." He coughed again, and with his hand indicated a glass on his bed stand. Müller handed over the glass and von Reinhardt took a sip of water, which seemed to calm the cough somewhat. He smiled wanly, and whispered. "You talk for a while, Wolfgang. Bring me up to date on the proceedings at headquarters. For as Cicero says, 'The gods attend to great matters, they neglect small ones.' Tell me what the general-gods are up to, Wolfgang." He leaned back against his pillow weakly.

"I've half a mind to call the nurse anyway, Günter," Müller said. "That cough doesn't sound at all good to me. But if you'll lie quiet and sip your water, I'll tell you everything I know."

Von Reinhardt nodded, smiled, and took a sip of water, which seemed to relax him somewhat. Müller watched him carefully, then decided it was safe to bring him up to date on the situation at headquarters.

"Well, everybody seems to be getting along fine as nearly as I can tell," he said. "General Eisenhower offered Rommel the chancellorship of Germany under a new government."

"And our good Desert Fox turned him down, I presume?" whispered von Reinhardt, leaning his head back on his pillow and closing his eyes.

"How did you know?" said Müller. "It came as a surprise to everyone else. Has somebody been here before me to tell you what happened."

"No, no," von Reinhardt replied. "It was logical. As our new führer says, 'My honor is my loyalty.' Even though it's just an SS motto, it's something that weighs all too heavily on Rommel. His feelings of personal disgrace are running very deep right now. He could not possibly accept such an honor unless he felt worthy, and how can a traitor and surrendering coward possibly feel worthy?"

Müller was shocked. "He isn't either of those things!"

"I know that, and you know that, but right now he doesn't know that. There is war in his soul, because every choice leads to betrayal of at least one of the ideals he has held throughout his life. It's difficult. As Montaigne says, 'Any person of honor chooses rather to lose his honor than to lose his conscience.' But that does not make such a choice easy." Von Reinhardt's voice began to crack, and he took another sip of water.

Müller thought for a minute. "I guess that's right, but it's unfair."

"So it is," replied von Reinhardt. "What else?"

As Müller began to provide a rundown of the morning's other events, a voice interrupted in American-accented German. "Excuse me, gentlemen." It was Porter, the American newspaperman.

Müller stood up. "He's not very well; he can hardly talk."

Porter nodded. "I came by mostly because I had never thanked him properly for capturing me a few days ago. This has been the most important few days of my life, and if Oberst von Reinhardt hadn't thought I'd be of some use as a translator, I would have missed the whole thing and be stuck in a cage with a bunch of American soldiers waiting for release."

"You're welcome," whispered von Reinhardt. "If you wish to repay me, I feel cut off from the world here in my hospital bed. My friend Wolfgang has been filling me in on the various discussions and meetings in headquarters. If your reporter sources have provided you with additional information, I would love to hear it."

Müller shook his head. "He can't stop being an intelligence officer, you know. He really should be resting."

"I think I understand him, though," replied Porter. "I feel the same way about being a newspaperman. In fact, your friend would make a great reporter if he chose. When the war is over, if you'd like to join the Associated Press, look me up in Berlin, okay?"

"Thank you," whispered von Reinhardt. "When the war is over, I'll have to think about earning an honest living."

"I didn't say anything about an *honest* living," laughed Porter. "I'm talking about the news game. So, friend Wolfgang, what news have you heard? They're starting to bar the doors against me in case I snoop in areas they aren't yet ready to make public."

"Watch yourself carefully, Wolfgang," added von Reinhardt. "You don't want to inadvertently tell top-secret information to the enemy."

Müller was startled—for a moment he found himself looking at Porter suspiciously—and then he realized his leg was being pulled and he laughed. "I was going to say that we were all now on the same side, but then I realized that what you meant was that the press itself was the enemy."

"That's not fair," replied Porter, half in jest. "We of the press only report the facts!"

"Beware of facts," von Reinhardt interjected. "As Nietzsche says, 'There are no facts, only interpretations.' Right now, it's hard to say what exactly the facts happen to be."

"You're in the hospital with a wound," retorted Porter. "That's a fact. Rommel surrendered. That's a fact."

"Interpretations. Did Rommel actually surrender? Certainly not in a traditional sense. And I am in a hospital and I have a wound, but it was not a hospital but a battle zone just a short while ago. That's the trouble with newspapers. They deal only with now. 'Now' has no permanence and no meaning other than that which history gives it—and history is even more about interpretation than is 'now.'"

"Forget what I said about a job after the war, von Reinhardt," snorted Porter. "I can just see sending you on a story and getting back a philosophy dissertation instead. And I bet you're hell on deadlines."

"Perspective, my dear Porter, perspective is everything. And now, my friends, I think I hear the rustle of the nurse, and that tells me I must rest."

"Good-bye, Günter. I'll come back tomorrow," said Müller solicitously.

"Hey, I was only kidding, von Reinhardt," added Porter. "You're a good guy, and I'm grateful."

But von Reinhardt's eyes were closed, and neither visitor could tell whether he had fallen asleep or was merely feigning.

3 JANUARY 1945

NINETEENTH ARMORED DIVISION FORWARD
HEADQUARTERS, DINANT, BELGIUM, 0530 HOURS GMT

A night's sleep and a bath were precious commodities. Civilians didn't really appreciate them, thought Frank Ballard as he finished shaving. He rinsed the remaining soap off his chin and felt the smooth skin with a pleasure that completed what two cups of coffee had begun. In short, he felt as if he were becoming human again.

He stepped outside, into the cold, crisp morning air that seemed unreal, impossibly peaceful. The din of combat had ceased at last, and the cries of the injured and dying had faded into silence. The rubble-filled streets and the occasional growl of a tank engine were the only reminders that he was still in the middle of a war—some kind of war, anyway, even if the major details, such as who they were fighting against, had yet to be clearly defined.

It was odd to be alive, he thought. He'd nearly died in the Somme last summer—by rights he was already living on borrowed time. In Dinant he'd lived when his tank was hit, though all his crew except for his sergeant had perished. And yet Frank Ballard was alive, a few scratches the extent of his wounds. What was it that had enabled him to survive? Was he just lucky, "dumb lucky" as he thought of it? Or was there some special protection granted to him by fate, or by Almighty God? He shrugged away the silent questions, accepting, for now, the reality that let him walk into this cold, quiet morning.

He stopped, lit a cigarette, looked around him. Standing in the window of a destroyed shop was his girlfriend, the mannequin who'd kept him company during the twenty-four hours of battle. She had survived along with him. That made her special.

Ballard took a deep drag from his cigarette and exhaled. It was good to be alive, true, but it was hard to feel that he deserved to feel this way. His CO had died in the battle, died to stop the German advance in its tracks. So many of his subordinates, good and brave men, had given their lives in the same cause. But not him, not Frank Ballard.

He began walking, passing a Sherman that had burned up in the battle, the smell of gasoline and burned flesh mixing with his smoke. He was getting to a point where he hardly noticed the smell.

Stamping his boots on the cobblestones outside the temporary Nineteenth

Armored HQ to knock mud and slush off, he opened the door. Stale heat and different smells greeted him as he entered the building.

General Wakefield looked up as he entered. "Siddown," he growled around his cigar. "Get some sleep?"

"Yes, sir," Ballard replied. "And you?"

Wakefield grunted a yes. Silently, he indicated a percolator, and Ballard helped himself to a cup, his third, black and bitter.

"Good morning, gentlemen," a cheery Bob Jackson said as he entered the headquarters. "And how are you on this fine spring morning?" Jackson had the annoying habit of looking freshly pressed, clean, and comfortable regardless of the circumstances.

Wakefield's grunt sounded about as cheerful as Ballard felt. "Morning, Bob," he said. He indicated the coffee pot and Jackson nodded. Ballard turned the spigot to dispense a second cup and passed it over.

"Ahh, nectar of the gods," said Jackson, taking the cup and inhaling the steam with relish. "A day like this makes me long for summer days in Richmond. This strange white stuff you get around here—I guess you Yankees are used to it, but those of us from God's country find we can live without it. Brrr!" he shivered.

"Siddown, Bob," said Wakefield. "We're moving out in half an hour. But before we go, I've got a few changes to make."

"Yes, sir," replied Jackson, utterly at ease. "Will we single-handedly be fighting all of Sixth Panzer Army today?" he asked with an innocent expression.

Ballard's stifled laugh turned into a snort. "Then what would we do for an encore?" he asked.

Jackson was just about to launch into an extended joke, but Wakefield stepped in. "I've got to rebuild CCA. SHAEF says because of all the press, you get to be Rommel's personal escort, Frank."

Jackson's eyebrows went up at that remark. "And where precisely shall we get the necessary replacements?" he asked, a slight edge in his voice. There was only one obvious place for Wakefield to get replacements to quickly beef up CCA.

Wakefield took a puff on his cigar, let it out. "CCB. We'll fill CCB out from reserves and the repple-depple. Frank, Georgie Patton and Rommel are both pretty impressed with you. I've recommended you for a Silver Star. While you're waiting, you get an eagle, effective today." Ballard would trade in the silver oak leaf of a lieutenant colonel for the eagle of a full colonel.

"Congratulations, Frank! Well deserved and long overdue," said Jackson in a hearty voice, reaching over to shake Ballard's hand. "And I guess this means you'll be buying drinks at the officers' club tonight." This was a traditional ritual upon promotion—though where, in battered Dinant, they'd find an officers' club was a moot point.

Wakefield shook Frank's hand as well, a grin forming around his ever-present cigar. "And, while we're at it, you get confirmed as CO of CCA permanently."

"Thank you, General," Ballard said, stunned. He'd half expected to get command of CCA at least temporarily, but to get a promotion, a medal, and a command all at once was a little breathtaking.

"Figure out what you need to get to full strength and take it from CCB," Wakefield said. He was still grinning.

Bob Jackson's grin, however, was getting a little stretched. "Now, General," he said in his smoothest voice. "I think Frank Ballard well deserves his command, but I seem to recall that Combat Command B has been keeping pretty busy on its own."

"Yeah?" growled Wakefield. "You want a medal, too?"

Jackson was taken aback at the implied insult. "Now, General, I don't rightly think that's a fair . . ."

Wakefield interrupted. "Anyway, you're not in command of CCB any more."

Jackson was on his feet, angry and ready to argue. "What in hell do you mean—" he started, but then noticed that Wakefield's grin had grown larger and larger. He paused, his intended tirade on hold for a moment.

Wakefield reached up and unpinned the star from his right shoulder. "You're now XO of Nineteenth Armored, Bob. How do you like them apples, General Jackson?" He handed the star to Jackson. "How about sharing one of your eagles with Frank?"

Jackson let out a long, slow breath. "God damn, General. I sure didn't see this coming. Sure, Frank can have an eagle. And I guess this means I'll be buying the drinks tonight." His own grin now matched that of his commanding officer.

Wakefield pulled a small box out of his pocket. "No, I will," he grinned, showing his officers the two stars of a major general. "But we'll have to take a rain check. The Old Man wants us to be up to the Westwall in three days, and into Germany by the day after that. At the latest. That, gentlemen, means that we've got some work to do."

KAMPFGRUPPE PEIPER, FIRST SS PANZER DIVISION "LEIBSTANDARTE ADOLF HITLER," SAINT-VITH, BELGIUM, 1321 HOURS GMT

It was inspection time again. Carl-Heinz gestured at Digger to feign being asleep when the doctor came in. As usual, Dr. Schlüter nodded at each patient, and looked sharply at Carl-Heinz as soon as he saw Digger. The hidden message was clear: *How could you put all of us at risk?*

Well, the deed was long since done, and now it was a matter of surviving each day. Schlüter moved efficiently through the trucks of the wounded, prioritizing the cases and treating them as well as limited supplies would allow. The supply of fresh bandages was low; he had a medical orderly boil old bandages to make them sterile again, and then used them, stains, tears, and all, on the wounds of his patients.

Some of his fellow soldiers had returned to duty, and new patients joined the rolling hospital on a regular basis. This allowed Carl-Heinz to get a little information of how the war was progressing, and to hear the occasional rumor about the location and fate of the Desert Fox.

Today, however, Obersturmbannführer Peiper had decided to join Schlüter on his rounds. Peiper, one half of his face handsome and unmarked, the other half hideously scarred, was there primarily to visit his own wounded. His attitude toward the Wehrmacht soldiers he had "liberated" from Allied control was different. "This one looks fit enough for duty, *nicht wahr?*" he said.

Schlüter, intimidated by Peiper but unwilling to compromise his best medical judgment, demurred. "A few more days to allow the final healing. He could fight, but he would be vulnerable to any strain. Better to wait until he can take his place in the line without that risk."

Peiper made a noncommittal "mmm" sound, and continued. "You— what's the matter with you?" he asked Carl-Heinz.

"Belly wound, sir," Carl-Heinz replied. "Coming along well, sir. I'll be ready to return to duty shortly."

The impression of eagerness worked. Peiper again made an "mmm" sound, but this time with less skepticism. "What's your background?" he asked the feldwebel.

"Panzers, sir—Panzer Lehr to be specific. I'm also a good mechanic."

"Well, feldwebel, you'll find the Leibstandarte keeps a higher standard than Panzer Lehr, but you might fit in."

There was nothing Carl-Heinz wanted less, but he put a big gap-toothed smile on his face. "That would be great, sir," he said with forced cheerfulness.

Somewhat mollified, Peiper turned away to leave, then looked back, a puzzled expression on his face. "This one—he's been here since the hospital. What's his problem?"

"Leg wound," said Schlüter, picking up the chart to conceal the sudden concern on his face. This was the one patient he didn't want Peiper to notice. "Also eye damage and throat strain."

"Throat strain?"

"Yes, sir." Schlüter felt the beginnings of sweat breaking out.

Peiper looked at the silent patient. "Laryngitis?"

"Basically, sir."

"For more than a week?"

"Well—yes, sir."

"Mmm." He looked more closely at the patient. "How is your voice today?" he asked.

The silent patient looked up at the Waffen-SS officer, smiled and nodded.

Peiper darted a suspicious look at the doctor, then back at the patient. "If you are nodding, your voice must be fine. Say something."

Again a smile, but no speech.

"An odd type of laryngitis," he murmured. Schlüter fought to keep his hands from trembling. Carl-Heinz looked over at the patient warningly.

"Doctor, it seems as if not only his speech is impaired, but also his hearing. Does your chart indicate this?" Peiper's voice was silky smooth.

"Well, yes . . . yes, I think it might . . ."

"*Might?*" Peiper's voice cracked like a whip. "Don't you know?"

"I—I have a lot of patients . . ." Schlüter said weakly.

Peiper turned back to the patient. "Would you like me to put another bullet in that leg of yours?" he asked, smiling broadly and nodding his head up and down in a friendly manner.

The patient turned his head toward Carl-Heinz, then back up to Peiper, and smiled again.

Peiper rounded on the doctor with sudden fury. "Doctor, why do I have the distinct impression that you have been concealing a prisoner of war as a German patient?"

Schlüter had no idea what to say; he stammered weakly and then fell silent.

"So! I gave orders that all Allied patients were to be killed. Did you disobey my direct order, or . . ." Peiper suddenly noticed Carl-Heinz gesturing. "Or did you have help? You—feldwebel! What's your name?"

"Clausen, Carl-Heinz, sir."

"Clausen . . . Clausen . . . where have I heard that name before? Wait a minute! Panzer Lehr, that's right! You were the driver of the panzer in that picture, weren't you?" A picture of Carl-Heinz's tank, numerous soldiers riding on top, was one of the well-known images of the war, as Normandy-based troops escaped the Falaise.

Slowly, Carl-Heinz nodded.

"And afterward . . ." Peiper suddenly pounded his fist into his other palm. "That's right! You became Rommel's personal driver!" He laughed, not prettily. "Well, well. Rommel's personal driver, and a panzer hero. Under other circumstances, the Leibstandarte Adolf Hitler would be pleased to use you. But this prisoner here—" Peiper kicked him in his wounded leg, drawing a gasp of pain. "You are accused of sheltering an enemy soldier. That's a serious offense. Rommel's driver should have known better . . . unless you've been infected with the same strain of cowardice as your boss!"

"Wie heissen Sie?" Peiper barked at the prisoner.

Realizing he was now found out, Digger O'Dell answered the way a prisoner of war was supposed to. "O'Dell, Staff Sergeant Franklin. United States Army Air Force. Serial number T-zero-zero-one-nine-two-one-six-five."

"American. And a *terrorflieger* to boot." Peiper grinned. "And out of uniform. That makes you a spy, my fine fellow. And we are entitled to shoot spies." He made a pistol of his thumb and finger, pointed it at Digger, and made a bang sound.

Carl-Heinz began to protest, but Peiper shut him up with a glare. "I could kill you as well for treason. And as for you, Doctor—" He left the threat uncompleted.

Schlüter was shaking as Peiper stuck his head out of the back of the truck. "Guard! I need a guard here on the double!" In minutes, several SS soldiers showed up. Peiper turned back to his victims. "It's your lucky day. I received a directive from Berlin yesterday about *terrorfliegers*. Because of their atrocities against our civilians, our führer has decided that they are criminals, not prisoners of war. And as particularly odious criminals, they are now being sent to a very special place, and it's not a comfortable prisoner-of-war camp, either! You, Clausen, fall into the category of traitor, and traitors are sent to the same place. You both can learn firsthand how we deal with criminal scum in modern Germany!" Peiper gave instructions to the guards, and both Clausen and O'Dell were pulled roughly from the truck and thrown to the ground. Peiper kicked hard at Digger's wounded leg, drawing a gasp of pain.

"And as for you, Doctor," Peiper said menacingly, "you've earned a trip to the same destination, but I need you here. I can't allow this behavior to go unpunished, however." He gestured at the burly SS guards. "I'm going to have these men teach all three of you a lesson you'll never forget." Peiper turned to the guards. "Work them over, but don't kill them. And the doctor still has to work, so leave his hands alone." Schlüter looked with increasing terror at the two huge guards who grabbed him by the arms.

"Jawohl, Herr Obersturmbannführer!" the guards replied, grinning.

Peiper hit Schlüter across the face once, twice, then a third time, each with all his strength. "You are a doctor of the Third Reich, and your job is to return combatants to duty. Got it?"

Blood welling from a split lip, the doctor gasped out a terrified "Yes, sir." His eyes pleaded with the SS officer, but Peiper only smiled.

4 JANUARY 1945

HEADQUARTERS, FIRST BELORUSSIAN FRONT, WARSAW, POLAND, 1034 HOURS GMT

"So, *Colonel* Krigoff, you have come to us from Moscow? In order to ensure that the army functions as effectively, militarily and politically, as possible?"

General-Armii Petrovsky, commander of the Second Guards Tank Army, asked the question with no trace of irony in his voice. But when Alyosha Krigoff considered the words, contemplated the man's condescending manner, and evaluated the chaotic bustle of the headquarters staff, he felt certain that the army commander was mocking him.

For now, he would take the honorable route, and ignore the taunt. It would not, however, be forgotten.

"Yes, Comrade General! But please consider me a mere assistant, one who will do what he can to aid your commendable efforts to obliterate the foes of World Communism!"

"Ah, yes," said Petrovksy, with a sigh. He looked tired, Krigoff thought, and his nose was an unnatural, unhealthy red in color. Too much vodka, perhaps? "The foes of World Communism, indeed."

Now Krigoff was certain that he was being mocked. He was in no mood to accept this kind of treatment, at least not from an army officer, even the general of a mighty army. Krigoff was tired from three sleepless nights on a crowded train, hungry from a lack of any decent food, and sore from the uncomfortable ride on the hard wooden seat. Furthermore, he had been separated from Paulina at Kiev Station—her westward train had departed two hours later than his—and after arriving at the front had been forced to push his way through a chaos of trucks, horses, shouting sergeants, and marching, heavily laden troops, just to reach this building where he had been ordered to report.

Though he was assigned to the staff of the tank army, he had been required to come to the front HQ building first. This was a battered hotel, just east of the Vistula River, and it had been overrun with Soviet officers in the last six months. Such damage as the war had failed to inflict seemed to have been delivered by the hands of the new occupants: walls had been knocked down, heavy communications cables draped through windows and across the floors, and the stink of unwashed bodies seemed to have seeped into the very woodwork. He had masked his distaste, and reported with due respect to his army commander, who was working at a small desk in a small room on the second floor, but now his temper was reaching its limit.

"I refer, of course, to the Nazis, Comrade General," he said archly. "I came here with the understanding that you were about to commence an attack against them. Or do you not consider them the foes of World Communism—and Mother Russia—after all?"

Instead of snapping back, as he expected Petrovsky to do, the veteran army commander rubbed his high forehead with a sturdy, short-fingered hand, and sighed heavily.

"Attack the Nazis. Yes, Colonel, we will attack the Nazis here, just as we attacked them at Moscow and Stalingrad, at Kursk and Kiev and all the rest of the places scarred by this war. We will cross the Vistula and trap them in Warsaw or push them out of Poland. Then we will chase them into their own cursed fatherland, and root them out of their holes like the venomous snakes that they are. Now that you are here, of course, this will all be accomplished with ease."

"I will do my duty to the best of my ability, General," Krigoff retorted stiffly. "If you will give me my orders, I will be out of your way at once."

"Orders? Yes, of course. Take your kit and go to my own headquarters—we're in a manor, ten kilometers down the road from here. Report to General-Leitenant Yeremko, my chief of intelligence, and he will find something for you to do."

"Yes, Comrade General!" Krigoff honored the army commander with a salute, even as he viewed the old man with contempt. Perhaps Petrovsky had been a fine soldier in his day, but that day had passed like the fading of the summer. At the same time, he was a little surprised, when he thought about it, that the man wouldn't have made a little more of an effort to be polite to a subordinate just arrived from Moscow. When he pondered the fact the truth seemed to be obvious: Petrovsky just didn't care anymore.

Now, Krigoff had his own problems. Ten kilometers was not a long distance, but it was farther than he intended to walk. He went down to the hotel lobby, which seemed to be a clearinghouse of frenzied activity. Making his way to the kitchen, he was able to acquire a sandwich—a slab of tough sausage and a thick slice of onion between a couple of pieces of brown bread—and that helped a little. Some further checking revealed a truck loaded with radio equipment, already revving up for the drive to the tank army HQ, and he was able to fling his pack over the tailgate and then climb up in the cab to ride with the driver.

He took a look at the flat and battle-scarred Polish countryside as they lurched along a rutted, frost-hardened road. There were peasants' cottages scattered about, and each of them was at the very least pocked with bullet holes, if not damaged or destroyed by the impact of high explosives. The few trees he saw were skeletal and leafless, and though this was the winter norm he could tell by the torn bark and ripped or shattered trunks that many of them had suffered from the campaigns that had swept across this country with such brutality over the last six years.

The manor house of army headquarters proved to be a country home that had once belonged to a wealthy Polish merchant—a Jew, the driver explained to him, spitting. General Yeremko and the intelligence unit occupied a large parlor and a trophy room. Heads of boar and deer, as well as a snarling bear, adorned the walls; now these were draped with the wires connecting to several large radios that had been set up against the walls.

"Krigoff, eh? From Moscow?" Yeremko was a slender man with a pinched face and narrow, penetrating eyes. His age was apparent in his parchment-yellow skin, and the thin wisps of hair that were plastered across his scalp. He eyed the colonel suspiciously, but he, clearly, had the sense not to immediately alienate this new and potentially well-connected officer.

"I am at your service, Comrade General!" Krigoff declared in response.

"Well, you'll be sleeping in a tent like most of the rest of us. But we'll have you working so hard that you won't have to worry about that very much. There are four weeks of work left to do, and—who knows?—perhaps four or five days before this show gets started."

Krigoff noted the harried look of the intelligence general, the sallow complexion and the way his eyes darted nervously this way and that. Clearly the man was unstable, perhaps dangerously so.

"Have you ever been in a plane?" asked Yeremko abruptly.

"Yes, Comrade General," Krigoff lied. "I am fond of flying." The latter part was vaguely true, insofar as he had always hoped for a chance to get up in an airplane.

"Good. For now, I want you to study reconnaissance photos; we're trying to pick out the Nazi strong points before we attack. With luck, our artillery will knock out one in ten of them, before the infantry has to take out the rest. So every one you find means a few Russian lives saved, when the attack gets under way."

"I understand," Krigoff replied.

"Of course, all of these photos have been looked over by a hundred good men already. But every new set of eyes is useful. I need you to compare the shots from last week to those taken yesterday—we're looking for changes, anything different. That will be a sign that the Nazis have been at work, and we'll have the specialists take a look, try to decide what sort of work that might have been."

"Indeed, General. If necessary, I will take to the air myself, of course," he added.

Yeremko nodded. "That time will come—when the attack gets under way, I'll have you and a few other officers flying over the battlefield. That's the way of war, today—get us the reports at once, and we can keep our men alive for a few days longer."

Krigoff nodded, his face impassive though he was troubled by these words. Like Petrovsky, General Yeremko seemed to be placing an undue emphasis on coddling his men, keeping them alive even at the cost of delaying the progress of the offensive. It was a distressing sign of the war-weariness that might prove to be endemic among these veteran officers.

He was still thinking about this as he made his way to the tent that an aide showed him, a shelter he would share with four other colonels. He was relieved to find a cot there, for he had not looked forward to the thought of sleeping on the ground.

Before he entered, he took another look around, at the chaos of men and machines that would, in a few days, be unleashed against the Nazi devils. How would these men function? Would they be as aggressive as necessary?

Yes, thought Krigoff, eventually they would. But it was a good thing that he was here.

TWELFTH INFANTRY DIVISION HEADQUARTERS, CLERVAUX, LUXEMBOURG, 1357 HOURS GMT

"Pull over here," General Patton said, and Sergeant Mims turned the jeep into the stone-paved courtyard of a small inn. The standard of the Twelfth Infantry Division, one of Third Army's veteran formations, was draped from the upper window, marking the building as the headquarters of the fast-moving unit—for today, at least.

"Ten-hut!" shouted a sergeant on the headquarters staff as Patton stalked through the door. The general was pleased but unsurprised to see men hard at work throughout the great room of the inn. Maps were spread upon tables, and kerosene lanterns suspended from the rafters gave the place an uncanny brightness.

"As you were," Patton said, and the men quickly resumed their duties. He approached the table with the largest map, as two captains stood aside to give him room.

"Welcome to the Twelfth, sir," declared one. "General Hooper will be sorry he missed you—he's up with the recon unit, checking out the road down into Dasburg."

"Good for him," Patton said. That was the kind of thing he liked to hear. He fixed an eye upon the captain. "Tell me, what's your situation?"

"We've got a perimeter set up around Clervaux, General, and we have detachments moving off the road in both directions, getting set up on every piece of high ground between here and the German border. It's going well— that is, we haven't had any Krauts shooting at us for the last day, though there are plenty that seem willing to surrender."

"Good. Most of them know their war is over—at least, when it comes to fighting Uncle Sam. It's the cocksucking SS bastards that are going to give us trouble, but I think they're bugging out for the Westwall now. What do you hear from Fourth Armored?"

That tank-heavy division had been ordered to secure the breach in the fortified border that was represented by the small city of Dasburg. Patton's last report had indicated that CCB of the Fourth was moving into the burg, but he was anxious for further details.

"It sounds good, General," said the other captain. "They've pushed all the way through the town and across the river. They have the high ground on the far bank, and are ready to let the rest of us through."

"Excellent! If I remember right, Nineteenth Armored should be coming along in a day or so. I want the road held open—they have top transportation priority. As soon as they get into Germany, the rest of you wonderful boys are going to be right on their heels. We'll spread out through the Rhineland, and make a run for the river with ten divisions. Those Nazi sons of bitches won't know whether we're going to punch them in the teeth or kick them in the ass!"

He noted that the rest of the staff had stopped their work to listen, and this pleased him. He knew it was good for the morale of his army to see its general. More important, he tried very hard to make sure that these men understood the fighting mentality that lay at the heart of Third Army, and the need for speed that would see them succeed where no other force in the history of warfare would even dare to try.

"We're ready to move out, General!" said the first captain enthusiastically. "As soon as the Nineteenth Armored goes through, we'll be right on their heels!"

"Good, good," said Patton, turning to leave. At the door he stopped, and favored the staff with a grin. "We'll take a few bottles of Belgian beer with us—and by the time we've finished them, we'll all be pissing into the Rhine!"

5 JANUARY 1945

KAMPFGRUPPE PEIPER, NORTHERN APPROACH TO DASBURG, GERMANY, 1553 HOURS GMT

Jochen Peiper had found that he could use the pain from his facial wound, a constant searing fire that penetrated deep into his skull, as a focusing agent. For more than a day he had remained awake, guiding his racing column through the narrow, tree-flanked roads of the Ardennes as they raced out of Saint-Vith and back toward the German border. When fatigue threatened to drag him into sleep he simply slapped himself, right on the raw red wound. The blow inevitably provoked a fresh wave of pain along with an ooze of blood—and enough adrenaline to keep him going for another hour. He could see the medical disapproval in Dr. Schlüter's eyes when he inspected the wound—underneath the naked fear, of course. The doctor would not trifle with him again.

He had sent the last of his wounded away, and made certain that the traitorous driver and American terrorflieger had been shipped to Germany under an SS guard. Treating terrorfliegers as if they were common criminals was a good idea of the führer's, Peiper thought. And sending Rommel's driver along was a delightful bonus. Perhaps he would arrange to get a photograph of Clausen after he had been sufficiently chastised, and send it to the Desert Fox. Let him know there was a personal price for treason. Now, relieved of the need to carry along the added burden of noncombatants, he had ordered his fully mechanized column to race along at top speed.

Finally they began to descend into the valley of the Our River, which here formed the border between Luxembourg and his native Deutschland. The kampfgruppe approached the city from the north, still on the east side of the river, while Peiper ordered his signalmen to try and get some information on the status of the city itself.

When no radio reports were available, his motorcycle reconnaissance units raced toward the town while he ordered his panzergrenadiere to dismount from their trucks.

"I want you to be ready to close off the east road, in case the Americans come that way. Alternately, you might have to fight your way into the city, if some of Rommel's traitors are here before us," he warned the oberst in charge of the battalion, a replacement Peiper had never met before.

"Heil Himmler!" the man replied, snapping a salute before taking his place in the command armored car, a squat vehicle with bulging tires and an array of antennae. He headed down the river road with engine roaring, while the infantry advanced at a trot in the wake of the speeding motorcycles.

While he waited for word from the scouts, Peiper walked along the line of tanks, barely noticed how all of them had pulled off of the road into the dense cover of the pine forest. These men were veterans; no one needed to remind them of the ever-present menace of Allied air power.

It was a modest collection of armor: a dozen Panthers and about fifty Mark IVs. He was just as happy not to have any of the lumbering Tigers in his kampfgruppe—they slowed down the whole column, and were too damned big for most of the bridges in this hilly, gorge-crossed countryside. But he couldn't help feeling that this force was too small for the task at hand—he should have had a full division, at least! Of course, Dietrich had informed him that even the SS divisions still loyal to the Fatherland numbered barely more than this in strength. Fortunately, one SS soldier was worth a dozen of any enemy.

He was distracted by a racket of small-arms fire—carbines and the rip of an American BAR. Moments later a heavy machine gun, .50-caliber, started to chatter, and soon an entire cacophony of weapons crackled down the road.

"*Scheisse!*" he snapped. Americans here, in Dasburg? He had anticipated encountering some treacherous Germans, probably a few old volksgrenadierie who had lost the will to fight, but this was an unpleasant surprise. Could the Yank bastards have really moved that fast?

Any doubts were quickly buried as the distinctive, woofing blast of 75mm tank guns joined the fray. The Americans were here, with armor! All along the column his tankers were scrambling back into their panzers, while the infantry oberst was barking orders to his company commanders, sending more men to quickly reinforce the scouting patrols. Peiper stalked up to him, pleased that the man was taking aggressive action.

"Send everyone you've got!" he ordered. "My tanks will follow. We have to breach this screen, get into the Westwall!"

"*Jawohl, Herr Obersturmbannführer!*" declared the man; Peiper was racing away before the fellow could stiffen his arm into the reflexive salute.

"Go! Go! Go!" barked the kampfgruppe commander, racing along the line of his tanks. Several panzers were already moving out, and his own driver rolled the Panther forward as he saw Peiper running up. He seized the rail and lifted himself on to the deck with an exertion that brought tears to his good eye; momentarily he wondered if he had torn the stitches in his face.

But he had no time for self-pity. He slid through the hatch in the turret, sitting so that his head and shoulders emerged from the top of the tank. He was exposed here, but he needed to see, needed to understand what was happening.

Fire blossomed in the road before him as a panzer exploded. The following vehicle advanced to press against the flaming hull. The engine growled as the driver gunned his throttle, shoving the burning hulk sideways until it toppled into the ditch. Then the makeshift bulldozer advanced quickly, snapping off a shot from its main gun, roaring downhill along the tree-shrouded road.

Two seconds later that tank exploded, like the first hit by some as-yet-unseen gun. Peiper grimaced, suspecting that the Americans had placed some tank destroyers along the road. The situation called for patience, an envelopment—ideally, some air power—but all of those things called for, at the bare minimum, time. And that was one resource he did not possess.

He slid down into the turret and picked up his microphone. "Go!" he shouted over the radio. "Find them—kill them!"

His own gunner snapped off a shot, the turret echoing as the spent shell popped out of the chamber. Bullets clattered against the armored hull, the hail of battle rising to a deafening roar. Clasping his eye to the periscope, Peiper tried to see what was happening.

At least six of his panzers were burning, the wrecks perched like hellish obstacles on the narrow road. The armored column still advanced by snaking around those destroyed tanks that could not be pushed out of the way. He heard his own men shooting back, saw a welcome burst of flame emerge from the woods up ahead—they had spotted one of the tank destroyers, exacted the first measure of vengeance!

Small-arms fire crackled in the woods and he knew the panzergrenadiere were pressing forward. Another American tank exploded, and he saw more of the tank destroyers—they looked like Shermans, except the turrets were blocky and open on top—maneuvering in the cover of the trees.

"There!" he barked, clapping his gunner on the shoulder. The man had an armor-piercing round loaded, and squinted into the shadows. He pulled the trigger and the Panther's main gun barked; almost immediately, another billow of fire brightened the shadows in the tree-lined gorge.

"The bastards are running!" Peiper crowed. He saw the German infantry rush forward, sweeping through the gorge where three American tank destroyers burned. A few GIs were there, holding up their hands—as if the SS had time for prisoners! By the time the command tank rolled past, their foolishness had been terminated by the bursts of a few Schmeissers.

Now Peiper could see the road into the small city, with its precious bridges still intact, leading to the forested ridges across the valley and the solid fortifications of the Westwall. Perhaps it was not too late—perhaps they could reach that fortified border and hold those ramparts against the Americans.

A shot banged off the turret in a clang that punched his ears with a physical blow. He screamed, deafened so that he couldn't hear his gunner cry out behind him. A dim awareness: That was a dud shot; an explosion would have killed him.

Others were not so lucky. He saw more of his panzers explode, including two of the precious Panthers. Only vaguely did he become aware that they were being fired on from the flanks.

"Ambush! It's a trap!" The words crackled over the radio as, all along the column, his tankers figured out the awful truth. They had pushed their way through an initial roadblock, but their headlong approach now brought them under the guns of the lethal American artillery, a dozen or more guns emplaced on the high ground to their flank. The enemy gunners were able to sight directly against the side of the column, sending powerful shells blasting into the panzers where the armor plate was thin.

"Back—fall back!" Peiper shouted, hating the words but knowing there was no alternative—to press on was to lead his command into annihilation.

The infantry screened the panzers like true veterans, as the armored behemoths backed up the narrow road, guns blazing as they again sought the shelter of the dense woods. Ten minutes later they were under cover, and though American shells continued to explode around them the enemy was using the much less accurate indirect fire now, no longer shooting straight at targets that the gunners could observe. Even so, the barrage was intense, and Peiper knew that he could not stay here for long.

"Kraus!" he called, recognizing the captain from the reconnaissance company "Where is the next bridge across the Our?"

"Eight or ten kilometers north, sir—there is a span that will hold the weight of a Panther."

Peiper looked back down the road to Dasburg. The Americans were here, in strength, and that could only mean that they had already breached the Westwall. The change in tactics was as necessary as it was bitterly distasteful to him.

"Very well—lead us there, at once."

As the column pulled further into the woods, sorting itself into a road march again, he was already pulling out the maps. The Westwall was lost, that was certain—for a line with a major breach in it was no line at all. Instead, he looked to the east, through the tangled terrain of Germany. The only tactic was obvious: They would have to race the Americans into the Fatherland, and then they would have to hold them at the Rhine.

6 JANUARY 1945

NEUE REICHSKANZLEI, BERLIN, 0700 HOURS GMT

Berlin was dark outside, but it hardly mattered inside the tightly sealed inner office occupied by the führer. There, it was dark all the time, except for the single desk lamp that illuminated Heinrich Himmler's work surface. As usual, there were endless reports to review, endless decisions to make—couldn't his subordinates handle *anything* without his help? And then there were meetings. Paperwork and meetings, paperwork and meetings—the life of any leader.

"*Generalfeldmarschall Keitel, Generalfeldmarschall Mödel und Generaloberst Jodl, mein Führer,*" announced his secretary.

"Good morning, gentlemen," Himmler said to his most senior Wehrmacht officers. "Do you bring me good news today for a change?"

Keitel immediately started to stammer out an optimistic view of the current situation, but Mödel interrupted smoothly. "Führer, we bring you a realistic assessment that is not devoid of hope."

Himmler looked sharply at him. "Well, if that's not code for more Wehrmacht pessimism and defeatism, then I'll be glad to hear it."

"I don't think it is," interjected Jodl.

"From you, I believe it," said Himmler irritably. "Well, let's hear this realistic assessment that contains hope."

"Very well," Mödel replied. Moving to Himmler's conference table, he unrolled a large map and placed weights on each corner. "The key strategic issue before us is time. The longer we delay, the greater the likelihood that the former allies of East and West will find cause to struggle among themselves, the greater the likelihood that a populace tired of war will settle for a negotiated peace. Even a peace under less than completely favorable conditions allows us time to rebuild. We are, after all, destined to be a Thousand-Year Reich. What is a matter of a generation or two to us? That is one of the greatest advantages we have over the Americans, in particular. They have no history to speak of."

"All right," nodded Himmler. "Time. That was the motive behind our temporary peace with the Soviet Union. That time is about to expire. How do we get more?"

Mödel made a short bow in the direction of the führer, acknowledging his observation. "We must first stabilize the Western Front, then strike back toward the east, forcing the Soviets to exhaust their supplies, then counterattack in the west once again. The perverse advantage of our setbacks in recent years is that our internal lines of mobility are much shorter. Although we must now move at night because of air-superiority issues, we can still move. Once we get past the current Soviet offensive period, we have an opportunity to force a decent settlement in the west. The odds are not entirely in our favor, but the strategy, as I said earlier, is not without hope. That is what OKW proposes."

Himmler canvassed the two other senior officers with his eyes and saw their nods of agreement. Keitel's opinion counted for little—the man would applaud anything once it was clear the führer wanted it. Jodl, on the other hand, combined patriotism and loyalty with a somewhat better sense of realism. And Mödel—well, the Führer's Fireman was clearly the best man for this job. "Very well. I accept this plan, but with one important addition. I don't see any plan for ensuring that forces on the Western Front don't suddenly decide to join Rommel and the other traitors. Forces in the east, I think we can all agree, are unlikely to see switching sides as a practical option." He smiled thinly at his own joke. Keitel chuckled in sycophantic chorus.

Mödel looked at his map, his pointer touching the various military headquarters. "Each major unit has political officers appointed to it. All have exemplary Party credentials. I think we can rely on them taking direct action in the event of any threatened disloyalty."

"As Brigadeführer Bücher did?" Himmler replied in a silky voice.

Mödel raised his eyebrows. "Sir, Brigadeführer Bücher was a brave man, but remember that what happened was then without precedent. Everyone knows what happened, which means everyone is far more prepared. It would be far more difficult for anyone else to do what Rommel did—it would take only one brave officer and a pistol to stop attempted treason, and no commander could be so secure as to believe all his officers would follow a surrender initiative without resistance."

Himmler considered this argument for a moment. Then he shook his head. "It's not enough. Political officers are known. A treasonous commander would simply have political officers shot before any announcement took place. No, I'm afraid that the security of the Reich demands more. Much more."

"What do you propose?" asked Mödel. Suspicion and resistance were clearly written on his face. These Wehrmacht generals didn't understand state security, didn't understand politics, didn't understand the messiness of this business. Their problems were clean and straightforward, not like Himmler's. All the big problems rested on his shoulders.

The Führer of the Third Reich looked at his most senior generals. "A conspiracy to surrender a large military command needs a number of people. No single officer can do it alone. Rommel had a staff who largely hero-worshipped him. This, and of course the element of surprise, allowed him to succeed. Even then, he could not achieve the surrender of Sixth Panzer Army, and that was because loyal officers in that army were able to take action. Therefore, no commanding officer can be allowed to surround himself with sycophants, yes-men, and personal loyalists. I order, therefore, that the senior staff of all officers at the grade of colonel and above be switched randomly. All senior officers will have to work with a staff of strangers. This will prevent the kind of trust necessary for a conspiracy to surrender." Himmler looked at Mödel, waiting for the argument he knew would come.

"But mein Führer," Mödel protested, right on cue. "This move will dramatically hamper military effectiveness. Commanders need staff on whom they can rely utterly, and that kind of relationship is built over time. If staff is transferred, operations will be hampered."

Himmler smiled. "If we were going on the offensive in the West, I might agree. As it happens, you yourself have stated that your plan is one of delay and defense. That requires far less communication. In any event, the danger to our cause of losing another army or even a division is far greater than the theoretical disadvantages of hampered communication within the senior command staff."

Mödel looked back down at his map as he gathered his thoughts. "I'm afraid I have to agree with you, mein Führer," he said, shaking his head, "even though this goes against virtually everything I was ever taught about leadership. However, one fundamental characteristic of war is that the unexpected happens and must be integrated into plans, and this situation is nothing if not unexpected."

Himmler smiled. It was unusual for a Wehrmacht general to be actually convinced that Himmler was correct in something. Normally, they grumbled, protested, and sometimes grudgingly gave in, but Mödel actually saw the wisdom in Himmler's decision. Well, Mödel was a smart man, and as führer, Himmler was prepared to recognize the man. "Very good. I thank you. Your plan is a masterful response to a difficult situation, and I appreciate the creativity with which you responded to the facts. So often I am confronted with premature hopelessness in my generals. You at least know the difference between difficult and hopeless."

Mödel straightened slightly, showing Himmler that everyone responded well to praise. "An auspicious start to the morning. May the rest of the day continue to provide the same. Thank you, gentlemen."

Himmler jotted notes in a thin, spidery hand. Mödel could not be expected to handle the security issues himself; that was not in his area of expertise. Gestapo would oversee the reassignment of staff officers in Army Groups G and H, the two main forces Mödel would use to hold the Westwall. He could not prevent treachery and cowardice, but he could certainly make the price high, he thought.

"Obergruppenführer Dietrich, sir," his secretary announced. Himmler removed his eyeglasses and polished them on his handkerchief. He was still annoyed at Dietrich's stupidity at being maneuvered out of command of Sixth Panzer Army, and it was important that he not show it too clearly. Dietrich was too ignorant to be an ideologue—Party philosophy was too deep for him. He had simply fallen under the charismatic spell of Adolf Hitler and devoted himself to Hitler's service. Now that Himmler was the führer, it suited him to bind the man's loyalty to himself, for Dietrich was useful. But *lieber Gott!* the man was stupid. "Sepp, how are you," Himmler said, his mouth curving in a thin smile.

"Good morning, Führer," Dietrich replied, saluting in proper *sieg-heil* fashion and taking off his hat.

Himmler returned the salute and gestured toward a chair. "Sit down. Bring me up to date. How many of our brave troops have you extracted from the traitor's clutches?"

"Most of them, yes, most of them," replied Dietrich, his battered face nodding up and down. He sat with his legs apart, both hands holding his hat in his lap. "Most of them that didn't surrender, you know."

Yes, I know, you bleeding idiot, Himmler thought, and jotted another note. "I've appointed Model as Commander in Chief West. He has overall responsibility for stabilizing the Western Front."

"Model? Good man, Model. Good choice. The Führer's Fireman, you know," said Dietrich. "If anybody can do it, he can. Difficult job, though. Difficult." He shook his head sadly. "It's a bad time."

Himmler took his glasses off again so he wouldn't have to look at Dietrich's slack-jawed expression. The old soldier had always annoyed him, and yet he was good with the troops. As long as he could be surrounded with competent staff, he was useful. And right now, the Reich couldn't afford to spare any talent, no matter how modest. "Yes, Sepp, I understand. Now, we need to talk about what comes next, after the remnants of Sixth Panzer Army and any other Army Group B forces have successfully been returned to our control."

"Next?" Dietrich stopped to think. "They'll go into the Westwall, won't they?"

"Yes," replied Himmler with exaggerated patience. "They'll go into the Westwall. Most of them, anyway. And there they will continue to hold against the Western Allies. Meanwhile, our Eastern Front will be commanded by Generaloberst Jodl as he defends against the renewed Soviet advance."

"Jodl's a good man, too," Dietrich added helpfully.

"I'm glad you approve," Himmler replied acidly. "In any event, Sixth Panzer Army's role will be to set up a defensive posture along the Elbe to form an additional layer to continue to slow the US and British advance."

"The Elbe?" Dietrich thought for a moment. "The Soviets are the bigger danger. We both know that. Shouldn't we deploy along the Oder to fight them?"

"No," Himmler said slowly. "I want you on the Elbe. Jodl is responsible for defense in the east. He has a good plan."

Dietrich could not be shaken from his path quite so easily. "He still needs more troops. And the Soviets are the biggest danger to Germany. We should be along the Oder."

"No. And that's an order. You will coordinate with Generalfeldmarschall Mödel on this, but the basic strategy is that as he stabilizes the front, your forces will withdraw through German lines, cross the Rhine, then cross the Elbe and form a new defensive line there. You'll receive detailed orders on this point. The forces you have to work with will be those you're able to extract from Army Group B, so the more you get, the more you'll have. Understand?"

"Jawohl, mein Führer," Dietrich replied, "but I still believe . . ."

"And I still believe that you will defend the Elbe. Thank you, Sepp. That will be all."

"Yes, sir," replied Dietrich, but the stubborn look on his face told Himmler that he was not convinced. Well, no matter, as long as the man followed orders—and he knew how to follow orders.

CCA, DASBURG, GERMANY, 0711 GMT

Frank Ballard jolted awake with a sense of panic, then realized he had just dozed off, again, in the command seat of his rumbling Sherman. It had been three days since he had actually slept in a bed or even caught more than a few minutes of uninterrupted slumber. When he ran his hand across the rough stubble on his chin he knew that his shave and shower on the morning of his promotion were but dim memories, lost in the haze of war.

But CCA, which now comprised virtually all of the fighting strength of the Nineteenth Armored division, was making great time. By late afternoon of the fourth they had roared into newly recaptured Bastogne, where he had learned that Americans of the Fourth Armored Division, aided by some friendly Germans of the Volksgrenadierie, had opened the road all the way to the German border.

The next stop for Nineteenth Armored was Dasburg, where they would slip through the Westwall and enter Germany proper. After an all-night run through the winding and hilly roads of the Ardennes, they rolled down the road into this border city, entering from the west. The picturesque town was located on the narrow river in a deep valley, and as they approached Ballard could see smoke lingering to his left. Obviously, there had been fighting here yesterday—but just as obviously there was an American flag flying over the city's main hall, and emplacements of Sherman tanks and GIs guarding the approaches.

A helpful MP guided him toward the HQ compound, and while he sent the reconnaissance company and a detachment of Shermans through the city to take up positions on the far side of the river Ballard directed his driver toward the compound. Here they stopped to refuel, and he dismounted to learn what he could.

"You there, Major!" he called, to the first ranking officer he saw.

"Major Weber, Colonel. What can I do for our pals from the Nineteenth Armored?"

"Colonel Ballard, CCA. If you can tell me the situation in a hundred words or less, I'll buy you a case of champagne when we get to Berlin."

"My pleasure, Colonel. Can I interest you in some eggs and bacon while we're at it? They were expecting you, and I think the kitchen has put out a few extra helpings."

This was the best news Ballard had heard since getting his eagle. He sent the men of his HQ company toward the outdoor mess "hall" set up at the edge of the HQ compound, and gladly took a plate of hot food himself while he listened to Weber speak.

"We came from Bastogne, the day before yesterday. Things changed pretty fast for us in the last week of '44. The bastards were entrenched in the hills south of there," Weber explained. "Even with Georgie himself cracking the whip, we were having a helluva time trying to fight our way into Bastogne. Then we get word over the radio—the Krauts surrendered, and we were supposed to march right in! Heard you boys in Dinant had a little to do with that development—nice work."

"Thanks," Ballard mumbled around a mouthful of eggs.

"Well, let me tell you, we came into Bastogne with our heads down and our guns loaded. But the Kraut general—he was acting CO of the Twenty-sixth Volksgrenadiers; I guess their chief got killed in some fracas with his own men—handed over the whole town without a shot. Said he was acting on orders of Rommel himself. To hear the old guy talk, that was the next best thing to God."

"I've met the man," Ballard replied. "Impressive, even when he's supposed to be a POW."

"But he isn't really, is he?" the major had asked. "Seems like he's actually got some Krauts working on our side." He frowned and Ballard felt again the strangeness of the current arrangement.

"That's supposed to be the way it's working," Ballard allowed.

"Well, they got us into Dasburg without any trouble," Weber continued. "Now, we have our CCA across the river, holding a five-mile stretch of the Westwall. Don't know what's happening north or south of here, but if you want a road into Germany, we've got it."

"Then Rommel was as good as his word, again. He said he'd try to get us through the Westwall, and it sounds like he came through," Frank noted. "Though I'm still wanting to keep a close eye on my flanks."

"Yeah, I know the feeling," Weber said cheerfully. "But, we've got scouts as far east as Bitburg—that's halfway to Trier. The road is good, and it's open."

"Let's hope it stays that way," Ballard had noted, wolfing the last bite of his breakfast. His driver waved, signaling that the Sherman had been refueled. "The Old Man will probably want us across the Rhine by tomorrow."

Weber's eyes widened at that, his mouth twisting into a wry smile. "You guys in the Nineteenth did some nice running in France—see if you can't set a new record here in Kraut country."

"Wish us luck," Frank Ballard replied. "And thanks for the chow."

The dawn had broken clear and cold around them, and a whole new country awaited as the tank engine roared to life. Ballard's stomach felt full for the first time in days, and he wished he could take a minute to enjoy the feeling. He saw a pretty young girl—a German girl, no doubt—looking out the window of a nearby house, and he grinned at her and waved. Not surprisingly, she darted back behind the sill, though he had the sense she was still watching from within the shadowed room. Who was she? He wondered about that, wanted to meet her, just to hear the pleasant sound of a female voice.

But Smiggy's reconnaissance company was somewhere up ahead. Beyond was Trier, the Moselle Valley, and the road to the Rhine.

He knew that he had better get going.

7 JANUARY 1945

HEADQUARTERS, FIRST BELORUSSIAN FRONT, NEAR WARSAW, POLAND, 1148 HOURS GMT

Marshal Georgi Konstantinovich Zhukov, commander of the First Belorussian Front of the Army of the Union of Soviet Socialist Republics, flipped through the last few pages of the mammoth supply report and slammed the cover shut. "Good," he said. His voice was deep and gruff. Zhukov was a short, square-built man with a high forehead. His rough demeanor and powerful stature gave him a bearlike appearance, appropriate to the Rodina he served. "Supplies and reinforcements are at their fullest levels. Unfortunately, the damned Germans are probably saying the same thing right now."

"Those that aren't being pounded into the dirt by American bombers," Marshal Ivan Stepanovich Konev, commander of the First Ukranian Front, replied. The two Soviet marshals were meeting here, on the estate of a former Polish nobleman, to coordinate their planning work. Colonel Alyosha Krigoff stood among two score officers, including generals in command of entire armies, staff officers charged with coordination between fronts of hundreds of thousands of soldiers, and intelligence staffers who were responsible for assessing and reporting on the enemy's capabilities. He was one of only a few colonels here, attending because General Yeremko was ill. General Petrovsky had grudgingly brought Krigoff in the veteran intelligence officer's stead. Now the two of them, like all the others except the two esteemed front commanders, remained silent, listening attentively.

Soon, the mighty juggernaut of the Soviet Union would once again roll forward, crushing everything in its path. Neither marshal wanted to wait any longer, but the order from Moscow had not yet been received. Krigoff was surprised by how eager he himself was to see this great army hurl itself, once more, against the fascist foe.

Zhukov laughed. It was not a pleasant sound. "You're right. The Nazi bastards still have a war going on, and one of their own just turned chicken on them. That must be a kick in the pants for Himmler, don't you think?"

Konev stood up and walked over to the samovar to draw himself another cup of tea. He took a heaping spoonful of strawberry preserves and stirred it in, then took a sip, taking a deep breath of the hot steam at the same time. "I'm surprised Rommel is the only one. The rest can't be so stupid as to think they still have any sort of chance. Going over to the Americans and British is the only way for most of them to save their own lives. Now that Hitler is dead and rotting in his grave, what else makes them hold on?"

Zhukov scratched his chest. "They're soldiers, I guess. That makes them blind and stupid. They can't imagine any alternatives except win or lose."

Konev laughed. "I guess that makes us blind and stupid as well. We couldn't imagine any alternatives, and our situation was nearly as bleak not that long ago."

"That's exactly what I mean. We're all blind and stupid. Sometimes that makes us stronger." Zhukov's gaze roamed across the faces of the assembled staff officers, came to rest on Krigoff's—at least, that's how it seemed to the colonel. "Perhaps not all of us," amended the general. "Some of us see more than others."

"I despise that stubbornness in an enemy. It will make the Germans stronger when we push forward," Konev remarked.

"I'm afraid it will," Zhukov replied. "It won't change the outcome, but it will affect how much more blood we shed for Mother Russia. Look at the maps our intelligence people have drawn up. The Germans have dug in all along the Oder. This will be a difficult river crossing to make."

"I never thought I'd say this," said Konev, "but there are days I miss Adolf Hitler."

Krigoff's eyes almost widened in surprise before he exerted his self-control to mask the reaction. Now *that* was a remark to remember; he went over it in his mind, so that he could jot it down verbatim after the meeting.

Zhukov chuckled in response. "I know what you mean. He'd give orders to keep his overwhelmed units from retreating and send orders to his generals to defend 'fortresses' that had no protection. There were times he was as much an ally as our good friend General Winter." The cruel Russian winter, and the muddy season that preceded and followed it every year, had done a great deal to hamper the German war effort ever since Operation Barbarossa had bogged down on the approach to Moscow in late 1941.

The two generals looked up as a signals officer, himself a colonel, knocked on the door and hesitantly entered the room. "Comrade General?" he addressed Zhukov. "There is a communiqué from the Kremlin."

The general snatched the missive without formality and eagerly read the page of text.

"Well, one more dead fascist is a good fascist," replied Konev, taking his turn to look at the staff officers while his superior perused the missive. "Sometimes killing can make the world a better place."

Did his attention linger on me? Was he speaking to me? Krigoff couldn't help wondering, and tried to suppress a stab of paranoid fear. "When all the fascists are dead, the world will be much improved," concluded the front commander, as Zhukov put down the message, his face breaking into a broad grin.

"Then we're going to have the chance to improve the world, quite a bit," said the venerable general. "This is the order we have been waiting for." He glanced at his watch. "Execute Operations Plan Alpha immediately. Air strikes against German positions will commence this afternoon, and I want a full-scale artillery bombardment going by dusk. The tanks will roll as soon as it is dark. Comrades, once again, we are at war."

9 JANUARY 1945

THIRD ARMY FORWARD HEADQUARTERS (MOBILE),
TRIER, GERMANY, 1830 HOURS GMT
Rommel looked out the smeared-glass side window of the jeep, at the country-side that didn't look so very different from the forests and swales of Belgium or France. But it was different—this was Germany.

This was home.

He pondered how, exactly, he returned here. Was it as a traitor? A liberator? Conqueror? All of the above, in some measure or another, he supposed. He did feel like a stranger, a foreigner in his own fatherland. And he came here, rode the wave of a whole tide of foreigners, these amazing and energetic Americans.

They were racing everywhere, it seemed. Throughout Belgium the roads had been jammed with columns of trucks, jeeps, tanks, and troops, all moving toward the front. The Westwall was breached in a gap a hundred miles wide, and all those men were flowing into Germany, surging toward the Rhine.

On a purely military basis, he remained amazed at how rapidly the American columns physically moved across the ground. The HQ unit that was his destination served as a prime example: there were hundreds of men, dozens of trucks full of equipment and supplies, and when it was up and running it was like a busy and crowded office building. Yet the staff could set up or tear down that office in about an hour, and load it up for transport in less time than that. With a roar of engines and cloud of dust, the HQ was a motorized column racing down the road to the next city, or the one after that.

There seemed to be plenty of gasoline for all of these vehicles, and ample food for the men, and even for POWs and displaced civilians. As to American equipment, he believed that the Yanks made up for in quantity what they might have lacked in quality. The Sherman tanks were light and undergunned by the standards of modern German armor, doomed in a face-to-face shootout with a Panther or Tiger. But at the same time Rommel acknowledged that they were fast and reliable, so nimble that they could move across all types of terrain, and light enough to cross rivers on bridges that would never support even a Panther tank, much less one of the gargantuan Tigers. Furthermore, there seemed to be hundreds of the things, everywhere he looked. Speidel had remarked earlier, only half in jest, that the Yankees must be growing their tanks on the vast steppes of the North American heartland. After his experiences in the past month, Rommel was forced to agree.

The Desert Fox had been driven to Trier in a closed jeep by an American driver, and as they made their way through the narrow streets, crowded with military traffic, he saw that this town—gateway to Germany going back to Roman times—had been given over, completely, to American control.

Third Army MPs were busy steering traffic through the town, all of it the olive drab of American military, and most of it heading east. Rommel's driver apologized as they were halted for more than ten minutes, while an apparently endless column of Shermans rolled past on the main avenue through the city. The field marshal found it telling that, even as the great column rolled speedily along, there was enough traffic in the side streets that each of them became thronged with waiting vehicles. As the last of the M4s passed, each driver stepped on the gas, to be challenged by a chorus of MP whistles and shouts.

Only by jockeying through a tight turn, then dashing down an alley, did the jeep driver finally break free of the crush. He turned back onto the thoroughfare with a screech of tires, and then pulled into the elegant, semicircular driveway of the grand and venerable Hotel Trier.

"This is the HQ building, for today anyway, General," the driver said in his passable German. Rommel ignored the mistake in rank, knowing that the Americans had no field marshal in their military hierarchy. "I'm supposed to drop you here."

"Thank you," Rommel replied, getting out of the small car and stretching. His back was sore and his legs stiff, but he shook off the travel kinks and entered the large lobby, returning the salute of the MP who stood outside the door. The room was a rather jarring contrast of military functionality and Baroque overindulgence. There were great, floor-to-ceiling mirrors along one lofty wall, with vivid tapestries framed by marble columns. In between were tangles of radio and power cables, plain tables, and functional folding chairs.

His arrival didn't seem to cause much of a stir. That was interesting, he reflected—perhaps it might be possible for the Wehrmacht and the American army to work together after all. Instinctively he went to the table, where a large map—depicting Germany from the Westwall to the Rhine—was spread. Everything had an air of transience. Several tables were simply sheets of plywood laid across sawhorses, while the radio consoles across the room resembled a jungle of hastily laid wiring and cables. He knew that the HQ staff had moved in here a few hours ago; by tomorrow, or perhaps the day after, they would be back on the road.

He had hoped to find Patton here, but was informed that the Third Army commander had blown through the temporary headquarters like a winter squall. He was up at the front, supervising the fast-moving spearheads of his armor divisions. Rommel nodded in understanding, and in fact wished that he could be doing the same thing.

One of Third Army's senior intelligence officers, a one-star, was emerging from a small office adjacent to the lobby, and he greeted the field marshal warmly in German.

"General Patton asked me to show you every hospitality if you should visit. I am sorry not to have greeted you when you arrived, but I was just finishing up in the decoding room," he said, with a glance at the door that had just closed behind him. "And I've got good news, Field Marshal! Frank Ballard of the Nineteenth is already twenty miles down the Moselle Valley. We have four more divisions through the Westwall, and they're driving to the east and north. It looks like your Seventh Army is going along with the surrender. So our own Seventh—that's General Patch—can move into the Palatinate south of here."

"Good. I expected as much, in that arena. I have been in regular contact with General Brandenburger, and he has been willing to follow my orders," Rommel declared. "What is the latest word on Sixth Panzerarmee?" While he greatly disliked asking that question of an American officer, no matter how polite, the current status of those forces was continuously on his mind.

Here the American general's good cheer wavered slightly. "They're giving First Army and the Brits a helluva tussle—they still hold the Westwall north of Dasburg, all the way to the sea. Our only breakthroughs are from here south."

"So the valley of the Moselle is the best route, the only fast route, to the Rhine."

"Right. The main threat seems to be here—" The general marked a line from Bitburg to Koblenz, which was a shorter distance than the Moselle Valley route. "There are several SS-kampfgruppe racing eastward. Panzer Lehr is in pursuit, but the Nazi panzers have slipped away for now. There's a chance they could reach the Rhine before us, and if they do we won't get the crossing without a nasty fight."

"Big news, men!" This shout came from the radio room, where a colonel rushed into the room waving a piece of paper. He skidded to stop when he saw Rommel, then threw up a quick salute. "Hello, Field Marshal," he said hastily. "Um, this can wait."

"Spill it, Joe," the general said quickly. "The field marshal is in this with us, remember?"

"Yes, sir," Joe replied. He held up the paper. "Intelligence reports are in from some of the Polish resistance. They report that the Red Army has opened fire—a helluva bombardment, along a hundred miles of the Vistula. Looks like the Russians are getting back into the game."

Rommel nodded, unsurprised. He saw the same kind of acceptance on the faces of the American staff officers all around him. Indeed, they had expected the attack for so long that it was almost a relief to know, at last, what Stalin was planning to do.

"Well, looks like the race is on," the American said after a moment. "We'd better get busy."

"I'll head up to Panzer Lehr," Rommel said. "It may be that I can help with logistics, up there. It's important to get as many of your troops through the Westwall as possible—we need to reach the Rhine before the SS can blow bridges and form some kind of defensive front."

"Right, sir. General Patton has already ordered the Nineteenth to aim for Koblenz, with Fourth Armored moving up right behind. You know what kind of speed they can maintain. We have two divisions driving north, moving up behind the Westwall, trying to roll up Dietrich's flank. Unfortunately, the mobile SS elements seem to already have bugged out."

Rommel nodded, concerned but hopeful. The day promised another clear sky, and he was learning to think of that as a *good* thing—the tactical air forces would have free rein, and that should only help the Shermans as they raced for the river.

This was a race, he knew, that the Americans—and his loyal Germans—very much had to win.

10 JANUARY 1945

PANZER BATTALION, TWELFTH SS PANZER DIVISION "HITLERJUGEND," BITBURG, GERMANY, 0842 HOURS GMT

The battalion command post had been set up on a small yard, with a Panther tank parked nearby. The engine hatch was open, with a mechanic leaning in so far that his head and both arms were invisible inside of the compartment.

"Hauptsturmführer Friedrich?" Lukas Vogel asked, standing at attention as he reported to his new commander. He was an officer now, but the enlisted man's reflexes were still with him—he felt a little bit awkward dealing with higher rank. The SS captain to whom he was reporting was scarred on one cheek, and his eyes were a watery clear blue. He was balding on top, and his uniform was dirty. He hadn't shaved in a few days. Lukas ran his eyes over the man's decorations. The Panzer Assault Badge with silver wreath signified twenty-five separate days of armor combat. That didn't seem like a lot to Lukas. After twenty-five days of action, he would just be getting started. The captain also wore a silver Wound Badge, which meant he'd been wounded three times. He had obviously seen action, and seemed somewhat the worse for wear. *When I've seen that much action, I'll still know how to keep my uniform pressed and look tike a German officer,* Lukas thought.

"Yes . . . Untersturmführer . . . ?" The panzer officer looked up from his map table with mild interest, eyebrows rising as he saw the second lieutenant's badge newly pinned to the young man's brand-new and ill-fitting uniform collar.

"Vogel, sir. I have been assigned to your battalion by Obersturmbann-führer Schultz. That is, my men and I, sir. I was sent to the division by General Dietrich himself," he added, reaching for the worn sheet of paper written by Dietrich's aide-de-camp.

"Dietrich, eh?" Friedrich looked at the boy with slightly greater interest.

"Yes, sir." Lukas waited for Friedrich to ask him how he knew the general, but instead Friedrich motioned toward a pile of papers and Lukas dropped his document on top of the pile. "All right, Vogel. I can use you." He looked toward the street, where Hans Braun and the other boys were waiting outside the truck. "Do you come with that truck?" he asked.

"Yes, sir," Lukas declared.

"Good. You will need it shortly. Do you have small arms?"

"Some, Hauptsturmführer. We have three carbines and a Schmeisser, also four grenades left. However, our ammunition for the carbines and the machine pistol is all gone."

"Draw what you need from my quartermaster—you'll find him in the stables behind that inn." Friedrich pointed at a large stone building down the street. "And be ready to move out in an hour."

"Yes sir! And, thank you, sir!" Lukas declared, stiffening his arm in a salute that Friedrich acknowledged with a flip of his hand. *Another officer who doesn't give a shit any longer,* Lukas thought.

"This is our new unit," he reported to Hans as his sturmscharführer and the other boys gathered around him. "Fritzi, you bring the truck. The rest of you, come with me."

As they walked down the narrow street Lukas noticed other panzers tucked into alcoves and sheds, always where they would be out of sight from the air. The tanks looked battered but serviceable, manned by hard eyed young soldiers who watched the newcomers with expressions ranging from bored to skeptical. He saw only a few trucks, and one yard contained a dozen horses and some wooden wagons. He saw a tank with its track off, several men working to make the repair, while other men were carrying crates of heavy ammunition—rounds for the tanks' main guns, he guessed. A welder's torch flared brightly within the shadows of a large shed. There was an easy familiarity these men displayed toward their companions and their equipment, and this made Lukas feel woefully unprepared.

"Notice the age differences?" Hans said. "The officers and senior enlisted are all ancient—at least thirty years old!"

"Yeah," replied Lukas. "I bet a lot of them are wounded or washed out, sent over here to let us do all the fighting."

"Hey, at least we get into the war for real," Hans replied, slapping his superior officer on the back. "You've brought us this far, mein Untersturmführer! We'll go the rest of the way together."

"Thanks, Hans" Lukas replied. "We'll take care of our boys and win this war yet."

They found the stables Friedrich had indicated, and Lukas approached an old, skinny man he assumed to be the quartermaster.

"Hauptsturmführer Friedrich sent me to get weapons and ammunition for my men," Lukas explained.

"For your men, eh, Untersturmführer?" said the man, with a casual look at the group. "Are you sure you're old enough to shoot them?" He grinned, showing missing teeth.

"We will fight for the Fatherland—and we will die, if necessary!" declared the young officer indignantly. *Old fart,* he thought. Then he realized that it might not do to antagonize the quartermaster, so he adopted a slightly softer tone. "But we would do a better job of it if we were properly armed. Can you help us?"

The old sergeant cracked a grin at that, and stepped aside to gesture toward a stack of crates within the stable. "Take what you need," he said. "There's plenty for everybody—just don't load yourselves down so much that you can't move."

The young soldiers entered the building and looked around in awe, recognizing grenades, ammunition crates, and several different kinds of firearms. Lukas had a memory of Christmas morning, some years before, when his father had presented him with his first folding knife. Now he claimed a Schmeisser machine pistol for Hans and a Luger sidearm for himself. Fritzi came along with the truck, and as they were loading up boxes of ammo Lukas realized why there were so many extra guns: These had been gathered from dead soldiers.

After his detachment was fully armed, he found a kitchen and saw that the boys got some food: thin broth, brown bread, and—wonder of wonders!— fresh milk. By the time they were finished, Captain Friedrich came along and told them it was time to move. Lukas heard tank engines roaring to life, saw the horse-drawn wagons, each loaded with a dozen panzergrenadiere, rolling down the streets toward the east end of town. He and Hans loaded his boys onto the truck as Friedrich came over.

"We've been ordered to Koblenz," the captain said, leaning in the driver's window. He had bad breath.

"Koblenz?" Lukas was surprised; he knew that the Rhine city was far behind the front. He knew better than to question the order, but Friedrich smiled a cold smile and filled him in.

"It seems the Americans are on their way to the Rhine, and they aren't wasting time—are you prepared to hurry?"

"Yes, Herr Hauptsturmführer—we will get to Koblenz before them!"

"Indeed, my boy, we have to—since once we get there, we will have to turn around and fight."

"I am ready to do that, too," promised the young untersturmführer.

"You've heard the tale of the little Dutch boy and the dike?" asked the captain. "The fellow had to stick his finger in the hole to keep the dam from washing away?"

Puzzled, Lukas answered in the affirmative.

"Well, good. Because right now, the Rhine is our dike. And you, my lad, you and the rest of the Hitlerjugend division, including me—"

"Yes, Hauptsturmführer?"

"Well, we are the finger."

HEADQUARTERS, FIRST BELORUSSIAN FRONT,
WARSAW, POLAND, 0933 HOURS GMT

The Polish capital had absorbed a lot of punishment over the previous six years of war. First had come the German invasion of 1939, culminating in the battle for this city. This was followed by brutal Nazi repression of rebellion, first against the Jews in their squalid ghetto, then—just the previous summer—by the Poles who mistakenly viewed the Soviet advance, and the death of Adolf Hitler, as harbingers of freedom. Naturally, they had been crushed.

Just as well, thought Alyosha Krigoff. The last thing the Soviets wanted, in this city that would soon be part of the growing Soviet empire, was a bunch of freedom-minded Polish nationals expecting to control their own country. Of course, there would be Poles in charge of the Polish government, but they would be Party-member Poles selected by Chairman Stalin himself.

Now that decision loomed near. More than a thousand guns, a whole galaxy of artillery, pounded Warsaw into an even finer grade of rubble. Soviet engineers quickly laid bridges across the Vistula, and Marshal Zhukov sent his armored columns surging westward, around the city and toward the prize of Berlin and all the rest of Germany. Meanwhile, more tanks and a great wave of infantry moved into what was left of the historic city.

Krigoff had a box seat for this epic show. He rode in the observation seat of the small scout plane, watching the strings of ubiquitous T-34 tanks as the rumbling vehicles pushed through that moonscape of ruins like files of ants seeking food. Fires blossomed throughout the ruins, smoke billowing upward in black columns while buildings tumbled and streets vanished beneath ever-growing mountains of debris.

Even better, he had been able to secure a very special passenger for this dramatic view. Paulina Koninin had been working with the documentary crew attached to front headquarters, and when an influential colonel of intelligence—himself—had requested that she personally accompany him on this reconnaissance flight, her director had been only too thrilled to let her come along. He'd given Krigoff a knowing look, of course, but Krigoff didn't mind. She sat in the second observer's seat, behind Krigoff, and when he looked back he saw that she was busily snapping pictures of the vast sweep of destruction.

"Glorious, is it not?" he asked, grinning over his shoulder.

She heard him and lowered the camera long enough to favor him with a smile. "Yes, Comrade Colonel!" she replied with a nod.

The only failure, thus far, had been the rockets that had been designed from the German specifications. They had been used shortly after dawn, and Krigoff had watched in dismay as the strange, birdlike missiles had roared out of the eastern sky. He had spotted five of them, each trailing a plume of smoke. They had soared past at high speed, and he had seen the fire spewing from their tails. But then one, and soon after a second, had flamed out, tumbling down before they even reached the target. The first had fallen with a fiery explosion right into the midst of a Soviet tank column, while the second had vanished with a pathetic splash into the Vistula.

He had watched the other three breathlessly, knowing they had been targeted against a large fortress near the southern edge of the city. Two had overshot the area completely, vanishing into the distance, while the third had plummeted to the ground at least a mile from the intended destination. The resulting explosion had been spectacular, but Krigoff could already see that the weapons lacked the accuracy to have much use on the battlefield.

Nevertheless, he was awed, and thrilled, to think of the destructive power that was now being brought to bear against the Nazi war machine. There could be no greater manifestation of might on the planet than the great tide now advancing westward. Tanks, hundreds of them within his own line of sight right now, rolled onward as armored testament to the might of Soviet industry. Vast flights of aircraft dove against the German positions, dropping bombs and strafing relentlessly, emblematic of the Soviet ruthlessness and resolve. And the men, more than a million of them fueling this great offensive, were the ultimate proof of communism's manifest destiny. How could any force, any group of nations, stand against such a wave of historical inevitability?

In truth, they could not. With a tight, almost wolfish grin, Krigoff pressed his binoculars to his eyes and studied the city—or, more properly, the battlefield, he thought with a wry laugh. It was a city once, and might be a city again, but now it was only a killing ground.

He spotted a factory, the shell of a building standing as a makeshift fortress at the junction of the Vistula and a smaller tributary stream. Soviet tanks lined the perimeter of the location, firing at point-blank range with their guns. Krigoff knew the place could be plastered by artillery, and for a moment he longed for the authority to call in such a barrage. But his observations were in the service of a higher calling: He would report only to the chairman. Somewhere else, however, an artillery liaison officer did his job, and batteries arrayed on the east side of the river opened up a devastating barrage. He saw the muzzle flashes, knew instinctively that their target was below.

"Would you like a better look?" he asked Paulina.

She nodded, her one eye alive with the fire of battle; clearly she was enjoying this as much as Krigoff. Ah, she was a rare treasure, a Soviet gem! Paulina reached for the movie camera that she had brought along, and started winding the spring while Krigoff tapped the pilot on his shoulder. The colonel gestured when the man turned to look.

"Down there—fly closer," Krigoff ordered.

If the flier had any reservations, he understood his role well enough to conceal them. He merely nodded and put the plane, a small Piper provided by American Lend Lease, into a steep dive.

Krigoff couldn't suppress a giggle of sheer delight as they swept toward the factory and saw the place dissolve in a hail of high explosives. Fire ballooned upward, a great mushroom cloud, as some store of fuel or arms was ignited. The aircraft lurched to the side, the pilot cursing as he veered around the fireball, while Krigoff pressed his face to the glass window and stared in wonder and delight. His binoculars dangled from his neck, forgotten—at last he was close to the action, where he belonged. Once more he looked at Paulina, saw that her hands were steady, her attention rapt as she recorded a reel of movie film.

In another minute they were past the front and over the enemy positions. He saw a few gray vehicles, German panzers, moving away from the river, and watched with satisfaction as a pair of Sturmoviks, red stars bright on their wings, swept downward, releasing bombs that fell to earth like tiny eggs. Flame blossomed again, and he relished the sight of a tank upended, tossed like a child's toy on a demolished street.

"Back," he declared, sneering at the pilot's expression of relief. "I will be speaking to the chairman personally, to let him know that the attack is progressing very well indeed."

He watched, with no attempt to conceal his satisfaction, as the flier's face drained of blood, leaving his expression as wan and pale as any sheet.

11 JANUARY 1945

KAMPFGRUPPE PEIPER, EIFEL (NORTH OF MOSELLE VALLEY), GERMANY, 1023 HOURS GMT

"We've located five tanks, Panzer IVs, hull down on the next ridge," reported the scout. "They're backed up by an eighty-eight, and have the whole road covered."

"Panzer Lehr?" Peiper asked, his scarred face flaming red hot at the thought of these traitorous bastards standing between him and the river that had become his Holy Grail.

"It would seem so. The prisoners we took yesterday were all from the Lehr," reported the young lieutenant, who still straddled his idling motorcycle. His goggles were raised above the bill of his peaked SS officer's cap, the circular outlines clear in the white flesh surrounding his eyes. The rest of his face was red and raw, the marks of windburn and frostbite.

Peiper nodded in acknowledgment, satisfied that those prisoners, at least, had paid the price for treachery. He only wished that the rest of the Wehrmacht could have witnessed the example of ten men, their throats constricted by coiled wire, slowly strangling to death in the snow.

"Rommel has sent them here to stop us," he muttered. "And if you've found five, there are at least ten, and a few more guns, that have yet to show themselves,"

The untersturmführer, sensing that Peiper was talking to himself, made no reply as the panzer commander pulled himself out of the hatch and perched on the edge of the turret for a moment, thinking. Then Peiper stepped to the deck of the Panther's hull and hopped to the ground in a leap that should have been easy, but still sent a stab of pain searing through his wounded face.

As always, he used that pain to focus, to help him gather his thoughts and his resolve. Striding fast, he passed a dozen panzers idling along the shoulder of the bluff-side road, until he reached the bend. Here he could see that the road dipped through a broad ravine and then climbed toward a ridge on the far side. All of the terrain was thickly forested, except for a clearing of farmland down in the ravine.

"The . . . enemy tanks are over there," said the scout, who had followed the colonel up to this vantage. He indicated the crest of the next ridge.

"You are right to call them 'enemy,' " Peiper said, sensing the man's hesitation.

"They have betrayed everything that our führer has made right and holy. There is no death too painful for them."

"Yes, Herr Obersturmbannführer, of course."

Peiper's communications officer was nearby, and he gestured the fellow forward. "Have you had contact with the Hitlerjugend division?"

"Yes, Herr Obersturmbannführer. They have made good time—they are approaching Koblenz from the north. It seems they have moved too fast for the Panzer Lehr to get in their way."

"Good. Then we shall take our time, and see that this roadblock is destroyed." The decision was easy, knowing that their SS compatriots were close to the key city. Peiper's job would be to remove this threat from their flank and rear, and he knew just how to go about that. "Dismount the panzergrenadiere and start an enveloping attack, sweeping around to the left," he ordered. "Set up our own antitank guns on this crest, and if one of those bastards so much as twitches, I want him blasted to hell!"

Quickly officers and men hurried to obey his bidding. He went back to his command tank, anticipating the coming carnage with satisfaction.

12 JANUARY 1945

ARMEEGRUPPE FIELD HOSPITAL, DINANT, BELGIUM, 1317 HOURS GMT

"You can't get out of bed. Doctor's orders," the officious nurse said. She folded her arms and glared at her disobedient patient.

Günter von Reinhardt put his right leg gingerly on the floor. This was the first time since his wounding he'd sat upright, and the new perspective made him dizzy. He looked at the nurse and smiled ingratiatingly. "I'm afraid that I have orders that supersede them," he replied. He placed his left leg on the floor, generating another wave of dizziness. His punctured lung had trouble sucking in enough air, and he felt a need to cough, which he dreaded. Coughing hurt.

The patient's body language was perfectly clear to the nurse. "You see?" she said in triumph. "You're not ready to get up." Sensing victory, she switched her tone from peremptory to soothing. "Now, why don't you just lie down quietly and get some rest. You'll be fit for duty soon enough." She pulled down the bedcovers to make it easy for him, but as she approached, he used her shoulder to pull him to a standing position.

Immediately, the cough he was trying to suppress hit him fully. He grabbed the headboard to keep himself from collapsing as a sharp edge of pain cut through his lungs. The nurse tut-tutted as she held his shoulders. "See? You're not healed yet. Let's get back into bed now and let medicine and nature take its course."

As the painful spasm ran its course, von Reinhardt looked at the hand he'd used to cup his mouth. There were flecks of red in it. He wiped his palm with a tissue. "I'm sorry," he said firmly, "but I must return to my duty. The field marshal has requested that I do so immediately."

A mere field marshal wasn't enough to intimidate this nurse. She was so strong, von Reinhardt had seen her lift patients from bed to rolling cart single-handedly. If it came to hand-to-hand combat between this woman and the Desert Fox, von Reinhardt suspected the nurse would win. The thought amused him and he cracked a small smile.

The smile annoyed the nurse. "Stay here," she ordered peremptorily. "I will get the doctor, and then you will see that you must return to bed immediately." She wheeled around and left.

Von Reinhardt inspected himself in the small mirror above the tiny washbasin across from his bed. His long, angular face seemed unusually drawn, revealing the skull shape underneath. His jet black hair had grown longer during his hospital stay, one lock falling over his forehead in a manner reminiscent of his late führer's. The nurses who bathed him had shaved him as well, and the skin of his cheeks was still smooth.

The gauntness of his face, however, startled him. It made him look as if he'd aged decades in the last month. In a way, he had. He felt ancient.

He splashed a little cold water on his face, patted it dry, and looked at himself once again. Better. He straightened up to attention, but that triggered another round of agonizing coughing and some blood to spit into the sink.

A voice behind him said, "What's this I hear about you wanting to leave our lovely hotel to return to the battlefield?" Dr. Caroselli, a short, plump Italian who had remained—not entirely of his own free will—in the service of the Germans after his country's surrender, was the replacement for the kidnapped Dr. Schlüter. Caroselli's Mediterranean cheerfulness seemed out of place in the very German atmosphere of the field hospital.

"Why, this is a battlefield, nor am I out of it," murmured von Reinhardt in response, splashing more water on his face.

Caroselli threw up his hands in mock outrage. "Are you comparing my fine hospital to Hell, Herr Oberst? Yes, yes, I know the reference. Ah, the man thinks he is the only one with a classical education! *Doctor Faustus*—pah, too easy! Your mind is clearly not up to the challenge of the outside world. There is the proof you belong back in bed. Rest! That's what you need! Take the time to think up a real stumper for me—you haven't succeeded yet!"

Von Reinhardt could not help but smile at the excitable physician. "Herr Doktor Major, you're clearly right. If I fail to stump a man like you, it's a sign that my mind is truly in a weakened condition." The two men had traded friendly insults over the last weeks. It was one of von Reinhardt's few pleasures during the long, enforced rest. "Nevertheless, this weak mind is required in the service of our great field marshal, and regardless of the state of my health, I must go."

Caroselli threw up his hands again. "Another sick person flees the hospital! What about the damage to my reputation? Did you ever think about that? Has it occurred to you that if people leave my care before they are well, and then get worse, I will get the blame? Here, lie down again. Rest. Get better for another week. I'll talk to Rommel myself. He seems like a reasonable man."

"It might be a good idea. He's quite used to working for Italians," replied von Reinhardt. During the majority of the North African campaign, in which Rommel acquired his "Desert Fox" nickname, his nominal superior as theater commander was Italian. Rommel retained the right of appeal directly to

Berlin, however, and tended only to follow those orders or directives with which he agreed in the first place.

Caroselli laughed. "See? When he was under Italian command, he was able to accomplish great things! Perhaps you should take that to heart, and return to bed so you can get better."

Von Reinhardt could recognize the seriousness under the doctor's joking manner. "At this moment, my services are required elsewhere. Otherwise, I would without hesitation stay safely in the hospital." He cracked a grin. "After all, where else will I find a physician who so beautifully embodies Voltaire's thoughts about medicine?"

There was a pause, and then Caroselli shook his head. "All right, Herr Oberst. It looks like you stumped me. I'll probably regret asking, but what thoughts are those?"

With an innocent expression on his face, von Reinhardt replied, "'The art of medicine consists of amusing the patient while nature cures the disease.'"

Caroselli roared with laughter. "Too true, too true! All right, you ungrateful wretch. But take it easy, okay? I don't want to see you back here any time soon."

"No more than I want to be here, I can assure you of that," von Reinhardt replied. He paused. "With all sincerity, I thank you for your excellent care."

"Go! Go!" Caroselli said, arms waving wildly. "I could hope for a better advertisement of the quality of my medical care, but a soldier takes what a soldier can get." He grabbed von Reinhardt's hands in both of his own, shook them violently, then patted him on the back. The physically reticent von Reinhardt returned a pat to Caroselli's upper arm, then went to find his uniform.

"Oberst Günter von Reinhardt to see the field marshal," he told the headquarters feldwebel.

"He's expecting you, sir. Go right in," replied the feldwebel.

To von Reinhardt's surprise, Rommel had company—important company. Dr. Carl Goerdeler had once been mayor of Leipzig, had been an anti-Nazi activist since the beginning, and was now newly established as the acting chancellor of the provisional German government. Von Reinhardt saluted, and Rommel motioned for him to sit.

"How are you feeling?" the Desert Fox asked.

"Quite well, thank you," lied von Reinhardt, hoping that the pain he was feeling wasn't reflected on his face. The walk across the compound had left him dizzy and gasping for breath; his collapsed lung felt as if it were on fire.

Evidently the lie was not obvious, or alternately the Desert Fox was choosing not to see it, because Rommel merely nodded in response.

Chancellor Goerdeler was looking at him with an expression of contempt. "So, this is the man who took over negotiations with the Soviets after von Ribbentrop's collapse?" he asked Rommel. From the redness in Goerdeler's face and the tense body language, von Reinhardt got the idea that these two men had been arguing before he arrived.

"That's right," replied Rommel. The field marshal's hands were folded neatly on his desk. The cold look in his eye and the unusually calm timbre of his voice were storm signals well known to the officers who served under the Desert Fox. It was time to run for cover, von Reinhardt noted, but he couldn't run and the chancellor couldn't see the approaching hurricane. He turned toward Goerdeler to hear his response.

Goerdeler turned toward von Reinhardt for the first time and spoke with a voice heavy with sarcasm and dislike. "So you are the man who preserved Himmler's option to continue the war while giving away German rocket technology to our worst enemy?"

The attack stung. Von Reinhardt had considered this point several times on his own. He had understood the Faustian bargain he was making; the true character of the Nazi leadership had by then become fully evident to him. Yet it was his nation, his uniform, and his duty. Should that have been enough to overcome his moral sensibilities, or was it only that few options were available to him? Or—and this was a thought he dared not dwell on too deeply—was his appetite for cleverness and the game so strong that he had played to win for no better reason than that it amused him?

In any event, the chancellor's question was clearly legitimate, and the implied attack not inappropriate. Although von Reinhardt could identify several quotes appropriate to the occasion, he decided that the moment for the *mot juste* was not present. He looked directly at Goerdeler. "Yes, sir, I am," he stated quietly.

"Proud of it, are you?" snapped the chancellor nastily. "Do you know that, even as we speak, the Soviet hordes are sweeping across Poland? They have breached the armistice line along its full length, and are driving for the heart of the Fatherland!"

"You ask if I am proud of that accomplishment?" Von Reinhardt took a moment to think over the question. It was complicated, but he didn't think the chancellor would be interested in a detailed analysis. "Overall, yes, sir, I am," he replied. "It was a bad choice, but it was the least bad option I could find at the time."

That put Goerdeler off guard for a moment. "Bad choice, eh?" he grumbled. "Damned right it was a bad choice. Perpetuating the Nazi regime, arming the Soviet Union . . . " He shook his head. "And you want this man to crawl back into bed with his former masters to betray your new allies?" he snapped at Rommel.

Rommel's lips tightened slightly, but he didn't react otherwise. That was interesting. Rommel didn't brook back talk well, even from his nominal superiors. "Yes, Chancellor. Oberst von Reinhardt has a back-channel opportunity to enter into dialogue with Berlin, and I have hopes that we can achieve our mutual objective with minimum bloodshed."

"By letting those criminals get away scot-free?" Goerdeler's voice broke into a shout. "No! No!" he said, punctuating each with his fist pounding on the arm of his chair. "Not under the auspices of my government, and not by stabbing our allies in the back."

Von Reinhardt looked at the two men—Rommel quietly angry and nearing his own explosion, Goerdeler completely enraged. "May I ask a question?" he interjected, keeping his own voice mild.

Both men turned to look at him. Not waiting for formal permission, von Reinhardt exploited his temporary opportunity. "Is it fair for me to conclude from what I just heard that you are considering whether I should open back-channel negotiations with the Nazi leadership, offering them freedom and escape in exchange for the surrender of Berlin?"

Rommel nodded. "Yes, Oberst von Reinhardt. That is what we are discussing."

"Then this discussion is over!" Goerdeler snapped, folding his arms across his chest in a defiant manner. "I am the chancellor, and I forbid any such approach. I do not want it brought up again, Field Marshal."

Seeing the expression on the Desert Fox's face, von Reinhardt rushed to fill the breach once again. "Chancellor, we may be able to reach a deal that is less drastic. Remember, their alternatives are not too good."

"No! The joint policy of all the Allies is to stand for unconditional surrender. Nothing else."

"If I recall, Chancellor," von Reinhardt riposted, "that demand was originally established as a way to reassure Stalin that the western Allies would not seek a separate peace. And 'unconditional surrender,' in any event, always means whatever the negotiators and their governments wish it to mean."

Goerdeler's face narrowed in complete contempt. "So. You weasel-word the principles of our allies. That tells me my judgment of you is correct. You are nothing but an opportunist. You negotiate for the Nazis and bring them what they want, then you switch over to the winning side and offer your former masters a smarmy thing—a peace utterly without honor. No. This cannot be done. It is a matter of the highest principle. The Nazi government must be crushed by military force and all those who have participated in it must be punished. You have no idea the atrocities that have been carried out by Hitlerian functionaries—self-serving and cynical toadies like yourself." He turned back to Rommel. "I am the chancellor and I have made the decision. That is the end of it."

He moved to stand up, but Rommel fixed him with a cold stare. "Sit down," he said, his voice still quiet but filled with menace. Goerdeler sat.

"You are the chancellor of a government that exists only in the imagination," Rommel said, his voice cold as iron. "The only real part of the government is this army, and it is my army. If you doubt me, try to take me out of it and see whether the soldiers will still follow your lead."

"Don't you threaten me! Mutiny, and I'll see you rotting in jail!" Goerdeler wasn't planning to give an inch.

Rommel's eyes flashed angrily. "You're a puppet running a fake paper government. You had better realize who you're dealing with, and understand that *I* run this army. Not you, not some paper-shuffling group of bureaucrats without a government. You're nothing without me and my army, and you had damned well better remember it."

Von Reinhardt winced a little at Rommel's bluntness, and wished he could teach the man greater subtlety. Everything he was saying was true, of course, but it was impolitic. Rommel's army needed a civilian government for its legitimacy, and Germany would require a functioning new administration to replace the old. The two men needed each other, but neither seemed able to settle for less than complete power.

"They will obey lawful orders," Goerdeler said, but his voice was less strong. "No man is indispensable. Not even the Desert Fox."

Rommel smiled, but only with his mouth. He could recognize that he now had his opponent in retreat. "Chancellor, you can speak the words, but remember that it is I whom you expect to perform the dirty work. You want me to lead this army into war against our own countrymen, for Germans to kill Germans. You want me to kill Germans to achieve your objectives. Well, I won't, if it can possibly be helped. If the Nazis can be removed from power by peaceful or diplomatic means, then I don't have to kill as many Germans."

"I expect you to obey lawful orders and work alongside our allies!" Goerdeler responded. "You cannot let the murderous Nazi scum escape their just punishments!"

"And how many others shall I punish on the way?" asked Rommel. It was time for the coup de grâce. Clearly he held the victory in his hands. "Chancellor, let's get this straight between us. This army is mine. It's not yours. It goes where I want it to go, it fights whom I want it to fight. I command this army by virtue of the loyalty of its soldiers to me. Not to you, not to the paper government you represent, but to me. I will lead this army as I see fit. If you want others to see you as technically in control of the army, I don't object, but understand me very clearly. I give the orders."

Goerdeler looked ready to fire the Desert Fox on the spot, but he paused. It was obvious that Rommel was not bluffing. "I see," he said, the coldness in his voice echoing Rommel's. "So you are, after all, the megalomaniac we all feared you would be. When Speidel first recruited you, there was a deep disagreement as to whether you would be part of a democratic government, or whether you would turn yourself into another tin-pot dictator. You have shown your true colors today, and I will remember it." He stood up to leave. The Desert Fox remained seated.

Von Reinhardt stood up. He could not leave this dangerous breach untouched. "Chancellor," von Reinhardt interjected, urgency in his voice. "I beg you to think carefully before you speak or act. Field Marshal Rommel is not a new dictator in the making, and doesn't wish to be. He's right that you can't ask this army to make war against its own fatherland. It's not just the field marshal, it's the soldiers as well. They didn't sign on for this. Can you truly expect them to shoulder the burden of killing their countrymen and fellow soldiers?"

Von Reinhardt could see the chancellor thinking, calming down. Goerdeler was a good politician. He understood the realities of power, and he understood the political necessity of getting along with his own opposition. He and Rommel could fight—would fight—but at the end, they had to present a solid front together for the sake of their mutual objective. It was easier for Goerdeler to see this than Rommel. Von Reinhardt resumed his persuasion, ignoring the pain that threatened to clamp his chest in a fiery vise.

"We must get this war over with quickly, or else the Soviets will take over everything. There is the old Russian story of the sled being pursued by wolves. In the bargain I made, I threw some food off the back to slow down the wolves, but all I could do was slow them down a little. They must be stopped. Let the field marshal stop them. Other things can wait, and it will be different when you occupy Berlin."

Goerdeler looked at von Reinhardt closely, seeing more of him than before. He grunted, and shook his head slowly from side to side. "I don't see that you've left me much choice. Very well—for now. But I warn you. Both of you. The crimes of the Nazi government are much larger than either of you imagine. If you let the leaders get away, the outcry of the world will do more damage to Germany than would a military offensive." He turned and left.

Von Reinhardt sat down again, slowly so as to minimize the pain in his chest.

"A good job," Rommel said. "You handled him well."

Von Reinhardt nodded his acknowledgment. "He has a point, of course, as you no doubt know," he observed.

"Yes, I know. I've heard some of the stories. I'm sure they're exaggerated like all rumors, but if the stories are even fractionally true, it's terrible. I'd like to bring those responsible to justice as much as anyone," Rommel replied. "But I have to address first things first."

Von Reinhardt had heard the stories, too. Some of them were so outrageous, so enormous, it was hard to conceive how they possibly could be true. But even if they were only partly true, it would be bad enough. *That, however, is a matter for another day,* the intelligence officer thought. For now, the issue was ending the civil war as quickly and as bloodlessly as possible.

"Now let's talk about you making an approach to Himmler," Rommel said. The two men leaned forward and began to plan.

13 JANUARY 1945

PANZER BATTALION, TWELFTH SS PANZER DIVISION "HITLERJUGEND," KOBLENZ, GERMANY, 1540 HOURS GMT

"You—Untersturmführer Vogel!"

"Yes, Hauptsturmführer!" Lukas replied, hopping out of the passenger seat of the truck as they came to a rolling stop on the Koblenz waterfront. Captain Friedrich was deploying his men and his few tanks along a stretch of warehouses on a low bluff, just a few hundred meters from the great river.

"I want you to take your men and garrison this tanning plant. You will have support from a panzer to your left, and a light antitank gun in that smokehouse to your right. You must hold this line at all costs."

Lukas saluted. He could see the girdered span of a railroad bridge nearby, and another, a highway bridge leading across the Rhine a kilometer or so to the south. "Are the engineers going to blow the bridges?" he asked, as Friedrich took off his cap and rubbed a grimy hand across his forehead.

"No—we're not going to destroy the bridges!" snapped the captain. "We must *hold* them, keep the Americans off, so that the Panzerarmee can get across the river! We can't very well defend the Reich if we leave the Panzerarmee on the other side, can we?"

"Hold them, yes sir!" replied Lukas, embarrassed. "You can count on us, sir!"

Friedrich drew a breath and shook his head, looking like a very old man—until he placed his cap back on his head and was once more transformed into a resolute veteran of the SS. "I'm glad I can count on you, Lukas . . . glad, because I have no choice. The future of the Fatherland rests upon what we can do, right here." He placed his hand on Lukas' shoulder, then patted him gently.

The captain went away then, stalking along the outside of the tanning factory, no doubt inspecting the rest of his positions. Lukas looked at the building, which seemed very large to try and hold with a dozen boys. But he would do it . . . they would hold it, or die trying.

Because, as Friedrich had said, they had no choice.

THE WHITE HOUSE, WASHINGTON, D.C., 2203 HOURS GMT

It was a few minutes after five o'clock. Civil-service Washington was shutting down pretty much like clockwork, packed trolley cars carrying the occupants of the Federal Triangle complex up Pennsylvania Avenue toward Georgetown and up Fourteenth Street toward Thomas Circle and their respective residential neighborhoods. The city was dark and cold; the remnants of a two-week-old snowstorm clung to shadowed corners of buildings.

Other corners of official Washington continued, random offices casting their lights into the city's darkness. In the Executive Office Building next to the White House, Hartnell Stone was entering the state of mind in which additional coffee no longer contributed additional wakefulness; he found himself crossing out more words than he was adding to a summary report of troop movement data. He stubbed out his cigarette and was about to start another when the intercom buzzer rang. "Mr. Stone? The President would like to see you."

"On my way." He took the steps down to the basement quickly, two or three at a time, then walked briskly through the tunnel that connected the Executive Office Building to the basement of the White House. Climbing two acts of stairs, he entered a carpeted hallway on the ground level.

Grace Tully, the president's personal secretary, looked up as Hartnell entered the president's outer office. "Go right in. He's expecting you."

"What's going on? Can you give me a heads-up?"

Tully grinned. "Nothing bad, Hartnell. Go on in. He won't eat you."

The Oval Office, like the upstairs Oval Study, reflected the personal style of this president. Overflowing inboxes, ten aides—including both Stimson and Hull—having eight simultaneous conversations, with Roosevelt in the middle of the whirlwind. With the president's growing ill health, the whirlwind was being tamed somewhat by his staff, though FDR was notoriously difficult to manage. A doctor and two nurses sat nearby, pretending to be invisible as the president listened and spoke, read memoranda and jotted notes at the bottom. The presence of people gave him much-needed energy, and he looked surprisingly hale even after a long day's work.

Roosevelt glanced up and saw Stone enter. "Hartnell, my boy! Come in, come in! Just in time for cocktail hour, isn't it? Why don't we take this upstairs and splice the mainbrace, eh?" He grinned, his cigarette holder clenched firmly between his teeth, and signaled to his valet. While the president and his valet traveled upstairs by elevator, the rest of the party—quickly sorted by Grace Tully into those who had continued purpose with the president and those who did not—walked up the wide center staircase to the residential level.

It was traditional for FDR to serve as mixmaster for the presidential cocktail hour in the Oval Study. He made drinks for the two Cabinet officers and for himself, then allowed someone else to take over. Although this time was officially labeled as a cocktail hour, the Oval Study hours were as much work time as the daylight hours in the White House, and would often go on until midnight, although of late this was no longer the case.

Hartnell nursed a gin and tonic as he waited his turn. He understood the rhythms of this White House well enough to know that he had in fact been summoned for a purpose, and he would learn that purpose whenever it suited FDR to get around to it. What's more, his assignment might or might not have anything to do with his official areas of expertise, such as they were. FDR did not like his assistants turning into subject-matter experts; he preferred to keep them generalists by throwing them at random targets. It was stressful, but it was certainly educational.

"Hartnell, my lad?"

"Yes, Mr. President?"

"Tired of this DC winter?"

"A bit, sir."

"Ready for a little jaunt? Something warm and exotic, maybe with a few bathing beauties?"

"Well, that sounds pretty good, sir."

"Sounds pretty good to me, too. Too bad you won't find any where you're going, eh, Cordell?" FDR winked at his secretary of state.

Cordell Hull chuckled. "Well, I understand that Moscow has an event where people swim naked in the river in the middle of winter, but that's as close as you'd get to bathing beauties, I'm afraid."

"Moscow?" Hartnell interjected.

"I think I need to send a little personal letter to Uncle Joe, and I want it hand-delivered," FDR said. "Teletype is a bit impersonal, you know. You'll be the courier, and you'll go along with Averrell when he delivers the note." W. Averrell Harriman was the U.S. Ambassador to the Soviet Union. FDR leaned forward. "Hartnell, what I need you to do is to be my eyes and ears. Averrell is a fine and smart man and he's going to do all the heavy lifting. You're going to be watching for the small stuff. I want you to get a feeling for what's going on—I want you to be able to make me feel like I'm there. I want to know what people sound like, I want to know what expression is on their faces—everything. It's important. Understand?"

"I think so, sir. I heard a German word once. *Fingerspitzengefühl*. It was used to describe Rommel. It means 'intuition in your fingertips.' You can't be there, so you want me to see if I can be your fingertips."

"Finger-spitting fool? Is that the word? Well, close enough. Sounds about right." FDR looked over at Hull. "Not bad. The boy's got promise. Okay, Hartnell. Be my fingertips. Make me feel what it's like to be there. I know Uncle Joe pretty well, and I think I know which way he's going to jump, but the warning signs are subtle. Watch him very well. Notice everything and tell me all about it. I'll have a letter waiting for you with Grace first thing in the morning and then you're off to Moscow."

"Bathing beauties and all," Hartnell added.

FDR grinned. "Find a bathing beauty in Moscow in January and I'll let you replace Wild Bill Donovan as head of OSS."

Stone laughed. "It's a deal, Mr. President."

15 JANUARY 1945

EN ROUTE TO BERLIN, GERMANY, 0941 HOURS GMT

The checkpoint guard did not have three heads, but Günter von Reinhardt recognized echoes of the mythical dog Cerberus, guardian of the river Styx—in this incarnation, the Rhine—in the feldgrau Waffen-SS uniform. He passed over his papers, had a predictable argument with the officer in charge about his status as an emissary, and was finally waved through into what passed for Hades—the bombed landscape of his fatherland.

He started to take a deep breath, but caught himself before he triggered yet another bout of painful, bloody coughing, and satisfied himself by waving the driver onward toward Berlin.

It was odd thinking of Berlin as the enemy capital; it hadn't been that many months earlier when he stood in Führer Himmler's office to receive his orders assigning him to Armeegruppe B and Operation Fuchs am Rhein. Now he was returning as the secret emissary of Erwin Rommel to negotiate for the surrender of the government of the Third Reich. Even for a man with von Reinhardt's appreciation of irony, that was rich.

This was a back-channel operation, complete with mutual deniability, which meant that von Reinhardt was running significant risks without the protection normally accorded to diplomats. From the first opening of communication all the way through, he would be on his own.

One would imagine that reaching an opposing enemy commander in a war zone in order to arrange secret talks would be quite difficult. It had amused Günter von Reinhardt that all he had had to do was to pick up a telephone and make the call. After all, the complete telecommunications apparatus of the German Republican Army, formerly Armeegruppe B, was built around communicating with other German forces.

The private office used for all top-secret transmissions had long been his preserve as an intelligence officer. There was even an Enigma coding machine available for his use. Of course, the armies of the Third Reich now knew that the Enigma machine was available for enemy use, so the valuable code machine was no longer used. Von Reinhardt had imagined that his Allied counterparts would have wanted the code machine as their first order of business. Their calm in the face of that temptation told him what he had suspected: the Allies already had the secret of Enigma. Well, no matter.

He shifted his position in the back seat of the staff car. It was hard for him to get comfortable; he knew the doctor was right and that it was premature for him to leave the hospital. The legendary German autobahns still were bumpy enough for him to feel each minuscule irregularity in his chest. He only hoped he wouldn't have to cough again.

It had taken him a few hours of working his way through the telephone screens surrounding Führer Himmler to reach the man himself, ensconced in his black-draped Chancellery office like a snake deep in his den. And then came a bout of verbal fencing—also predictable—in which two people who clearly loathed one another pretended to a civility pregnant with hostility. Then to the mechanics of arranging a passage through the lines, with von Reinhardt, as the lower-ranking negotiator, responsible for the transit.

His first way station was the headquarters of Armeegruppe H, one of the reinforcement army groups originally intended to exploit the Fuchs am Rhein gains. Fortunately, von Reinhardt had a slight personal acquaintance with the commanding officer, Generaloberst Karl Student.

"Good to see you, Günter! Sit down!" said the general as von Reinhardt was escorted in.

"Good to see you, too, Herr Generaloberst," he replied.

"So you're now an Allied diplomat, I understand," said the general, gesturing to an aide to fetch coffee.

Von Reinhardt watched as the aide left the room. "Safe to talk?" he asked.

"God only knows," shrugged Student. "Our Gestapo friends are everywhere. So I assume they hear everything I say and go about my business as usual. Why worry? Are you planning to ask me to join Rommel's new . . . what are you calling it? Oh, yes. The German Republican Army. Has a sort of Weimar ring to it, doesn't it?"

Von Reinhardt smiled. "I'd never dream of asking a fine German officer of your stature to switch sides." Raising a finger to his lips, he pulled an envelope from his pocket and passed it across to Student, who took it, a quizzical smile on his face, and slipped it into his own pocket.

"A good thing, too," replied Student. "I take my soldier's oath quite seriously, you know. I don't change out of pique or because one of my plans fell through. You know, Walther Mödel had some fairly harsh words to say about your baby field marshal. He thought if Rommel had any courage, he would have shot himself, rather than put Himmler to the trouble of having it done for him. But that's Rommel, isn't it? Quite a complainer, that one. Knew how to suck up, though. That's how he got all his promotions so young."

The aide returned with coffee, and von Reinhardt sipped quietly from his cup. "I won't argue with you about Rommel," he said. "Frankly, he'd probably agree with most of what you said—he's pretty harsh on himself. But I think what he's doing is best for Germany. Remember our late führer's dictum, that Germany will either be a world power or will not be at all. It's to prevent the latter outcome that Rommel acted."

"Fighting for your own side is what's best for Germany," Student replied firmly, but he patted his breast pocket, where he had placed von Reinhardt's letter. "But here I'm keeping you and the führer expects you in Berlin. May I furnish you with escorts?"

"I'd be grateful, Herr Generaloberst. Thanks."

Student walked him out of the headquarters personally and saw him into his staff car. "Thanks for dropping by, von Reinhardt. Look forward to seeing you again soon."

"I, too," he replied, and nodded to his driver.

As they sped away, now escorted by Wehrmacht motorcycles, von Reinhardt wondered if the seed he had just planted would bear fruit. There was another quotation from Adolf Hitler that fit, also from *Mein Kampf*: "As soon as by one's own propaganda even a glimpse of right on the other side is admitted, the cause for doubting one's own right is laid." If he had shown Student a "glimpse of right" on his side, perhaps that would grow into doubt.

16 JANUARY 1945

CCA, APPROACHING KOBLENZ, GERMANY, 1739 HOURS GMT

It was sunset on Frank Ballard's tenth day in Germany, and he was aware that the terrain was changing around him more rapidly with every mile. They were approaching the mouth of the Moselle Valley, where that dark river flowed into the Rhine. For days they had rolled along between forested ridges, bypassing small, almost medieval towns, but they were now entering a region where factories were as common as farms. The land was flat, and the vast landscapes of forest had been reduced to clumps of isolated woods between roads, hamlets, farms, and industry.

The headquarters company of CCA pulled into the yard of one such factory, where the fuel trucks had formed an impromptu depot. As the vehicles took on gas, Ballard climbed out and spread his well-worn map on the hood of a jeep. They were close, now—damned close—to Koblenz and that great prize, the only river crossing that really mattered.

He was taking a drink from his canteen when a jeep came racing up the road and turned into the depot yard. Ballard recognized one of Smiggy's corporals, and waved a salute as the man jumped out of his vehicle and raced up to the combat command CO.

"What do you see up there?" asked the colonel.

"We caught sight of one tank down in the city," the man reported breathlessly. "But we've moved in past the first downhill run, and haven't taken any fire. We're going in as fast as we can, Colonel, with the first company of tanks right behind us. It looks like if we get any trouble it won't be until we're closer to the river."

"Well, be careful and keep your eyes open," Ballard suggested—unnecessarily, he knew, though it made him feel better to give the advice. "We want to get across those bridges as soon as possible."

"Aye, aye, Colonel!" replied the corporal, quickly heading back to his vehicle.

As he was leaving, another group of jeeps and trucks pulled up, these coming along the road Ballard had been following from the west. He recognized the headquarters company of his artillery battalion, and ambled over to greet Major Diaz as he scrambled out of a half track.

"How long has it been since you've been shot at?" Ballard asked Diaz.

"A few snipers here and there," the major acknowledged with a shrug.

"They get their heads down pretty fast when we give 'em direct fire from a couple of one-oh-fives."

Ballard nodded. "I can't help feeling like we're missing something—like it shouldn't be this easy."

"Maybe it won't be," Diaz suggested. "But it's not far to the river, is it?"

"Not far at all." Ballard folded up the map, saw that the fueling hoses were being rolled away from the last of his tanks. "Headquarters—mount up!" he called.

"Well, I'll keep my guns ready," Diaz pledged. "You go get 'em, Colonel!"

Ballard reviewed the advance, tried to plan for any obstacles. Sure, the tanks and infantry of the combat command were already penetrating the outskirts of the city, with little resistance reported so far. But Diaz was right—surely it wouldn't be this easy? With these thoughts weighing on his mind, Ballard's command tank rumbled off, following a road leading into the heart of Koblenz. He sat atop the turret, looking around and listening for sounds of combat.

He had seen a lot of damaged cities in the course of this war, but he was surprised at the extent of the destruction here. This was the work of heavy bombers, he knew—mountains of brick and concrete and dust rising as high as two-story buildings flanked the sides of this street, marking places where tall structures must have stood.

A half hour later he heard a screeching call over his radio.

"Eyes One, calling Barnyard Ten. Spot me, ten o'clock, up the hill."

He recognized Smiggy's voice and, looking to his left, caught sight of his recon officer waving from beside a blasted wall on a side street. Ballard instructed his driver to head that way, and the Sherman nimbly skirted several piles of bricks, lurching through a bomb crater as it climbed the road.

The tank halted a dozen paces away and Ballard pulled himself out of the turret, then hopped down to the street. The reconnaissance captain's face was split by a wide grin, and Ballard felt a flash of hope. "Whatcha got?" he asked.

"Take a look at that, Colonel," Smiggy said, turning to peer over the wall, which at this point dipped down to chin height. Ballard leaned into the gap and looked, saw the glorious sight of sunlight reflecting from a wide band of water.

"Is that what I think it is?" he asked.

Captain Smiggs nodded proudly. "Yup, Colonel. You can call all those generals and field marshals, and tell 'em that we've got a bead on the Rhine."

Ballard was still looking, eyes ranging to right and left. "I count two bridges still standing!" he declared.

"And there's one more, just out of sight around the bend," Smiggy replied. "If we can keep moving, we can be across that river by the end of the day!"

It seemed too easy, too tempting a thought . . . but once again Ballard allowed himself to hope that, very soon now, this goddamned war would be over. No sooner had he let the hope creep into his thoughts than it was dashed by the sounds of guns—*lots* of guns—coming from the city, near the waterfront. It was small-arms fire, but it denoted a pretty tough level of resistance.

"Shit," Smiggy grunted. "Sounds like trouble, Colonel."

Ballard could hear that for himself, as machine guns and several tank cannon added their notes to the chorus of battle. He cursed silently as he saw one of his Shermans go up in a plume of orange fire and black smoke. Other tanks hastily reversed, rolling back to the cover of a railroad embankment. He heard the distinctive crack of an 88 and saw another M4 explode. The CCA armor was shooting back now, machine guns and infantry rifles coming into play, but it took only a moment's study to see that the headlong advance had been brought, at least temporarily, to a halt.

"HQ—move out!" Ballard called, sprinting back to his own tank. He had been right, dammit, and he hated to be right about stuff like this.

But the speedy race against no opposition had, in fact, been too good to last.

17 JANUARY 1945

**THIRD ARMY FORWARD HEADQUARTERS, TRIER,
GERMANY, 0745 HOURS GMT**

"Well, Field Marshal, I've got word that Nineteenth Armored reached the outskirts of Koblenz last night," General Patton declared, his face split by a wide
grin. "They're having to fight their way into town, but they report progress.
Fourth Armored is on their south flank, only a day away from the Rhine, and
the Twelfth Infantry is making damned good time to the north. By God, I'm
proud of these men!"

"You have good cause to be, General." Rommel was surprised by the wave
of relief he felt. "I am glad that my loyal troops were able to provide passage
along the Moselle. Any word of the SS elements?"

Patton scowled, as he always did when reminded that not all of the enemy
troops had perceived reality the same way Rommel did. It was almost as
though the American general took the thought as a personal insult.

And it is *personal, at least to me,* he realized in the same breath. He,
Rommel, was the man who had issued the orders to surrender. Those officers
of the SS were his subordinates, and yet they had disobeyed the order, even
acted criminally to kill those loyal soldiers who had simply tried to do their
duty. Even now the memories infuriated him, clenching his jaw and tightening
his hands into fists. He looked down at the map, trying to conceal his anger
from his American counterpart.

"Well, you know about Panzer Lehr holding up those columns," Patton said.

"Yes," Rommel replied tightly. Another bitter blow: He had sent those
brave men to do their duty, and one battalion had managed to race ahead of
several SS-kampfgruppe. The outnumbered Wehrmacht panzers had taken a
blocking position across the high road to Koblenz, holding up the Nazis for
hours. In the end, however, SS troops under Jochen Peiper had encircled the
Panzer Lehr formation, wiping it out nearly to the last man. "Their sacrifice
bought us most of a day."

"And the SS tanks are still north of the city—at least the ones we know
about. There's been no word about the Twelfth SS Panzers yet. Can't say I'm
wild about fighting children."

"Neither am I, General Patton," Rommel replied. "I'm afraid, though, that
young boys often feel themselves to be invulnerable, and they see the world
entirely in black and white, with no shades of gray."

"Well, they'll be like a newspaper soon," chuckled Patton. "Black and white and red all over." Rommel looked puzzled at the joke. "We haven't heard about any direct resistance in the city, either," Patton continued. "Best of all, they've got at least three bridges in sight—'advancing on waterfront' was Frank Ballard's exact phrase."

"Good," Rommel replied. "If you can get your tanks across the river, I think we will prevent anything Sixth Panzer Army can do to stop us."

"It's still a long way to Berlin," Patton warned, though the glint in his eye suggested that he viewed that distance more as an opportunity than an obstacle.

"As long as we can beat the Soviets there," commented Rommel.

"You got that right, Field Marshal," replied the American general. "Damned if you don't have that right."

A signals officer, a colonel, approached with a sheet of paper and an apprehensive frown. "What is it, Budge?" asked Patton.

"Word from Nineteenth Armored, just in," the colonel reported. "Seems they've run into some opposition—they're only a mile from the river, but they have SS tanks and panzergrenadiere dug in before them."

"Frank is hitting the bastards hard, isn't he?" the American general snapped.

"Yessir. Sounds like he's using artillery, some of it direct fire. And he's sending his tanks right at them, trying to break through."

"Well, that's what he should be doing. I like our chances," declared Patton.

"Any word on what formation is blocking the path."

"Yes, Field Marshal . . ." The colonel called Budge squinted, scanned farther down his sheet of paper. "Looks like it's the Twelfth SS Panzer Division."

"Well, we know where they went, the sons of bitches," growled Patton.

"*Ach du lieber Gott,*" Rommel said, shaking his head. "The children. Sepp Dietrich wasted no time in getting the Hitler Youth Division out of Luxembourg."

"Well, they'll be the Hitler Dead Division inside of an hour," Patton remarked with certainty. "At least, they will if Frankie Ballard has anything to say about it."

UNITED STATES EMBASSY, MOSCOW, USSR,
0800 HOURS GMT

It was eleven o'clock in the morning Moscow time, but to Hartnell Stone's travel-weary body, it was still the middle of the previous night Washington time. Even with the highest level of wartime priority, traveling nearly halfway around the world was hugely punishing.

He had landed in Moscow seven hours previously and checked in at the Hotel Nationale, next door to the embassy on Mochovaya, just across Red Square from the Kremlin itself. The bed was hard and lumpy, though that hadn't posed much of a problem after having tried to sleep sitting up in an air-plane seat for hour after hour. The constant droning of the engine was still with him; when he lay down, it still felt as though the room were vibrating and moving underneath him. Although he was exhausted, it was difficult for him to drop off to sleep, since his body kept telling him that it was too early. Once it got to sleep, he had found it difficult to wake up, and had barely made it next door in time for his early meeting.

Marine guards outside the embassy checked his identification before admitting him; he signed in again at the front desk, and waited patiently for the escort who led him to the ambassador's office. Ambassador Harriman had a great view of the Kremlin, but Hartnell had a more immediate interest in the hot coffee the secretary brought on a silver tray. "Welcome to Moscow, Stone," the ambassador said, shaking his hand. "Have a seat."

"Thank you, sir," Hartnell said.

"How's your father?"

"Well, sir. I went to Somerset over Christmas and saw him then, along with the family." Stone's father had been connected to the Roosevelt circles for many years, and was well known to most of the major players in the administration.

"Good, good," Harriman said. "It's been a bit chilly in Moscow lately, and I'm not referring to the weather, either."

"I understand, sir. I gather the president hasn't been very happy about it either."

"Damned right. But Stalin thinks that he's got the right—and the might—to write his own ticket, and on a practical level I'm not so sure he's wrong. When the climate was a little friendlier, I've watched the Soviet army on the move, and I have to tell you, I've never seen anything like it in my life. Hell, I haven't *imagined* anything like it in my life. I understand you worked for a while on the Overlord plans at SHAEF headquarters in London."

"Yes, sir, I did."

"Tell me, what's the full U.S. Army authorized military strength?"

"As I recall, sir, about ninety full divisions—not that we're quite at that level."

"And that's Atlantic *and* Pacific, right? How about the British?"

"Around twenty-seven divisions, sir."

"And the Germans? Know how many they fielded overall?"

Stone had to think for a minute. "I studied what they had in the West that might oppose the invasion, but I don't know the grand total."

Harriman grinned and leaned forward. "Well, I do. Two hundred and sixty, my boy. Two hundred and sixty. And here's what's truly amazing—the Soviets dwarf even that number. There's no precedent for it."

"But what about strategic bombing? What about superior weapons and training?"

"Well, I'll give you some edge for that, but never as much as the generals will tell you. They like their pretty shiny toys, the generals do, and they'll always tell you that pretty shiny toys mean that one of our boys will whip ten, twenty, even fifty of the other side's boys. Don't underestimate sheer weight of numbers, my lad, and make no mistake, the Soviets have a huge superiority in that department." Harriman leaned back. "So then, Hartnell Stone. Can you tell me why the president thinks we can walk across the street and tell Uncle Joe to steer clear of Berlin and expect him to knuckle under?"

"Honestly, sir, I don't know. But he seems pretty confident."

Harriman looked out the window and sighed. "I've known Franklin for a long time. I think he trusts me about as far as he trusts anyone. But that isn't much. He's got more things up his sleeve than any other ten people I know. The hell of it is, he may have some piece of god-knows-what magic, or he may be engaged in some colossal bluff, and either way he can look you or me straight in the eye and tell us anything he likes and make us believe he knows what he's talking about." He looked back at Hartnell. "Sometimes he's right. Hell, often he's right. But you can't always count on it. And so in a couple of hours we're going to walk across the street and you're going to hand your little letter to Uncle Joe and we're going to look him in the face and act like we know what the hell we're talking about. How's your poker game?"

"Middling, sir."

"Uncle Joe's a little better than middling. You're pretty tired, right?"

"Yes, sir."

"Good. Tired is good. Think about how exhausted you are from your trip. Think about how nervous you are about meeting Stalin. That will help cover up any nervousness about thinking you're playing a big hand of nothing and pretending it's a royal flush. Understand?"

"Yes, sir. My father told me that it was better to emphasize a small flaw to pull attention away from a bigger one."

"Your father's a smart man. Always was."

"Thank you, sir."

"Now that we've got the first order of business out of the way, let's get to the next item," Harriman said, lighting up a cigar. "How's the president holding up? I'm hearing some disturbing news, that he's not sleeping well, that he's having to cancel a lot of meetings, that the doctors are getting worried. What are you hearing?"

Hartnell looked at the ambassador. *I guess my poker playing starts here,* he thought. "I don't know what you've heard, Ambassador, but the president looks in good health and good spirits as far as I can see. He's sleeping well to the best of my knowledge, and I do some of the overnight shifts . . ."

18 JANUARY 1945

"Shoot, dammit!" shouted Lukas. He could see the American soldiers, scuttling low like bugs, darting across the railroad embankment, diving toward a drainage ditch where they disappeared from view. They were out of the effective range of Vogel's Luger pistol, and it seemed like too many of his men—his boys—were hunkering under cover, unwilling to shoot their weapons.

He couldn't blame them, really. They had been under attack for more than twenty-four hours straight, now. Not his little platoon, exactly—the Americans were just now coming in sight of the tanning factory—but they could feel the battle raging nearby. The firing had moved closer, the Germans slowly giving ground against the press of enemy attackers. The Americans had tanks coming from every direction, jabos that strafed and bombed the Germans wherever they tried to stand, a seemingly uncountable number of artillery pieces arrayed somewhere out of sight, capable of sending punishing barrages that landed with uncanny accuracy.

Yet still Lukas had kept his boys alive, most of them, anyway. He put his hand on the young soldier's shoulder, forced him to meet his eyes. "Look, Fritzi. They're coming to get us. There are lots of them, and if we don't shoot at them, nothing is going to stop them. It's not even us they want—it's those bridges, that river—our fatherland!"

The boy, Fritzi, stared wide-eyed at his young lieutenant, his carbine clutched to his chest with white-knuckled fingers. Lukas cursed to himself, wanting to slap the fellow across his thin, pale face. Instead, he leaned close, spoke directly into Fritzi's ear.

"Those Amis will kill you, sure enough, if you don't start shooting." He smacked the boy's hands where they were wrapped around his rifle stock, tried to be reassuring. "You know how to use this thing. There they are; now pick it up and shoot!"

"O-Okay, Lukas," stammered Fritzi, shaking his head as if to clear away a fog. He twisted on the floor and rose to a kneeling position so that he could sight the weapon out the second-floor window of the tanning factory, and squeezed off a shot.

"Good boy," whispered Vogel, clapping the frightened youngster on the shoulder. "Keep shooting, and they'll have to hide from you."

Fritzi fired several more rounds in quick succession, and Lukas crawled on to inspect the rest of his makeshift platoon. They were not being pressed too hard, yet, thanks largely to the antitank gun and the Mark IV panzer positioned to either side of this battered factory. As to his own men, he had done the best he could. He wondered if that was good enough. He remembered what General Dietrich had told him, about his responsibility for "his boys." He was beginning to understand what it meant to be in command.

He found Josef at another second-floor window, two dozen meters from Fritzi. One of the biggest boys in the platoon, Josef was full of bluster when he talked. Now he was showing that same spirit, rising to the window, squeezing off several rounds from his rifle, then dropping down out of sight for a few moments as American bullets plunked into the brick outer wall. Once in a while a slug would enter the open window, and Lukas could hear it zing around in the factory.

"Do you have enough ammo?" he asked Josef. The boy scowled, and clapped his large—and still stuffed—duffel, then pulled out another box of rounds.

"Enough for today," he said, calmly feeding bullets into his magazine. "But you might check on Paulo; he wasn't carrying so many."

Paulo had the last window on the second floor, to the far right of the factory, and Lukas was going to do just that. Keeping low, he left the long room where Fritzi and Josef held down the fort, then hurried down the hallway to the small storage room where Paulo was.

He was approaching the door when a loud explosion shook the floor under his feet, sending him flying against the far wall. He tried to keep his balance, but his wobbling body fell to the floor anyway. Blinking, Lukas coughed on a cloud of dust, realized the debris—and the explosion—had originated in the room where he had left Paulo.

Forcing himself to his feet, balancing on shaking and unsteady legs, he stumbled into that room and tried to wave away the smoke and dust obscuring his vision. The first thing he saw was a large swath of brightness where the small window had been. A hole had been blasted in the wall, probably by a tank round. Grimacing and spitting out the dust that gritted in his teeth, he ducked low.

"Paulo!" he called, not really expecting an answer.

He found the boy, or rather, the boy's legs, emerging from beneath a heavy shelf that had toppled over his body above the waist. A pool of red ran down beside the legs. Touching the still calf, shouting the name again, Lukas confirmed his fear: Paulo was dead. "Oh god," he moaned. He had seen dead men before, but this was one of his. He felt sick. Then he felt mad.

"Fucking Americans!" Lukas cried. He peered out the irregular hole in the wall, saw more Americans scuttling forward, using the oblong boxes of some large equipment for cover. They were still too far away to hit with his pistol, but he shot angrily at the moving figures. "Bastards! I'll kill every fucking one of you!" He couldn't help noticing that they were much closer than they had been only a few minutes before.

Grimly Lukas made his way back toward the stairs, stopping only to tell Josef what had happened, and to encourage Fritzi to keep shooting. Satisfied that they would do what they could, he descended the open stairway and went to the factory's corner office, where Hans Braun was stationed.

The young sturmscharführer squeezed off a burst from his Schmeisser machine pistol, shooting out the window as Lukas came through the door. Hans pulled back from his firing portal as an answering burst of small-arms fire riddled the frame and the surrounding wall.

"I don't know, Lukas," Hans admitted, his face ashen. "There sure are a lot of them."

"You know what Hauptsturmführer Friedrich said: We have to hold them here, so that General Dietrich can get the SS panzers across the river."

"Yes, I know. And I'm trying!" Hans looked as though he was going to cry.

"I know you are—you're a brave soldier," Lukas said, giving him a pat on the shoulder. God, was this what being an officer was like? For the first time he thought of Friedrich's Panzer Assault Badge. Twenty-five days of this? He didn't want to stand up and look calm any longer; he felt just like Hans and wanted someone to console him. More bullets chattered through the window, leaving puffs of dust where they struck, and passed through the office walls. "Just keep shooting—I'm going to see what it looks like outside."

"Okay, Lukas. Come and tell me what you see, won't you?"

"Sure," replied the young lieutenant.

He made his way to the side door of the factory, where he could see the panzer that was giving them flank protection. The armored vehicle looked tough, even indestructible, as it blazed away with its main gun, using the rubble of a knocked-down wall as protection for all but its squat turret. The corner of the tanning factory provided cover from the American tanks that were still trying to fight across the railroad embankment, and a large concrete blockhouse across the alley loomed like a mountain on the other side of the tank.

The panzer's coaxial machine gun chattered, and Lukas leaned out far enough to see American GIs diving for cover; one of them twisted in the air and toppled, and the young officer choked out a quiet hurrah. One bastard down. When the gun ceased, however, he heard another sound, the wailing drone that he had come to recognize within his first few days near the front.

Jabos! He looked up to see three or four dive bombers screaming toward him, daring to fly very low. They were so close that he could see the bomb break free from the lead plane, seeming to plummet directly toward him. Lukas lurched away from the doorway, panic fueling his flight as he raced into the factory, then threw himself down behind a heavy tanning press.

The concussive blast outside the door was the loudest, most terrible thing he had ever experienced. Debris and shrapnel slashed through the air, much of it clattering against the metal press he hid behind. He was deafened, and looked up in the strange silence to see a dense cloud of smoke churning through the building. As that settled he saw that the doorway where he had been standing was gone, replaced by a gaping hole.

Stumbling over broken beams and shattered brick, he made his way to that entry, looking for the tank. His bearings were off and he wondered if he had gone to the wrong door, since he couldn't even see the broken wall that had concealed the panzer. But there was the big concrete blockhouse, though a corner of it had been smashed away. Where the tank had been there was only a crater.

Now the American infantry advanced in a rush. Lukas drew his Luger and fired several shots, not sure if he hit anyone as the troops again ducked down. "Bastards!" he screamed again. A fusillade of gunfire spattered around the gaping hole where the door had been, but the young officer was already gone, stumbling through the factory, trying to get to the office where Hans Braun was fighting.

He heard shooting and realized that his hearing was coming back. Two boys, Fritzi and Josef, were tumbling down the stairs from the second floor. Shapes darkened the windows at the ground level, and he saw a fruit-shaped object come sailing into the big room.

"Grenade!" he shouted, throwing himself down again.

The missile exploded with a dull crack and then Fritzi was screaming, kneeling over Josef's motionless body. The GIs wasted no time in following up the attack, tumbling through several windows at once, guns blazing. Fritzi went down, blood spurting from the ruin that was once his eye, his mouth still opened to utter a scream that would never emerge.

Hans appeared in the door of the office. One American spun around, his carbine raised, but Lukas got him with a shot from his pistol. Another grenade exploded and the young officer was down, felt something heavy crash on top of him. It was the lid from the big press, he realized, straining to breathe. He was momentarily pinned, although apparently uninjured.

He watched in horror as Hans dropped his machine pistol and raised his hands—not, not Hans! Not his sturmscharführer! But the Americans had him, were already herding him toward the gap where the bomb had blasted away the doorway. Hans was crying, and Lukas felt like doing the same thing. He had failed, he knew, failed Captain Friedrich and General Dietrich, failed his boys, failed his countrymen and failed his fatherland.

Still Lukas couldn't move. His gun was somewhere nearby, but he couldn't even shift enough to pick it up. He could only watch as Hans approached the ring of light outlining the door.

"Hey, Kraut—eat shit! You fuckers killed Joey!" snarled one of the Americans. He raised his carbine and cracked off a single shot, and Hans Braun toppled forward to lie motionless in the rubble of the alley.

Lukas lowered his head then, still unable to draw a full breath. "I'm sorry, Hans," he whispered. He wanted to scream, but he knew that meant instant death. Instead, he focused every iota of his being on revenge. He would live, live to take revenge on everyone who killed his boys, everyone who invaded his fatherland, every enemy of Germany. He lay still in the battered factory, grieving in silent rage, as the troops, the battle, the war passed him by.

19 JANUARY 1945

CCA, KOBLENZ, GERMANY, 0655 HOURS GMT

Frank Ballard looked down as the Sherman rolled through the last defensive position. The Rhine was visible, a shimmering band in the morning light, the goal of weeks of campaigning, and a day and a half of savage battle. Yet he felt no elation, just the weariness of one more battle finished, with who knew how many unknown challenges lying thick on the road ahead.

He passed a few prisoners, SS troops mustered out of a corner police station that had been turned into a makeshift blockhouse. Ballard was shocked to see that the Germans who had held them up for the last hour were nothing more than boys.

"Sergeant!" he shouted, as he saw a veteran NCO pushing several prisoners into an alley behind the building.

The man looked up, annoyance flashing in his eyes for a second before he straightened up and lifted his tommy gun to a semblance of port arms. "Sir?" he replied in a sharp bark.

"See that those prisoners make it to the marshaling yard. They have POW processing set up there, next to the stockade. Then get back to your unit!"

"Yessir, of course, sir!" replied the sergeant. He shoved one of the young men roughly in the back. "You there—move along, quick now! *Schnell*, see?"

Ballard hoped his order would be obeyed. It was common enough, he knew, for prisoners to get shot "accidentally" in the immediate aftermath of battle, especially when their captors had lost friends in the fight. The colonel himself had witnessed such acts, and he understood the motivations and had a hard time fastening blame. Still, when the enemy was a bunch of kids, it seemed even more wrong. He hoped that he might have put a stop, at least temporarily, to the practice.

For now, he had more important things demanding his attention. Already CCA infantry was crossing the Rhine on two bridges. Engineers were inspecting the spans, and reported that charges had not even been set. Obviously, the Americans had gotten here faster than any of the SS had expected. Idly it occurred to him that, once again, the Nineteenth Armored had scored an historic victory—the first Americans to cross the Rhine! He knew that Fourth Armored, on his right, and the Twelfth Infantry, on his left, would doubtless be pulling up to the water barrier within a day, perhaps even a matter of hours. Knowing Patton, he suspected that all of Third Army would be hurled across the river within a few days, leaving the Seventh Army to the south and the First, in the north, to clean up the rest of the Krauts on this side of the Rhine. From the way things had gone during his race to the river, he suspected—and believed—that those men wouldn't have a lot of bloody work in front of them.

An hour later Ballard's own tank was rolling across the bridge. He sat high in the turret, looking at the deep waters rolling past below. The east bank drew closer, and already he could see his Shermans spreading out, establishing a bridgehead. They had beaten the Nazis in the most important race. It looked to Frank Ballard as though there was nothing standing in their way, nothing at all between here and Berlin.

KAMPFGRUPPE PEIPER, MOSELLE VALLEY, GERMANY, 1501 HOURS GMT

Sturmbannführer Werner Potchke brought him the final bad news. "We can't get forward, Obersturmbannführer. The Americans have cut the road to the bridges. We can see them sending their tanks across already."

Jochen Peiper felt his ruined face twisting under the strain of this lost battle. He was close to his goal, close to crossing the Rhine with his kampfgruppe largely intact, in spite of all that the Allies and their pet traitor Rommel could throw at him. At that moment he hated Potschke for bringing him the bad news, hated every man in the kampfgruppe for failing the Reich, hated himself for not somehow triumphing over all odds.

He had begun this offensive with a task force of five thousand men and eight hundred vehicles, over one hundred of which were tanks. As the spearhead unit, his men had seen the toughest fighting, and with the attack on Dinant as well, his task force had suffered greatly. He now had around fifteen hundred men and twenty-eight tanks, as well as eighty or so additional vehicles. The Reich needed those tanks, and now it wouldn't get them. What was left of his kampfgruppe would shortly be reduced to infantry.

From his command position atop his Panther, he looked at the bedraggled remnants of what had been the finest fighting force the Third Reich had ever put in the field. Many of the men wore warm boots, pants, and coats looted from dead and wounded American soldiers. They hadn't taken clothes from prisoners—they hadn't taken any prisoners. His men had better things to do.

At each stop, his headquarters team set up a small command post, which basically consisted of a tent mostly filled with radio equipment, a folding table, and chairs. Because of the bitter cold, they built a blazing fire with scavenged wood; even so, a man dared not go without gloves for long. "What have we got?" Peiper shouted down from his perch.

"The usual sets of orders," came the reply. That meant one set of orders from General Dietrich and one set of orders from the fake Rommel government, still claiming command over all of Army Group B's forces.

"Throw the Rommel shit into the fire! No, wait. Let me read it. Maybe it will tell me what those hurensohnnen are up to." He jumped down from the tank.

There was nothing particularly revealing or insightful in the message originating with Rommel. Peiper wouldn't mind reading all of Rommel's message traffic, but his kampfgruppe didn't have the organic intelligence capability necessary; that was at the division level, and with everyone on the move, good intelligence was hard to produce. He looked at the orders coming from Dietrich carefully. It had occurred to him almost immediately that sending orders purporting to be from the other side would be a good tactic; in the general chaos it seemed no one had had the initiative or focus to send out fake orders, but he wanted to take no chances.

Because everyone had the same authentication codes, he had to interpret the order in light of common sense, but this order posed no problem. He was directed to move his kampfgruppe across the Rhine, with his equipment if possible, without it if necessary, re-form with his division or else report to higher headquarters. Common sense. There was another order, this one to report to General Dietrich in person as soon as possible. Again, he planned to do that anyway, so fraud and communication sabotage was not an issue.

His problem was how to do it. The strategic situation looked bleak. He did not have enough military might to force an opposed crossing. He and some of his men might make it across the Rhine by abandoning their vehicles, but even then they would need a covering action.

His eyes fell on Major Potchke again. "Yes, sir?" Potchke said.

"Werner, the division has to get across the Rhine," he said heavily.

Potchke's face went wooden. "Yes, sir," he replied.

"Our kampfgruppe was to blaze the way, but you tell me that we're stopped here."

"I'm afraid so," Potchke replied.

"And the Allies are coming."

"Yes."

"On foot and in small bands most of us can cross the Rhine over the next few days. Vehicles and equipment must be abandoned and rendered useless to the enemy."

"Yes, sir."

Peiper paused. "We're going to need a holding action to give the rest of us some breathing room and a head start."

Potchke's emotionless voice responded, "Yes, sir."

"We need twenty-four hours. After that, everyone goes." Both men knew that was a face-saving lie. There was virtually no chance that Werner Potchke could hold out that long. This was a stand and die order. "Decide what you need and who you need, Werner. All equipment and ammunition is yours. If

any of the other division elements reach here, they can reinforce you, but I suspect they will be abandoning vehicles short of here, because the enemy is closing in on all sides."

"Yes, sir," Potchke replied.

Peiper stood awkwardly for a minute. He had sent men to their deaths
many times, but most often when the guns were blazing. In the incongruous
snowy peace of this January morning, it seemed out of place. "I have orders
from General Dietrich. I have to leave," he said, and his voice was hollow. He
was not afraid of death, but because he was not going to die here and now, he
felt ashamed, embarrassed.

Soon his dwindled command was divided between Task Force Potchke,
who would build a defense to draw in and slow down the attacking Americans, and Task Force Diefenthal, under Hauptsturmführer Josef Diefenthal,
consisting of soldiers on foot who would make their way to the Rhine and
cross as best they could.

As for Peiper, he had orders, and for the first time in years he would travel
alone. He commandeered a motorcycle that belonged to one of his couriers,
climbed aboard, and took a moment to refresh his memory of the controls.
Satisfied, he gunned the throttle and felt the welcome rush of acceleration. It
gave him pleasure to be moving with such speed, such freedom, to leave the
chaos and failure of this terrible campaign behind.

He would find a bridge, somewhere north of Koblenz, and he would cross
the river and travel east. Alone, on this fast machine, he would make good time.
He would reunite with General Dietrich and take on a new mission. No matter
what, he knew that when all others dropped away, he would remain faithful to
the cause, to the passion that ruled his life. He had to get across the Rhine.

ASSOCIATED PRESS NEWSWIRE, 1900 HOURS GMT

FLASH/BULLETIN
PARIS BUREAU, JANUARY 19, 1900 GMT
COPY 01 ALLIES CROSS THE RHINE
DISTRIBUTION: ALL STATIONS

PARIS, JANUARY 19, 1945 (AP) BY CHUCK PORTER
ALLIED FORCES TODAY PENETRATED THE FINAL BARRIER PROTECTING THE
GERMAN HEARTLAND! AS FORWARD ELEMENTS OF THE UNITED STATES
THIRD ARMY CROSSED THE RHINE RIVER AT KOBLENZ, GERMANY,
DEFEATING HEAVY OPPOSITION IN THE FORM OF THE NAZI 12TH SS PANZER
DIVISION, GENERAL OF THE ARMIES DWIGHT D. EISENHOWER DECLARED
TODAY "A WATERSHED DAY IN THE LIBERATION OF GERMANY FROM THE
YOKE OF ITS NAZI MASTERS."

IN LONDON, PRIME MINISTER WINSTON CHURCHILL PRAISED THE
COURAGE OF "THE BRAVE MEN OF OUR ALLIED ARMED FORCES, WHO,
FROM THE BEACHES OF NORMANDY THROUGH THE FORESTS OF THE
ARDENNES, AND NOW ACROSS THE RHINE RIVER ITSELF, HAVE WITH
INDOMITABLE WILL SET A NEW COURSE FOR HUMAN DESTINY."

IN TRIER, GERMANY, CHANCELLOR CARL GOERDELER OF THE PROVI-
SIONAL GERMAN REPUBLIC GAVE THANKS TO THE ALLIES FOR THEIR
BRAVE SERVICE IN THE LIBERATION OF HIS PEOPLE FROM THE NAZI
TYRANNY, AND CALLED UPON THE GOVERNMENT IN BERLIN TO LAY DOWN
ITS ARMS IN UNCONDITIONAL SURRENDER AND AVOID SPILLING ANY MORE
BLOOD IN A LOST CAUSE.

WHILE SCATTERED FIGHTING CONTINUES IN AND AROUND THE CITY
OF KOBLENZ, UNITED STATES THIRD ARMY HEADQUARTERS REPORTS THAT
THE OCCUPATION OF KOBLENZ IS SECURE, THE BRIDGES ARE CAPTURED,
AND ALLIED FORCES, INCLUDING THE GERMAN REPUBLICAN ARMY UNDER
FIELD MARSHAL ERWIN ROMMEL, WILL CROSS OVER BEGINNING TONIGHT
AND CONTINUING FOR SEVERAL DAYS.

OTHER RHINE CROSSINGS ARE EXPECTED TO BE MADE IN THE NEXT
FEW DAYS, EXPANDING THE NUMBER AND RANGE OF ALLIED FORCES PEN-
ETRATING THE GERMAN HEARTLAND.

MORE

AP PAR 333548 JF/011145

Excerpt from *War's Final Fury*, by Professor Jared Gruenwald

The sweep through the Rhineland to a crossing of the great river
itself by Patton's Third Army, coupled with Rommel's German Republican Army, broke the final defensive barrier on Himmler's western flank
with a brutal and decisive blow. The American armored divisions reached
the river so quickly that the SS units simply could not react in time. When
CCA of the 19th Armored Division crossed at Koblenz and, a day later,
the 4th Armored crossed a few miles south to strike at Wiesbaden, the
whole illusion of a defensible front was shattered.

The remnants of the SS units that survived the campaign were forced
to make their own crossings of the wide river, often just ahead of the
American units that were spreading out along the east bank. Although the
positions north of the Ruhr Valley remained strong, holding the British
and the northern half of Bradley's army group in check, the breakthroughs
in the south were too vast, too sweeping, to allow for any containment.

Eisenhower's decision to strike out for the political prize of Berlin was audacious, and would fuel many of the events over the next months. It created a direct challenge to the Russians, who were no longer viewed as part of the Great Alliance, and this was a challenge that Stalin could not afford to ignore. Though the Western Allies were in total command of the air, and fully mechanized in all aspects of their land armies, they had barely a quarter as many men as the Red Army could bring to bear from the east. It was not a gamble that the Western governments would make lightly.

In his typical fashion, however, Patton was not concerned with such strategic details. Nor was he content to allow his units to simply consolidate the initial gains while the rest of the Allied forces came up in support. Sensing the crucial weakness of his enemy, he hurled his forces to the east and north in a broad hook that raced ever closer toward the prize of the German capital. Rommel's German forces accompanied this advance, which of course would lead to the surprising developments in the Thuringer Wald.

But even before then, Himmler's difficulties reached their crisis. With the renewal of the Soviet offensive in the east, Germany was once again trapped between the jaws of two implacable enemies—enemies that were not just focused on destroying Nazis, but were now engaged in a deadly race with each other.

Besides the now-dashed hope that Rommel's western offensive would succeed, there were few other opportunities for Germany to exploit. However, there was some cause for hope. In the months of buildup to Operation Fuchs am Rhein, Field Marshals Alfred Jodl and Walther Mödel were busy rebuilding the shattered Eastern Front. Finally freed from the shackles of Adolf Hitler's irrational demands, such as the infamous "fortress" order, the two field marshals were able to use the interval of peace to create new, fortified lines drawn on the basis of what was defensible—an "Eastwall" of sorts to parallel the Westwall that had successfully delayed the western Allied advance. Of course, the eastern line lacked the extensive fortifications and gun emplacements that characterized the "Siegfried Line" along Germany's western border. The most significant work had been done in East Prussia, where the approaches to Konigsberg were now guarded by extensive and modern pillboxes, tank traps, and strong points.

Even so, the initial Soviet advances met with stunning success. The line of the Vistula was crossed in multiple places, and Warsaw was quickly gobbled up by the Red Army. They barely slowed their pace as they raced toward the west, crossing the prewar border between Poland and Germany and preparing to close in on Berlin itself. . . .

OPERATION EASTWALL

1 FEBRUARY –
26 FEBRUARY 1945

The art of leadership . . . consists in consolidating the attention of the people against a single adversary and taking care that nothing will split up that attention . . . The leader of genius must have the ability to make different opponents appear as if they belonged to one category.

—Adolf Hitler
Mein Kampf (1925)

1 FEBRUARY 1945

NEUE REICHSKANZLEI, BERLIN, 1000 HOURS GMT

The ritualistic display was intended to intimidate him, and on some levels, Günter von Reinhardt admitted to himself, it worked quite well. Marched within a square of goose-stepping SS-Totenkopf guards, he felt as if he were being escorted off to one of the infamous concentration camps—the *Totenkopfverbände,* or death's-head units, had that as their primary responsibility. Himmler's use of death's-head guards for personal bodyguard and ceremonial escorts was a signal, and not a pleasant one to contemplate.

Guards flanking the double doors into Himmler's inner sanctum snapped to attention at their approach, and opened the doors with military precision. Von Reinhardt always admired precision, even under these circumstances.

The room was dark, blackout curtains drawn tight, the only illumination a lamp on the desk of the Third Reich's second führer, Heinrich Himmler. Two more guards flanked the führer, their faces shadowed, giving them the look of demons. Only the death's head insignia gleamed white on their collars. Von Reinhardt noticed that there were no chairs visible in the room other than the one occupied by Himmler. The man expected him to negotiate standing up. Well, the opening gambit in a negotiation was almost always an emotional one.

Von Reinhardt turned to one of the guards. "Fetch me a chair," he commanded. The guard stood stony and silent, as well he should. This wasn't his initiative.

After a moment, von Reinhardt turned to the man who had once been his führer. "I'm only recently out of my hospital bed," he said in as cheerful a tone as he could muster. His voice echoed in the room—it was a space calling for whispers. "I'm afraid I need a chair. Have your guard fetch one."

Himmler's voice had a sibilant, almost snakelike quality to it. "And why should I provide a seat for a traitor standing before me?"

Von Reinhardt chuckled. "Is this how we are to negotiate? If so, I can go back and make my report without wasting either of our time further." He turned to go. As he expected, the death's-head guards barred his way.

"You won't be leaving without my say-so," Himmler snarled.

"Of course not," von Reinhardt acknowledged. "But my failure to return will constitute a report all by itself, you know. I'm here because I'm expendable, barely out of the hospital bed Bücher put me in. Holding me, torturing me, or even killing me won't have any effect—except on me, of course, and I can't say I find the prospects enthralling. If we're here to do business, have your guards fetch me a chair, or have them drag me away. It's your call."

Himmler stood up, enraged, and pounded his fist on the table. "You damned insolent traitor! How dare you talk to your führer this way?"

"It's premature to decide whether I'm a traitor, Herr Reichsführer. Treason, as the Englishman Sir John Harington put it, never prospers. 'What's the reason? For if it prosper, none dare call it treason.' " He smiled. This kind of verbal fencing actually relaxed him. He had called Himmler's play. Now the führer could either negotiate or have him taken away, and the latter didn't advance Himmler's interests. He waited, calmly meeting the cold stare through the führer's round glasses.

Suddenly, Himmler laughed. It was a thin, high-pitched cackle, very incongrous for the position he held. " 'None dare call it treason'! Ha-ha-ha! It's too bad our late führer couldn't have heard that back in the old days. Of course, maybe he did. Welcome back to Berlin, Oberst von Reinhardt." He walked around the desk to shake his hand. Suddenly a chair materialized out of the shadows, and a uniformed orderly was on hand to fetch coffee.

First the threat, and now the gracious hospitality. This negotiation would proceed along traditional lines. There would be time for discussion; then suddenly there would appear to be an unbridgeable impasse, and threats would return. He knew the pattern well. But here in the middle of the snake's lair he realized something else: The pattern worked, even on the mind of someone coolly logical and well prepared. He took a sip of coffee and tried to smile, hoping the beads of sweat on his back and face were not apparent.

LONDON, ENGLAND, 1800 HOURS GMT

"Good evening, Mr. Philby," the secretary said.

"Good evening. See you in the A.M.," Philby replied. He fastened his overcoat, retrieved his umbrella from its stand, picked up his hat and briefcase, and walked down the hall to the elevator with measured stride. He pressed the Down button with the tip of his umbrella, nodded to two men from the documents section who were also leaving promptly at six o'clock, and entered the elevator with them. The elevator stopped on two intervening floors. On the first of the two stops, a female secretary joined them; on the second stop, a British army major entered. On the ground floor, Philby hung back as the lady exited first, followed by the two documents staffers. The major and Philby each gestured at the other, but Philby, having entered on the higher floor, prevailed, and the major exited, leaving Philby as the last off.

There was a small queue at the guard's desk to exit the building, fed by a second elevator as well as by first-floor and basement offices. Philby took his turn in the queue and, when he reached the head of the queue, snapped open his briefcase without waiting to be asked, showed the document-release authorizations inside, signed the exit log, replied to the guard's pleasant "Good night, Mr. Philby," and turned right onto Baker Street.

Philby's measured stride took him back to Marylebone Road, across the divided street, then left four blocks to the intersection with Lisson Grove. There he paused for a moment, waiting for the light to change. As he waited, the tip of his umbrella probed the metal plate at the base of the streetlight. A wad of gum was stuck to the right edge of the plate. The light changed, and Philby stepped off the curb to cross Lisson Grove.

There was a message waiting for him. His cutouts left and picked up messages for him at a series of rotating drops, which he changed on a regular basis, and left notifications at other points, which also changed regularly. Philby rather enjoyed the methodical discipline of tradecraft, and practiced it with rigor.

He dined alone at a neighborhood curry house and took a stroll about the park after dinner, all part of his normal routine. In the process of his walk, however, he retrieved a small envelope from underneath a water fountain as he took a brief sip. He continued his walk, for the fresh air and exercise was good for him, and returned to his flat within a few minutes of eight-thirty.

He washed his hands, hung up his coat, removed his necktie, unlaced his shoes, and made himself a cup of hot cocoa, mostly milk, then turned on his desk lamp and sat down to decode his message, using a dog-eared schoolboy copy of Caesar's *Gallic Wars* as the cipher key. Within a few minutes, he had a clean copy of his message ready to read.

> WHEELCHAIR HAS WARNED URSA MAJOR THAT INTENDED HOLIDAY
> DESTINATION IS NOT AVAILABLE. REPORT SOONEST ON ALL WHEEL-
> CHAIR AND CIGAR PLANS FOR HOLIDAY RESORT ACTIVITIES. HIGHEST
> PRIORITY.

"Wheelchair" was FDR, "Ursa Major" Stalin, "Cigar" Churchill, and everybody's favorite "holiday destination" was Berlin. So, FDR was warning Stalin to stay out of Berlin, was he? Pretty obviously, the forces on the ground were not enough to back up such strong language, but with so many secret weapons projects, there was always the possibility that not all the available forces were currently visible. A ground war between the Western Allies and the Soviet Union would favor the Soviet Union, but the strategic bombing and air superiority advantage of the United States in particular balanced the equation somewhat. Still, it did not seem to Philby that an intelligent man would find it wise to issue ultimatums to Stalin under the present circumstances.

He would begin to nose around a bit in the morning. In the meantime, he took the message, his worksheet, and three or four sheets of paper from the pad on which he worked, and burned them in his ashtray, then flushed the ashes down the loo. He turned off the desk lamp, then sat down in his reading chair, turned on that lamp, unsnapped his briefcase, and began reading the various documents he'd brought home with him. Thirty or so more minutes of reading for pleasure while smoking his pipe, and then to bed. All in all, a normal and productive day. Kim Philby smiled.

REMNANT OF HITLERJUGEND PANZER DIVISION, APPROACHING TANGERMUNDE, GERMANY, 1954 HOURS GMT

The little village had been plastered by a dozen or more bombs at some point during the winter. Lukas Vogel assumed that the Allies had been simply trying to make another statement about their brutal mastery of the skies, and the landscape, of Germany.

"Ach, nein," suggested Hauptsturmführer Friedrich, waving his hand dismissively at the notion. "Probably a bomber was shot up, losing power . . . the terrorflieger bastard dumped his bombs to lighten the plane, and so what if there was a village below him?"

"But the whole town square—blown apart?" asked the young Nazi. "That's more than just chance!"

His commander shrugged, his eyes narrowing as he squinted through the ruins. The two men were alone, standing in the narrow lane that led through this anonymous hamlet. "Not the whole square—look, that tavern escaped with only a few scratches!"

Friedrich's pace picked up immediately as he strode across the cratered town square toward a corner of buildings that had escaped relatively unscathed. Suppressing a sigh, Lukas followed along. He had seen the inside of many taverns during the last few days, as he and the few surviving comrades of his division had been making their way, on foot, across Germany. Every town had a bar, of course, and he privately reflected that Friedrich seemed to have stopped in most of them.

Out of more than ten thousand troops in the division at the beginning of the Ardennes offensive—with Rommel's treason, Lukas no longer thought of it as Operation Fuchs am Rhein—fewer than a thousand had survived through to the defense of Koblenz. None of Lukas' panzergrenadiere had survived, a thought he kept pushed away from his mind, though it threatened to overtake his thoughts almost hourly.

Over the course of that bleak, frigid march, the other surviving men and boys had drifted away one by one, sometimes slipping off in the night, at other times simply collapsing and refusing to continue. Now, not even a week after they had crossed the Rhine in the midnight shuttle run of a small boat they had commandeered, only the captain and the loyal young lieutenant were left.

"*Hallo!*" shouted Friedrich, pushing open the dark oaken door. Not surprisingly, there was no answer—to the best of Lukas' guess, the entire village seemed to be abandoned.

"No one here," Friedrich said, shaking his head in disgust. Then he brightened. "That means the drinks are on the house!"

This was no change from any other place, of course—the SS captain had refused to pay for any of the food or lodging the soldiers had claimed from their countrymen. This circumstance only seemed fair to Lukas, for men who had been risking their lives for years in the desperate defense of Germany. Still, he had been shocked several nights ago, when Friedrich had pulled his sidearm and shot dead a grandfatherly old innkeeper who had dared to ask for a few reichsmarks in exchange for a night of food, drink, and lodging.

The captain stalked behind the bar, loudly opening several cupboards and cursing in disgust before he pushed back into a storage room. Lukas clomped over to the fireplace, and found some kindling and logs. Quickly he stacked them into a fire, and had touched one of his last matches to the wood before the captain emerged, wiping the foam of a beer from his lips.

Friedrich threw his empty bottle across the room, where it shattered in the corner, but he had several more of the brown glass containers cradled in his left arm. He came over to the fire and sat next to Lukas on the bench that the young soldier had pulled up. "Here," he said, offering one of the beers.

Lukas grasped the bottle and took a long pull. Beer was liquid, beer was food, and for occasional moments, beer was forgetfulness. It felt fine, washing his parched gullet and at least starting to fill his rumbling belly.

"What day is it?" the young soldier asked, suddenly thinking of something.

Friedrich squinted, draining his second beer; that bottle joined the first in the shards of the corner. "It's the eighteenth, I think. Why?"

Lukas shrugged, reluctant to tell the truth. "No reason," he said. "I just wondered."

January 18, 1945 . . . it was his sixteenth birthday. But he would keep that news to himself. He felt a sense of satisfaction as he, too, emptied his bottle and threw it across the room.

Friedrich had already started on his third, and Lukas knew better than to ask him to share. Instead, he got up, reluctantly leaving the warmth that was starting to spread from the growing fire. He rummaged in the same storeroom the captain had searched, and finally came out with a whole crate, twelve large bottles, of beer.

"See if you can find us some food," Friedrich said, after they had each finished another.

Lukas nodded. Next to the storeroom he located the small kitchen, which had mostly been emptied when the owners had departed. There was a loaf of bread, but mold had rendered it inedible even by his nearly starving standards.

But then he found a stairway, descended into the cellar, and—treasure!—found a ring of blutwurst hanging in the cold room. He came back up and found a frying pan, then cut the blood sausage into inch-long lengths. Soon the chunks of dark ground meat were sizzling and dancing in the cast-iron skillet. When they were fully blackened he pulled the pan out of the fire, and the two soldiers took turns spearing the links on their knives, enjoying the rich, crunchy taste of the well-crisped meat.

By this time they had finished half of the crate of beer, and Lukas felt a pleasant warmth and lethargy creeping over him. He silently toasted his birthday in the crackling flames.

Friedrich was staring into the fire, his head shaking sadly. He looked at his dirty hands, wrapped around the brown bottle, and suddenly he was weeping silently, fat tears rolling down his chapped, weathered face. Abruptly he straightened up, shifted so that he was staring at Lukas with a strangely intense expression.

"Tell me, Luka'—di'jou have a girl, back home, 'fore the war?" he asked, blinking as he tried to focus his eyes.

The young soldier shook his head. He had been only thirteen when he had gone off to join the army, and hadn't thought much about girls one way or another.

"Me . . . I 'idn't have a girl, either," said Friedrich, almost sleepily. He leaned forward, out of balance, arresting himself by placing his left hand on the young officer's knee. The older man squeezed so hard that it hurt, but Lukas did not dare to squirm away, certain that such a gesture would have caused the captain to fall right to the floor.

"No girls fer me . . . they just trouble," said Friedrich, shaking his head. His beer bottle slipped from his right hand to shatter on the slate floor. "Need 'nother beer," he said, suddenly pushing off of Lukas' knee to sit up straight.

Relieved to be freed from the captain's grip, Lukas rose and pulled two more bottles from the case. He finally pried them open, though he was having a great deal of difficulty with the caps. The room was spinning, and suddenly the rich sausage in his belly was not feeling as good as it had a short time before.

He sat down, aware that Friedrich had moved very close. The captain threw an arm around the young man's shoulders, and once again he was crying. Lukas raised the bottle, took a drink, and knew immediately that he had made a mistake. He leaped to his feet and lunged for the door, barely making it outside. He leaned over the porch railing and puked in the snow. He felt Friedrich's hands on his shoulder and heard a strange moaning sound from his lips.

3 FEBRUARY 1945

KÖNIGSPLATZ, BERLIN, GERMANY, 2134 HOURS GMT
"Stop the car, right here," ordered Jochen Peiper.

"Ja, Herr Obersturmbannführer," said his driver, pulling the armored car over to the side of the wide, yet empty, boulevard. The SS officer pushed open the door and heaved himself out of the vehicle, finally drawing a breath of air in this once grand, now ravaged city. His destination lay just across the square, but he wasn't yet ready to enter the forbidding building, to go through the inevitably unpleasant interview awaiting him.

"Turn the engine off—but wait for me here," said Peiper. The driver nodded and obeyed. Peiper took a few steps away, and when the thrumming motor ceased running he was stunned at the overwhelming silence surrounding him, right in the middle of Berlin. The Tiergarten, to the south, was silent and dark, missing all of the frivolity and activity of peacetime, even lacking the purposeful congregations of citizens that had gathered there during the early, successful, years of war. It was like a ghost forest now, grim and oppressive.

He found himself strolling under the canopy of trees, shivering in the cold night. He saw the armored car, steaming but silent, across the street; except for that, he might have convinced himself that he was all alone, in some supernatural expanse of a Grimm Brothers' forest.

Now he was here, in Berlin, and this had been his objective for a very long time. But the reality was anticlimactic, disappointing, even depressing. He knew that he had to shake this feeling away before he went to see Himmler.

It had been a harrowing trip across the nation. He recalled the details of war, of flight, and survival as if it were a story that had happened to someone else, a long time ago—though he had lived the journey, and it had taken less than a week. After the Americans had punched through to the Rhine at Koblenz, Peiper and the few remaining men of his kampfgruppe had made their way across the Rhine by boat. Two days later, after an interval of frigid eastward trekking, they had come upon a Wehrmacht patrol that had been using the squat, ugly armored car. When the sergeant in charge had refused to hand over the car, Peiper shot him between the eyes. The rest of the detachment had vanished into the woods, and the SS survivors claimed the vehicle as their due.

There was room for only four, so he selected three of his men to come with him, and left the rest with orders to reach Berlin any way they could. Making their way northeast across the country, they had driven at night, traveling more like bandits than officers of the national military. Every day they pillaged fuel and food from the citizenry or from small units of the home defense forces or Wehrmacht, often at gunpoint. One of his men had been killed when a company of stubborn volksgrenadierie had refused to part with their precious cans of fuel. The rest of those fools, old men and beardless boys armed with World War I vintage rifles, had been slaughtered by the ruthless SS veterans in revenge.

Peiper snorted with contempt at the memory, the steam of his breath bursting from his nostrils as if in reassurance that he was still alive. They had been weaklings and cowards, those so-called Germans—unfit to call this great country their fatherland. Why couldn't they *see?* The Third Reich needed resolute heroes, now more than ever, if the nation was not to be plunged into a nearly inconceivable era of slavery and subjugation.

He looked up at the Reichstag, dark and forbidding, yet solid and grandiose as well. There pulsed the heartbeat of the nation. He refused to wonder about the strength of that pulse, about the life expectancy of the Nazi government—for that pulse, and that life span, were his own, as well.

For a long time, as the night got colder and darker, Jochen Peiper sat on the bench in the Tiergarten, staring at the nerve center of the Third Reich barely a hundred meters away. His master was in there, and it was Peiper's duty to report to Himmler, to tell him of the valiant but ultimately failed attempt to hold at the Rhine. He must seek new orders, new duties, tasks that would give Germany—and himself—some chance of survival as a true Teutonic state, not the puppet of Russian and American masters.

But for now, he couldn't make himself move. Instead, he simply stared, not seeing, not feeling, not caring.

Only when the air-raid sirens started to wail did he get up and shamble toward the Reichstag. He would find Himmler, and get his orders, and the war would go on.

The Neue Reichstag showed damage, but had not been destroyed. Its many windows were mostly broken or boarded up; blackout curtains covered all the openings. He wandered around its periphery for a while before encountering guards who could let him inside, and he had to make the inevitable stops at lower levels of command before being admitted to the inner sanctum. Fortunately, he was quite familiar with the routine and with many of its players, and was able to get coffee and a cot to doss on, as well as an orderly to wake him up with enough time to wash and straighten up before being ushered into the führer's presence.

When he was awakened, he had no idea what time it was. In the world behind the blackout curtains, there was no external cue. Day or night, it was

all the same. He washed in a small bathroom, straightened his uniform as best
he could, shaved with difficulty over his scar tissue, and then allowed himself
to be escorted. It would be the first time he'd seen Himmler as führer; he had
been aide-de-camp to Himmler as Reichsführer-SS from 1938 until 1941, then
had spent the rest of his military career with the Leibstandarte Adolf Hitler—
a division that now no longer existed.

"Jochen—how good to see you, my boy," Heinrich Himmler said, getting
up from behind his desk and coming around to greet him.

Peiper saluted in his most formal manner, then shook the führer's proffered hand. "It is good to see you, too, sir. It's been a long time."

"Too long. This terrible war has so many consequences, but one is that
there is no time to keep up with dear friends. I am delighted that you survived
the terrible events of the past month. What a horrible shock this treason has
been! And without my trusted Peiper at the front, how much worse could have
happened! Here, sit down, sit down. Have you been well taken care of?"

"Very well, mein Führer, thank you."

"Good. Now, Jochen, tell me what happened."

For an hour, Peiper gave his report as Himmler asked questions. Heinrich
Himmler was not primarily a great soldier, but he was enormously insightful
about people and politics, and Peiper provided as much detail as possible on
the personalities and situations he had encountered. Finally, he hit the part he
most dreaded sharing.

"As we approached Koblenz, we found that the Allies had managed to get
across first. We could not cross the Rhine, and therefore destroyed our vehicles, and the remaining forces of my kampfgruppe and other kampfgruppe of
the LSSAH slipped across the river as best we could. Our division no longer
exists as a fighting unit. This fills me with utter shame, mein Führer."

Himmler sat and looked at him. "Jochen, the leading edge of the attacking
force was farthest from safety. In addition, I tasked you with the additional
role of making a raid on Rommel's headquarters in Dinant. Had you not done
so, but concentrated all your efforts on getting the unit back across, could you
have done so?"

Peiper thought, not wishing to dodge the responsibility. "It is possible, sir,
but . . ."

"Enough. It was a great sacrifice, but one that was necessary. The one
part that we did not plan for was to have two-thirds of our attacking force
turn traitor on us. For that, you cannot be faulted as a commanding officer.
You did the best you could." Himmler turned back to his desk, and picked up
two boxes.

"For your heroism in confronting the potential mutiny at Sixth Army
headquarters, for your daring raid on Army Group B headquarters, and your
exceptional work in the near-extrication of the LSSAH from an impossible sit-

uation, I award you Swords for your Knights Cross," Himmler said, snapping open the first box and handing it to Peiper.

Peiper took the box. "Sir, I—I . . . Thank you, mein Führer!"

"And now for your next assignment, for our war goes on, and brave men are needed many places at once. The Das Reich division has a new commanding officer, Gruppenführer Werner Ostendorff. I am promoting you to standartenführer and assigning you as second-in-command of Das Reich." The Second SS Panzer Division was known as "Das Reich." Himmler handed Peiper the second box. In it were new collar insignia for his new rank as SS colonel. "It's time for us to worry about the Slavs again," Himmler said.

HEADQUARTERS, SECOND GUARDS TANK ARMY, WLOCLAWEK, POLAND, 2255 HOURS GMT

Colonel Krigoff walked through the quiet bivouac of the army headquarters. His boots crunched the brittle frost on the ground, and his breath steamed in the air. Tents were pitched all around the wide field, shelters for the enlisted men and lesser officers of the army's intelligence section, while the large farmhouse occupied by the generals was shuttered tightly, smoke puffing from the chimney.

Krigoff knew that General Yeremko was in there. The commander of the battalion had disappeared through the door hours ago, leaving the real work to his underlings. No doubt he had finished his vodka and gone to sleep. The colonel grimaced in disgust; he knew there was still work to do, and it would fall to him to take care of it.

He entered the communications trailer, and the enlisted radio operator, knowing Krigoff's routine, made a polite excuse and departed. The colonel sat down and tapped out his message, his daily report about the operations of the tank army.

DESTINATION MOSCOW
KREMLIN, SECTION 34
TO THE ATTENTION OF POLITICAL MARSHAL NIKOLAY BULGANIN
RE: PROGRESS OF SECOND GUARDS TANK ARMY, 3 FEBRUARY 1945
COMRADE BULGANIN:

OUR FORCES MADE SIGNIFICANT HEADWAY THROUGH THE CRUMBLING DEFENSES OF THE NAZIS. AFTER STRIKING WESTWARD ALONG THE NORTH BANK OF THE VISTULA SINCE WARSAW, GENERAL PETROVSKY HAS AT LAST BEGUN TO SEND SPEARHEADS SOUTH OF THE RIVER, THOUGH THESE CROSSINGS ARE ACCOMPLISHED ONLY WITH GREAT PREPARATION AND VERY DELIBERATE PROCEDURES—PROCEDURES THAT, AS USUAL, SEEM INCLINED TO PRESERVE THE LIVES OF THE MEN AT THE COST OF THE SPEED OF THE ADVANCE.

HOWEVER, IT MUST BE REPORTED THAT THE ENEMY IS YIELDING TO US
IN EVERY SECTOR OF THE FRONT. WE MAINTAIN A SPEARHEAD THAT SEEMS
TO BE SPLITTING BETWEEN THE FORCES OF NAZI ARMY GROUP A AND
ARMY GROUP CENTRE. THERE IS AN EXPECTATION THAT COMRADE GEN-
ERAL ROKOSSOVSKY'S NORTHERN THRUST WILL ISOLATE THE LATTER FOR-
MATION IN THE VICINITY OF EAST PRUSSIA BEFORE THE END OF THE
MONTH. INDEED, THAT ESTIMABLE GENERAL SEEMS DETERMINED TO
ACCOMPLISH THIS ENCIRCLEMENT, THOUGH HE IS REMINDED REGULARLY
BY HIS COMMISSAR SECTION THAT THE TRUE OBJECTIVE OF THIS CAM-
PAIGN IS THE CAPTURE OF BERLIN. AS HAS HAPPENED SO OFTEN IN THIS
GREAT PATRIOTIC WAR, THE EFFORTS OF THE MILITARY MEN SEEM TO LIE IN
DIRECTIONS THAT ARE NOT NECESSARILY IN FULL COORDINATION WITH
THE AIMS OF THE STATE, AND THE CHAIRMAN.

OUR OWN FORCES, UNDER COMRADE MARSHAL ZHUKOV, HAVE MAIN-
TAINED A STRONG AXIS IN THE DIRECTION OF BERLIN. INDEED, IT IS THE
FRONT COMMANDER HIMSELF, I BELIEVE, WHO HAS FINALLY PRESSED
COMRADE GENERAL PETROVSKY INTO PUSHING ELEMENTS OF HIS ARMY
ACROSS THE VISTULA—FOR THAT IS BUT A PRELIMINARY OBSTACLE
TO OUR CARRYING THE WAR INTO THE HEART OF THE NAZI
HOMELAND.

I KNOW THAT YOU WILL AVAIL YOURSELF OF STATISTICS REGARDING
PERSONNEL LOSSES AND TERRITORIAL GAINS AS PROVIDED BY THE COM-
MISSAR SECTION, SO AS USUAL I WILL NOT BURDEN YOU WITH THOSE
DETAILS—EXCEPT AS TO REPORT THAT THE CITY OF WLOCLAWEK (ACROSS
THE VISTULA FROM OUR CURRENT POSITION) SEEMS POORLY DEFENDED,
AND RIPE FOR LIBERATION. THERE, UNLIKE IN WARSAW, THE ELEMENTS OF
POLISH RESISTANCE SEEM TO EXHIBIT A BENT OF PROPER COMMUNIST
IDEOLOGY; IT MAY BE THAT WE SHALL BE ABLE TO TAKE ADVANTAGE OF
THAT, AND EMPLOY THESE MEN AS WILLING AND PRESUMPTIVELY LOYAL
ALLIES TO OUR OWN OCCUPATION.

FROM HERE, THE LINE OF POZNAN KUSTRIN-AN-DER-ODER-BERLIN
LIES BEFORE US. I SHALL ENDEAVOR TO UPDATE YOU DAILY, INSOFAR AS
POSSIBLE, AS SECOND GUARDS TANK ARMY FOLLOWS THIS LINE, DRIVING
LIKE A SPEAR INTO THE VERY HEART OF THE THIRD REICH.

> SIGNED: POLKOVNIK ALEXIS PETROVICH KRIGOFF,
> DEPUTY CHIEF OF INTELLIGENCE,
> SECOND GUARDS TANK ARMY

After he sent the message he sat back, thinking. He went to the door and
looked out, studying the house where General Yeremko was sleeping. Krigoff
could almost hear the old man snoring, and he spit into the snow in disgust.

There was much work to do, and it saddened him that such a tired old fool was nominally in charge of those tasks.

How long would that state of affairs last? Krigoff pondered the question, and slowly a sly smile crept onto his face. The communications sergeant looked at him quizzically, wondering if he should return to his post, but the colonel of intelligence held up a hand: *Wait.*

Still thinking about Yeremko, Krigoff went back to the radio and took the seat. He reached forward to begin a new transmission:

For the eyes of the Chairman, alone . . .

5 FEBRUARY 1945

419TH ARMORED INFANTRY BATTALION, FOURTH ARMORED DIVISION, WESER RIVER, GERMANY, 0934 HOURS GMT

"What the hell do you mean, 'deploying your infantry'?" demanded George Patton, his reed-thin voice grating through the headquarters company of Combat Command B of the Fourth Armored. All the work came to a standstill as officers and enlisted men alike stared in awe and fear at the army commander. "Are all of your tanks out of gas?"

"No, General!" snapped the colonel in charge. To his credit, he glared at the army commander, allowing no hint of hesitation in his voice. "But there is at least one Tiger dug in down there, covering the approach to the river and the bridge. We have a better chance of taking him out with a flanking maneuver than a direct attack. The terrain is no good for tanks, so the only way to get around the son of a bitch is to send men on foot. I've ordered the men to deploy with all possible haste—but I'm not taking the risk of throwing lives away when we can smoke the bastard out with a little patience, and a dose of tactics!"

"*One* Tiger?" Patton waved his hand at the column of Shermans on the road, halted now, with engines idling loudly. "You have twenty-five tanks I can see from here! And that's probably the only fucking Kraut son of a bitch between you and Berlin! Now get moving!"

Patton felt his eyes bulging out, knew his face was taking on a sheen of redness that did not bode well for the health of his heart. He also knew that this was an effective look for him—it invariably provoked hasty obedience in whatever hapless underling he chose to fix those bulging eyes upon.

Thus, he was surprised almost to the point of speechlessness when the stubborn colonel refused to back down. "With respect, General, I lost ten men and two Shermans—my front units, with me since Normandy! And that fucking Kraut will pick off God knows how many more of them if we charge down the road. It won't take long to get him from the flanks, to plant a satchel charge right on his turret, for Chrissakes!"

"*If* they don't blow the goddamn bridge while you're dicking around with this penny-ante bullshit! We have a schedule to meet!" shouted the army general. "If you can't meet it, then I will find someone else who will! When we get to Berlin, do you want to find the fucking Russians waiting for us? Colonel, I am ordering you to take that bridge—now!"

The colonel glared, trembling for a moment as emotions ranging from outrage to grief raced across his features. Finally he replied, his voice dead level.

"Yes, *sir*, General Patton!"

"Good! These boys of yours will get the job done. And dammit, you know
that the sooner we can finish this war, the more men's lives we'll save. Remember, speed—always *speed!*" Patton barked.

The colonel had already picked up his microphone. He didn't look at the
general as he issued his orders. "This is Dogpatch One to all Abners. Get these
tanks moving, on the double! Blow up that fucking Tiger, cross this fucking
river, and get some miles behind you before the sun sets!"

Patton nodded, then stalked away from the compound of parked trucks,
hopping into his jeep without a backward look.

"Where to, General Patton, sir?" asked his driver, the ever-loyal Sergeant
Mims.

"Take me back to HQ, Johnny," said the army commander wearily. He had
a headache, and he felt tired all over. He shook his head. "I tell you, the wheels
would fall off this goddamned army if I didn't personally see that they were
bolted on."

An hour later the jeep pulled into the little village square where Third
Army had established a command post for today's operations. As they had
done ever since crossing the Rhine, the men of the army HQ staff were constantly on the move, setting up a new CP every day or two so they could keep
up with the fast-moving spearheads of Patton's armor. More and more of
Germany was rolling past beneath their tracks, and each day brought encounters with only a few stubborn Nazis, like the men in the Tiger back at the river
crossing. But the roads were bad for the most part, especially with the country
still under the grip of winter weather, and the rough terrain proved troublesome as well. All of these factors seemed to combine with almost malicious
purpose to keep him from that cherished objective, Berlin.

"General, the reporters have been here for the last couple of days. They're
wondering if you'd have time for a word?" Colonel Wallace, the liaison officer,
spoke to Patton tentatively as the Third Army commander hopped out of the
jeep.

Patton looked toward the small group of civilians, notebooks and pens at
the ready, who were standing outside of the small inn that was serving as the
temporary command post of the army. "What the hell," he snorted. "Now is as
good a time as any."

He stalked over to the group, enjoying the sudden frenzy as they rushed
forward, flipping pages in their notebooks, gathering around like a flock
of young birds hungry for a tempting morsel of worm. "It'll have to be quick,
fellows—and lady," he added, nodding and smiling at the female reporter from
Life magazine. "I have a war to win."

"General?" shouted one writer. Patton knew he worked for the *New York Times,* and eyed him warily. "Do you think the war is almost over?"

"Hell," barked the general, "this war *is* over—these Nazis bastards are beat, and they know it. Of course, we have some bigger fish to fry, and I hope we don't lose track of that."

"Do you mean the Russians, General?" asked another writer, scribbling madly.

Patton recognized the man, Chuck Porter—a fellow who had been a pretty straight shooter in his stories about Rommel's surrender. Still, the general snorted contemptuously for effect. "You're not going to get me to walk into any traps," he declared. "Let's just say, those bastards know who they are— and they better know that we're coming for 'em!"

"Are you going for Berlin, General? Is that a clear objective now?" pressed Porter.

"Hell, yes," he replied. "Berlin *is* Germany any sonuvabitch with a sense of history knows that. And—don't quote me on this—we're going to get there before any cocksucking communist faggot even gets a look at the place."

With that, he stalked toward the headquarters building. Colonel Wallace, looking a little pale, came trotting along behind.

"Lew," Patton said with a grin, as they entered the command post, "I think that went pretty well."

11 FEBRUARY 1945

BRANDENBURG GATE, BERLIN, GERMANY, 1104 HOURS GMT

It wasn't until the huge, arched gate rose before him that Lukas Vogel finally realized where he was. He had been walking for years, it seemed, and for the last few days he hadn't had anything to eat. His boots were worn through, his feet wrapped in shreds of leather that he had scrounged from a bombed tailor shop, and frostbite had chapped the skin of his face and numbed his fingers so that he could hardly clench his hand into a fist.

He had still been able to hold his knife, though. Two nights earlier, when Hauptsturmführer Friedrich had finished his beer and repeatedly tried to crawl into the bedroll with the young soldier, it had been the knife that greeted the older officer. Lukas hadn't waited to see if Friedrich had lived or died; he had simply rolled up his kit and started trudging east through the midnight frost.

Now he was here. In fact, he hadn't even noticed when he had first entered the city. He had simply kept walking, until his footsteps had carried him onto the Charlottenburger Chaussée and the great arch, symbol of German might, rose before him.

Only then did it occur to him that he really didn't know where to go. General Dietrich had assigned him to the Hitlerjugend, the Twelfth SS Panzer Division, but for all Lukas knew he was the only surviving member of that unit—at least, the only one who hadn't fallen into American hands. And of those prisoners, he assumed that most of them had been butchered, just like poor Hans, who had only wanted to surrender. Every time he thought of that boy, shot down in cold blood, he felt a burst of rising hatred. At first he had wanted to cry, but that feeling was gone . . . now he just wanted revenge.

He saw several SS soldiers standing casually around one of the pillars of the gate; if they were on guard duty, they didn't seem to be taking their job very seriously. Still, their uniforms were a welcome sign of familiarity, and Lukas forced himself to an erect, military posture as he walked over to them.

The men watched as he approached. They looked like real veterans, unkempt but businesslike, Schmeissers slung casually from their shoulders, eyes hooded and wary. One of them who was seated on a bench took note of the officer's insignia on Lukas' shoulder, and smirked slightly. He pushed himself to his feet with almost contemptuous ease, and raised a hand in the Nazi salute.

"Heil Himmler, Herr Untersturmführer!" he said, as the rest of the detachment—a half-dozen strong—mirrored the salute and came to some semblance of attention.

"Heil Himmler—at ease," said the youth, embarrassed. Looking at the sunken eyes, seeing several fingers blackened by frostbite, he felt like an imposter. Surely these men had been enduring the brutal Russian winter, probably as far back as '41, while Lukas was still scheming for ways to get out of school. He had no right to command soldiers such as these.

But one of the others was taking note of the unit insignia on Lukas Vogel's collar, and nodded in a manner of respect. "You're with the Hitlerjugend division?" he said. "We hear you gave the Americans a hell of a fight."

Lukas shook his head, again feeling that sense of shame. "We couldn't stop them," he admitted. "Tell me, are there any others of the division that have reached Berlin?"

The men looked at each other, shrugging shoulders and shaking heads before the original speaker—a corporal, who no longer looked contemptuous—replied. "We thought the whole unit had been wiped out on the Rhine. How did you get to Berlin?"

"I walked here," Lukas admitted, ashamed that he couldn't at least have come away with an armored car or a motorcycle. "I had to take a rowboat across the river," he said apologetically.

"Well, you fought like men," the corporal said.

"Are replacements gathering somewhere in the city?" asked the young officer. "I would like to report."

Now it was the guards who looked sheepish. "There's not much going on," the corporal said.

One of the others spoke up. "Word is that General Dietrich is trying to muster a defensive force just across the river," he said. "He has a couple of companies of SS panzers, a battalion of troops."

"We'd be over there ourselves," said the corporal, eager to explain. "Except we have orders to keep an eye on the gate."

"General Sepp Dietrich?" Lukas brightened immediately as the men nodded in affirmation. "Thanks—he'll know what to do. Tell me, how do I find him?"

"Pardon me, O mighty Untersturmführer, but what makes you think a man of General Dietrich's rank and status will find the time to let you kiss his hairy ass?" The corporal laughed raucously, and the guards joined in.

Lukas started to get angry, but he was too tired and cold. "He gave me these in the first place," he said, pointing to his insignia of rank. "For leading men out of a unit that was going over to Rommel."

The corporal's eyebrows raised, and the laughter stopped. "No shit? You actually know General Dietrich?"

Lukas nodded. "He was in Saint-Vith when we got there. He was standing on a corner talking to Obersturmbannführer Peiper."

"*Peiper?* Come on, boy, don't piss on my leg and tell me it's raining."

"No, he was there. Lots of units were coming in through Saint-Vith. It was very confusing. They were trying to sort everyone out. That's why he talked to me."

The guard shook his head. "If that ain't the damndest story—meaning no disrespect, sir. Well, perhaps the general will find time for you after all. And— hey, we really didn't mean to give you a hard time or anything, but if the general has room for a few more men, remember us, okay?"

Lukas got the directions—it was another two kilometers of walking, but that meant next to nothing to him. When he started toward the bridge over the River Spree, his step was lighter than it had been in a hundred miles.

NORTH BANK OF THE WARTA RIVER, POLAND, 1322 HOURS GMT

"You are Colonel Alexis Petrovich Krigoff?"

Krigoff examined the speaker, one of four men in black trench coats and clean, dark fedoras. They were from the NKVD, he knew at once, and—like any sensible Russian—he felt a tremor of nervousness in his belly as he made the identification. But he forced himself to remain outwardly calm, reassuring himself that they couldn't possibly be after him.

"I am Krigoff," he replied. He gestured with the sheaf of communiqués in his hand, the parcel that he had been carrying over to the army headquarters truck. "I am busy with important matters of army intelligence—what do you want?"

He was pleased to see the man's look of apology; the colonel had guessed right, and in fact these secret policemen obviously did not want to antagonize him.

"Forgive the interruption, Comrade Colonel. I was told to seek you out, to have you accompany us on our mission. We were hoping that you could take us to General Yeremko."

"Of course. I understand that the work of the state is more important than all other functions. It so happens that we may find the general at my intended destination in any event."

He led the four agents of across the muddy field. All of the headquarters encampments were like this, these days—the army was moving forward so fast that even the generals often slept in the backs of the trucks. Having fractured the initial German defensive line, they were rushing through Poland, drawing near to the prewar border with Germany. Only one more geographic obstacle, the Oder River, lay between the Red Army and Berlin.

The spokesman for the NKVD officers fell into stride beside Krigoff. Like all such, he looked dour and humorless, and Alyosha forced his own face to match that expression. Inside, however, he wanted to do handsprings. His note to the chairman had apparently provoked a very quick response, and he was delighted that he would be able to see this matter carried through to its conclusion.

"General Yeremko?" he called, knocking at the door of the large trailer that served as the office of the intelligence chief.

"Ah, Alexis Petrovich—come in," said Yeremko cheerfully. The old man had some color in his cheeks again, and in fact looked better than he had in days. "That was a nice bit of analysis you did. . . ." His voice trailed off when he saw the agents follow his subordinate through the door.

"These men are here to see you," Krigoff said, dispassionately. In point of fact, it occurred to him that he might have actually liked Yeremko, under other circumstances. Now, in wartime, with the responsibilities of national welfare on his shoulders, this was a luxury he could not allow himself to indulge.

"General Yeremko," said the NKVD spokesman, stepping forward. "We have instructions to escort you back to Moscow. Your hard work is being rewarded, and you shall have the chance to get some much-needed rest."

Yeremko was looking not at the speaker, but at Alyosha. The old man's eyes had the same expression Krigoff, when he had been a boy, had seen in the eyes of a puppy. The mongrel had come to him, once too often, to beg for food. Alyosha had kicked the dog away, and had gotten this same look in return. He winced; it was not a pleasant memory, and it angered him that this pathetic and incompetent old fool would bring it up at a time like this—a time that would be celebrated as Krigoff's own, personal triumph.

"Can I have a moment to collect my things?" asked the general sadly.

The NKVD agent shook his head. "I am sure that your replacement will have them sent along in good order," he said stiffly. "If that should prove necessary."

Yeremko's shoulders slumped, but he nodded in understanding and reached for his jacket and fur hat. As he pulled them on the bulky garments somehow made him seem even smaller.

"May I ask—who is to replace me as head of the intelligence section?"

"Yes," echoed Krigoff. "Who is the new chief?"

The agent pulled a paper out of his pocket and handed it to Alyosha. "Comrade Colonel, these are the instructions of no less than the chairman himself. You are to assume your new post, at once."

Only when Yeremko was led away, flanked on both sides by the four agents, did Krigoff allow himself that thin smile. This was a great victory, he knew, even though it meant much more work for him, greater responsibilities. He could get to those tasks in short order.

Then he would find Paulina, and tell her. He was already planning a small celebration.

15 FEBRUARY 1945

ARMEEGRUPPE H HEADQUARTERS, OUTSKIRTS OF FRANKFURT AM MAIN, GERMANY, 2236 HOURS GMT

The Douglas C-47 Dakota transport had been hastily painted with the new colors and insignia of the German Republican Army; for the sake of convenience, these had temporarily been established as the prewar Weimar standards. On a night mission like this, insignia hardly mattered. The plane was flying without lights in an overcast sky—the classic case of the black cat in the coal cellar at midnight.

Not much was left of the Luftwaffe in the old Armeegruppe B area of operation (minus Sixth Panzer Army, of course), and the Americans had eagerly "borrowed" most of the surviving Me-262 jet fighters to start the process of reverse engineering. In exchange, however, Rommel was able to count on American air support—a luxury that only those who had been on the receiving end of air superiority could appreciate fully—and even had a few American planes transferred into his army.

The transport pilot was an American captain seconded to the Germans, and the German operational commander rode in the copilot's seat. He could fly, but hadn't received more than a quick checkout in the C-47. He could spot, however.

"There!" The German commander pointed. Although the German spoke only a few words of English and vice versa, that was enough for this mission. Two parallel lines of lights pointed the way to their temporary runway.

The C-47 landed bumpily on the grassy field between lines of burning flares, cutting its twin engines as soon as it touched down, and rolled to a stop. Shadowy figures ran toward the plane, local partisans drafted for this special operation. The rear door swung open, and a line of black-clad commandos exited. Their faces were painted black; black knit hats were pulled over their hair.

The ground leader, a German man in civilian clothes, spoke rapidly. "We have two trucks waiting for you."

"Good," replied the erstwile copilot and team leader, also in German. "Drivers?"

"Wehrmacht uniforms, also ready."

"Good. We have less than half an hour to reach the headquarters compound."

"That should not be a problem. The traffic is virtually nonexistent."

"Let's go."

The commandos and several of the escorts moved off into the nearby woods separating the field from the road where the trucks were waiting. Their engines cranked as the men approached. The remaining partisans stayed behind. On a signal that the trucks had pulled away safely, the C-47 pilot started his engines again, swiveled the plane around, and started his takeoff taxi. Much lighter with the load delivered, the Dakota lifted quickly off the ground and started its return flight.

There was little need for conversation as the trucks rumbled toward the Armeegruppe H headquarters, an older military compound that dated back to World War I. The mission commander reviewed his maps as much to deal with pre-mission jitters as with any actual uncertainty about his plan. Large sections of the compound had been softened up by bomber raids over the past year, and it was relatively easy to sneak into broken sections of the fence in spite of guard patrols.

The mission commander divided his team into pairs. Each had a name and a location. Silently, they moved off. The commander and his partner had two names on their list. The first, an SS-Brigadeführer, had a house on Generals' Row. There was only a single sentry so far behind the lines, and he was removed easily. Then into the house, up stairs that creaked—not loudly enough to wake a sound sleeper, but agonizingly loud for the people climbing the stairs—and to the master bedroom. And then came an end to subtlety: one hard kick and the door flew open. A sleepy brigadeführer and his mistress woke, startled and disoriented.

The commandos had orders to capture, not kill, if possible, and so while the commander held his Schmeisser at the ready, his partner took cuffs from a black satchel and locked the brigadeführer to the bed stanchion. A rough gag shoved into his mouth stopped the sputtering, confused protests.

The terrified mistress, however, had not been anticipated. "We're not going to hurt you," the mission commander said, but who would believe an armed man in black bursting into one's bedroom? He stifled her scream with his gloved hand, but she bit him, hard, and struggled to escape. It took both commandos to subdue her, to tie her to the other side of the bed and gag her. She glared at them with murder in her eyes.

"Maybe she should be the SS officer, *hein*?" the mission commander said to the immobilized brigadeführer, who had just now woken up enough to sputter helplessly through his gag. "Good fighter, that one." He saluted the imprisoned woman. "Someone will be along in a few hours," he said, and the two men headed for their next destination, further along Generals' Row.

The second sentry posed no more problems than the first, but instead of quietly opening the door, the mission commander knocked once, paused, then three more times. With that, the door opened, and a Wehrmacht officer wearing colonel-general insignia came out.

"Herr Generaloberst!" said the mission commander, coming to attention and saluting.

"Welcome to Armeegruppe H headquarters. Have all my troublesome officers been immobilized?"

"In progress now. We're here to protect you."

"Damn straight. I don't fancy ending up like Heinz Guderian." Generaloberst Karl Student grinned in the darkness. "I guess this means it's official—Armeegruppe H has just joined the German Republican Army." He reached out his hand.

"Welcome to the winning team, General," said the mission commander, shaking it.

17 FEBRUARY 1945

NINETEENTH ARMORED DIVISION, WEST OF WEIMAR, GERMANY, 0612 HOURS GMT

"This is General Custer calling for Major Reno. Do you read?"

Ballard winced at the code names he and Smiggy were using for the day. They had seemed kind of amusing at first, but the present was turning out to be just a little too close to the past for his comfort. The connection was undeniably apt, however, for if any U.S. Army unit was venturing into the equivalent of Indian country right now, it was the Nineteenth Armored.

How long had it been since they'd had a good, American presence on their left flank? More than two weeks, by Ballard's reckoning. And during that time they had done nothing but race onward, as fast as they possibly could. Once again, good old Nineteenth Armored was forming the vanguard of Third Army. That army was spreading out across the country, liberating towns in Germany even more quickly than they had in France. Ballard knew that the US Seventh Army and the French First Army had crossed the Rhine south of them, and these forces were moving strongly through the Black Forest, driving on Nuremberg and Munich. Hodges' First Army, too, had crossed the great river barrier, and was moving into north Germany, though its front remained a hundred miles or more behind Third Army's. Farther to the north the Nazis had kept control of their armed forces, and were making a staunch defense of the Ruhr Valley and the north German plain against British and Canadian forces.

Of course, there were good, solid German units on Ballard's left flank, most notably Rommel's favored Panzer Lehr. Just a month ago Ballard's men had been engaged in a knock-down, drag-out battle with that same unit, and now they were protecting each other from the rogue units of SS and loyalist Wehrmacht that still made the German countryside a dangerous place.

As if to underscore his thoughts, Ballard heard a crackling chatter of machine-gun fire in the distance, underscored by the crump of several tank or antitank guns. At least one of them was a deadly 88, the colonel could tell by the sharp crack of sound.

"General Custer—this is Major Reno!" the radio chattered into life.

"This is Custer—go ahead," snapped Ballard anxiously.

"We have a strong defensive position in front of us," Smiggy reported. "One 88 with a commanding view of the road and the fields—no good cover, and I have a report of tanks moving around my left. Can you get some guns on the bastards?"

"I'll patch you through to Crazy Horse," Ballard responded, using the code name for Major Diaz and the artillery battalion. "They're not far back—if you can give him some coordinates, he should be able to help you out."

Meanwhile, the Sherman tanks of CCA were breaking off of the road in near-instinctive reaction, pushing through a copse of light woods that provided little serious obstacle to the churning M4s. Ballard sat in the turret of his command tank and, for the time being, simply watched. These were veterans, these men of the Nineteenth Armored, and they knew what to do and how to do it.

For the first phase of the fight, they gave ground—stubbornly—and allowed the Germans to reveal their strength and dispositions. The American tanks fired rapidly, high explosive shells exploding in the woods. The Germans played it cautiously, firing from concealment, but pressing forward with enough armor to convince Ballard that he was facing his first major enemy formation since the Rhine crossing. One of the Shermans exploded in an orange billow of fire, and several more kicked into reverse, rolling backward through the trampled saplings, firing as they retreated.

At the same time the tanks of his second company were moving quickly. He saw them disappear into a little draw, driving over the lip of the embankment and dropping out of sight one after the other, and he knew that they had discovered some sort of road—or even a forest cart path; the nimble tanks didn't need much of an avenue to make headway—leading around the enemy flank. The tanks of Company A retreated only far enough to conceal their hulls behind the raised roadway, and from here they blazed away furiously. Now the tankers were loading armor-piercing rounds, and at least one scored a direct hit on a panzer pushing through the ravaged woods.

Moments later, artillery shells screamed overhead and plunged into the lightly forested terrain, sending rippling shock waves through the air and great bursts of fire, smoke, dirt, and splintered timber showering through the air. Ballard could sense the hesitation in the German tanks, which couldn't have numbered more than an understrength company. Still, it was a little startling to encounter even this much of an enemy force, after the days of open-field running that had brought them already halfway to Berlin.

But now the momentum of the attack was clearly broken. At least two more panzers were burning, struck by some combination of Sherman antitank rounds or lucky artillery strikes. His infantry, firing with small arms and a few .50-caliber machine guns, had forced the German troops to ground. Everywhere the enemy was seeking shelter, the men more concerned with saving their own lives than pressing home the offensive against the American veterans.

It was time for the coup de grâce.

"This is General Custer, for Wild Bill—come in, Wild Bill."

"This is Wild Bill, General. What do you want me to do?" Captain Kelly, of his infantry company, asked the question in his Boston twang.

"Time to take the action home—can you get your boys up and moving?"

"Roger, General Custer—we'll be at them in a minute."

"Sitting Bull, this is Custer. Are you in position?" Next he got in touch with the captain in charge of Armor Company B, and learned that the Shermans that had vanished into the woods had moved far past the German armor, and were ready to smash the enemy in the rear.

"All right, Sitting Bull, Wild Bill, let's get this wagon train on the road!"

The counterattack unfolded in textbook fashion. The German tanks were using a low ridge as cover but a half-dozen speedy Shermans burst from the woods directly behind them, coming up on the panzers and knocking out two of them with the first volley of shots. The others quickly withdrew, driving wildly along the crest of the ridge, then skidding down into a ravine on the far side. The whole platoon was composed of obsolete Mark IIIs, a sign of just how far down into the barrel these Nazi bastards were scraping.

Only that 88 was providing a serious threat, and Ballard had his driver move forward so that he could get a look as his infantry crawled forward down a long, deep ditch, looking to take the antitank gun in the flank. The GIs moved quickly but carefully, and he was pleased to see that they were avoiding casualties even as they drew ever closer to the gun, which was dug in behind the stone wall of a small farmyard.

Even so, Ballard was surprised by how quickly the shooting stopped; he expected that it would take another fifteen minutes before his men could have brought the defensive position under direct fire. But he saw Germans coming forward with their hands up, and his own men advancing to take them prisoner. Their morale must have been even lower than he had thought.

He was even more surprised when the radio again chattered, Smiggy sounding quite surprised, although quite pleased as well. He even forgot to employ the code.

"Colonel, you won't believe this, but the sons of bitches are surrendering! We have a hundred prisoners already, and more of them are coming out of the woods with their hands up!"

"More than a hundred?" Ballard said, surprised in his own right. "Are we bagging a whole battalion?"

"Actually," Smiggy said, chuckling, "from what this captain is telling me— mind you, my German's not so good, and his English is worse—it sounds like the whole of Army Group H has just gotten orders to hand over their weapons, and turn themselves in to the first Americans they can find."

Ballard whistled, and put down the microphone. He could see whole columns of Germans coming into view, far more than the hundred men of

Smiggy's first estimate. He'd seen plenty of things, good and bad, in this war, but this was one of the most memorable.

"Move out," he told his driver, and the Sherman started to rumble forward, as the prisoners were gathering themselves into long, disciplined ranks.

"I'll be damned" was all the colonel could think to say.

THE WHITE HOUSE, WASHINGTON, DC, 1630 HOURS GMT

General Leslie Groves passed easily through White House security. It was, he noted with dry amusement, much less strict than the security surrounding several of his own facilities. He signed in, showed his military identification card, allowed the uniformed Secret Service guards to inspect his briefcase, pinned on his access badge, and waited for the escort to take him to see the president. He wasn't patted down; he could think of two or three different ways he could have smuggled a pistol in. He had no intention of doing so; he always looked at any building with an eye to how its security could be compromised. It was part of his job.

As he was escorted into a working office area, no one covered up papers or folders and file drawers were open. One file cabinet actually had its key sticking in its lock! He would have been giving out demerits, if not courts-martial, right and left if any facility of his had been so careless about security procedures, but then this was the civilian world, for all that the president was his commander in chief.

The difference in discipline was one way the White House stood apart from Leslie Groves' world. The other one that struck him most strongly was its age. The Pentagon, where Groves kept his main office, was brand new. All the facilities of the Manhattan Project were new. The White House was old. Not only old, but run-down, worn, even shabby. There were holes in the carpet. Areas of paint were peeling. Much of the furniture was secondhand. The upholstery had tears in it. The first time he'd ever been in the White House it had come as a great shock to him, a shattering of an illusion he hadn't been aware he held.

In the secretarial area outside the Oval Office, one of the president's staff was fitting a stencil onto a mimeograph, an A. B. Dick drum-ink machine that had seen better days. She pressed the ink lever a few times and began to turn the crank. Dissatisfied with the first few copies, she kept pressing the ink lever, until suddenly the ink can burst, and thick black mimeograph ink oozed over the machine, her hands, and onto her dress. "Damn it!" she said, jumping back. "Look at this! My dress is ruined!" She ran out of the room to try to wipe off as much ink as she could.

Grace Tully, the president's personal secretary, had gone over to see what could be salvaged from the mimeograph disaster when she saw Groves. "Oh—good afternoon, General Groves. Sorry about this little mess. After you finish the project you're working on, maybe you can turn your attention to copying technology."

Groves laughed. "Oh, I'm afraid that's far too difficult for me. I'd better stay with simpler challenges. But I do agree there's got to be a better way."

"I don't blame you. The president's running a little late today, but the people in there need to be shooed out anyway. Why don't you just go right on in?"

"Thank you, ma'am," Groves replied.

The chaos outside was nothing compared with the chaos inside. Groves had figured out that this was President Roosevelt's preferred style of management, but it still seemed somehow improper as far as he was concerned. There were several conversations going on at cross-purposes, including two telephone conversations, neither currently involving the president himself. A large stack of papers resided in the inbox, and the stack seemed to be growing rather than shrinking. But what alarmed Groves most of all was the way Roosevelt seemed to have shrunk since their last meeting. He was failing fast. The human dynamo that once could thrive in the center of the whirlwind was now unable to control it, and the people surrounding the president could not step past their own individual agendas to serve him properly. Roosevelt had always refused to appoint a chief of staff, but he needed one desperately. This job was going to kill him, and he needed to survive a few more months at least. The way he was going, that seemed unlikely to Groves.

He stepped forward. "Mr. President. I'm your twelve-thirty appointment," he said in full parade voice, coming to attention, cap under his arm. Everyone else stopped talking and looked at him.

He stared at each one in turn, and slowly, one by one, they made their exits. "Gotta go," said one of the men on the phone, and the other quickly hung up as well. Finally, the room was down to Groves, FDR, and one man who did not budge. The man wore a Navy captain's uniform.

"Who are you, Captain, if I may ask?" asked Groves.

"His doctor, sir," replied the Navy captain.

"Are you cleared for Top Secret, Captain?" asked Groves.

"He's cleared for anything I'm cleared for," said FDR in a weak voice. "It's okay, Leslie. I've got his firstborn locked up in a safe place." He smiled. "Sit down."

"Thank you, sir," said Groves.

"We already know what we're going to talk about, don't we?" FDR said. He managed a slight smile. "I'm a little tired today, so I thought we'd cut out the middleman."

"All right, Mr. President. You're going to tell me how much you need me to have the bomb ready more quickly, and I'm going to tell you how we're already pushing ahead as fast, if not faster than humanly possible. You're going to ask me to go faster, and I'm going to tell you I'll do everything I can, but there's only so much that can be done. Is that about right?"

"I like the military mind, Leslie. Right to the point, don't beat around the bush, don't waste time. I believe you. I believe you'll do the best any human being can possibly do, and I am as confident today as I have been from the start that this program is in the best of hands. Thank you Leslie. Thank you very much."

"No thumbscrews today, Mr. President?" Groves asked.

FDR laughed, but the laugh turned into a cough. "I'm fresh out of thumbscrews. I'm going to have to order Third Army and the German Republican forces into Berlin, where they'll be sticking out like a thumb. The Soviets will be able to surround them, and we won't be able to shore up their position. There's only one thing that will get them out, if the Soviets decide to get sticky about it. I can slow things down with talk-talk, but only for a while. Then, I hope I'll have something available to use to pry them out. April, I think it will be." He reached forward and patted Groves on the hand. "You'll do your best. I know it."

"April." Groves shook his head. It was an impossible deadline. The old man had twisted his arm again. Somehow, he'd have to find a way to shave even more time out of his project. He had no idea if it would even be physically possible.

Groves looked at the dying old man in the wheelchair. He fit well with the shabby old White House. Yet this man had, through little else than force of will, shaped the greatest coalition the world had ever seen to fight the biggest war in history. He had, in the process, changed the direction of Leslie Groves' life and made him responsible for the most complex scientific and engineering project ever undertaken. He started to chuckle.

"Thought of a good joke, Leslie? I could use a laugh," FDR said.

"I just realized, sir, that I was only working on the second-most-powerful weapon in this war."

"Oh? What's the first?"

"I'm looking at him, sir."

LONDON, ENGLAND, 2000 HOURS GMT

It's been observed to the point of cliché that government agencies view their internal competitors with more dismay than their national enemies. When Kim Philby, officially employed by MI-6, the Secret Intelligence Service, needed to examine matters on British soil—the turf of MI-5, the British Security Service—on behalf of his true employers, the Communist Party of the Soviet Union, he knew that he was crossing into enemy territory, and would need to move with extreme caution.

As part of that caution, Philby followed the sort of routine that would lull

potentially suspicious observers. He left his office at the same time most evenings, unless a major operation was in progress or the work demands were
otherwise unusually high. He ate dinner at one of a small number of restau-
rants in his neighborhood, Indian one night, a chop house another, a pub with
two or three acquaintances still another. He had a walk after dinner, weather
permitting, did some reading or paperwork back in his flat, turned out the
lights at a reasonable hour, and got a good night's sleep.

He had enough variety to make a normal life, but not enough to give any
hypothetical observer cause to work hard to keep tabs on him. Within his limited universe, he had eight message drops, twelve alert points, and three preset
escape routes, should he have to leave in a hurry.

Dinner and walk complete, Philby turned on the lamp on his desk, drew
out a pad of lined paper, and began a methodical ticking off of points.

He viewed his tasking with some skepticism. In the normal course of his
duties, he was privy to a fair amount of daily information about the size and
scope of Allied forces. While there was a substantial level of detail available
only on a "need to know" basis, he didn't need to know it for the purposes of
his current mission, which was to assess the overall level of the Western Allies'
ability to take and hold Berlin against determined Soviet opposition. As long
as the general information was reasonably accurate, it would serve.

Were there major resources capable of affecting the outcome of a Berlin
campaign not part of the generally available information? If so, what kinds of
resources would they be? He began to jot notes as he thought. The first and most
obvious type of hidden resource would be a secret weapon of some sort. There
were always secret weapons of one sort or another under development. Most
of them tended to fizzle out, which was the nature of scientific research. Of the
ones that entered production and service, the majority tended to prove somewhat less world-shaking than originally advertised. A few, such as radar, were
truly revolutionary.

Another resource would be the shifting of forces from one theater of war to
another, either delaying action on another front, or possibly discovering that the
other front required far fewer forces than originally thought. The shocking surrender of Army Group H the previous day would allow Rommel's army group
and Bradley's army group to move forward at a greater rate. Sir Miles Dempsey's
mostly British and Canadian Twenty-first Army Group, in the north—Dempsey
had replaced the late Field Marshal Montgomery—still faced the German Army
Group G in the north, but would tomorrow bring news that Army Group G had
also surrendered? If not, perhaps he could find a way to complicate any such
action, slow up any movement on that front. He jotted notes in outline order,
checking them in order of action. For many items, he knew the answers already;
for a few, he would begin his investigations tomorrow.

Back to secret weapons. He jotted down a list of projects with which he had some familiarity. He could relatively easily check into the status of those projects; with previous knowledge came a lessening of suspicion when curiosity intruded. If there did turn out to be a secret weapon serious enough to alter the military balance, however, random questioning would be greeted with far less generosity. How, then, to probe for secret weapons without triggering a dangerous response?

He decided on a strategy by knowledge area. For a potential field such as rocketry, for example, he would identify and call upon a well-known and elderly figure in the field, one unlikely to be personally selected to work on such a project, but one likely instead to be part of the field's gossip chain. Philby had a well-developed sixth sense; it came with the job. He could listen to general chatter and from what was said (and frequently from what was not said) draw surprising amounts of insight.

A famous contemporary poster cautioned against chatting with strangers. It read, "Loose Lips Sink Ships." Most people laughed at it, thinking it a rather silly exercise in wartime paranoia. But Philby knew better. All he needed to do was be at the right party, in the right company, and idle chatter would form itself into patterns, almost as if by magic. And from there would come clues and eventually conclusions.

By nine-fifteen Philby had finished his lists. It took him approximately ten minutes to memorize them, then he carefully burned his working papers and once again flushed the ashes. He turned his desk light off and his reading lamp on, then lit his pipe. He picked up Gibbon where he had left off the previous night, and exchanged the worries of the twentieth century for the challenges of the second.

18 FEBRUARY 1945

NEUE REICHSKANZLEI, BERLIN, 1022 HOURS GMT

"You lying, double-crossing bastard! I'll kill you for this! I'll tear your fucking heart still bleeding from your chest and shove it down your throat!" Heinrich Himmler's thin voice screeched his rage. His round, chinless face was red and swollen; his eyes bugged out beneath his wire-rim glasses. "You come here and sit in this office after suborning the treason of yet another of my generals!" The Führer of the Third Reich was standing right in front of Günter von Reinhardt as he screamed into his face. Himmler was much shorter than the aristocratic von Reinhardt and had to tilt his head back to look at him. They were close enough for bits of spittle to hit von Reinhardt's face.

"General Student's change of allegience had nothing to do with me," von Reinhardt lied. He worked to keep his voice calm, but firm, as he argued. "Do you think I'm the only intelligence officer or agent Field Marshal Rommel has? Or do you think I'm stupid enough to put myself in your clutches right after the act? Besides, even if it were me, do you expect our side to implement a truce during these negotiations? I note that Army Group G continues to fight in the north. Should I take that as evidence of your bad faith?"

"Don't talk to me about 'bad faith,' you contemptible little slug!" screamed Himmler in return. "You're the traitor here, and so is your master Rommel! You're an offense in the eyes of Germany! You're unworthy to call yourself a German officer! You oath-breaking, lying *Hurensohn!*"

Von Reinhardt could tell he was centimeters away from being shot. Having already been shot, he was not happy about repeating the prospect; on the other hand, a certain dread of the unknown was now missing. His chest ached terribly, and he felt faint under the physical and emotional strains of his position. In a way, that helped him cope better with his current situation.

He looked at the screaming führer and was momentarily reminded of seeing Adolf Hitler in a similar rage. Fortunately, he was no longer subordinate to either man. Putting all the forcefulness into his voice that he could, he stated firmly, "This is business. It is not personal. We are resolving the future of Germany as well as the future of Heinrich Himmler." It was the first time he had ever spoken Himmler's surname aloud.

"The future of Germany? National Socialism is the future of Germany! The Third Reich is the future of Germany!" Himmler's tantrum, if anything, actually increased in volume. Unlike their earlier encounter, this temper was not faked, not calculated. That was dangerous for everyone concerned.

"That may be so, but the future you are discussing is a long-term future, not a short-term one. If you do not manage the short term correctly, there will not be a long term. Do you want to save your cause and save your life?"

The discipline of difficult negotiation was to focus on the interest of the other party, not merely on one's own interest. Only if the other party saw an advantage to be obtained could a negotiated solution possibly work. An angry opponent was a disadvantage to both sides because an angry opponent was often more interested in harming the other party than in helping himself. The Nazis had always been more interested in hurting their enemies than in helping themselves. That was one of their fatal flaws.

"I don't need your help to save National Socialism, you treasonous, scheming bastard! I'll make you pay for this! You'll beg me to die before it's over!"

"What will Rommel do if he has to kill Germans in order to reach Berlin and take over? What will he do to you if he gets his hands on you? You ordered him killed, remember?" When an adversary crowds your personal space, it may be cultural, it may be deliberate, but either way, one must never back up. Move forward, bring yourself even closer.

There—he saw a small chink in the führer's armor with his last gambit, a flicker of doubt in Himmler's eyes. He sought to exploit his opening. "You need time, you need resources to rebuild, you need to escape the trap of this city. It's the only way left in which you can still win. Let's work together to get you safely away. Rommel has an open road until he reaches the outskirts of Berlin. You don't want to fall into Rommel's clutches. Trust me."

"Trust you? Trust you! Why should I trust a lying traitor?" The screaming was weakening now. The question about trust was no longer rhetorical. "Prove to me that I can trust you" meant "I want what you are offering," and that meant the game had changed once again.

"You can only trust what you can guarantee, Reichsführer," von Reinhardt said in softer, more soothing tones. "I don't ask for trust, I offer proof."

"It's a good thing," grumbled Himmler. "I still don't trust you."

"Of course not," replied von Reinhardt. "This is business. That's why you were smart to have Peiper open this channel in the first place. You've always understood what's at stake." Flattery is inexpensive. The smarter the other person feels, the more relaxed he becomes, the more receptive to the process.

"Yes, that's right, that's right," said Himmler, moving behind his desk but not sitting, walking back and forth. "What do you propose?"

Von Reinhardt sat down, relieved to have the initial gambit over. He would have to take care that his sense of relief and the accompanying euphoria did not weaken his discipline and judgment. One danger in this kind of negotiation was that by identifying with the interests and goals of the other party, one could get swept away in the eagerness to reach agreement. That's why it was wise to make someone other than the front-line negotiator responsible for the final decision. The final decision would be Rommel's. Still, he wanted to return with a workable deal.

"Let's start with both of our goals. Field Marshal Rommel's goal is simple: Berlin, so he can defend Germany against the Slavic hordes. You want to preserve the promise of National Socialism, which requires you and other important members of the government to have privacy, wealth, and an opportunity to rebuild. This cannot be achieved in Berlin, where the options are Rommel and the Western Allies or Marshal Zhukov and his Communist thugs. You cannot leave Berlin safely without cooperation from at least one of those parties. You must carry real liquid wealth, mostly gold, of an amount that will fill several trucks. You need safe conducts and a place to go, one that does not expose you to an easy double-cross. Do I understand correctly?"

The hook had been fully set, von Reinhardt could see. This gave him quite a lot of satisfaction, but now he would have to reel this big fish in slowly and carefully. He kept his face carefully neutral, his eyes continually studying his opponent's expressions and body language.

Himmler continued to pace. "I know where to go; there is a safe haven. There is wealth already stockpiled, but it's not enough. I will need more. And there are people—people I'll need. I can choose them. Yes, yes, I understand I am struggling against difficult odds, but I've known that even before the führer died. But there is still a chance, still a chance . . ."

Von Reinhardt was surprised to notice that Himmler was essentially talking to himself. But that was a very good sign, because it meant that "I want what you are offering" had now trumped "Prove to me I can trust you." The desire created its own proof, and the mechanism was von Reinhardt's understanding of Himmler's goals. Von Reinhardt had to struggle to keep a smile off his face. Instead: empathy, eye contact, head nodding up and down in the same rhythm as the führer paced behind his desk.

"There is still a chance, Reichsführer. What you want is quite possible, and in everyone's best interest. Let's see if we can work out the details together."

"Very well," replied Himmler, a slight absentmindedness in his voice revealing that he was still looking inward at his own vision. Suddenly, though, Himmler looked up, looked sharply at von Reinhardt, and von Reinhardt could feel the probing stare. "You *were* the right man for the Soviet mission, weren't you? You're very skilled. I wish you were still on my side."

In the compliment was a warning: *Don't take me for granted or assume I'm too dumb to understand what you're doing.* Von Reinhardt could hear it clearly. "When the interests of the different parties are aligned, we're all on the same side," he replied, and that seemed to be the right thing to say, because

Himmler sat down in the high-backed chair behind his desk and leaned forward. "Tell me what you have in mind."

Von Reinhardt leaned forward as well and began to talk.

THIRD ARMY MOBILE HQ, CROSSROADS IN THE
THÜRINGER WALD, GERMANY, 1110 HOURS GMT

The jeeps roared up the steep road, following the twisting switchbacks between frowning bluffs lined with dark firs. Snow lay heavy across the ground, drifts mounded especially deep in the sunless depths of the primordial woods. One by one, the drivers backed off the gas as they neared the crest of the ridge. The middle jeep turned out of the narrow road to park in a natural overlook next to a large Mercedes staff car while the other two jeeps continued on. Maintaining an army on the move had something in common with cowboys moving a herd across the plains; the jeeps were the outriders, rounding up stragglers and strays and keeping the dogies rollin'.

A flag with three white stars fluttered from the fender of the jeep that stopped. General George S. Patton pushed himself from the front seat of that vehicle, nodding as he took in the vista of rolling hills and dark pine forests. He raised his binoculars and scrutinized the road before them, for the several kilometers it remained visible before the next ridge. A Sherman tank was visible before him, though it quickly disappeared around a gentle bend. On the far horizon he saw a string of half-tracks cresting the elevation and rapidly vanishing from sight on the other side.

Pronouncing himself satisfied, the general strode to the shoulder of the road, unzipped his trousers, and relieved himself. When he had finished, he planted his fists on his hips and looked around. Ahead of him, at the very edge of the ridge, stood a man in a leather trench coat holding a pad of paper, watching the moving line of vehicles and sketching. Patton walked toward him. It was Rommel.

"Nice spot for a couple of tourists," Patton joked. "This is a fine view!"

"Indeed," replied the Desert Fox. "There is good hunting in these woods— for deer and boar, during better times."

"Right now, it's open season on Nazis," the American general replied. "But the bastards seem to be pretty scarce. That's the tail end of Fourth Armored up there, and I can barely keep up with them. Maybe all of Himmler's boys have gone to ground for good."

Rommel nodded hopefully. "We haven't encountered any resistance stronger than a platoon since crossing the river. I am beginning to think we'll have an open road for as far as General Eisenhower wants us to go."

"The real prize is out there," Patton said, pointing unerringly on a line east by northeast. "I've been hammering at Ike to turn us loose, send us all the way to Berlin, but he keeps hemming and hawing."

"We will go to Berlin, General Patton. One way or another. You have my word on it," said Rommel with certainty in his voice.

"Yeah? I hope you're right. But listen, Rommel—Do you mind if I call you Rommel?"

"Not at all. I will call you Patton. Unless you prefer George . . . or is it 'Georgie'?"

Patton laughed. "Patton suits me fine. Thanks. But listen, Rommel—Berlin is only the first stop. You know where I want to go?"

"Where?"

"I want to kick the commie bastards all the way back to Moscow."

Rommel continued to sketch. "It's a nice thought, but personally, I would be satisfied merely keeping them out of Germany."

"Why? Don't you know that they'll be back? They won't rest until every inch of Europe is red."

"Perhaps. But Europe has seen so much war, so much destruction, that I'm afraid it cannot take very much more. If you're dead, it makes little difference whose flag flies over your grave. Another major war on top of everything else the twentieth century has given us, and there would be no victor."

"That's pretty defeatist, Rommel. I'm surprised at you."

Rommel chuckled. "Remember, Patton, my friend, I have been defeated. Of course, when it comes to war, I have been the most fortunate of men. I went through the First World War without experiencing trench warfare and the Second World War without experiencing the Russian Front." He finished his sketch and turned over the page.

"I didn't know you were an artist," Patton said.

"I'm not," Rommel replied. "I do a little sketching, it's true, but it's mostly to fix the picture in my mind." The pencil sketch was rough, with quick outlines for vehicles and men. The men were articulated stick figures, but quite animated. The scene was surprisingly vivid, showing a military operation in progress.

"That's pretty good," Patton observed.

"Thank you," Rommel replied. "I make the drawings and write a daily summary that forms the raw material for the books I plan to write when this is over. I will return to the war academy, I expect, and spend my remaining years writing and teaching the operational arts of war. I look forward to it. I seem to have an aptitude for the craft of making war, but had that not been my calling, I think I would have made a fine engineer and been quite satisfied with that life."

Patton looked out over the ridge. "I suppose I'll write a book and teach as well, but I'm not looking forward to it at all."

"No?"

"No. Ever seen a greyhound dog?"

"A racing hound, right?"

"Yep. Bred for one purpose, not good for anything else. That's me. My entire life is about this. When it's over, I'm just marking time till I die. If I'm lucky, I get killed by the last bullet."

"It's a great shame, my friend, that you were not born German. You Americans have come over here late in the war with the aim of finishing it. With huge armies and immense power, you move through any obstacle, and you don't have the opportunities for creativity that come only to those who are short of resources. You would have gotten your appetite better satisfied as a German."

"You're damn right, Rommel. I admire you people, I really do. You planned and fought a war against the rest of the world put together and damn near won. A hell of an accomplishment. A *hell* of an accomplishment."

"In the area of military strategy and tactics, I thank you for your compliment. I'm afraid, though, that Germany has much to answer for in other spheres—aggression against its neighbors, inhumanity against its own citizens and civilians among its neighbors . . ."

Patton waved his hand. "Liberal bullshit, if you ask me. But, hell, let's not talk politics. That's not what they hire generals to do, anyway, right?"

"Exactly. Taking Berlin, on the other hand, is exactly what generals are here to do."

Patton laughed. "You got that right, Rommel. Shit, the Brits are still taking their sweet time crossing the river up north, while we've ripped the belly of the country open." Patton knew that the British offensive was facing much heavier opposition than his own advance; still, that knowledge did not to diminish the delight he took in the comparison. "We should take Berlin, then come back and help Dempsey mop up around the Ruhr." General Sir Miles Dempsey, who had been commanding the British Second Army, had been promoted to field marshal and taken command of the Twenty-first Army Group after the death of Montgomery during the Fuchs am Rhein offensive. "Last time I talked to Ike, he sounded like he was coming around to that idea. Now that the fucking communists are back in this game, I think he's starting to see that we could have some real problems if we *don't* get to Berlin first."

Rommel smiled at that, but tactfully made no reply.

"Well, another day or two of this, and then we'll get to some open country, right?" Patton remarked. "Then we can really let these hounds loose to run."

"Ah, the hunt, again," replied the German. He gestured to the vehicles waiting with idling engines. "Then perhaps we should get back to our saddles?"

"I like the way you think—and the way you make war," General Patton agreed, shaking Rommel's hand before turning back to his jeep. "Let's do this again in a few days! Maybe by then the Big Boss will have come to his senses—and we can plan a parade in front of the Reichstag!"

"It would be my pleasure," the field marshal replied, with a little bow and a click of his heels. The two commanders returned to their vehicles. Rommel stood at the door of his staff car as Patton climbed into his jeep. The Desert Fox saluted again as the three jeeps roared into motion, one after the other starting down the next descending slope.

EXCERPT FROM WAR'S FINAL FURY,
BY PROFESSOR JARED GRUENWALD

Field Marshal Walther Mödel had taken every precaution to keep his commanders from switching sides, recognizing the temptation posed by Rommel's German Republican Army. Senior staff were shuffled to keep any general from having a completely trustworthy team; the Gestapo routinely bugged all headquarters offices; random transfers of key personnel were routine. Even at troop levels, SS troops were mixed in with regular Wehrmacht troops and even Volksgrenadier units, serving the classic medieval function of shooting those who would either retreat or surrender.

Mödel fully recognized the extent to which this would hamper military operations, but the alternative—as shown in the defection of Army Group H—was catastrophic.

Mödel, who committed suicide shortly after the Army Group H defection in order to avoid capture—"A field marshal worthy of his oath never becomes a captive or a pawn of his enemy," read his suicide note in a thinly veiled stab at Rommel—was a brilliant military officer, but had been dealt a losing hand.

In spite of all his precautions, there was a slow but steady hemorrhage of individuals and small units moving to the other side. To complicate Rommel's life, Mödel even arranged decoy defections—spies and saboteurs. This forced the German Republican Army to be more cautious in accepting surrenders. With the inevitable misunderstandings, it became understood that there were dangers involved in trying to change sides.

The full story of the surrender of Army Group H did not come out until well after the war. The officer/diplomat Günter von Reinhardt, who had been instrumental in the Soviet pact of the previous year, passed through Army Group H headquarters several times while on secret visits to Berlin on behalf of Rommel. Although both Army Group H commander Colonel-General Karl Student and von Reinhardt denied any collusion at the time, the two men had literally passed notes to one another under the very nose of the Gestapo. Student had identified those officers who might resist the surrender, and these officers were taken prisoner before the surrender was announced.

Although Mödel went to his death thinking of himself as a failure, the odds against his success were so high that it is unreasonable to judge this failure harshly. He tried to hold together an unstable front made of disaffected troops who saw a clear opportunity to join the winning team and still regard themselves as patriots. That initiative was surely doomed from the outset.

With Army Group H gone, only Army Group G (Upper Rhine) remained to give battle in the west, resisting the British and American armies who were battling toward the industrial heartland of the Ruhr. Because of the large number of SS divisions in Army Group G, it continued to resist, giving ground only slowly, but even its motivation was substantially diminished by the realization that Rommel now had a completely open road to Berlin.

OPERATION
WOLKENBRAND
18 FEBRUARY –
26 FEBRUARY 1945

On Wednesday, March 22, 1933, the first Concentration Camp will be opened in the vicinity of Dachau. It can accommodate 5,000 people. We have adopted this measure, undeterred by paltry scruples, in the conviction that our action will help restore calm in our country, and is in the best interests of our people.

—Heinrich Himmler
Commissioner of Police for the City of Munich
Munchner Neusten Nachrichten
March 21, 1933

18 FEBRUARY 1945

APPROACHING RAMSIA, THÜRINGEN, GERMANY, 0246 HOURS GMT

The jeep's headlights stabbed at the blanketing fog but failed to penetrate far. Snow patches on the road reflected and diffused what little light did penetrate, giving the illusion of driving through a ghostly tunnel. The jeep careered around a curve, going much too fast for weather conditions. Smiggy could barely keep his map spread out on his lap, and the beam of his flashlight danced up and down with the motion of the jeep.

"Hey there's a sign. Slow down," the recon captain ordered.

"Gotcha, Cap'n," replied the driver, a corporal named McConnell. As he began to brake, he waved his hand high in the air, signaling the other jeeps in the patrol to brake as well.

As the jeep slowed down, Smiggy checked his compass and then played his flashlight over the sign. "All right. Looks like the sign's in the right place." Altering road signs was a traditional way to confuse invaders. "We'll turn right and head past Ettersburg and on into Weimar." He picked up his walkie-talkie. "Hodad One to Big Kahuna."

"Big Kahuna, go ahead," came the crackling reply from his headquarters unit. Lieutenant Bucklin was holding down the fort coordinating reports. Smiggy liked being out at the edge of the recon area. He sometimes felt he had a sixth sense about the terrain, but it was only active when he was out there. When he briefed Major Keegan, the new G-2, he always enjoyed the "I was there" part best, because he could see the embarrassment on Keegan's face— the man was a chair warmer of the worst sort. Smiggy had originally thought the same of Sanger, Keegan's predecessor, but he'd finally decided the man had balls. Keegan had none. Smiggy was sure.

He toggled the walkie-talkie again. "Clear approach as far as Ramsia. Ettersburg next check in about fifteen minutes. Nothing going on here. What do you have?"

"Reports clear to Ottstedt and south, Hodad One. God knows how many kids with rifles, but no force concentration."

"Copy on the kids with rifles, Big Kahuna. They won't come out till the day shift. Thanks for the update. Hodad One out." Kids—Hitler Youth—were the biggest resistance the advancing Allies were facing. In the towns and cities, the Germans were waving American and prewar German flags as the Allied forces rumbled through. They loved all the Allies, but they loved Rommel the best. Smiggy had started thinking of Rommel as Ike's pet Nazi, a turncoat glory hound, and the way people made a big deal over him made Smiggy ill.

It was a running joke that there weren't any German Nazis other than the kids. The adults fawned over the troops like liberated Frenchmen. You'd think *they'd* been the oppressed victims of the war. But the kids were bad enough. Some of them were good shots, and none of them would surrender. Soldiers had to go in and kill them, and killing kids—even kids who were trying to kill you—was not the kind of war story you planned to tell your grandchildren.

Smiggy's recon battalion was screening ahead of the advancing German Republican Army and the American Nineteenth Armored, making sure there weren't any pockets of serious resistance left. So far, it had been a quiet night. "Let's go," he said to McConnell, and the jeep sped up again, leading his patrol deeper into the fog.

KONZENTRATIONSLAGER BUCHENWALD, THÜRINGEN, GERMANY, 0330 HOURS GMT

When you're playing poker and you can't spot the sucker, it's you. Digger O'Dell was a serious poker player, but he was never the sucker, though people often assumed—until they lost enough money—that the tall, slow-talking North Carolina boy would be an easy mark. Digger had what poker players call alligator blood: When the pressure was on, he always stayed calm. Here in Hell, his alligator blood was all that was keeping him alive. Stay low, stay out of sight, stay out of trouble, stay alive. He watched everything through carefully expressionless eyes, and played every small angle he could get.

A sudden shriek of wind from an opened door sliced through his thin blanket and woke him up. It was just the Russian prisoners on their morning rounds. They came early every morning to take away the dead. They stripped their clothes away to give to new inmates and wrote serial numbers on the corpses with black markers. Proper record keeping was necessary regardless of the circumstances.

There were new dead every morning. Sometimes it was from injury, more often it was illness, but a good amount of the time it was just the endless cold. You could tell, a lot of the time, when someone had just plain given up and died. Death was the only sure escape from Hell.

The door closed, cutting off the wind, but it was still nearly freezing inside. The cold had settled in for good, it seemed. Digger O'Dell wondered why everybody said Hell was hot. As far as he was concerned, it was cold. Cold was crueler. Digger knew that spring would eventually come and the cold would be banished, but it would come too late for him. A six-month veteran of the camp was already an old-timer; most of his colleagues would be long since dead. Digger was good at staying alive, but in Hell fate would always catch up with you sooner or later.

The barracks nominally had heat—there was a camp furnace that doubled as a crematorium—but it was minimal and intermittent. The hut where the Allied prisoners lived had a small heater of its own, a big metal barrel with a fire in it, at least whenever they had a few sticks of wood. Some days there was wood and other days there was none. There had been a little wood last night, but it had burned itself out sometime during the darkness, and by now the only temperature difference between inside the hut and the camp outside was the wind.

When Digger and Clausen were first turned over, he'd been surprised at first to find other Allied airmen in the camp, and asked why.

"We're terrorfliegers, haven't you heard?" said the ranking Allied officer, Leftenant Kirby, an Australian Lancaster pilot with a thick accent. "We're not honest soldiers; we're fucking war criminals. POW status is too good for the likes of us, mate." Most of the Allied inmates, all shot-down aviators, had made it to supposed safety with the French Resistance, but were caught in a massive roundup. A few more than 150 of them had been sent here so far. As far as they knew, they were all officially "missing and presumed dead." The Geneva Convention didn't apply in Hell.

The Allies—mostly American, but British, Canadian, and Australian as well—tended to stick together, and were normally assigned to the same slave-labor details, sometimes to factories and sometimes to farms. They didn't associate with the other inmates, but there wasn't a lot of energy for socializing anyway. They all shuffled through their duties in the same sleepwalking style as the less-privileged inmates, and their life expectancy was only a little better.

At first, the Allied prisoners had wanted to throw Carl-Heinz Clausen out of their barracks, but Digger held firm. "He's a good guy. He saved my life." So "Digger's Nazi" was kept around. Clausen could only do a little work, but Digger with his gimp leg covered for both of them as best he could. About a week ago, Clausen had gotten pneumonia in his poorly healed lung, and it was clear to Digger that the stocky German sergeant was going to be another janitorial job for the Russians within a few days at the most. He was running a high, delirious fever, high enough that he warmed Digger at night more than did the pitifully small fire.

If the Russians were here, roll call would be coming up soon. Digger hated to get up early—he'd miss the trumpet of doom if it came before ten o'clock—but with his still-aching leg he needed a good head start to end up in the relative safety of the middle of the pack. Besides, he had Clausen to worry about. The stocky feldwebel was still shivering as he'd done all night. Digger was half surprised he was still breathing. He slid his legs off the edge of the bunk he shared with four others, and started manhandling Clausen's inert form to pull him out of bed.

Roll call was hours of standing at attention outside in the frigid February weather, and God only knew what new fun and games the Nazis would introduce. Most prisoners would be sent on slave-labor details or to one of the subcamps—there were more than a hundred. The ones found "unsuitable for work" would be taken away for disposal, or often beaten to death on the spot. Daily there were executions or disciplinary whippings to witness, or maybe some casual brutality by some SS guard who just felt like it. Inmates would drop and fall from disease or exhaustion and then get beaten to death while the rest of them watched.

Suddenly the door opened from the outside, letting in a new blast of frigid wind that made Digger's teeth ache. The SS guards started screaming, *"Heraus! Schnell! Schnell!"* There were nearly nine hundred prisoners in the barracks, so there was always a jam at the door. Digger planned to be in the middle of the crowd; less chance of being randomly clubbed by a guard that way.

"Come on," Digger said urgently, shaking the feverish German. "Wake up. Roll call. *Schnell!*" Clausen's eyes opened, but did not focus. Digger wasn't sure Clausen even knew where he was anymore—not that that was necessarily a bad thing. But the German sergeant did get up. Digger held up Clausen with his arm and leaned against him with his bum leg, and they shuffled and hopped into the crowd squeezing through the door, successfully avoiding the guards.

The wind outside the barracks whipped through the thin prison garments everyone wore. Even the SS guards in their heavy coats were cold, and that made Digger hope roll call wouldn't be too terrible. If he watched carefully and kept moving, perhaps he and Clausen could dodge the work details for yet another day. They lined up, standing at attention, palms facing up—anything even slightly resembling a fist was punishable by death on the spot. Again, Digger had located a spot in the middle of the pack to minimize the chances of being singled out.

Damn. The guards were thick on the ground this morning, even in the terrible weather, and they were doing a selection. Whatever they were selecting for, Digger knew it wasn't anything he wanted part of. So far, they hadn't used captured Allied airmen for anything except heavy-labor details, but Digger wasn't counting on that being permanent policy.

The pattern quickly became clear. It was the Jews again. They normally got the shittiest end of the shit stick—the worst jobs, worst punishments, worst food, worst barracks. For the last week or so, they'd been rounding up Jews, thousands of them, men, women, and even children—there were children even here in Hell—walking skeletons for the most part, herding them into boxcars to be taken somewhere else. Where else he didn't know, and didn't want to.

He'd asked the Australian lieutenant if they were just being taken to a new slave-labor detail. The lieutenant had shaken his head slowly. Digger found it hard to believe that there were worse places than Buchenwald, but evidently that was the case.

The daily pile of dead normally included large numbers of Jews. All the prisoners were being worked to death, but the Jews faster than the rest. A couple of camp epidemics combined with the weather had sent the death rate sky high; there were nearly a thousand frozen bodies—corpsicles, the Americans called them—stacked like cordwood outside the furnace building. The crematorium couldn't keep up with demand.

The one virtue of the bitter cold was that the corpses didn't rot before they could be put into the furnace. The bodies were blue-gray and looked like mannequins.

While most of the SS guards were herding Jews, others were moving down the roll-call ranks in Digger's direction, closer and closer. Digger noticed the pattern—it was a sick-call selection. In most cases, sick call would be where he wanted to be, but here the best you could get was shoved into an infirmary barracks where you'd probably die sooner—no point in feeding the sick; they couldn't work anyway. And he knew that both he and Clausen would be thrown in. Carefully, he looked from side to side, looking for any escape.

The guards were about ten men away from him. One prisoner—Digger had seen him around, but didn't know him—was shivering uncontrollably. A guard shouted at him. The prisoner didn't respond quickly or fully enough, so the guard clubbed him in the head. He dropped to his knees. The prisoner tried weakly to fend off the blows, but the club hit again and again, cracking his skull so blood and brains were revealed, killing him. The blood began to well out, mixing with the mud, and then another prisoner—this one from the block next door, a German Communist—screamed and began running toward the fence.

They called that "suicide by guards." Two different guards fired submachine guns, stitching a line of bullet holes through the prison garment, sending the inmate sprawling facedown into the mud. Several other guards turned momentarily to watch, and Digger saw his opportunity. With alligator calm, he took a step backward, the dazed and feverish Clausen responding automatically, like a dance partner, then slipped to the other side of the guards, before both returned to attention. Several of the prisoners looked at him, but Digger's face continued expressionless and neutral. Soon enough everyone had returned to watching the selecting guards.

They'd escaped the sort. He'd won one more day in Hell for himself and Clausen. It wasn't much of a prize, but he wasn't going to give up yet. There was another game tonight, and still another one tomorrow.

GERMAN REPUBLICAN ARMY FORWARD
HEADQUARTERS, NEAR ERFURT, THÜRINGEN,
GERMANY, 0600 HOURS GMT

"Guten Morgen, meine Herren," said the Desert Fox with a cheerful grin, emerging from his office freshly dressed, washed, and shaved, and already at least two hours into his workday. "Glad you could make it on such a fine winter morning." The regular daily staff meeting always started at 0600 promptly, and the assembled officers began moving into the conference room for the morning's briefing. Rommel's new chief of staff, General von Manteuffel, made sure that people were assembled, and that the meeting moved along. It was an efficient headquarters.

Reid Sanger, not an early-morning riser by choice, slipped into the back of the conference room just as Rommel started the meeting and sat down next to his Nineteenth Armored compatriots Wakefield, Ballard, and Jackson. The three American officers now had their own translator, a sergeant, relieving Sanger of that extra duty.

Sanger was embarrassed at trailing his colleagues into the conference room. For a while, he kept trying to get to his desk before Rommel arrived in the morning, but it was futile. He suspected that Rommel's batman kept an eye on any challengers to "first in" status and woke the field marshal accordingly. Now, he had simply surrendered to the inevitable and contented himself by arriving at the morning meeting on time—or in this case, he amended silently, about a minute late.

Although he was not technically under Rommel's command, he caught the field marshal's good eye looking at him. Rommel always knew who was in on time and who was not. Sanger felt any disapproval on Rommel's part all too personally, so he quietly took his seat and flipped his notepad to the first blank page.

The agenda for the day was the agenda for most of the last few weeks—how to keep the German Republican Army moving forward. Armies, like other massive objects, have inertia. Making an army move is all too similar to prodding a reluctant mule. Wheeled and tracked vehicles give the impression of instant mobility, but tracked vehicles notoriously break down and wheeled vehicles require daily loading and unloading. Massive troop movements demand rail, but there was little unwrecked rail to be had throughout Germany. The Desert Fox was used to leading from the front, but now his days were spent speeding from unit to unit, pushing, nagging, and yelling at the laggards to load up and move out, to hurry forward in a huge, snarled game of leapfrog across a Germany newly devoid of its defenders.

Whether it was true relief at their liberation or merely cynical ingratiation with the new regime, wherever Rommel went he was greeted with crowds cheering, lining the streets, celebrating the New Germany and the new leader.

While the motives of the "liberated" Germans were subject to question, the motive of Rommel was obvious: he was enjoying himself to the limit.

Accompanied by his own personal motion-picture crew—a custom he had begun in North Africa—he was the daily star of his own newsreel. The running joke had it that he turned down the opportunity to be Chancellor of Germany because it was a demotion. That sort of popularity, Sanger observed, breeds enemies.

Sanger, as military liaison officer, was often the contact point for people wanting to complain about the Desert Fox. Only two days ago, Omar Bradley himself had shown up to "have a friendly chat." Nominally, the German Republican Army was an independent army-group command; in practice, they were moving on Third Army's front and so took operational guidance as a part of Bradley's Twelfth Army Group. The strange status of Rommel reflected itself in a confusing T/O.

Bradley's arrival had come as a surprise. The general, a quiet, homely man in a permanently wrinkled uniform, suddenly stuck his head into the office. "Sanger? Got a minute?"

Sanger, startled, immediately stood and saluted. "Of course, General. Come in. Coffee?" Sanger made a mental note to tell Sergeant Wilson, his secretary, to do a better job of warning him when the big brass were around. Of course, most of the brass liked the pomp and circumstance of command, so he usually got plenty of warning. That gave him a chance to kill the fatted calf. But there were a few senior officers who liked to sneak around without their escorts—they thought it improved their influence.

Bradley came in, sat down, waved off the offer of coffee, and lit up a cigarette. "How's the liaison role coming along, Sanger?"

"Great, sir, thank you. It's challenging, but very, very educational."

Bradley smiled crookedly, and absentmindedly stuck a finger up his nose. "Got a good relationship with Rommel? Can you tell him things he doesn't want to hear?"

"Well, to some extent, I suppose," Sanger said without strong assurance. If Rommel wanted to hear you, even a hint worked, but if he didn't, it was difficult to get through.

Bradley grinned and leaned forward. In a confidential tone, he said, "I bet it's easier than telling Georgie something *he* doesn't want to hear."

Sanger's meetings with Patton had given him the same impression. "I suspect you're right, sir. But is there something Rommel particularly needs to hear about?"

Bradley took out his finger and wiped it on his pants. "His victory laps."

"Sorry?"

"Victory laps. The way he shows up whenever we advance into a new town to catch all the glory before any of it escapes."

"Begging the general's pardon, but I think there's a bit more to it than that," Sanger replied carefully. He understood the complaint; it wasn't the first time he'd heard it. Rommel was certainly human enough to welcome—even to solicit—publicity, but there was a lot more on his agenda.

Bradley nodded. "Oh, I know. Get the people on the side of the new team and all that. He's already started his campaign to be first elected postwar chancellor. Don't get me wrong. I don't mind him becoming chancellor; Germany could do a lot worse—hell, *is* doing a lot worse. But he's forgetting that he was on the losing side and switched over at the last minute. This isn't *his* victory. It's ours, and a lot of us generals are going to have to find real jobs pretty soon. That means a lot of people are looking for good press, and Rommel's got the AP in his hip pocket."

"Chuck Porter does manage to pay us a visit fairly regularly," replied Sanger. "But if I understand you correctly, sir, you really just want him to have a little lower profile."

"Right on the money, Sanger. Can you do it?"

"Honestly, I'm not sure, sir. I can broach the subject with him, but I don't know what he'll do."

"Thought that might be the case," replied Bradley. "Stubbornness seems to be a good part of what makes a general a general. Maybe I'll stick my head in for a minute. If that's all right with you—I don't like making end runs around the chain of command unless it's unavoidable."

"Of course, sir," responded Sanger. "I appreciate you keeping me in the loop."

"Not a problem," said Bradley, standing up and sticking out his hand. "Good to see you, Sanger."

"Good to see you, too, sir." Sanger shook hands. "Drop by any time."

Sanger would have given his eyeteeth to know exactly how the Bradley-Rommel dialogue came out, but Bradley had taken along his own translator to avoid putting Sanger in an embarrassing position. There hadn't been any evident fireworks, and Rommel appeared to be starting the morning in a good mood, so presumably the message had been received and understood. Whether it would be accepted, he'd find out shortly. Reporters flocked to Rommel like hungry pigeons to a peanut vendor, and they were difficult to shake loose. But perhaps the Desert Fox would invite a few American generals to accompany him on parade. Sharing the wealth a little bit would go a long way to quieting down the resentment, and Rommel's underlying strategic objective would still be on track.

"Our next objective is Weimar," Rommel announced, snapping his pointer against the large wall map. Weimar, home of Goethe and Schiller, as well as home to the Weimar Republic that had preceded the rise of National Socialism, was an important cultural location. Accordingly, Rommel was eager that no additional damage be done during the "liberation" of the city.

Ballard spoke up. "Field Marshal, our reconnaissance company has been screening ahead. As of the last radio check at five hundred hours this morning, it looks as if we won't be facing any military opposition, except for snipers and normal hazards." Even that was a matter of some concern; a sniper bullet had passed less than two feet from Rommel's head just a few days ago.

"Thank you, Oberst Ballard," Rommel replied. "I have some confirmations from our own scouting forces as well. Therefore, we will not be expecting military resistance as we move. We should plan on motoring through Weimar officially tomorrow, which means we need forces in there today. I suggest that Panzer Lehr take care of today's work, and I would like the U.S. Nineteenth Armored to lead tomorrow morning's official parade. General Wakefield, will you do me the honor of riding with me? My staff car is a little larger than a jeep, but we can take your jeep if you prefer." Rommel's smile seemed genuine and unforced.

Sanger thought he was probably the only man in the room who knew that this was not exactly a spontaneous gesture. Then he looked over at Wakefield, who, he suddenly realized, was an old friend of Bradley's, and then he wasn't nearly so sure.

"Okay by me," said Wakefield in his usual gruff voice. "I don't care which car we use."

"Very well," smiled Rommel. "Gentlemen, we have another long day ahead of us, and it is slipping away even as we speak. Let us adjourn until this evening."

As the meeting began to break up, Sanger struggled through the crowd of officers in the direction of Rommel. Rommel nodded at his approach. "Ah, Sanger. Will you accompany us today?"

Riding with Rommel was an honor, but it was also a chore calling for a cast-iron butt. Rommel might cover a hundred miles or more in a day, making multiple stops often not long enough to take a piss, with meals uncertain. "Of course, sir," Sanger replied. "Thank you, sir."

There were a variety of necessary conversations that took place at the meeting's end, and today they dragged out for about half an hour. Sanger's pen flew over his notepad as he made a list of the hundred and one details he would have to handle today. The paperwork part of this job was a nutbuster, and driving around with Rommel would take the whole day. What the hell, that's what the night shift was for, he thought. At least he slept in a bed and not in a hole.

His sergeant slipped into the room to tap him on the shoulder. "Excuse me, Colonel. There's a call for you. Captain Smiggs of the CCA recon battalion. Says it's urgent."

"All right, Wilson. I'm coming."

Rommel was deep in another conversation, so Sanger slipped away. The call was being patched through from a radio, so the reception was filled with static. "Hello, Smiggy. Reid Sanger here. What can I do for you?"

The distorted, crackle-filled voice was filled with anger. "Pardon my French, Sanger, but you can get that goddamned Nazi you work for down here on the double."

"Say again?" replied Sanger.

"Rommel. You'd better get him down here, and fast. We're near Ettersburg."

"What's the matter?"

"Sanger, you've got to see this for yourself. And I've got to see the look on Rommel's face when he sees it. Trust me. Get down here, and fast."

"I need more information."

"God damn it, I'm not fucking kidding," Smiggy said with unusual rage. "This is important. If you think I'm bullshitting after you see this, then you can have my ass. Okay?"

"Okay, okay. I'll get him there. Near Ettersburg?"

"Yeah. Railroad tracks crossing the Ettersburg road coming up from Weimar." He read out some map coordinates and Sanger noted them down. "And listen, Sanger," Smiggy added.

"Yeah, Smiggy?"

"This is big shit, understand?"

"I understand, Smiggy. See you soon. Sanger out," the intelligence officer replied, shaking his head silently. He had no idea what the short captain was up to. However, Rommel would be spending all day in the car anyway, so they might as well head to Ettersburg.

NEAR ETTERSBURG, THÜRINGEN, GERMANY, 0609 HOURS GMT

Only a few minutes after Rommel's staff meeting began, Smiggy's radio had crackled. "There's a train just departing from Ettersburg."

The reconnaissance captain acknowledged the transmission. This was good news. Although the Allied strategic-bombing campaign had done its best to destroy German rail capacity, some links and routes remained in operation, especially at night and in the early-morning hours. Working rail was essential to moving huge forces across the map, so the mission had now changed from destroying rail to capturing rolling stock and preserving track from further destruction.

Smiggy liked hijacking trains. It made him feel like a member of the old Hole in the Wall Gang. He loved Westerns. He spread his map across his lap, folding and refolding the worn paper, and ran his finger along the rail line looking for a suitable crossroads . . . there! He picked up the mike again and read out the necessary coordinates. "Let's go, Jack!" he said to his driver. "It's time to head 'em off at the pass!"

He had about ten minutes to set up the ambush. It was fairly simple. A small satchel charge to twist about thirty feet of track into a modern-art sculpture, a few jeeps mounting .50-caliber machine guns to pick off any hostiles, and all his riflemen behind good cover. Even if this were a troop transport, which was unlikely based on the lack of forces in the area, it would be hard as hell for them to get into position to fight back. Hurling grenades into tightly packed passenger cars took care of opposition before it got started.

The sound of the locomotive could be heard in the distance, quiet at first and then growing louder. Smiggy grinned with nervous anticipation. He didn't get a lot of direct combat opportunities; his role was mostly to run away from any potential fights and call in the big guns. But this little incident belonged completely to him.

The tracks curved left just about fifty yards from where the satchel charge was wired to the tracks, something Smiggy had considered when picking the spot. No sense giving the enemy a lot of advance warning. There was the beginning of a glimmer of dawn, and as the chugging grew louder he could see a billow of whitish smoke from the locomotive. "Heads up, boys," he called out. "It's showtime!"

A yellow glow began to illuminate the curve, growing brighter, and then became a stabbing light as the locomotive rounded the final curve. Smiggy's dark-adapted eyes took a few seconds to clear, and then he saw the huge locomotive. It had a silvered circular plate on front rather than the traditional matte black iron, and at the two-o'clock and ten-o'clock positions swastika flags protruded. It was a military train, no doubt about it. It let out a long whistle as the engineer neared the intersection, and Smiggy could hear the growing chugging sound of the locomotive.

"Now!" Smiggy called, and the satchel charge exploded, shredding the metal rails into splintered wreckage. The engineer had enough time to blow his whistle again and pull his steam brakes, but not enough time to slow his train. The locomotive hit the twisted track, lurched over on its right side, then crashed down, its weight flattening the rails underneath it. But the front wheels had already left the track and the engine was yawing around. The coal tender pushed into the locomotive's side, tipping it sideways, but the lighter tender, not the massive locomotive, flipped on its side. Behind it, the first of the cars crashed into the obstacle created by engine and tender. Made of lighter wood, the boxcar splintered, shattered, and fell on its side, its doors bursting open. Behind it the other cars folded, accordion-style, tipping and collapsing, crashing and tearing themselves apart.

His men opened fire on both sides, raking the engineer's compartment of the locomotive before turning their fire on the line of boxcars following. In the dim and confusing mixture of headlight, smoke, and beginnings of daylight, Smiggy saw what appeared to be a few shapes jumping down and fleeing into the woods. To his surprise, there was no return fire. "Cease firing!" he called, and after a few seconds the din of gunfire waned. A little leftover ringing in his ears was the only sound in a suddenly silent world.

He signaled to his men to move up. Taking a train was a little bit like taking a house. Some men provided cover while others inched forward. You never knew what the house or train would contain. There might be a heavily armed squad or maybe just one lone wounded guy firing out of desperation, so you were always careful opening the Crackerjack box. Smiggy didn't like getting any of his men killed.

As the first men moved closer to the train, still nothing. No sign of defenders; no return fire, however weak. Two of his men reached the engineer's cab; one covered while the other clambered up the ladder and disappeared into the compartment. A moment later, his hand stuck out the open window, waving. All secure. A hand held up with one finger, then turning to thumbs-down. One dead man, no one else.

But there was movement from the first.

As the men worked their way forward, the "all clear" signal came through, and Smiggy approached the train. Following the engine, the coal tender had scattered its contents across the snow. Then came an empty passenger car that should have been full of soldiers. There were signs of recent habitation: a few empty coffee cups, a left-behind single glove. These must have been the shapes Smiggy had seen fleeing in the dim light. They might not have been able to put up a great resistance, but they should have fought back, Smiggy mused. "What's going on?" he wondered aloud.

Suddenly a loud voice began shouting, "Cap'n! Cap'n! Jesus Christ, you've got to see this. There are thousands of 'em! Thousands!"

Smiggy quickly clambered out of the passenger car and looked in the direction of the yelling soldier. At first, he couldn't quite make sense of the scene.

The doors of the first shattered boxcar had been torn off by the crash, and what appeared to be mannequins, stiff and blue, dressed in black and white striped prison garb, began spilling out. It took a few seconds for Smiggy to realize they were corpses, and a few seconds more to see that in the mounds of dead bodies there were a few still alive. And then he began to notice that many of the dead and those struggling to their feet were women and even children who had been stuffed into the cars like cattle, crowded together with no room to move.

Then came shouts from the next boxcar, and the next, and all semblance of military discipline came apart suddenly as Smiggy's small unit was utterly overwhelmed by masses of dead and dying.

It was still freezing outside, a fact that had momentarily escaped Smiggy in his heavy winter-issue jacket. He realized that there was no heat in the box-cars. While that mattered no longer to the dead, Smiggy realized that the living needed heat, and needed it now.

"Awright!" he shouted. "Attention!"

His men slowly stopped what they were doing long enough to look at him. "These people need heat and they need it now. We got coal and we got boxcars made of wood. Tear 'em down, use satchel charges if you have to, and set 'em on fire. Now!"

As his men began to shift their attention from the immense and over-whelming scene to the immediate task of building a fire, Smiggy turned to his corporal. "McConnell—get on the horn to Lieutenant Bucklin and tell him to light a fire under the rest of the division. We need medics and we need food and we need blankets and we need them ten minutes ago. If you get any shit, tell him I said so and if he doesn't get those fuckers moving inside of ten min-utes I'll rip his balls off and feed them to him."

A skeletal woman, resembling a zombie more than a human, moved toward Smiggy, hands reaching for him, clutching him. He pulled off his jacket and gave it to her, then found that ten more of the barely living were clustering around, grasping for his jacket. One tore his coat away from the woman he'd given it to. He nearly punched the thief, but realized that the needs were equally great. "What have we got? Any food? Blankets? Cloth? Check your vehicles. Everything they can use, give it to them." He pulled one set of grasp-ing hands off his arm. It was easy; they had no strength.

Herding the prisoners away from the boxcar was difficult; it was terrible but it was the only shelter they had from the steadily increasing wind. He spoke no German, other than a little GI pidgin, and *"Raus! Nein! Schoko-lade!"* didn't go very far. The satchel charge that demolished the car terrified the survivors; a few fled into the woods and he never saw them again. But then the wrecked lumber was dragged into a growing bonfire hot enough to allow the coal to burn as well, and slowly the terrified prisoners drew closer to the warmth.

Smiggy was not by nature a violent man. He liked speed and he liked adventure, but combat and blood were not his thing. But this made him angry in a way he'd never felt before. He wanted to kill someone—anyone—who was responsible for this.

Then he thought of Rommel. Smiggy wanted to rub his Kraut face right in the mess. "Those fucking Nazis did this," he thought aloud, "and they are by god going to pay." He would call Sanger, get the Desert Fox down here. Smiggy was sure he could look into Rommel's eyes and know if that Kraut bas-tard knew about this. And if he did, Smiggy planned to shoot the son of a bitch dead on the spot.

NEUE REICHSKANZLEI, BERLIN, 0644 HOURS GMT

Heinrich Himmler also started work early in the morning. The telephone calls normally did not begin until after 0600 Berlin time, and the earlier time allowed him to focus on planning and organization. His large office—it had been Hitler's—was completely dark except for the single banker's lamp on his desk. Inside the small pool of yellowish light, the small round-faced man with a weak chin slowly shuffled the papers that represented the world at war.

Although he had reached an agreement with Rommel through the intermediary von Reinhardt—he hoped he lived long enough to wipe the supercilious smile off the face of that smug know-it-all bastard—Heinrich Himmler had lived his life so far by keeping all his options open. And, after all, the strength of his negotiating position was affected by how good his other options looked.

Alas, the documents in front of him did not look promising. The war in the east had fully restarted, and he agreed with the recommendation of his generals to concentrate forces on that front, essentially abandoning the west. The west was lost anyway, between the traitors Rommel and now Student. The Allied advance was inevitable, but there were ways to slow it down somewhat.

Rommel's infantile and unrealistic desire to spare the lives of German soldiers and civilians was a weakness that could be exploited. Such bourgeois concerns were a sign of decadence, in his judgment. Himmler's intelligence sources—not to mention his personal knowledge of the man—informed him that Rommel's slow pace on the unopposed front, combined with his evident inability to resist the news camera, was sowing some discord among his erstwhile allies. This was good.

Of course, part of Rommel's slow pace had to do with their secret agreement. Rommel was giving Himmler time to get organized for his agreed-to escape from Berlin. Himmler would not decide until the very last minute what he would do, but he planned to have everything in readiness for an instant departure. Certain key officials and aides had been briefed into the escape plan as well; still others would not be told until the last minute so as to lower the likelihood of leaks.

The next report was an update on Operation Wolkenbrand. He adjusted the thin-rimmed glasses to read the report in detail. This was an important operation, and nothing must go wrong with it.

While it was necessary to rid the Fatherland of the sniveling, conspiring Jews, sentimentalists often balked at the necessary actions. Himmler was not a sentimentalist. He had taken action, and although the great work was not yet finished, it was well begun. The Reich would not fall back into the hands of Jewish bankers and degenerate Jewish entertainers and all those who would weaken the German soul, even if a few Jews escaped his grasp. But the work must be kept secret from those who could not or would not understand, and so Operation Wolkenbrand.

The first part of the operation was to transport Jews still in the labor camps to the east, where the manufacturing and processing facilities were in place to dispose of them neatly and finally, and with a minimum of force or personal involvement. Then it would be necessary to dismantle and hide the structures of the extermination camps, covering up all direct evidence. Afterward, it would only be necessary to deny. Others would take up the false story for their own purposes, reading the record for the smallest ambiguities and using those to argue that the entire structure was rotten. Even those offering the true story would have motives to achieve thereby, allowing their testimony to be attacked as biased. In the midst of argument, the objective truth would forever remain controversial. The art of propaganda had been forever advanced by the Nazi leadership, and truth—whatever that was—would have to look out for itself.

He inspected the map showing the progress of the enemy in the west. They were approaching Ettersburg, somewhat more quickly than expected. But he had a report that the last major shipment of Jews from that facility had taken place. Now it was a normal labor camp; there might be Jews left, but not in such numbers as to raise unusual suspicions. He was glad that the camp commander had been so efficient, and made another note on the report that he was to be commended.

With the west under control for now, he turned his attention to the east. There were still ways to sow additional confusion, to hamper the inevitable Soviet advance somewhat, and to move ahead with his new plan—a plan that would turn the tables on von Reinhardt, Rommel, and all his enemies, and give him yet another option and avenue to exploit.

They think they are good enough to bring me down, he thought with satisfaction, *but the world underestimates the genius of Heinrich Himmler.*

RAIL CROSSING, ETTERSBURGER STRASSE, BETWEEN WEIMAR AND ETTERSBURG, 0912 HOURS GMT

The field marshal stoically examined the battlefield. A raging bonfire sent light and smoke high into the sky; people sat huddled around it, dwarfed by the conflagration. Corpses littered the narrow path alongside the tracks. Medics circulated around the living as arriving soldiers unloaded trucks of emergency supplies.

The locomotive and a few empty cars had been pulled to the other side of Ettersburger Strasse; soldiers were demolishing the other railcars to add the wood to the pyre. The smoke, flame, and scattered dead reminded Rommel of the aftermath of the many battles he'd witnessed. The scene was appropriate for a major battle; but this had been only a minor skirmish. Yet it looked and felt far worse.

The American captain, Smiggs, was looking at him with hate-filled eyes, as if he were personally responsible for this horror. He could tell that Sanger was softening the translation of the captain's situation report; the sound of the captain's voice carried the true meaning quite clearly. He could not blame the captain for his reaction, but neither could he afford to recognize it officially.

Captain Smiggs had meant for Rommel to come upon this scene as a complete surprise, but a secret of this nature could not be kept long. His urgent requests for help had roused large portions of Rommel's headquarters. Rommel knew the outline of the situation even before he got in his staff car. The plans of the day had been overtaken by events, as was frequently the case in war.

"After he radioed in his need for support, the captain pulled his company in, secured the perimeter, and offered what aid and comfort he could to the survivors until the trucks began to arrive," Sanger finished translating.

"Please tell the captain that he acted with commendable dispatch and creativity under extremely difficult circumstances," Rommel replied.

In response, Smiggs turned his head and spat on the ground; then his eyes fastened back on the field marshal with undimmed rage. Sanger did not translate his next remark, nor did Rommel need him to.

Rommel was no sentimentalist. War was hard and people suffered, even innocent people. The necessity of the state must trump concerns for the individual, and though necessary acts might sometimes be deplorable, yet they must be done with efficiency and dispatch. Even so, honor must be maintained, and there were always rules, even under the most extreme of circumstances. From what he had learned, mostly from Hans Speidel, once his chief of staff, now the defense minister of the new provisional government, the Nazis had gone far beyond what was acceptable.

"Mass murder." The words did not sound right, even in his head. He knew the führer—both of them—and did not believe that especially Adolf Hitler was capable of this, although he had been told emphatically that he was mistaken. Himmler's role, on the other hand, was far easier for Rommel to believe. The man was a barbarian. Evidently thousands, perhaps tens of thousands, of innocents had been sent to their death at the hands of the SS. That was why he had forbidden his son Manfred to join the Waffen-SS, even though the SS divisions normally got the best equipment and the most challenging assignments.

But this train had come from somewhere. "Colonel Sanger, please ask the captain if he has had time to trace back the rail line to its origins."

No, the captain had been otherwise occupied, came the reply. But the question had clearly piqued his interest, and he excused himself momentarily to fetch a map. This was the way to deal with such anger, Rommel knew. Focus attention on the next step, on the next action, and change anger into forward motion. Energy can neither be created nor destroyed, but it can be channeled and it can be transformed.

The American terrain maps used a different coordinate grid, but Rommel was an old hand at reading maps of any sort. Captain Smiggs spread the map out on the hood of his jeep and the field marshal looked down at it, quickly locating their current position. He ran his finger backward along the rail line, and thumped his finger on the map.

"Here, in the woods," Rommel said. "This is the logical place to look. See where a road enters the forest? It's known as the Buchenwald, the Beech Forest. There are tracks here as well. Where the track and this road intersect, I believe we'll find the origin of this train."

The captain started issuing orders, but Rommel called a halt. "I suspect we'll need a larger attack force than we have here. And the force should be German. Honor demands it."

When Sanger translated the final part, the American captain exploded with more language that Sanger did not need to translate. Rommel stood under the verbal onslaught for a moment, then added, "I will need a reconnaissance force as well. I believe the captain has earned that right if he wishes." He paused to get Smiggs' acceptance of the assignment.

When the captain nodded okay, Rommel then added in a firm tone of voice, "Listen to me, Captain Smiggs. On this mission, you will behave in a soldierly way, you will control your emotions, and you will follow orders. Is that clear?" He locked eyes with the captain and held him in his gaze as Sanger translated.

At first, the captain attempted to stare him down, but even with Rommel's one damaged eye, the field marshal's force of will was superior. Captain Smiggs broke first. "Yes, sir," he replied sullenly.

"Good. Turn over your duties here and then come back for your new assignment. I will order the remaining forces to meet us at once."

As Rommel turned back to his staff car, the first flakes of snow began to fall.

KONZENTRATIONSLAGER BUCHENWALD, THÜRINGEN, GERMANY, 1640 HOURS GMT

A couple of the guards liked to throw the dinner bread into the mud so they could beat the prisoners as they scrambled for their food. With Digger's bum leg and Clausen farther gone by the minute, it wasn't worth it. Digger had managed to keep hidden most of the day, but he knew that both their time was running out.

The snow had interrupted some of the daily guard routine, which was one good thing about it. It also kept down some of the smell and covered up the corpsicles, and you could eat it. It was the cleanest water he'd had in weeks.

There was something going on, and Digger wanted to know what it was. The early-morning train had taken away thousands of Jews, and it looked like they were loading a second one. Why transport them somewhere else when they were certainly going to die here soon enough? Only one explanation made sense to Digger—the cavalry was coming—but he didn't want to get his hopes up too much. If it was coming, it better get here soon, because he didn't have much time left.

SS-Oberführer Hermann Pister glanced briefly out his office window and noticed that the snow was beginning to stick. This was both good and bad news. The good was that it would likely slow up the Allied advance; the bad was that it would hamper his own escape. He was ready to leave; it was quite clear that falling into Allied hands would be a disaster. But he had his duties to perform. Operation Wolkenbrand required him to eliminate certain pieces of evidence, and afterward, he and his Waffen-SS soldiers would depart.

The first trainload of Jews had been shipped out; another was loading. Information on the camps to which they were being sent was to remain completely secret. He had hoped that the backlog of bodies to be cremated would have been reduced, but the poor weather had not only slowed down cremation, but increased the number of dead.

He stopped for a minute and looked out the window again, longer this time. The snow was coming down steadily. His work here was futile; he knew that. Whatever information he could successfully eliminate would be nothing compared with all the evidence that remained. Some of his men were already deserting, hoping to blend back into the civilian population.

Pister could not see his camp any longer in the dark and the snow. There had been over sixty-eight thousand people crowded into this camp and its sub-camps, far more than it was designed to hold. He had gotten rid of nearly twenty thousand Jews. There were still Allied soldiers here. Should he have them disposed of? Would finding them add to the expected Allied anger? So many decisions. He had thought himself far too professional to share the fate of Karl Koch, his predecessor, whose criminality (not to mention his wife Ilse's sadism) got him executed by the SS at Auschwitz. But he didn't think the Allies would consider his administration of the camp ultimately that much different.

He turned to look back over his office. Piles of paper were stacked, ready to go into the furnace along with some more bodies. *To hell with it,* he thought. He had devoted his life to the Nazi cause, and he had more than done his duty to his führer and his fatherland. Now there was nothing left. It was time to go. He left the papers where they were, grabbed his greatcoat from the rack, and headed for his quarters to pack.

NORTH OF ETTERSBURG MOUNTAIN, 1717 HOURS GMT

Americans tend to think of football when they think of teamwork. Germans think instead of a symphony orchestra. From the orchestra you can extract and organize teams of any combination depending on the immediate goal.

"So tell me," Frank Ballard whispered to Reid Sanger, "how come it takes a German five-star field marshal to plan an operation involving maybe two companies?"

"Because he happens to be here," whispered Sanger with a shrug. There really wasn't another reason, he thought, although Ballard certainly had a point. Here was the commander of the free Germans standing in a poorly heated tent, looking at unrolled maps under lantern light while giving orders to two colonels, one major, and a captain who was still scowling from his day with the captured train.

Rommel was looking a little haggard, Sanger noted. His scarred eye was twitching and fluid was running from it. A doctor should look at it, and soon—if the field marshal would ever slow down. Rommel's batman, Günther, tried to take care of him, but Rommel tended to ignore any information he didn't want to hear. Sanger had never met the man called Mutti, Rommel's vanished driver, but heard that Mutti was about the only person who could keep the man under control. As for Sanger, he was supposed to be a military liaison but frequently found himself drafted into an ADC role. Rommel had a tendency to coopt anybody in his orbit on behalf of whatever mission he was pursuing.

"All right," Rommel was saying in German. "Of the two approaches shown on the map, we can only use the northern approach for now. By tomorrow we will have secured Weimar and the southern approach would be workable, but tomorrow is longer than I want to wait. I want this camp liberated tonight." The map of the area only showed a forest, but Rommel pointed to a spot right in its middle. "Here is a hill, about five hundred meters high. The camp is on the hilltop, and guard towers surround it. It will be difficult to approach with an element of surprise, but this snowstorm will be to our advantage." Sanger stepped forward and translated, then Rommel began again.

"The Smiggs Detachment, consisting of the reconnaissance company supplemented by an infantry company, establishes a perimeter around the camp and uses suppressive fire against the guard towers and against any breakout attempts." Sanger watched the expression on Smiggy's face. Still angry, but won over and ready to fight. "I have also designated the second battalion of Nine-hundred-and-second Panzergrenadiers as the Kranz Detachment." Rommel had encountered this advance unit of Panzer Lehr division and simply coopted it for this new mission.

Hauptmann Kranz of the 902nd, a short man with jet black hair grown thin on top, eyes distorted through Coca-Cola-bottle glasses, clicked his heels in acknowledgment. *"Jawohl, mein Generalfeldmarschall!"*

"Kranz Detachment advances in strength up the northern road, uses panzerfausts to destroy the entrance gate, and occupies the camp." Sanger translated for the English-speaking Allied listeners.

The tent flap opened, letting in a gust of wind that rattled the papers and nearly extinguished the lantern. Sanger looked up sharply, then noticed it was Müller, the supply officer.

"Ex-Excuse me for being delayed, mein Generalfeldmarschall," the pudgy colonel said. His round glasses had completely fogged over as he entered the somewhat warmer tent, and he fumbled with them, trying to wipe them clean, as he spoke. "I-I just received your message, and . . ."

Rommel held up his hand and smiled. "I know you got here as fast as you could. Müller, I have a special need of you tonight. You know about the train that Captain Smiggs here discovered."

"Yes, of course, sir. Horrible! Simply horrible! I've been shifting first-aid and food supplies to them." Müller shook his head in wonderment. "For once, there is no problem with quantities, only with transportation and speed."

"There may be thousands more, even tens of thousands, here in this area. It's the camp from which the train came. We're going to take it tonight, and I need food, medicine, and clothing coming as fast as possible."

Müller placed the glasses back on his nose and blinked. His eyes were a watery blue. "I thought it might be something like that, mein Generalfeld-marschall. I've started the planning already." He held up a clipboard.

"Good man," Rommel said. "It's going to be a long night, I'm afraid, but this weather not only helps conceal our attack, it also poses a grave danger to those in the camp who are still alive."

"I'll do my very best," Müller replied, his eyes wide. Rommel had quickly discovered that in spite of the man's nervousness around authority, if he was treated gently, he could produce fine results. Sanger had seen plenty of evidence of Rommel's notorious temper, but with this supply officer who had saved the field marshal's life, the Desert Fox had adjusted his style to get results. That made Sanger wonder how much of Rommel's temper was an act.

As Müller left, Rommel turned back to his soldiers in the tent. His gaze grew stern, his one good eye steely. "The watchword for this battle is safety for the prisoners. For that reason, we move with dispatch and silence, and we fire cleanly at targets we identify. Nighttime battles greatly increase the danger of friendly fire. Keep control of your units, especially when your soldiers see things that anger them." Rommel paused, then added, "I promise you there will be a reckoning and an opportunity for justice—but after the prisoners have been saved."

"Now, Kranz," the field marshal continued, "I have an idea how we can improve the stealthiness of our initial approach. . . ."

KONZENTRATIONSLAGER BUCHENWALD,
1805 HOURS GMT

"Fucking snowstorm," groused the Totenkopf-SS guard as he swiveled his searchlight to scan the northern approach road. "I can't see a damned thing. There could be ten thousand Americans fifty meters ahead, and they might as well be in Norway."

"Don't even joke about ten thousand Americans, Jürgen," the second tower guard said. He was pacing back and forth in the narrow space, periodically slapping his arms to his sides in an effort to get warm. "Those bastards will be here too fucking soon, and I don't want to be here when they show up."

Jürgen swung the light around into the camp compound in a cursory fashion. In this weather, anyone caught outside would die of exposure before the tower's machine gun could do its job. "You think it's time to leave, Karl?"

"It's getting time. As soon as this weather clears up, I think we'll all be pulled back. The führer can't afford to throw away trained SS veterans. Besides, even if we walked away today, it's not like these prisoners are going to live much longer. All we have to do is shut down the furnace and by the time the Americans get here, there will be nothing left but frozen stiffs."

"I suppose," Karl replied in a skeptical tone of voice. "Fucking Jews. Trouble when they're alive, and trouble even when they're dead. It'll be a better world when the Jews are all together in Hell."

"You've got that right," agreed Jürgen. "I'll be glad when we're off tower duty. Maybe we'll get the furnace room—at least it will be warm!"

"As long as we don't have early-morning roll-call duty, I'll be satisfied," Karl replied. "Hey—what's that?" He swiveled the searchlight again.

"What? I don't see anything," said Jürgen, leaning over the side, staring into the snow. "Probably just your imagination. There's nothing out there, believe me."

The sound of a truck motor could be heard in the distance, faintly at first, then louder. "Hey, hear that? That's not just imagination, Jürgen."

Jürgen listened for a moment. "You're right. Sounds like a truck. What kind of stupid fucker comes driving up here in the middle of a blizzard? Either it's a very special prisoner drop, or—hey, maybe it's a convoy to come take us back to Berlin!"

"Yeah. Maybe it's a limo driven by the führer himself," said Karl sarcastically. "Not a chance. It's just a prisoner drop-off." Karl picked up the telephone. "Hey, Oberschütze Metzger," he said loudly—the telephone was of low quality. "There's a truck carrying prisoners coming up to the gate. Better open up!" He swiveled the searchlight onto the truck—SS markings; all in order. The great gates swung open and the truck revved its engine to push through the snow and into the gates.

Before the gates could close, a new sound was heard. "Jesus Christ, Karl—that's gunfire!" said Jürgen. Karl swung the light again, this time down inside the wide-open gates. The truck was disgorging soldiers armed with machine pistols, tearing into the SS camp guards. Quickly, Jürgen manned the machine gun, aimed it down, and fired a burst at the truck.

Then there was more noise. "The fucking Americans—or maybe that *arschloch* traitor Rommel—they're here!" shouted Karl. "I'll call the commandant."

As he picked up the telephone again, he could see tanks and half-tracks approaching, far more than a single machine gun could handle. But at least he'd take some enemy with him, he thought.

There was a sudden burst of light on his right, followed by a shattering explosion. Karl looked over to see the second main guard tower collapsing, its observation platform consumed with fire. One of the tower guards—Karl couldn't tell whom—jumped from the blazing wreckage. His greatcoat was on fire.

That was enough. "Let's get the fuck out of here!" he shouted to Jürgen. He pulled open the trapdoor and both men tried to squeeze in, fighting to be first out of the tower.

Neither of them saw or heard the mortar shell that exploded at the base of their tower.

"Move! Move! Move!" shouted the feldwebel. Klaus Bäker's heart was beating fast as he scrambled toward the rear of the truck. His bayonet was fixed and pointing up in the confined quarters; he didn't like being around all these jabbing knives and was thankful his pack served as padding for any overeager soldiers behind him.

His eyes were dark-adapted from the last hour spent waiting as the truck struggled through the snowstorm. Then there was the long moment of suspense, sitting helplessly in the dark like the soldiers in the Trojan horse so long ago, waiting for the enemy to pull them into their own fortress. The searchlights from the guard towers had swept across the truck; he could see the light through the canvas. His hands were sweaty in their thin gloves; it was funny how they could be icy cold at the same time. Time seemed to stop for a long while, until he thought anything, including close combat with bayonets, was better than continuing to sit in the dark truck.

Then came the command and suddenly time sped up again. He jumped from the truck when his time came and was blinded as the searchlight swept over him. Disoriented, he couldn't tell friend from foe. The uniforms, the helmets, the insignia were so alike as to be indistinguishable in the intermittent light. He lowered his rifle into attack position, then saw a guard with a machine pistol that stuttered, sending a spray of bullets into the attackers.

Bäker dropped into the snow, lifted his rifle and squeezed off a shot, missed, fired again. There was a scream and the machine-pistol soldier dropped; Bäker could not tell if he had killed or merely wounded him.

Another stutter of machine-gun fire, this one louder, coming from the guard towers. He felt like an exposed bug under the searchlights and scrambled through the wet snow toward the shelter of the truck body. *Mortar— come on, mortar!* he thought, willing the shell to fire itself, and then there was an explosion, the first shell falling short, the second one on target, and the tower exploded in a sudden flare of white light. The searchlight stayed on for a brief time; then there was darkness from the first tower. Bäker crouched, brought his rifle to his shoulder again, and began to fire from the cover of the truck. There were screams, all in German, and there was no way to tell friend from foe in the new dark.

One searchlight continued to stab into the snow outside the compound. Bäker heard a loud roar and turned his head briefly to see a massive Panzer V bearing down on the camp like a leviathan from the distant past. Then the dark was punctuated by another flash of explosive fire. The second guard tower exploded, and the Panzer V was swallowed up by the darkness.

The camp guards were firing in retreat, holing up inside one of the barracks. "*Schnell!* After them!" yelled the feldwebel, and Bäker began running, began yelling with the others, charging across the compound through the deepening snow. His rifle barked, and again, but he didn't have a target in mind. There was firing coming his way again, and he dived forward, splattering into the snow and mud. Others around him fell as well; he couldn't tell if any of them had been hit. He began to snake forward on his belly, rifle forward, until he found a few garbage cans he could hide behind, then up on his knee, rifle to his shoulder. He could see shadow figures at the barracks windows and he shot into them randomly.

And then there were shouts: "Truce! Truce! We surrender! Don't shoot us! We surrender!" Bäker's hands were shaking as he saw the surrendering guards coming out, still unrecognizeable shadows, with hands held high or clasped over their helmets. The feldwebel shouted his orders, "Single file! Keep your hands in the air!," and then shouted at his men to surround the survivors, march them into a barbed-wire area where normally prisoners were received.

Bäker's heart began to calm. He was soaking wet from the snow and the mud, and his arm hurt. He must have wrenched it when he fell, he thought, and reached in to find that the liquid was warm, not cold. *Jesus Christ, I'm bleeding!* he thought in horror, and then he shouted aloud "I'm shot! I'm wounded!" until the feldwebel came over. He couldn't stop shouting until the feldwebel slapped him, and then he was terrified. "Am I going to die?" he asked, and the feldwebel replied, "God damn it, it's just a shoulder wound, but if you don't shut up and get hold of yourself I'll fucking kill you. Got it?"

*   *   *

Hermann Pister, the camp commandant, took a final look around his quarters. He had packed everything he needed; the boot of his staff car was full. His driver was waiting; the engine was warmed up. Driving away in a heavy snowfall was a bit dangerous, but waiting until the weather cleared was probably more risky.

"All right," he said to himself, rubbing his hands together. "Time to leave."

He heard the gunfire and mortar explosions as he left his quarters. "Damn it!" he said. The enemy was already at his gates. They, like he, must have seen the opportunity in the snowstorm. But all the noise was from the north. The Allies hadn't captured Weimar yet, so they couldn't have approached from that direction. Time to move south, he thought. Opening the door to his car, he said, "Change of plans. We are leaving to the south, along the Blutstrasse." The Blutstrasse, or Street of Blood, was the name the prisoners had given the main camp access road.

"*Jawohl, mein Oberführer,*" the driver said. He was glad to be leaving as well.

The wheels of the car spun in the snow and mud before getting traction. Pister leaned forward, momentarily anxious, although he was normally quite self-controlled. His driver ground the gears rather badly, and then finally the car began to move. Once out of the gate, the road was bumpy but straight, and they would pick up speed. With luck, he would be in Berlin by midmorning tomorrow.

The car stopped at the gate, and Pister rolled down his window impatiently. "Open up! Open up! Can't you see who I am?"

He stared up into an ugly, unshaven face with a toothless smile—the teeth had been broken off and nothing but stumps remained. Suddenly he realized that this was not one of his guards, but a prisoner—a Russian, by the look of him.

"Drive! Drive! *Schnell,* you idiot! Break through the gate! Get us out of here!" Pister shouted at his driver. The driver floored the gas pedal, but that only sent the wheels into another spin, and in a moment the driver's door was wrenched open and all Pister could see was an arm jerking the driver out into the snow.

He tried to roll his window up and lock his door, but the Russian's arm blocked the glass. He pulled hard at the door handle, but the arms outside the car were stronger. His door too was wrenched open, and he felt strong arms pull him out and into the snow.

In the light from the guard shack, he briefly saw a body slumped forward. There was another body facedown in the snow, stripped of its coat and looking incongruously cold.

"Please . . . I can get you money, safe passage, whatever you want! I'm too important for you to kill. I can be very useful! Very useful!" As he babbled out reasons for the prisoners to spare his life, he suddenly wondered if any of them spoke enough German to understand him. "Money! Freedom! I can help you!" he said, simplifying the message.

"So, Commandant Pister, you can help us?" A deep voice, speaking in German but with a very thick Russian accent. "And we should spare your life for your help?"

"Yes, yes! I have money, some in the car, but I can get more. I can prepare passes for you, help you get your freedom!" He was relieved—someone was going to be rational, going to be sensible, going to make a deal. He forced himself to get calm; an overanxious bargainer had little leverage.

Pister stood up, brushed the snow from his coat, prepared to deal. Then he got a look at his captor—the man had suffered severe burns; one eye and most of his face were gone. Like the other Russian, his teeth were either rotten or broken, and Pister noticed that one arm hung limp. The Russian leader saw Pister look at him. "Not so pretty, yes?" he said. "You Germans did this. And now it's our turn." He had a camp knife, mostly rusted scrap metal, and with it he slashed Pister across the face, cutting into his eye.

The commandant screamed, tried to run, but a foot tripped him and he fell facedown in the snow. The cold gave him momentary relief, but then he felt hands grab him, turn him over, and the Russian knelt on top of him, grinning as he brought the camp knife down again and again.

Digger O'Dell scraped a handful of snow off the sill outside the broken window to try to lower Clausen's fever. "Just let the fucking German die," growled Kirby, the senior POW officer. "It's going to happen anyway, so don't waste your time."

Digger ignored him, and took the snow back to his bunk, wrapping it in a bit of scrounged cloth and placing the improvised cold compress on Clausen's head. In spite of the snow and cold, Clausen's fever had spiked even higher.

"You're sleeping on the fucking wet spot, you hear me, Digger?" snarled one of his bunkmates.

Digger grinned. "Hell, I used to sleep with three younger brothers. Water ain't nothing compared to sleeping in piss." He continued working on Clausen. There wasn't much he could do, but it beat just sitting around and waiting for the man to die.

The first mortar explosion rocked the room. "What the fuck was that?" the bunkmate asked.

Digger was already on his way back to the window, but by the time he was there, a crowd of prisoners was trying to peer out. "Hot damn, it looks like the war done got here at last," crowed one soldier.

"About fucking time," came the grunted reply.

Kirby was on his feet. "Men, if the cavalry has arrived, as you Americans put it, we had better do our share in this."

"With what?" a sarcastic voice called out. "Our bare hands?"

"Do you want our friendly SS guards to make their escape unharmed, or become POWs according to *our* standards of treatment?"

"Fuck, no!" The chorus of replies grew in volume.

"Do we want to show our friendly Nazis what we can do?"

"Yeah!" "Hell, yeah!" "Goddamn right!" "Let's cut those bastards' balls off and feed 'em to them!"

"Right!" Kirby called out loudly. "Take anything you can turn into a weapon, and let's go!"

The camp adminstration building had an ornate Art Deco door, but it was splintered into nothing by a grenade. Rommel, escorted by several machine-pistol-bearing enlisted men, strode into the room. "Deserted, damn it!" he snarled. "We're too late." There were desks in the open room, papers neatly put away. Rommel pulled open a drawer filled with punch cards, and pulled one out. He peered at the pattern of holes. "A man's life and death . . ." he murmured. There was a Hollerith tabulating machine behind a half window in the next office.

Angrily, he strode toward the door leading to the commandant's private office, kicking it open with his boot. It, too, was empty. "The bastard got away. How did that happen? Did he get warning of our attack?" He turned around, glaring, looking for someone to blame.

"I-I don't think so," quavered Müller. "It would have taken hours to clean out a space like this. We-We weren't even near when this work started."

Rommel stared angrily for a moment, then said, "I suppose you're right. It was certainly no secret that we would be here eventually. All right, Müller. This is your new office space. Take the people you need and get this place cleaned up."

Müller looked around silently, then said, "Y-Yes, sir."

Rommel clasped him on the shoulder, calming himself. "This is an impossible job I'm giving you, Müller. You must do your very best with it; these people depend on you."

The supply officer took a deep breath, straightened up, and replied, "Yes, sir. I'll do everything that can be done."

"Good man," Rommel said, then turned to the feldwebel in charge of his escort. "I need Kranz and Smiggs at once. Resistance should be over shortly; it looks like the officers have fled. Let's move our forces into the camp as quickly as possible."

Rommel did not notice as Müller left the building.

*   *   *

Chaos had overtaken the camp. Groups of prisoners hunted down surviving guards as soldiers tried to get them to return to their barracks. Calls in German, in English, and in Russian went largely unheeded. Digger wasn't particularly interested in revenge, though. It was medical treatment he needed. The guards could wait for another day.

Holding Clausen tightly, two thin blankets wrapped around them both, he grabbed at one of the invading soldiers. "Hey, you—my buddy needs medical help. Me-di-cal help. *Hilfen? Bitte, hilfen.*"

"*Gehen Sie zurück!*" the soldier replied, gesturing at the barracks.

"No. Listen to me. This man—German. Needs doctor! Doc-tor!"

"*Rein Jetzt!*" Another gesture.

"Listen, buddy. I need help. Now."

The soldier shoved Digger, nearly pushing him off balance with his bad leg. Although gaunt from poor rations, Digger was still a strong man. He reached out, grabbed the soldier by the collar, and pulled him close. "Help. Now. *Verstehen?*" His German still had a Southern accent to it.

The soldier was about to push again, when suddenly an officer appeared. "*Was ist los hier?*" Müller asked.

The soldier tried to explain, but Digger got there first. "This man. German. Deutsch. Needs medical attention. Doc-tor. *Helfen. Ja?*"

Müller shined his flashlight at the strange American and his companion. The American blinked in the sudden light. Then Müller looked at the other man, delirious, nearly dead. "*Mein Gott!*" he whispered. "It's Mutti!"

BLOCK 66, KONZENTRATIONSLAGER BUCHENWALD, 2024 HOURS GMT

The night and the snow could conceal some of the visual horror, but it was the smell that Sanger was never able to forget.

Rommel's escort could barely contain themselves; it took all of Sanger's willpower to keep him from gagging. The Desert Fox himself looked on stoically, his face wooden. Sanger had observed that this was a dangerous early warning sign of Rommel's ferocious temper.

Rommel seemed determined to visit each building, to see each atrocity at firsthand. He said little, marching with long strides from block to block (as the prisoner barracks were called).

It was easy to recognize the kapos, the senior prisoners who translated Totenkopf-SS directives into action. They were the ones whose throats had been freshly cut. The first time they came upon a prisoner who had died in this fashion, Rommel had asked, "What happened here?"

A gaunt, dirty, unshaven prisoner stepped forward out of the pack. "He committed suicide," the prisoner said sullenly.

Rommel looked at him thoughtfully for a moment. "I see," he said.

The guards who had not yet been killed or captured were in hiding. If Rommel's men did not find them, Sanger suspected that the prisoners would.

In each building there were many near death; there were dead in several of the buildings that had not yet been taken away for disposal.

"What building is this?" Rommel asked as they approached the next barracks.

One of his escorts shined a flashlight on the number. "Block 66, General-feldmarschall." He opened the door and shined a light in.

It was full of children.

Silent, staring, solemn—gaunt and ragged children, bruised and malnour-ished, many with open sores and some with mutilations. Unlike the adult bar-racks, where the prisoners knew that liberation was here, these children saw only uniforms, and that was no different from their everyday lives.

Because of Rommel's tendency for interminable car tours, Sanger had got-ten in the habit of stuffing a few Hershey bars in his briefcase. He knelt down, opened the briefcase, and pulled one out. He held it toward a young boy who appeared to be about four years old. The boy cringed away. "Chocolate," Sanger said in a quiet, soothing tone. No response.

After a moment, Sanger realized that the boy had never heard the word before and did not recognize the package. He unwrapped it, broke off a piece, handed it over. The boy scurried away behind an older boy, who was perhaps seven. Sanger reached out with the chocolate square and offered it to the older boy. "It's good," he said in German.

The boy took it and then gulped it down in a single bite. Sanger offered him another piece, which he chewed more slowly and with evident delight. He tried again with the four-year-old, but still no reaction.

Meanwhile, the guards shone their flashlights around the room. *"Du lieber Gott,"* one whispered. His light had revealed shackles on the far wall, from which four bruised and beaten children hung by their wrists, unmoving. Dried blood streaked their faces and the rags they wore.

Children cringed away as two soldiers ran the length of the barracks toward the hanging children. *"Sie sind tot,"* they called back. They were dead.

Sanger closed his eyes for a moment, and then he heard another noise.

"Gerade Stehen! Hände auf den Kopf!" the soldiers called. There was a brief scuffle. They had found camp guards. All the remaining soldiers had weapons out, moving to protect their field marshal.

Rommel's face darkened. "Bring them here. Now," he ordered. His voice was low, almost guttural.

His men dragged two SS guards to him, and threw them down at his feet.

"Sir! You've got to protect us! The prisoners—they're murdering every-body! We're Germans, sir! Germans! Just like you!"

"Like me? Then God help Germany, because I want no part of you,"

Rommel growled, his voice nearly choking, and drew his officer's Walther from its holster.

"Sir, stop!" said Sanger, standing up. "You can't shoot them without a trial."

Rommel turned to look at him. He was enraged, livid. He spoke slowly, his rage growing with each word. "A trial? Did they give these children a trial? Animals like this don't deserve a trial."

"You're right, sir," said Sanger, moving in between Rommel and the guards. "They don't deserve a trial. But these children do."

"Get out of my way, Colonel, before I shoot you," growled Rommel, and pointed his pistol at Sanger's face. "Now."

Sanger didn't budge. Looking the Desert Fox directly in the eye, he stammered out his argument. "This has to be part of the record. What they did here. What we see. It's got to be documented. They don't deserve a trial, but the world has to know the truth about this. This has to be done by the book. Not for their sake, but for everyone else." Sanger had never been this close to death and his body was shaking.

The pistol was inches from his face and the expression on Rommel's face made him think of flames. They stood together for a long time, and then Rommel lowered his gun. His eyes never left Sanger's face as he said, "Take them away and put them in a cage somewhere. We'll give them a fair trial and then we'll kill them by the book. Does that meet with your approval, Herr Oberst?" The last was a sarcastic snarl.

"Yes, sir," Sanger replied, standing at rigid attention. His lips were thin and white. As Rommel's knifelike gaze pinned him to the spot, the soldiers pulled the SS guards to their feet and prepared to hustle them out the door.

"Stop!" Rommel ordered. "The guards—they have warm clothes. Strip them. Give the clothes to the children. All of you. Give them your coats. Now."

Sanger took off his coat at once and started a pile. It was cold in the barracks, even with his uniform jacket on. He took that off, too. A pile of coats grew as other soldiers contributed their own. The Totenkopf guards were stripped to their underwear before being roughly hauled away.

"Food. Food and blankets. Bring them to me," Rommel ordered as the soldiers left. When only Sanger was left, Rommel said in a low and harsh voice, "If you ever interfere with me again, I'll shoot you where you stand. Is that clear?"

"Yes, sir." Sanger stood his ground.

"Then get out of my sight."

With that, the field marshal turned away, and took a slow, deep breath. Then he slowly took off his coat and then his uniform jacket. He knelt down on the floor and began unpinning the decorations. Holding each one in his open palm, he offered his medals to first one child, then another, until one took his gift. Then he took another medal, and repeated the process. The children looked at him, some with dulled, expressionless eyes, some with cringing fear, but with wordless coaxing, he distributed all his medals. Then he gave his coat to one child, a rail-thin girl with matted hair, and his jacket to another.

Sanger stepped outside.

He shuddered as the frigid air rushed into his lungs; he felt weak and drained. He had ruined his relationship with the Desert Fox over the fate of two men who clearly deserved to die and by the most horrible means available. He hadn't felt like this since he was in his teens and resigned from his cousins' Hitler Youth chapter in Augsburg. More friendships sacrificed on the altar of morality.

He pulled out a pack of cigarettes and tapped one into his shaking hand. His gloved thumb couldn't work the wheel on his Zippo, but when he took off his glove, he dropped his cigarettes into the snow. Gathering them back up, he tried again to light his cigarette, but this time the wind blew it out.

A hand reached out with a flame in it. "Here, Colonel. Let me help you."

It was Captain Kranz, the battalion commander from Panzer Lehr that Rommel had drafted for this assignment.

"Thanks," said Sanger, taking a deep pull off his cigarette, enjoying the feel of the warm smoke entering his lungs. The frigid air was not nearly as terrible now that he was out of the barracks.

"I was looking for the field marshal, and overheard you. Don't worry. He'll calm down and realize that you were right. People don't stay on his shit list unless they really deserve it. Although, I must say shooting those scum on the spot does seem like a very good idea."

"Hell, I agree. I wanted to shoot the bastards myself," said Sanger. He didn't believe Kranz was right about Rommel's shit list, but he was glad of the thought. He held out his cigarette pack to the captain. Kranz took a Lucky Strike and lit it. "Is the camp secure?"

"As secure as we can make it under the circumstances. We need supplies and medical personnel more than anything. This is going to be the world's nastiest cleanup job, I suspect."

"Until we find the rest of the camps," Sanger replied.

"You think there are more?"

"Quite a few more. I've seen the photographs and heard some of the stories. This evidently isn't even the worst."

"*Scheisse.* When it comes time to execute those *Hurensohne,* I want a piece of them myself," Kranz growled.

"You'll have to stand in line," replied Sanger.

A figure in a thick coat was running toward them. "Where's the field marshal? I've got to see him now!" It was Müller, the supply officer.

"He's inside," said Sanger, "but I wouldn't interrupt him right now. He's found the barracks with the children."

"Children? *Here?* Oh, my god!" Müller gasped, stunned. Then he collected himself. "But I have to see him."

"Why?"

"We've found Mutti."

"Here?"

"Yes, here in the camp."

"Oh, my god," Sanger echoed.

19 FEBRUARY 1945

UNITED STATES EMBASSY, MOSCOW, USSR,
0600 HOURS GMT
It was still dark at nine o'clock in the morning Moscow time. Hartnell Stone looked out the ambassador's window at the colorful lit onion domes of the Kremlin across Red Square.

"Ready to visit the bear in his den again?" Averrell Harriman said.

"Yes, sir," Hartnell replied. He drank the remainder of his cup of coffee and put it down on the tray. "Why do you think he hasn't replied to the president's letter?"

"You've got to understand one important difference between the United States and almost every other nation in the world—time. We're the youngest major nation in the world. We've got less than five hundred years of total history, and only about three hundred years of serious history. We've been a nation less than two hundred years. In Europe, they call that 'contemporary studies.' You think that because we've been sitting around waiting for an answer for almost three weeks that we've been waiting forever. Stalin doesn't have to play on our schedule, and so he doesn't. Berlin isn't an immediate issue, so why deal with it yet? So, we'll go to round two and see what happens, but don't be surprised if the answer is 'nothing much.' It won't be the first time."

"Then why go?"

"The Russians are the world's greatest chess players, but the world's greatest poker players are Americans. Stalin is going to lay out his plan, whatever it is, with subtle steps and a long time horizon. What we're going to do is look at personality and psychology and see how we can read it and influence it, and that's our strategy for winning. Either way, it's time to make another move on the chessboard or bet another round in the poker game. Neither Stalin nor we are in a hurry. If one of us gets in a hurry, that one loses."

Stone looked at the senior diplomat. "But you still don't know what cards you have in your hand."

Harriman smiled. "In this kind of poker, that's not always the most important knowledge. Besides, you play what you have, not what you wish you had. By the way, here's some diplomatic advice for you. Always take a leak before entering a long meeting. Your ability to negotiate is a function of the capacity of your bladder." The ambassador picked up his briefcase.

"Do you follow your own advice?" Stone asked.

"Always," Harriman replied.

Stone felt his nose hairs freeze as he paced the ambassador across the square. The Soviet guards recognized Harriman, snapped to attention, and opened the courtyard gate. A military escort awaited them inside the building, took their coats, then marched ahead of them with precision, boot heels clicking on the polished floor. They followed the escort through a wide corridor and up a formal staircase, then along another corridor lined with statuary and portraiture that Stone wished he had time to admire properly.

Midway down the corridor, another set of guards flanked large double doors made of dark wood. At the escort's approach, they snapped to attention, and opened the doors. A receptionist stood, and welcomed the visitors in English. "The chairman is ready to see you now," she said, and opened another door leading to Stalin's official inner office.

The office was immense, with a long carpet leading to an elevated platform where Stalin sat at a large desk. There was a conversation area with a sofa and several chairs around a blazing fireplace, a conference table, and several cupboards. The chairman stood as Harriman and Stone entered. "Good morning, good morning," Stalin boomed in a cheerful voice. "Welcome! How are you? Please, sit down. Tea?" He gestured to his receptionist, who drew cups of tea for each of the three from an ornate silver samovar, flavoring each with a spoonful of strawberry jam. A translator stood behind Stalin's chair.

"Thank you, Chairman Stalin. How have you been?"

"Oh, busy, always busy. The paperwork never stops, you know. As long as a tree stands anywhere in the world, someone will chop it down and pulp it so they can write a memorandum asking for more funding." He laughed at his own joke. "In this respect, I think there is probably no difference between capitalism and communism, am I right?"

Harriman laughed. "I am sure you are right. It is the bane of my existence as well."

"Oh, before I forget," Stalin said. "I have a gift for President Roosevelt. A small thing, but it may amuse him." He walked back to his desk and picked up a small envelope. "He collects postage stamps, and this is a ten-kopek stamp from 1858, the very first Russian postage stamp."

"Oh, really?" Harriman opened the envelope to look at the stamp. In the center it had the Romanov eagle in white surrounded by a blue oval, with a printed black drape and "10" in each corner. "Very nice. Thank you. I know the president will appreciate it very much."

"Good, good. I worry about him all the time, you know. Such a great man, and a dear friend. How is his health?"

"I hear he's in excellent health. His doctors want him to slow down a bit, but that's all."

"Bah, doctors want everybody to slow down a little bit. And eat less and drink less and fornicate less and basically eliminate all joy from life. And for what? Sooner or later we all die, right? Right."

"That reminds me of a Mark Twain story you might like," Harriman said.

"Ah, Mark Twain. I like him. He would have made a good Russian, I think. Tell me the story."

"It seems that Mark Twain caught pneumonia. When the doctor visited, he saw Mark Twain smoking a cigar. He asked, 'How many of those do you smoke each day?' Twain said, 'Oh, a dozen or so.' And the doctor said, 'I see a bottle of whiskey. How much do you drink?' Twain said, 'I'm a moderate drinker, only a bottle or so a day.' The doctor said, 'If you'll temporarily give up drinking and smoking, you'll recover quickly.' Twain followed the doctor's advice, and got well. Later, a woman he knew got pneumonia, and Twain told her that if she temporarily stopped drinking whiskey and smoking cigars, she'd get well. She said, 'I don't drink whiskey, and I don't smoke cigars.' And you know, she died. The moral is, you need a few vices to serve as ballast to throw overboard in case of emergency."

Stalin laughed. "She died!" He slapped his leg so hard he nearly spilled his tea cup. "Ah, your Mark Twain is so funny. She died! Hilarious! Well, if you will allow me vodka instead of whiskey, then I shall live a very long time indeed." He continued to chuckle for a few minutes. "Well, my friend, how can I help you this fine day?"

"We should talk about Germany and the end of the war. Last time we talked, I gave you a letter from President Roosevelt having to do with Berlin. We had expected a reply, and having received none, it is time to ask more directly."

"But all that was long since settled," Stalin said with a shrug. "We talked in Teheran, and all was decided. Nothing has changed as far as I can see. The Nazis are finished, except for a few scurrying cockroaches that we'll crush over the next couple of months. You gave me that letter from President Roosevelt about Berlin, and that's why I asked you about his health. Surely, only ill health would explain how he could have forgotten the arrangements he had previously made with me."

"Refresh my memory, Chairman. Which arrangements were those?"

"I'm shocked, Harriman. You know those as well as I do. I'm talking about postwar spheres of influence in Germany. Our plans to make sure that those criminal bastards don't rise up again and give us a third world war to fight."

"Oh, *those* spheres of influence. But you had canceled those, as far as we were concerned."

Stalin looked innocently shocked. "Canceled them? I did no such thing."

"Your separate peace with Germany. After you warned us so stringently against even thinking about such an action, you turned around and did it to us."

Stalin threw up his hands. "Harriman, how can you say such a thing to me? We've been good friends for such a long time, I thought surely you and Roosevelt would understand perfectly how little that temporary armistice meant. It was nothing, really. It surely was nothing that would in any way abrogate the arrangements we had so carefully established at Casablanca and Teheran."

"I'm afraid that we regarded it as something far more serious."

"Oh, my dear Harriman, you're sadly mistaken. Sadly mistaken! Frankly, our decision was based primarily on the practical reality that our supply situation was such that we could not continue to advance for several months until we were able to build up our stores again. Getting a peace out of the stupid Germans saved Soviet lives at no cost to the war effort, as we would be unable to act anyway."

"It freed them up to move against us in the west."

Stalin frowned. "And this means what? That you in the west now have suffered one one-hundredth part of what we have suffered from the Germans? You Americans have never sufficiently appreciated the extent to which it has been the Soviet Union who has suffered most in the war, the Soviet Union who has fought most in this war, the Soviet Union who has made it possible for your armies to move as rapidly and as successfully, the Soviet Union who has borne the burden. We took a well-deserved rest, we fooled the Germans into leaving us alone for a few months, we came back into the war effort and are moving forward on the original timetable, and with all of that you want to use this as an occasion to cheat us out of our rightful share of the spoils and our rightful role in ensuring that the German hydra does not have a chance to grow multiple heads and return to menace us again? Make no mistake—it is us they will menace again first, not you."

"You took Norway and Greece."

"So, you think we should be satisfied with whatever crumbs you want to dole out to us from the victory table? Who appointed you Tsar of all the Russias? We liberated two nations ahead of the Allied schedule, removed the Nazi yoke from their backs, and you want to act as if this is a *bad* thing? Don't be ridiculous. Do you realize what kind of shape these nations are in? What kind of shape our nation is in? The burden of rebuilding, of reconstruction, is immense. It will be greater by far than the cost of fighting the war itself. Taking on additional nations is a liability more than an asset. But like you Americans, we Soviets have a responsibility to the world, and we will shoulder our burdens as you do.

"But I must tell you, my good friend Averrell—we will not take a backseat to you in your big fine country that has no bomb craters in it, that cannot count even a mere million dead, that has all its factories and power plants intact and running. No, my friend. This little pretend armistice means nothing. Forget it. It never happened. It changes nothing as far as agreements at Casablanca and at Teheran.

"And as for Berlin?" Stalin leaned forward, his mouth smiling and wide beneath his mustache. "Berlin is the capital of Germany. Germany must never pose a threat again to the Soviet Union. No nation other than the Soviet Union can guarantee that essential fact. So, you must tell President Roosevelt that our agreement still stands.

"Berlin—and all of the eastern part of Germany—will be ours."

LONDON, ENGLAND, 1938 HOURS GMT

Tube alloys. It was rather pathetic, Kim Philby thought as he worked at the desk in his flat. This was what came of allowing amateurs in the serious business of intelligence tradecraft. Having evidently once read Poe's "Purloined Letter," these amateurs had missed the essential point—it was just as much an error to call too little attention to the letter as it was to call too much to it.

The Directorate of Tube Alloys, part of the Department of Scientific and Industrial Research, simply had far too highly credentialed a team for a project with so pathetically minor a name. Sir John Anderson, lord president of the council, was involved, for goodness' sake, and a senior executive of Imperial Chemical Industries served as the directorate's managing director.

If in fact the project had something to do with tube alloys, its management would have developed a more exciting name to enable it to compete for funding: the Directorate of Advanced Missile Survivability, for example, or possibly the Directorate of Impervious Armor. No, it was clear that something important was being concealed under "tube alloys," and something that had gone on for a long time—since 1941, in fact. The longer such a program operated, the more likely that its result was not some chimera, but a real weapon, a real potential danger.

A misleading project identity was only a first line of defense, Philby recognized. Like an ordinary door lock or the ignition on an automobile, its intent was not to discourage the serious professional, but only to warn off the dilettante, the casual thief or intruder, the unobservant. Penetrating this initial line of defense was not something that created much risk for Philby, but he was certain that additional defenses would surround such a program. Fortunately, if the same amateurism that characterized the naming of the program had helped design the additional defenses, he would be in good shape. Still, it never did any harm to overestimate one's opponent, and he resolved not to lessen his personal security. He planned to be in this game for a long time to come.

Continuing to jot notes on his pad, he summarized his process and results to date and began to list the next questions and steps. His first step had been a survey of current programs and projects. This was fairly straightforward research, involving little direct risk. While there were black projects—so secret that even their names were classified—most secret projects were hidden in the same way as "tube alloys," buried under ordinary-sounding names and dropped into general lists. It was not a bad approach, in general, though it wouldn't stand up to a Kim Philby. Fortunately, there weren't many Kim Philbys out there.

While "tube alloys" was his best candidate, he had five or six other projects that he needed to probe a bit. Depending on the yield from his next probes, his target might change, but for now, he would continue on the course of highest probability.

Of course, the next question was to discover what "tube alloys" really concealed. For that, Kim Philby would draw upon years of personal contacts and relationships throughout government, contacts built from family, from public school and university, from clubs, from positions held, from the web of social class and education that knit the capitalist class structure together. He had developed a large network of agents, many of whom he had recruited to the Communist cause, others who were utterly unaware of their role. As usual, he used the tools of the system he planned to destroy against its own structure, the thought of which never grew tiresome or stale.

A good first step would be to look at the personnel records and organizational structure of the project. Who was who and how did they fit together?

Of course, lifting the personnel records of a classified government program, especially one that served as a cover for an even more secret program, was a dodgy exercise under the best of circumstances. From Kim Philby's perspective, it was complicated further because it crossed over the respective spheres of influence between MI-5 and MI-6. Because Philby had no intention of sacrificing his cover and his career over this mission, regardless of its importance, he needed plausible deniability should his inquiries receive unwanted scrutiny, which was all too possible no matter how well he ran this operation.

He needed two things: first, a legitimate excuse for the inquiry that was connected with his own operational area, and second, "trade goods" with which to bargain for reciprocal cooperation from the rival service. The second usually posed no problem. The number of favors each service needed from the other tended to be large, and as was the case in bureaucracies, formal requests had to go up the chain to cross over, then down to operational levels, where they automatically enjoyed far lower priority than requests generated internally. Only peer-to-peer requests received active support, and the lack of direct peer-to-peer channels frustrated cooperation and tended to increase mutual hostility. He would have to pay for the cooperation he needed, but he had the necessary currency.

For the legitimate excuse, he needed to create an ostensible German intelligence thrust at "tube alloys," which would necessitate his own investigation as part of turning or defeating the threat. This was a matter of simulating incoming traffic from his network of agents over a period of time—a few weeks would suffice—allowing him to build a case and generate a memorandum, for surely nothing in this world was real without a memorandum to certify its reality.

As Deputy Chief of Section 5 of MI-6, Philby was high enough to arrange direct peer-to-peer contact with MI-5. He had relationships of long standing, and by offering his own services in support, soon he would be in possession of the critical details of the Directorate of Tube Alloys.

And then he would have enough information to justify a report to Moscow.

His next steps developed, he decided that this day was done. Time to burn his notes, take up his pipe, and do some pleasant reading before bedtime.

HEADQUARTERS, SECOND GUARDS TANK ARMY, EAST OF POZNAN, POLAND, 1954 HOURS GMT

Colonel Krigoff took a breath of the cold night air and willed the frigid temperature to cool his nerves. Nevertheless, he felt sweaty and agitated, almost giddy, as he approached the gate of the compound where the staff officers were encamped. He had been called from his trailer office by a sentry, who had reported to him—breathlessly—that there was a *woman* asking to see him. That, he assumed, could only mean one thing.

Indeed, Paulina Koninin was pacing restlessly outside the gate. She smiled nervously when she saw him approaching, even stood at a semblance of attention as he spoke to the captain of the guard post.

"She is an official visitor," the colonel explained. "I assume you have already checked her identification papers?"

"Yes, Comrade Colonel! She has proper documentation, as a member of the State Film Bureau, but no pass for this compound. As you know, regulations require—"

"Yes, of course, an official escort. You did well to summon me immediately." Krigoff nodded at the man, then turned to Paulina, his expression forcibly masked to conceal his current state of delight from the lower-ranking officer. "Comrade Koninin, would you care to join me in the officers' mess? It is somewhat warm in there, at least, and at this hour we will be able to talk, uninterrupted."

"Thank you very much, Comrade Colonel," she said, coming through the gate. Feeling rather dashing, he extended his arm, and felt a tingle of delight as she took his elbow. They walked through the compound, which had once been a village square but was now surrounded only by a few tattered walls indicating where buildings had stood. The vehicles of the army headquarters, massive trucks and heavy trailers, were parked around the periphery, looming larger than the small houses they replaced. The ground was covered in slush, which the two Russians easily kicked out of the way, their worn boots slick and wet.

The officers' mess was simply a large, walled tent. A sentry pulled aside the door flap and they entered, immediately surrounded by humid warmth. Kerosene lanterns cast enough light to illuminate long tables and benches, with a few groups of men sitting here and there, engaged in quiet chat or sharing bottles of vodka. Two large coal stoves radiated heat, and they sat beside the nearest of these while Krigoff sent an orderly for two cups of tea.

"Forgive me for coming to see you like this," Paulina said, tugging at her eyepatch and nervously looking around the cavernous enclosure.

"Nonsense! It is always a pleasure to see you!" he replied at once. This was the truth, and in fact he didn't really care *why* she wanted to see him; he was just glad she was here. He waited for her to speak, enjoying the faint flush that seemed to color her ruddy, weather-chapped cheek.

"Perhaps you know that the State Film Bureau is assigning photographers to cover the advance of Comrade Marshal Zhukov's armies?" she said tentatively. "Of course, the objectives of the operation are secret. I in no way wish to breach this security!"

"Of course not," Krigoff said soothingly. "But I do know that the heroic exploits of the Red Army are subjects of historical interest, and it is important that they be recorded. As to the First Belorussian Front—well, you certainly know that I am with the Second Guards Tank Army, and that we form the spearhead of Comrade Marshal Zhukov's advance."

"Yes, I do know that. There is a crew that will be assigned to accompany the leading elements of your army, as a matter of fact. My superiors are currently making these selections. However, the director bears some outdated ideas regarding the respective roles of his female photographers, and it is becoming apparent to me that he has me in mind for some rear-echelon task, instead."

Krigoff felt a rush of indignation sweep through him, and he almost pounded his fist on the table. Instead, he leaned closer and, feeling exceptionally daring, reached out to take her hand. "That would be an outrage!" he snapped. "I was with you in the airplane over Warsaw—I saw your courage, your steadiness firsthand!"

"I was hoping you would remember that," she said, with a reassuring squeeze of his fingers.

"Tell me, is there something I can do that might help? I cannot countenance such a waste of your skills, especially for a fatuous concern like this— does your director not understand the important role that the women of Russia have played in this great war?"

"I believe that he knows," she said. "But I am not sure he approves."

With a shake of his head, Krigoff all but condemned the man to a lifetime in the gulag—though that could come later. For now, he would deal with the immediate problem. "I will speak to my commissar," he told her. "And specifically ask that you be assigned to our headquarters. If necessary, I will personally see that you have a place with the leading battalion of our tank army!"

"Thank you, Alexis Petrovich—"

"Please, call me Alyosha . . . Paulina," he said, staring into her one eye, wondering if she could perceive the passion burning within him. It was not merely the passion of a man for a woman, of course—although that passion was certainly present—but the passion of two people toward a cause that was destined to transcend all of human history.

She squeezed his hand again, and he knew that she understood. He smiled, and led her from the mess back toward his quarters.

509TH COMPOSITE BOMBING GROUP, WENDOVER FIELD, UTAH, USA, 2345 HOURS GMT

General Groves got out of the car and stretched. He liked this place—it was perfect for the purpose it served. The great salt flats of this remote valley extended to the horizon to the north and south, allowing for smooth runways many miles long, with clear, unobstructed flying space beyond. To the east and west the ridges of dry mountain ranges framed this very secret base, served to keep operations safe from prying eyes.

Nearby, a line of B-29s was arrayed beside a hangar, while farther off another one of the big, silver bombers revved its engines for takeoff. Groves stood still and watched the sleek aircraft rumble down the runway, looking oddly stilted on its tripod of landing gear. The takeoff ran for more than two miles, bringing the bomber right past the general. He turned and watched, waiting for it to rise from the ground, following the image of the long metallic wings shimmering in the late-afternoon heat over the desert—until there was a slight falter in the pitch of the big Wright engines.

"Damn," he muttered under his breath, knowing that takeoff was aborted. The bomber was clearly slowing down now; it would idle back here over the next hour, and the ground crew would go to work on the temperamental engines one more time. How long would it be before they got those bugs worked out?

"General Groves. We've been expecting you, sir. Would you like to come inside?"

He turned to see that Colonel Tibbets had come up behind him. The commander of the 509th led the visiting general into a spartan office at the end of a Quonset hut. They sat on hard folding chairs, across from each other at a small desk, and Groves knew the colonel well enough to understand that he wouldn't be getting a drink stronger than a Coke.

"When can we move out, General?" asked Tibbets, sort of plaintively. "We've been training here for near six months now! I understand they have space set aside for us on one of those Marianas bases—Tinian, right? General, these men deserve to get into the war before this whole thing is over! Now I hear the marines have landed on Iwo Jima—look at the map! Are we going to let the foot soldiers win this war—and God knows how many of them get killed—when we could do it from the air?"

"Relax, Paul." Groves was not in the mood for his subordinate's zealotry. "Yeah, we have Iwo—and it was a bloodbath. And there's space for the Five-oh-ninth on Tinian. The plan, last I heard, is still to get you guys over there. But the gadget's not going to be ready for months, yet—"

"Still, we can practice with the dummies! You had the pumpkins made, didn't you?"

"Yes. You convinced me to have all seventy-five made. I still don't like the idea of dropping them outside of the country, though. You can get plenty of practice right here in Utah. And if that's not big enough, I can get you Nevada, too."

Tibbets pursed his lips and drew a breath through his nose. Any normal man would have resorted to profanity at this point, but not the devout colonel. "Then, what is the holdup? What can you do about it?"

Groves leaned forward, and looked the pilot right in the eyes. He kept his voice low, and Tibbets shifted in his chair, moving closer to hear. "There is a chance—just a chance, right now—that the Five-oh-ninth will be needed in Europe."

The colonel's eyes widened. "You don't mean . . . ? But the Germans, they're finished, right?"

Without wavering his gaze, the general continued. "It is possible that Japan will not be the greatest enemy facing us by the end of this year. And if that's the case, Paul, then this country is going to need you. And I mean, *really* need you."

20 FEBRUARY 1945

SHAEF HEADQUARTERS, REIMS, FRANCE,
0817 HOURS GMT

Eisenhower looked out the window at the railway station. He drummed his fingers on the desk. "What the hell is the matter with Rommel? Dammit, we've got to get the goddamn Germans moving eastward again, or else we're going to be looking straight in the face of a Russian occupation!"

"Ike, this concentration-camp thing has thrown everybody for a loop," Bradley replied. "We knew it was there, but nobody could imagine what it was going to look like close up. And Rommel . . . well, hell, Ike, how would you feel if this was a marine-run prison camp in Louisiana?"

Eisenhower stretched his neck and reached a hand back to rub a sore spot. "Dammit, I understand," he said. "It was unbelievable. And you're right. If I discovered it was Americans behaving like that, I don't know what the hell I would do. Jesus Christ, how *could* the Nazis do something like that? There were *children* in that place. Children!" He threw up his hands in disgust.

Bradley nodded. "I'm seeing some of the preliminary reports from last night. It looks like there's another one outside Munich—Dachau, I think they called it. And, if you can believe it, they say the worst ones are all in Poland. That means the Soviets will find them first, and God knows what kind of prop-aganda they'll put out."

"Lampshades made of human skin—barbaric!" Eisenhower shook his head. "But what are we going to do about Rommel? I understand he's just ordered everybody to stand still or help clean up the camp."

"That's right," Bradley replied. "Von Manteuffel's chief of staff, and so he's technically running things. It's a Junker-style army, you know, where the chief of staff basically keeps things moving while the Prussian aristocrat struts around the front lines and looks brave. Rommel, of course, is a lot more hands-on than most, but even so, he's laid down the law. Von Manteuffel's not planning to move unless it's on Rommel's say-so. And Rommel isn't saying so."

"So, what is Rommel doing? Carting food and dead bodies?"

"That's about the size of it. He's basically taking over as latrine orderly for the camp, shoveling shit and sweeping the barracks. I expect he'll put himself on KP next and we'll find him peeling potatoes." Bradley shook his head, disgusted.

"Oh, hell, Brad, I can understand it all right, even sympathize to some extent. But we can't afford to have him do a whole atonement production. We need him back in action. He ain't exactly Gandhi, you know."

"Don't let Winston hear you say that," said Bradley, grinning. It was well known that Churchill strongly disliked Gandhi and his movement for Indian independence.

"We've got to go talk to him," Eisenhower said, swiveling around and placing both hands on his desk. "Tell him what he has to do. Hell, maybe we can tell him that getting moving is the best way to liberate the rest of these camps. Find the guilty and lock them up. Whaddaya think?"

"Worth a shot. We've got to do something."

"I'll have Kay drive us there right after lunch. Dammit, I've got to see this for myself." Eisenhower's voice became firmer as he made a decision.

"Yeah. I think I probably need to see this too," Bradley replied. "What else have you got?"

Eisenhower shuffled through a few more papers and came up with a memo. "From the president. See what you make of it."

Bradley ran his eyes quickly over the memorandum, and picked out the important section.

I HAVE INFORMED PREMIER STALIN THAT UNDER NO CIRCUMSTANCES ARE SOVIET TROOPS TO ENTER BERLIN. AS A RESULT OF THE SOVIET/GERMAN SEPARATE PEACE, PREVIOUS AGREEMENTS AMONG THE ALLIES WITH RESPECT TO POST-WAR AREAS OF OCCUPATION NO LONGER APPLY. NOW THAT THE SOVIETS HAVE RESUMED HOSTILITIES AGAINST THE NAZI FORCES, THEY MAY CONTINUE TO ADVANCE AGAINST OPPOSITION, BUT ONLY AS FAR AS THE ODER RIVER. YOU WILL OCCUPY BERLIN AS SOON AS PRACTICAL, AND ENSURE THAT SOVIET FORCES FOLLOW THE GUIDELINES SET FORTH ABOVE.

Bradley shook his head. "So, we're going to walk into Berlin and when Zhukov and his boys show up, we're going to say 'Shoo!'?"

"Yep. That's what it looks like."

"And you expect them to turn around and walk back across the Oder like good little Russians?"

"That's what the president expects to happen, at least according to this memo."

"Well, goddamn, Ike! Have you talked to General Marshall about this?"

"As soon as I got it."

"And what did Marshall have to say?"

"He seems to be of the opinion that they'll go peacefully." Ike swiveled around to look out the window again. "Which means there's something big that Washington has up its sleeve that they're not telling us about."

"Won't be the first time," Bradley said.

"Nor the last."

"What do you suppose it is?"

"I'm guessing it's some superweapon. There's been talk, you know."

"Yeah, I've heard a rumor or two myself. But how super can a super-weapon really be? Those Nazi V-1 and V-2 rockets were fairly nasty, but didn't mean a damn thing as far as the war effort was concerned. Those Messer-schmitt jet fighters shut down the bombing campaign for a little bit, but not for very long. If Washington has a superweapon big enough to scare the Sovi-ets back to the steppes, it's got to be a hell of a lot bigger than the V-2 and the Me-262s put together. Think they've got anything that big, or have the lab boys talked up some big, fancy scheme that will never work on the battle-field?"

"Hell if I know, Brad. But I think you and I probably need to start planning on the idea that this thing, whatever it is, won't work half as well as Washing-ton thinks it will, and figure out how we can kick a pissed-off Soviet army back across the Oder if we have to. In the meantime, I'll talk to General Marshall and see if I can pin down a few more details about what we've got up our sleeve."

"Which means we better get Rommel back in action, and fast," replied Brad.

"And figure out how to describe this to Georgie in such a way so he doesn't get into a premature shooting war until we've got ourselves into a posi-tion we can defend," Eisenhower added.

21 FEBRUARY 1945

**MAIN CAMP, KONZENTRATIONSLAGER BUCHENWALD,
1507 HOURS GMT**

The Desert Fox waited patiently in line with the other enlisted men behind the supply truck, standing stoic and silent in the frigid air. When his turn came, he took the heavy crate in his arms, and turned back toward the medical barracks, trudging heavily through the dirty snow. With one foot, he pushed open the wooden door and twisted himself to get the awkward crate through the narrow opening. His grip slipped slightly, and the crate began to teeter dangerously in his arms. The feldwebel checking in the crates stepped forward to help him, but the cold look on Rommel's face made him step back. Straining, Rommel pulled his heavy burden up, lifted it high, and placed it on the growing pile of unloaded supplies. He took one deep breath, straightened up, then turned to go outside for the next crate.

As he pulled open the door, another man was entering, staggering under the load of his crate. It was Sanger, in immediate danger of losing the heavy box. Rommel held the door as Sanger twisted himself inside, then left without saying a word. Unlike the Desert Fox, Sanger did not object to the feldwebel's assistance with the heavy crate, and his load was shortly added to the pile.

On his way out the door, Sanger found an American lieutenant waiting for him. "Colonel? General Eisenhower is here and would like to see you."

"Jeez, I look like shit," he said, looking down at himself. He was wearing fatigues with a heavy coat, two pair of long underwear, a hat with earflaps, and everything was filthy. "Do I have an opportunity to change, or does the general need me immediately?"

The lieutenant, a headquarters type who was immaculate in his own uniform, except for the snow-mud mix that was staining his spit-shined shoes, looked Sanger up and down with a disdainful air. "Sir, my guess is the general would prefer to see you sooner rather than later." His body language suggested that he was glad that *he* would never be caught like that when a senior officer wanted to see him, but at this point Sanger didn't care.

"All right," Sanger replied. "Lead on, Macduff," he misquoted.

"The name's Wright, sir," the lieutenant corrected.

Sanger grinned wearily. "Lead on, MacWright," he amended, ignoring a look from the lieutenant that suggested he had a screw loose.

*　　*　　*

"Lieutenant Colonel Sanger, reporting as ordered, sir!" he said, coming to attention in his dirty clothes.

"At ease, Sanger," Eisenhower replied. "I see you've been working hard." The general didn't seem to be angry about his unmilitary dress, and Sanger took that as a very good sign.

"I figured staying near the field marshal was my job, and he's not letting anybody near him who isn't working," Sanger replied.

Eisenhower looked over at Bradley for a moment, then turned back to Sanger. "Will he talk to me?"

Sanger grimaced. "I don't think so, sir. He's not talking to anyone right now."

"How about you?"

There was a long pause. "Sir, he got pretty angry with me on the night we liberated this camp, and hasn't spoken to me since."

"What happened?"

"He was about to shoot a couple of the SS guards who were running the children's barracks, and I stopped him."

"For God's sake, why?"

"They needed a court-martial before they could get a formal execution."

Eisenhower looked at him. "Well, I'm glad you respect the military justice system," he said with a hint of sarcasm, "but why on earth would you get involved in that? Hell, it was still a combat zone at the time. Not that I'm suggesting that makes it okay or anything, but still . . ."

"Sir, this situation must be formally investigated for the record of history." Sanger stood at rigid attention.

Eisenhower leaned back in his chair and looked sideways at Bradley. "Well, I suppose I understand that. I hate to ask, Sanger, but has your effectiveness as liaison officer come to an end?"

Sanger thought for a moment. "I really don't know, sir. I'd like a few more days to find out, with the general's permission."

"You've done a good job so far, son," Eisenhower said. "If you can straighten things out with Rommel, I'm happy for you to stay on. But if you can't, you need to tell me before I have to find out officially on my own. Understand me?"

"Yes, sir," Sanger answered. "Thank you, sir."

"So, is he just not talking to you, or not talking to anyone?"

"Not to anyone, as far as I can tell. He did have a few words with von Manteuffel, but he made von Manteuffel help him sweep out one of the blocks while they were talking."

"Really?" chuckled Eisenhower. "That must have been a sight."

"I'm afraid that if you want to talk to him, you may have to do the same thing."

"Are you suggesting that the Supreme Commander go on KP?" Bradley interjected.

"Begging the general's pardon, but I guess I am, sir," replied Sanger. "That's the best advice I've got, anyway."

Eisenhower laughed. "Well, hell, I haven't done any real work in years. It'll be good for me. How about you, Brad? Up for a little work today?"

Bradley sighed. "First Patton, then Montgomery, and now Rommel. I've never had to do so much work just to get somebody to settle down and listen for a while. All right, let's do it. Sanger, the general and I need some work clothes."

The hospital block had really only served as a waiting room for death. Hundreds of bodies, infected, wounded, septic, filthy, had been jammed in, four or five to a bunk, to die. The death rate was so high that sometimes two or three days' worth of dead would be waiting for collection. Everyone who could be moved had been moved as quickly as possible to something approaching regular military hospital conditions, but transporting and setting up a hospital took time. It was time the inmates of Buchenwald didn't have.

For the rescuers, assignment to that barracks was the worst of the jobs. The odor was foul, and with each breath you inhaled God only knew what soup of germs. The wounds had festered; maggots crawled from the bodies of the recently dead that had not yet been removed for disposal.

Dwight Eisenhower, Supreme Allied Commander, lifted his mop to right shoulder arms, picked up his bucket, and went inside. His eyes didn't take long to adjust from the gloomy gray outdoor weather, and he surveyed the long, open barracks. The Desert Fox looked up from his mop, then looked back down, face expressionless, eyes dead. Eisenhower sighed, put his bucket down, dunked his mop into the soapy water, and began to clean.

THIRD ARMY HEADQUARTERS, ERFURT, GERMANY, 2212 HOURS GMT

"You did *what*?" asked Patton incredulously.

"Mopped out a barracks," the Supreme Commander repeated. "Hell of an afternoon. My back will be sore for a week. I'm not used to this anymore. How about you, Brad?"

Omar Bradley sat down heavily in one of Patton's office chairs. "I'm whipped."

"Did he *talk* to you?" Patton asked.

"Yep. A little, at least. Didn't get very far with him, though," Eisenhower replied. "Interesting man. I spent a lot of time thinking about the psych reports G-2 did on him way back when. 'Intuitive,' 'brilliant,' 'brittle,' and 'temperamental' are a few words that came to mind."

"Sounds like a fucking prima donna, if you ask me," growled Patton.

Bradley let out a guffaw. "Talk about the pot calling the kettle black!"

"At least I haven't asked you to mop any fucking floors," retorted Patton.

"Georgie, maybe it comes with being a genius. You and Rommel, right? Maybe being brilliant in commanding armor means you have to be a little nuts, right?" laughed Eisenhower.

Patton grinned. "Okay, maybe that explains me and Rommel, but then how do you account for Monty?"

With that, all three generals began to laugh. "Hell, George, it's bad form to speak ill of the dead," Eisenhower said, still laughing.

Bradley wiped his eyes. "Jeezus, I needed that. Not a whole lot of laughs these days."

"You said it," Eisenhower replied. "And we've still got to figure out how we're going to get Rommel back up on his horse and back to work. Georgie, you got any ideas?"

Patton shook his head. "Damned if I'm going to go mop barracks just to kiss a goddamn German general's hairy ass. If you'll forgive me for saying so, that's just fucking stupid."

"You don't have to go mop, George," said Eisenhower wearily, the day catching up with him. "Although it might do you some good. I'm not sorry we did it, and maybe we have to give Rommel another couple of days before we decide to take some different action. It's a hell of a mess there, George. I've never seen anything like it."

"Well, neither have I," Patton said with a growl in his voice. "It's fucking awful."

"I agree," Eisenhower replied, stifling a yawn. "George, we really just dropped by to borrow a couple of cots for the night. I don't feel like riding all the way back to Reims before I can stretch out."

"I got the best hotel in town, all ready for you," said Patton with expansive generosity. "You want the bridal suite?" he leered, obviously thinking about the very attractive Kay Summersby.

Eisenhower chose not to respond to Patton's sally. "Right now, even a GI standard-issue cot would be fine."

Realizing he might have slipped over the line, Patton switched to unctuous charm. "Well, then, how about a little medicinal pick-me-up after a hard day's work."

"I wouldn't say no to that, Georgie."

"Great!" Patton opened a cabinet door to a shelf lined with liquor. "I've got some damn fine cognac here."

"Sounds good," said Eisenhower, suppressing a yawn. "Good for you, too, Brad?" he asked his companion.

But Bradley had nodded off to sleep.

U.S. ARMY FIELD HOSPITAL, ETTERSBURG, GERMANY,
2217 HOURS GMT

"How is he, Doctor?" the Desert Fox asked in a quiet voice.

"He's doing well. The man must have the constitution of an ox. Between his earlier unhealed wound and the exposure in the camp, it's a miracle he is alive. Frankly, I'm surprised at the rate with which he's healing. Today, I caught him quizzing one of the orderlies about the state of your health, and it was all I could do to keep him from getting up to take care of you."

Rommel looked down at the sleeping feldwebel and smiled. "He's a good man."

"A lot of these boys are good men," the doctor agreed. "Now that you're here, though, I can do something I promised Clausen. Let me look at that eye of yours."

Rommel shoved the doctor's prying hands aside. "I have no time for that. I'm fine."

"Do you want to be responsible for Clausen getting out of bed in the morning?" growled the doctor. "If I can't tell him that I checked you out, there's going to be hell to pay in this ward. Understand?"

Rommel's dour face yielded a small smile. "Oh, all right. Do what you must, but do it quickly. It's a hell of an army where the field marshals take orders from the feldwebels, *nicht wahr?*" He fidgeted as the doctor took off his patch, looked and prodded at him. "Damn it! That hurt."

"Infection. You need to stay out of the camp for a few days and get treated."

"Impossible, Doctor," Rommel replied firmly.

The doctor shook his head. "You may lose that eye altogether," he said. "I hate like hell to do this, but I'll put some ointment on it and let you go. But when you come back, I want another look. Okay?"

Rommel sighed. "Very well, Doctor. May I sit with Clausen for a while?"

"Good idea for both of you. You need to sit down, and a sick man benefits from company. I'll pull a chair over for you. I'll be making rounds for a while yet, so I'll check back every once in a while. If you feel like getting a bit of sleep, I can scrounge up a bed."

"Thank you, Doctor." Rommel sat in the chair and looked at the sleeping feldwebel. Clausen was a stocky man normally, but his flesh sagged from weeks of near-starvation. His mouth was open as he slept; the pronounced gap between his front teeth quite visible. But what Rommel noticed most was the expression of contentment, the smile across Clausen's broad face. How could he manage to be happy in the face of so much misery, Rommel wondered to himself.

"I imagine that you did everything you could to improve the situation until you got so sick you could no longer move," Rommel said quietly to the sleeping man, putting his hand on Clausen's shoulder. "Did you give your food to the children? If it was possible, I'm sure you did. Did you rig up some mechanical device to improve life in the barracks? How is it that one man can stay so engaged with life under the most appalling circumstances, when others sicken and die? It's a talent I fear I lack completely."

He sat quietly for a time, but his mind kept racing around a narrow track. He could not let go of his feelings of anger, of frustration, of self-loathing; he could not find in himself any particle of Clausen's peace. Finally, he decided it was time to go, to work himself until his body was forced to sleep, taking his mind temporarily with it. He stood.

"Field Marshal?" It was Clausen, voice only slightly louder than a whisper. The feldwebel's eyes opened.

"Shh," Rommel said. "I apologize. I did not mean to wake you."

"You didn't wake me," Clausen replied. "Please don't worry. Sit, if you have time. You look tired. Have you been taking care of yourself? Doing your exercises? Eating well?"

Rommel smiled, sat down. "None of the above, I'm afraid."

"Then I'll get the doctor here. The kitchen must have someone in it; we'll order you some food. It's important for you to eat well. You're still recovering from your wounds, you know." Clausen fumbled for the cord that would summon a nurse or doctor.

"Don't disturb anyone for now," Rommel said, patting Clausen on the arm. "If it makes you feel better, I give you my oath that I will find something to eat as soon as I leave. All right?"

"Good." Clausen sank back into his bed. "Now that I'm awake I can arrange for people to take care of you until I'm fully back on the job."

"Ah, Clausen, I don't know how I ever managed to live without you. Even my dear wife doesn't take care of me the way you do."

"How is she? Has she managed to get to you? How about your son?" Again, Clausen struggled to get up, to take some action.

"All well. Lucie and Manfred reached Bitburg safely, and I had men in place to bring them out. They have temporarily gone to England. I've sent Günther along with them." Rommel's batman Herbert Günther had been with him for many years, and was nearly a member of the family.

"Good, good," Clausen replied. "I'm glad. Günther will take good care of them."

"Yes, I know he will. And soon every member of the Rommel family will have a good caretaker. Keep resting so you can come back to duty strong and ready. This is an awful place, and I'm very glad you have survived it."

"It wasn't so bad, at least for me. But the others . . . Field Marshal, did you find the children?"

The children. "Yes. I found—" A huge lump swelled in his throat, and he was unable to finish his sentence. He tried again. "I found—" He was choking on his own voice. He could not speak. The lump was so large it felt as if it was about to burst from his throat, tear him apart. For the first time in many years, he felt the hot flush of tears burning in his eyes. It shamed him.

"They're all right, aren't they?" Clausen asked, concern in his voice.

"All right? How could—" He paused, tried again. "How could anyone—" He stopped. The tears had welled in his eyes in spite of everything he could do to stop them. They burned.

Clausen reached over, touched his hand in concern. "It's not your fault."

"Not my fault? Not my fault? How can you say that?" The words began to spill over the lump. "I was a field marshal in the service of the Third Reich. I was fighting to support the people who did this!"

"But you didn't know."

"I did, don't you understand? I chose not to, but I did. Maybe not in the beginning, but I did. I did. God help me, I did." He buried his face in his hands. His shoulders heaved with silent sobs.

"You didn't know," Clausen said again. "You couldn't."

Rommel looked up. His eyes were red, but dry. "I chose not to know. In the beginning, there were only a few cases of abuse, and I could believe that as the Nazis settled into power, even that would go away. Every nation has some of this behavior, and in an imperfect world, we accept it. Then came the Nuremberg laws that restricted the Jews, but I understood that was a temporary situation and in the end, it would just mean that people would be moved to new locations where like would be with like. Then I was in North Africa, and all that came to me was the occasional rumor, and rumors can easily be disregarded."

His voice grew steadily more controlled. "Then I returned from North Africa and started to learn who Adolf Hitler really was, but I resisted that knowledge because he had always been kind and supportive to me personally, at least until the end of the African campaign."

"But there were more rumors. These were harder to ignore, but I had sworn a soldier's oath of loyalty. I was a servant of the state and not its master. It was my duty to follow my orders, and these other matters were none of my business. And then came more rumors, but they were so ridiculous, so absurd, that no sensible person could possibly give them credence. Thousands dead? Millions? War is hard and bad things happen; I knew that. I did my duty. It's taken me this long to figure out what my duty really is."

"But you switched sides ultimately," Clausen argued. "You liberated this camp and these people. You are doing what is right."

"I didn't switch sides for the victims; I switched sides for one reason— Germany's leadership was losing the war. I'm still not fighting on the right side." He shook his head. "I thought of myself as a man of honor, a man dedicated to duty and to virtue. But I have betrayed everything."

Clausen said nothing. Rommel's eyes were unfocused, distant.

"I found the children's barracks shortly after we took the camp," he said quietly. "There were guards. I wanted to kill them. I wanted to kill myself. But there were all the children, looking at me. They knew. I wore a German uniform. They knew. I took off my coat, and tried to hand it to a child, but he shrank from me. He knew. So I sat down and took the insignia off the coat. I handed them to one child. The insignia were bright and shiny. She took them. When the coat was clean, one of the children finally took it."

"So, I—" He paused again. The lump had returned. "I . . . took off my jacket and began to unpin my medals. I gave them all away. I didn't want them anymore. I even gave away my *Pour Le Merite*." The *Pour Le Merite* was the Imperial German equivalent of the Congressional Medal of Honor. Rommel had won the medal, normally reserved only for generals, as a lieutenant at Caporetto in World War I. "I climbed five mountains and captured ten thousand Italian soldiers to earn that medal because I was angry that someone else had gotten credit for my ascent of Mount Cosna." Rommel shook his head. "But it doesn't matter anymore. Nothing matters anymore."

"The children matter," Clausen said slowly.

"Yes, the children matter." Rommel put his face back down in his hands, and this time the tears flowed more easily.

23 FEBRUARY 1945

MAIN CAMP, KONZENTRATIONSLAGER BUCHENWALD, 0752 HOURS GMT

Chuck Porter ditched the press-pool escort as soon as he had a chance, and went looking for someone he knew. This story was huge; it was crowding everything else off the page. He needed an original slant, a different perspective. He needed to talk to the Desert Fox.

Of course, so did everybody else, and the Desert Fox wasn't talking to anybody. And that story—Rommel doing some strange sort of penance in the middle of a hellish prison camp ripped right out of the Spanish Inquisition—was the story he needed.

Porter figured the best way to go about it was to get access to his friends and trade on his personal relationships. Nothing much embarrassed him when he was after a story.

He was surprised to find Müller, the supply officer who had saved Rommel's life, occupying the old camp commandant's office. All the former camp offices and barracks were occupied by the liberating forces. Müller, though, was buried three feet deep in paperwork. Günter von Reinhardt was working some private mission, and no one knew where he was. Porter sniffed a story there, but maybe later.

The one person he did find was Reid Sanger, the officer who had replaced him as acting translator for Rommel's surrender. Sanger was occupying a small office that could barely accommodate a desk and a military-issue cot in the corner.

"Sanger?" Porter called out as he stuck his head into the office.

Reid Sanger stood up, slid his fingers through his disheveled blond hair. "Porter! Good to see you, though not surprising, I guess. This sure is the story now, isn't it?"

Porter stepped in, shook hands. He was aware that Sanger had been promoted to the liaison-officer role with Rommel, and that was just the inside track he needed. "Yep. I bet everybody's here."

"I guess. I actually saw Margaret Bourke-White taking pictures. I used to see her stuff in *Life*. I think she's the biggest nonmilitary celebrity I've ever met."

"Peg? Is she here?" Porter asked with studied casualness. He remembered an embarrassing dinner prewar in Paris, where he'd gotten seriously drunk and made an ill-received pass at the well-known photojournalist.

"Sure. You know her?"

"We've met. But, hey, listen, Sanger. The Desert Fox remembers me, right? I helped him out when he needed me. I know he's off-limits right now, but do you think he could spare a few minutes for an old buddy?"

Sanger laughed. "Nice try, Porter. But it's no way, no how. I'm sorry."

"Come *on,* Sanger. Tell him it's me, his old friend Chuck Porter. Didn't I do right by him in the surrender negotiations? Didn't I put him first and my story second? He owes me one. Just ask him. What harm could that do? All he could say is no, and he might say yes. How about it?"

"Porter, I'm truly sorry, but I can't. It's completely and absolutely out of the question. If there was any way, I'd help you, but there is just no way. None."

"So, I'll take that as a maybe," Porter replied. "And while we're waiting for you to arrange my interview with Rommel, maybe you could walk me around a little bit? I'm supposed to be on a leash with the rest of the press corps, but if I'm with the liaison officer to the German Republican Army, that would be all right, wouldn't it? Unless you're too busy doing liaison work . . . What the hell *is* liaison work, anyway?"

"Mostly going to meetings," said Sanger, his face suddenly blank.

Porter could tell that Sanger was holding something back. That was okay. Porter would keep prying and sooner or later something would break loose. "So, too busy to spend some time with an old friend?"

Sanger laughed and shook his head. "Okay, you win. Let's go for a walk and I'll tell you everything I can. But don't screw me, okay?"

"Screw you? Would I screw an old friend?" Porter spread his arms wide to show he meant no harm.

"Not unless it would make a good story," replied Sanger cynically.

"I am deeply wounded and hurt by your suspicious nature," Porter said, putting his hand over his heart. "But I guess the suspicious nature comes from being an intelligence officer."

"You got it," said Sanger. He grabbed his hat and overcoat and began to bundle up. "It's still colder than a witch's tit out there."

"Don't I know it," Porter replied. "Let's hold the next war someplace warm, okay?"

"I'll get right on it."

"Okay."

When they stepped outside of the long, low building, Porter immediately hugged himself even inside his thick coat. "God damn, it's cold. Brrr!"

"Imagine all you had on was a shirt and pants, maybe shoes," Sanger said. "That's what most of the prisoners had. They were worked between ten and fourteen hours a day and fed maybe a few pieces of bread and some soup.

Technically it was soup. Mostly it was hot water with a few chopped-up vegetables in each barrel."

Porter looked at the barbed-wire fence that separated the administrative area from the main prisoner compound. Near the main gate he saw the burned wreckage of a couple of guard towers. The remaining guard posts were manned. "How come you have guards? Worried about escapes?"

"Not as such," Sanger said. "Some prisoners have been doling out a little freelance justice on the former guards, but our guards are mostly keeping supplies secure. These people are starving, but if they eat too much too quickly, they get sick, they can't keep it down, and the shock can actually kill them."

"Eating can kill them?" Porter shook his head in noncomprehension.

"Most of them are on the edge of dying, and they've got to take it slow and easy, build up their strength. We're feeding them as fast as the doctors say they can take it. Warm clothes, heat, medical care—those things they can use immediately."

"Are they still dying?"

"Yeah. Twenty or thirty a day." Sanger shook his head sadly. "It's a damned shame, but there is nothing we can do for some of the worst cases. They're already dead, but still walking around until their bodies finally stop. You know, almost none of these people have been here more than six months. Hardly anyone lasts longer than that under these conditions."

As they approached the main gate, the German MP saluted Sanger, and opened the gate to admit the two men to the main compound. Although the cold kept the smell somewhat in check, it was still powerful. "Jesus," Porter said, putting his hand over his nose and mouth.

"Yeah, it's bad. It's better than it was, though," Sanger said. The remains of the last snowstorm had mixed with the mud to create a brown, crunchy expanse. Aside from soldiers and medical personnel, no one was out in the compound.

"How many people were in here?" Porter asked.

"At the height, about sixty-eight thousand. But that's not just here; there are over a hundred subcamps, most of them close to places where the prisoners were assigned to work. Still, it got quite overcrowded. When this camp was liberated, there were around twenty thousand people actually here. A couple of trainloads of Jews had been transported toward the East."

"I've been hearing about that. The death camps, right?"

"Evidently. Between you and me and the fencepost, the intel groups have known about the camps for a while, mostly from aerial photography. Now, Buchenwald is only a concentration camp. That's a combination of prison, torture of political prisoners, and management of slave labor. People died here—lots of people—but they were worked to death or beaten to death or killed after they were unable to work any more. Death was a by-product. The death camps, on the other hand, don't furnish slave labor. They're simply killing factories, processing plants. There's at least one in occupied Poland that is both a death camp and a concentration camp, but most of the camps are one or the other."

Porter shook his head. "How many dead?"

"We keep revising the likely death toll upward, but we won't know for sure until we can get everywhere. But it looks like well over a million victims just in the death camps, besides all the people that got worked to death here. Call it at least two million as a low-end estimate; the final number could end up a hell of a lot higher."

"And they were mostly Jews?"

"At the death camps, the vast majority are Jews. Concentration camps get more variety, but still a lot of Jews. There aren't a lot here right now, but that's because they tended to be worked to death faster, and a lot of them were cleaned out before we came. One thing is clear, though. The Nazis have been doing their level best to kill every single Jew in Europe. Men, women, children . . . everybody."

"Jesus Christ," Porter said.

"He was a Jew, too," Sanger observed.

"What's the story, though? Why Jews? Any particular reason?"

"Well, the Nazis believe that everything that ever went wrong in their country was the fault of the Jews and the International Zionist Conspiracy, whatever the hell that is. Communism, high interest rates, the loss of World War I—for all I know, the common cold and hangnails. Himmler was in charge of the mechanics of the operation, but it was Hitler's passion. When the war turned against him, the killing sped up. He was determined to get that job finished even if he lost the war. Hitler's dead, but as I said, it was Himmler's operation and he's still doing his level best to finish it."

"You mentioned kids. I heard there were children here."

Sanger shivered in his heavy coat. "Hundreds. They were not in as bad shape as some of the grownups. It looks like the women starved themselves even more to get at least some food to the kids. They were worked, though, just like grownups, and beaten and killed and abused in pretty much the same way. Well, in other ways, too." Sanger stopped walking, his eyes unfocused as he spoke.

"Listen, Sanger, seeing this stuff must have been hell, I know," Porter said sympathetically.

Sanger turned to Porter. "Yeah. But not as bad as living it." His voice was flat.

There was a commotion at one of the barracks. Sanger immediately began striding in that direction. Porter had to take about a step and a half for every pace of the taller man. Two German guards were marching someone out of one of the buildings. It was a woman, holding a large-format camera in her hands. Porter recognized her at once. Margaret Bourke-White had been traveling with Third Army throughout Europe.

"Sie können nicht Fotographien hier nehmen!" one of the guards was shouting as he tried to take her camera away.

"Hey! Hands off the merchandise!" she shouted. "No! *Nein! Hände weg!*" The German guards continued to shout.

"What is the matter here?" Sanger asked the guards in German.

"Hi, Peg," Porter said. "How are you?"

"Oh, hi, Chuck! Long time no see. How they hanging?" Bourke-White replied, still holding tightly onto her camera.

"This woman has taken a photograph of Generalfeldmarschall Rommel without authorization!" the guard said indignantly in German.

Sanger nodded. "I see."

"She must be turned over to the appropriate authorities for punishment!" continued the guard.

"I will see to it that the correct action is taken," replied Sanger. "Will that be satisfactory to you?"

"Most satisfactory, Herr Oberst!" replied the guard, saluting. He was nervous and started a sieg-heil salute without thinking, then, embarrassed, switched to a conventional salute. Sanger returned the salute in a punctilious manner, then switched to English.

"I have agreed to turn you over to the appropriate authorities," he said to the photographer.

"Oh, yeah? And who exactly would those be?"

"Those would be me," Sanger said. "If that's okay with you."

"Honey, if you can get these apes to get their hands off my camera, that will be just fine."

"Of course." He spoke in German briefly. "Now, if you don't mind coming with me?"

"I've got the shot, so it's okay by me."

"Thank you," Sanger replied.

"So, you got to Rommel?" Porter asked. His tone was friendly and casual, but he was significantly pissed off and more than a little jealous.

"I got within flashbulb range, anyway," she said. "They don't have to stay still long for me to do my job. It was Rommel and General Bradley. They were humping boxes in a line of enlisted men. It's going to be a hell of a photograph. A hell of a photograph!" Her eyes were shining.

"So, what's he look like right now?" asked Porter.

"He's just another dogface, except older and more scarred than most. I got a great shot. Real human-interest stuff." She was obviously pleased with herself. "Listen, Colonel . . ."

"Sanger. Reid Sanger."

". . . Colonel Reid Sanger, what's the story?"

"It's simple. Field Marshal Rommel wants to set an example and show the depths of his concern for the terrible situation here. General Bradley and some other senior Allied officers also felt the same way."

"Sounds like a quote direct from the press release," mocked Porter.

"I wrote the press release," Sanger replied calmly.

"I guess that explains it, then," said Porter. "That's the story?"

"That's the story. Nothing else. I think he sets a great example, don't you? I'm putting in six hours a day myself," Sanger added.

Porter looked at the tall, thin officer. "You? Yeah? When do you get the rest of your work done?"

"I put in a couple of hours at my desk in the morning through morning staff meeting, then go to work. Then I finish up paperwork after dinner."

"Getting much sleep?" asked Porter.

"Enough," replied Sanger.

Porter looked at him. The tall officer looked tired. "Maybe I should interview you."

"Nah. I'm not the story, and I don't intend to be the story. You want to interview somebody? Interview Colonel Müller. Bring him something to eat and talk him into taking a break. He needs one, anyway. He may not look like much, but he's got a lot more on the ball than you'd think. He's a real hero."

"Well, the man who saved Rommel's life should be good for a few more column inches," Porter said. "Speaking of lifesaving, I heard another interesting rumor. I know there were Americans here, but I heard that Rommel's driver was a prisoner here, too."

"Mutti? Yeah. Müller found him, in fact. Feverish, nearly dead. He was obviously stuck here as a Nazi slap at Rommel. Rommel sat up next to his hospital bed for several hours last night. Terrible thing. He had saved an American airman back in the Army Group B hospital that was raided, back in Dinant, and the American airman had kept him alive here in Buchenwald. Feldwebel Clausen can't talk yet, but you could track down the American. His name's O'Dell. There are a lot of stories here, not just Rommel. Look around. Miss Bourke-White?"

"Yeah, honey?" replied the photographer.

"Please go where you like and photograph what you like, but stay out of Rommel's way. I won't be able to help you again. Next time you lose the camera and the film. That's unofficial, but I mean it."

Margaret Bourke-White looked at Sanger for a moment, then nodded. "Okay, sweetie. I gotcha. Hey, just a second!" She lifted up her camera, popped in a big blue flashbulb, and pointed at Sanger. "Look over there, toward that guard tower. Okay?" The flash left him seeing double images for a few seconds. "Good. Thanks a lot."

"Thank *you*, Miss Bourke-White."

"The name's Peg, sweetie."

HEADQUARTERS, SECOND GUARDS TANK ARMY, POZNAN, POLAND, 1555 HOURS GMT

Colonel Krigoff was beside himself with frustration. He could *see* the walls of the ancient Polish fort, not two miles away from him, and he could *hear* the chatter of German machine guns snapping away from those very ramparts. And yet, nothing was being done about it. Poznan, like all these other filthy Polish towns, was merely an obstacle on the road to Berlin, and it was maddening to think that it was being allowed to delay the inevitable tide that was the Red Army.

The solution seemed obvious, even to a combat neophyte such as Krigoff: A thunderous barrage of artillery should blanket the fortress and the surrounding terrain. He had seen on several occasions the lethal, destructive storm of such firepower, and he was distressed and annoyed with the commander of the tank army, General Petrovsky, for failing to employ such a sound tactic. Instead, Petrovsky seemed inclined to let his armored spearheads slip around the rear of the fortress, while his infantry was closing in for a painstaking assault.

In good conscience, Krigoff could not allow this lapse to pass unchallenged. Though the general was currently busy with his staff officers, all of them studying the situation through binoculars from the upper story of this old manor house, he pressed forward, noting without surprise that the other officers stepped back to allow him the access to the division commander that he required—and that he deserved.

"General! This delay is unconscionable. Don't you realize that the First Guards Division is already moving around to the south? Why do you not have your guns concentrate on the objective? Blow it off the face of the earth!"

"Listen to me, Colonel, and I will explain it one more time," growled Petrovsky, the bearlike man—unlike his subordinate staff—failing to display fear, or even a decent measure of respect, to the intelligence officer who had already denounced one superior officer to the NKVD. "You cannot see them from here, but I have a thousand men advancing in the very shadow of that fort—a battalion that has been with me through Stalingrad, Kursk, and a host of other battles. Perhaps you've heard of some of those fights? We beat the Nazis in each of them!" His tone was acid, but Krigoff, while mentally recording each word, managed to keep his face impassive. The colonel made no reply, nor was one expected.

"Those men have lived through hell, five times over or more. They are within sight of the end of the war now, and I will not sacrifice them on the altar of haste. Rest assured, this fort will fall, and it will fall in good time—but *do not* tell me how to capture it!"

Krigoff stood rigid, his jaw clenched. There were many arguments he could make: Those men, those lives, were nothing compared to the goals of the state! How dare this mere soldier try to elevate them thus, when none other than Chairman Stalin himself had demanded that speed be of the utmost importance in this campaign?

But the colonel was pragmatic enough to realize that these arguments would carry no weight with this grizzled warrior, that it might even place Alyosha Krigoff himself in some physical danger should he press the matter now. He would accept, not defeat, but the necessity of a tactical withdrawal.

"Very well, Comrade General," he declared, with a crisp salute. "I shall return to my duties, and await the harvest of intelligence that our *eventual*"— he couldn't resist that one word—"capture of Poznan will inevitably yield."

Petrovsky was already ignoring him, binoculars pressed to his eyes as he scrutinized his precious infantry, the soldiers who would have been endangered by the thunderous barrage Krigoff so desperately desired. The colonel of intelligence departed, stiffly marching down the stairs from the overlook. He returned to his trailer, which had been parked in the lee of this shell-blasted manor for more than a day. There was nothing for him to do, not until they took some prisoners, or gained some ground that would yield useful data—the uniform insignia of slain Nazis, for example—to the intelligence staff.

But Krigoff couldn't just sit here, not under these circumstances. Finally he got up, left through the small door, and started toward the radio truck.

Perhaps it was time to send another report to Chairman Stalin.

24 FEBRUARY 1945

COMMANDANT'S OFFICE, KONZENTRATIONSLAGER BUCHENWALD, 0840 HOURS GMT

Wolfgang Müller sometimes bit his fingernails. Over the last three days, he had bitten them down to the quick. In spite of shipments of food and medicine and blankets and warm clothes, the liberated Buchenwald prisoners were still dying at a rate of twenty or more a day. That was lower than a day ago, but still a huge number. It struck him as horribly unfair. They had survived so much, and then died after they had been freed. It seemed oddly ungrateful of them.

Moving from German shortages to Allied plenty was a big adjustment—when he put together a requisition, he got what he ordered. He had to learn new forms and new procedures, of course, but that was something he could do well. What took more getting used to was the special clout his position gave him. The Desert Fox himself had made it clear that no military priorities would stand in the way of taking care of the prisoners of Buchenwald. And the Americans—including Eisenhower himself—after they toured the camp, or stayed to work, added their own indorsements to the orders.

Still, his days were long and full of details, and no matter how much he did, he felt it was little enough. He took a sip of coffee—another luxury was real American coffee—and began leafing through the sheaves of paper required for his next requisition.

A voice interrupted. "Did you know that Goethe himself once used this place as his private retreat?"

Müller looked up in surprise. A tall, dark-haired man with sharp features stood in the door. He wore a plain but pressed Wehrmacht officer's uniform with bare patches where the swastika and other Nazi insignia used to go. His face was drawn and tired, and he walked with a cane. "Günter! When did you get here?"

Von Reinhardt sat down in the visitor's chair, and leaned his cane against the desk. "Just now, Wolfgang. I have been driving places I should not drive and talking to people I should not know." He reached over the desk to steal one of Müller's cigarettes. It, too, was American-issue. "Shortly, I must find our dear field marshal and bring him up to date on all the news. But I see that you have become the new camp commandant."

"Don't even say that as a joke, Günter," retorted Müller. "This is the most horrible thing I've ever seen. We bring in food, but the prisoners can't keep it down. We had to put armed guards around it to keep prisoners from eating what would make them sick, or even kill them. People are still dying every day in spite of the medicine we bring in."

"Didn't you deal with this when you were at Peenemünde?" asked von Reinhardt. Müller's work with the V-1 and V-2 rocket programs was the assignment of which he was most proud.

"You mean, uh, slave labor," Müller replied. He looked down at his desk. "Yes, it was used in construction of the underground factories. But I didn't have anything to do with that part."

Von Reinhardt nodded. "I understand. But you did know about it."

"Yes, I did know," Müller said. He looked up, his face stricken. "Does that really make me guilty of this? I couldn't do anything about it; I wasn't involved in it."

"Now, that is a question worthy of the man who spent his summers here. Look out the window at that tree. The large one, the oak tree."

"I see it."

"That's Goethe's oak. He was another Wolfgang, just like you. He sat under it—the great man himself—and thought great thoughts. Some of them might apply to this problem."

Müller grinned weakly. "And you know these great thoughts, of course?"

Von Reinhardt grinned in return. "Well, I've read a little Goethe in my time. I'm not sure he will be of much comfort, though. 'We are never deceived, we deceive ourselves,' he wrote. You—and I, and the Desert Fox, and many of us—have strained not to know about some of the darker elements in our war. We cannot make excuses for that; Goethe tells us it is our own fault.

"He also observed, 'National hatred is something peculiar. You will always find it strongest and most violent where there is the lowest degree of culture.' That one is quite ironic, sitting near the city of Weimar as we are. I suspect Goethe was wrong on that point. In our Germany, high culture seems to exist side by side with the most uncivilized brutality. One does not excuse the other, however. The story of Weimar will forever be entangled with this place, I'm afraid. Perhaps such a juxtaposition is for the best."

Von Reinhardt looked out the window at Goethe's oak. The thick glass reflected his image, a ghost superimposed upon the strong leafless branches. "How about this? 'We do not have to visit a madhouse to find disordered minds; our planet is the mental institution of the universe.' I am not sure that's quite fair in the current circumstances, because the sin with which we are now wrestling is peculiar to the German people, and especially the German military, of this time. Though I must add, wreaking horror on one's fellow human beings is a time-honored profession unbounded by nationhood."

"Does he have any advice about what to do?" asked Müller. "You can describe a situation all day long, but what is the right thing to do?"

Von Reinhardt thought some more, then said, "I think Goethe only repeats wisdom you seem to have already acted upon. 'There is one elementary truth: that the moment one definitely commits oneself, then providence moves too. A whole stream of events issues from the decision, raising in one's favor all manner of unforeseen incidents, meetings and material assistance which no man could have dreamed would have come his way. Whatever you can do or dream you can, begin it now.' That's abridged, by the way. There was more to the quote."

"No doubt," replied Müller dryly. "And this means?"

Von Reinhardt gestured at Müller's desk. "You have committed yourself. Providence is moving, and things you cannot dream will come your way as a result. But, my friend, you have already revealed yourself as a man of action."

"So are you," said Müller, defensively.

"You're a good influence on me, then," replied von Reinhardt. "And, speaking of men of action, where might I find our Desert Fox?"

Müller paused, took off his glasses and polished them. He shook his head slowly. "You won't believe it, Günter. He's working as a laborer, taking the dirtiest and filthiest jobs for himself. He won't listen to anybody; he won't do his real job. He makes anyone who wants to talk to him work the same way, and half the time he still won't talk to them!"

Von Reinhardt bit his lower lip. "I should not be surprised at this. It is too bad that the field marshal does not have more interest in great literature. It would help him in the current situation."

"Uh, Günter—how would that help, exactly?" Müller thought his friend had some strange ideas from time to time.

"It would, among other things, help him understand that his situation, though painful, is not unique. This provides perspective. You see, he's lost his honor and is trying to get it back."

"I know you've said that before. We've talked about this. I still think it's silly. Field Marshal Rommel is an honorable man, and he has acted honorably in every respect."

" 'So are they all, all honorable men,' " murmured von Reinhardt, but Müller continued speaking on top of him.

"And this is really not his fault, except to the extent that it's all of our faults. Really, though, it's not that much our fault—it's the fault of the people who did it."

"On the contrary, I think it is all our faults in a core sense. It's his, and mine, and even yours. The only ones who can claim true innocence in this matter are those who could not have known about it, and those who did know and worked actively against it. All the rest of us are culpable, and we are all dishonored. Coming on top of Rommel's feelings of dishonor for the surrender, one cannot be surprised that he found an extreme solution. It may yet turn out for the best."

"There's still a war going on, you know," responded Müller acridly. "And he's not fighting it."

"Perhaps he's fighting a different war."

"That may be so, but the Americans and the British and our German Republican government are all up in arms because Rommel has stopped moving. The entire army is working to clean this situation up! It's important, but it's not the only thing going on!" Müller raised his hands in frustration. "Nobody can reason with him!"

Von Reinhardt tapped his cigarette into Müller's ashtray. "Tell me everything," he said.

"My god, where do I begin?" Müller asked. "Well, let's see. Rommel discovered the children's barracks and I found Mutti—"

"How is he?"

"Out of danger, but still very sick. He would not have lasted very much longer." Müller shook his head. "Rommel then sent troops out to both Ettersburg and Weimar, and ordered every citizen to tour the camps. Do you know, some people laughed and joked? Rommel arrested them and put them in one of the barracks. They are now part of the cleanup crew. Only a few joked—especially after the word got out. There was crying, and several people got sick. And . . ." He hesitated. "The mayor of Ettersburg and his wife committed suicide."

"Showing that they were, in the final analysis, honorable," von Reinhardt interjected.

"I suppose, but it's still horrible. There's enough death and suffering already. And there are reporters and photographers everywhere."

"Our friend Mr. Porter?"

"Oh, yes, he's here. He actually interviewed me for his story. I've never been part of a news story before. And an attractive American woman took my picture. She says it will appear in *Life*. What is that?"

"It's an American magazine with many photographs," von Reinhardt replied. "Congratulations. You're not only part of a news story, but part of history as well. One day you'll be in a book about this camp, possibly with that very photograph included."

Müller shivered. "No, thank you. I don't care to go down in history linked to this place."

"But you are, like it or not."

"I suppose, but—*oh, mein Gott!* What a horrible legacy." He shook his head and continued. "And there have been some criminal trials of the guards and officers . . . at least of those who managed to escape from the prisoners. I can't blame the prisoners at all, of course, but there were quite a few camp personnel who . . . er . . . cut themselves shaving, if you know what I mean." He drew a line across his throat with his index finger and made a *skrrt* sound.

"Probably that was far too merciful an end for them."

"I think that's right. We hanged a few of the SS guards yesterday, but with ropes. There were scaffolds set up with barbed-wire nooses. I thought we should have used those instead, but we did it by the book. It was still horrible to witness. Frankly, I expect to have nightmares about this place for the rest of my life."

"Demonstrating that you, too, have honor," von Reinhardt added. "I'll see you again before I leave, all right?"

"Yes, please. Now I've got to get the rest of this procurement documentation finished. Filling out forms is a strange way to be virtuous, is it not?"

Von Reinhardt laughed. "In today's world, I suspect filling out forms may be the biggest weapon both for good and for evil."

TRANSPORTATION DEPOT, ARMY GROUP CENTER, EAST OF BERLIN, GERMANY, 1020 HOURS GMT

"Ah, Lukas, my boy, I see you are finding your way toward the war, again."

"Generaloberst Dietrich!" Lukas Vogel snapped to attention, feeling a rush of excitement as he recognized the great man, and even more excitement because the great man recognized him. Dietrich was accompanied by several SS staff officers as he toured the chaotic scene of this great marshaling yard. Tanks were being repaired all around, and trucks rumbled bearing equipment, ammunition, and men to their new assignments. But the young soldier only had eyes for the man who had treated him so honorably in Saint-Vith.

"That is, yes sir! Standartenführer Peiper has assigned me to a company of panzergrenadiere in the Second SS Panzer Division! We are marching to the Oder—we will stop the Russians there, General, or die trying!"

Lukas could have gone on—he had so much to say, and Dietrich had always seemed like a good listener—but some growing kernel of military discipline held his tongue. Instead, he looked closely at the general, and was startled and upset to see how old the man looked, a little more than a month after Lukas had first laid eyes upon him. If anything, the young lieutenant's explanation of his intention only seemed to make the general look even older, and sadder.

Time had passed in a whirlwind since Lukas had walked into Berlin. A few days ago he had found General Dietrich right where the Brandenburg guards had promised that he would, in the marshaling fields across the Spree River. The general had recognized him, with a little reminder about the truck and the stolen money Lukas had turned over in Saint-Vith, and had been pleased to assign him to the Second SS Panzer Division "Das Reich." This was another veteran formation, though it was badly in need of reinforcements. Lukas had heard a rumor that there were only twenty tanks in the whole division, and even though he well knew the fighting prowess of the SS panzer men, that seemed like a terribly small number to put up against a horde of Russians. But of course, he was willing to go. When he learned that Jochen Peiper, one of the heroes of Dinant, had been promoted to SS-Standartenführer, or full colonel, and was second-in-command of the division, Lukas had felt as though destiny was guiding him toward a second chance at victory.

"So, let me think . . . Das Reich is going to Küstrin-an-der-Oder, are you not?" asked Dietrich conversationally.

"Yes, Herr Generaloberst! We are to depart within the hour."

"That is an important city, you know. The Russians will be there soon, on the other side of the Oder. Do you know, they will be only eighty kilometers from Berlin then? That is only an hour's drive, on a good road."

"We will make sure the road is very, very bad," pledged the young soldier. "They will not get across the river. Or, as I promised, Generaloberst, we will die trying to stop them!" It seemed like the right thing to say, and it was the truth.

"You are a brave soldier," Dietrich said gravely, placing a hand on his shoulder. "I know you will do what's right—but do me a favor, Untersturm-führer Vogel, will you?"

"Yes, Generaloberst—of course!" stammered Lukas.

"Try not to die."

The old man looked even sadder as he walked away.

BLOCK 24, KONZENTRATIONSLAGER BUCHENWALD, 2139 HOURS GMT

The rule seemed to be that if you wished to speak with Rommel, you had to work. That was not so unreasonable, von Reinhardt thought, but it quickly turned out to be impractical. When he attempted to wield a broom, the dust stirred up immediately sent him into a fit of coughing so strong that he doubled over and collapsed. One of the medical officers took a look at him and exiled him from the barracks. He was embarrassed at receiving medical attention in an environment where so many were suffering far worse than he, but at least he had made a good-faith attempt and was fairly sure Rommel had noticed.

He waited until late afternoon outside Sanger's office for the liaison officer to return. This did not distress him; he had books with him and there was so little leisure time available for reading. He managed to catch Sanger right before he headed for the shower and a fresh change of clothes, and learned from him the approximate time Rommel stopped working. As a result, it was quite late when von Reinhardt returned to the prison compound and the barracks where Rommel was sleeping.

"Generalfeldmarschall?"

"Ah, von Reinhardt," replied the Desert Fox in a weary tone. He was sitting on the edge of a bottom bunk and had just taken off his shoes. His clothes were matted with dirt. The room was cold, and there was no blanket on the bed. "I saw you earlier. How are you feeling."

"Well enough, sir, thank you. I regretted not being able to continue."

"I understand. Thank you for making the attempt. How was Berlin?" Rommel gestured to the bunk across from his own; von Reinhardt sat, and lifted his briefcase to his lap.

Von Reinhardt grinned ruefully as he snapped open the catches on his briefcase. "I'm afraid that I must report that my mission was a complete success. I have in these papers all the arrangements for a deal that is, I can see, no longer appropriate."

"You save me the trouble of telling you. I'm sorry. A few days ago, there was nothing more important than bringing this war to an immediate close, even at the cost of letting the high Nazi command escape. But as you can see around you, that no longer is a morally legitimate option."

"I fully understand. Nevertheless, I knew I had to bring you the report."

"Of course. And I appreciate the hard work and personal risk, even though it has been overtaken by events."

"Thank you, sir."

The two men sat in silence together in the cold, bare barracks. Then Rommel said, anguish in his voice, "How could they *do* this?"

"It's incomprehensible. For once, I cannot find anything meaningful the great minds of history have to say about it. I can think of numerous quotes about man's savagery, but they only describe it; they don't explain it. I thought of Goethe—did you know that this place is Goethe's summer retreat?"

"Really? How curious."

"Strangely, yes. The great oak tree in the administration compound, you may remember?"

"Yes."

"That is known as Goethe's oak. Great thoughts were thought under that tree."

"What an odd mind you have—I don't mean that as an insult . . ."

Von Reinhardt laughed. "I've been told that before, and I don't take it as an insult. But even Goethe doesn't add much to our knowledge or understanding of the situation. No one does. This is beyond sense."

"So what do I do now?"

"What you can. That's all any of us can do." And suddenly von Reinhardt realized what it was that he now had to do.

25 FEBRUARY 1945

CREMATORIUM, KONZENTRATIONSLAGER
BUCHENWALD, 0952 HOURS GMT

Sanger was not particularly religious, but he felt the dead deserved some respect, some acknowledgment. After he slammed shut the furnace door, he stood at attention and saluted before heading out for the next body.

As he turned around, he saw Rommel standing in front of him. Like Sanger, Rommel was shirtless. His body was a patchwork of scar tissue. Much of it was from the strafing attack that had nearly killed him about seven months ago, but Rommel had experienced numerous wounds in his two wars.

The field marshal paused when he saw Sanger saluting, and after Sanger finished, Rommel began moving his body into position. It had terrible slash wounds and bruises on it; one of the arms was twisted into a completely unnatural position. As a result, it was particularly awkward to handle, and slipped. Sanger caught the body before it fell to the floor, and helped Rommel get it into the furnace. Like Sanger, Rommel then came to attention and saluted.

Afterward, he said, "Thank you, Sanger."

"You're welcome, Field Marshal."

There was an awkward pause; then Rommel said, obviously trying to make conversation, "Those burn scars on your neck and shoulders—how did you get them?"

Sanger reached up to touch his neck. His burn scars went from the middle of his neck down over his left shoulder and onto his back, covering about a square foot of total skin surface. "Aboard Luftschiff Zeppelin 129. The *Hindenberg*." He remembered the awful pain quite well, but he also liked the feeling of having been a part of such an historic event.

"Really?" Rommel was quite interested. "You were on the final flight?"

"Yes, sir." Sanger was gratified at the reaction. "I spent my last year of high school in Augsburg, and flew back to the States aboard the *Hindenberg*." He paused, looked into the furnace flames and remembered the flames that had scarred him, and the young Nazi officer who had saved his life.

"You were in Germany. That must be the source of your language skills. Your family is German, I presume?"

"Yes, my parents are first-generation immigrants, from the Augsburg area, a little town called Haunstetten. I stayed with cousins when I was there. That's when I worked for you before."

"You were Hitlerjugend?"

"Yes, sir. You were its military adviser at the time."

"It was an assignment that didn't last long. Von Schirach and I had different views of how to build character in young men." Rommel chuckled ruefully. Baldur von Schirach was the Hitler Youth analogue to Robert Baden-Powell.

"My parents were active in the Bund. We were all big fans of the führer at the beginning. That's why I went over; I expected to stay and become part of National Socialism and the transformation of Germany."

"You didn't stay," observed Rommel. "Why not?"

Sanger paused for a long time, looking into the flames. "The Nuremberg laws had already been passed. Although Krystallnacht happened later, we often went to the Jewish neighborhoods looking for trouble. At first I went just as a way to fit in, but one night we went too far . . ."

Sanger could still hear the screams, see the broken glass and the blood trickling from the old man's skull from the rocks he had thrown. He still didn't know whether the unconscious man had lived; the blood had pooled quickly. He shook his head to free it from the memories that still gave him nightmares.

"So," Rommel said, interrupting his reverie. "I think I understand. You personally committed violence against some Jews, blamed the Hitler Youth for leading you on, then returned to the United States and personally declared war on Nazi Germany well in advance of your countrymen. Is that about right?" The field marshal's voice was harsh, sarcastic.

Sanger looked up, surprised at the Desert Fox's tone. He thought a minute, then acknowledged the truth. "Well, yes, sir, I suppose that is about right. Except that I know the responsibility was mine, not anybody else's."

"It's good that you remember that. But still, you wage war against your own people to atone for your individual crime. Although, I must add it looks as if your war has gone quite well, Colonel Sanger," Rommel observed dryly.

The condemnation Sanger heard in Rommel's voice confused him. Certainly Sanger had condemned himself many times, but when he had shared the story of his actions with others, they had mostly tried to excuse his behavior. "I tried to talk with my cousins about what I had done, what we had done together, but they couldn't see anything wrong with it. They thought they were acting on behalf of the Party."

"You don't agree. You feel your moral judgment in this matter is superior, and you are willing to judge and condemn your elders and even your own people on nothing stronger than your personal ideas of right and wrong." Rommel's statements were blunt, almost monotone.

Again, the harshness in Rommel's tone surprised him. He supposed that this meant that his relationship with the Desert Fox was at an end. It was not the first time he had lost friends over this issue, though the loss saddened him.

He would inform Eisenhower that the time had come to replace him as liaison officer. Nevertheless, he was firm in his principles.

He looked Rommel straight in the eye. "As a matter of fact, sir, I do. That's exactly right." Sanger straightened up. He felt stronger, standing once again on firm ground. "I suppose that in this area, I don't particularly care what anybody else thinks."

Rommel nodded. "But you still have trouble forgiving yourself for your crime," the field marshal prompted. His voice was softer now; his one good eye was fixed on Sanger. The fire reflected and glistened in his sweat.

Sanger felt that something important was going on, but he couldn't tell what it was, as if Rommel was having another conversation at the same time that somehow didn't include him. "Yes, sir, I do." That, too, was a fact.

"Good!" The field marshal slapped his hand on the empty cart in triumph. Rommel's voice was so loud it rode over the roar of the flames, startling Sanger. "You deserve to feel guilt. Such conduct is absolutely unforgivable. Shameful! Disgraceful!"

Sanger was shocked and somewhat hurt at Rommel's response. He felt embarrassed and small in the field marshal's eyes. He glanced up. Rommel appeared almost smug, calm, as if he had settled something. He was smiling widely.

"Yes, you were right to declare war, Colonel Sanger. But it will not lift a single gram of your guilt and dishonor. Not today, not in all the remaining days of your life. It excuses nothing. It forgives nothing. If it were otherwise, all the work would only be an exercise in selfishness. Do you understand?" Rommel's tone had changed, lower, but intense, willing him to understand.

Sanger chewed on Rommel's words for a moment. Yes, that was right. If his effort were merely a tool to obtain forgiveness, it would be tainted. The work, the atonement needed to be an end in itself, not a means to a selfish end. He nodded, then replied, "I do understand, Herr Generalfeldmarschall. You're right. Thank you, sir."

Rommel's sweat-stained scarred face flickered in the light of the furnaces. "For what?" His voice was friendly, but dismissive. The conversation had obviously become too emotional for Rommel's tastes. "I did nothing. We should get back to work, not stand around talking." With that, he began wheeling his cart toward the outer room.

Suddenly, the Desert Fox cried out, clasped his hand to his face, covering his bad eye. "Aaah!" he gasped, the pain overwhelming his normal stoic self-discipline.

"What is it?" asked Sanger, rushing to him.

Rommel looked in Sanger's direction, his face taut with pain, his body bending over. "My eye," he said through clenched teeth. A sudden spasm wracked his body, and he dropped to his knees.

Sanger knelt beside him. "Help! Medic!" he shouted. "It's Field Marshal Rommel! He needs help!"

HEADQUARTERS, SECOND GUARDS TANK ARMY, GERMAN/POLISH BORDER DUE WEST OF POZNAN, 1202 HOURS GMT

In the end the Soviet armored spearheads had swept around the fortified city of Poznan and rolled onward, leaving the task of reducing the vast emplacements to the following waves of infantry. The place was inevitably doomed, but to Krigoff it still seemed like the army had wasted a criminal amount of time in the fruitless attack. Even the thunderous artillery barrage, when Petrovsky had at last withdrawn his infantry and ordered the guns to open up, had failed to significantly impact the enemy firepower emanating from the huge concrete fort. The Germans had replied with not just small arms and automatic weapons, but artillery of their own that had somehow been sheltered in the vast emplacements of the redoubt.

This return fire had seemed like an almost personal affront to the colonel of the intelligence section. The guns had been audible for a long time, even within the tin compartment of his trailer, and Krigoff had brooded—not over the insolence of those vicious, but doomed, Nazis, but instead over the stubborn refusal of his army commander to follow the necessary course of action.

To Krigoff, of course, the failure of the bombardment was not proof that the idea of such an artillery attack had been wrong, but that the army general had been too slow to order the guns to open up. Surely if the barrage had commenced in a timely fashion, and the infantry had been pushed to advance under the horrific storm of explosions so that they could have capitalized on the enemy's disarray, the outcome would have been different.

He had been rebuked by the general, but Krigoff had no regrets about speaking up. If the same situation was to come up again, he resolved that he would not fail to press home the point.

For now, he sat in his lurching trailer, following the vanguard of the tank army as it rolled along the rutted roads of western Poland. He thought of Paulina, riding in a T-34 tank with one of the army's lead battalions, and hoped that she was safe. He knew that she was fearless, but he had personally spoken with the battalion commander. Without the photographer's knowledge, he had enjoined the colonel to make sure that she was granted the opportunity to take fine pictures, but at the same time was protected from harm. The CO had promised to do his best, and Krigoff had let it be known that success was the only acceptable option.

With nothing else to do for the moment, he got out the map. Within an hour they would cross over the prewar border between Germany and Poland; the army's spearheads were already ten kilometers inside the enemy fatherland.

That border was a symbol, but it was only a small relic of the past. Krigoff imagined a future where the arbitrary lines between states were barely acknowledged, as all of Europe—and, eventually, the world—came to accept the doctrines of Lenin and Marx, the theories that had been proven so exceptionally effective in the hands of a true leader like Stalin.

Soon they would reach the Oder River, and Zhukov had already declared his intention to push across that barrier with all possible haste. Krigoff looked forward to that accomplishment, for beyond the river it was only a short distance, eighty kilometers or so, to the heart of Germany itself.

And even then, Berlin would be just the beginning. . . .

26 FEBRUARY 1945

KONZENTRATIONSLAGER BUCHENWALD,
1900 HOURS GMT
"Is he well enough to attend this meeting?" Chancellor Goerdeler asked. "I understand he was unconscious for several hours today."

Sanger hung back as the chancellor and the defense minister chatted so he could eavesdrop more effectively. Although everyone knew he was fully bilingual, his American uniform served to make Germans sometimes less guarded when they spoke in their native tongue. Most of the big shots had their own translators anyway, relieving him of that duty for tonight's meeting.

Hans Spiedel, the defense minister, replied, "I've never seen medical opinion stop Generalfeldmarschall Rommel from doing anything. If he can stand, he will be here. But that's not enough. He is a man of his own mind, and does not easily put aside his opinion to accept that of someone else. It won't be enough to get him to obey. He has to want to do this or it will not work."

"Should we consider replacing him?"

"Goodness, no! Besides his undeniable military genius, he serves as a magnet, pulling soldiers from the other side. And his fame helps win over the citizenry."

The reference to Rommel's fame obviously didn't sit well with the chancellor. The officials of the provisional German government weren't united on much, but they all agreed that Rommel's fame and reputation was eclipsing their own, and none of them liked it. The Desert Fox was, after all, a recent convert to the cause, not one who had truly paid his dues. Spiedel, who seemed born to the political arts, was kept busy nearly full-time just smoothing over ruffled diplomatic feathers. It seemed odd to Sanger that people who didn't even yet have their country pacified would be spending their time jockeying for relative position, but that was altogether too common a behavior in people of any nationality. Politics seemed to him a fundamental characteristic of what human beings were all about.

As Eisenhower approached, Spiedel slipped directly into heavily accented English. "Good evening, General," he said, reaching out his hand. "Forgive me. I haven't been a civilian in a long time, and my hand wants to go into an automatic salute."

Eisenhower laughed. "It's hard to make the adjustment, I know."

The room was filling up with the big brass: Eisenhower and Bradley,

Goerdeler and Spiedel, Patton, and a smattering of colonels—Sanger himself, Müller, and von Reinhardt. The civilians wore suits, the American officers wore their pinks-and-greens, and the German officers still wore Wehrmacht dress uniforms, omitting only decorations and insignia containing the swastika. They hadn't had time to make new uniforms; the only evidence of their new affiliations were armbands with the letters DDR, for Deutsche Demokratische Republik, the provisional name of the new government.

Von Reinhardt was sitting while the rest of them stood; his face was stretched and pale and he was obviously in some discomfort. The cigarette smoke was already thick, and it was irritating the wounded man's injured lungs. Müller had arranged coffee and a small assortment of cakes, but was the only one who had helped himself to something to eat. The others drank only coffee or did without.

Only the guest of honor—Rommel himself—was missing. As Sanger maneuvered himself into a good position to watch the proceedings, he tried to figure out what was going on. Goerdeler wouldn't object if Rommel took himself out of the picture altogether, as long as he got to appoint his successor. Spiedel was weaving a spiderweb of control, manipulating everyone, including Rommel himself.

Eisenhower was full of bonhomie, but his babyish face and open manner masked a subtle and powerful intelligence. Patton was telling an off-color story to Bradley and laughing uproariously at his own punch lines. He had the edginess of someone who expected the current process to be a waste of his time. Bradley's body language was reserved. Sanger wondered if Patton knew how much he put others into a defensive mode and how much that tended to cost him—if Patton did understand, it was clear he didn't care. Müller, the supply officer, looked awkward and out of place. He had filled his cup of coffee too close to the brim and some had fallen on his tunic. There were other food spots there, too.

Aside from the pain clearly evident on von Reinhardt's face, the intelligence-officer-turned-diplomat seemed pulled into himself, watching. Sanger had the feeling that von Reinhardt had a few cards to play, and was waiting for an opportunity.

"Good evening, gentlemen. Are you waiting for me?"

The voice at the door was sharp and penetrating, although not particularly loud. It was a "general's voice," the tone of command that all leaders need but not all leaders have. It drew everyone's attention to the door.

The Desert Fox stood framed in the opening, his face solemn, left eye covered with a fresh bandage, the marks of battle scars and wounds clear. His uniform was unadorned, without medals or rank insignia; it was dirty from manual labor.

Chancellor Goerdeler, as the technically highest-ranking member of the group, tried to open. "How are you doing, Generalfeldmarschall? We're all quite concerned . . ."

Rommel moved forward abruptly. "You're all concerned that I seem to be fighting the wrong war in the wrong way. Correct? You find my working here, trying to save these prisoners who have been savaged by our own fatherland, to be wasteful when I could be out adding to the death toll of this war." He gathered in the room with his remaining good eye. "I have just learned from my American doctor that I have become blind in one eye from the wounds I sustained last summer, exacerbated by infections and dirt from our current surroundings. My scholarly friend von Reinhardt reminded me that an eye is the traditional price one pays for wisdom, for that is what the god Odin paid for his."

Von Reinhardt nodded solemnly at this. He was a strange bird, thought Sanger—an intelligence officer who thought that his business was actually intelligence. Not many military officers would think to give their commanders lectures on Norse mythology.

"I don't know whether I have gained wisdom, but I do know that I see what has happened here in a new light. I'm sure many of my countrymen will want to say that this was not us, but rather the doing of our Nazi masters. That is not sufficient. We are Germans and patriots, and therefore this belongs to us. This camp, and the others we have not yet found, is German property, not merely Nazi property, for the difference is one fit only for lawyers. There is no cause, no work in Germany today more important than this, because our honor is the only true value a people can have. Ours is here, in the dirt, and must be reclaimed from the dirt."

It was Patton—indeed, it had to be Patton, Sanger thought—who interrupted Rommel's speech. Patton was the only major Allied officer who had come to the camp but who had not done some KP duty. "Hold on just a goddamned minute, Rommel. I agree with you that this is a pretty fucking awful mess, and that you Germans have responsibility for cleaning this up. But you can't just forget the lines of Soviet bastards rolling westward. If you just swap Nazis for Commies, you haven't made things better. And if you think your buddies mistreat prisoners, just wait until that son of a bitch Stalin starts in. He'll give Buchenwald a run for its money in the competition to be Hell on earth."

"Now, just a minute, Georgie," interjected Bradley. "I think we ought to hear Rommel out before we . . ."

"Brad, we're here to lay it out in black-and-white for Rommel, and I don't think he's the sort of man who likes people to pussyfoot around. What do you say, Rommel? Do you want it straight, or do you want it political?" The unstoppable force paused for a minute. Sanger noticed that Rommel was having trouble controlling a smile.

"General Patton," Rommel said in his most formal voice, which sounded odd in contrast to his dirty clothing, "I always prefer straight talk from men I respect. I am just as aware as you of the threat the Soviet Union poses. In fact, I have more intimate knowledge of them because so many of my colleagues in the armed forces of the Reich have been doing battle in the East for years. And I am mindful of what you are saying. But what we have here is unprecedented. War, as we all know, is often terrible, and the suffering of innocents is not unusual. That is why we have laws and customs of war, to lessen its savagery. What we see around us is not only horrific and inhumane, but also criminal. That crime must be expiated."

Eisenhower stepped forward, as if to separate the two men. "Field Marshal Rommel, I completely agree with you about the ethical and legal issues here. This matter demands our deepest concern. But we are officers in a military organization trying to prosecute a just war and bring it to an honorable finish. We have doctors, investigators, social-service teams, and many other resources available to help with this situation. This assignment is important, but it isn't a task calling for the full capabilities of the man who commanded Army Group Africa. We can find capable people for this work. If you'll forgive me for saying so, we can find people more capable than you—or I. It is not your job."

Rommel gave a short military bow, acknowledging Eisenhower's speech. "In fact, most of the logistical work is already being ably handled by Colonel Müller." The pudgy colonel reddened. "You're right that much of the work can be done by others, and that others may be able to do it better. But there is one job that I'm afraid only I can do."

The pause grew in length, until Eisenhower felt compelled to ask, "And what is that job, Field Marshal? Manual laborer?"

"Exactly, General Eisenhower." He stood, waiting. The pause grew longer again.

"Manual fucking laborer!" Patton could no longer contain himself. "So you've decided to wallow in shit and claim you're on a moral high horse, when your failure to command your troops is condemning your countrymen to Soviet slavery? God *damn* it, Rommel! If you want to tear your shirt and wear sackcloth and ashes, then I suggest you get the fucking hell out of my way and I'll go fight the Russians for you. Jeezus!" He threw up his arms in melodramatic disgust.

"Put a sock in it, George," said Eisenhower with deceptive mildness. Bradley added the force of a restraining hand on Patton's arm.

"Perhaps another German can best speak to this," interjected Goerdeler. "You see, Herr Generalfeldmarschall, those of us in the resistance are as horrified by the evil we see all around us as you are, but we are less surprised, because we have known about this for years. You were in North Africa, carrying on warfare in a manner consistent with German honor, and because you are an honorable man, you tend to assume that honor is a common character-istic. I'm afraid that isn't true. You yourself finally reached the point where your soldier's oath to the führer had to be set aside because of your deeper loy-alty to the German people and to humanity.

"Our good name as Germans has been befouled with mass murder, and the worst crimes have not yet been exposed to the light of day. The extermina-tion of Jews and others continues even as we speak, and military action is needed—now. There will come time for acts of contrition. But this madness must be ended, and quickly. We need the Desert Fox to return to his station at the head of the free German military, to liberate this nation from Nazi domi-nation, and to stop this madness."

Rommel bowed in acknowledgment. "Herr Chancellor, when I took on these new responsibilities for the provisional government, it was my deepest hope and prayer that I would be able to get Germans to lay down their arms, to switch sides, to bring an end to the Third Reich with as few additional casu-alties as possible. Now you are asking me to wage the cruelest sort of war on my own people, for the leaders of the Reich well understand that there is no longer any surrender to be had now that this crime has been revealed. How can I do this? Hans," he said, turning to Spiedel, "what do you think I should do?"

Spiedel looked down at the floor. "Erwin," he said quietly, "you are my field marshal, and I will be with you whatever you choose. If it is war against our own, I will stand with you, or if you want me to go back into the camp and continue to perform manual labor at your side, I will stand with you there as well."

"Of all the pansy-ass bullshit I've ever heard, this takes the cake!" Patton could no longer contain himself. "Do you think for one minute that any of the sadistic bastards who built these camps shed one tear or had one minute of conscience over what they did? So instead of tracking these bastards down and putting a personal bullet through their miserable fucking heads, you're going to stick your heads in the sand and be oh-so-noble? You're a soldier, goddamn it, not a fucking pussy! So as one soldier to another, it's time to suck it up and get back on the fucking goddamned horse! Jesus Christ!" Patton looked heavenward, as if he was looking for immediate confirmation from above.

"Dammit, George, I said to put a sock in it," growled Eisenhower. "Field Marshal, I appreciate your dilemma, but I must tell you that General Patton has an important point, even when put in somewhat less than diplomatic lan-guage. We can certainly prosecute the end of this war without you and your army group, but for a variety of reasons I'm sure you understand, it would be far better to continue with the plan that's got us this far."

The Desert Fox surveyed the group in front of him. His one good eye was sharp and clear, and Sanger noticed that he did not seem fazed by the opposi-tion in front of him. "All of you, I think, view the events here and at the other camps as quite serious, but something less than world-shaking. I, on the other hand, believe we have entered an entirely new world with evil on a scale not heretofore seen. Because this is unprecedented, the appropriateness of normal behavior is subject to rethinking. I am not convinced that what seems obvious is necessarily correct. Sanger, you have worked with me these past few days. What is your opinion?"

Sanger was surprised to see himself called upon in this company; he had expected to be confined to the role of observer, a role that suited him fine. "Sir, I will be fighting this particular war for the rest of my life, in whatever role I can get." The confidence in his own voice surprised himself.

"Thank you, Sanger," Rommel answered. "And you, Oberst von Reinhardt? I suppose you have a quote for us?" Sanger could see that most of the room hoped von Reinhardt would have the good sense to keep his mouth shut.

But the sharp-faced diplomat was ready. "As you know, Generalfeld-marschall, I have been engaged in private negotiations with Führer Himmler in hopes of achieving a surrender." This surprised several of the Americans in the room, although Sanger had figured it out some time ago. It was, after all, only logical. "The price of personal safety and freedom that he asked for himself seemed to me to be in the best interests of everyone. That was until I saw this camp. And, yes, sir, I do have a quote for you."

Sanger found the young aristocrat hard to read. Von Reinhardt was a lat-eral thinker, and those were difficult to predict. He kept his fingers crossed that von Reinhardt would say the right thing.

Von Reinhardt looked directly at the Desert Fox as he spoke slowly, enun-ciating clearly, as the various translators whispered into the ears of their prin-cipals. "The quote is this: 'If God wills that this war continue until every drop of blood drawn by the lash shall be paid by another drawn with the sword, as was said three thousand years ago, so still it must be said, "The judgments of the Lord are true and righteous altogether."'"

Sanger well remembered the words of Lincoln's Second Inaugural. On a family vacation trip from New Jersey to Washington, DC, he had stood inside the Lincoln Memorial and read those same words chiseled into the wall. He was not surprised that some of the German faces looked puzzled, but he was sur-prised that a few American faces were blank as well. And Sanger seemed to be the only one who noticed that by comparing the concentration camps to American slavery, von Reinhardt was giving a backhanded slap to the Americans.

"'Until every drop of blood drawn by the lash shall be paid by another drawn by the sword . . .' I see." Rommel stood in thought for a moment, but Sanger could see in his posture that the battle-scarred soldier had made up his mind.

"Very well," the Desert Fox announced. "We will turn responsibility for these victims over to the authorities best suited to assist them, and take up the sword once again. We will wage this necessary war so that the German people can engage in the serious business of resolving this horrific matter. There will be a high price to pay for these crimes, a price that the German people as a whole must shoulder. There is no forgiveness and there is no expiation, but there is the opportunity to work." It was then that Sanger realized who Rommel had been really talking to in the furnace room.

"The time for battle is upon us."

As the various attendees came forward in turn to shake Rommel's hand and welcome his return to command, Sanger noticed von Reinhardt pull himself slowly and painfully from his seat and head, unnoticed by anyone else, for the door.

EXCERPT FROM *WAR'S FINAL FURY*,
BY PROFESSOR JARED GRUENWALD

The extent of what subsequently became known as the Holocaust was not revealed all at the same time. The liberation of the Buchenwald and Dachau concentration camps created shock around the world. Unfortunately, the majority of the death camps, including Auschwitz/Birkenau, the largest, were located in Poland. As a result, it was the Soviet Union, rather than the Western Allies, who first discovered the full scale of the atrocities.

This meant that acknowledgment of the Holocaust got caught up in the politics of anti-Communism, and from there came the phenomenon known as "Holocaust Denial." All those facts that came from behind Soviet lines were dismissed as propaganda designed to legitimize the Soviet advance. Difficulties in getting fully independent observers to the sites, the time delays involved, and the various concealment activities practiced by the Nazis themselves as part of Operation Wolkenbrand, all created enough muddiness in the data to allow those with a political interest in denial of the Holocaust to argue that it was not "proven" sufficiently.

Of course, all those with understanding of how the process of history works know that muddiness at the detail level is the common experience of all history, and that minor discrepancies in the historical record are not in themselves sufficient to disprove the larger picture.

The critical days in February of 1945 spent by Rommel in the Buchenwald camp had an immense impact on Germany's postwar destiny, and on the postwar shape of the world itself. Some of the ripples of that period showed up mere days later. . . .

OPERATION
ECLIPSE

7 – 31 MARCH 1945

War has seldom brought anything for any of the people engaged in it. But the people aren't usually asked. Once war has begun, you go on fighting simply to get the best you can out of it. But what when there is no more to be got? Then it's better to stop it at once. And that, you see, is our position today, except we are fighting an enemy in the East before whom there can be no surrender. There it's a matter of fighting for our lives, and that complicates the issue. What we should do now is to see to it that our Western enemies occupy the whole of Central Europe and keep the Russians outside our borders.

—Field Marshal Erwin Rommel
August 1944

7 MARCH 1945

HEADQUARTERS, SIXTH PANZER ARMY, MAGDEBURG, GERMANY, 0625 HOURS GMT

The autobahn was a marvelous road, parallel strips of asphalt rippling smoothly across the countryside. Departing from Berlin via Potsdam, the road arched across a long bridge, spanning one of the city's broad lakes, before rolling through hill and forest toward the Elbe. The highway system was another of Hitler's innovations, one of the things that had offered such promise of a greater Germany as the Nazi party bore the nation into the future. Wide and smooth, graded through the steep hills, with multiple lanes in both directions, the autobahn had been a key factor for the movement of armies and supplies throughout the country.

Now that road allowed the big Mercedes staff car to rumble westward at better than a hundred kilometers per hour. In the backseat, SS General Sepp Dietrich kept his mind focused on the possibilities of that road as he watched the forests and pastures of his fatherland roll past. His panzer army was activated now, some fifteen divisions—at least in name—having been mustered around the capital, now awaiting his orders for deployment. This autobahn was just one of many roads that the führer had ordered Dietrich to use, in order to move that army up to the Elbe, where they were expected to stand firm against Eisenhower's armies.

Soon the outskirts of Magdeburg began to clutter the landscape: Here was a cluster of factory chimneys in a gray, flat valley, there a railroad siding with tracks hastily laid right in the midst of a dense evergreen forest. The bridge over the tracks was still intact, though Dietrich suspected it would be bombed by the time the Allied armies were close enough to give this area the attention demanded by imminent operations. Now, at least, the great highway gave an illusion of perfection, and the installations below looked like toys, model trains and cars down on the solid surface of German soil.

Dietrich had no illusions about the role of his reconstituted, but very much understrength, panzerarmee. Most of his divisions were manned by elderly, unfit, or youthful and untried soldiers. The few veteran units he had were mere shadows of their once mighty shapes, battalion-strength remnants of formerly great divisions. He knew that these formations would fight furiously, but they were woefully understrength—the First SS Panzer Division, for example, had less than thirty tanks.

Even so, these men—and boys; he sighed as he remembered the boys—would fight bravely. Dietrich was not an introspective man, but he could not help thinking about *why* these German soldiers would battle with such courage. For a long time, since the Munich days, many years before Adolf Hitler had come to power, Dietrich had believed that the Nazis gave his country reason to be proud, reason to be strong, reason to fight and, if necessary, die. Now he was not so certain.

Certainly many in his panzer army would die. While they did so, holding this line of the Elbe River, they would hold up the Americans and the British for some days, maybe even weeks. Would that help Germany win the war? Dietrich snorted at the notion. This war was lost, beyond any doubt. He had realized that when he had first heard of Rommel's surrender in Belgium. The Americans, the British, the Russians—hell, even the French!—would carve up his homeland in whatever fashion they desired. Who knew—perhaps the Soviets and the Western Allies would go right to war with each other, using the battered corpse of Germany as their battlefield.

So it was all a question of time and place—when and where would his men die? The battle he had been ordered to fight, here west of Berlin, would accomplish one thing. It would allow the Soviet Army to claim Berlin, the great capital of old Prussia, the shattered center of whatever Germany was to become. Dietrich had had a lot of trouble sleeping, during the recent weeks. Late at night, he regularly stared at the ceiling and wondered what kind of nation this war would leave behind. The Nazis were finished, he could see, though they would not go quietly. This mighty war machine was still capable of determined, lethal resistance. These fifteen divisions, ragtag and motley as they were, could hold the line of this deep, fast river for many bloody days.

Was that a thing worth spending the lives of his men and boys to accomplish? The answer was so obvious that Dietrich made his decision without even a measure of guilt.

"We are coming to the advance field headquarters, Herr General," said his driver, slowing down and pulling onto a roadway that angled down and away from the main highway. The Panzerarmee staff had spread camouflage nets through a small grove of evergreens, masking a large clearing on the ground where a number of trucks were parked. Radio antennae and a few antiaircraft guns bristled from the makeshift compound, and several SS guards snapped to attention as the car rumbled to a halt. One, a tall sturmscharführer, quickly pulled open the door and saluted as Dietrich pulled himself out.

Feeling very weary, the SS general started toward the large command tent, then brightened as he saw a familiar officer emerge.

"Greetings, Herr Gruppenführer," said Colonel Peiper, his scar still as ghastly as it had been in Saint-Vith. "My division is fueled and armed; we're waiting only for darkness before we move out."

"Ah, yes, Colonel. Your tanks are too precious to risk losing any of them on the way to the battlefield." Dietrich thought of that broad highway he had just traversed, taking the chance to travel by himself during daylight. Certainly any column of German armored vehicles would be irresistable targets to the Allied air forces.

"I quite agree, sir."

"There is just one change to those orders," Dietrich said. "You are the first in the panzerarmee to hear of this change, but the orders will be made general in the next hour."

"Yes, Herr Gruppenführer. And what would that change be?" asked Peiper.

"You will be going east, not west, out of Berlin." Dietrich was calm; he felt more right about this command than any other he had issued through his career. "I want your division to deploy in Küstrin, astride the Berlin road. You will be the next—perhaps the last—stumbling block in the way of the Russian advance."

"Of course, my general!" Peiper raised his hand in a salute, though his good eye was clouded by doubt. Finally he voiced his concern. "I was under the impression that we were to be the only force on the Elbe. If you send your panzerarmee east, will that not leave Berlin terribly open to the west, in the face of the American attack?"

"Yes," said Dietrich, shaking his head, then shrugging his shoulders. "Yes. I'm afraid it will."

8 MARCH 1945

THIRD ARMY MOBILE HEADQUARTERS, DESSAU, GERMANY, 1440 HOURS GMT

Patton and the Desert Fox stood on the hotel balcony overlooking the valley of the Elbe River, which twisted into the distance to the right and left below them. The steeple of an ancient church jutted incongruously upward from a mass of rubble, dozens of square blocks that had been bombed to oblivion. Beyond, a stretch of green pine trees marked a park that had been miraculously spared during the aerial bombing campaign. There, the snow had melted off the ground, and the evergreens stood out in stark relief against the gray and brown of the surrounding ruin.

Rommel had returned to an officer's uniform, but one devoid of insignia of any sort, a plain suit and cap in Wehrmacht feldgrau. His blind eye was covered with a black patch. "Still no insignia, Rommel?" Patton asked. Sanger, standing to the side, translated.

The Desert Fox shook his head. "No. Not at the present, at least."

"Then how the hell do you expect people to know you're a field marshal?"

Rommel smiled slightly and looked Patton straight in the eyes. "They'll know when they see people obeying my orders. How do they know you're a general? Because of *that?*" He gestured at Patton's splendor: silver helmet with three stars, jodhpurs, ivory-handled pistols.

Patton laughed in return. "Point taken. I guess not. They know when they see people following my orders." Rommel nodded in satisfaction.

An orderly came out onto the balcony. "General Patton, sir? I have General Eisenhower on the phone. If you'll follow me, sir—"

Patton was already moving, and the orderly hastened to lead him through the lobby and into the manager's office, with Rommel and Sanger following close on his heels. The field marshal and the liaison officer halted outside the office, until the American general waved them in while he took the receiver of the phone. The orderly quickly departed and pulled the door shut behind him.

"George, Ike here."

Patton grimaced unconsciously, hoping that the gamble he and Rommel were taking would pay off. "Yes, General," he said, surprising even himself when he referred to SHAEF by rank instead of his ubiquitous nickname.

"Well, you're going to be a very happy man," said the Supreme Commander in his matter-of-fact Midwestern tone. "I've just spoken to none other than the president himself. He sends his congratulations, by the way, and his best wishes." There was an agonizing pause. "And, Georgie . . . ?"

"Hot damn—it's Berlin, right?" Patton's voice rose in excitement, and he saw Rommel nod in satisfaction—the field marshal didn't need a translator to understand the topic of the conversation.

"Yes, George—he thinks that all bets are off, as far as the Russians go. They're back in this thing whole hog, and this time we're not treating them as allies. You need to get there ahead of them, and in enough strength not to be pushed out. How soon can you get your vanguard across the Elbe?"

Patton looked out the office window. There were many bridges in this medieval city, and several of them were visible from here. All of them were choked with eastbound traffic, mostly columns of Shermans and American trucks, though one span had been dedicated to the German Republican Army, and was dotted with panzer Mark IVs and a few Panther tanks. On the far bank, the columns were winding through the outskirts of the city, the leading elements already vanishing into the countryside beyond.

Some details, Patton thought with a wicked grin, didn't need to be shared with the high command.

"Well, Ike, it'll take some time to get an entire army moving, but I think we can get started pretty quickly," he promised, crossing his fingers behind his back.

"Good," said the Supreme Commander. "Then, Godspeed to you, Georgie—the eyes of the world are going to be watching for the winner of this race."

"Ike, this is the sprint I've been waiting for all my life—you can bet your ass we're going to finish first!" He put his hand over the mouthpiece, whispered to Rommel: "The word is 'Go.'"

Eisenhower continued speaking. "But listen: We don't want a shooting war with the Russians—I can't stress that point strongly enough. I've seen the figures—they have ten times as many men as we do, and an even greater advantage in tanks. So this is a race, but it's not a war—understand? Get to Berlin first, you stay there, and keep them out. But if anything goes wrong, Berlin is theirs, at least for a while, got it? No matter what, you stop when you get to the Russian lines. We'll let the situation develop from there."

"Yes, Ike—I understand." Patton was certain Ike's figures about Soviet strength were exaggerated—hell, the Supreme Commander probably bought into that same commie propaganda that fooled everyone else—but he was also certain it wasn't going to be an issue. This *was* in fact a race, and there was no faster army on earth than his own Third.

"What's the latest word on where the damned Russkis are right now?"

"They're pulling up to the Oder along a front that's a hundred miles or more wide. They're closer to Berlin than you are—within fifty miles at Küstrin, whereas it looks like you have a good hundred or more to go. But they have that river in front of them, and it looks like the Waffen-SS is going to do us a favor for once, and try to hold them there."

"All right, Ike—we're off! And give my compliments back to the president when you see him, will you?"

"Certainly, Georgie. Give 'em hell!"

"You know I will, General." Patton hung up the receiver. "We got permission to go!" He crowed.

Rommel laughed. "I see that you have the same healthy respect for orders and the chain of command that I do."

"It's easier to get forgiveness than permission," Patton replied, grinning.

The three men made their way through the lobby and back upstairs. When they emerged onto the balcony again, it seemed that the day was brighter and warmer than any since they had crossed into Germany. The sun was shining and there was actually a promise of spring in the air.

Patton gestured to the three huge columns that were still rumbling across the bridges, through the far side of Dessau, and onward toward Berlin. "We have Fourth Armored on the right, Panzer Lehr in the middle, and Nineteenth Armored on the left. Pretty damn good spearhead, if I say so myself."

"Yes," Rommel agreed, through Sanger. "They'll be able to handle anything Himmler's SS remnants try to do. As to the Russians, how many more divisions ready to cross as soon as the bridges are opened up for more traffic?"

"I have three more—two infantry and another armor—waiting outside the city for the columns to clear out. They can be across by tomorrow, I think, and I want my whole army on the other side of the Elbe by the end of the week. We can set up a bulletproof ring around Berlin—no commie bastard will get within twenty miles of the place! And you have, what, another panzer division and an infantry division ready?"

The Desert Fox nodded. "At least that. As Armeegruppe H makes the transition to the DDR side, that should give us at least another two mobile divisions within the week. Perhaps I should send some of them around to the north, make our front a little more broad?"

"Good idea," Patton agreed. He looked across the river, toward the three tank-heavy formations at the heart of the drive. "But the key to this thing will be those boys, right there. As Ike said, this is a race—and one we can't afford to lose."

BROADCAST HOUSE, BERLIN, GERMANY, 1700 HOURS GMT

"Good evening. This is your führer, speaking to you tonight from Broadcast House in Berlin. I am addressing you this evening about a matter of great importance, to set the record straight about the conduct of your government, your party, and your fatherland.

"You may have heard some shocking allegations regarding concentration camps where the enemies of our nation have been imprisoned. Those allegations are false, misleading, and libelous propaganda aimed at weakening the bonds between People and State. Tonight, I will tell you the truth." Himmler took a deep breath, drinking primly from a glass of water. He pursed his lips, annoyed to see that his hand was shaking. With great concentration he inhaled through his nostrils, slowly exhaled, and leaned in toward the microphone again.

"Germany has been attacked viciously, both inside and out, by those who wish to see the Aryan race subjugated to the mongrel peoples of the world. In particular, the Elders of Zion, the international cartel of bankers they control, and their agents the Communists, see in our proud people the primary challenge to their goal of world domination.

"We have been forced to defend ourselves and to gain for the people of Germany what history and justice demand—room for our people and freedom from that domination. We have waged war only in self-defense, only to provide us with the freedom that is our birthright, only to give us a chance at survival." He was feeling more confidence now, and allowed himself the glimmer of a smile. His speechwriter had done a good job—in truth, who needed Goebbels, anyway? The man had always been overrated.

"To that end, we have arrested the enemies of the Third Reich, and imprisoned them—as all nations of the world imprison criminals and traitors. Have we treated them unfairly or harshly? No, no, a thousand times no! They have been placed in prisons where they have been receiving good food each day, a place to sleep, and appropriate care. Even when our own people have been called upon to make sacrifices, we have paid working prisoners in a currency called lagergeld, with which they can purchase the luxuries of life. We have done so because we are a humane people.

"But what of these accusations of barbaric living conditions? Those, dear countrymen, were created by the prisoners themselves! We furnished them clean barracks and they chose to live in squalor. They have fought among themselves, lived like filthy pigs, prostituted themselves to each other, and in spite of all our care and attention, have chosen to reveal themselves as they truly are. Our hands are clean and our conscience is pure.

"With other prisoners, alien to our race and foreign to our people, such as Jews and Gypsies, we have, at great cost, found them room to resettle and build their own lives, free from outside interference. But the Soviet Bolsheviks have attacked them, killed their women and children, and brutalized the survivors. The Mongol horde returns across the steppes, and with it comes brutality such as the civilized world has never seen.

"The proof of this you will have shortly, for I predict you will hear the Soviets claim in their propaganda that there are death camps in the territories they have captured. Indeed, there are death camps, but they are not German death camps. They are the creation of the Soviets themselves, in their own mission to rid the world of those whom they find inimical to their Slavic temperament.

"Those who set themselves up as our enemies have been motivated by envy—envy of our character, of our purity, of our strength. In spite of all our enemies may do, the Third Reich will never crumble, never falter, never die. As Führer of the Third Reich, I call upon all of you to continue your unwavering support of your fatherland, and resist with all your might, and we will yet prevail!

"Thank you and good night."

Heinrich Himmler knew full well that he was not the orator that Adolf Hitler had been. Speaking, even on the radio, was exhausting to him, calling on all his reserves of emotional energy. His face beaded with sweat, he moved into the dark control room, where an aide waited with a towel and another glass of water. He wiped his face and quickly drank the water.

"A masterful performance," the radio engineer said. "It will inspire the people." Himmler nodded his thanks, too tired even to reply.

He walked down the single flight of steps to his waiting limousine. The SS driver opened the door, saluting smartly at his approach. Himmler slid into the backseat, where his ADC awaited. "You have a visitor at the chancellery, mein Führer," he said.

"Who is it?"

"Rommel's envoy, von Reinhardt."

Von Reinhardt was waiting at the new chancellery when Himmler arrived. The aristocratic officer was seated in a chair in the outer office, and rose to his feet with visible effort, bracing himself on both arms, as the führer walked past.

"I'm rather surprised to see you," Himmler said coldly. "I would have thought your master would be far too shocked by political reality to continue our dialogue." He walked to the bar in his office to fix himself a drink. He did not offer one to his visitor, who merely turned to follow the führer with his eyes.

"You're right," replied von Reinhardt. "The deal with the Desert Fox is, as you no doubt realize, completely cancelled by the reality of Buchenwald. I daresay if he were here now, he would strangle you with his bare hands."

"Let us stick to practical matters." Himmler waved away the idle threat. "To what do I owe the pleasure of your company?"

"A deal that can lead to escape for you is still possible—if you are prepared to negotiate with me."

Himmler stopped, his drink nearly to his mouth. "You? Have you gone freelance, then?" His eyes blinked behind the small, wire-rimmed glasses.

"Yes. I still think the outlines of the deal we reached together are in the best interests of the Fatherland. Rommel, an idealist, feels that bringing you to justice is the most important thing of all."

"And you don't? Funny. I would have thought you, too, would have that mystical reverence for justice." The führer gulped from his glass. He was not a frequent drinker, but now the burn of the fine cognac was soothing to his stomach, and helped to clear his mind.

"Justice is a matter for the gods to sort out. Whether or not you receive justice will have no benefit to a single victim of the camps. This is a fact of 'political reality,' as you yourself might be inclined to observe."

Himmler smiled. "I'm glad you understand that. Our party has written large upon the face of history, and nothing can undo what we have written."

"That's correct. The world will never be the same because of the Third Reich's rise . . . and fall. So it is silly to worry about the past. Only the future can be affected by our actions in the present."

"And you an historian." Himmler took a sip, sat down in his chair. "I am beginning to see where you would take the long view. Please, continue."

"Being interested in history does not automatically make one a hopeless idealist, you know." The colonel walked slowly over to the bar. "May I?" he asked, leaning against the rail. Himmler gestured with his hand, and von Reinhardt dropped a few ice cubes in a glass, poured himself a drink from the same decanter the führer had used.

"How very interesting you are, von Reinhardt. It's a shame you aren't still on my side."

"I'm on Germany's side, if that means anything to you."

"It depends, I suppose, on what you mean by 'Germany.' I am still the lawful leader of this nation, you will remember. My power is not to be scorned, nor treated lightly."

"I intend no scorn. I simply mean that having you depart peacefully and quickly is in everyone's best interest. Even Rommel, though I don't think he'll be able to understand that harsh truth. For a pragmatic man, our Desert Fox does have that surprisingly deep streak of idealism."

"So, you're willing to help the poor, beleaguered Nazi high command escape, are you?"

"Yes." Von Reinhardt slowly raised his glass to his lips, sighed deeply, then added: "For a price."

Himmler took another sip of his drink. "Am I now to believe that you are for sale to the highest bidder? Is this how you show your interest in the Fatherland? Or do you have such a low opinion of my insight and intelligence that you expect to fool me by pretending to be dishonest? Come now, von Reinhardt."

"I'm not for sale. But there is a price to pay."

"Money? Women? Art? What do you want?"

"Money."

Himmler shook his head and smiled. "No, no, von Reinhardt. You cannot convince me that what you want is money."

"Not money for me." Von Reinhardt moved slowly back to his chair, used his free hand to brace his arm, and slowly lowered himself back to the seat.

"For whom, then?" Himmler was intrigued. He went to his huge black desk and sat down, facing his visitor expectantly.

"For the victims of the camps."

"Ahh." Himmler put his fingers together as a steeple. "For the victims of the camps. How much money?"

"Twenty million marks. Gold, I should think. Yes, gold is the only way it would work. I am certain that you have a lot of it stashed around, here and there—you know, just in case. . . ."

"Gold. Of course you would want it in gold. Very practical." Himmler laughed. It was a brittle sound. "Keep talking. I find this conversation quite entertaining." He took another long drink, vaguely annoyed when the glass was empty. Yet he felt relaxed, and masterful.

"You have the Soviets approaching Berlin on one side and the Western Allies approaching on the other. Within a week they will be bickering over the bones of your capital—surely you realize that. The skies above you are dominated by your enemies, and the troops on the ground are so numerous that you will never reach either the Eagle's Nest or Switzerland or any other place of refuge without help. You might escape as a single man in disguise, but that will hardly meet your needs. First, your face is too well known, and the risk of accidental discovery high. Second, it would not suffice you to escape if you cannot bring with you wealth sufficient to reestablish yourself and the key members of government and Party and hope to rebuild. Shall I continue?"

"Go on." Himmler waved his hand languorously.

"You will have to escape by car or truck. To do it the right way you would need a convoy. Yourself, a small bodyguard, communications equipment, and all the gold you have here in Berlin. I imagine there's still a fairly tidy sum available to you. You would head south for a while and then go either toward Berchtesgarten or Switzerland, unless there's another place available for you to hide. Simultaneously, you would send out of Berlin all the other key officials in small groups and in civilian clothing, so they could make their own way to your rendezvous point. From there, you would bribe and maneuver your way to a safe haven. South America seems like a good bet, I would think. Perhaps the only place on earth where you might have a chance to live as a free—not to mention, very wealthy—man."

"Amusing. And how would this convoy avoid contact with my enemies? As you mentioned, the Allied armies are thick across the ground."

"I'm still an intelligence officer with appropriate security clearance. I would provide you with detailed maps and troop movements, and could see that operational orders are issued to keep the enemy out of your way while giving the illusion that the front was still well protected. Of course, you will need to move quickly, but there are still opportunities for you. Neither your eastern nor your western enemies have yet approached Czechoslovakia. From there, you will have a clear road to the Alps. I'd suggest you prerecord some more radio addresses and have them broadcast to conceal the moment of your departure."

Himmler began drumming his fingers on the tabletop. Should he consider this offer seriously, or not? He looked at von Reinhardt. As usual, the man was the picture of equanimity. He couldn't read him, and that fact was not to Himmler's liking. "Let us discuss—quite hypothetically, of course—the possibility that you are planning some sort of double-cross. Naturally, I cannot simply leave my payment with you, and trust you to carry out your part of the bargain."

"It's always wise to consider the option of a double-cross, Reichsführer. With all respect, I consider that possibility in reverse, as well. I think it should be possible to create a set of consequences that would make it in neither one of our interests to double-cross the other. We will need to place the twenty million marks in one location and keep a hostage in another, so that your complete and successful escape releases both the money and the hostage."

Himmler looked at von Reinhardt with more seriousness. "Would you be the hostage?"

Von Reinhardt paused, took a sip of his cognac, and smiled at Himmler. "Yes. It would not be my first choice of roles, but if it's a necessity, yes, I would agree to be your hostage."

"Twenty million marks for my freedom and a chance to start over. I must think on it. For now, I want you to stay the night. My guards will see that you have a comfortable room—one with a stout lock on the outside of the door, of course. We'll talk tomorrow."

"Very well, Reichsführer. But you must know that time is of the essence."

"So it is. We will speak tomorrow."

9 MARCH 1945

FORWARD ELEMENTS OF SECOND SS PANZER DIVISION
"DAS REICH," KÜSTRIN, GERMANY, 0247 HOURS GMT

Lukas woke up and looked out the rear of the truck, realizing that the division had entered another city. He knew even before the vehicle started to slow down that this was their destination. In another minute they had come to a halt, and even in the darkness he could make out the truck behind them pulling up close and also stopping.

Within the canopied cargo compartment of this vehicle, he sensed the watching, patient eyes of his men, the twelve veteran panzer grenadiers that Peiper had assigned to him. They were his own platoon of tough SS veterans, and he desperately wanted to prove himself worthy of their respect. Only the whites of the men's eyes were visible in the almost lightless compartment, but to Lukas they seemed penetrating and keen, as if they could look right into his soul. Every one of these men was older than he was. He resolved that he would prove himself worthy to these heroes of the SS, who were so very different— so much more serious, weary, and yet quietly capable—from the boys who had formed his first command.

"Dismount—*schnell!*" came the order from outside of the truck.

"You heard—let's go," Lukas said, holding back the canvas flap so that the men could climb down to the ground. After the humid, drowsy warmth of the cabin, the chilly night air against his face felt bracing and invigorating, and he was instantly wide awake. A moment later Lukas followed the last of the enlisted men in spilling out of the truck.

Quickly, instinctively, he checked his weapons. His Schmeisser machine pistol was slung across his chest, and many extra clips of ammunition weighted him down as they were slung from pouches at his belt and on his back. His sidearm, a battered but capable Walther claimed from the equipment depot, was secure in its holster on his right hip, with several extra clips for that weapon fastened to his belt. On his left side he wore his knife, the same blade he had carried throughout the war, and the worn hilt felt smooth and comforting when he reflexively wrapped his fingers around it.

"Form up," he called, as he heard other officers and sergeants shouting the same thing. "Check your weapons." He was not certain if the latter command was necessary or not, but he wanted the men to know that he was thinking.

"What about the grenades, Herr Obersturmführer?" asked one of the privates. When Peiper had given Lukas his new assignment, he had also given him a promotion from second lieutenant to first lieutenant.

Lukas knew that there were two crates of the explosive devices, affectionately termed "potato mashers," in the back of the truck. He pointed to the four largest men. "You two, and you two, each take a crate. We'll carry them along in the boxes, until we get closer to the front." He was gratified when the men reached into the truck without hesitation, following his orders to pull out the heavy cases.

The night sky was overcast, and the city dark, so he relied on his ears to decipher what was going on around him. He could hear the rumbling engines of tanks, was even able to identify the deeper thrum of a Panther against the rattle of the more numerous Mark IVs. The Second SS Panzer Division might be understrength, but it was still a lethal formation.

Next Lukas tried to get his bearings. He had never been this far east before, but he understood the geography that Standartenführer Peiper had explained to his officers: Küstrin was a city on the Oder River that stood astride the most direct route from Poland to Berlin. It was here that the Russians were expected to make their first great push, and here that Führer Himmler had dispatched his most loyal troops. It was hard to see much in the night, but he perceived mounds of rubble on both sides of the road, and a few tall walls that looked like they might have been intact buildings—though most likely these were just façades that had survived the bombing and shelling. He didn't know where the river was, but he assumed that it wouldn't be far.

He saw flashes of matches here and there as the troops started to light up ersatz cigarettes near the front of the column. The trail of sparkling lights moved back, and he saw that a tall officer in a peaked SS cap was coming along the line of trucks.

"Have a smoke and a piss, men," he was saying. "We'll move out in a few minutes. From here we're on foot—these trucks are needed to go back to Berlin and bring up a few more of our friends. You don't want to hog all the glory for yourselves, do you?"

By now Lukas recognized Peiper's voice, and it made him feel better to know that the colonel was so near. One of the troops nearby struck a match as he passed, and the tall Standartenführer looked down at the young officer and smiled, a tight look that was almost a grimace. His scarred face was etched in fire, and he looked very fierce—like a mythical warrior, thought Lukas.

"Ready to go to work again, Obersturmführer Vogel?" he asked.

"Yes, sir!" Lukas promised.

"Good. We'll be putting your grenadiers into some buildings near the waterfront. I'll want you to wait there, but be ready to move out at a moment's notice. Understand?"

"Yes, Colonel," pledged the young soldier, his manner solemn and serious as he suspected a veteran's should be.

"Good man," said Peiper, and then he was gone.

A few minutes later they started to march. As dawn came to this blasted city, it was somewhat heartening to see the great number of SS soldiers around Lukas. This was the equivalent of a great panzerarmee, including many divisions of tanks, as well as thousands of battle-hardened soldiers. It was hard to imagine that the Russians could force their way across a wide, deep river when the bank was held by men like these. And vividly Lukas remembered the promise he had made to General Dietrich himself:

They would stop the Red Army here, or they would die trying.

OSWIECIM, POLAND, 1014 HOURS GMT

The Red Army major looked up at the metal gate and its sign, "Arbeit Macht Frei," and shivered. Although he was a veteran of Stalingrad and thought he had seen all there was to see of man's inhumanity to man, he now knew there were numerous chapters still left to witness. He turned to his captain. "I think this is rather beyond our authority as well as our capability. Captain Spalko, I want you to get to army-level headquarters with this as soon as possible. Get to the highest-ranking officer you can reach and explain the situation. Come back if possible, but if you receive different orders, you will of course follow them."

"Yes, sir," replied the captain. "But Major—"

"Yes?"

"What if they don't believe me? I mean, I don't know if I'd believe it if someone told me about this."

The major looked at the gates and at the camp behind the gates. "Damned if I know. Do the best you can."

"Yes, sir."

SHAEF, REIMS, FRANCE, 1045 HOURS GMT

The cathedral tower rising above the central square of this French city bore the scars of many wars, but still loomed proud and straight, certainly the most dramatic building in this small city in northeast France. It was far from the most important, however.

That distinction fell to a three-story building of undistinguished architecture, in a quiet district of back streets near the railroad station. A small sign identified the place as the College Moderne et Technique, and in the prewar years more than a thousand young men had attended here, studying various technical trades. Now the large structure held only the most crucial sections of the Supreme Headquarters of the Allied Expeditionary Forces; the rest of the vast command hierarchy was spread throughout the city, wherever they could find room.

The Supreme Commander had chosen for his own office a small classroom on the second floor of the building. It had two windows overlooking the street, though even after the gray dawn these were still covered by blackout curtains. The general—or "the General," as he was known through the HQ—had put his desk on the old teacher's station, on a platform slightly higher than the floor of the room. The only other furniture in the room consisted of a few battered, but comfortable chairs.

General Dwight Eisenhower was nearing the end of a pack of cigarettes, and he was vaguely irritated that it was not yet nine in the morning. He had opened the package with his first cup of coffee, some four hours earlier. He shrugged and flicked his lighter one more time; he had more important things on his mind than cigarette consumption, right now. He stepped off the platform and paced the length of the classroom, then returned to his desk. He stared at the telephones, wondering when—not if, since he had already made up his mind—he should give the order.

Of course, he acknowledged that it was not entirely his decision to make. He had made his recommendation, sent it off to the Combined Chiefs of Staff, and expected an answer shortly.

As if on cue, there was a knock on the door followed immediately by the entry of Ike's chief of staff, General Walter Bedell Smith. He greeted the Supreme Commander cheerfully.

"Ah, Beetle. I take it you've got my cable?"

"Came in less than an hour ago, sir." He opened his blue leather folder and pulled out a sheet of paper, reaching to lay it on the desk. Eisenhower snatched it up before it came into contact with the surface. His eyes went right to the meat of the message:

REGARDING OPERATION ECLIPSE, YOUR RECOMMENDATION ACCEPTED BY
PRESIDENT AND COMBINED CHIEFS. YOU ARE AUTHORIZED TO PROCEED AT
THE EARLIEST POSSIBLE MOMENT. INDICATIONS ARE THAT UNCLE JOE IS
PLAYING FOR THE SAME TROPHY, SO EMPHASIZE THAT TIME IS OF THE
ESSENCE.

GOOD LUCK, AND GODSPEED.

GENERAL GEORGE C. MARSHALL,
CHIEF OF STAFF
UNITED STATES ARMY

Eisenhower exhaled a long stream of smoke through his nose. He was a cautious commander as a rule, and not by nature a gambling man—except of course when it came to D-Day, which had been to his way of thinking the biggest gamble of the entire war. Now he was authorized to take another chance, with an operation that would certainly have unexpected consequences. Given the Russian betrayal, with their armistice of 1944, it was a chance that the United States of America was willing to take.

He pushed a button on his intercom. "Send in Looie Brereton and his division COs," he told Sergeant Summersby.

A few moments later General Lewis Brereton, commander of the First Allied Airborne Army, entered, accompanied by five generals, each a commander of an airborne division or brigade, the components of the airborne army. Their troops were elite, and could travel to battle by parachute, glider, or—once an airfield had been seized by initial lander—transport aircraft. All of them were itching to get back into the war. Since their key use during the Normandy invasion, they had been relegated to use as reinforcement and reserve troops.

Two of them, Generals Maxwell Taylor and James Gavin, commanded the veteran American divisions, the Eighty-second "All-American" Division, and the 101st "Screaming Eagles," respectively. Eisenhower knew and trusted them, and had a very high regard for their troops. Both formations had been instrumental in insuring the success of the D-Day landings, and had provided crucial reinforcements during Rommel's great offensive in December. In the latter case the airborne soldiers had been trucked to the battlefield, and the Supreme Commander knew they were itching for a chance to fulfill their proper role one more time; that is, to drop out of the sky to claim objectives in advance of the ground troops.

"Men," Ike began, pulling down a map of Germany from a rollup on the wall. "You're going to be out in front of the whole damned expeditionary force, this time." The Supreme Commander's finger pointed to the map, while he watched the generals, pleased to see the light of excitement and possibility kindled in every man's eye.

"You're going to drop into Berlin, and hold the place until Third Army and the rest of Twelfth Army Group can get up there to take over."

"Hot damn, General!" declared Taylor. "This is the chance we've been waiting for!"

"It's a big job. Max, your boys will be assigned to these major airfields— Gatow and Staaken, with the airfield at Schönwald as a tertiary objective. Jim, the All-Americans are to take Tempelhof—that's practically inside the city limits—and Rangdor airfields." Eisenhower went on to round out the plans: A British brigade would take the large airport at Oranienburg, while more Brits and a reserve brigade of expatriate Polish paratroopers would serve as reinforcements.

"This will be a daylight drop. Some of the Krauts can be expected to resist, at least those in the SS. We have hopes that the Wehrmacht units will be willing to surrender, in the hopes that we, and not the Russians, will get control of their country after the war."

"Are my boys going to get into the show?" asked General Eldridge Chapman, commander of the newly arrived Thirteenth Airborne Division. Chapman's division had been created in August of 1943, activated on Friday the thirteenth in fact, and his unblooded officers were eager to prove their mettle.

"You'll be going in the second wave," the Supreme Commander explained. "Your paratroop regiment will be dropped where we need reinforcements, and your two glider regiments will land at Tempelhof, as soon as Jim's boys get the runways cleared."

Eisenhower turned the briefing over to his staff officers and stood back, chain-smoking while he watched the rapt eyes of the airborne generals. This was the chance they had been waiting for, and he saw the determination and excitement in their expressions. Good, he thought—they would need all that, and more.

For this whole Operation Eclipse was a gamble, and Dwight Eisenhower was not by nature a gambling man. His greatest roll of the dice had occurred nine months earlier, when he had sent an invasion force across the English Channel in the face of a worrisome weather report, and the tenacious defense of Field Marshal Erwin Rommel. That gamble had paid off, in spades.

But could he be that lucky again?

CCA, NINETEENTH ARMORED DIVISION, EAST OF DESSAU, GERMANY, 1207 HOURS GMT

Frank Ballard took a whiff of the pine trees, relished the fragrance that was so thick in the air. The nearly constant overcast had blown over with the dawn, and despite the wintry season, a rare day of clear skies and sunshine had him thinking of spring. Wet snow still lay deep in the woods to either side of the road, but on the southward-facing banks and shallow hillsides the sun had almost completely eradicated the seasonal blanket. Idly he wondered which would happen first: the snowmelt, or the end of World War II.

Certainly, the prospects for bringing the war to a close were looking good, far better than they had at any time since the attack on Pearl Harbor. It had been seven full days since CCA had lost a man to enemy action—though, sadly, a corporal had been killed and a private paralyzed with a broken neck when a jeep had rolled off of a slippery road.

But there had been no letup in the speed of the advance, which was reminiscent of those heady days in France, during August of the last summer. After the lightning crossing of the Elbe at Dessau, CCA and the rest of Nineteenth Armored had raced northeast, knowing that the rest of Third Army, as well as friendly German forces, were advancing on their flanks. Organized resistance seemed to have come to an end, and even the vexing snipers had faded into the countryside.

As if to challenge his complacency, a rattle of gunfire distracted him.

Ballard flinched reflexively, almost ducking down through the hatch of his turret. But the shots were distant, and were almost instantaneously amplified by a
barrage of machine guns from CCA vehicles. Two tanks chimed in with HE
rounds and the colonel saw a small house and nearby shed, perched on a hillside with a good view of the road, vanish in a cloud of fire and smoke.

He looked down the road, saw no signs of excitement—no one was calling
for the medic, or aiding a wounded man. Good . . . looked like the CCA luck
was holding. Still, the shots, probably resulting from an amateurish attempt at
an ambush, provided a pointed reminder that the war was still on and that he,
Frank Ballard, still had a job to do.

Leaning out of the tank as it rolled forward, he looked along the column,
trying to understand the source of the disturbance. He saw an infantry sergeant explaining something to the commander of one of the tanks that had just
blasted the building, and directed his own driver to pull off next to the NCO.

"What happened, Sergeant?" Ballard asked, shouting over the rumbling of
his tank's engine.

The man shook his head in embarrassment. "One of my boys, one of the
replacements, thought he saw something moving up there and took a few
shots. Naturally, the rest of the company chimed in. Turns out it was only a
cow, coming around that farmhouse. Poor ol' Bessie never had a chance."

"Hey, Colonel?" called the other Sherman's commander, a sergeant who
had been with the unit since Normandy. "How 'bout I send some boys up there
and see if we can round up some steaks for dinner?"

Ballard laughed at the thought, but shook his head. "Sorry, Buck. But
we're in a race, remember—no time for a barbecue!"

Buck waved good-naturedly and reached down to tell his driver to keep
moving. Ballard's tank fell in behind as a gap opened, almost magically, in the
tight rank of Shermans on the road. One thing about being the CO, he
reflected—you never had to wait for the column to make room for you.

A jeep skittered along the shoulder of the road, coming back against the
flow of the tank traffic, and he recognized Captain Smiggs. The recon officer's
driver nimbly backed the four-wheel-drive vehicle down into the ditch, facing
the road, and when the command tank rolled past the little car lurched onto
the shoulder and raced along beside; the two officers could talk this way without any delay in the advance, though the jeep driver was forced to wrestle with
the steering wheel as he drove through the mountains of slush and mud kicked
up by the column of Shermans.

"See anything interesting up there?" Ballard shouted down.

"Met one of Rommel's scouts at the next crossroads," Smiggy called back.
"We should veer right there—that'll lead us past Potsdam. Sounds like Fourth
Armored and Panzer Lehr are getting into a traffic jam on the outskirts of the
place, so the right turn will let us skirt around the city."

"Straight to Berlin, that's what we want," Ballard said with a smile.

Indeed, when General Wakefield had caught up to them at the end of the previous day and given them the go-ahead, the old man had been unusually enthusiastic. Apparently some of Patton's fire was rubbing off on the normally stodgy division commander. In any event, Berlin was a prize that had achieved almost mythical status in the minds of the GIs of Third Army. Now it was their objective, assigned by no less an entity than the president himself.

Ballard found himself grinning at the very thought.

"What's so funny?" Smiggs called out.

The colonel just shook his head. "I was just thinking about how strange this war is," he replied. "We fight our way through France, and now that we're in the enemy's home country we're racing along like it's a Sunday road rally!"

"Tally ho!" Smiggy shouted, mocking a British accent as his jeep sped away.

The column continued on, but it was only a few minutes later when Ballard was tapped by his radioman, who was down inside the turret. "Colonel—it's General Wakefield on he horn for you."

Ballard took the headset and microphone but stayed on top of the turret. This was too nice of a day to climb down into that metal cocoon, even if he did have the division CO talking to him. "This is Texas One—good afternoon, Dallas," he said.

The big man's voice came through clearly, and the colonel had no trouble hearing. "Texas One, there's a small plane en route to you. Set up a landing field marked with smoke, and let me know when you take delivery," said Wakefield in his deep growl.

"Roger, Dallas, we're on the job," Ballard said cheerfully. "Anything you can tell me about what it's carrying?"

"It may involve some diversion of forces," Wakefield said. "Do you copy?"

"Diversion of forces, Dallas? But we're twenty-five miles from—" He paused a moment while he tried to remember the code word for Berlin. "—from Birthday! We could be having dinner there tonight!"

"You can still be at the birthday party," Wakefield said sternly. "At least most of you nineteen Texans. We have Arizona and Iowa still en route—you won't be lonely. Dallas out."

"Arizona" was today's code word for the Fourth Armored Division, and Iowa represented Panzer Lehr of the German Republican Army. Ballard lowered the mike and asked his radioman to switch to the combat command's channel.

There were smooth pastures all over the place, and Ballard picked one that had a good approach into the wind, with no trees to block an aircraft as it came in to land. He brushed aside the questions of his officers as they clamored for an explanation, telling them to take advantage of the break to heat up some rations or to get out and stretch their legs.

As soon as the time interval had passed, he had one of his Shermans fire a couple of smoke rounds, one at each end of the proposed runway. Not only did they mark the spot, but the plumes trailing away from the impacts provided a good gauge of wind speed and direction for the pilot. For a few minutes nothing happened, and as the breeze finally dispersed the markers he had another two rounds fired. No sooner had these exploded than he heard the droning of a small aircraft engine, nothing like the powerful thrum of a fighter or dive bomber.

Soon the craft was in sight, a high-winged Piper with stilt-like tripod landing gear and oversized windows around the compartment. The pilot made a low pass, then circled around until he was flying into the wind. He dropped lower, almost stalling, then set down on the bare ground, bumping along for only a hundred yards or so—barely a quarter of the available distance—before coming to a halt.

One man, an American officer, got out of the passenger door and started across the field toward the Sherman tanks parked beside the road. Ballard climbed out of his turret and started away from the column, wanting to talk to the fellow with some degree of privacy. Even before he had taken a dozen steps, the Piper was turning around in the field, engine revving as it started a takeoff run. By the time the newcomer was close enough for Ballard to identify him, the plane was back in the air, heading west.

"Sanger, how the hell are you?" he said, as the two men shook hands.

"It's good to see you again, Frank. Got some place where we can talk? And can you ask Smiggy to join us?"

Ballard gestured to a deserted farmhouse he'd commandeered. In a few minutes, the two men were seated at a kitchen table, a fire roaring in an old stove. "Frank, before we get started, I want you to know that this is a little bit off the reservation. I talked to General Wakefield before I flew here, but this is an operation that doesn't have top brass approval, and we could all end up with our tits in the wringer. If we're unlucky, we'll freeze our asses out here in the cold and waste time and men when we could be in Berlin."

"And if we're lucky?"

"We'll put the bag on a top Nazi bugging out of Berlin with a shitload of gold and what he thinks is a get-out-of-jail-free card from one of Rommel's top men. It's one of those double-double-double-cross situations."

Smiggy grinned. "Is the man big on the camp operations side?"

"The biggest."

"Count me in." He pulled his service .45 from its holster, twirled it expertly, and slipped it back in.

Ballard spoke up. "Okay. What do you need?"

"I need enough forces to cover these roads and intersections . . ."

11 MARCH 1945

PRIVATE APARTMENTS OF HEINRICH HIMMLER, BERLIN, 0341 HOURS GMT

Heinrich Himmler prowled through the darkened rooms readying himself for his departure.

The arrangements had been made. Günter von Reinhardt would travel as a hostage with the escaping convoy. The Prussian colonel had marked a clear route on the maps, and had shown copies of the movement orders issued to the affected Allied units. At a point in Bavaria near Berchtesgarten, von Reinhardt would be released—and from there Himmler could plan his own route undetected.

Below the release point were American units. To get through that screen, von Reinhardt would have to issue additional orders. That was his protection. He would be left with one armored car filled with twenty million marks of gold and two SS guards. When a coded radio transmission was received stating that Himmler had gotten through the lines, the SS guards were to release von Reinhardt and the gold and make their own escape. A possibility still existed of a double-cross, but that far south, Himmler believed he had an excellent chance of avoiding capture. Not wishing to leave anything to chance, he had made arrangements to split his convoy immediately on the other side of the line, so that von Reinhardt could not betray his location the moment he was again free. To ensure his safety, the SS guards would kill von Reinhardt upon receipt of still another code, and would attempt to liberate the gold. If they failed, well, money was only money.

Foolish of von Reinhardt to think he could outwit Heinrich Himmler. Himmler had had a thousand opponents, many of whom had been considered intelligent. He had outwitted them all, and most of them were dead now.

South America? He wondered what it would be like. Certainly there would be many changes, but he would have numerous loyal companions around him as well, and plenty of money. Though money was no substitute for power, it was certainly better than poverty. Perhaps one day it could be the means of a return to power . . . that was something to think about, to hope for, in the long term.

His thoughts turned to von Reinhardt again. Imagine, taking that kind of risk for mere money—funds that he intended to give away! Himmler shook his head at the mere idea. But the Reichsführer did understand von Reinhardt's unsentimental assessment that a Nazi abdication was probably best for Germany, and perhaps he was willing to sacrifice himself, a true patriot in the end. The money was simply a red herring, though he wouldn't mind getting it if he could. Himmler wondered if von Reinhardt would end up keeping it for himself. He was willing to bet that the sight of so much untraceable gold would tempt even the imperturbable aristocrat.

There. He was packed and ready, and there were only a few more things to do. He took his gun from his holster and screwed a silencer onto the barrel. He placed it in the top desk drawer, then sat down and reached for the buzzer. One must never leave loose ends hanging, he thought to himself.

Moments later his aide-de-camp, Captain Wolter, came in. "Yes, Herr Reichsführer?" asked the capable, if unimaginative, bureaucrat.

"Bring your staff attendants in here, please," Himmler said.

Soon the two sergeants, one a lanky Silesian who had joined the SS as a lad, the other a sturdy female who had worked as the Reichsführer's secretary since before the war, joined Wolter in standing before Himmler's desk.

"You have undoubtedly noticed that there are some changes going on around here, have you not?" he asked them.

It was the captain who spoke. "We stand ready to obey your orders, Herr Reichsführer, in any capacity you desire us to serve."

"Certainly. I am glad to hear it." Himmler knew that the man spoke the truth, but at the same time he couldn't know exactly what they understood about his plans: the great amount of gold that had been brought from various underground vaults, the plans, even the maps and travel arrangements that were so crucial to the secrecy of the operation. The Reichsführer opened the desk drawer.

"I order you to attention," he barked.

Immediately the three staffers stood rigidly, eyes fixed on the wall above and behind Himmler's head. "You have served the Reich well, all three of you . . ." His hand went into the drawer, felt the cool hilt of the Luger.

"Your loyalty deserves a reward," he continued, bringing up the gun.

The silencer worked well, though by the third shot the baffles had begun to wear, and the last bullet exploded outward with an audible "whoof" of force.

But there was nobody left to hear . . . nobody except Himmler himself, who started to return the gun to the drawer, then remembered that his wife was waiting for him upstairs in the bedroom.

"No loose ends," he reminded himself, pocketing the weapon before he walked out of the office, closing and locking the door behind him.

12 MARCH 1945

142ND TANK BATTALION, SECOND GUARDS TANK ARMY, APPROACHING KÜSTRIN, GERMANY, 1341 HOURS GMT

Colonel Alexis Krigoff had never ridden on a tank before, and he found the sensation strangely exhilarating, and at the same time frightening. He had heard and watched the mighty T-34s rumble past on many occasions, both on parade and on the battlefield. He was prepared for the noise, but he had never imagined that the machines would jolt and rock so much, merely from the motion of rumbling down a road. At first he had been determined to ride outside the hull, where the view would be best, but he had quickly realized that he would very likely get thrown to the ground—an ignominious fate that he ruled as completely unacceptable.

So he had ordered the young lieutenant who was acting as his chauffeur to climb down inside the T-34. The intelligence colonel took his place at the hatch atop the squat, functional turret. He propped himself on the commander's seat with his upper torso outside of the metal shell, and allowed the ring of the small opening to provide at least some support around his midriff. There was a light machine gun mounted right next to him, and he secretly hoped that he would get a chance to use it to mow down some Nazi infantry.

This battalion was one of the leading elements of Zhukov's Front, and Petrovsky's Second Guards Tank Army. Ahead of him he could count ten more T-34s, but beyond that lay the terrain of as-yet-unconquered Germany. It gave him a thrill to know that he was now in the vanguard of the epic advance.

Some distance to the right, following a parallel road—really nothing more than a farm track—he could see the second company of the 142nd Battalion. Beyond them were additional columns of tanks, and when they crested a low elevation he could see them stretching for miles across the flat, open countryside. To the left was another tank division, and he knew that there was yet another beyond that one.

In fact, he found himself thinking about the big picture of this whole campaign, and he grinned fiercely at the knowledge. Petrovsky's army numbered some twelve divisions, four of which were armored. Zhukov's First Belorussian Front, in turn, was comprised of three great armies—Petrovsky's, plus two more. Beyond that, there were three additional fronts—one to the north and two to the south—all driving relentlessly forward, all striving to wipe the scourge of Nazism from the face of Europe.

While he had been riding in his trailer, Krigoff had spent a great deal of his time studying the maps. He knew that this division, on the direct road into Küstrin, was on the straightest line toward the great prize of this campaign: Berlin. The city of Küstrin-an-der-Oder, which was already visible on the horizon before him, lay only eighty kilometers from the German capital. If they could cross that river and quickly race onward, it was conceivable that Krigoff and the Second Guards Tank Army could be in Berlin by sometime tomorrow. He delighted at the thought of waiting for the Americans there, with the Red Army already in possession of the objective that Patton and Eisenhower had striven toward for so long.

In his most secret thoughts, he imagined another fantasy—a circumstance whereby the Americans and their British allies would provoke the Red Army into an attack. The Russians would sweep through the weakling capitalist armies, Krigoff knew. He was certain that Stalin was eager to send this mammoth war machine against the capitalists, the traditional enemies of communism. Many times, with private glee, he had looked at broader scale maps of Europe, imagining the glorious spread of communism as the Soviet military machine swept across Germany, driving the Allied rabble before it. They wouldn't stop, not even at the Rhine, he knew; instead, they would charge westward, across the Low Countries, through France, all the way to the ultimate barrier of the Atlantic Ocean.

What a continent this would be! The whole cradle of civilization, everything from the Pacific Ocean and Siberia across the largest landmass of the world, under the rule of the great man who sat in the Kremlin, the man who had appointed Krigoff to this important task, this historic opportunity. Perhaps it would take a long time, longer even than Krigoff's lifetime, to spread the doctrine of Marx to the Americas, or through the teeming populations of China and India. But if he could live to see the hammer and sickle flying over Berlin, over Paris and London and Rome and Madrid, then he would die a happy man. And he, and the rest of the world, would know beyond doubt that the spread of communism was an inevitability, the true destiny of the planet.

He twisted around on the uncomfortable metal chair. In the tank immediately to the rear rode Paulina Koninin, though he couldn't see her, as she was currently down inside the hull. An hour earlier he had watched her scramble out and jump down to the ground, when the battalion had come upon a German antitank emplacement; he had been awestruck and terrified as she snapped pictures of the swift counterattack, as the Russian armor closed in on the doomed position and plastered it with high-explosive shells. There had been no enemy survivors, and though the battalion had lost its two lead tanks, the surviving vehicles wasted no time in resuming the advance. After the fast firefight, Paulina had favored him with that tight smile, holding up her camera like it was a trophy before she had climbed back into the tank.

He had been spending as much time as possible talking to her, admiring her courage, her passionate belief in the Soviet system. Her technical skills, too, impressed him. When he had remarked on her photographs she had given him a picture of Stalin himself that she had taken, a shot in which the chairman looked avuncular and charming as he sat at a small tea table, a mischievous sparkle in his eyes. Krigoff had liked the picture so much that he had asked for another copy, which he had given to Petrovsky as a gift—and also as a subtle reminder of where the true power lay in this vast military machine.

It had been her tales of such engagements that had convinced him that he, too, needed to be up here with the vanguard. He had assigned his assistant, Major Rokov, a solid staff officer, to take over the affairs of the Intelligence Section, manning the communications center in the trailer so that Colonel Krigoff could get out here for a firsthand look at the war. It had been one of the best decisions he had ever made—there was no comparing this to the aloof contemplation of the battlefield such as he had gained from the small airplane over Warsaw. He had been baptized by fire, had known the thrill of combat, and he relished the thought of the upcoming battles. If it wasn't for the delays that would necessarily have entailed, he would have allowed himself to hope for some stiff German resistance at the Oder, just so that he could get the experience of a true, savage engagement.

As if in answer to his musings, an artillery shell exploded in the field before him, not too far from the road. More shells plummeted downward, sending cascades of turf and ice blasting into the air on both sides of the column. Obviously, the Germans had this road under observation, and had sighted their guns with care. Several blasts erupted at once, and chunks of dirt cascaded downward, spattering across the road—several of them actually landed on the foredeck of Krigoff's tank.

Where was the Red Air Force? He scanned the skies in vexation, then relaxed as he saw a phalanx of dive bombers, fifty or sixty of them, growling out of the east. The single-engine planes roared overhead, the drone of their engines thrumming even through the hammering of the tank motors and the sporadic bursts of artillery. They would find the German guns, Krigoff knew, and allowed himself a moment's wistful reflection, a longing that he could be up there with them.

But here, this was where the action was, where the fight would be resolved. He grinned as another round of artillery shells plastered the landscape, and then he felt the tank lurch beneath him—as if the driver had heard the explosions, and flinched. He felt someone tugging at his leg and looked down in annoyance to see the worried face of the young lieutenant.

"Comrade Colonel?"

"What is it?" he snapped.

"Perhaps it would be good if you climbed down inside the hull. The danger from shrapnel is real, and you have very much of your body exposed. It would be much safer down here."

Krigoff looked at the man in contempt. "I want to see what's happening," he retorted. "I will stay where I—"

The next blast was so close that the concussion drove the air from the colonel's lungs, as if forcing his words back down his throat. A spray of pebbles and dirt slashed across his face, stinging his skin and darkening his vision. He was terrified at the thought that he had been blinded, but in moments he blinked away the grit and was stunned to see that a T-34 several tanks ahead of his own had been pushed right over onto its side by the blast. The armored behemoth looked helpless and stricken as flames started to rise from the engine compartment. A man pushed open the turret hatch and started to climb out—awkwardly, as with the tank on its side the upper portion of the hatch tried to press down and hold him in. Then the ammunition inside the turret exploded, sending a column of fire' out of the hatch and blasting the soldier like a projectile. Krigoff watched in awe as the fellow flew a hundred meters just above the ground, then tumbled and bounced like a rag doll until at last he lay still.

More shells exploded, closer now, and the colonel reasoned that, in truth, it would make no sense to get himself killed just so that he could watch this violent display. He lowered the seat until just his head, protected by the steel bowl of his helmet, was outside of the hatch. But he would not go all the way down—instead, he peered over the rim of the hatch, watching the steady onslaught of Soviet arms. This was just too good to miss.

The young lieutenant looked at the colonel, then shook his head. There was a panoramic targeting scope just in front of the commander's seat.

SECOND SS PANZER DIVISION, KÜSTRIN, GERMANY, 1401 HOURS GMT

"Obersturmführer Vogel!"

"Yes, Standartenführer Peiper!" Lukas had been sitting on the ground with his back to the brick wall, but he instantly climbed to his feet and snapped to attention, glad to have something to take his mind off the shelling. He and his platoon of lean, hollow-eyed panzergrenadiere had been waiting for more than a day in a rubble-strewn alley no more than two blocks from the Oder River. The Russian artillery had been pounding the city throughout that time, and every few minutes an explosion would erupt close enough that the men could see rubble raining down on one side or another of their scant shelter.

The Das Reich division was steadily diminishing in size. To call it a division was a courtesy—its actual strength was less than battalion-sized by now. Standartenführer Peiper was now commanding officer—Gruppenführer Ostendorff had been killed in action.

"It's time to earn your pay," said the veteran SS colonel, his scarred face looking eerily like a death's-head as he gave the young soldier a grim smile. He was standing tall in the entrance to the alley, his hands on his hips; he barely even flinched as a shell exploded half a block away.

"What are your orders, *mein Standartenführer*?" asked Lukas, tingling with excitement and fear.

"We are taking a company of panzers across the bridge, and I need infantry support," replied the commander. "Bring your platoon and fall in with the rest of these men; stay close behind the tanks while we're out in the open— they'll be your best protection against small arms fire. Once we get to the far side, spread out to the left and engage any Russian infantry that you come across. Keep your heads down—there's a whole division of Russian tanks coming this way."

"Yes sir!" Lukas raised a hand in a sieg-heil salute, even as he wondered why the Germans would be advancing across the river. It had been his understanding that they were going to try and hold the line of the Oder against the enemy attack, not go on the offensive. But the panzers rolled past, first a dozen Mark IVs, then the Panther commander by Peiper himself.

When that tank rolled forward, Lukas and his men came out of the alley and advanced at a jog. In a minute they were in the open, climbing the easy grade that led to the span across the Oder. They crouched instinctively as bullets whined overhead and more shells burst over the water of the dark, frigid river.

Lukas got an idea of why they were crossing the river as he saw several burly engineers hauling packages of TNT and detonators down the bank, to disappear under the bridge. They were preparing the span for demolition, he understood; it would be his job, and Peiper's, to hold up the Russians long enough so that the crossing could be properly mined. Would they let them come back before they blew it? He shrugged away the question as soon as it occurred to him, ashamed for thinking such a selfish thought.

Two minutes later they were across, having lost no one to the enemy fire. The Panther's engine growled and chugged as the driver downshifted, then started to drive up the steep road leading out of the valley. The grenadiers slowed the pace of their advance, bunching up behind the steel behemoth, still crouching as they made their way up the street. The tank crawled over an obstacle of shattered stone and the men scrambled after, and soon they reached the crest. The road continued on, past an array of ruined buildings and out across a flat, barren steppe, but here Peiper's panzer turned off the road.

Lukas led his men after, then watched as the Panther turned, jockeyed back and forth a few times, then rumbled forward to the concealment of a notch between the ruins of two stone buildings. The wicked barrel pointed eastward, but the remnants of the walls rose high enough to mask every part of the tank below the level of the gun from the direction of the enemy's approach.

"Deploy in this building," Lukas ordered, grateful that, with these veterans, he would not have to assign a specific position to each soldier. Indeed, the SS panzergrenadiere scrambled over the rubble of the front wall and quickly spread out within the gaping, roofless shell of what had once been a warehouse or large store.

He was about to follow when he saw the Panther's hatch open up to reveal Jochen Peiper's head and shoulders. The SS colonel waved him over, so he trotted through the broken street to stand beside the tank's fender.

"We'll need to hold them for at least a few hours, maybe the rest of the day," the colonel said.

"*Jawohl, mein Standartenführer!* Long enough for the engineers to set charges on the bridge, I presume?"

Peiper smiled. "Smart soldier, you are. Yes, that's the reason. We had it mined to blow like all the others, but the artillery barrage shook loose the main charge and dropped it into the river. So they have to redo the whole thing."

"You can count on me, sir!" Lukas pledged.

"I know I can, my boy—I know I can," replied Peiper.

Lukas thought that he sounded kind of sad when he said it.

142ND TANK BATTALION, SECOND GUARDS TANK ARMY, KÜSTRIN, GERMANY, 1410 HOURS GMT

Alyosha Krigoff put his head down only reluctantly, and felt the concussion of the explosion through the ground on which he lay. Next to him, Paulina Koninin failed to display that caution, remaining upright to see and photograph above the rim of the muddy ditch in which they had taken shelter.

Abruptly she cursed, finally dropping into the foxhole and clutching her bleeding hand. Her eye was wide with concern.

"Are you all right?" asked the colonel worriedly. He saw the blood and gasped. "You're wounded!"

She exhaled a sigh of relief and held up her camera so that the blood dripped down her arm, and not onto the lens of her precious instrument. "I was afraid the body was cracked open," she explained. "That would have ruined a fine roll of film—such pictures!"

"What about your hand?" asked Krigoff, a little awed by her dedication to her craft. After all, German artillery had zeroed in on their position, and shells continued to rain down on them, exploding on all sides. Their survival under these circumstances was not something that could be taken for granted. His own tank had been crippled, a track blown off by an enemy shot. Krigoff had leaped into this ditch when the lieutenant informed him that his advance was over, and he had found Paulina down here, poking her head up to snap picture after picture.

"Oh, that—just a flesh wound," she explained, at last examining the injury. "A lucky piece of shrapnel must have gotten me." Indeed, the colonel could see that her little finger was torn open along half its length, and his stomach churned as he saw a white flash within the nasty gash that could only be the bone of her finger.

"We should get you to an aid station," he blurted, shocked by this real proof of war.

"For this?" she scoffed. She rolled onto her back in the muddy hole, resting her camera on her belly as she reached into her side pouch and came out with a dirty handkerchief. She wrapped her little finger alongside the ring and middle fingers of the same hand, then used her other hand and her teeth to tie the cloth into a tight wrap. She picked up her camera again and manipulated some of the controls, then flashed him a grin. "There—I can still focus, and shoot!"

Krigoff's own sense of focus was growing more than a little fuzzy. The chaos of the battlefield was making it very hard for him to think, to process information in the calm and rational manner that his role as army intelligence officer required. The artillery had been bad enough, but now those guns had been joined by a chorus of antitank weapons, and even several powerful cannon that Paulina had suggested must be German tanks. Briefly, he longed for the shelter of the armored turret that had protected him in the T-34.

He looked toward that tank, which squatted all by itself in the road, the other vehicles of the column having rolled into the field when they started coming under antitank fire. No less than a dozen Russian tanks were burning around him, though the T-34s were firing boldly back against the mostly hidden enemy. The damaged tank looked particularly vulnerable, since the track had been shattered on the right front, and several of the bogey wheels in the suspension were nothing more than twisted sprockets.

But the gun was still firing. Krigoff felt a grudging measure of admiration for the young lieutenant, who had insisted upon staying with his crippled vehicle. The colonel watched the turret swivel slightly, bringing the long cannon around in a small traverse. The gunner made an adjustment, depressing that barrel slightly so that it was just parallel to the ground, and then the tank spat out a round, fire flashing from the muzzle, instantaneously replaced with a waft of black smoke.

As Krigoff was watching he saw a white flash, so bright that the light lingered even when he closed his eyes. A second later he felt the blast and heard the explosion. Blinking, he strained to see, and was finally able to make out details again. The turret of the crippled T-34 was unrecognizable, as half of it had been blown away. The gun was canted off at a crazy angle, and the colonel could look right into the crew compartment. There was no sign of the lieutenant, and—to judge from the violence of the explosion—Krigoff was pretty certain that no part of him would ever be found.

"Damned 88!" cursed Paulina, shaking her head, then rolling onto her stomach, crawling up to the lip of the ditch, and staring in the direction of the enemy emplacements.

"What?" asked Krigoff, forcing himself to lift himself up to her level. He could make out nothing in the smoke and gray rubble of the city's outskirts.

"It's an antitank gun," she said. "Actually, antiaircraft by design, but it's a cursed good tank killer and these bastards know how to use them."

"Oh, yes, I remember," Krigoff acknowledged, embarrassed that he had forgotten such a detail in the heat of the moment. He heard that loud crack again, and another T-34 blew up, sending a plume of fire rising thirty or forty feet into the sky.

"It must be over there, behind that wall," Paulina said. "I can't see it for sure." She raised her camera, pressing the viewer against her good eye, and snapped another picture. "I think there's still a bridge standing down there— that's probably why they're fighting so hard on this side of the river."

Krigoff had no idea which wall she was talking about; everything looked the same to him, more like an expanse of rubble strewn along the horizon than any recognizable structure. But a bridge—that was crucial news! He looked to the side, where still more Russian tanks were catching fire. None of them were advancing any more, and in fact he saw several of the T-34s starting to back away, though they moved in reverse so that their guns could keep up the steady barrage of fire against the enemy line.

"How can you see a bridge?" he asked. "I can't even see down into the valley!"

She rolled over until she was lying right beside him, and pointed with her good hand. He followed the line of her finger. "Those are the towers of a bridge stanchion," she said. "Of course, there's no guarantee that the road—or rail, perhaps—is still there, but it's a good sign that the piers are in place. And why else would they be fighting here, when they could just fall back and use the river for protection?"

"Why else, indeed," Krigoff thought. In fact, her suggestion made perfect sense. His heart was pounding, not in fear but excitement. A bridge across the Oder—a bridge to Berlin!

"Shit!" Paulina snapped in irritation.

"What is it? Are you wounded again?"

She shook her head and held up the camera. "That shrapnel broke the rewinder. I've shot up this whole roll, and I can't open it up out here to change my film or I'll lose all these pictures."

Alyosha felt a surge of relief. "I have to get back to headquarters and report to General Petrovsky, tell him about this bridge," he said. "Come with me—certainly there'll be a place you can use as a darkroom."

"Might as well," she agreed. "I can't do any good out here until I get some fresh film in my camera."

For an hour they crawled through the cold, slushy ditch, gradually moving away from the German lines. Finally they were beyond the range of the shelling, and they stood up to start walking. Krigoff saw a scout car racing past, and waved it down.

"Yes, Comrade Colonel?" asked the driver, a young Siberian.

"I need to get to army headquarters! Take me there at once!"

The driver nodded agreeably, and pointed to the door on the other side of the cab. "Hop in," he said. Ten seconds later they were racing toward the rear.

LONDON, ENGLAND, 1422 HOURS GMT

"Ah, Philby, old man. Good to see you. Rather beastly weather, what?" Ian Weatherspoon was a portly, tweedy man who sported a bushy mustache that completely covered his upper lip. He was one of those men whose handshake was a fundamental test of masculine prowess; Kim Philby extracted his own fingers from the grip ahead of certain injury.

"W-Weatherspoon. Good to s-see you as well. Thanks for making t-time."

"Always have time for you. Sit down, sit down. What's all this about Jerry taking interest in one of our programs?"

Philby sat down, placed his briefcase upon his lap, snapped open the catches, and extracted a file folder. He opened it, pulled out a single sheet of paper, and passed it across the desk. "This is an extract f-from a report we received—the source is pro-protected, of course—"

"Of course, of course," Weatherspoon agreed, taking the paper.

"Our friends in Peenemünde—you know, that's the Jerry m-missile program—evidently are showing some interest in one of our research programs that goes by the name of . . . let me see . . ." Philby looked down at the folder. ". . . 'tube alloys.' It seems they have a mole inside the program who has been feeding them some useful information." Philby glanced up. Weatherspoon's ruddy complexion had gone pale. Pay dirt! He had had to guess what part of the German apparatus would most alarm the "tube alloys" people, and had settled on the German missile program as the most interested party. Whatever "tube alloys" was hiding, it was a weapon that could be used in conjunction with a missile.

"Are you sure about this?"

Philby gave a casual shrug. "As sure as anything can be in the intelligence game, you know. At least h-half of what we get is p-pure garbage. The t-trouble is, we never know w-which half." He laughed. Weatherspoon was too upset to join him in the joke. Very good. Very good indeed.

"How can we help?" Weatherspoon asked.

"First, I wanted to put you on a-alert, just in case there's s-something here. S-Second, I thought I might l-look through some p-personnel lists, if it's not t-too much trouble? The best way to catch a mole is to salt some special information with a likely person and then see if that information m-makes it across. T-Try it with different people and different bits of information, and as Bob's your uncle, there's your mole."

"Yes, yes, of course. Thanks, old man. I don't mind telling you, if 'tube alloys' were to be compromised, it could be serious. Quite serious. Can't say much about it, but it's important."

"Well, I'm glad for once that MI-6 and MI-5 can work on the same side of the street. Now, you mentioned on the telephone that you had a few problems in the other direction where I might be of some small assistance . . ."

Some time later, after Philby had left, Ian Weatherspoon made a telephone call. "Sir, I received an inquiry today concerning 'tube alloys.' . . . Yes, sir. . . . It was from Mr. Kim Philby. He's deputy chief of Section 5, MI-6. . . . Yes, that Philby. . . . He says there's a German mole in the project and information is traveling to the German missile program at Peenemünde. . . . Yes, sir. . . . He wanted personnel records, sir. . . . Key technical staff. . . . I did provide them as he requested, sir. . . . Yes, the contact seemed legitimate enough to me, but your standing orders were that any contact be reported and that all contacts were to be investigated. Therefore, I ordered surveillance to be placed on him. I hope that was in order, sir. . . . Thank you, sir. . . . Yes, I'll keep the surveillance going, sir, and report any subsequent contacts. . . . I agree, sir. The likelihood is that Philby is on the up-and-up, but better safe than sorry, eh? . . . Yes, sir. . . . Thank you, sir. . . . Good-bye."

SECOND SS PANZER DIVISION, KÜSTRIN, GERMANY, 1554 HOURS GMT

The drone of a hundred airplane engines penetrated the din of shelling, shouts, and small-arms fire. Lukas was looking at the sky when his corporal, a lanky twenty-year-old from East Prussia, grabbed him by the arm and threw him onto the pile of rubble that formed their makeshift foxhole. Ten seconds later the ground shook so hard that he was lifted into the air. He tumbled back onto the jagged bricks, cursing as the sharp edges tore at his face and hands. Shrapnel whistled over his head, jagged steel making eerie wailing sounds as it tore through the air.

"Thanks. You saved—" Lukas turned toward the corporal and saw the man's eyes, open but sightless, staring in his direction. Stunned, the young soldier reached for the fellow's shoulder, and when he tugged slightly the lifeless corpse rolled over to reveal a gory mess at the back of his skull.

"Goddammit!" he cursed, rolling on his back to shake a fist at the Soviet fliers. Guilt surged within him, for he suspected the corporal would not have perished, had he not raised himself up to save his young lieutenant from the same fate. A lump tightened in his throat, but Lukas would not let himself cry.

He stared skyward, amazed at the number of winged shapes that seemed to be breaking downward, plummeting directly toward him. The dive bombers came on in waves of ten or twenty, winging over from high altitude, plunging toward the earth with earsplitting screams, releasing their bombs like little turds when it seemed as though the aircraft must plunge straight into the ground. But the pilots were skilled; they pulled their Sturmoviks out of the nearly suicidal dives and roared away, a hundred meters above the ground, as their lethal loads slammed into the ruined terrain on the outskirts of Küstrin.

Each wave of explosions rippled through the air and ground, louder and far more violent than the most furious thunderstorm. This was worse than any artillery barrage, and not just because the bombs were bigger than the shells fired by even the heaviest guns. To Lukas, there was something maddeningly purposeful in the vicious fliers, for he knew that each bomb was delivered personally by an enemy pilot. He wanted to blast the sky, empty the magazine of his machine pistol, but he withheld this irrational impulse, knowing that—as close as they looked—the planes were flying too high for him to offer any threat whatsoever. Instead, he vowed to make his bullets count, when the Soviet infantry came advancing across this hellish wasteland.

But he truly wondered if the Red Army would even have to attack, so potent, so powerfully destructive was this deadly bombardment. He saw Peiper's panzer, still crouched between the ruined buildings, now covered with a layer of bricks and dust cast by the relentless explosions. He ducked and pressed his face into the ground, his hands over his head, when the bombs struck nearby, and his back and shoulders were bruised from the rain of debris that came tumbling out of the sky after each crunching blast.

More roars filled his ears as another wave, and then another, of the horrible airplanes swept down. Some of the pilots were exceptionally hateful; they flew through the bombardment of their comrades, strafing, sending streams of whining bullets and explosive cannon shells into the ruins where the German infantry and armor sought shelter—shelter that didn't actually exist.

How many airplanes did they have? Lukas couldn't even begin to imagine. It seemed as though the same bombers must be circling around, dropping new explosives with each pass, but he didn't think this was the case. In fact, when one flight flew low overhead he saw that each Sturmovik carried but one of the deadly bombs under its belly. There were just so many of them that they could keep sending fresh aircraft into the fray, while those that had dropped their payloads had enough time to return to their airbases, rearm, and come back to maintain the uninterrupted onslaught.

A frightening thought occurred to him: What if the enemy infantry was using the cover of this bombardment to creep closer, ready to lunge forward in a great human wave and wipe out these few shell-shocked Germans who stood between them and the precious bridge? He looked around. The men of his platoon were invisible, each having wormed his way as deep into a hole as he possibly could. He didn't even know if any of them were still alive, though it seemed logical that, since he had survived, some of them had made it too. But certainly none of them were keeping watch against the approach of Soviet troops.

Resolutely, Lukas decided to look for himself. He crept out of his hole, pressing flat against the broken ground as a bomb exploded nearby, then crawling forward and upward until he reached the top of the pile of bricks he had been using for shelter. Lying flat, he raised his head just high enough to look over to the other side. His hand was on his knife, as he half expected some Mongol infantrymen to be lurking there, waiting to spring forward with fixed bayonets and savage Asian battle cries.

There was no human being in sight. Instead, he saw a landscape of terribly broken ground, shell holes and craters eliminating even the traces of what kinds of buildings, gardens, and streets might have been there before the war. He couldn't see more than one or two hundred meters; beyond that the smoke and dust was so thick that there could have been a hundred tanks lurking there, and he wouldn't have seen a single turret. Somewhat relieved, but still uncertain, he slid back down the pile of bricks and curled into his small foxhole next to the lifeless corporal.

He tried to reassure himself: If the Russians sent troops to advance through this storm of explosions, they would have to find men who were either insanely brave or criminally stupid. From what he'd heard of the Soviet army, however, neither of these categories seemed likely to be in short supply. He resolved to take frequent trips to the crest of his little pile of rubble, and to keep his machine pistol handy.

Time passed like a nightmare that would never end. Eventually Lukas became numb to the danger of instant death, deafened to the chaotic thunder of explosions that formed such a claustrophobic perimeter around his world. The shock of each blast seemed like part of normal life, a violent backdrop to an existence that could not possibly last more than a few minutes, an hour at the most. He looked up, but couldn't see the planes that still roared overhead, and realized that it was getting dark. That seemed right—nightmares should happen at night, after all.

For a while he lay on his back and stared at the dark, glowering sky. Only gradually did the realization come to him: There were no more bombs, and all the aircraft engines were fading away as the last flight of Sturmoviks winged back to their bases. The sound continued to grow more faint, and there was no sign of a fresh wave of aerial attackers. He shook his head, trying to think, and then he understood. If he couldn't see the bombers, then they couldn't see their targets, either.

Suddenly the night seemed like a very beautiful thing.

His pleasant reflection was interrupted by a rattle of small arms fire, a German machine gun from some other platoon opening up, several hundred meters away. Of course—now the Red Army would come! Quickly he pushed himself out of his foxhole to climb up the hill of broken bricks, peering over the top to try and discern movement in the thickening dusk. All around, the men of his platoon were coming out, doing the same thing, rifles at the ready as each veteran panzergrenadier sought a good firing position.

For a long time Lukas stared into the darkness, which was nearly complete by now. He heard shooting on both sides, but couldn't see anything that looked like a target, and he didn't want to waste his ammunition firing at figments of his imagination. The main gun of Peiper's tank suddenly cracked off a round and he saw a blast of fire as a Soviet tank was hit. The stricken T-34 went off like a Roman candle, glowing sparks cascading into the sky and scattering across the bumpy, irregular terrain of the battlefield. In that surge of light he saw plenty of targets, Russian soldiers who—knowing they were illuminated—threw themselves to the ground and instantly vanished into the natural foxholes created by the crushing bombardment and the earlier artillery barrage.

Suddenly a bright light burst into view, a flare fired from a German gun on the other side of the river. Lukas was ready, and he squeezed off a burst from his Schmeisser, scattering a detachment of enemy infantry. Many of them fell, and though he didn't know if they were hit or were just taking cover, his instincts told him that his aim had been good.

The Panther fired again, a high explosive shell this time that exploded near where Lukas had been aiming. He heard screams of pain out there and he all but snarled in satisfaction, delighted that the enemy was being made to suffer some of the same punishment their hated jabos had inflicted on the defending Germans.

The Russians seemed to have gone to ground for the time being, as the flare slowly drifted lower, suspended by a parachute. Lukas took advantage of the respite to scramble back down, then to make his way along the position of his men. He found most of them, learned that two more men plus his corporal had been killed by the bombing.

"Go check on Wolfgang," one suggested, pointing to a niche in the rubble.

Lukas went to look and found a man with a ghastly wound in his leg and hip.

"Wolfgang? How are you feeling?" he asked.

The man grimaced, then lifted his gun. "I can still see, still shoot. I'm a good soldier."

"Yes, you are," Lukas said, awed. "You can't walk on that, can you?"

"Don't plan on going anywhere," Wolfgang said, his next breath a gasp of sudden pain.

"Well, when we pull back, we're taking you with us," Lukas promised. He saw that the man's comrades had bandaged the wound as best they could, and the tough grenadier showed the officer that he had found a perch for his rifle. Lying prone, he was able to squeeze off a shot or two every time a target presented itself.

One more of the men was curled up in his foxhole, and when Lukas asked him if he was hurt he began to cry, sobbing like a baby. The young officer tried cajoling and threatening, everything he could think of to get the fellow to come out, but the grenadier simply cradled his head in his hands and rocked back and forth, uttering long, agonized wails. Repressing an angry urge to simply shoot the man for cowardice, Lukas at last left him alone and went back to his own vantage, the brick pile that was near the center of his platoon's little section of front.

He took stock of the situation. They had eight fighting men left, plus himself—though one was wounded and immobile. All of the soldiers had carbines, and he had his machine pistol. These were good soldiers, and they could hold here for a long time, and kill a lot of Russians while they did it. That was the best he could hope for now.

Another flare sparked in the air and he started to shoot, raking the stream of his bullets across the crests of the rough ground. The Panther fired again, and another Soviet tank burst into flames. Several return shots flew out of the darkness, armor piercing shells punching into the rocky walls around Peiper's Panther. None of them seemed to do any damage.

Lukas wiped the sweat from his eyes. It occurred to him that he should be getting hungry, but he wasn't interested in food. Instead, he reached for another clip of ammunition, jammed it into the stock of his machine pistol, drew a deep breath, and waited for his next target to appear.

HEADQUARTERS, SECOND GUARDS TANK ARMY, KÜSTRIN, GERMANY, 1917 HOURS GMT

"Comrade General!" Colonel Krigoff spoke sharply, determined to make himself heard.

A moment ago he had left Paulina outside the door flap of this tent that served as the headquarters conference room, where the army general was still poring over the map. A few of the army staff officers were present and they all watched as the colonel strode forward.

Paulina, who had reloaded her camera, had told him that she would wait for him outside, but he rather wished she was here, to see him in action. He felt very brave, inflamed by the passion of his true belief.

"I don't have time for you now!" snapped General Petrovsky. He was meeting with his staff in the mess-hall tent, since no surviving building nearby was large enough to hold the group of two dozen officers. Maps were spread across the central dining table, illuminated by lanterns turned up to their full brightness. The lesser officers, a few generals and many colonels, watched warily as the army commander addressed his young colonel of intelligence. "Can't you see I have a battle to win?"

"Do you suppose you will win it by holding your tanks back here and letting the Germans die of old age?" retorted the colonel. "There is a bridge still standing across the Oder—I have seen it myself!" Alyosha felt good, proud and brave, about being able to make this honest declaration. He glared as the general snapped back at him.

"Of course there's a bridge there! Did it occur to you, supposedly an intelligence officer, that I have aircraft reconnaissance to tell me about little details like that? We're doing everything we can to take it, but we lost forty tanks trying to bull through in the afternoon. There's an entire panzer division dug in, right in our path—so now we're trying to bomb the bastards off the face of the earth!"

"The tanks pulled back too soon," Krigoff charged. "How do you know they couldn't have done it with another push? Now the Nazis will blow that bridge up any minute—you must get on with the attack!"

"Dammit, Colonel—I have had enough out of you!" roared Petrovsky, his voice like the bellow of a furious bear. "You may have the ear of Comrade Chairman Stalin himself, but you are a menace on the battlefield! I could listen to you, and have a thousand more men that would never go home after the war, never see their women and their babies again!"

Krigoff was about to snap back with a retort when the general waved a hand wildly, somehow stifling the words in the colonel's throat. Petrovsky was gesturing to a picture on the table next to the map, and Alyosha saw a photograph there—the picture of Stalin he had given to his commander a few days before.

"Do you think I don't know that you had General Yeremko removed?" growled Petrovsky. "He was a good man, loyal to the state, and he had served with valor since Leningrad in '41! He trusted you, and you betrayed him!"

"He was old and sick, unable to do his job," Krigoff retorted. "I merely—"

"Leave me!" snapped the general. Alyosha was about to refuse when he realized that Petrovsky was talking to his staff officers, not to his colonel of intelligence. The other officers left and the army general fixed Krigoff with a murderous glare.

"Old and sick, eh?" The voice was low, again like that angry bear. "You goddamned little *peesa,* you make me sick—toadies like you, all in service of the great man!" A *peesa* was a polite penis, all smooth surface just waiting to insert itself in any vacant hole. The general took up the picture of Stalin, looked straight at Krigoff, and spit right into the chairman's face. "That's what I think of you—and of him! And if you think you will tattle in Moscow of my feelings, you should know, Comrade Colonel Krigoff, that I have friends there too. And it may be that my word will be taken instead of yours, within those halls of power."

"Comrade General . . ." Krigoff didn't know what to say. He was shocked by the man's desecration of the symbol of state might, and he wondered if Petrovsky might be losing his mind. At the same time, the man had been shrewd enough to send his staff officers away, so that there were no witnesses to his political heresy.

"Guards!" Petrovsky's roar was a blast of sound, riding over the colonel's arguments. Immediately four sergeants, each armed with a submachine gun, stepped into the tent. "Take the comrade colonel away, and lock him up in the prison truck! He is guilty of treason against the state. I will deal with him later!"

"You will lose this battle!" shrieked Krigoff in disbelief. "This bridge will be destroyed, the advance to Berlin criminally delayed!"

"Bah, we will cross on a bridge of our own making if the Germans destroy this one. Tomorrow, or the day after, we will have our victory."

"Tomorrow, Comrade General—" the colonel shouted as the guards took his arms and dragged him toward the door of the tent. "Tomorrow will be too late!"

REICHS CHANCELLERY, BERLIN, GERMANY, 2309 HOURS GMT

The five armored cars rumbled to a halt before the colonnaded façade of the great building, and a dozen SS guards spilled out, machine pistols at the ready. They formed a twin rank leading from the front entrance down the stairs to the lead vehicle, facing outward, weapons cocked and ready.

The doors opened and a party of six men came out. Four of them were guards, armed and uniformed like the men who had arrived in the armored cars. The fifth was a nondescript man with round, wire-rimmed glasses and a nervous, pinched expression. The last was a tall, aristocratic officer in the gray uniform of a Wehrmacht colonel. He walked with a cane and leaned on the arm of one of the guards as the party made its way down the long flight of marble steps.

"Hurry!" demanded Heinrich Himmler, turning to glare at von Reinhardt. "Get in the car!"

For once, von Reinhardt seemed unable to muster a quote or a clever remark, the führer reflected with a sneer of disdain. Indeed, it seemed like all he could do just to keep his feet moving as the guards, none too gently, pulled him across the wide sidewalk and pushed him toward the door of the second car in line.

"Wait! Search him again!" ordered the Reichsführer.

The colonel stood listlessly as two guards patted him down thoroughly. "No weapon, not even a pencil or a pen," one of them reported.

"Very well—get in the car," snapped Himmler.

Von Reinhardt was pushed none too gently through the open door. Himmler and two of the guards followed, the four men sitting in the small compartment on two facing seats while another pair of guards entered the cab.

"*Macht schnell!*" snapped Himmler, rapping on the panel that separated the back of the car from the driver's compartment. He was rewarded with the roar of an engine, and in moments the car lurched away from the curb, following the lead car and trailed by three other vehicles as the convoy began to make its way southward through the dark, silent city.

13 MARCH 1945

SECOND SS PANZER DIVISION, KÜSTRIN, GERMANY, 0420 HOURS GMT

Near midnight Lukas had realized that he was going through his ammunition very quickly, and he decided that he would have to be more careful in his selection of targets. An ordnance platoon had come around with a resupply earlier in the evening, but there was no guarantee that they would be back before dawn. And this battle, it seemed, would be resolved in the dark of the night.

For a time there was a lull, and Lukas let his head fall forward onto his forearm. He almost fell asleep, then jerked upward with a start as a rattle of machine gun fire burst through the night. This was the coaxial gun on Peiper's tank, chattering loudly as it sent a burst toward the no-man's-land of the cratered landscape. Russians were moving there, hundreds of them charging forward, ignoring the dead who fell out of their ranks in ever increasing numbers.

Lukas fired his Schmeisser, raking the enemy troops with a long burst until the last of his ammunition was exhausted. Finally he dropped the machine pistol, rolled down the ridge of his makeshift breastwork, and picked up the carbine that had been carried by his corporal. He crawled back up the pile of rubble and kept firing, taking care to aim with each shot, as he had been taught.

The Panther, hull down in the rubble between two houses, fired round after round of armor-piercing ammo into the darkness. Somehow Peiper must have been able to see, because several of these shots found Russian tanks, setting off fiery explosions, leaving the T-34s as burning hulks spewing flames that brightened the battlefield for dozens of meters in every direction.

Lukas saw an enemy soldier silhouetted against one of these ghastly flares. Even as the man dove for cover the young officer shot, saw his target flinch and roll over as the bullet struck home. But more tanks were visible now, at least a dozen illuminated by the fire. These opened up against his platoon, firing high explosive shells that blasted violently into the rubble, and sent shards of stone and steel zinging through the air.

The Panther blasted away again and another Russian tank exploded, and then the night was full of sounds—gunfire and explosions, the curses of wounded and dying men, the bark of Lukas' own rifle as he fired as fast as he could jack another bullet into the chamber. He heard a ghostly voice like something from a dream, as if his father was calling him in from the woods at the end of the day. It was a pleasant sound, and he concentrated on it, instead of the chaos of combat sounds. He fired again, loaded another clip, and still there was that distant voice.

He was distracted when someone slapped his arm, and looked around to see that one of his men had crawled over to him and was trying to get his attention.

"What is it?" asked the young officer.

"There," said the grenadier, pointing toward the hulking, battered Panther. "Vogel—come here!"

The voice—it wasn't a dream at all! Instead, it was Peiper calling to him from the hatch of the Panther. Staying low, Lukas scrambled over to the big panzer, coming up to the fender and looking apologetically upward. "I'm sorry, mein Standartenführer! I didn't know—"

Peiper waved his excuses away. "Listen, I have just talked to a runner from division HQ. The charges are taking longer than they anticipated, but they are going to try and blow the bridge just after dawn. I want you to take your platoon and bug out of here, do you understand? Get back across the bridge, and wait for me there!"

"Leave you here, sir?" Lukas was surprised, and strangely reluctant to go.

"Use the darkness, son! Remember, you are an officer—responsible for the lives of your men. Now get them together, and fall back. Do you understand?"

"Yes, sir!" Lukas saluted.

Peiper was right, of course—he, Lukas Vogel, Obersturmführer of the SS, was responsible for these men. He felt a flash of shame as he realized that he hadn't even learned their names; now at least three of them were dead.

His sense of shame grew as he jogged back to the position, and one by one collected the men from their foxholes. Two more had been killed in the firefight, but the survivors helped Wolfgang—the man whose leg had been shattered in the aerial bombardment—to rise up onto his good leg. With a comrade on each shoulder, he started hobbling back toward the bridge.

Lukas waited until all of them had started to fall back, and then he came along behind—halting for a moment, then running back to retrieve the Schmeisser he had dropped after his ammo was exhausted. He jogged along, careful not to trip on the broken ground, trying to make out the road descending into the river valley, leading toward the bridge.

He heard the crack of the Panther's gun when he was just below the crest, and stopped to look back. He saw Peiper, tall above the turret hatch, holding binoculars to his eyes as he studied the enemy positions in the sporadic light of fire and flare. Those lights faded into darkness once again, and the SS colonel was gone.

US ARMY AIR FORCE TRANSPORT COMMAND
AIRFIELD, NEAR METZ, FRANCE, 0430 GMT

Chuck Porter made his way from the briefing room, through the equipment hangar, and out onto the crushed-gravel surface of the taxiway. The sky was still dark, but all around him the great Allied air armada was thrumming and roaring with life, with energy, with barely restrained anticipation.

He had learned in the briefing that this field was one of more than three dozen installations throughout England and France, each of which was a scene of similar controlled chaos on this chilly spring morning. Twin-engine Dakota transports were rumbling from their places along the flight line, while paratroopers were lined up just back from the runways, already organized into their single-plane "sticks." One by one these files of men advanced to the doors in the C-47 fuselages. Each soldier was loaded with more than a hundred pounds of equipment, but they pulled themselves up and through the hatch with only a small assist from the jumpmaster—the NCO who was in charge of seeing the parachutists safely out the door over the jump zone.

A captain was directing traffic as air crew and paratroopers were milling around near the hangars. Porter went up to the man and waited for him to finish directing a couple of lieutenants toward their unit.

"Hello, Captain," said the reporter. "Can you point me toward A Company, Captain Dickens' plane?"

"Who the hell are you?"

"Sorry—press, Chuck Porter with the AP." He showed his pass, and the order sheet authorizing his passage on the transport.

"Shit. Now we're sending reporters along! You know you're taking a place that could be used by a real fighting man?"

"General Gavin assured me that he had enough transport for the Eighty-second Division, plus one reporter," Porter said, hoping that the name of the division commander might carry a little weight with this pompous little martinet.

It worked. The captain grimaced, but pointed. "Dickens is over there, second Dakota from the end of the line. Don't get in the way."

"I won't," Porter promised, his muttered addendum—"jackass"—lost in the roar of powerful aircraft engines.

He made his way to the transport, double-checked the number, and climbed aboard after the last of the paratroopers. The interior of the fuselage was a tangle of men and equipment, the soldiers sitting with their backs against the outer shell, their legs extending into the middle of the deck. Apologizing, and stepping carefully, Porter made his way to the front of the cabin, just behind the cockpit. He found Dickens seated there, poring over a map; the captain flashed him a grin as the reporter settled into the narrow gap beside him.

"Ah, Porter. I was afraid you overslept, and were going to miss the ride."

"I wouldn't miss this for the world, Captain," Porter said. "Parachutes over Berlin—this might be the last big adventure of the war."

"I wouldn't count on it," the soldier, a veteran of landings in Sicily and Normandy, said. "Who knows what the Russians are going to think of this whole project?"

"At least you guys will be on the ground before they hear about it," Porter replied.

He felt a little guilty. After all, he would be coming back here for a hot meal and a warm bed tonight, while the rest of these men would be on the ground in war-torn Berlin. Some of them would be wounded, others dead.

"Well, do your best to make us look good," Dickens said, as if reading the reporter's mind. Porter laughed at the joke, not entirely sure if the paratrooper was kidding.

The flight to Berlin would take a couple of hours. He had been briefed on the mission, knew that the All-Americans—the nickname of the Eighty-second Airborne Division—were charged with seizing Tempelhof airport, the largest network of airfields in the Berlin area. Other Allied airborne soldiers would try to capture other airports, a ring of them surrounding the German capital. Once the paratroops were on the ground and the airfields secured, a train of transport aircraft would begin to haul in supplies, weaponry, and reinforcements. By tomorrow night, Operation Eclipse would be over.

The day was sunny, though the inside of the metal tube was cold and very loud. Porter found that if he twisted around in the seat he could get a pretty good view out of one of the oval windows lining each side of the C-47. He could see the starboard engine and the blur of the big propeller; beyond, there was a scattering of cotton-ball clouds, sparse enough to provide a good view of the countryside. For a time they flew above a region of densely forested hills, marked by occasional outcrops of weathered stone. Gradually the ground gave way to a patchwork of fields, greening only slowly in the wake of the harsh winter. Looking ahead, he could make out a broad strip of water, a cluster of industrial buildings sprawling along the bank beside a medieval town.

"That's the Rhine!" he called out, tapping Dickens on the shoulder.

The captain looked at his watch. "Right on schedule!" he shouted back, the words barely audible over the drone of the engines and the rattling of wing against the aluminum frame.

The landscape of Germany didn't look all that different from France, or England—or parts of New York or Pennsylvania—he reflected. He saw no signs of enemy fighters or antiaircraft as they droned on, passing another great river he guessed to be the Elbe.

He saw the twin ribbon of a great highway, and knew this was one of the legendary autobahns. They flew along, parallel to the road, and he guessed that it would lead them all the way to Berlin. Soon the character of the land began to change: He saw more factories, a network of railroad lines—though there were still great swaths of forest and dazzling blue stretches of lakes to break up the appearance of civilization.

Now the first puffs of smoke began to appear, and he knew that a few German guns were opening up. The bursts were spread out far in front and off to the side, appearing to be silent and harmless. But there were many of them, and as the Dakota flew on they grew closer and closer.

The outskirts of the city were below them. Some of the explosions were near enough that he could hear the blasts, sharp *cracks* against the background din of the aircraft.

Porter told himself that the antiaircraft fire was light. With his face pressed to the glass of the round window, he could see only a few blasts of black smoke. They were distant and, against the backdrop of the roaring engines, soundless, yet he knew that each one had the potential to bring sudden and very violent death to a plane full of men.

He felt a tap on his shoulder, looked to see Dickens leaning close. The captain shouted in his ear, pointing to the horizon toward their course.

"That's one of those antiaircraft towers!" he shouted. "They were plastered by bombers, but they're still shooting."

The reporter could easily make out the sinister structure. It was like a square block of concrete, many stories high and apparently a full city block around. It was shrouded in smoke now, with bright flashes sparkling across the roof and sides. Numerous tactical fighters strafed and bombed the tower, like insects buzzing around a picnic box. Porter could see more of those black puffs now, higher in the sky. He felt a chill as he realized that the German gunners were ignoring the direct threat of the strafing fighters to direct their fire against the precious transports.

A C-47 not more than a mile away suddenly lurched, angling downward from the formation, flames trailing from a stricken engine. Porter watched in horrified fascination as the troopers started to fling themselves from the jump door. . . . One . . . two . . . three men made it out before the plane flipped onto its back and spiraled away.

It was only then that he noticed the sky filling with parachutes, white silk canopies bursting into view across the whole of his view. They drifted downward with deceptive gentleness, suggesting nothing like an army on the attack.

Porter stared out of his small window, wishing he could have a view of a broader section of the sky. Everywhere he looked he could see parachutes, a rain of fighting soldiers that seemed like it must be an overwhelming force. These were elite soldiers, he knew, a select few drawn from large numbers of volunteers. Each man carried his ammunition and full kit, as well as a portion of the company ordnance, whether that be a portion of a light machine gun, extra ammo for the gun, or any of the components of the bazookas and rockets that were supposed to serve as a defense against enemy armor.

Even so, he knew that these men landed, and entered combat, with significant disadvantages. They had no armor, no artillery to speak of—though there were a few small pieces that would land in the first wave of gliders—and no way to retreat. Furthermore, they were at the mercy of the wind and the not-necessarily-perfect accuracy of the pilots and jumpmasters. Even those who landed exactly where they were supposed to had to avoid trees, buildings, water, and enemy soldiers.

Porter's attention whipped around at a new sound, and he saw that the door at the back of the plane had been thrown open by the jumpmaster. The soldiers had stood up while he had been looking out the window, and he saw that each man had clicked a sturdy strap, his static line, to a cable running down the center top of the fuselage. The first man stood in the door, while the jumpmaster held his hands to his earphones, concentrating on some message unheard by the reporter.

Abruptly the man looked up and clapped the first paratrooper on the shoulder. With both hands braced on the sides the door, the soldier leaned forward and leaped into space. The next came right after, the whole stick moving down the plane with precision and impressive speed.

"Good luck!" Porter shouted, as Dickens turned back to give him a wave. The reporter raised his fingers, a V for victory, and then the captain was gone, the last man through the door. The jumpmaster started to pull the portal shut, but Porter had already turned around, once again pressing his face against the glass of the window.

142ND TANK BATTALION, SECOND GUARDS TANK ARMY, KÜSTRIN, GERMANY, 0609 HOURS GMT

The prison truck was a large armored vehicle with a steel shell of a trailer, two small, barred windows, and a single door securely locked on the outside. There was enough room inside of the compartment to hold twenty or more men, but for now Colonel Alexis Krigoff was the only prisoner. He had been handled roughly by Petrovsky's headquarters guards, who literally tossed him through the open door and then slammed it, loudly, behind him.

After testing the barrier and finding that it had indeed been securely locked, Krigoff sat on the floor with his back to the wall and brooded on the injustices that had brought him here. Petrovsky was a stubborn reactionary fool, and he would pay for his arrogance, his contemptible dismissal of a true envoy of the state, not to mention for his desecrating the likeness of Chairman Stalin himself. That act was the single most horrifying thing Alyosha Krigoff had ever witnessed. The colonel spent more than an hour imagining the ways, many of them quite creative, in which the general could be made to suffer.

But gradually, as his thoughts twisted on, he began to have some doubts. Petrovsky had made it clear that he would deny that the spitting gesture had occurred. He was in fact a highly regarded soldier who had been decorated by Stalin personally. He was a good friend of Zhukov, who was perhaps the only general in the Red Army whose reputation made him if not quite untouchable, at least the closest thing to it. If it came down to an argument of wills between Petrovsky and Krigoff, could the young colonel truly be certain that his word would be accepted over that of the veteran army commander? Certainly Krigoff had earned the ear, and even the trust, of the chairman, but Stalin's loyalty had been known to be fickle in the past . . . might it prove to be so in Krigoff's case, as well?

That was a very frightening thought indeed.

Eventually the inactivity and the brooding drove him to move, and he started to pace around the long, featureless metal box. He went to one of the windows and looked out, saw only the black night of the German plain. On the other side he noticed a sergeant standing on duty, wearing the sidearm and the cap of a military policeman.

"*Serzhant!*" Krigoff hissed, pressing his face against the bars of his cell. The man made no verbal response, but a twitch in his posture revealed that he had heard the summons. "You are making a terrible mistake—see me released from here, and I will see that Chairman Stalin personally hears of your good judgment."

The soldier spun about to glare at him. "I have served General Petrovsky since the first weeks of the war. It may interest you to know that he, too, has the chairman's ear. I should not want to be in your shoes when word of your insubordination reaches Moscow!" He laughed, a short, nasty bark of sound.

Krigoff slumped back from the window. This was bad, as bad as it could be. In despair he slid down the wall until he was again seated on the floor, holding his head in his hands.

It was some time later that he heard talking outside of his cell, and he was apprehensive—though curious—when the door suddenly swung open. He recognized the commissar officer standing there as Major Rokov, his adjutant from the intelligence office, and he took this as a good sign.

"Comrade Major Rokov—you are a welcome sight," Krigoff said, pushing himself to his feet, squinting against the daylight that was starting to brighten the outside world.

"I have good news, Comrade Colonel," said the major, standing back to reveal another person who had accompanied him.

"Paulina—that is, Comrade Koninin!" exclaimed the colonel, as the woman reached out a hand to help him down from the trailer's door. Just beyond he saw the sergeant he had spoken to earlier; the man's face was pale, and his forehead was slick with sweat.

"Comrade Colonel!" said the sergeant. "Please forgive me—I did not understand the situation, not at all. I made a terrible mistake!"

"What is the situation?" Krigoff asked, turning first to Major Rokov, then to Paulina.

"The situation is that I have taken a picture of Comrade General Petrovsky," Paulina said with a tight smile. "He is holding a picture of Chairman Stalin—the chairman he professes to admire so much."

"And in this picture . . . ?" Krigoff let the question hang in the air, sensing good news in the offing, but not knowing what that news could be.

"I was looking through a gap in the wall of the tent. There was good light on him as he rebuked you, and I had my camera ready. He is spitting on the picture," Paulina said. "The focus is good, and the shutter speed fast," she added with true photographer's pride. "I caught his spittle in midair."

SPANDAU, BERLIN SUBURBS, GERMANY, 0611 HOURS GMT

General Patton was in his element, as he stood in the back of his command jeep—the canopy was folded down despite the spring chill—and acknowledged the cheers of his men. He was passing through the Twelfth Infantry Division, a forward unit where the men had debarked from their trucks and were advancing in file along the shoulder of the road. The general held his salute for a mile or more, as man after man turned to face the road and snap his fingers to the front of his helmet. It was after he passed that the whoops and shouts—"See you in Berlin, General!"—rang out, and the sound thrilled him, filled him to bursting with a sense of fierce pride.

Everywhere the lead elements of Third Army were streaming into Berlin, while overhead the train of C-47 transports extended in a sky-spanning bridge. In his heart Patton knew there had never in history been such a splendid display of American military might, and it touched him to his soul to know that he was in command.

He had felt a flicker of resentment, of course, when Ike informed him of the great airborne drop. But the idea made too much sense, and appealed enough to Patton's own sense of adventure, to hold him at bay for long. In minutes he had been embracing the idea, adding elements. When the transport aircraft returned tomorrow, they would carry supplies, heavy guns, jeeps—and now, with Patton's suggestion, a large ration of fuel for the tanks and trucks that would spread out to make Berlin an impregnable fortress.

The fact that their potential attacker was now the Red Army was an interesting detail, captivating to Patton's sense of history. Yet it did not change the fundamental tactics that had made Third Army such an unqualified success.

He turned his attention back to the sky. Now passed a glider regiment, a string of powerless aircraft, one trailing behind each Dakota on a long cable. Some of the transports came from France, others from Belgium and England, combining into a river of aircraft as they droned above the racing columns of Third Army.

When the command car reached the top of a low hill, with a wide expanse of parkland and small houses ahead, Patton ordered Sergeant Mims to pull over. He got out of the car, rested his hands on the butts of his twin pistols, and stared eastward in amazement. The parachutes drifting downward reminded George Patton of milkweed pods, drifting on a summer breeze near the marsh. One of the western airfields, no doubt. His men would be there in an hour.

A German command car, distinguished as friendly by the white star on the door, pulled up and a colonel got out. Patton recognized the man from Rommel's staff, and sharply returned his salute.

"I am happy to find you, Herr General. The field marshal would like to extend an invitation for you to visit him at his new command post, in Spandau."

"Spandau?" Patton's eyebrows rose in shock, before he got control of his features. "How the hell did he get there already?" he demanded.

"Panzer Lehr hit a long stretch of open road," the colonel replied with a tight smile. "I believe the field marshal was riding in a motorcycle sidecar for much of the way."

Patton laughed ruefully, then climbed back into the jeep. "Lead on," he said, moments before the jeep roared, tires spinning, after the big Mercedes.

Twenty minutes later they pulled into the large square at the center of the city, one of many lesser burgs gathered around the skirts of greater Berlin. Rommel's flag flew from the city hall, and Patton found him supervising the arrangement of the radios in what had once been a large waiting room.

Only when he clasped the German's hand in a firm shake did Patton fully experience the wave of relief.

"Looks like we beat the Red Army here, after all."

"Not by much," Rommel replied. "They've pushed through north and south of the autobahn, well across the Oder. It's only in Küstrin that they've been held up—by some SS panzers, of all things."

"First time those bastards have done *me* any favors," Patton snapped.

He turned his attention to the map. "These are the latest deployments from SHAEF," the field marshal explained. "Ninth Army and the Brits have got the Ruhr encircled, but they're two hundred miles away from here. Hodges is coming up, but First Army has the whole of central Germany to cover—they won't be any direct support to us for at least a week."

The rest of the Allied armies, Alexander Patch's Seventh and the French First, were needed in the south; indeed, they faced an exceptional amount of German territory because of Patton's lunge to the northeast.

"Well, my twelve divisions are coming up—I'm keeping three of them deployed to hold the best routes to the west. If the Reds come up to us, we're going to hope that they stop—but that'll be up to diplomats, not soldiers."

"I would like to offer a suggestion," Rommel said.

"Go ahead—shoot."

"I have three divisions of the Republican Army in the western approaches of Berlin. Send them into the city, where they can be used to keep order and calm the populace. If they are not in direct contact with Russian troops, there's no chance of an unfortunate incident."

"I'd like to," Patton said. "But we're still coming up to the south—I don't have anyone to put north, and you can see from your map that Zhukov is coming like gangbusters."

"Then I will get on the move," replied the German field marshal. "Since I don't think we want the Red Army to hold a victory party on our supply line."

"No," replied the American. "No, that wouldn't be good at all."

EAST BANK OF ODER, KÜSTRIN, GERMANY, 0615 HOURS GMT

"Go!" called Peiper to his driver. "Full reverse, now—let's get out of here!"

The Panther rolled backward, lurching and jerking as it rumbled over the broken rock and debris left by the shelling and bombardment. The driver swiftly spun the vehicle to the side, and then stepped on the gas.

Peiper held on with both hands as they rumbled up over the pile of rubble that had once been a house. He wasn't even sure he could find the street leading down to the bridge, but he knew he had only a few minutes to cross the span before the reset demolition charges went off.

"There—turn right," he ordered, and the driver obeyed.

The shell smashed into the body of the tank, an armor piercing round fired by a T-34 that neither Peiper nor his driver had seen. Fire flashed through the compartment, incinerating the driver and radioman in the first flash of ignition. A shell exploded in the turret, shrapnel tearing through the body of the gunner, and Peiper cried out in pain as burning metal lanced through his leg.

He pushed at the hatch, flipping it open, fearing the flames. But when he tried to rise up he found that his foot was caught, imprisoned in a twisted nest of steel formed by the wreckage of the gunner's seat. Furiously he twisted and pulled, each gesture resulting in excruciating pain, but moving him no closer to freedom. He was caught like a fox in a spring-powered trap.

There would be no escape for him.

SECOND SS PANZER DIVISION, KÜSTRIN, GERMANY, 0701 HOURS GMT

Daylight crept from the east as Lukas was making his way down the road toward the bridge. Sporadic artillery fire was falling on the city, but it didn't seem close enough to worry about. He was more concerned about the return of the jabos, but for now there was neither sound nor sight of Russian aircraft.

Ahead of him the men of his platoon moved resolutely along, even crippled Hans swinging along at good speed between two of his comrades. Lukas was holding back, as their officer wanting to insure that they had the chance to reach safety first.

Abruptly, a machine gun chattered up the hill, the slugs kicking up dust and stone fragments on the road. Lukas ran for all he was worth, as the men, too, hastened onto the bridge. He heard a bullet zing past his ear, felt the hot sparks on his cheek as another slug chipped into a concrete pillar and cast a shower of shards against his skin. His feet pounded across the pavement, past the girders of the bridge supports. The waters flowed past below, dark and deep and forbidding.

Finally he was across the bridge. His men took shelter immediately behind a low wall of the sidewalk, but Lukas urged them on, into the ruin of the city itself. As soon as they approached the first cross street, the young officer darted to the side, tumbling down the steep embankment of the approach ramp, and started crawling through the rubble, looking for the engineer in charge of the demolition.

He found the man in a niche beside the dock, ready to press down the T-shaped handle of his detonator.

"Colonel Peiper is still over there!" Lukas protested.

"Sorry kid—I have my orders." The engineer shook his head. "The bridge is ready to blow—and the goddamned Russians will be starting across any minute."

He pressed down on his lever, and the valley of the Oder shuddered to a powerful boom, a crash of sound that echoed up and down the river like the lingering thunder of a an early spring storm.

SKY OVER TEMPELHOF AIRPORT, BERLIN, 0812 GMT

Porter reluctantly turned away from the window when he felt the tap on his shoulder. The jumpmaster leaned in and yelled into his ear. "We're going to be heading back, now."

The reporter nodded, and set down the notebook—his second one—with its pages of hasty notes. "Thanks for the sightseeing tour," he shouted back. The sergeant smiled acknowledgment and returned to the cockpit.

Porter swung around and resumed his observations. There were no parachutes visible in his immediate vicinity—the first wave of the All-Americans had touched ground more than half an hour ago—but the view of the city and the sky had held him entranced for all that time.

A group of P-51s dove past, a mile or so away. The six Mustangs plummeted toward the ground, and Porter watched them strafe a concrete enclosure near the end of largest runway of Tempelhof airport. He spotted a flash of flame followed by a plume of smoke and debris, and knew that the nimble fighters were dropping bombs on an enemy position—no doubt they had been called in by radio, to support the battling paratroopers on the ground.

Farther away, the great square bulk of the antiaircraft tower near the Reichstag was shrouded in smoke, having been pummeled by more bombs than Porter could have counted. Somehow, it was still functioning: guns flashed from the apertures that he glimpsed between the shifting clouds of murk, and the deadly black puffs still erupted across the sky.

Drawing a deep breath, Porter reflected with awe on the scene he had witnessed. The paradrop had been the most stirring sight he had ever seen, and he was already working out the terminology of his story in his mind. How to convey that awe-inspiring sense of might, in a way that the readers back home could share his sense of wonder?

He was slammed against the side of the fuselage then, assailed by the loudest noise he had ever heard. For a moment he could see nothing except flashing lights, his head throbbing from the impact into the sheet metal of the aircraft body. As the pain faded he still couldn't see, though he felt the seat lurch beneath him, a very frightening sensation of the big transport plane sliding sideways through the air.

Vaguely he wondered if he had been hit, if blood or wounds obscured his vision. Tentatively touching his face, he was surprised and relieved to find that his GI-issue helmet had slid forward, down to the bridge of his nose. Pushing it up, he gawked in shock and a sudden, squeezing sensation of fear.

The big radial engine, that droning image of power on the wing, was torn and flaming. The propeller was a bent stick, and orange flames billowed from the cowling, and through the gashes in the metal housing. Porter's face was pressed against the window, and he realized that gravity had a lot to do with this: the plane was virtually on its side, and he was looking straight down at the ground.

Strangely, Chuck Porter wasn't terribly afraid. In fact, some cool rational part of his mind was suggesting, strongly, that he should be terrified, but his reporter's instincts were in control. He studied the wing, noting that some of the outer surface seemed to have been blasted away by the explosion that had damaged the engine. Gradually the horizon was coming up; he realized that the pilot was righting the plane, though they were losing altitude fast.

He saw the jumpmaster, coming back from the cockpit. The man grabbed the overhead cable for balance, and gestured Porter toward a chair against the bulkhead wall, a few feet forward of his window. "Sit there and strap yourself in!" the sergeant shouted. "We're going down!"

With that, he turned and pulled himself back through the door. Porter looked out the window again. The ground was closer now, coming up fast. He glanced at the chair, saw that he wouldn't be able to see anything from up there, and decided to stay right where he was. He wrapped a couple of straps around his waist, and found a buckle that secured the belt, but kept his body twisted around so that he could continue to observe.

The Dakota was leveled out, now, obviously limping along on one engine. They continued to descend, flying at barely a thousand feet over a large cemetery, dropping closer and closer to the ground. Abruptly there was a runway in view—Tempelhof! He saw GIs scattering to either side of the wide, paved strip, and was mildly relieved that no one seemed to be shooting at them.

Clearly the pilot intended to put the plane down. The reporter couldn't see beneath the wing, wondered if the landing gear had dropped—until he saw the C-47's shadow in profile, with no suggestion of any wheels hanging below. They were gliding low over the tarmac, thirty, twenty, only ten feet, when sudden silence engulfed him. There was still the rattle of the wind and speed, of course, but he knew the pilot must have cut the remaining engine.

A moment later he felt a sharp jolt, a shock that hurled him sideways until the belt cinched painfully around his middle brought him to a sharp stop. Gasping for breath, he heard a terrible shriek of metal, smelled smoke and ozone with the awful, gritty taste of sooty fire. But still he looked: They were skidding on the plane's belly, sparks streaming from beneath the wings. It seemed to take forever, but finally the big C-47 came to a halt. Porter was out of his seat before the jumpmaster came back, and together the two men raced to the rear door, pushed it open, and jumped the five or six feet down to the runway.

Porter rolled away, grimacing from the pain of a twisted ankle, then looked up into the curious face of a helmeted paratrooper.

"Welcome to Templehof airport, sir," said the private, with a wink. "Property of the All-Americans. I guess we're open for passenger service."

EAST BANK OF ODER, KÜSTRIN, GERMANY, 1020 HOURS GMT

As soon as he heard the explosion Peiper knew that the last bridge over the Oder had been blown, and he allowed unconsciousness to claim him. It was a merciful relief from the pain of his mangled foot, and the burns where the short-lived fire had seared his skin.

He awakened some time later, startled by an ominous change in the level of noise. The shelling that had been so intense and so nearby had shifted far away; he could still hear the guns, but the barrels and their targets were many kilometers away. He was half out of the turret, but trapped so tightly that he could neither get out nor climb back inside the tank.

More significantly, the small-arms fire that had chattered throughout the night and the bleak, gray morning had fallen away entirely. That could only mean that the Russians had abandoned their advance—an inconceivable thought—or that all of the other Germans on this side of the river were dead.

Peiper cursed weakly—why did he have to remain alive? He squirmed within the metal trap of the tank's turret, but the twisted metal where the shell had punctured the armor still held his foot in a vise of steel. His pistol had been knocked from his belt and lay on the floor of the tank turret, two meters away but beyond the reach of his straining hand. He knew beyond any shadow of doubt that if he could have reached the gun, he would have put a bullet into his brain.

Instead, he could only wait for the Russians.

A half-hour later he saw the first of the enemy infantry coming through the smoke. They were short men, crude and savage compared to the Aryan ideal of which Peiper was such a splendid example. Or had been a splendid example, he reflected ruefully, before his face had been blasted open and his foot twisted and broken in the grip of twisted metal.

He tried lunging upward when one of the Soviet riflemen was close, expecting that the sudden gesture would provoke a merciful, fatal gunshot. Instead, the man seemed to sense the Nazi's helplessness, for he looked up at the trapped SS officer and grinned widely, displaying a mouth with more gaps than actual teeth. His face was oriental and swarthy, and Peiper guessed that the fellow was one of the hardy Siberian troops that made up so much of Stalin's army. How appropriate, he thought in despair: The Mongol hordes were once again riding across the civilized peoples of Europe.

The soldier jabbered something at him and gestured with the barrel of his rifle. Peiper tried to spit, but his mouth was too dry to muster even a fleck of saliva.

LONDON, ENGLAND, 1016 HOURS GMT

"Operator, may I help you?" came a somewhat nasal voice over the telephone line.

"Yes, I'm trying to locate a Mr. W. G. Marley." Kim Philby drummed his fingers on his desktop and looked out his office window as he waited for the reply.

"I have no listing for a W. G. Marley at this exchange."

"I see. Thank you."

"You're welcome," the operator replied, then disconnected.

Eight names on the personnel list, and eight names no longer with addresses or telephone numbers on the exchange. Quite mysterious. Philby no longer had any doubt that he had found the right program, but he did not yet know the details of the program, or what it concealed.

The danger to himself multiplied with each step in the process. He needed to discover where the names on his list had gone, and indeed find out more about each of the names, but if someone found him crawling about the countryside snooping into the affairs of these people, it would be dashed hard to explain, German mole or not. It was time for some help. He would activate his personal network of agents, and at the same time prepare a message for his Soviet handlers, letting them know the status of the work and assigning them some of the necessary tasks. Let them do some of the legwork and report back to him for a change. On his way home, he would mark the lamppost to let them know a message had been placed in the drop box.

It was raining and a little bit past six o'clock. A small trickle of people were still departing from 64 Baker Street. Two men sat in the small Morris across the street. "There he is," the man in the passenger seat said.

"Right, then," said the driver, and started the engine.

Traffic was dense enough that it was no challenge to drive slower than foot traffic. The walking man easily reached Marylebone ahead of the Morris, and on the green signal crossed the street. The Morris briefly swung ahead as it turned left, then was stuck in traffic again. "Got him?"

"Yes, there he goes. Right on schedule. Punctual man, what?"

"Very regular."

The passenger focused binoculars on the walking man, even though he was only a few feet away.

"You think he's something really special, eh?"

"If he's any kind of double agent, he's likely to be a very good one, now, isn't he?"

"I suppose. It's more likely that he isn't any kind of double agent at all, though."

"Here now, hold on, hold on." It was at the corner of Marylebone and Lisson Grove. The walking man stopped, put his foot up on the base of a lamppost, leaned over, as if to tie an unlaced shoe. "Well, I'll be damned. He is a bleedin' spy. He just left a marker at the base of that lamppost, cool as anything, right in the middle of a crowd of people. My, my, Mr. Philby. We are a professional, now, aren't we."

"Are you sure? You can't see anything in this rain, now can you?"

"That's why I brought my binocs, lad, that's why I brought my binocs. If he tried anything, I'd need to look close up, like, and that's it. I'll bet pounds to shillings that if we go back and look at the base of that lamppost we'll see something—a piece of tape or a matchbox or something. Mark my words, someone is going to come round to look at it, and when he does, he'll know that Mr. Philby has left a message for him."

"So, do we go arrest Mr. Philby now?"

"Oh, no, not at all. Wouldn't do. We'll need a lot more evidence, and even then, identified spies are often more useful left alone than arrested and punished. No, our Mr. Philby, I'm quite sure, is a very bad man, but he may yet be able to serve king and country, whether he wants to or not."

SHAEF, REIMS, FRANCE, 2345 HOURS GMT

The ashtray had been emptied and refilled again, Ike noted absently, crushing out another cigarette. His eyes went to the map that had remained on the wall, taunting him with promise and danger, throughout this long day. Pins and flags had been thrust into many places on the map, marking the reports of the successful landings, but there were still many questions remaining to be answered.

"We have Tempelhof and Gatow," he recited to himself. "And Patton and Rommel are in Spandau, already. But what of Oranienburg?" He cursed to himself, lit another cigarette, then looked up as Beetle Smith came in.

"The Brits have done it, too, General," said the hardworking chief of staff. "Oranienburg is secure; we can bring in the first of the supply planes just after dawn."

"Well, Beetle, it looks like we pulled it off," suggested the Supreme Commander, not entirely sure of his own words. "Any word from the Russians?"

"No communications. We do know that they're advancing north and south of the city, but so far they haven't made any move to attack our boys."

"Well," Ike said, exhaling a long plume of smoke. "Let's hope they continue to show that kind of good sense!"

14 MARCH 1945

**RURAL HIGHWAY #47, EAST OF LUCKENWALDE,
GERMANY, 0101 HOURS GMT**

The convoy of armored cars was moving too slowly for Heinrich Himmler's taste, but he was forced to accept the pace. The driver had pointed out, in tones that the Führer of the Third Reich normally would not have tolerated, that the narrow and winding road, coupled with the need to drive without headlights, had of necessity slowed the procession to a painstaking crawl. He turned in irritation to confront the hostage, who had the audacity to sleep during this tense passage.

"Wake up!" snapped Himmler, slapping von Reinhardt on the shoulder. He took some satisfaction from the wince of pain evident on the tall man's face as his head jerked forward and, ever so slowly, he opened his eyes and peered around.

"What is it?" asked the aristocratic Prussian.

"You are sure this is the right road?" Himmler pressed. "Remember, if we encounter trouble, you are the first one to die!"

"That is a fact that I am not likely to forget," von Reinhardt noted with a maddening lack of passion. "As to whether we are on the right road, I cannot say—perhaps you noticed that I was sleeping?"

"Bah," Himmler snorted, turning to look out the window. That was worse than useless; all he could see was the forested countryside, wherein even the trees seemed to lurch and sway with menace. He saw a tall pine swaying in the wind and recoiled; it was too easy to imagine some nightmarish creature lunging forward to attack him.

"Is your driver following the directions I provided?" asked von Reinhardt.

"Of course," snapped the führer.

"Then I should say you have nothing to worry about. As I explained, this route was carefully arranged to carry you between the enemy spearheads. Once it's light out, we'll pick up speed, and we'll be in Czechoslovakia by the following night. There, you will have neither Americans nor Russians to worry about."

Any reply Himmler would have made was stifled by a sudden burst of small-arms fire. The car in front of them lurched, spun off the road, and toppled onto its side in the ditch.

"What is going on?" shrieked the leader of the Third Reich.

"Americans!" cried the guard sitting next to the driver. He scrambled upward to man the light machine gun in the small turret overhead. The gun chattered, but that was nothing compared with the cacophony of noise outside. Weapons were flashing, and a hail of bullets rattled against the armored car's exterior. The gunner suddenly cried out and slumped down, falling into the compartment of the car, and Himmler gagged as he saw that half the man's face had been blown away—although he had ordered the deaths of millions, the führer was often squeamish at the sight of blood.

"You bastard!" he cried, turned to von Reinhardt, who was still watching him with that calm expression.

There was another explosion and the vehicle lurched, a sickening jolt that slammed Himmler into the door, then sent him tumbling against the Prussian colonel. Furiously he punched at von Reinhardt, who tried to lift his arms but was too weak to deflect the blows. Light flashed outside, and another blast jolted the car, bringing bile of terror rising into the führer's gullet.

He drew a breath and was suddenly aware that they were not moving. "Why have you stopped?" he shouted to the driver. "Go!"

"We are disabled, mein Führer," said the guard apologetically. "I think they have destroyed our front wheels."

"Keep trying!" cried Himmler, raising his fist to punch at the man through the panel dividing the cab from the rear compartment. Before the blow could land, the driver slumped forward, blood oozing out of his ear. There was a bullet hole in the thick window behind him, and several men with guns were gathering around the car. Soldiers—American soldiers!

Von Reinhardt was looking at him, his eyes strangely penetrating, his lips locked in a half smile. The effort to defend himself seemed to have drained all of his strength.

In that instant Himmler understood that he had been betrayed. He turned to the remaining guard. "Give me your gun!" he demanded, reaching out to pluck the weapon from the man's hand, turning around to train it on von Reinhardt.

"Don't you understand—I warned you that you would die if you betrayed me! You are my hostage!"

"Call this a bishop's sacrifice leading to checkmate," von Reinhardt said, leaning back in the seat, his eyes half closed. "Our mutual friend Rommel not only believes in the ends of justice, but also the means. This kind of trap is not his style—but it does work for me. As Goethe observed, 'A great deal may be done by severity, more by love, but most by clear discernment and impartial justice.' Rommel would have done you justice; I add the clear discernment. This plan achieves the original end of a rapid Nazi departure with fewer deaths and achieves the additional end of justice richly served. All for the sacrifice of a mere bishop. A bishop is not much of a sacrifice to make, *nicht wahr?*"

Somehow, his pallid lips creased into a semblance of a smile—an expression of smug satisfaction that remained on his face even as Himmler shot twice, then two more times, sending the bullets directly into the Prussian's heart.

By this time the doors of the armored car were being pulled open and voices—voices speaking *English*—were making harsh demands.

HEADQUARTERS, SECOND GUARDS TANK ARMY, KÜSTRIN, GERMANY, 0209 HOURS GMT

Colonel Krigoff walked into the conference room accompanied by Major Rokov and several enlisted men from the commissar's security staff. He stood at attention, facing down General Petrovsky, who straightened up from his leaning posture over the map table and confronted his intelligence officer with an icy glare.

"Did you forget that I placed you under arrest?" he asked.

"Your orders were countermanded by a higher authority," Krigoff retorted.

"I am the authority in this army! Or, perhaps, did Comrade Marshal Zhukov hear your cries for help and come to rescue you—like Rapunzel taken from her lofty tower?" snapped the commander of the Second Guards Tank Army.

"I represent an authority superior even to our esteemed front commander," the colonel declared calmly. "I am an emissary of the chairman, himself. And there is no doubt how Comrade Chairman Stalin will react when he sees one of his trusted agents arrested by a general—a general who is in the process of failing to capture the most important objective of the war. Even in the prison truck one can hear the sound of a crucial bridge being demolished." The latter statement was not quite true; it was Major Rokov who had told him of the successful German defense, but it seemed like an effective bit of verbal flourish.

That stab, Krigoff saw, had struck home. A sheen of sweat covered Petrovsky's brow, though the temperature in the mess tent was not far above freezing.

The general recovered his composure and snorted in disgust. "We will cross this river soon enough, and I myself will lead these troops into Berlin."

"This army will cross the river, Comrade General—that fact is as inevitable as World Communism. But I would not be so confident about you being in front of those troops."

Krigoff looked at the black-and-white photograph he had in his hand. Paulina had been right: the focus was excellent, as was the image of Comrade Stalin in the picture Petrovsky was holding. The general's face, too, was clearly visible, as was his expression of disgust and the gob of saliva, which Paulina had in fact caught in midair.

With a grin of triumph, the colonel threw the picture onto the table so that it slid across the surface and came to rest in front of Petrovsky.

The blood slowly drained from Petrovsky's face as he recognized the picture and, no doubt, recalled the incident of his contemptuous remark. He looked around the conference table as if seeking assistance from one of the generals on his staff. All of them, Krigoff was pleased to note, kept their faces studiously on the map; none raised their eyes to meet their commander's gaze.

"How did you get this?" croaked the commander of Second Guards Tank Army.

Paulina Koninin entered the mess tent, her camera held at the ready, the bloody bandage still wrapped around the fingers of her left hand. "Comrade Colonel Krigoff was wrongly accused," she said. "And I myself heard the general's comments, and saw his despicable gesture regarding our glorious chairman. These of course are merely matters of record, but they will certainly be produced in your trial."

"My trial? On what charges?" demanded the general, his tone a hoarse rasp. It was a silly question and no doubt he knew it; formal charges were purely optional in the NKVD-directed trials of Stalinist Russia. Nevertheless, Krigoff took some delight in answering.

"Charges of contempt for our leader, just for a beginning. I am sure that the public presentation will focus on your military incompetence—of extreme caution in the face of grand opportunity! Of costing the Red Army the chance for an historic victory!" Krigoff's voice fell to a hiss. "Do you know that Allied Radio is reporting that the Americans are already planning a victory parade through the heart of Berlin for tomorrow? That victory should have been *ours,* Comrade General!"

With an almost bestial snarl, Petrovsky groped for his sidearm, which was in a buckled holster at his hip. The safety cover was stubborn and he pulled at the flap several times, while Krigoff stared in growing horror, unable to force himself to move in the face of this utterly unexpected development. This was not right—truly, the man *was* mad!

A moment later the general drew his gun, pointing the weapon directly at Alexis Krigoff.

In that instant the colonel, proud appointee of the chairman himself, felt his bladder go weak and his knees start to tremble. He raised his hands, recognizing the gesture for the pathetic futility that it was. The pistol cracked, the sound incredibly loud in the confined space.

But one of the guards accompanying the major had acted quickly, grabbing the general's arm so that the shot went wild. With a moan of relief Krigoff scrambled to his feet and fled through the door, acutely conscious of his wet pants. He heard the sound of another gunshot and flinched, tumbling to the ground in his terror. "Did he shoot me?" he cried to Rokov, who was standing in the doorway of the large tent.

"No. Comrade General Petrovsky has taken his own life," replied the major.

He was looking down at the sodden Krigoff, and his expression was unreadable.

TASK FORCE SANGER, RURAL HIGHWAY #47, EAST OF LUCKENWALDE, GERMANY, 1200 HOURS GMT

"So, you got him, son," said General Wakefield.

"Yes, sir," Sanger replied. Now that the capture was over, he felt empty. All the emotion seemed to have drained out of him.

The prisoner was under twenty-four-hour guard by a full platoon of armed, watchful veterans—men who would have relished a chance to use Führer Heinrich Himmler for target practice. As a consequence, the former leader of the Third Reich was trying very hard not to attract any attention. He remained in the back of a half-track, hands and feet shackled. Wakefield had driven to Luckenwalde as soon as the word had come down. Sanger had set up shop in an old farmhouse, where he had a good fire going. Wakefield had made himself comfortable at a rough-hewn wooden table in front of the fire, a mug of coffee in one hand and a cigar in the other. Sanger stood, fidgeting and pacing, unable to stay still.

"What do you want to do with him?" Wakefield asked.

"What do I *want* to do with him, or what *should* I do with him?"

Wakefield chuckled. "Whichever."

"I *want* to shoot the son of a bitch an inch at a time and see if I can make him feel a hundredth part of the pain he's dished out. I *should* turn him over to SHAEF and hope they do the right thing. Whatever that is."

"You think they'll do the right thing at SHAEF?" Wakefield chewed on his cigar.

"I don't know. There isn't a lot of precedent here. Whatever gets done will have a lot of politics in it. And whatever gets done will be done with one eye looking east."

"At the Rooskis."

"Yep."

Wakefield waited, puffing contentedly on his cigar. Finally Sanger spoke again. "What do you think, General?"

Wakefield grunted. "Hell, I don't know. Won't make a difference to the dead, if that's what you're asking, and he ain't in shape to do more damage to the living. It's over for him." Wakefield looked directly at Sanger and puffed on his cigar. "Revenge is poor comfort, boy. You want it simple, tell Smiggy to take care of things and go for a walk. You want to pass the buck, turn him over to SHAEF. He won't go free. If he does, someone will track him down and kill him sooner or later. You feel like it, kill him yourself. Write down 'Shot while trying to escape.' Doesn't matter. Won't make you feel better, at least not for more than a few minutes."

"Then what should I *do?*" Sanger said in an anguished voice.

"Don't get your tits in a wringer about it, for one thing," replied Wakefield. He took a swig of coffee and puffed on his cigar as he watched Sanger pace back and forth. "Gonna wear yourself out that way. You worry too much, boy. Worry never did a damn thing for anybody. Make a decision. It's either right or it's wrong. Worrying won't change it. Look at me." The general grinned. His teeth were yellow. "Often wrong, but never unsure. Hell, you want some advice, I'll give you some, okay?"

"I'd be grateful, General."

"Wait till you hear it, son, then tell me if you're grateful," Wakefield said. He scratched his leg. "All right. What good is he?"

"Who? Himmler?"

"Yeah, Himmler. Who do you think I was talking about, Sally Rand?"

"Well, you just told me he couldn't do anything anymore."

"I said he couldn't do any more *damage,* at least with anything other than his mouth. What *good* is he?"

"Well—I—I don't know," Sanger said. He thought for a moment. "I haven't looked at it that way."

Wakefield stood up and picked up his coat. "That's my advice. If he isn't any good, get rid of him, either to SHAEF or like I said. If he is, then use him."

"I'm going to have to think about that for a while, sir," Sanger said. "But I have an idea what you're talking about."

Wakefield nodded as he pulled on his leather jacket and put his helmet back on. "Good habit, thinking. Always like to encourage it in a young officer." He opened the door. "Jesus, it's cold out there and my goddamned hemorrhoids are killing me. I'm getting too old for this." He clamped his stogie between his teeth as he returned Sanger's salute, then he was gone.

LONDON, ENGLAND, 2127 HOURS GMT

"Ah, yes. You look a likely lad. Are you going to sit on that bench? No? Walking by again?" The man in the passenger seat peered through his binoculars. It was not raining this night, but it was damp and the car window kept fogging up.

"Are you going to ask that of everyone who walks by that bleedin' bench all night?" the driver growled. He had little to do on this stakeout and was bored.

"Oh, laddie, it's excitin' to watch professionals at work. It's like a cricket match, it is. Subtleties of play, professionalism, style. Our friend Mr. Philby is an artist. If there were a World Cup, he'd be a contender."

"I'm a rugby man, meself," replied the other. He rubbed his hands together in his woolen gloves. They were still cold.

"Here comes another, strolling along the path, umbrella furled. A lady walks by . . . he does *not* tip his hat. Not quite the pucca sahib, is he? Two points off, mate, for unsportsmanlike conduct. Not the same quality of gentleman as our Mr. Philby, are you? But wait! What's this? He's sitting down! Is this just a coincidence? A happenstance? Oh, no, it isn't. I see a hand slipping underneath the bench. Yes, and here it is clutching a folded newspaper. We've got our quarry, yes we do. Briefcase comes up, ah, here it comes . . . yes, the envelope inside the newspaper is slipped into the briefcase, and now another envelope comes up to replace it, yes—not quite up to the master's standards, but adequate, fully adequate. . . . Now, briefcase drops between legs in front, paper up, read an article or two by the light of the lamppost, just in case, yes, throw off suspicion, no need to hurry, and now we're done, paper is folded, paper returned underneath bench! We're done! All right, me bucko, time to find out where you call home."

The driver started up the car and slowly crept into traffic. The passenger picked up a rather heavy walkie-talkie. "This is Unit Four. The pigeon is returning to his roost. Repeat, the pigeon is returning to his roost."

A crackle of static, then, "Roger. All units copy."

There was an underground entrance three blocks away, and to no one's surprise, the pigeon headed down into it. There, another agent was waiting to pick up the tail, and so forth in a slow shuffle through the city. Unit Four was able to rejoin the party at the other end of the tube journey, just in time to learn the pigeon's roost. "Gor blimey," whispered the driver.

"Well, now," said the passenger, as the pigeon entered the gates of the Soviet Embassy.

15 MARCH 1945

THE KREMLIN, MOSCOW, USSR, 0500 HOURS GMT

The State Defense Committee met each morning to conduct a daily briefing and review of the military and strategic situation. It was often a meeting that engendered nervousness among some of its participants, especially when there was bad news to be given.

Although the conference table was large, the cavernous room dwarfed it. A square of old carpet underneath the table was the only floor covering; boots and shoes echoed in the chamber as the principals entered for the meeting. Stalin sat at the head of the table. A quick scan of the faces let him know that this morning's news would be bleak. Of course, with news this discouraging, the general outlines were already well known before the meeting started.

"Good morning, comrades," the chairman said.

"Good morning, Comrade Chairman," they choroused in return.

Attendance at this meeting was somewhat irregular. Molotov, the foreign minister, was present, as was Beria, head of the NKVD, and Bulganin, the defense minister. Stalin, in addition to his other portfolios, served as people's commissar for defense, the most senior military post, but various deputies and military officers provided additional support at these meetings.

Stalin looked at the faces around the table and smiled. He could see the visible relaxation that resulted. Good. For the moment, he needed people to focus on solutions, not on preserving their own skins. If later he needed examples to help others focus more effectively, then so be it. "We have two topics this morning. The first has to do with the large camp that our troops discovered in Poland—the one called Auschwitz. The second topic is Berlin. Let us talk first about Auschwitz."

Bulganin spoke first. "Comrade Chairman, we heard about the various atrocities that were perpetuated at the Nazi camp known as Buchenwald, which the capitalist forces uncovered a few weeks ago. It now seems that those atrocities were minor indeed compared to those being committed in Nazi camps in occupied Poland. The largest of these camps, it seems, is the camp known as Auschwitz, located near the Polish community of Oswiecim. While it provides slave labor for various factories, it is primarily a factory for mass extermination of Jews. Some of the facilities were wrecked by German troops as they evacuated ahead of our advancing forces, but enough remains to reconstruct what went on. The scale of the program is quite unprecedented."

None of the men around the table were strangers to mass killings for political reasons, but as Bulganin passed around photographs and documentation, there was silence.

"We have known that the Germans were unprincipled, savage barbarians," Stalin said, "but even so, this exceeds our understanding. This effort, Nikolai Aleksandrovich, was aimed, you say, at the Jews?"

"At Auschwitz, nearly exclusively," Nikolai Aleksandrovich Bulganin replied. "The Nazis, however, had a long list of enemies. The Jews headed the list, and it seems that the first objective of this program was the complete extermination of every Jew in Europe. Eventually, I suppose, every Jew in the world, if they got that far. Gypsies, homosexuals, some other religious groups would come next."

"Communists?"

"I would imagine that Hitler and Himmler would have happily held open the gas-chamber doors for every communist, whatever race or nationality. Plus, while they were at it, every Slav, every Georgian, every Russian. I do not think those gas chambers would have stopped operation for a very long time, if the Nazis had their way."

Stalin shook his head. "When I was in Teheran, meeting with Roosevelt and Churchill, I told them that it was of the highest importance that Germany after the war must be rendered so powerless that it could never again threaten the world. To that end, I proposed that fifty thousand, and maybe even a hundred thousand senior German officers be liquidated. I see now that I was sadly mistaken. I am too softhearted, my friends. That number is far too modest. But now we have this camp. How can we use it to help convince the rest of the world of the importance of crushing the Germans so they can never possibly rise again? Our relations with the Americans are strained, and the British have never been trustworthy."

"The capitalists will want to discredit anything that we bring forward that does not suit their own purposes," Beria observed.

"True," Molotov replied. "But this is a technical problem in the organization and dissemination of propaganda. It is not so much how to *be* objective, for in this case being objective serves our purpose, but how to *appear* objective. We must appear to be cooperative in this sphere even if we conflict with the capitalists in other spheres. I have people who can work on this and put together a good strategy."

"Very well," said Stalin. "Do so. Topic two. Berlin."

Silence.

Stalin laughed. "My comrades, it's hardly the end of the world. It's not even the end of the week. It's only pawn to king four, and we can capture en passant if we choose."

He saw a nodding head among his generals and pointed to him. The general spoke. "Yes, Comrade Chairman, it's true. Even with the bridges across the Oder destroyed, there is no longer any effective resistance. Our armies are bridging even as we speak, and soon we'll have forces sufficient to envelop the relatively small Western force—a mere pawn, as you say—in its Berlin outpost. Our only real concern has been avoiding direct conflict with the capitalists, per our standing orders. That can change at a moment's notice."

"Good! Very good! Now, I did hear you say that the bridges across the Oder were all destroyed? I think I recall hearing that one *might* have been captured?"

"Yes, sir. Second Guards Tank Army, under the command of Colonel General Petrovsky, failed to take a bridge in time. The general took his own life right before he was to be taken into custody."

"Ah, I see. A man who understood his own failure. Alas, he should have remembered that his life did not belong to him, but rather to the state. Now, if it should be necessary to make the lesson more official, someone else will have to suffer in his place. Wasteful of him. So, you are confident that we have the military force to take Berlin. Can we hold it against the capitalists?"

"Without a doubt, Comrade Chairman," replied the general. "The ratio of forces is substantially in our favor, even neglecting the dictum that the defensive form of warfare is stronger than the offensive."

"But the capitalists outweigh us in air power, do they not?" interjected Lavrenty Pavlovich Beria, head of NKVD.

"They do, Lavrenty Pavlovich, but . . ." The general shrugged.

"We are already aware that the capitalists have large numbers of bombers and large numbers of bombs, and this has been taken into account," said Stalin. "On the ground, our armed forces outnumber theirs by a substantial margin, enough so that we could push on to the Atlantic Ocean if we chose. In the air, we do not enjoy the same strength. Very well; we will not push our borders to the Atlantic quite yet. But how can superior air power keep us from taking Berlin, or holding it once we take it? Enough bombs to dislodge us from Berlin would have the effect of destroying Berlin, in which case the capitalists would take possession of a crater—a crater without Germans in it, mind you. Our forces would still be so spread out across eastern Germany that even very many bombs could not kill them. Perhaps I am growing old and stupid, comrades, but for the life of me, I cannot see much threat here. Can any of you enlighten me? Is there some danger here I do not see? In all sincerity, comrades, if you can find a flaw in this, let me know at once."

Stalin looked around. One of his ministers had raised a finger. "Yes, Viacheslav Mikhailovich? Please, let me have the benefit of your analysis."

Viacheslav Mikhailovich Molotov, foreign minister of the Soviet Union, was old enough and senior enough that he could speak with relative freedom on these matters. "I do not think there is a flaw in your military analysis, Josef Vissarionovich. I am thinking only of the right steps to follow in the process. We can take Berlin; we can hold Berlin. The capitalists can drop many smaller bombs on our troops." He shrugged fatalistically.

"But following the Great Patriotic War immediately with another war with the capitalists of the West would not be my first choice," Molotov continued. "When the cannons cease fire in this war, there will be much to do. We must rebuild here in the Soviet Union. We have missile technology from Germany, and I am certain that Lavrenty Pavlovich will bring us any new military secrets that turn out to be worth having. At the same time, we have accomplished two of the greatest foreign-policy objectives of our land, dating even back to the tsars. We have Greece, a warm-water port on the Mediterranean. We have Norway, for access to the Atlantic Ocean. In addition, we have most of eastern Europe, regardless of whether Berlin falls ultimately to us or not. We need a time of peace in order to take advantage of the opportunities these new lands provide us."

"Your recommendation?"

"Encircle Berlin, fortify positions in eastern Germany, and make talk-talk. Make Berlin the objective you will not compromise, and eventually yield on Berlin in exchange for a fully demilitarized Germany, recognition of the People's Republics of Norway and Greece, occupation of large portions of eastern Germany, et cetera, et cetera. Let the Americans and the British play the endgame of the last war. We shall play the opening moves of the next war, so that our pieces are in the most advantageous of positions."

"Comments?" Stalin asked.

A senior general, a holder of the Order of the Soviet Union, spoke up. "Comrade Chairman, I want to go back to Allied air power again. Assuming for the moment that it is as superior as claimed, what if it were to be used not on our forces, not on Berlin, but on, say, Moscow?"

"I will speak to that," replied Molotov. Stalin nodded.

"That is certainly a military option, Comrade General. From a diplomatic perspective, it would be a declaration of full-scale war between the capitalist West and the Soviet Union. A struggle for Berlin, even if it should turn into a battle, could be localized at a level short of a full-scale war. For the reasons I just outlined, that is not only in the current best interests of the Soviet Union, but for similar reasons is in the current best interests of the capitalists as well. They will want to sell us tools and machinery for our rebuilding, for we are that most precious thing, a market."

Molotov took a sip of water and continued. "The capitalists can bomb Moscow when they choose, as we are at liberty to send our bombers against

Paris or London at a whim. However, such an act would be a declaration of total war, of the sort that could not be contained once it had been unleashed. I do not believe they wish this, at least at the present time."

The old general looked at the foreign minister. "I do not mean to give offense, but did you not have the same opinion about Germany?"

Everyone at the table watched the two men. This was turning into a serious duel. Men had lost their lives for less. Molotov's face had gone expressionless. "Comrade General, in the matter of Adolf Hitler, I made a mistake. I was aware that he was a treacherous snake. I was not aware, unfortunately, that he was a stupid *svoloch.*" The untranslatable Russian insult had a meaning somewhere on the spectrum between "jerk" and "asshole," and was not the sort of word normally heard in meetings of the State Defense Committee. "I thought he would have attacked us earlier in the year, or failing that, I thought we would be safe until the next year. I could not imagine him stupid enough to forget our fine ally General Winter. Perhaps I am wrong this time, but I do not see our capitalist opponents having the same level of stupidity as our late unlamented führer." He looked around the table. "It is my opinion that they fight for Berlin or they do not fight for Berlin, but they do not start a wholesale war with the Soviet Union without substantial provocation or clearly logical gains to be had."

"Thank you, Foreign Minister," the old general said. "Cogently argued."

Molotov inclined his head graciously.

"Very good," said Stalin. "This is a constructive and forward-looking approach. I am to see the American ambassador tomorrow, but I think I shall cancel that and put him off until the encirclement of Berlin is complete. Then we will start talking. I am not yet happy with the idea of giving up Berlin under any circumstances, but I will consider the foreign minister's arguments and let the situation move forward. Since the foreign minister's recommendation is to begin by making Berlin a nonnegotiable demand, this fits the strategy so far."

Stalin's eyes covered the faces of his attendees, reading in their carefully controlled expressions a sense of their real ideas. "In the meantime, the two fronts in Germany are to move forward with the encirclement of Berlin. Avoid direct combat with Western Allied troops to the extent possible, but move forward even if opposed. NKVD will step up production of diplomatic intelligence, where possible influencing negotiation positions of our capitalist partners. Physical takeover of Norway and Greece continues as highest priorities. Comments? No? This meeting is adjourned."

KÖNIGSPLATZ, BERLIN, GERMANY, 1229 HOURS GMT

"Nothing like a good military parade, eh, Field Marshal?" asked General George Patton, grinning in boyish glee as he saw the column of Sherman tanks rumbling past the reviewing stand. The M4s were battered and war-weary, many of them showing the dents and scuffs that were proof of a long and bitter campaign, but these only made him more proud than ever. Following the tanks came a column of marching infantry, who began to sing loudly to the tune of the "Colonel Bogey March," whistling the chorus between each verse,

"Hitler, he only had one ball,
Göring, he had two but very small,
Himmler had something simm'ler,
But poor old Goebbels had no balls at all.

Frankfurt has only one beer hall,
Stuttgart, die Mädchen all on call,
Munich, vee lift our tunich,
To show vee Nazis have no balls at all."

Rommel, who was long familiar with the bawdy songs of both Axis and Allied forces, pretended not to understand the lyrics. He looked at Patton, who could hardly contain his grin at getting away with the joke, then looked meaningfully at General Bayerlein, who was on the reviewing stand with him. Bayerlein nodded and spoke to his own ADC, who slipped quickly away. Bayerlein had once served as Rommel's chief of staff, and knew well enough that Rommel would not stand for being shown up by the American general. That was well and good, for Bayerlein himself felt the same way. Following the example of his commander, Bayerlein had removed most of his own medals and insignia, all those containing a swastika—which, under the Third Reich, had included the vast majority—so that the German officers looked plain next to the bedecked Americans and other Allied officers present.

"Indeed, General," Rommel replied, looking innocently at Patton. "This is your Fourth Armored Division, I believe?"

"Yes . . . yes it is. One of my best units, been with me since Normandy, you know." Patton was slightly nonplussed that Rommel seemed unaware how Patton had pulled a fast one on him.

"I know," said the Desert Fox. "I remember them well. Ah, and here comes the Panzer Lehr." The rumbling of German panzers followed behind the marching American infantry. He smiled, certain that a few seconds was all Bayerlein would need.

Patton gestured expansively. "You know, those Panthers are nice tanks. I wouldn't mind a company or two of them for Third Army."

"Perhaps you will have a chance to command them," Rommel said. "It is hard to say what the future will hold. If you had told me two months ago that you and I would be standing here, side by side, I would have had you locked in a ward for the mentally unbalanced."

Patton laughed loud and long at that, and naturally all of the other staff officers in the bleachers joined in the gaiety, though they couldn't have heard the field marshal's remark.

A company of panzergrenadiere followed the rumbling Panther tanks. As they passed the reviewing stand, they, too, began to sing. Rommel smiled in satisfaction. Bayerlein had picked up his cue properly. His soldiers would not take second place to Patton's men, no, sir! He watched Patton's face as his men sang the "Panzerlied," the theme song of the panzer forces. He had a translator provide Patton with a running English translation of the lyrics.

"Whether it storms or snows, whether the sun smiles on us,
The day blazing hot or icy-cold the night,
Dusty are our faces, but cheerful are our minds,
Our Panzer roars in the stormy wind.

With thundering engine, as fast as the lightning,
Toward the enemy protected in the Panzer,
Ahead of the comrades in combat all alone,
So we thrust deeply into the enemy lines.

With roadblocks and tanks the enemy slows us down,
We laugh at the roadblocks and drive around them,
And if he shakes his hand furiously, enraged,
We search for paths that nobody found before.

And if faithless luck abandons us one day,
And we don't return to the homeland,
The deadly bullet hits us, we meet the fate,
Then the Panzer is our honorable grave."

Patton looked suitably impressed at the marching men and the singing, and Rommel was satisfied that the honor of his forces had been maintained. Flags and bands came past next. Across the street, through the vast park of the Tiergarten, citizens of Berlin watched warily, relieved but not exactly joyous. Only when Rommel came forward and gave them a wave did they break into loud, persistent cheers.

Slowly, still limping on his leg that would never quite heal, the Desert Fox followed the other generals from the reviewing stand. Berlin was theirs.

ASSOCIATED PRESS NEWSWIRE,
1600 HOURS GMT

FLASH/BULLETIN
PARIS BUREAU, 15 MARCH, 1500 GMT
COPY 01 VICTORY OVER NAZI GERMANY!
DISTRIBUTION: ALL STATIONS

PARIS, 15 MARCH (AP) BY CHUCK PORTER
WITH A TRIUMPHANT PARADE OF ALLIED TROOPS THROUGH THE STREETS
OF BERLIN, THE WAR WITH NAZI GERMANY HAS FINALLY ENDED.

AT 0800 HOURS BERLIN TIME, COLONEL-GENERAL SEPP DIETRICH,
NAZI MILITARY COMMANDER FOR THE CITY OF BERLIN, FORMALLY SURREN-
DERED THE CITY TO THE WESTERN ALLIES, REPRESENTED BY LIEUTENANT
GENERAL GEORGE PATTON OF THE UNITED STATES AND FIELD MARSHAL
ERWIN ROMMEL OF THE GERMAN REPUBLIC.

SIMULTANEOUSLY, COMMANDERS OF THE NAZI ARMY GROUP G, THE
LAST MAJOR OPERATING NAZI MILITARY FORCE IN THE WEST, SURREN-
DERED TODAY TO THE 21ST ARMY GROUP UNDER THE COMMAND OF
BRITISH FIELD MARSHAL SIR MILES DEMPSEY, ENDING FORMAL NAZI RESIS-
TANCE IN THE WEST.

SOME NAZI FORCES CONTINUE TO FIGHT DEFENSIVE ACTIONS
AGAINST ADVANCING SOVIET FORCES IN THE EAST, BUT HAVE YIELDED TO
WESTERN ALLIED FORCES TAKING OVER THEIR POSITIONS.

CIVILIAN OFFICIALS OF THE NAZI REGIME, INCLUDING FUERHER
HEINRICH HIMMLER, HAD ALREADY FLED THE CITY BEFORE THE ARRIVAL
OF ALLIED TROOPS. UNCONFIRMED REPORTS SAY THAT HIMMLER HAS
BEEN CAPTURED SOUTH OF THE CITY NEAR THE CZECHOSLOVAKIAN BOR-
DER. WHEREABOUTS OF OTHER TOP NAZI OFFICIALS ARE NOT YET KNOWN,
BUT SHAEF OFFICIALS EXPRESSED CONFIDENCE THAT MOST WILL BE CAP-
TURED WITHIN A FEW DAYS.

CONTINUED PEACE TALKS WITH SOVIET OFFICIALS IN MOSCOW AND
WITH FRONT LINE COMMANDERS ARE TAKING PLACE AROUND THE CLOCK.
SOVIET, BRITISH AND U.S. OFFICIALS HAVE ALL EXPRESSED THEIR DESIRE
FOR PEACE IN THE REGION . . .

MORE

AP PAR 334639 RZ/021445

16 MARCH 1945

**POW COMPOUND, HQ SECOND GUARDS TANK ARMY,
KÜSTRIN, GERMANY, 1018 HOURS GMT**

The makeshift compound for captured enemy soldiers stank of blood and shit
and piss and fear. Medical attention was not always available even for Soviet
troops, so much less was available for captured Nazis, who were left to rot and
fester in their own waste. The POW area was a commandeered farm. The
holding pen was a barnyard, its fence reinforced with barbed wire and
patrolled by guards. Some barrels filled with scraps of wood and leftover oil
served as sources of heat; scraps and leftovers from the mess tent were taken
over and given to the prisoners for their meals. The barn was used as an interrogation center, the milking stalls pressed into offices where German-speaking
interrogators took down information and made dispositions. Transport to
more formal POW camps, reeducation centers, gulags, or other destinations
would take place over periods ranging from days to weeks after the battle;
there were numerous activities that took higher priority. However, as trains
returned empty, loading them with prisoners took advantage of otherwise
wasted space.

Colonel Alexis Krigoff did not normally like going to the prisoner compound, because it was smelly and dirty, but it was one of the areas under his
command, and proper military procedure demanded that he make the rounds
periodically. He wore older boots and clothing that could get dirty, for there
was no way to ensure that he could remain clean. Paulina had expressed some
interest in photographing the prisoners, but Krigoff had done his best to discourage her. Although this process was fully in accordance with Marxist-
Leninist doctrine, it was not something for the squeamish. We all eat meat and
the butcher is a comrade, but that does not mean we would all enjoy seeing
him at his work. Frankly, some of the necessary activities even turned Krigoff's
stomach from time to time.

Lieutenant Jerozlaus Kraichin was just stepping out of one of the stalls.
Krigoff could just see the shadowy figure of a Nazi prisoner slumped against a
wall. He had been rather badly wounded, Krigoff could see, with damage to
right arm and leg. Kraichin saluted when he saw Krigoff. "Comrade Colonel!"

"As you were, Lieutenant. That man—an officer?"

"Yes, very interesting, too. He's a Nazi celebrity."

"Really?"

"Yes, if you're interested, Colonel."

"Sure. Tell me about him." Krigoff knew very little about Germans or Nazis as actual individuals.

"He was only giving name, rank, serial number, but as he's Waffen-SS, there's quite a lot of information to be gotten from the uniform, you know." Krigoff didn't know, but he nodded anyway. Kraichin continued. "The Nazis we overran were the remnants of the Second SS Panzer Division 'Das Reich.' They were originally one of the most elite panzer units, especially in the beginning. But this man had an embroidered cuff from the First SS Panzer Division 'Leibstandarte Adolf Hitler,' which means he was in that division. His name is Peiper, and he was a leading Nazi in the Mscha campaign. A very nasty man."

"Good we've got him, then." Krigoff didn't care what the lieutenant was prattling on about; the man might have been a big Nazi fighter, but he was a helpless prisoner now, and the Nazi fangs had all been pulled.

The lieutenant smiled. "I want to put him in for reeducation, sir."

"Why on earth? If he's such a top Nazi, can he be bent to our ways?"

"Oh, yes, I think he can. You know that Nazi stands for National Socialism, of course." Krigoff remembered hearing that, but it had never really occurred to him to think about it, so he nodded once again. "It actually was originally a socialist party, until Hitler and his thugs took it over. They kept the name, even though they purged the socialist elements from within. They did keep a sense of dialectic and a bit of a sense of class struggle—all this nonsense about the Jews was a way to displace class hostility. Originally, it was anti-aristocrat, but the Jews were turned into a symbol of aristocracy, a hidden aristocracy, if you will."

"This is all interesting," said Krigoff in a voice suggesting that it was anything but, "but what has this to do with your pet Nazi celebrity here?"

"This man is already sensitized to indoctrination. Men like this don't bend easily, but they do break. With reeducation, he could be turned into a good communist, then sent to work for the greater good of the proletariat, say in Siberia. He can serve his remaining days on earth helping to repair what he fought so hard to destroy. Justice, yes?"

Krigoff nodded. "A little elaborate, but if it pleases you, go right ahead. Killing the man's probably easier, but as long as you make sure your plan works, it has my approval." It didn't matter to Krigoff, and if that sort of thing improved his lieutenant's efficiency, all well and good.

He went into the stall and looked at the man. He had been handsome once, though half his face had been terribly scarred. His uniform was torn and dirty; his arm and leg wounds were open and festering somewhat. He might or might not live long enough to be reeducated; either way, he was due for a lot of pain. His eyes had gone dull, though Krigoff could detect a feral spark of hate underneath. He wouldn't want to meet this one healthy and armed. No matter; this was one fewer Nazi with which the world needed to contend.

He moved on to the next stall.

LONDON, ENGLAND, 1351 HOURS GMT

"Kim Philby a Soviet double agent? You've got to be out of your mind! That's the most ridiculous statement I've ever heard."

"Nevertheless, Minister, the evidence is rather damning. He has passed a list of personnel on the Tube Alloys project to someone who has been identified as a Soviet agent."

"Nonsense. First, you must have made a mistake. Second, even if it's true, I'm certain there is some sound, reasonable explanation for this. He's probably running some complicated scheme for our side, you know."

"That is possible, Minister. In any event, we don't propose arresting him, or anything like that, certainly not at present."

"No? Then what's all the fuss about?"

"If we assume for the moment that he is somehow working for the Soviets as a spy, an identified enemy agent is quite useful. It's the ones we don't know about who are really troublesome. We don't mind Stalin learning of the existence of the atomic bomb—in fact, he was informed about the project in Casablanca by the prime minister himself. In fact, we might do well to have him believe we have more of them and that they are far more successful than may be the actual case."

"Mmm. Go on, then."

"We would be quite concerned if we believed Stalin—or anyone else—was learning how to construct such a bomb for himself, but that's not at issue here. We'd like to make sure that Philby receives the information he seeks—suitably edited to meet our purposes, of course—and successfully transmits that information to the Soviet Union. We'll monitor the document flow; now that we know where the drop-offs are located, we'll slip in, copy and replace the transmissions between Philby and his Soviet contacts. Anything too dangerous can be stopped or edited. We'll learn through our own intelligence sources there whether the doctored information is getting through, and that, of course, will be the final confirmation of Philby's true role."

"I still say that's rubbish, but I can't fault the plan. Go ahead, then. If you find ironclad proof that Philby's a traitor, then when the time comes, I assume you'll take appropriate action against him."

"Yes, when he ceases to be useful."

"Dirty business, this. You'd better be damned sure you're right before you make any move against Philby. I mean, do you know who his *father* is?"

"Yes, Minister. Thank you for your time."

18 MARCH 1945

HQ, FIRST BELORUSSIAN FRONT, FRANKFURT-AN-DER-ODER, GERMANY, 1008 HOURS GMT

Marshal Zhukov looked grim, and Colonel Alexis Krigoff did his best to shrink into the back row of officers, mostly division and army-level generals of the First Ukrainian and First Belorussian fronts. They had been summoned to learn the details of the great soldier's new plan.

"The delay at the Oder has proved to be disadvantageous," the marshal reported bluntly. "While the Nazis were fighting us tooth and claw, they were also opening the back door to their capital, inviting their new friends in the West to take up housekeeping in Berlin."

There was only silence among the gathered officers, all of whom had heard this truth in some level of detail. In addition to General Petrovsky, who had committed suicide as a result of his attack's failure, two other division leaders and the general commanding the First Shock Army had been relieved, sent back to Moscow in disgrace. Krigoff had been more than happy to go along with the story about Petrovsky's fate—a story that was remarkably close to the truth, when he got right down to it—and had reasoned that there was no reason to provide to the NKVD additional details on the general's last confrontation.

"Our latest information indicates that most of Patton's Third Army has moved into Berlin; some nine divisions taking positions around the capital. They are accompanied by at least three Wehrmacht divisions under the command of Rommel. There are also numerous airborne troops, parachute and glider units, that have landed in and around the city—perhaps as many as four full divisions of elite soldiers. Marshal Konev—will you continue?"

"Thank you, Comrade Marshal." Konev, a square and stocky man with the build of a wrestler, fixed a glare on the gathered officers. "As you have heard, we are facing something like fifteen divisions of fascist and capitalist troops in the city itself. The American general, Eisenhower, has filled Berlin with these troops, and herein we may find the enemy's weakness."

The marshal gestured to a large map that an aide had unrolled for him, the graphic image hanging like a tapestry on the wall. "This is the road from Küstrin to Berlin. It is fully blocked, and guarded by antitank emplacements and heavy fortifications. Here, here, and here"—he snapped his pointer to the north and south of the great city—"are strong defensive positions. Comrade

Chairman Stalin has indicated that it is not his wish that we commence attacking the Americans in these positions."

Now his pointer trailed, almost sensually, along two threadlike marks on the map, roads connecting Berlin to the regions of western Germany.

"The enemy is bringing supplies into the city along the A-two autobahn and another road, Reich Highway Twenty-Four." Neither of them is well protected, and if we can cut them both, the city and its garrison will be cut off from the rest of Eisenhower's armies.

"But the Americans are in a state of flux, and we must strike quickly, before the rest of their armies can come up to support Patton. We have two great fronts poised to commence the attack. But there is an additional consideration." Here Konev paused for effect, and Krigoff—as well as his fellow officers— anxiously waited to hear what that consideration was.

"The chairman, in his wisdom, has determined that this is not the moment to embark upon a wholesale war against the West. This is not a reflection on his faith in our prowess—Comrade Stalin has told me, personally, that he knows we would prevail in such a contest. Rather, it a question of diplomacy and timing. And besides, why should we go to the effort of annihilating the enemy, when we can attain the same geographic objectives with patience, and maneuver. Comrade Marshal Zhukov, would you care to conclude the session?"

"Indeed. Well stated, Comrade Marshal." The great soldier came forward and took the pointer, but he did not face the map. Instead, he looked at his men. "We will test the mettle of these Yankees," he said, "but not with a direct attack. The key are these two roads, the highway and the autobahn, by which Patton is still connected to his headquarters." Now he turned, and indicated Reich Highway Twenty-Four.

"This road, to the south, will be seized by a paratroop attack. Intelligence shows that it is very lightly defended, logically enough since it is forty or fifty miles from our current positions. We have reason to believe that the Allies, despite their own use of the airborne tactic in seizing Berlin, will not be prepared for such a move on our part. We will drop a full division along the road, reinforced with a second of glider-borne troops. They will have to hold their ground until Marshal Konev's spearheads come up, forty-eight hours after the drop.

"In the meantime, my own front will attack—aggressively—in the north, and close off the last supply route into Berlin. But we will not trigger the next war—because we will not smash into American troops. Instead, we will hit the Germans, here." He indicated the region directly north of Berlin, where a swastika marked the position on the map. "Rommel has three divisions in line here, and we will obliterate them." Zhukov smiled, thinly. "This may be my last chance to kill large numbers of Germans in my lifetime. I intend to make the most of it."

Krigoff joined in the round of hearty chuckles that greeted the marshal's gallows humor.

"Attacking a day after our own offensive begins, Marshal Konev's men will jump off without artillery preparation, as soon as the parachutists drop on the highway. There are few American troops that far south—yet—and any that he encounters will be brushed aside. The First Ukrainian Front will sweep around the city to the south, while my own Belorussian Front with take the northern route. In less than three day's time, we will meet between these two roads."

The marshal waited as the officers absorbed the plan, murmurs of approval rumbling quietly from one man to the next. The scheme was elegant, and did not seem to require a great deal of murderous combat. Rather, it required a certain element of finesse that had not been a character of Red Army operations. Still, Krigoff felt certain that it would work. And once those fifteen divisions were trapped in Berlin, he could see that the Soviet Union would have a very strong bargaining position.

Krigoff returned to the division HQ, which occupied the same tent compound as a week earlier, when Petrovsky had killed himself. The new CO was General Benko, who had been Petrovsky's XO, and he looked up nervously as the colonel of intelligence came into the room. He had been treating Krigoff with considerable respect, ever since his promotion, and the young officer was pleased with this development.

"What did Comrade Marshal Zhukov have to say?" asked Benko deferentially.

Krigoff explained the plan as he remembered it, knowing that the front's official marching orders would be coming soon. "I expect that we will be in the secondary wave of advance," he guessed. "Since the main thrust of our attack will come from south of here, near Frankfurt-an-der-Oder. With luck, we will have a key role in closing the trap around the Yankee dogs."

"Yes, yes! That would be splendid, indeed," agreed the general, who then remembered some matters requiring his urgent attention and beat a hasty retreat.

Krigoff found Paulina in the officers' mess tent, where, since the incident with Petrovsky, she had been warmly welcomed by the men.

"Comrade Colonel!" she said, her one eye brightening at Krigoff's entrance.

He felt a great happiness at her reaction, an immense outpouring of gratitude for her loyalty, courage . . . and, to be truthful with himself, with her discretion. She had never rebuked him for his blatant explosion of fear when it looked as though Petrovsky had been ready to shoot the colonel. If she had noticed his shameful wetting of himself—he had tried to mask his stained trousers with the ubiquitous mud—she had never mentioned the fact.

"Come with me," he said, gallantly offering her his arm. He led her from the dark, smoky tent and into the cold night. The stars were bright in the cloudless sky, and he gestured toward the river, unseen but felt by both of them from the dense mist that seemed to be rising from the ground.

"Soon," he said, relishing the squeeze of her fingers on his arm. "Soon, we will cross that river, and then the war will be won."

21 MARCH 1945

REICHSTAG BUILDING, THIRD ARMY HEADQUARTERS, 1222 HOURS GMT

The crump of artillery was distant, but deep and resonant enough to indicate a truly massive bombardment. Reports started to filter into Third Army headquarters in the middle of the morning, and by the time, a few hours later, that General Patton came down the wide hall to the great conference room, there were dispatches arriving almost on a minute by minute basis.

"What's the word?" asked the army commander, displaying a fierce scowl. His trousers were spattered with mud, from the personal reconnaissance he had performed for half the morning. He had been unable to confirm the full scope of the attack, so had returned to HQ for a full briefing. Most of his division commanders were here, as were Looie Brereton—overall commander of the Airborne Corps—and Max Taylor and Jim Gavin, the division COs of the 101st and Eighty-second Airborne, respectively. Von Manteuffel was here, too, representing the Germans; Patton knew that Rommel would be out in the field, checking firsthand on the situation as it developed.

"Well?" Patton snapped finally, his voice rising into an irritated squawk. "Who's going to be first with the bad news—or is there anything good to report?"

"It's a concentrated attack against Rommel's men," Reid Sanger told him bluntly.

General Patton looked at the map that had been hastily spread across the broad table. Sanger indicated the area directly north of the city. "Judging by the artillery concentration, they're coming with at least an army. They have their guns lined up practically wheel to wheel for a twenty-mile front here. They have an aggressive combat air patrol up, and our recon aircraft have been reluctant to fly into that nest of Sturmoviks and MiGs. Not to mention some Curtises and a few other planes that came from the good ol' USA."

"Ah, Lend Lease," Patton said sarcastically. "Kind of changes the tone of it, when that stuff is shooting at us now. But we have to sleep in the bed we've got." He turned his attention back to the map.

"We need more protection on that flank," he said curtly. He directed his remarks at General Brereton, who was in command of the Seventeenth Airborne Corps, including all of the parachute and glider troops that had dropped into the city. "Do you have the Hundred-and-first available, to move up to support Rommel?"

"Well, we'd leave a gap on the northwest quadrant. I can get them in motion, but you'll need to bring someone else up to fill the gap."

"Dammit!" snapped Patton. "We don't have anyone else! Hell, there are a thousand Russian tanks just east of Berlin, and another thousand to the southeast. If we start jockeying our defenses around, we'll just weaken another sector."

The Third Army general gritted his teeth, and tried to swallow his immense frustration. This was not the kind of operation he favored: a relatively static defense against crushing attack. He wanted speed, maneuver, surprise! Yet none of those options was particularly useful in their present fix.

Brereton spoke up. "I know General Eisenhower was concerned that, if Zhukov attacked, we would have enough strength here to trip him up—at least until the rest of the army group can move up in support. Can we do that?"

Patton looked at the map again. "Max, if you can move a regiment up here, you can be in position to support if the Russkis break through Rommel and turn south." The army general's finger traced the line of the autobahn. "I have a feeling they're after this road."

"At least we still have this Highway Twenty-Four down here," Sanger pointed out. "Even if they get the autobahn, they're still forty miles away from each side of our supply line."

The general studied that truth, as it was displayed on the map. "Yeah, they'd have to fight through Nineteenth Armored to get to Highway Twenty-Four. And with that distance, we'd have time to react, to give the bastards a real bloody nose. Any sign of trouble down there, to the south?"

"No sir," General Wakefield said. "I talked to Ballard and Jackson both within the hour—so quiet you could hear a pin drop down there."

"Well then," Patton concluded, feeling a little better. He turned to von Manteuffel and spoke bluntly. "It's a local attack, designed apparently to punish our German allies, and perhaps threaten part of our supply line. I think, for the time being, we will hope that Field Marshal Rommel is up to the challenge. Can you convey to him our best wishes for a dramatic victory—and ask him to tell me right away if he's going to need more help."

143RD PANZER BATTALION, PANZER LEHR DIVISION, SPANDAU, GERMANY, 1422 HOURS GMT

He might have been in Africa again, if not for the soggy mud and the gray skies. Those details didn't matter, as the Desert Fox rode in his open staff car, his driver steering unerringly toward the sound of the guns. They were forced to detour, away from the route they had been using for the last few days, since that road was now under direct fire from Russian guns. As they circled down this secondary track, approaching the battalion from the rear, Rommel tried to evaluate what was happening.

The Soviet attack was bad, he knew simply from the volume of the fire, and the fact that it was continuing to move westward. Soon he came to a couple of dazed panzergrenadiers, one supporting the other as they limped out of the underbrush and onto the roadway. The weaker man had a bloody gash in his left leg, and that half of his face was blackened with soot and, perhaps, burned skin.

"Stop!" Rommel commanded, bracing himself as the driver braked hastily to bring the car to a halt beside the soldiers.

The two men gaped up at him momentarily. The strongest one brought his hand up to his forehead in a salute. "H-Herr Generalfeldmarschall!" he stammered. "The Russians are attacking!"

Rommel passed over the obvious truth. "I see you are with the Hundred-and-forty-third Battalion. What is your situation?"

"We were shelled, sir, for an hour—they came down like rain, or hail! Half my platoon was killed. Then came the tanks, T-34s mostly but some big monsters in among them. We had two panzers left, and both were taken out immediately. Finally we ran. . . . Franz and I are the only two to make it out, I think."

The field marshal nodded, even as he looked around. There was a wooded area shrouded in smoke, to the east. This road was banked, a meter or more above the flat ground, and there were no visible obstacles for several kilometers to the west. "Stay here—move Franz into the ditch on the other side of the road. I'll send a medic back for him, and try to get a few more troops to help you out. We can't let the Russians past this road—understand?"

"*Jawohl, Herr Generalfeldmarschall!*" If the man had any misgivings about holding, for the time being alone, a stretch of road against a Soviet tank division, he displayed none of them.

"Good man," said Rommel. "And good luck!"

They were off in a roar, heading toward a small crossroads north of Oranienburg, where Panzer Lehr had its field headquarters. Within three kilometers, Rommel knew they would never make it. They had encountered more shell-shocked survivors, and the field marshal ordered all of them to set up a line based in the ditch to the west of this road. But by the time they crested a low hill, the smoke and noise of the battle had moved so far west that it blocked the path before them.

Rommel stood in the car, his binoculars pressed to his eyes as he scanned the low ground before them. He saw tanks crossing the road, moving from his right to his left, and he could barely make out the red-star insignia on the turrets of the nearest. In the fields to his left he spotted several Tigers, awkwardly exposed on the flat ground—the few patches of brush only rose high enough to screen the tracks of the big tanks. These were firing steadily, and one after another of the Soviet T-34s burst into flame as they rolled down off the road and into the ditch. No less than a dozen were burning right before him, but that seemed to have no effect on the fifty or more that Rommel could see rolling into view.

The enemy tanks were emerging from a massive bank of white smoke that billowed from the forested land to the east. The smokescreen all but obscured the edge of the forest, but Rommel could see the tiny figures of Red Army infantry emerging from the murk. There were waves of them, coming at a rapid trot, hastening to keep up with the first wave of tanks. More of the armored behemoths streamed into view as well, two files of them within his view. As they emerged into the clear terrain the tanks maneuvered like veterans, expanding from their road columns into lines of ten or twelve of them abreast. They rolled forward with guns blazing.

The Desert Fox shifted his glasses to the west, bypassing the Tigers and seeking other points of resistance. He located a light antitank gun firing between two pine trees from the front yard of a small cottage. Here and there were small groups of panzergrenadiere, a machine gun nest set up in a barn, a couple of stone houses rendered into strong points. Even as he watched, two of the houses were blasted to pieces by the guns of Russian tanks, while the leading line of Soviet infantry swarmed across the road. A hundred men fell to the German machine gun, but the vast gap in the line was almost immediately filled by the next wave, who simply picked up the pace of their advance.

"Sir—we need to get to cover!"

Rommel glanced at the driver in irritation. The man was pointing at the sky, gesturing urgently. The field marshal nodded, seizing the bar before him with both hands. He would not sit down, though. Instead, he looked upward, wincing as he made out the specks of aircraft. More of the dreaded jabos, this time marked with the same red-star insignia as those tanks.

The car squealed through a hard left turn, lurching down through the ditch, pulling back onto the road facing toward Berlin. "Wait!" ordered Rommel, still watching the action.

The dive bombers were not coming toward him, he realized. There were hundreds of them, but they all seemed to be focused on the battle in the low valley. They roared lower, and bombs fell away, plummeting lethally into the ground and then erupting in fountains of dirt and smoke and debris. The two Tigers disappeared in the blasts, and for a short time the whole field was obscured. Some of the Soviets were blown apart by their own bombs; not even this seemed to give any pause to the advancing horde.

As the wave of jabos passed, Rommel was amazed to see that one of the Tigers was still firing. The huge tank was almost invisible beneath a layer of mud, dirt cast by near-missing bombs, but its main gun blasted shot after shot toward the Russian T-34s.

Until the field marshal heard the crack of a new gun, a sharp and gut-churning sound. The Tiger vanished in a blast of fire; when the smoke cleared, he could see that the turret had been blasted off with almost surgical precision. The killer tank rolled forward, dwarfing the T-34s, even looming higher and wider than the great Tiger.

This was one of the mighty KV5 tanks, the Desert Fox realized. Disdained as too slow and heavy for the modern battlefield, they clearly had their place in a fight like this. Looking more closely, Rommel spotted several more of the giants among the swarm of enemy armor.

"Drive," he ordered. "We have to get down to the switchboard at Oranienburg and let General Patton know what's happening."

Even then he didn't sit. Instead, he twisted painfully around for another look at the field, now completely overrun. He remembered something about that big tank, the KV5.

The Soviets called it the "Stalin."

SHAEF, REIMS, FRANCE, 1605 HOURS GMT

Ike was pacing around in his office, corralled here because this was the place everyone brought information. That was the one thing he needed now, the only thing he could act on. Unfortunately, both information and opportunities for action seemed to be in very short supply.

He crushed out his cigarette and looked up as his chief of staff came in.

"What have you got for me, Beetle?"

General Smith shook his head, and the Supreme Commander could not help grimacing.

"They're still limiting their attacks to the German units," reported Beetle, handing over the latest dispatches. "But they've all but obliterated Panzer Lehr, and Rommel's infantry is badly broken. Zhukov has closed Highway One-Thirty-Five to us, but we still have Number Twenty-Four and the autobahn."

"That's a damned tenuous lifeline for a whole army," Ike growled. "But they're not close to Twenty-four yet, are they?"

"No. And the British Sixth Airborne has set up a line south of Highway One-Thirty-Five. They won't be enough to stop the Russians, if they continue on—but at least they'll let us know if Stalin wants to start a full-fledged war."

"Dammit!" snapped the Supreme Commander, the word sharp as a steel blade. He hated it when the other guy held all the decision-making cards. But that was the case, right now.

"How long till Hodges and Simpson can get up there?" The American First and Ninth armies, now moving eastward from the Ruhr, were the only units in position to offer Patton any support.

"A matter of three days, for Hodges to get there in strength. Simpson is a day or two behind him."

"Then we'll just have to hope that Uncle Joe isn't ready to go for the kill," Ike declared, lighting another cigarette. He didn't want to speak the rest of the thought, but he knew that, if Stalin wanted the kill, Patton and Rommel were dead.

22 MARCH 1945

FRITZ SCHLOSS PARK, BERLIN, 0932 HOURS GMT
George Patton climbed out of his jeep, his throat tight with emotion. All around were the battered remnants of formations that had fought valiantly against an overwhelming storm of force. These men were German, not American, but they had fought as a part of Patton's command, and his heart broke at the proof of their suffering.

Some of them were still coming down the road from Oranienburg, limping, supporting their comrades. Others were collapsed in various stages of exhaustion. The seriously wounded had been moved into hospitals, but those with minor hurts waited here listlessly for their next assignment.

Rommel was visible at the other side of the broad field, talking to a group of men, then moving on to another. Patton could see that the Desert Fox left his men standing a little taller, looking a little better, after just a few words.

Finally the field marshal came over to the American general. Patton guessed that the Desert Fox had not been to sleep; he had heard that Rommel had been driving around, gathering the shattered elements of his three divisions, pulling them back to the northern environs of the city.

"Zhukov has cut the highway, hasn't he?" Rommel said; a young aide translated for him.

"Yep. Got word before dawn. British Airborne troops have a line south of the road, and it looks like they're stopping short of that."

The field marshal shook his head. His face was stained with soot and grime, and his injured eye was watering, seemed red and inflamed. Uncharacteristically, Rommel took off his hat and rubbed a hand over the sweaty strands of his thinning hair.

"We still have the autobahn, and Highway Twenty-Four," Patton said, going for the positive news. "The Russians are forty miles away from them."

"For now," Rommel noted, and Patton felt the chill of that truth in his own gut.

HEADQUARTERS, FIRST BELORUSSIAN FRONT,
ORANIENBURG, GERMANY, 1622 HOURS GMT
Krigoff put his arm around Paulina's shoulders, thrilled to the touch as she melded close to him. The spring night had descended, bringing a blanket of

moist and chilly air, but the young colonel felt only the heat of his personal, and political, passions.

"It was a great victory," she said, gesturing to the shattered, burned-out hulks of German tanks that dotted the ground. "But only against the Germans? Do we not dare to attack all of the capitalist lackeys?"

Krigoff allowed himself a private chuckle. "Ah, do not judge prematurely," he said. "I think you will see that, tomorrow, Comrade Marshal Zhukov has a little surprise planned for our former allies."

She pulled away from him. He wondered at first if it was a playful gesture, then saw that she was walking toward one of the burned-out panzers, apparently deep in thought. He followed, biting back his impatience, and was surprised when she spun suddenly to face him.

"It is a parachute attack?" she asked bluntly.

He was taken aback. "I—I am not at liberty to say!" He found the beginnings of outrage. "We shouldn't even be having this discussion—"

"Oh, it's all right," she said. "I know some officers in the Fifty-second Parachute Battalion. They are mindful of security, but I could see that something is up."

Krigoff was torn between a stern sense of security, a desire to impress Paulina with his own knowledge, and a surprising, deep-seated storm of jealousy that had erupted when she mentioned the parachute officers. He tried to settle on a middle ground.

"Of course, we all have to be aware of security considerations. But I can see that I am giving you no new information if I but confirm that your observations, your instincts, may well be correct. I trust that these parachute officers have been quarantined, if they are about to embark on a mission?"

"Oh, quite," she said, then surprised him again by leaning upward to kiss him, lightly, on the lips.

23 MARCH 1945

**FORTY-FOURTH MOBILE RADAR STATION, TEMPELHOF
AIRPORT, BERLIN, GERMANY, 0454 HOURS GMT**

"Captain! You'd better have a look at this!"

Chuck Porter heard the alarm in the sergeant's voice, and ambled over to the office door, trying to be unobtrusive as he listened. Fortunately, the men of the Eighty-second had accepted him as a regular feature around their HQ and other offices, so he had relatively free run of the great airport, which—now that the runways had been cleared—had been the landing point for a steady string of transport aircraft.

"Whattya got, Mac?" asked the duty officer, ambling over to have a look. There was a low whistle of amazement. "What the hell is going on? There must be a thousand bogies, to make the screen wash out like that!" The captain swiveled, shouted across the large office, which was located atop the terminal at the airport. "Jake—what's the weather? Anything funky going on east of here? Rainstorms? Big fronts? Anything?"

"No, captain. Clear skies—can't even see a cloud out there."

"Shit. Mac, what do you make of it?"

The operator shook his head. "I don't know, Captain. But if I had to guess, I'd say the Russians are putting a helluva lot of planes in the air. And they look to be coming this way."

"All right." The captain was moving across the room now, but Porter could still hear him in his agitation. "Get me Third Army HQ on the horn!" he was shouting. "We've got a big problem over here. . . ."

SHAEF, REIMS, FRANCE, 0620 HOURS GMT

"They're tracking the column. They have a count of more than a thousand multiengine aircraft, and at least that many fighters flying as escort. Right now, their course seems to be taking them south of Berlin, General," Beetle Smith reported to the Supreme Commander.

"What the hell are they up to?" Eisenhower fumed.

American and British fighters had been scrambling in waves ever since the first reports had come in from Third Army. Naturally, they had first expected a bombing raid against the besieged cities, and there were some five hundred P-51s flying circles over the German capital right now, ready to start shooting if this proved to be a Russian air raid. But that, at least, seemed not to be the case.

"Any visual confirmation yet?" Ike asked.

"Reports are that a few pilots have started to close it, but they've been jockeyed aside by Russki fighters who get right in their path. Our boys have dived away, rather than risk the collisions."

"We need more information! In the meantime, get every fighter we have into the air. I want this formation shadowed every mile of their flight path. And try again to get through to Zhukov's headquarters—and to our boys in London! See if they can learn anything out of the embassy in Moscow, anything at all about what's happening."

The door opened. Kay Summersby came in with a sheet of paper. "Sorry to interrupt, General, but this looks important."

"Thanks, Irish," Ike said, warming enough to offer a smile while he took the newest report.

"Damn, this is a new wrinkle!" he declared, passing the page to Beetle Smith. "A couple of our flyboys threw caution to the winds and went flying right through the Russian formation."

"Transport planes? A thousand transports, in a sky train?" Smith looked puzzled. "And they're not going to Berlin. Look at this position—they're already west of the city."

"This has got to be an airborne operation," Eisenhower said. "But what's the objective?"

Summersby was just leaving, but stepped aside to let another orderly come into the room, with yet another report.

"What is it?" demanded Ike.

"The Russian planes are turning north," the sergeant reported, glancing over the text. "They're west of Potsdam, but now changing course."

"They're after Highway Twenty-Four!" the Supreme Commander deduced immediately. His heart sunk at the thought of the quandary facing him: Surely those planes were filled with thousands of Russians soldiers, and they were relatively defenseless now. If the P-51s tore into them, who knew how many would die? Certainly the landing would be disrupted, and . . .

And Zhukov would have the best excuse he could ask for to attack. He could claim that the Americans had fired the first shots—indeed, had massacred his airborne troops—and he could roll in, crush Third Army, and claim Berlin for his own.

If the American fighters didn't attack? Ike looked at the map. Clearly he stood to lose another of the roads leading into Berlin, leaving only the autobahn as a supply link. But still, there might not be a shooting war, not yet.

"What are your orders, General?"

He realized that Beetle Smith was watching him, and once again the Supreme Commander felt the ultimate loneliness of his position. He sighed, threw the dispatch onto the floor in disgust.

"Keep an eye on the bastards, as close as possible without triggering accidents. But don't start shooting yet. We're going to see what Uncle Joe is up to."

FORTY-FOURTH RESUPPLY COMPANY, HIGHWAY
TWENTY-FOUR, GERMANY, 0630 HOURS GMT

Mickey Davis was a master scrounger. He was an old corporal—he had been sergeant, twice, busted back to private both times—and he was content with his role in this man's army. Now he was driving a two-ton truck, a very nice improvement over the jeep that had been his faithful steed for most of the drive across Germany. But he had learned that, with a truck, his capacity for cargo—and, hence, profit—was dramatically improved.

Corporal Davis had been fortunate enough to get a job that was well in line with his talents. He was actually an official scrounger for his supply company, and neither his platoon sergeant nor his company commander were inclined to ask him too many questions about how he got his work done. That was just the way Davis liked it, because it gave him the freedom to do what he was doing today.

The big truck rumbled along the highway, going toward Berlin. In the back he had several radios, a dozen crates of rations, and twenty jerry cans filled with gasoline, all castoff material that he had found along the highway, in vehicles that had broken down and been left behind by the convoys of the Red Ball Express—the great trucking caravans that hauled supplies from the great ports, especially Antwerp, to the far-flung spearheads of the Allied Expeditionary Forces. That cargo, he could claim truthfully, was just proof that he was doing his job, making sure that nothing too valuable got left behind.

His real treasure was stored in a couple of cases up near the cab, plain crates marked TOOLS. One of them was completely filled with cigarettes, which were already becoming the currency of choice in postwar Europe. With them, he could buy women, beer, or anything else from Germans, and they weren't bad for bargaining with the Brits, either. The second crate was even more valuable, however: That one rattled slightly from the bottles of fine brandy stacked there. It had a false bottom, with something like ten thousand dollars' worth of gold and silver concealed beneath that; the booty of a few of his most lucrative transactions during the last nine months.

Mickey Davis would not be coming home from this war a poor man.

He spotted another target up ahead, a truck much like his own that was parked on the shoulder of the road, with the hood up. Probably just overheated, Davis figured, but the boys in the express were in too much of a hurry to take time out for such details. No doubt the driver hopped into another vehicle—Davis was unique, in that he usually traveled alone—and ridden on to Berlin, where he would report the breakdown. Sooner or later a maintenance crew would arrive to either fix the truck where it sat, or haul it to some motor pool for more involved work.

That suited Mickey just fine; he only needed five minutes with the broken-down truck in order to do his job. He slowed down, pulled over, and braked to a stop a dozen feet behind the other truck. The canvas flap on the back was loosely tied, but there was no sign of anyone left behind to guard it. That was not a surprise; what German civilian in his right mind was going to mess with the US Army?

He climbed right in the back and looked around, cursing as he saw that the bed of the truck had been picked pretty clean. Pushing back the flap, he was about to jump out and go around to check the cab when he heard the sound of an engine. He looked up and down the highway, couldn't see anyone coming, but the sound continued to swell. Not just one engine, he realized, but lots of them.

When he looked up, he saw the airplanes, a great train of them growling through the clear blue sky. He had never been big on aircraft identification—that was too much like studying—but he guessed these were Allied bombers, returning from some raid or another. Maybe the war wasn't quite as much over as he thought it was.

Then he saw the parachutes, scores, then hundreds of them popping into sight. They were clearly arrayed above the highway, and as they drifted earthward Davis figured that he was in the middle of some kind of huge drill. Several soldiers landed very nearby, crunching into the ground with force that seemed like it should have broken their legs. But they bounced to their feet, reaching for their rifles as if this was a real battlefield situation.

It was only then that Mickey started to notice some odd differences. Their uniforms were not quite olive drab, and those guns—he had never seen rifles like that before.

"Hey, guys," he said, waving his hand and walking toward them. "What's going "

He never heard the gunshot, nor felt the bullet that killed him.

COMMUNIST CITIZENS' CELL #435, POTSDAM, GERMANY, 1734 HOURS GMT

Franz Grubhof had been waiting for this moment for more years than he could remember . . . since before the start of the war, before even the ascendancy of Hitler to the rulership of Germany. Grubhof was a dedicated communist, and he had spent nearly a lifetime nourishing, cherishing that belief, and waiting for the day when he could strike a blow in the name of his cause.

That day had arrived.

His orders had been delivered by the man who was now in the rowboat with him, the stranger who had known the proper passwords—"Red sky tonight?"—and thus had been welcomed into Grubhof's little apartment. From there they had gone to a boathouse on one of Potsdam's many lakes, where they had encountered other members of the cell. They had paired up, two men—or women; Franz had noticed a couple of females among the two dozen provocateurs—per boat. Concealed in picnic baskets beneath the seats were strange packages, with timers. Grubhof knew that these were bombs.

Now, as they glided across the dark waters, he began to understand their target. There was a large span of concrete overhead, a causeway that ran for more than a mile through this shallow lake. Over that span passed the autobahn, the main highway connecting Berlin to the west.

Under that span, poking carefully among the sturdy concrete pilings, were twelve little rowboats, and twenty-four dedicated German communists.

NINETEENTH ARMORED DIVISION, LUCKENWALDE, GERMANY, 1735 HOURS GMT

"What the hell?" Frank Ballard charged out of the mess tent and looked to the south. Men were coming out of all the division's buildings, looking in the same direction.

The sound of guns was loud, and all too close. "There must be a thousand pieces shooting down there," murmured Major Diaz, with his artillerist's ear. "They're plastering the fields south of town."

"We don't have anyone down there, now, do we?" asked Ballard, knowing that any unfortunate persons caught in the blast zone were most likely already dead.

"Not that I know of. Smiggy's men pulled back a few days ago—they're still in the city."

Ballard nodded. Smiggs was not his concern, not right now. "Get me some eyes out there," he called, and a couple of privates took off in jeeps. "The rest of the combat command is going on full alert."

An hour later he had his report: The barrage was intense, and it was slowly creeping northward, toward Luckenwalde—and the bivouac area of the Nineteenth Armored. Now the rounds were falling among the sheds and cottages at the fringe of the little town, and Ballard ordered his pickets to back up, out of harm's way.

"Do you want me to start shooting back?" asked Diaz, getting ready to head back to his batteries, which were posted in several fields north of town.

Ballard, who had been unable to get through to Third Army HQ, shook his head. "You said they're shooting a thousand guns at us? I don't think they'd even notice your fifteen barrels shooting back. No, we're going to have to skedaddle out of here."

In fifteen minutes CCA was on the move, all the men riding in trucks, jeeps, and half-tracks, or on top of the tanks. They pulled out slowly, but within a few minutes after their departure the whole center of Luckenwalde was under fire. From a nearby hilltop Ballard watched the buildings that had been his HQ and mess hall for the last week get blasted into kindling.

"It's like they're herding us away, but not trying to kill us," he told Wakefield, when they finally established a radio connection.

"Well, hell. Stay out in front of the barrage, but try to keep an eye on 'em," the division CO replied. "We've lost two of our three roads into Berlin. The only one left is the autobahn, and you can bet your ass we're going to fight for it if they get that far."

The formation withdrew to the north throughout the night, and the barrage chased after them. No one was killed, but the forward progress of the Russian shelling was inexorable, and frustrating. By dawn, Ballard's HQ company was coming up on one of the lakes of Potsdam. He could see the long bridge of the autobahn before him, stretching across the placid water, and he knew they would have to be prepared to fight.

He was just about to order his men into deployments when he heard a massive explosion behind him. Ballard whirled, worried that the Russian attack had gotten behind him. There was no sign of anything, except a cloud of smoke drifting across the water. Only when that smoke started to clear did he realize the stark truth:

The autobahn bridge was gone.

25 MARCH 1945

SHAEF, REIMS, FRANCE, 0437 HOURS GMT

"We don't have a single road into Berlin, is that right?" the Supreme Commander asked tiredly, rubbing his forehead. He had not been to bed, even as the dispatches from Berlin had slowed to a trickle through the long, dark night. But neither had there been any news that substantially changed the situation.

"I'm afraid not, General," said Beetle Smith. "The Reds overran Highway One-Thirty-Five with Zhukov's attack. Their paratroops grabbed Highway Twenty-Four, and they're fortifying like crazy, until the ground troops get up."

"And the autobahn was destroyed by goddamn communist saboteurs?" Ike demanded, already knowing the answer.

"Well, the long bridge is gone, yes sir. And with Konev's men moving up from the south, it will be impossible for us to rebuild it in the foreseeable future."

"So General Patton and Third Army—not to mention all the airborne troops, and a million German civilians—are surrounded by the Red Army. Cut off. Trapped." He spat each painful word, and they were as harsh on his ears as they were on his tongue. Smith didn't answer, and Ike drew a breath and continued.

"What we do have are airfields—at least a dozen landing strips within the ring, right?"

"Including Tempelhof and Gatow, sir, a couple of large airports."

"Then that is our supply line. We're going to feed those soldiers and civilians, and arm and resupply our boys, by air. At least until we see how this thing sorts out. Get me all the transport commands—I don't care who you have to wake up. Better get ahold of Harris and the rest of the bomber generals, too. Before this thing is over, we might be using B-17s to haul grain."

"Right away, General. Harris is already here, and the rest will be landing at Reims by dawn."

General Eisenhower looked at the map, then turned his eyes to the sky that was still dark outside of his office window. It seemed that this war had changed a great deal since the sun had gone down the night before.

He could only wonder what the new day would bring.

27 MARCH 1945

POTSDAM, GERMANY, 0935 HOURS GMT

There were relatively few intact buildings in the city center, and that was a good argument for holding the truce meeting there—low risk of ambush. A Russian and an American Third Army crew had prepared the area overnight; there were white flags, a conference table, coffee service, the basics. Armed troops bristled along the edges like porcupine quills as the principals arrived: Zhukov and Konev from the Soviet side, along with two aides and a translator; Rommel and Patton from the SHAEF side with the same. Sanger felt lucky to have wangled a spot—but as the cars pulled out into no-man's-land he wondered if he had outsmarted himself. It was mighty lonely and exposed out there.

There was a cease-fire in place; now they needed to make it official. The business of modern siegecraft now included the business of establishing a secure telephone link between the military headquarters of the opposing forces, making sure that it was monitored twenty-four hours a day, ensuring that minor incidents didn't boil up into major ones, agreeing on protocols, even planning future meetings. Of course, most of the future meetings wouldn't involve nearly so many stars.

The body language among the generals was very interesting. Zhukov and Patton were somewhat alike, as were Konev and Rommel. The resemblances were not close, but they were there. Zhukov and Patton were men who might have fought on the same side, had things worked out differently—though Patton was clear and unambiguous in his hatred of the Soviets. And Rommel was still an enemy even after changing sides, though an enemy who had never fought a Russian before.

The men got down to work.

PENTAGON, WASHINGTON, D.C., 1405 HOURS GMT

General Groves looked up as the secretary of war came through the door.

"Yes, Mr. Secretary?"

"You've heard the details about Berlin?"

"Yes, sir." Nobody in the Pentagon had been talking about anything else for the last four days. "Patton is surrounded, but we're keeping Third Army supplied by air. So far as it stands, we and the Russkis are not yet in a shooting war. Is that about it?"

"The high points, yes," said Secretary Stimson, dryly. "I've just been to see the president."

Groves raised his eyebrows, not because it was unusual for the secretary of war to visit his chief executive, but because the clear implication seemed to be that this meeting had something to do with him. Or at least, with his gadget.

"I've got the preliminary crews out on Tinian," Groves said, referring to one of the Pacific islands, captured last year, that provided a bombing base for B-29s within range of the Japanese homeland. "But I'm guessing you'll be putting that operation on hold."

Stimson shook his head. "Not for sure, yet. Keep your boys at it, out in the Pacific. But we're going to need a contingency plan—bases, security personnel, a new scheme of operations—in case there's a change in the plan."

"A change," Groves said. "A big change, I take it?"

"The president doesn't know for sure. But depending on the actions of that old crook in the Kremlin, there's a chance that we'll need your gadget in Europe."

28 MARCH 1945

LONDON, ENGLAND, 2038 HOURS GMT

Kim Philby did not like odd feelings; it was too often the case that an odd feeling was the subconscious mind's early-stage detection of proto-clues. Yet ever since he had begun his probe of the secret project code-named Tube Alloys there was a growing sense that something was not quite right.

He did not ignore his feeling. He paid careful attention to individuals and cars on the street, looking for anyone unfamiliar to him who showed up more often than chance would allow. He made some random variations in his routine to see who, if anyone, would shift along with him. Nothing. That meant little, of course. It was easy to detect one or two people spying on you, but a large enough team could rotate members in and out so as to blend seamlessly into the urban environment.

He could not stop his work; he continued his methodical inquiry. However, he made sure that his passport and travel documents were easily accessible at all times, that he had sufficient liquidity for a rapid getaway, that his multiple preplanned escape routes were all still there. If he needed to, he could jump with a rapidity that would surprise even experienced professionals. He would not be brought easily to bay.

He finished his curry, sitting at a table facing the restaurant door, patted his mouth with his napkin, left money for bill and tip, took coat and umbrella from the stand, and walked out, tipping his hat to the lovely sari-clad hostess, wife of the proprietor.

It was the night for the park-bench drop, and the Lisson Grove lamppost had told him to expect a delivery there. He picked up an evening paper, and sat down to read for a good ten minutes before slipping his hand underneath to pull forth the waiting envelope. The reading time had given him ample opportunity to scan the area around him. Anyone could loiter unobtrusively for a minute or two; it was nearly impossible to stand around for ten minutes without being noticed. As far as Philby could see, there were no observers.

Another ten minutes of reading, and then he folded the paper neatly, envelope tucked invisibly inside, placed the paper underneath his arm, and sauntered back to his flat. At his desk, he opened the envelope and took out a sheaf of documents. It was the personnel information he'd been waiting for.

Fascinating. There were nearly thirty-five scientists on the list. While there were experts in gaseous diffusion, inorganic chemistry, and metallurgy, the most common specialty was nuclear physics. Even more fascinating, all thirty-five had vanished from Great Britain for unspecified destinations in America. No forwarding addresses in the States; any mail was to be forwarded through the Division of Tube Alloys.

Now, why would the States need thirty-five British scientists, mostly nuclear physicists? As to that, Kim Philby was fairly sure he had the answer without the need for further research. He was a man of many interests, widely read and happily curious. Not for him the artificial distinction between men of science and men of arts and letters. No, to be a man of the twentieth century required appreciation of both worlds, and to be a communist required an understanding of the new tools and technologies with which the proletariat revolution would be built.

One of those tools would be the atom. As swords could be pounded into sickles, the atom had potential both for peace and for war. Tube Alloys, then, was the British portion of what must be a joint Anglo-American quest for the ultimate weapon: the atomic bomb.

Yes, this was the answer to Chairman Stalin's question. This was the ace up FDR's sleeve. This was how the Western Allies expected to keep Berlin. Of course, Philby could expect a host of follow-on questions, but frankly, he could predict a number of them himself. He would write his report, then go to work on answering the questions he knew perfectly well he would be asked.

31 MARCH 1945

THE KREMLIN, MOSCOW, USSR, 1200 HOURS GMT
There was no samovar in evidence this time, Hartnell Stone noted. There was no gift for the president, no exchange of jokes or inquiries about health. This was purely business. Josef Stalin sat behind his desk and waited, silent as a stone, for the American ambassador and the Presidential envoy to sit down.

"Good afternoon, Chairman Stalin," Averrell Harriman finally said.

Stalin did not respond.

After a pause, Harriman handed over an envelope. "I bring you a formal protest from the government of the United States of America. Your troops have surrounded units of the United States Army and are interfering with our legitimate operations. We ask and require that these troops be removed immediately."

Stalin looked at the envelope on his desk, then back at the ambassador. Finally, he spoke. "The People's Army of the Union of the Soviet Socialist Republics has moved into territory of the criminal Nazi regime, a mutual declared enemy of both the Soviet Union and the United States of America, in accordance with the laws and customs of war, and in accordance with international agreements and treaties made with the United States in Casablanca and in Teheran. We have every right to be where we are. Your protest is noted, and it is rejected."

Hartnell studied the Soviet dictator's face. It was quite a contrast from their previous meeting. Stalin had previously appeared open and friendly, though with an inner core of steel. The man before him now was as stolid and unemotional as any cliché Russian—even if he was Georgian, not that Stone had ever met another Georgian to know what they were like.

He looked at Harriman. Interestingly enough, Harriman, who could also be friendly and open in his manner, was just as stoic and rigid in his own demeanor—two mechanical men repeating tape-recorded comments to one another.

Stalin continued to speak. "The State Defense Council of the Union of Soviet Socialist Republics now has a message for the United States of America. In light of previous agreements with the United States, and in light of recent discoveries in Poland, we have recognized a new German government as the legitimate postwar representatives of the German people. This provisional structure, the German People's Republic, has selected as its premier

Walter Ulbricht, and as its capital, the city of Berlin. This new government has dedicated itself to the goal of rooting out German criminality and aggression at all levels."

Stalin looked severely at Harriman and Stone. "We are aware that another provisional government has been declared, but it has no inherent legitimacy. Until full and free elections can be held, the German People's Republic will be the legitimate government in the portion of Germany now occupied by the Soviet Army. Accordingly, all foreign troops must vacate the city at once. The Soviet Army will provide guarantees of safe conduct for the withdrawal of forces."

Harriman stood up. "The United States of America has received your message, and I am confident that I can speak for the president when I say that this message is rejected utterly and in its entirety. Before I can speak further on this matter, I will have to withdraw for consultations with my government."

Stalin remained seated. "You may consult with your government, Ambassador Harriman. In the meantime, the status quo in Berlin and eastern Germany shall remain, in the absence of hostile or aggressive moves by your forces."

"Or yours, Chairman Stalin."

"That goes without saying. The Soviet Army will not commit provocative behavior. We do not wish war, Ambassador Harriman, but we will not allow our rights and interests to be trampled upon."

"Nor will we. Thank you for your time today, Chairman Stalin."

"Good day, Ambassador Harriman."

Excerpt from War's Final Fury,
by Professor Jared Gruenwald

The Siege of Berlin, as it came to be known, was a strange evolution in international relations, following as it did the five and a half years of near-total war that had torn apart the continent of Europe. The initial attack, a crushing blow delivered only to the German elements of the coalition force, was a deft stroke. To be sure, there were other casualties as the Soviet jaws closed around the city—several hundred American soldiers lost their lives in the short-lived defense of Berlin's lifelines, and the Red Army suffered at least comparable losses. But none of the clashes resulted in the kind of pitched and bloody battle that begins a war.

Once the ring had been closed, Marshal Zhukov—and Chairman Stalin, of course—was content to play a waiting game. He reinforced his encircling troops with tanks and infantry, and an almost incomprehensible massing of artillery. To the west of Berlin his troops established a line some thirty or forty kilometers wide, with entrenchments facing inward, toward the city, and outward, challenging the combined forces of American, British, and even a few French divisions, all drawn up to face the encircled city.

But for nearly thirteen weeks, nobody moved, nobody attacked. Sometimes it seemed as if nobody even dared to breathe.

There is little doubt that the Soviet juggernaut could have battled their way through the defenses established by Patton and his subordinate forces, should they have been commanded to proceed. After all, the numbers alone would have indicated such an outcome.

The defending forces included the combat elements of some fifteen divisions of Third Army (four of them armored divisions), as well as three airborne divisions (two American and one British), and the remains of the three divisions of the DDR army (one, Panzer Lehr, an armored division). Patton had overall command of the encircled forces, all of whom were veteran troops with good skills and plenty of equipment. Circumstances on the ground dictating administrative matters, the entire force was called the Army of Berlin, and numbered some 200,000 combat troops.

A brief note about command: Although Rommel held the superior rank, Patton was the actual commander. Most of the available forces were from Third Army, the supplies and reinforcements were all American, and Patton was an American rather than a defeated former foe. Nevertheless, face-saving had to be preserved. Patton was officially named SHAEF Commander in Berlin, and Rommel was Commander of the Army of Berlin, a shadow force. This role gave him the right to be consulted and the right to make suggestions. In a way, he was in the position of the Italian Commando Supremo who had been the titular head of the Afrika Korps. The difference was that while Rommel had little official power, he had the power that came from his knowledge and experience. When he spoke, others listened.

Facing this embattled force, however, were no less than two Red Army fronts—each the equivalent of a Western army group including some three armies in its order of battle. More than a million Soviet soldiers, with nearly three thousand tanks and a similar number of artillery pieces, were poised to commence the attack at a word from Moscow. More Soviet units—two additional fronts in Germany alone—were arrayed to face the major presence of Eisenhower's army groups. Here too, the Russians possessed clear superiority in tanks, guns, and men.

As every passing day seemed to bring additional reinforcements into the line, Stalin for these months of the siege remained content to allow his advantage to grow. In the meantime, diplomacy and brinksmanship came into play on a grand scale. And the Chairman of the Soviet Union became increasingly frustrated, and puzzled, as President Roosevelt seemed utterly unwilling to back down—even in the face of such obvious Russian superiority.

There was one area of military might in which the Soviets could not match the Western Allies, however, and that was in the air. The numbers of aircraft available to each side were approximately equal, with a small advantage going to Stalin. Qualitatively, however, the clear advantage fell to the Americans and their allies. The Soviets had no fighter capable of matching the P-51 Mustang in speed, maneuverability, or range; and by now the Mustang was the predominant fighter in the air forces of the Western Allies. The British continued to rely on their legendary, albeit updated, Spitfires, of course, and these, too, were superior to any of the Russian fighters.

There were even a few units of the reconstituted Luftwaffe available for the defense of Berlin. By the beginning of summer there were some one hundred Me-262 jet fighters in service, with more coming on line— including full squadrons turned over to the US Army Air Force and the RAF—as the months progressed. (None of these non-German units, however, had entered combat by July.)

Undoubtedly, it was this superiority in tactical air forces that allowed Eisenhower, with the blessings of Roosevelt and Churchill, to maintain the audacious program of supply and civilian evacuation that became known as the Berlin Airlift.

The first supply runs, escorted by some four fighters for every individual transport aircraft, were made within forty-eight hours of the surrounding of the city. As the Red Air Force allowed these missions to proceed, they were expanded until a veritable bridge of Dakota transports, enhanced by British and American heavy bombers pressed into emergency service, maintained a connection between the city and the democratic powers to the west.

The focal point for the airlift was the great hub of Tempelhof airport, of course, but there were many small fields around the periphery of the city, and none of them was overlooked in the vigorous efforts to resupply. For the first ten days, all efforts were directed toward bringing food and ammunition into the surrounded city. When it became clear that the Soviets would allow the planes to fly with only minimal interference, Patton—at Rommel's suggestion, it is reported—began to use the return flights to ferry noncombatants out of the city. In this manner, nearly a quarter of a million people were carried westward, out of the danger zone, during those three months of 1945.

It was a strange kind of stasis, unlike anything the world had ever seen before. Each of the great armies massed in central Europe possessed firepower and mobility far exceeding anything ever attained in the history of military endeavor. They were not active enemies, but the trust of their earlier alliance had been shattered by the Soviet betrayal of Summer 1944.

Indeed, even as matters in Germany were held at a stalemate, Soviet troops were securing their hold in a host of countries, including Norway, Poland, Bulgaria, Greece, Hungary, and Rumania. Governments of Communist sympathizers were established, often with the dubious validation of rigged, single-candidate "elections." And as Stalin tightened his hold on these formerly independent nations, it followed with perfect logic that he would expect to gain control of Germany—or at least the eastern portion of the country, including Berlin—before much more time could pass.

On this point, and with commendable firmness, both President Roosevelt and Prime Minister Churchill stood adamant. Emboldened, undoubtedly, by the knowledge—or the hope, at least—that the top-secret Manhattan Project was nearing fruition, the American president found the fortitude to stand up to Stalin's bluster, and for a long time the future of the siege seemed to be very much a matter of conjecture and doubt.

OPERATION
FAT MAN

30 JUNE – 12 JULY 1945

In recent years a new possibility—nuclear energy—has been discovered. Theoretical calculations show that, if a contemporary bomb can for example destroy a whole city block, an atomic bomb, even of small dimensions, if it can be realized, can easily annihilate a great capital city having a few million inhabitants.

—Russian physicist Peter Kapitza
October 1940

30 JUNE 1945

BERLIN, GERMANY, 0659 HOURS GMT

Carl-Heinz Clausen pressed his face to the window of the Dakota aircraft, shifted awkwardly in his seat—his feet were jammed into a tiny space between crates of canned hams—and grinned like a delighted schoolboy as the panorama of the great capital came into view. It was his first airplane flight, and one of the most thrilling experiences of his life.

He didn't know if the field marshal had pulled strings to get him one of the precious seats on this transport. After all, a hundred kilos of Carl-Heinz Clausen on the plane meant a hundred kilos of ham, or dried eggs, or flour, or any of dozens of other precious commodities that were not coming in to the besieged city on this flight. And *that* meant, of course, that he would have to work hard to make his presence in Berlin worthwhile.

But then, hard work was neither new nor unpleasant to him. Indeed, he relished the wholeness of his flesh again, the return of his strength, the capacity to make himself useful. He suspected that many of the prisoners who had been alive when the Americans had liberated Buchenwald would never again return to health—either physically, or mentally. He counted himself among the lucky ones, probably because he had been in there only a short time. Already the memories were starting to fade; instead, he could happily picture his daughters bouncing on his knees at home, or the walks he had taken through the orchard with Yetta during his convalescence. He could have stayed there, at home, for the rest of his life, and been a happy man—except for one thing:

He knew that the Desert Fox was still at war. So, as soon as he had felt whole again, he had fussed and complained, written letters, even made expensive phone calls to the new provisional government that was taking shape in Frankfurt. Who or what had taken those queries he didn't know, but three days ago the package had come in the mail: orders, and a plane ticket. He had taken off from Frankfurt before dawn, and now, in this dazzling summer morning, he was coming down in Berlin.

Already the tarmac at Tempelhof was rising to meet him. He studied the soldiers on the ground. They had looked like ants a few minutes ago; now they were recognizable as men, mostly in American uniforms, though he spotted several Wehrmacht tunics among them. There were US Army trucks, hundreds of them, all over the place, and at least two dozen transports like this big C-47 parked around the edges of the runways.

The Dakota touched down with a startling bump, then rolled for a long time before inching to a halt. Carl-Heinz followed a few other passengers, all American military, but there was a hold-up at the door of the plane. He heard some of the Yanks talking—"Do you know who *that* is?" "Really?" "No shit?"—before they moved on and cleared the steps. He had started to learn a little English while in the camp and in the hospital.

When he saw who had come to meet him, Carl-Heinz Clausen suddenly found himself too choked up to speak.

"You look good, my friend," said Rommel, clasping his former driver in a bear hug as the man tried awkwardly to salute. "And I am glad to see you!"

"B-But sir! Surely you have more important things to do than to meet a mere sergeant coming in on an early flight?"

The field marshal chuckled at the man's discomfiture. "Ach, we are in a siege here, Carl-Heinz. That doesn't keep a general busy the way a mobile battle does. Plus the enemy is not now, nor has he been for three months, attacking. And in any event, there are other important things to do at Tempelhof airport. Give me a few minutes, and I will think of some. Here, can I help you with that?" The field marshal indicated the small duffel that Carl-Heinz had slung over his shoulder—all the luggage he had dared to bring on the precious flight.

"No, sir! Thank you sir, but I can manage."

"How's the gut?"

"Seems to be good as new, sir. I can put away a plate of sauerkraut and schnitzel and ask for seconds. Don't have all my old weight back, but for this flight maybe that is a good thing."

Rommel grew serious, looking back at the C-47, which was already being unloaded by American soldiers—black men, Carl-Heinz observed with some interest. He had never seen a negro in the flesh before the Americans had come, and they were still unusual enough that he noticed. He had become particular friends with a hospital orderly, a black man from Alabama, who shared his talent and enthusiasm for creating mechanical devices. Between them, they had gone through the ward making self-adjusting trays for soldiers in traction, wheelchair seat lifts to allow patients to get themselves in and out of their own chairs, and adjustable crutches to ease arm strain.

Nearby, a file of passengers—German women and children, for the most part—formed a queue preparatory to boarding for the return flight. In the time since the plane had landed, at least five more aircraft had come in, including a big four-engine transport that was taxiing up nearby. More planes were circling the airport, with several lined up in the sky, approaching the runway in an aerial queue.

"We don't refuel them in Berlin, of course, because all the petrol would have to be airlifted in," the field marshal continued, speaking with pride.

"Instead, they carry enough for both legs. We get the cargo unloaded, the passengers on, and the plane takes off again. On a nice, clear day like this, we have them landing more than one a minute."

"It is a remarkable feat," the sergeant agreed. He had already thought of at least three technical improvements, but decided they would wait—at least a day or so. The field marshal's area had to be inspected first. Goodness knows what sort of mess he would find there.

"But come," Rommel said. "I have a car waiting. And believe it or not, we do have some work to do."

Wolfgang Müller looked up from his desk as the field marshal walked into the cluttered office. The supply officer was about to voice his vexation—the food shipments were still barely adequate, and he couldn't even *think* about the medical supplies—when he recognized the man behind the Desert Fox.

"Carl Heinz!" The colonel bounced up immediately, coming around the desk. He pumped the blushing sergeant's hand. "*Now* things will start getting done around here!"

"Thank you, Oberst Müller. It is good to see you! I understand, sir, that you were the one who found me in that . . . place?" He remembered nothing after the fever began.

"You are assigned to the headquarters staff, of course?" Müller asked Clausen, though he arched his eyebrows to look at Rommel.

"Of course," replied the field marshal. "In fact, for now you can go to the motor pool and get us a car. We have a meeting in thirty minutes." He smiled at Carl-Heinz. "How would you like to see the inside of the Reichstag?"

Colonel Reid Sanger had his new office in the great marbled halls of the building that had once been the center of power in the Third Reich and was now the headquarters for the Army of Berlin. He was reviewing the morning's dispatches from SHAEF, followed by the intelligence assessments from the front line units—those Third Army formations that were arrayed around the fringes of Berlin, facing off against the massed armies of the Soviet First Belorussian and First Ukranian fronts.

Through complex political face-saving arrangements, Patton was the actual commander of all SHAEF forces in Berlin, while Rommel, senior in rank, held a more advisory role as commander of the Army of Berlin. The arrangement worked well, because both men kept any arguments in private and presented a united front in public, and because Rommel understood the practical reality that Patton owned the vast majority of forces and the Americans controlled the supply line.

As liaison officer, Sanger was now the daily point of contact between Rommel's German Republican Army and all the other SHAEF forces in Berlin.

In his spare time, he had another function—serving as jailer for one special prisoner of war who was being held in what was once the führer's bunker in the Reichs Chancellery building.

The Reichs Chancellery was serving as administrative headquarters for the airlift operation and for city management, both staff-intensive operations. The two underground German military headquarters—Maybach I and Maybach II—that had housed OKW and OKH, were also being used as staff headquarters, communications centers because of their advanced communications technologies, and as backup command centers in case the battle grew hot again.

Sanger heard the distinctive squeak of Patton's voice in the hall—the two men had their offices quite close together—and it was time to go. The American colonel left his office, saw the Desert Fox coming, then smiled broadly as he saw the loyal German driver just beyond. Carl-Heinz was being greeted by everyone on the HQ staff, and was clearly embarrassed by the attention, so Sanger fell in behind the field marshal and strode into the briefing room.

The map on the wall depicted the same situation it had portrayed, with virtually no change, since the end of March. The Americans held the German capital, its suburbs, including Tempelhof, another major airport at Gatow, and several smaller landing strips. A small prong extended from the southwestern quadrant, where the Nineteenth Armored Division was holding the adjacent city of Potsdam, connecting to Berlin by a neck of land between two broad lakes. The Russians had the whole mess of them surrounded, with perhaps a mile-wide strip of unoccupied territory between them. In several locations, notably at Potsdam, and Spandau in the west, the Soviet positions thrust aggressively close, like hammerheads pointed into the heart of the great city.

General Patton came in and everyone stood at attention until he took his place at the front of the room. "Let's get started," said the CO of Third Army and SHAEF commander in Berlin.

General Zebediah Cook, Third Army's chief of intelligence, took over. "The airlift went well for the last twenty-four hours. No accidents, no weather delays. That means, of course, that we are bringing in as much food as we are eating. As well as a few little odds and ends—another eight thousand pounds of petrol, and three hundred rounds for the 155s."

"What does that bring us, for capacity on the big guns?" asked Patton. The 155s were the largest guns in the Third Army artillery section. The shell and powder for each shot weighed more than a hundred pounds; and if the Russians attacked, these guns would see nearly constant action.

"We could sustain intensive fire with all batteries for something like one day plus a couple of hours," Cook replied, after double-checking one of his sheets. His aide, Sanger's old nemesis Keegan, was serving as keeper of the files. Better yet, he was still only a major, which gave Sanger quite a bit of satisfaction. "After that, we'll be throwing the crockery at them."

Nobody laughed.

"What of the front line?" Patton interjected. "Another quiet night?"

General Cook nodded at General Wakefield. "Henry—you had something on that?"

The stocky general nodded, and pushed himself to his feet. "Probe in the Potsdam front last night. Good-sized commie patrol, ran into our pickets. Shots fired; ours and theirs. None of ours got hit; heard groans on their side. Found some blood when we checked it out this morning. Looks like the Reds took a few hits."

Patton grimaced, and gestured to the map. "I know you're sticking out like a sore thumb down there, Henry, but we need you to stay in position. If we fall back from Potsdam, they could snatch Gatow airport with one quick thrust— and that would cut our supply route by forty percent!"

"Got it. And so do my boys. They're dug in pretty damned well."

"Ah yes, not like those heady days of mobile operations, is it?" asked the army commander rhetorically—and a little wistfully, Sanger thought, as he turned his attention to the supply situation.

It was the middle of the afternoon by the time Henry Wakefield's jeep pulled up to the headquarters of his Combat Command A, in Potsdam. Ballard had set up his post in a sturdy building of concrete and steel that had once been a slaughterhouse. Now it made for a solid pillbox, with a ring of small windows on the second floor providing a good view in all directions.

"Any more trouble today?" the general asked Frank Ballard, finding the colonel at his desk—a long table that had once been used for dismembering pigs.

"We saw a few of their boys poking around in no man's land. Didn't shoot, 'cuz they didn't get too close. But I don't like it general. They've got us hemmed in tight, with water on two sides."

"The water guards your flanks," Wakefield grunted. "And Patton needs us here—this is one of the key places on the whole perimeter."

"We'll stay put," Ballard replied with a sigh. He saw Captain Smiggs enter the room, and remembered to add: "Say—do you have anything for the mail sack? Smiggy's going to run the letters out to the airport, get the bag onto an evening flight."

Wakefield shook his head. "Thanks for asking."

Captain Smiggs had a driver, but he preferred to be at the wheel himself. He guided the jeep down the Potsdamer Strasse, glad that the engineers had finally bulldozed the last of the debris out of the way. Berlin had been plastered pretty well by the Allied bomber campaign, and many neighborhoods had been reduced to rubble. Surprisingly enough, other, large parts of the city looked relatively untouched by the war.

So far, at least.

There were times when Smiggs thought that these German bastards were getting off too easy. He remembered Buchenwald—he would remember it, vividly, until the day he died—and he couldn't forget that these were the people, this was the society, that had allowed that to happen. Maybe they *should* let the Russians have them. He knew he wasn't the only man who felt that way.

But he still had a job to do. He turned at Schoneberg, made his way through the MP checkpoints as he approached Tempelhof. Weaving his jeep back and forth through traffic, he maneuvered around a long line of trucks, the big Dodges inching forward to collect precious supplies. There was a big gate at the far end of the line where the trucks rumbled through, carrying their cargo to various places in the city.

Smiggs made his way to the mail terminal. Here he handed over his sack to the busy clerk, and went back outside. The summer night was warm and humid. He knew that he should probably get back to CCA right away, but he couldn't make himself hurry, not on a night like this.

Instead, he stood at the fence around the tarmac, watching the sky as, one by one, the big transports took off. They flew with running lights, and he followed the diminishing brightness of the navigational beacons blinking, green and white, as the airplanes droned off toward the west.

FÜHRER BUNKER, BERLIN, GERMANY, 2302 HOURS GMT

The bunkers under the Reichs Chancellery had been prepared in 1944 for the führer and his closest associates so that they could survive and continue to command even when Berlin came under attack. The führer was in the bunker, but it was now being used as a prison, not as a command post. The military commander of Berlin was General George S. Patton, and his headquarters was in the Reichstag Building.

The construction had been a hurried project, never quite completed. The walls were slabs of gray concrete; they were damp and smelled of mildew. The ventilation system was noisy. The single prisoner did not complain, though it would not have mattered. These were officially executive quarters, and they were certainly secure enough.

Colonel Reid Sanger felt the best security was secrecy. The bunker's occupancy was secret; the area was kept low profile at all times. There were guards—all American troops, all troops who had seen the horrors of Buchenwald—at the entrances, all around the Chancellery Building, in fact. He had no fear of the relatively puny Himmler forcing his way out; he had somewhat greater fear of Nazi loyalists attempting to rescue their man.

Sanger had never thought of himself as suffering from claustrophobia, but the bunker was giving him a case of the fits. Forcing himself down the endless flights of concrete stairs became daily more difficult. He had difficulty breathing in the small conference room he used for his daily interrogation. But each day, accompanied by two guards, two secretaries, and a technician with a tape recorder, he interviewed Heinrich Himmler.

Himmler was willing enough to talk; the man had a boundless ego and his biggest fear seemed to be that someone else might get the credit for something he believed was his own. To hear him talk, he was the brains behind Hitler's throne, the source of inspiration, the builder that made ideas into cold, practical reality. He seemed to feed off Sanger's revulsion, laughing at him and mocking at him for his little-boy sensitivity at the pain and suffering. "No, Sanger, don't you understand? Women were even more important—after all, women breed, didn't you realize that? If Jews are to be eliminated, the women are the ones that *really* have to be exterminated. Without them, the male problem will take care of itself."

From time to time, Himmler would ask to have parts of the tape played back, to see if anything required amplification. When his memory failed him, he would recommend places Sanger might look for more details. It was as if Sanger were his biographer rather than his interrogator.

Sanger found himself spending more evenings at the O Club, with scotch his preferred choice of general anesthetic. As the siege grew longer, the club grew steadily better attended. Realizing that booze, however welcome, wasn't quite enough, he went up the chain. The first man he went to see was Henry Wakefield.

Wakefield listened passively, grunted, and said, "If it's a contest between you and Mr. Small-Balls—" Wakefield referred to Himmler by his nickname from the "Colonel Bogey March" lyric. "—he wins, because he don't care and you do. But if that's what you kept him for, you screwed up. It's his story you want, and it's his story you're getting. He may be proud of it, but you get to tell it. And you're on the winning side." He puffed on his cigar for a while, but that was all Sanger could get out of him.

Rommel started pacing up and down as Sanger laid out his problem. "At times like these I think perhaps I should have stayed as a barracks orderly at Buchenwald. A military operation, no matter how bleak the odds, is something I know how to handle. A moral issue of this dimension is completely beyond my capabilities. One moment, I think I should walk with you to the bunker and put a bullet through Himmler's head, and the next moment I think that is far too simple an answer for guilt that to some extent is shared by all of Germany. I do think you were right, back in the children's barracks that night, when you said that the story must be told and the record must be established. I don't believe that's enough, but I believe it's a necessary start. When this is over, we will need to have trials, I think—but we will also need something else, a truth court, whose job it will be to get everything on record."

"So much of the story, Field Marshal, is in the Soviet east now."

"Yes. Auschwitz. I've heard Buchenwald pales by comparison. I cannot imagine such a thing. I hate to admit it, but our Soviet enemies have justification. Great justification. We must stop them from taking over Germany, but at the same time, it may be that I must find a way to make a just peace with them, one that recognizes where the aggression began. Stalin is no saint, and the Soviet regime is not much improvement over the Nazis, but there is another of the problems that I must somehow attempt to solve."

"Not alone, Field Marshal. You have Americans and British, you have the Germans of the resistance, you have help."

Rommel stopped. "I'm not used to thinking in those terms. In the military sphere, my way of thinking is so unusual, I normally am all alone—I can give detailed orders, but the big picture resides in my head alone. I don't have the big picture here. Maybe I need to think and operate differently. I do know that this must be the final world war for Germany's sake. This nation will not survive another. I don't know if the world will survive another, especially if the technology increases as much as it has done from the first to the second."

"It looks like winning the peace will be as big a challenge as winning the war," Sanger said.

HQ, FIRST BELORUSSIAN FRONT, ORANIENBURG, GERMANY, 2359 HOURS GMT

Marshal Zhukov sat at his desk, the surface illuminated only by a single glaring lamp. His aide had just brought in the message, decoded less than ten minutes ago, and the marshal had sent the rest of his staff from the room. He would read this missive alone.

When the door was shut behind the last of his generals, he looked around, making sure there was no one lurking in the shadows with one last request, one more pressing need for the great soldier's time.

But he was alone. He drew a deep breath, and slowly slid the sheet of paper out of its envelope. He let it rest on the desk under the glare of the light, not touching it as he read.

FROM CHAIRMAN OF THE SUPREME SOVIET CONGRESS STALIN
TO MARSHAL ZHUKOV, COMMANDING OFFICER, FIRST
BELORUSSIAN FRONT
30 JUNE 1945

AMERICAN PRESIDENT REMAINS INTRACTABLE. NO MOVEMENT ON
MATTERS OF NEGOTIATION, RE: BERLIN. SUGGEST TIME APPROACHES FOR
OBJECT LESSON ON POWER OF RED ARMY. SUGGEST LESSON BE APPLIED

IN POTSDAM AREA, WITH GOAL GAIN CONTROL OF GATOW AIRPORT. PREPA-
RATIONS SHOULD COMMENCE AT ONCE. DO NOT—REPEAT, DO NOT—
INITIATE ACTIVITIES UNTIL SPECIFIC GO ORDERS ARE RECEIVED.

Zhukov looked around again—he was still alone—and snorted contemptuously. As usual, he had anticipated the chairman's demands. He had an
entire army, the Second Guards Tank Army, all but surrounding Potsdam. Just
last night he had ordered a probe of the American positions. These were, as
the marshal had expected, strong.

But they were also within easy range of more than one thousand Russian
guns, medium and heavy artillery batteries. The watery nature of the Potsdam
area created some difficulties for deployment, but his generals had worked out
a way to site all of these guns before the narrow isthmus held by one American
armored division.

Of course Zhukov would not act before the orders came from Moscow. He
was not, after all, a fool, nor was he suicidal. But he was sure of many things,
and one of them was this:

When orders came to attack, the Red Army would be ready.

1 JULY 1945

SKY ABOVE POTSDAM, GERMANY, 1034 HOURS GMT
Captain Frederick Douglass Robinson's head swiveled constantly as he scanned the airspace around his P-51. The Mustang's bubble canopy allowed for exceptional visibility, and the few clouds were of the white cotton ball variety, too small and insubstantial to conceal any serious threat.

Without breaking the rhythm of his scan, he grimaced at the cotton image—his grandfather and grandmother had worked themselves to death picking the stuff, and that legacy was a part of him, always lurking beneath the surface. His parents had made it out of Mississippi to Chicago, but how much better was that? His mother cleaned the houses of white women, and his father helped white men find comfortable seats on the Hiawatha Express train that ran up to Minneapolis and back.

Wouldn't they all be amazed if they could see him now? Even in the cockpit he sat ramrod straight, an unconscious effect of the self-discipline and pride that had brought him here.

Frederick Robinson—his squadmates invariably called him "Frederick"—had been an instant success at the Tuskegee school for fliers, a natural in the cockpit. His knack for leadership had made him squadron commander. And his keen eye and steady hand had, in the skies over Italy and Germany, made him an ace. He had earned the respect of officers, even white officers, with his competence and determination.

Most of his work had involved escorting American bombers into areas infested with enemy fighters. He had honed his eye on those flights, learned to spot the specks of dangerous attackers as they first came into view. He and his men would chase those attackers away, and—on a good day—send one or two of them flaming in. He took great pride in one fact: On all of those escort missions, they had never lost a single bomber.

But this was a different kind of war. For the last three months, he had been flying alongside the stream of transport aircraft that were Berlin's only lifeline. He had seen the Red fighters in great swarms, coming far closer to the transports than any German fighters had ever dared to approach Frederick Robinson's bombers. The orders from SHAEF to the American fighter pilots on these escort missions were clear: Do not start the shooting, but defend yourselves—and those precious transports—if the Russkis make the first move to attack.

So he had learned a whole new class of aircraft identification. He could spot the MiGs and the Yaks and the Laggs. And there seemed to be thousands of Ilyushins, the ubiquitous Sturmoviks that had been the scourge of the German army and the Luftwaffe for nearly four years. The older Ilyushins were slow, more like flying tanks than modern fighters. The newest Sturmovik, however, the IL-10, looked to have serious potential as an adversary to the Mustang. It was lighter and more maneuverable than any previous Soviet aircraft design, and even when the P-51s flew high-altitude cover—above twenty-five thousand feet—the Ilyushin 10s would be up there with them, Russian pilots glowering through the sky behind their oxygen masks.

Today Robinson and the three fellow pilots of his flight were at a lower altitude, right off the starboard wing of the transport stream. The Mustangs flew much faster than the big C-47s, of course, so the young captain and his three wingmen flew steadily past the Dakotas, overtaking the individual planes of the long column.

Overhead, to both sides, and underneath were Soviet fighters, often diving dangerously through the formation of transports, or coming up behind the American fighters in mock combat maneuvers. Robinson knew that there had in fact been a few accidents over the last months, a transport clipped by a diving MiG, and two or three instances of fighters colliding. There had been warning shots fired and tensions inflamed on each occasion, but quickly things had settled down again into the routine of the mainly bloodless siege.

Still, the Russians seemed exceptionally frisky today. The radio had been alive with warnings and curses all along the sky train. The four Tuskegee airmen had flown from a base in eastern France, and while they had not been close to a Soviet fighter today, Robinson's vigilance never relaxed, head always moving, eyes scanning.

Even so, it was his wingman, Cecil "Ceece" Hooper, who first spotted them.

"Red Star bogies, 'bout two 'clock low," he drawled, the sound of Alabama in the German sky.

Robinson saw the Russian fighters, a dozen or more of the IL-10s, flying parallel to the four Mustangs and climbing gradually. He checked the altimeter—it read 12,200 feet—and he reckoned the Soviets were two thousand feet below. They flew past a band of water, one of the wide lakes on the outskirts of Potsdam, and abruptly turned, still climbing, toward the sky train.

"Watch the bogies up there." One of the C-47 pilots put out the warning to his fellows.

"Got 'em spotted—bastards are cutting it close!" replied another.

Robinson clenched his teeth as he saw the Russian fighters wheel more tightly, spreading their formation as they arrowed through the line of Dakotas. They flew past the cockpits of two of the C-47s, one of which lurched crazily as the pilot flinched. The radio crackled loudly, indistinguishable shouts of outrage. The wobbly Dakota pulled back into line, but the captain could imagine the pilot's hands, clenched around the wheel to control the trembling, to manage the pulse of adrenalin.

On the far side of the sky train, the Russian planes banked around; it looked like they were going to come through again. Robinson looked over his shoulder. Ceece was watching him expectantly. The captain nodded, then used his throat mike to contact his two mates above and behind them.

"Time to earn our pay, fellows."

Immediately the four Mustangs growled through a coordinated turn. In pairs they dove beneath the train of C-47s, each wingman sticking to his leader. Smoothly they pulled up and leveled off, strung in a line now and directly between the Ilyushins and the defenseless transports.

The Russians roared in, spreading into pairs of their own. Four of the Sturmoviks converged on Frederick Douglass Robinson in the lead Mustang, but he held steady course. He turned to face them, a glare of challenge—I dare you!

At the last minute the Reds broke, two veering before him, two more taking the low road. At the same time the radio sparked, a single word in Cecil Hooper's surprised voice.

"Hey—"

Robinson felt the explosion even before he turned around to look. Two planes, an American and a Russian, tumbled wildly away from a smear of smoke and fire that lingered in the sky. Hooper was crashing, the plane engulfed in flames, no sign of a parachute. Fred Robinson cursed in disbelief, shock quickly replaced by fury.

"You sons of bitches!" He yanked on the stick, pulled up and around in the face of two more IL-10s. Both Soviet pilots twisted out of his way, probably shocked in their own right by the collision. Robinson didn't care; he pulled his nimble fighter around, and the nearest Russian maneuvered desperately to get out of the way.

Only then did the pilots see the Dakota. The window of the cockpit was right there, the pilot looking outward, eyes wide, mouth open in a soundless scream as the Ilyushin collided with the middle of the fuselage. Robinson's momentum pulled the Mustang down so he dove, trying to get underneath the crash.

The C-47 exploded, a massive fireball sending shock waves through the sky. One large piece, an engine, tumbled downward, right into Frederick Douglass Robinson's path. His last realization was that the falling engine still had a propeller attached.

FORWARD OBSERVATION POST, SECOND GUARDS TANK ARMY, POTSDAM, GERMANY, 1114 HOURS GMT

Colonel Krigoff had rushed outside when the first explosion had sounded. He watched, somewhere between thrilled and horrified, as squadrons of fighters roared into the smoking gap in the sky train. More planes fell, burning, and the American transports started to evade, many of them diving low.

Krigoff pressed his binoculars to his eyes, trying without success to follow the aerial melee. There were fighters shooting at each other all over the sky, as the battle seemed to be spreading quickly up and down the long column of aircraft. He heard more explosions, saw trails of black smoke as plane after plane burst into fire and plunged toward the ground.

After the first clash, he was bitterly disappointed to observe that the great majority of these doomed aircraft were Russian fighters. The Americans moved in with surprising speed, their nimble Mustangs driving the Soviets back. Still, the enemy was suffering too. Krigoff had counted at least ten of the transports destroyed, and the steady progress of the sky train was clearly broken.

"Colonel! Look out!" It was one of the lookouts—the man had the audacity to tug on Krigoff's arm.

He dropped his binoculars to rebuke the man, but he was instantly distracted by the view of a huge, four-engine transport plane, racing low across the ground—directly toward Krigoff! He dropped to his face, felt the air shudder as the big plane roared past, and lay there trembling.

"Get me front headquarters on the phone!" he snapped, realizing what must be done.

Instead, he got General Benko, CO of the Second Guards Tank Army. "What is it, Colonel Krigoff?" asked the general cautiously. "Can you see anything out there?"

"The Americans have started to attack!" Krigoff yelled. "Get Marshal Zhukov's headquarters! We must carry the alarm!"

"Are you sure? We tried to get a report, but all the phones are out. There is no word from front HQ."

"The phones are out?" This was the clincher, in Krigoff's mind. "Don't you see—it's saboteurs! Probably the damned Germans, took out our communications. I tell you, General, we have to strike back—now!"

Benko was no doubt mindful of his predecessor's fate. Still, he was hesitant to initiate dramatic action. "I think we need to wait for developments—"

"By then it will be too late!" shouted the colonel. "Our guns are sighted on the American positions—at least, give them a barrage!"

"Are you sure they are attacking?"

Krigoff wanted to tear his hair out. He looked around, counting at least a dozen pyres of black smoke rising into the air, just in this neighborhood of Potsdam. Even as he watched, a Sturmovik plummeted downward trailing a bright tail of fire. It splashed into the lake and vanished in a hiss of steam and spray.

"Yes—they are attacking everywhere I look! I tell you, General, I will not be held responsible for your hesitancy if you fail to act!"

Benko was silent for long moments. Finally, Krigoff heard him draw a breath, the sound rasping over the line. "Very well," said the general. "I will order my batteries to open fire."

CCA HQ BLOCKHOUSE, POTSDAM, GERMANY, 1200 HOURS GMT

"Everybody down!"

Frank Ballard didn't know who shouted the unnecessary command. All the officers and men in the blockhouse had ducked in unison as the sudden, shrieking wail of incoming Soviet shells screamed through the air. The explosions came from all around them, earthshaking impacts that rattled a radio off its shelf and brought a rain of plaster and debris falling from the old slaughterhouse's ceiling.

The next round of shells fell in the same pattern, and there was no mistaking the truth: CCA, and even the specific location of the HQ, were under direct attack. Ballard sprinted across the room as another rain of debris fell down. The signalman at the phone switchboard was under his table; sheepishly he crawled out when he saw his CO approaching.

"Get me General Wakefield—and tell him he'll want to patch through the Army HQ," Ballard shouted, over the din of continuing explosions. How many guns were firing at him, personally? There had to be at least a hundred!

"General?" he said, when the corporal handed him the receiver. "It looks like this is the real thing—the shit has hit the fan down here in Potsdam!"

SHAEF, REIMS, FRANCE, 1739 HOURS GMT

"General Marshall?" The Supreme Commander was on the telephone talking to his boss, their voices spanning an ocean.

"Yes, I have Secretary Stimson here with me," said the chief of staff of the U.S. Army. "What's going on over there?"

"Looks like the Russians have run out of patience. They've started an attack in the Potsdam area. We're taking heavy shelling, but Patton's men are holding their ground for now. There was an aerial battle too—they hit the sky train over Potsdam. We hit back, but not before we lost a dozen C-47s. By the end of the day, our fighters were getting control of the skies. We had a dozen escorts shot down—the flyboys claim they got a hundred Russkis, but you know how that goes."

"What about your line in Zhukov's HQ? Have you called the old SOB?"

"I've tried, General. But they've apparently cut off that connection—it seems to be a dead end. There's no way to get through to him. Dammit, I sure have a bad taste about our boys getting plastered like this. But there's no way to go toe to toe with them in an artillery duel. Can you authorize the release of the tactical air arm?"

"We're talking about that. You want to use air power to pound Zhukov's guns?"

"Yes." Ike was definite. "It's the only weapon we can put into play right now."

The Supreme Commander waited, hearing the soft buzz of conversation on the other end of the line.

"We'll get word to the president this morning. I think we can get you the air support, but we need to get his clearance. In the meantime, Patton will have to hold as best he can."

"Yes, sir, of course. But General?"

"What is it, Ike?"

"Listen, about that gadget you've been hinting about? If there's any truth to those rumors, I think we need it over here, right now. Looks like we are going to have to come up with some clout in the situation—you know Zhukov has enough tanks and guns to crush Berlin, if he sets his mind to it. So let's have that gadget sooner rather than later if it's humanly possible."

"I can't tell you for sure, but I can promise that I will express your thoughts to the president—I happen to agree with you, one hundred percent."

"Thanks, General. That's all for now."

"Keep in touch, Ike," said the chief of staff. A second later the connection was broken. Eisenhower lit another cigarette, stood up, and started to pace the circle around his office.

It's a wonder, he thought, that I haven't worn a rut into the goddamn floor.

US EMBASSY, MOSCOW, SOVIET UNION,
2234 HOURS GMT

"So, the chairman is not available for a meeting?"

Ambassador Harriman's voice was stiff, as cold as the ice of a Moscow winter, thought Hartnell Stone as he listened to his boss's side of the phone conversation with the Kremlin.

"Then I will speak to Foreign Minister Molotov. I see. You will leave messages for both men and for their assistants. Yes. Thank you. Good bye." He hung up the telephone. "Well, Hartnell, my lad, looks like no one's home right now."

"My god, don't they understand what's happening?"

"Probably not. I don't, not really. Do you?"

"It's a confusing mess."

"Oh. Then you *do* understand." Harriman laughed. "No, I'm not surprised at this. A little disheartened, but not surprised. As nearly as I can figure it, it goes like this. The battle starts. It's probably as a result of some dumb accident, but with a couple of hundred thousand trigger-happy maniacs on both sides, it doesn't take much for shooting to break out. They were having five or six minor incidents a day over in Berlin and were managing to keep the lid on. This time it doesn't work."

"Why not?"

"God only knows. Maybe the snafu spreads up the line. Maybe somebody's brother or cousin got killed and the relative is out for revenge. Maybe somebody sees a medal or a promotion to be had. Maybe it's just a string of coincidences. Won't be the first time. Or maybe it's not a coincidence. Maybe somebody's decided to take advantage of this one. But I still think it was an accidental start."

"Why?"

"We wouldn't have started it, not because we're necessarily so goody-goody, but because we don't have the strength to go on the offense. Not even Patton would think that. The Russians, on the other hand, do have the strength to start something, but my best guess is that they really don't want World War Three with us. At least not yet. When Stalin says that Russia has paid a much bigger price than we have in this war, he's right. Plus, if this were a deliberate, planned attack, it would look different. It would be more coordinated, probably on a wider front, backed by more troops, and probably with more noticeable preparation, not just a little local thing that spreads out.

"Now, exploiting an accident is not quite the same thing as planning a deliberate attack. If push comes to shove, they can claim we started it, and in the confusion and the fog, who knows? They might even be right—an accident could as easily happen on our side as on theirs. At least if they have to back down, or decide it's time to stop, they can use 'it was just a misunderstanding' as an excuse. So now we come back to the Kremlin. Stalin and Molotov get a call from me. Should they take the call or not? All right, Hartnell, explain it to me. What would you advise them if you were on the other team?"

Stone took a deep breath. "Yes, sir. Okay. The situation is, it's an accident, but they're exploiting it. They don't want World War Three, but they do want Berlin, and if they can get the upper hand and win a few more negotiating points, why not." He looked at Harriman for confirmation, but the American ambassador folded his hands across his chest and had on his best poker face. Stone wouldn't get a hint whether he was on or off the mark.

"So until this settles down and the smoke clears, there isn't anything he can gain by talking to us," Stone said. "His forces are clearly superior, but they still have to finish the job of taking Berlin. Afterward, he'll want to talk armistice and claim this whole thing was started by an American provocation, and he'll have some cockamamie piece of evidence to throw on the table. And as you say, it might even be the truth, though the claim's the same either way."

He thought for a minute, and then he nodded with understanding. "And then he's going to throw your own words back in your face." Harriman cocked an eyebrow at that. "Remember a few months ago, when you were telling him that the Teheran deal was off? He's going to grab the Teheran territory that you said he couldn't have, and a little bit more besides. Then he's going to tell you that he would have happily settled for the Teheran deal, except *you* were the one that threw it out, forcing him to this sad action."

Harriman nodded. "I think you've got it. Unless, of course," the ambassador added, "the president really is holding that ace up his sleeve he's been talking about. . . ."

2 JULY 1945

REICHSTAG BUILDING, BERLIN, GERMANY,
0544 HOURS GMT

Patton left strict orders that he be wakened immediately if there was any change in the situation, and went to bed after midnight, sleeping on a cot in an upstairs office of the huge building. No one disturbed him, but he still woke up before dawn. Taking only five minutes to shave and put on a clean shirt and slacks, he headed downstairs to the large conference room that had been turned into a command post for the Army of Berlin.

"They're still shelling the heck out of Nineteenth Armored, General," reported the major who had been supervising the dispatches through the early morning hours. "But there's been no movement, no firing, on any other sectors."

"Get me Henry Wakefield on the line. I need to know how his boys are holding up."

"Actually, sir, he's on his way to the HQ. Should be here within the next half-hour. He did tell me that they haven't given any ground, yet."

"Good." Patton concealed his worry with a hearty nod, then turned to look at the large map hanging on the wall. That provided no answers—and he had the damned thing memorized by now, anyway—so he stalked aimlessly around the room, looking over the shoulders of the three switchboard operators, going over the teletype reports from SHAEF. He was considerably relieved to see Hank Wakefield come through the door. The general looked hearty, if worried, and ambled over to the table where a large urn of coffee was percolating.

"They're bringing a shitstorm, Georgie," reported the CO of the Nineteenth Armored. "I don't think any American unit has ever come under this kind of artillery fire before. Bob Jackson had his boys dig in pretty well during the siege, so they're doing okay. But we've taken a lot of casualties, more than a hundred killed since the bastards started shooting. Can't we hit those guns with some bombers?"

"Ike has asked for clearance—I guess it has to go all the way to the president. But he's hoping to get use of the Nineteenth Air Force."

"Georgie, these are my boys," Wakefield said. The strain showed in the lines around his eyes as he fixed his gaze on his army commander. "I've had a lot of them since Normandy. I'm goddamned if I've got them all the way here just to make them sitting ducks for a bunch of fucking Russki guns." He looked at Patton, then said in a deceptively mild tone, "If you want to wait on some fucking chair warmers for permission, that's your business, but I thought Third Army took care of its own."

"Now listen here, you son of a bitch," Patton said, his own anger rising to the surface, "You know good and goddamn well that I am moving heaven and hell here. I have screamed at every fucking bastard I can get to take my phone call, and if I could reach my hand through the wires I'd have throttled five or six people by now. Got it? And if that ain't enough to suit you, hell, Henry, if Ike can't get us some air support, I'll climb into a goddamned transport and bomb the cocksucking Russian bastards myself! Does that fucking suit you?"

Wakefield nodded, pulled out a cigar, and lit it. "It's a start."

CCA HQ BLOCKHOUSE, POTSDAM, GERMANY, 0849 HOURS GMT

"That was General Wakefield." Ballard didn't try to soften the news; his men would realize the truth in any event. "No word yet on air support. But we can't afford to give ground. We're going to have to tough it out right where we are."

He didn't release the string of curses that rose in his throat, but it wasn't easy to meet the eyes of the men in his headquarters staff. They were down in what had been some kind of holding tank in the cellar of the slaughterhouse. Everyone was haggard, sweaty, and unshaven. The explosions of the enemy barrage were an unending background, sometimes near, other times right on top of them.

The building itself had been half demolished by the shelling of the last twenty-four hours. Ballard looked out periodically, and saw that this entire strip of Potsdam, where Nineteenth Armored had dug in, had been pounded severely.

As usual, CCA was the front line of the division, with CCB deployed in reserve. They were positioned along one side of a moderately wide city street, an avenue that extended from the wide Havel River on their left flank to a long lake, the Sacrower See, on the right. Over the months of the siege, the men had fortified positions in houses, down in cellars within stone and concrete buildings wherever possible. They had laid logs and timbers over their emplacements in anticipation of shelling, secured rear entrances and escape routes, scouted fields of fire, massed ammunition and supplies.

But nobody had expected anything like this. This was a version of hell, where steel and fire fell from the sky in a relentless rain, promising the threat of obliteration at any moment.

The door at the end of the long chamber opened, and Smiggy dropped down the steep iron steps, quickly pulling the hatch closed after him. His coat of dust looked dry and powdery, as compared to the oily film on the men who'd been cooped up in here for the last few hours.

"Any sign of troop movements?" Ballard asked.

Captain Smiggs shook his head. "Just the damned guns. They're coming from all along the southwest. I think most of the batteries are massed right in the middle of the city, on those open lawns by the resort hotels."

"All right—good work," Ballard said. "I'll go out in an hour."

"Hey, listen to that." Major Diaz, CO of the artillery battalion, held up a hand.

Ballard noticed it right away, the pounding of the guns abating, slowing to a sporadic blasting over the space of a minute or two.

"I see airplanes!" cried a PFC manning one of the watch stations around the upper rim of the HQ. "*Lots* of airplanes! They're our boys—attacking!"

Ballard was the first one up the ladder. He pushed his way through the hatch, out into the open air. Shell holes pocked the ground, and the high stone wall around the yard had been knocked down to half its height in a number of places. Rocks, bricks, timbers, and other debris—he stepped around a broken teapot, saw a cracked picture frame on the ground—were scattered everywhere, the litter of the long barrage.

In the sky, American fighter-bombers made a cloud as thick as the mosquitoes on a summer night, swarming down on the Soviet positions in wave after wave of devastating bombing runs. Other fighters battled through the air, dogfighting with the hundreds of Russian aircraft that were snarling into the fight. Now the sound of new explosions thundered through the air, vibrated in the ground . . .

But finally the explosives were falling on the other guys.

HQ, FIRST BELORUSSIAN FRONT, ORANIENBURG, GERMANY, 1344 HOURS GMT

"Do you mean to tell me that it was a plane crash that caused all this?" Marshal Zhukov's voice was low, but that only served to make the messenger— a two-star general from his communications section—more nervous.

"Yes, Comrade Marshal. An American fighter crashed, apparently as a result of a collision in the sky. It landed on our main exchange in the Potsdam area, knocking out not only our communications with the First Ukranian Front, but also our connection to the American SHAEF, in the west."

The marshal snorted, a sound of contempt. "And then this General . . . 'Benko' . . . of the Second Guards Tank Army decides to commence the attack?"

"That would seem to be the case, Comrade Marshal. There was a colonel of intelligence . . . a Colonel Krigoff . . . who was in an observation post, and reported signs of an American attack. Apparently he convinced the army CO that there was immediate danger."

"I remember this Krigoff," said Zhukov. "He has already cost me two generals. We will come back to him, but for now, tell me: What has been the American reaction to this sudden attack?"

"They have not withdrawn, and nor have they fired back. Perhaps they do not want to risk revealing their guns—we are facing a division here on the Potsdam isthmus, and even reinforced they won't have more than thirty or forty heavy artillery pieces. Benko opened up with something like a thousand guns, so the Americans might have realized that counterbattery fire would be futile."

"Sometimes *everything* is futile," breathed the great soldier under his breath.

"I beg the marshal's pardon?"

"Nothing. But tell me about the air battle."

"The American tactical bombers finally attacked this morning. We assume it took some time for their General Eisenhower to get authorization for the air strikes. Once they came in, they were furious—more than a thousand sorties in the first hour."

"Surely the Red Air Force intervened?"

"Of course, Comrade Marshal. Our own fighters flew heroic resistance, and as of this afternoon the air battle was still raging. We have lost many planes, also shot down many enemy aircraft."

"But in Potsdam, the Americans are sitting tight, eh? Then I think we should turn up the pressure a little bit. We will wait a day, perhaps, but then I shall have General Benko resume his bombardment after dark tomorrow, and move a few battalions of tanks forward by dawn We'll see how the Yankees like our T-34s."

"Yes, Comrade Marshal, at once!"

"Oh, and General?"

"Yes, sir?"

"Tell this Colonel Krigoff that I would like to see him."

LOS ALAMOS, NEW MEXICO, USA, 2232 HOURS GMT

Oppenheimer came into the lab, shaking his head in exasperation. The reaction was dramatic enough that many of the other men left their tables, microscopes, and Geiger counters to come over to the director.

"What is it?" asked James Conant, the young chemist who had been president of Harvard University at the start of the war.

"A call from Groves, of course. Excuse me, *General* Groves." The peevishness was not like the director, and served to further focus his men's attention on him.

"Well?" Conant pressed.

"They need the gadget in England, as soon as we can get it there. We aren't going to have time to do the Trinity test—the first test will be the first time it's used."

"That's ridiculous! You can't be serious! Impossible!" The objections, not surprisingly, came from all corners of the lab, enough of a hubbub that more people gathered in the hall outside the door.

"The shaped charges need more design, more testing!" protested Conant loudly. "We don't even know if we can make them work."

"They *have* to work," Oppenheimer said coolly. "It might be impossible— there are days when it seems this whole damned project is impossible! But we all joined this operation to help our country win the war. Now, by God, it looks like we have the chance to do just that."

3 JULY 1945

CCA, POTSDAM, GERMANY, 0550 HOURS GMT

It was after dawn before the final medical jeep pulled away, hauling the last of the wounded toward Third Army hospital. The dead, more than two hundred of them, had been claimed by the graves registration section. Ballard, for his part, had spent the last half of the night ensuring that the CCA positions that had been smashed during the barrage were patched together, reinforced if possible. Wakefield had sent up a company each of tank and infantry from CCB, and the colonel had integrated these into his defensive position.

That position had been in a relatively pastoral neighborhood, even after the Americans had moved in and made necessary defensive improvements, piling barricades, clearing fields of fire, and so forth. For three months they had stayed here among gardens, verdant trees, and clear reflecting pools. Following the barrage, the place had become a moonscape of rubble. None of the buildings were intact, though a few walls still stood, as well as many chimneys. Everything was coated with dust, and any standing water had been rendered into mud.

But those buildings, the shells of them that remained, had saved the lives of a lot of his men. If they had been in foxholes or trenches in the open, he couldn't imagine how many would have perished. As it was, two hundred killed out of four thousand was not terrible. Amazingly enough, only two tanks had been destroyed by the Soviet shelling, each by a direct hit. More than a score had broken treads or other damage, but by dawn feverishly working mechanics had repaired all of these.

Now, as Ballard made his way back to HQ, he looked at the brightening sky. During the previous day, the men of the Nineteenth Armored had cheered each successive wave of air strikes, thanking God and the flyboys for the respite from the shelling. He still couldn't quite believe that the guns had fallen silent like that, but it was not something he was inclined to question very much.

As the quiet continued through the long night, he found himself hoping that it had just been a crazy mistake, some fluke, not the start of another great war. It was a bad memory, certainly, and the reminders lay in the ruined landscape all around.

"Halt! Oh, sorry, Colonel." Ballard looked up to see one of the new guys, a green private from CCB, hunkered down in the rubble and pointing a rifle at him. Nervously the man turned his weapon away, while the colonel saw two of his comrades in the shadows nearby.

"No need to apologize—it's good to be alert."

He felt sorry for these fellows, knew they had just come over to Europe in time to get surrounded by the Russians. He told them to be careful, to keep their heads down, and to do what the veterans did.

Then he crossed his fingers, and suggested that they dig their foxholes a little deeper.

4 JULY 1945

HQ, FIRST BELORUSSIAN FRONT, ORANIENBURG, GERMANY, 0952 HOURS GMT

Marshal Zhukov seemed to be in a foul mood, an ugly enough mood that even his most loyal aides were afraid to go near him. Colonel Krigoff would have given anything to huddle with the aides, several rooms away from the great general, but he couldn't do that.

He, in fact, had been summoned to see the marshal in person.

He entered the office and saluted, waiting while the marshal finished a very leisurely read of some loose papers. Finally, Zhukov looked up, studied Krigoff's face for a minute, then allowed his gaze to slowly trail down the intelligence officer's body. Krigoff felt as though he was being measured for a coffin.

"Colonel Krigoff." The marshal sounded very tired, or very bored.

"Yes, Comrade Marshal Zhukov! Reporting as ordered, sir!"

"Do I understand that it was you who claimed the Americans were attacking, in the Potsdam sector three days ago?"

"Comrade Marshal, I can understand how my observations were misconstrued at army headquarters. Many airplanes were crashing in the area, and when I made this report, it was interpreted to mean that ... er ... I had observed enemy tanks in movement. I apologize for the error."

Krigoff didn't know if the NKVD was waiting outside the headquarters to take him away right now, or if Zhukov had some more imaginative punishment in mind. The colonel's knees felt weak, but he forced himself to stand straight and still. He was a dead man, he knew, awaiting only the means of his execution. For some reason, the knowledge left him strangely numb; he was surprised that his career had come to this, and still not sure how it had happened.

"It occurs to me that this might be an opportunity, a unique, and historical, opportunity," the marshal said slowly, pensively.

Of all the things Krigoff expected Zhukov to say, that one didn't even make the list. Still, he allowed himself to see a faint, wonderfully shimmering, thread of hope.

"I am afraid I do not understand, Comrade Marshal."

"It is not necessary for you to understand, Comrade Colonel. It is enough for you to know that, as of nightfall tonight, I shall order the bombardment to resume. The bombardment that was commenced because of your erroneous assertion."

"Yes, Comrade Marshal, of course." What did this mean?

"I have grown tired of this waiting game. We are in need of a resolution, and I am going to use you, Colonel Krigoff, to bring this about. We have resumed our bombardment in the night. This morning, the Americans will undoubtedly strike back with their tactical air forces. It so happens that our direct line of communications with SHAEF remains out—it will not be repaired, until I give the order.

"And when the American air forces come down on us again, I shall commence a general attack, around the entire perimeter of Berlin. We will not rest until every block, every building, every stone of that city is under our control. Do you understand?"

"Yes, Comrade Marshal!" Krigoff lied. How was he responsible for this?

"If the attack succeeds, and I believe it will, then there will be plenty of glory to go around. But if it fails . . ."

Suddenly the colonel of intelligence saw, with incredible clarity, the role he was to play.

"If it fails," Zhukov repeated, "then all the world shall know that the attack was only a little mistake.

"A mistake, Colonel Krigoff, made by *you*."

LOS ALAMOS, NEW MEXICO, USA, 2340 HOURS GMT

"Be careful with that!" General Groves snapped, as one of the men slipped on a stairway and almost dropped the toolbox he was carrying.

"Why don't you come outside, General?" said Robert Oppenheimer delicately. "I think we're just in the way, here." The director of the lab took the portly general by the arm and casually escorted him out of the hall and into the summer evening. The stars were brilliant, as they so often were atop this mesa, but neither of these men had any interest, tonight, in the view.

"I don't like this, sending it off without a test," Oppenheimer noted for approximately the two hundredth time.

"Me neither," Groves conceded. "But we don't have a—hey, watch that ramp! Dammit, you're going to roll it right onto its side!" Oppie trailed along, sighing in exasperation.

The general started toward the trucks, berating the forklift operator and everyone else who was in range. Sometimes a job could only get done right with direct supervision, and this seemed to be one of those times.

Finally, the components of the gadget were loaded into the three different trucks. One contained the plutonium core itself, the small lump of strange new metal that might—*might*—be compelled into a chain reaction by the right combination of pressures. The second truck contained a natural uranium tamper, a larger shell into which the core would be embedded. The third component, in the last truck, was the means of applying the pressure that might just cause the core to explode. This was a larger sphere of explosive, type Composition B, designed to be wrapped around the plutonium core. The theory was that this shaped charge would be so precise that it would compress the mass of the plutonium core enough to cause it to go critical—that is, to start a chain reaction that would result in the instantaneous release of God only knew how much energy. Of course, it had never been tried before, so they couldn't know for sure if it would work.

Finally the loads were packed, and cinched down, and inspected. A dozen jeeps and cars started out in advance of the truck convoy—they would lead the caravan all the way to Wendover, a ten- or twelve-hour drive—and another group of light vehicles would follow along behind. Groves, of course, would ride in the first truck.

"All right—I want two hundred feet between each truck. And we don't go faster than forty-five, got it? Everybody ready?"

The men, drivers, and mechanics and two armed guards for each truck mounted up as Groves walked around the vehicles for one last time. The plutonium and uranium elements, while key to the bomber, were relatively stable on their own. It was the last cargo, the sphere of high explosive, that presented the most danger of an accident. He looked up at the driver, who seemed calm enough in spite of everything.

"Be careful with that," Groves noted. "If you set that thing off, this will be one memorable Fourth of fucking July!"

5 JULY 1945

**HQ, THIRD ARMY, REICHSTAG BUILDING, BERLIN,
GERMANY, 0321 HOURS GMT**

"What's the bad news?" asked General Patton, striding into the command center, looking as if he'd had a good night's sleep—though Zebediah Cook knew he'd only retired a few hours before.

"I was just coming to get you, General," said the intelligence officer. "We're starting to get a picture of what's going on."

"I could hear the guns." Patton got right to the point, as usual. "Where are they attacking?"

"In Potsdam again, sir. The Nineteenth Armored is being shelled heavily. They opened up after midnight, and it's a general barrage. Initial reports have enemy armor moving up, as if they're taking attack positions. But they haven't moved against us yet."

"Well, by damn, we'll get the air force in there to plaster them as soon as the sun comes up. If they're going to play rough, we can give 'em the same thing back."

"I anticipated that order, sir. I have prepared a document with the coordinates, and the details—subject to your approval." Cook handed Patton a piece of paper.

Patton grinned as he read. "Just the way I'd have written it," he said with a nod. "Send it off. As soon as it's daylight, those commie bastards are going to feel the roof fall in!"

**HQ, FIRST BELORUSSIAN FRONT, ORANIENBURG,
GERMANY, 0952 HOURS GMT**

"Did the bombardment commence as directed?"

"Yes, Comrade Marshal," came the reply from the Second Guards Tank Guard liaison officer. "As you directed, a thousand guns opened up at midnight on the American armored division."

"And the tanks attacked at dawn? What progress?"

"Regretfully, Comrade Marshal, the Americans seem to be holding in place. The first wave of tanks was knocked out, and those following are having difficulty maneuvering in the city streets, blocked as they are by debris."

"And by our burning tanks," Zhukov said dryly. He no doubt surprised his listener when he continued. "But that is of no immediate concern. Tell me, what of the air battle?"

"The enemy commenced tactical attacks with the dawn, sir. Unfortunately, our own fighter forces seem to be standing off; I understand we suffered grievous losses yesterday. I regret to report—"

"Bah, that, too, is immaterial. The important thing is that the Americans are sending their bombers against us again? And they are, correct? Good. Now is the time to commence the general attack. Issue the necessary orders to all units."

Marshal Zhukov put the telephone back into its cradle, leaned back in his chair, crossed his hands over his belly, and smiled. The day was progressing nicely.

NAZI POW COMPOUND, BERLIN, GERMANY, 1235 HOURS GMT

"You don't have to be my prisoner, you know," Rommel said to Sepp Dietrich the day the old Waffen-SS general surrendered the city to him officially. "My offer of amnesty certainly includes you. After all, Sepp, you were ready to join me nearly a year ago, before my car got shot up, before I surrendered, before the assassination."

Dietrich shook his head, his boxer-battered face worn and tired. "Oh, I know, Rommel. But some of these kids, they won't think about giving up the old cause, even if it is dead, and some of my old Waffen-SS men, well . . . you don't want to give them amnesty, not so quickly anyway. Somebody has to be responsible for these boys. Somebody has to."

He laughed. "It's funny. Of all the people you'd expect to be the last Nazi officer standing, would you ever have picked me? But here I am: The last commandant of Berlin in the army of the Third Reich. The last commandant. Listen, we haven't always seen eye-to-eye, you and me. I'm an old man and I'm set in my ways, and I was never that smart to begin with. Never that smart. But I can handle a camp of resentful kids and angry beaten soldiers. Hell, it's just like it was right after the Great War, when we all started so very long ago. So long ago. Of course, I was one of those resentful kids and an angry soldier, too, then. A young sergeant major and not a bad mechanic, either. And look at me now! Look at me now!"

Dietrich laughed coarsely and punched Rommel in the arm. "I understand my boys and they understand me. My blood used to run hot like theirs, but now that I'm old it doesn't run so hot anymore. Not so hot anymore. I think it's better that way, though sometimes I miss the passion. Ah, for the days of a good drunk followed by a good fight and a bad woman, eh? Oh, never mind—that wasn't what you did even then, was it? No, you never did. You were one of the smart ones, one of the studious ones. We made fun of your type when we got drunk, but we knew who our betters were. We knew."

"Well, Sepp, if that's the duty you think you need to perform, it's yours. I'll put someone in charge officially, but you let him know what you need. If there's a problem, let me know. You know that everyone will have to make do under the circumstances, of course."

"Make do? What else have we Germans been doing for the last few years?" Dietrich laughed. "Frankly, my boys need work to do to keep them out of mischief. Got to keep them out of mischief. Once we get ourselves a POW facility put together, maybe we'll go fix up some places for civilians to live, if you don't mind. Fix up some houses, that would be a good thing."

"That's a fine idea. Thanks." As Rommel's staff car drove away, he turned to look at the old general rounding up his hardscrabble troops, many dressed in rags. Who would have thought that Sepp Dietrich, a bullyboy from the Freikorps days, would have turned into a decent man? He wasn't that old—not much older than Rommel—but he had lived hard. Age was partly a state of mind, and perhaps by that measure Dietrich really was old. Perhaps Rommel was getting old, too.

And maybe the old could change. The thought gave him hope.

Dietrich made morning rounds every day. With the beginnings of spring at hand, there were flashes of green amidst the rubble of Berlin that surrounded the barracks he and his men occupied. For the most part, his older troops were as glad as he to be finally finished with war. The younger men—boys, really—were eager to plan escapes, steal weapons, assault their captors, take up arms once again. Although it was the official duty of a POW to escape, Dietrich clamped down on such attempts as hard as he could, or assigned would-be escape groups to the leadership of someone he could trust to foul them up. He tried to find projects for his men to do, ways they could fix up their area, ways they could work to build shelters or make repairs to benefit the trapped civilians of Berlin. Anything to keep them busy, to keep them working.

"Good morning, General Dietrich," one of his barracks leaders said as he approached. His men were busy preparing a vegetable garden, and the boys stood at attention to salute.

"Good morning, Jürgen. Garden's looking good. Looking good. Don't forget me when you've got some good tomatoes going. I always love a fresh tomato, you know. Love a fresh tomato."

"Don't worry, sir. The first ripe tomato will be yours, I promise."

Dietrich smiled. "I'll hold you to that. Good work, boys. Good work."

By now, he'd learned most of the men's names, where they were from, what units they had served, and as they saluted him, he could greet them by name, tell them what a good job they were doing, help them feel good about the day.

Berlin was in ruins; Germany was in ruins; the Nazi dream for which he had worked his entire adult life was in ruins. But his boys were getting healthy and they were well fed and they had a roof over their heads, and maybe that was enough. Those who needed medical attention were being treated, and the worst cases had been airlifted out.

The worst part was that so many were gone. People he'd known since the Great War and the hard days of struggle that followed, people who'd fought alongside him for the years of the Second World War, and the children who'd followed him into the final battles. Kids like—what was his name? The boy he'd met in Saint-Vith who'd brought the other children out from under Rommel's nose, the boy he'd promoted then met again as he led them out against the Russians. He'd hoped the boy would have made it back to Berlin, but he wasn't in the camp. He was probably dead, but maybe he'd escaped and gone home to his mother. Dietrich hoped so, even if it was unlikely. It would be nice if a few people survived.

CCA, NINETEENTH ARMORED DIVISION, POTSDAM, GERMANY, 1545 HOURS GMT

Two Shermans squatted behind a stone wall, barrels extending over the barrier toward the long, debris-strewn street. One cracked off a shot, an armor-piercing round that struck the front of a T-34 rumbling out of a side street. The Russian tank burst into flame, as a couple of crewmen scrambled for their lives out of the turret hatch. They rolled off the hull and crawled back into the street from which they had just emerged.

But more Soviet infantry scuttled forward on the other side of the avenue, moving closer as soon as the American tank gun turned away, then vanishing into the mounds of rubble when the turret cranked back. The gunner put a high explosive round into one of those piles, scattering shards of gravel and steel in a lethal spray.

Ballard sat on the ground beside a shattered tavern, raising his head high enough so that he could see the two M-4s, as well as the street beyond. Beside him was Sergeant Kinney, with a radiophone for the colonel's communications—and a Thompson submachine gun for sport—and privates Sanderson and Duckett, who had come along as protection. The colonel heard a grinding of engines, looked to see two more Russian tanks roll into his field of vision. Halfway up a side street, they were screened from the view of the American tanks, and crept forward deliberately. The colonel was just about to give warning when he saw a GI run from the tavern, climb up on the tank, and shout to the crew.

Warned of the unseen threat, the two tanks pulled back. One traversed the long gun toward the gate of the square courtyard, while the other pushed into an alley, crunching over timbers and half-collapsed walls, seeking a new approach to the street. Ballard approved of the tactic—such mobility in a city was a dangerous, aggressive approach to the fight, but it was the only way they could wage the battle without giving steady ground in the face of the numerically superior foe.

"I've seen enough, boys. Let's get back to HQ. Stay in these backyards—I want to see how we're holding out in this next block."

One private led the way, rolling over the waist-high fence before the next yard. The sergeant and Ballard came next, the last PFC bringing up the rear. They repeated the process, and between each house Ballard looked across the street. The Soviets were active everywhere, often rushing into the open to draw fire.

A stutter of gunfire erupted before them and Ballard hit the ground.

"Sandy's hit!" growled Kinney. He popped up, holding his tommy gun at chest height, and blasted an extended burst into the next yard. Then he sprang forward, over a low hedge, and fired again.

Ballard's pistol was in his hand, but he plunged through the hedge instead of leaping it. He burst into another yard and saw Kinney, lying down behind a little garden wall and loading another clip into his Thompson. Two Russian soldiers, swarthy and almost Oriental-looking men, were rushing toward the sergeant's position, bayonets extended.

Some warrior's instinct propelled Ballard's hand, guided the notoriously inaccurate .45 toward the nearest Red. He fired once, pulled the gun down as it bucked, and shot again—even as he saw that his first bullet was knocking the man over backward. The second Soviet dropped into a crouch, bringing his carbine around toward the colonel. Holding his Colt in two hands now, Frank Ballard fired again and again, until he was sure that the bastard was down.

"Nice shooting, sir," said Kinney, with an amused grin, climbing to his feet with his submachine gun slung easily over his shoulder. "You pulled my fat out of the fire."

"I didn't know I had it in me," said Ballard, honestly.

They went to Private Sanderson—"Sandy"—and saw that he was hit in the thigh. The bullet had broken the bone, and it was an ugly but not mortal wound. Private Duckett was already applying a tourniquet, and the three of them were able to assist him back to headquarters—though they took a safer route, a full block away from the enemy.

Within the sturdy shell of the blockhouse Ballard found Hank Wakefield sitting in one of the few chairs. The general's helmet was off, and he held a rag to his head while a medic wrapped a bandage around his knee.

"What happened?" asked Ballard. He was shocked at the wan look on the CO's face. For the first time, he thought that Wakefield looked like every one of his years.

"Took some shrapnel through the door of my jeep," the general said with a game shrug. "It won't get me any time off of work."

Ballard chuckled; the old man would be okay. He grew serious immediately, however, as he made his report. "They're pressing us hard along the entire front, from the riverbank to the ponds. Tanks and infantry, waves of them. And that damned shelling—I guess you know about that, sir."

"Yeah. The flyboys can slow them down, but they can't shut them up."

"We'll hold 'em as long as we can, General. You know that. But there's a point that something's gotta give."

"I know that, son. I know. So do Patton and Rommel, for what it's worth—both of them talked to me after the briefing, told me to pass along the pat on the back. It's not much, but it's all they can send you, for now."

Ballard nodded. A pat on the back from the Desert Fox, and another from old Blood and Guts Georgie Patton himself.

There were worse rewards.

HQ, THIRD ARMY, REICHSTAG BUILDING, BERLIN, GERMANY, 2121 HOURS GMT

"It looks like a general attack, sir, around the whole perimeter," reported Zebediah Cook. "At least four tank or shock armies already identified, and aerial recon reports more of them massing behind the front. If they get a breakthrough—"

"You don't have to paint me a picture," Patton snapped. "Did the bastards take any ground?" He glared at the map on the wall of the command center, but the solid, inflexible ring gave him no information. There were no flanks to turn, no gaps to exploit; there was only dogged defense, where each determined hour of time was purchased in the blood of his men.

"I'm afraid so," Cook replied. "In the southeast they got a big jump, hit by surprise from Königs Wusterhausen. We used every one of the heavy guns to bring them to a stop—I estimate twenty-five percent of our 155 ammo was expended there. Plus the Reds took a helluva pounding from the sky. Unfortunately, they pushed a mile or so closer to Tempelhof before they bogged down."

"Unfortunate? Goddamned unacceptable is more like it! So, is there any good news?"

"We're winning the battle for control of the air," reported the intelligence chief. "For a couple of days the Russkis put a cloud of fighters up against our Mustangs. Best estimate is that the Reds got hammered at a ratio of better than five to one. A lot of American aces were made in the skies over Berlin, yesterday and today. By this afternoon, they were pretty much letting us fly wherever we wanted to go."

"Well, that's something," Patton admitted. Air superiority was a powerful advantage on the modern battlefield. But he knew with certainty that you couldn't take ground, or hold ground, with air power alone.

The truth was there, on that goddamned map: The Russians, with their overwhelming strength, were closing in on both Gatow and Tempelhof air-fields. If they got those, Third Army's tenuous supply line would be cut. This mighty fighting force, this thoroughbred of military accomplishment, would be forced to surrender.

George Patton knew that he would die before he saw that happen.

6 JULY 1945

HARRINGTON AIRFIELD, NORTHAMPTONSHIRE, ENGLAND, 0955 HOURS GMT

Kim Philby had seen heavy bombers before. Lancasters and Halifaxes and Liberators and Flying Fortresses were all familiar to him. But he had never seen anything quite like the Superfortress, or B-29, as the Americans called it. It was immense, a gleaming tube of polished aluminum nearly a hundred feet long—he couldn't help thinking of "tube alloys"— utterly unlike the greens, grays, and browns of the more traditional bomber fleets. The wings spanned 150 feet from tip to tip, and the immense tail towered above the top of the hangar beside it. This behemoth was destined for an outdoor life.

Behind the single Superfortress sitting on the tarmac, he saw a line of four more behind it, crowding a space normally filled by Liberator bombers. There were a few Liberators still on the field; the normally impressive B-24s of the 801st Bombardment Group looked puny compared to their new American cousins. Philby had been to this field before, although he did not make a regular habit of visiting American air bases—Harrington, though nominally Eighth Air Force, existed primarily to serve the U.S. Office of Strategic Services, his American counterparts, in various secret missions into Europe. Philby had availed himself of their services on more than one occasion.

"Quite something, eh, Philby?" Ian Weatherspoon slapped him on the back heartily. Weatherspoon had been responsible for getting Philby the invitation to see the newly arrived aircraft.

Philby straightened. He did not like being touched in a familiar way. However, Weatherspoon was an asset, and assets must always be humored. "Indeed. Quite. A bang-up job the Americans have done. Most of these have gone to the Pacific, I understand?"

"That's right." It was a new voice, deeper, with a markedly American accent. "Let me introduce myself. My name's Groves. Leslie Groves." Like Weatherspoon, Groves was a stout man, but much taller, towering over Philby himself. His hands were huge and his face was large and rectangular. He wore a U.S. Army uniform with the one star of a brigadier general, and a castle insignia that Philby recognized as belonging to the Corps of Engineers.

"General Groves, it's a pleasure to meet you. Philby's the name. Harold Philby, actually, but I'm generally known as Kim. I'm with the Secret Intelligence Service."

"Good to meet you, Philby. You're right. Most of these planes have gone to the Pacific. The missions there are generally much longer range, and the B-29 is the only aircraft capable of flying those missions. The B-17s and B-24s are great aircraft when the ranges involved are shorter, as they generally are in Europe."

"Then why . . ."

"Why have these here? The other distinguishing quality of the B-29 is its payload capacity. The package it will carry is just a bit bigger than a conventional bomb, and this is the only aircraft big enough to carry it to its target."

"I see. And does the package live up to its billing?" Philby asked.

Groves fell silent. "Until you see it," he said after a pause, "you cannot possibly understand it. It is beyond description."

Philby nodded. "I see. Or, rather, I should say that I don't see."

"If you'd like to follow me, gentlemen, the packages are in the hangar over there," Groves said, and marched off at a rapid military pace. In spite of Groves' bulk, Philby was challenged to keep pace. Weatherspoon started puffing after a few feet.

Inside the hangar, which was surrounded by guards, workmen had uncrated a line of twenty huge bombs, several times larger than the five-hundred-pound bombs that were standard for normal missions. Each bomb was over ten feet in length and nearly a yard in diameter. "They weigh nearly four tons apiece," commented Groves.

As he spoke, a forklift was trying to lift one of the units, but the weight caused the forklift to tip forward. The bomb rolled off and hit the floor with a crash that felt like an earthquake. "God damn it!" roared Groves. "Be careful!" Workers began scrambling over the dropped unit and the tilted forklift.

Philby had closed his eyes, expecting that moment to be his last, but Groves turned back to him and said, "Wasn't armed yet. They don't get armed until they're aboard the bomber. Until then, they're just big heavy pieces of metal. Wouldn't want to drop one on your foot, but other than that, they're not dangerous."

Philby took a deep breath. "Thought I heard the trumpet of doom there for a second."

Groves laughed. "I understand. I've been working with these things for years now, and there are days they still scare me."

"If I may, General," Philby asked, "I had the impression that there were limitations on production. I'm quite surprised—pleased, mind you, but surprised—to see so many bombs ready here."

Groves nodded. "You're absolutely right. Getting the production process started was immensely difficult, and getting one bomb ready took years. The trick is that once the process was up and running, we found that making more than one was far easier and quicker than we had expected. Not only do we have these, we still have enough for Tojo and his friends in the Pacific."

"Really?" said Philby. "That *is* impressive. The war will be over in a matter of weeks, then."

"One way or another," said Groves. "This is it. The fat lady—or Fat Man—has sung."

After Kim Philby had left, Lieutenant Colonel Paul W. Tibbets walked up to General Groves and said, "Bet you're glad I made you get me those extra pumpkins, now, aren't you?"

"Pumpkin" was the nickname for the dummy bombs used by Tibbets' group for target practice. Because of the difficulty and expense in manufacturing numerous duplicate bombs, Groves had initially vetoed Tibbets' request for seventy-five pumpkins as excessive, but when the assembly team pointed out that they needed practice as well, Groves had finally given in.

What he hadn't expected was to use the pumpkins to create a fake display for a suspected Soviet spy so that the spy could report to Moscow that the U.S. had at least twenty bombs in England plus an unspecified additional number in the Pacific.

The truth was a little more bleak: one untested unit here in England and two more undergoing final construction in the United States. This wasn't a war as much as it was the highest-stakes poker game in the history of the world.

"Yes, Paul," Groves said, "I'm glad you made me buy the extra pumpkins."

CCA, NINETEENTH ARMORED DIVISION, POTSDAM, GERMANY, 1225 HOURS GMT

The division artillery came into play in the center of the line. Diaz had his guns depress to fire directly at the Soviet tanks as they tried to push their way around the wrecks of their comrades. It was not that Ballard had lost all his Shermans, though more than thirty of the M-4s had been knocked out by now. Instead, it was that the big 105s were the only guns that had enough punch to stop the huge Russian tanks, the JS IIs and JS IIIs, collectively called the Stalins.

From his new command post Ballard had seen no less than four of the armored behemoths destroyed. Two of them were still smoking in the middle of an intersection, in death serving nicely as a roadblock. But there were still more of them rumbling through the smoky shadows farther away, looming over the ubiquitous T-34s. And always there was the infantry, the Red Army soldiers hurling themselves forward into the face of machine guns, tank cannons, rifles, and hand grenades.

They had broken through along the Havel riverfront, a bold attack in small boats helping to outflank the CCA position. The division reserve had moved up and stanched the flow, but the Soviet infantry had finally started to lever Nineteenth Armored out of its initial position. Now the colonel was managing a difficult retreat, trying to keep a line intact as they fell back one block at a time.

The battle had carried them into a residential district of mostly small houses, and each of these became a point of resistance, or a barrier behind which an American tank or self-propelled gun could find a moment's sanctuary. Each house had a tiny rear yard, often with nicely-groomed gardens, small gazebos, or fountains; invariably these were fenced from the neighboring yards by hedges, or walls of wood or brick. The population had long since fled, but there were reminders of people all over the place—a neat stack of laundry on a back porch, a rocking horse with one small, unbuckled shoe lying beside it.

A thunderous eruption of noise blasted along the line as the Soviet guns once again opened up. Houses, gardens, groves, arbors, and rocking horses vanished in a hail of dirt and debris, splinters of wood and metal and stone. The barrage thundered relentlessly, a hail of shells as the enemy tanks and infantry paused for a breather. Sensibly, they would let their artillery soften up the battered American defenders.

"Back—pull back!" Ballard called to all his units, hoping that most of the men could get out of the killing zone. They came into sight along the line, stumbling on foot as they broke for the cover of the next block. The tanks rolled over obstacles, turrets reversed to fire into the smoke at the unseen Russians.

"Save the ammo!" Ballard barked. "Mark your targets!"

They had reached the last strip of houses. Beyond was a stretch of open fields, parks, and sports venues, with a dense band of trees about a kilometer away. Ballard knew from months of scouting this position that the forest was thick, crossed with ravines and deadfalls, as well as many roads and hiking paths. He had long planned on it as his last line of defense, if he was to be driven out of Potsdam. For all its thickness, the woods was still bounded by the Havel on the left and the lake on the right; they had flank protection and some shelter against enemy fire. If they were pushed back through the woods, however, the country opened up; the enemy's superior numbers would swarm around and devour the Nineteenth Armored.

Ballard made the connection to Diaz, ordered him to get his big guns back first, then to set them up to cover the withdrawal of the rest of the division. Fortunately, the Soviet barrage continued—the thunderous curtain of explosions helped Ballard now because the smoke screened his withdrawal from enemy observation. Since the men of the Nineteenth had already pulled back far enough that they were out of the killing zone, the Red Army guns pulverized an uninhabited German neighborhood.

After Diaz had his batteries in position, Ballard sent the infantry across the fields. By now the curtain of enemy guns was beginning to lift, but the dogfaces made it to cover before the Russian troops came into view. Finally it was the tanks that crossed the field, Shermans once again with turrets trained to the rear, shooting on the run. Ballard saw three of them get hit and burn, but the rest made it to the shelter of the forest, lurching down through a shallow ditch, pushing noisily through the saplings at the fringe of the woods, filing along the tracks and trails. Like their CO, the men had spent the months of the siege getting to know the area. Now everyone had a predetermined fallback point, and the withdrawal went pretty smoothly—all things considered.

Ballard came in by jeep, following the main road—one of many that crossed all the way through this urban forest. At the first crossroads he stopped, startled by the sight of a German officer in a peaked leather cap—and even more surprised when he recognized him.

"Field Marshal Rommel. *Willkommen,*" he offered, shrugging apologetically at his German.

"*Danke schön,*" replied the Desert Fox. An aide stepped forward while he spoke again in German.

"The field marshal extends his admiration for your defense," said the aide in good, clipped English.

Ballard shook his head ruefully. "We lost our first line. I don't know how long we can hold here."

"I thought you Americans delivered some heavy artillery barrages, in Normandy," Rommel said, through the translator. He indicated the field, and battered Potsdam beyond. "We used to curse your guns, and wonder how any army could have so many batteries. I must say, those attacks were like pinpricks compared to this pummeling. These Russians, when they fire their guns like this, are like a force of nature, a flood."

"Yeah," Ballard admitted, beginning to feel his exhaustion. "And now, one more time, we've got to build a levee."

TEMPELHOF AIRPORT, BERLIN, GERMANY, 1815 HOURS GMT

The American fighters flew from bases outside of the siege for reasons of supply, but every now and then one of them would make an emergency landing at the big airport. Chuck Porter had been hanging out here since his arrival as the first official passenger on an incoming flight, and now that the battle had taken to the skies he was determined to get a firsthand account.

During the months of the siege he had been able to get press credentials that gave him almost free run of the huge airport, but one of the few areas that was off-limits was the barracks where the pilots who were stranded here found temporary accommodations. So the reporter found himself watching and taking notes on the first day's air battle, but he wasn't able to get the interview.

Stationed on the tower's observation deck, binoculars glued to his eyes, he watched the deadly dance being enacted in the skies over Berlin. He couldn't count who was winning or losing—the tiny fighters were virtually indistinguishable to him, unless they happened to be right overhead—but from the number of crashing aircraft he knew it was a frantic battle. He observed something like twenty different fighters come down to land on Tempelhof's wide runways during the day of July 5. Some of these were trailing smoke, and a few had landing gear problems, sliding in with screeching, fiery belly land-ings. One P-51 wobbled crazily as it came down. Before it could settle in for a landing, one wingtip dipped and scraped the tarmac, and the fighter cart-wheeled through a flaming explosion. Only the Mustang's engine came rolling out of the inferno; there was no point in asking if the pilot had made it.

Today was the second day of the big air battle, and as afternoon waned there were fewer than a dozen Mustangs that had made forced landings here. The fighting in the sky had grown visibly less intense, until by the afternoon it was hard to find a Russian plane up in the sky.

But Porter still wanted his interview. He had noticed that some of the damaged Mustangs were rolled off to a secondary hangar, behind the main terminal, and as afternoon waned into evening he decided that his best chance of meeting a fighter pilot was to go over there. First, he took the precaution of acquiring four large bottles of beer from the airport commissary, then he ambled over the pavement, showing his pass to the lone MP who ques-tioned him.

He found six Mustangs lined up, all of them looking a little battle-worn. They were inside, illuminated by electric lights, but there were only a couple of mechanics at work. Near one of the planes he saw a young officer, ruefully trailing his hands over the bullet holes in the engine compartment of the P-51.

"Lieutentant?" said Porter, approaching the fellow, reading the name on his tunic. "Wesling, is it?"

"What do you want?"

"You flying tonight?" Chuck nodded at the fighter, and the pilot grimaced.

"Not bloody likely. I'll be leaving Berlin tomorrow in the passenger seat of a Dakota—but when I get myself a new plane, you can bet I'll be back."

"Well, until then, maybe you'd like one of these?" Porter extended an opened beer bottle and the flier, who couldn't have been more than twenty years old, nodded agreeably and took a long pull. Suddenly he lowered the beer and looked at Porter skeptically.

"What's the catch?"

"No catch. But I *was* hoping you'd talk to me." Porter set his own beer down on the floor and pulled out his notepad. "You know, let the folks back home know what it was like to go toe to toe with the Red Air Force."

"You a reporter, huh?"

"Chief of the Paris Bureau of the Associated Press." That was usually good for a laugh around these parts, and Wesling was no exception.

"Paris? Damn, was *I* off course!"

"Temporary duty in Berlin—just like a lot of other Yanks. So tell me, how'd we fare?"

"We kicked their asses!" The lieutenant's face was suddenly alive. "I shot down two of the bastards myself, in those new Sturmoviks—the IL-10s."

"Good airplanes?"

The young man shrugged. "Better than some. But we can take them in speed, turning, and climbing. And I think our guys have more experience. Yesterday there were two aces made in my squadron alone! We shot down thirty-two of the bastards, between the twelve of us. Lost one of ours, a good guy, Kelly, from New York."

"And today?" Porter pressed, quickly scratching down the numbers, the name.

"Well, we didn't get as many 'cuz they didn't come out to fight, not after the early hours of the morning. Still, we got a dozen kills, including mine. Far as I know we didn't lose any planes—well, I guess you have to count me as shot down, now that you mention it. I never would have made it back to Frankfurt, anyway—lost all my oil pressure and had to glide her down here to Tempelhof."

"But it was your impression that we were winning the air battle?"

"Impression, hell, it's the truth. One reason I don't like being stuck here—I'm sure the boys are really whooping it up back at the base. I wish I was there."

"Well, here, knock yourself out," Porter said, offering the flier another beer. He made some more notes, happy that he could report that the air battle seemed to be won.

Now if only somebody would do something about their problems on the ground.

7 JULY 1945

HQ, THIRD ARMY, REICHSTAG BUILDING, BERLIN, GERMANY, 0651 HOURS GMT

"We have reports of Russian tanks within a mile of Tempelhof airport," reported the XO from the Forty-second Division. "They broke through in a couple of places, and we had to fall back—or we would have been surrounded."

"What about your boys, Henry?" Patton turned his glare to the CO of the Nineteenth Armored Division. "How are things in Potsdam?"

"Sorry to say, but we were pushed to the outskirts of Potsdam by yesterday night, General. They've got the urban part of the city—but there's a good bit of forest there; it was like a big park preserve. So Frank Ballard has his men set up with the woods for cover. As of twelve hours ago, and still holding, he's fought the Reds to a halt."

"Damn, they're doing a helluva job. But shoot straight, Hank. How long can they hang on before they break?"

"Best guess is just that, General: a guess. These men have been through hell. They've had more shells dropped on them in the last few days than any division I've ever heard of. I can't promise anything beyond another twenty-four hours."

"That's what I thought." Patton nodded, the point of decision passed.

"Get Ike on the phone. Tell him we need help now! If he can't give us anything, I'm not sure we can hold out for more than another day, before we lose both our airports. And once that happens, it's all over."

SHAEF, REIMS, FRANCE, 1231 HOURS GMT

"General Groves? This is the Supreme Commander. Yes, General, this is a secure line. Listen, we're going to need you to go into action on an emergency basis. Today, if possible, tomorrow at the latest. After that, I'm afraid it will be too late."

"I understand, General Eisenhower. And please know that we're doing everything we can. I've got my top men on this thing, and they're swarming all over it. But we . . . well, I know you have no time for excuses."

"No, General Groves. I understand about problems, about not having enough men, materials, time. But we all have to function anyway. And I tell you this, if we don't get a big helping hand out of your boys, this thing might be all over. And it won't be a happy ending."

"I understand, sir. There are too many connections to be made, too much assembly, for this thing to happen today. I will lay down my life, and the lives of my men, to get it up in the air by tomorrow morning. Now what, exactly, do you want me to do with it?"

"We'll get back to you with some target options, before dawn. I want to get General Patton's opinions on that. Can you give me an idea of the . . . effects we can expect?"

"You understand, sir, it has never been tested?"

"Of course, I know that."

"Then you understand these are estimates the whiz kids have come up with. But they know what they're talking about. General, picture an area at least a kilometer across. That is vaporized."

"Vaporized? You mean—?"

"Dust, General. Nothing left. Beyond that, for another kilometer perhaps, the blast will knock down buildings, toss trucks and tanks around, and burn like the fires of hell. Beyond that, it slowly fizzles out."

"And this is a *guess?*"

"Yes, sir. A good guess, made by smart people."

"Very well. I'll give you a place, and tomorrow morning you can drop the son of a bitch. Okay?"

"I read you loud and clear, General."

8 JULY 1945

HARRINGTON AIRFIELD, NORTHAMPTONSHIRE, ENGLAND, 0544 HOURS GMT

General Hap Arnold had said he wanted to be there when the balloon went up, which was certainly his privilege, so they waited until the olive drab Packard with the five-star flag arrived. The mission briefing wasn't much. Tibbets and his crew knew their business. They got a weather update and some last-minute information about Soviet artillery dispositions, and all that was subject to update by radio anyway.

Leslie Groves thought he ought to say something, but all that occurred to him was "Good luck, fellows," and that didn't sound much like "Damn the torpedoes" or "Fire when you see the whites of their eyes." From the look of it, Hap Arnold didn't have any glowing words for the history books, either. He went around and shook everybody's hand, and actually did say, "Good luck, fellows."

The nose art, reading ENOLA GAY after Colonel Tibbets' mother, was being painted on. Tibbets, as group commander, had pulled rank and assigned himself as mission commander and pilot, bumping the bomber's regular commander and pilot, who was livid at the name change. Everything was fresh and shiny and as new as could be. Near to it was the loading pit, where the bomb would be made ready.

The assembly crew had rolled the package out on the tarmac on a dolly, and they were going about the ticklish business of getting it all put together and wired in. This was the test shot and the money shot all rolled into one. Groves hoped to hell it would work. It didn't seem like the sort of thing he should be praying about.

They needed a hydraulic lift to take the bomb and its cradle from the dolly and lower it into the pit. As it engaged with the cradle, and lifted it six inches up, it suddenly jammed. The smell of burnt oil filled the air. "Shut the damned thing off! Now!" A crew of technicians swarmed over the lift, to no avail. A new machine had to be brought in, and then the problem arose of how to lower the cradle back onto the dolly. The solution, reached after fifteen minutes of argument, involved drilling into the hydraulic lines and draining fluid out. As the fluid drained, the forks dropped—but thudded down the last two inches. There was a sound of breaking glass, and a scream from one of the fusing technicians.

A brief inspection suggested that no irreparable damage had been done to the fusing mechanism. The new hydraulic lift was inserted, and this time it worked.

As the bomb and cradle left the dolly, the crew rolled it away. Next, the aircraft had to be towed into the exact position, because there was very little clearance. Slowly, the bomb and cradle was lifted into the open bomb bay. Wires and antennae hung all around the bomb.

The actual explosive package, two small hemispheres of plutonium, nickel-plated against corrosion, had developed blisters from trapped bits of plating solution. To avoid exposing the plutonium, the metallurgists had ground down only part of the blisters and smoothed the bumps with gold foil. The charges were made snug with wads of tissue and cellophane tape. All this had to be fit in. Outside, Leslie Groves paced back and forth, muttering to himself. "This isn't going to work. This isn't going to work." He drafted in his mind the letter of resignation he would have to write when the bombing mission had to be aborted.

There was a loud clank! inside the plane. "What the hell?" Groves shouted.

"Sorry!" came a voice from inside. "Dropped a screwdriver!"

Two hours turned into three. Three hours turned into four. The crew wandered back to the briefing room. The bombardier took a nap. Finally, the chief weaponeer, Deke Parsons, came over to Groves. "We've got it, but it's being held together with spit and chewing gum. I don't know if it'll survive takeoff, much less a bumpy ride. The only thing I can think of is for us to all go along to nursemaid the damn thing. It's the best chance we've got."

Groves looked at him, looked at the product of years of work. It all came down to this. Spit and chewing gum. He threw the cigarette he'd been smoking onto the tarmac and ground it out with his heel. "What the hell. Let's all go. This ain't the goddamn Enola Gay, it's the fucking Mickey Mouse Express."

To the eternal annoyance of Colonel Tibbets, not to mention all the trademark lawyers of the Walt Disney organization, Groves had the nose art repainted on the spot. The Mickey Mouse Express it was, and forever would be.

HQ, THIRD ARMY, REICHSTAG BUILDING, BERLIN, GERMANY, 0651 HOURS GMT

"I need to give Ike the target decision, now," said Patton. He was in a small conference room with Rommel and his division commanders. "They say that, if this thing goes off, it'll be a blast like the world has never known."

"Are they ready to take off in England?" asked Field Marshal Rommel.

"Not yet. They have some last-minute tinkering to do, and no one can even promise that the damned thing will work. I told them that it *has* to work! But they need to know: Where should they drop it?

"So, pertinent factors: We need to hit a concentration of Soviet forces, wipe out as many of the bastards as we can. A headquarters, a big one, might make a good target. Or artillery, one of those damn big concentrations of guns Zhukov is so fond of. And hopefully we need to secure at least one of our dangerous fronts."

"Tempelhof is our key site," suggested a general, CO of the Forty-fourth, the division that was being pushed pack toward that airport. "What about on the Third Shock Army?"

Instead of replying directly, Patton turned to his intelligence chief. "What does your information suggest, Cook?"

Zebediah Cook got up and went to the map. "Third Shock Army is pressing hard, but they're spread out along this arc, nearly twenty miles of frontage. Even if the bomb destroys everything in a one-mile radius—and that might be wishful thinking—it would only blow a gap in a small part of their line."

"No good. We need this to be hard-hitting, and decisive. Give me a better alternative."

Rommel pointed immediately to the isthmus of Potsdam, at the southwest corner of the besieged army. "Here the city streets and the lakes are funneling three tank divisions on parallel roads. They're going right past this green space—these are all palaces and resort hotels, above the lakeshore, but now their lawns have been turned into the biggest artillery concentration in the history of the world. If we can knock it out, we'll break the momentum of the Soviet attack toward Gatow airfield, too."

"Tempting," Patton allowed.

Sanger pulled down a rollup black-and-white picture, an enlargement of an aerial recon photo, and placed it on the table. "Here's a look at that part of Potsdam, taken yesterday. Reports overnight are that things haven't shifted much."

Rommel lifted a pointer and indicated a spot on the picture. "For a bonus, we've located the HQ of the Second Guards Tank Army, and the advance headquarters of Konev's First Ukrainian Front, in these two hotels. Adjacent to each other, it turns out. If we aim right—say, make a target point on this plaza, right here; it's white marble, with red-roofed buildings on three sides, and should be easy to spot from the sky—we'll at least take out the HQs and most of the guns, and we might do serious damage to these columns of armor. Those, incidentally, are the guns that have been turning Nineteenth Armored into hamburger for the last five days."

"Blow 'em off the face of the earth," said Henry Wakefield, forcefully. "It can't be soon enough to suit me."

"That's the place. All right. I'll send word to Ike, pronto," Patton said decisively, standing up and bringing the meeting to a close. Then he looked at Wakefield. "Better get a warning to your men, Hank. Even pull back a bit, get 'em under as much cover as possible beforehand. We'll set up a communication channel, patch us in to the plane, so we can give you a minute by minute countdown. All right?"

"General, one more thing," Zebediah Cook said, raising his eyebrows meaningfully.

"Oh, yeah," Patton remembered. "There's another warning, passed down from SHAEF. Hank, be sure your men know that you don't want to be looking at the son of a bitch when it goes off."

HARRINGTON AIRFIELD, NORTHAMPTONSHIRE, ENGLAND, 1122 HOURS GMT

Twelve B-29s stood ready on the tarmac of the huge airfield, the silver shapes looking like some kind of futuristic space-travel machines against the rows of olive-drab B-24s in the background. The sleek bombers were divided into four groups of three, and as trios they would fly four similar missions—each group traveling to a different target in the vicinity of Berlin. Three of the missions were decoys; one would carry the real gadget.

The charade was carried out even to the deployment of three of the pumpkins, the dummy bombs, so that if any enemy agent was somehow spying on the activity at the airstrip, he or she would not be able to identify the real mission aircraft. Now the dummies and the real gadget had each been loaded into its respective aircraft. The crew and weaponeers and General Leslie Groves all came along, walking out into the sun. The ground crews withdrew so that the mission could begin.

Like the other B-29s, the Mickey Mouse Express carried plenty of fuel for the trip, though much less than would have been required on the long Pacific Theater missions for which the plane was designed. With the bomb cradled in the large forward bomb bay, the crew prepared to climb in. Ladders led to hatches through both the forward landing gear bay and the bomb bay.

When Groves had announced his intention to ride along, Hap Arnold, of course, had tried to put his foot down, grounding the general on the grounds of everything from weight requirements to national security considerations. Groves had rebutted the first charge when the pilot assured them they had plenty of fuel, and even a half-dozen hefty officers would not have jeopardized the mission.

He dealt with the second by insisting that his expertise was crucial to the success of the mission. Arnold, even newer to the atomic warfare business than Groves, had lacked the in-depth knowledge that would have allowed him to dispute the claim. In the end, he had dourly insisted that Groves, if he had to bail out, would take steps to see that the Russians didn't capture him alive.

The general had willingly, and sincerely, agreed.

Standing below the silver metal belly of the plane, Groves confronted his dilemma. He could pull rank and take one of the seats in the cockpit, where the round dome of the B-29's nose was all windows. The view promised to be spectacular. But the access to the bomb bay, where the weapon would be prepared and armed while they flew at low altitude, preparatory to climbing to their bombing altitude of about thirty thousand feet, was limited to a hatch from a small "waist" compartment, aft of the bomb bay. The crew could get back and forth through the length of the plane—that compartment was connected to the cockpit by a long tunnel. Groves had been up there; he had seen the tunnel.

And there was not a snowball's chance in hell that at his current weight of three hundred pounds he would fit through it.

In the end there was only one choice, of course: He would ride in the back, with the gadget he had been shepherding along practically since he'd wrapped up the Pentagon project. He and the two weaponeers, Parsons and Freeman, climbed into the waist compartment and buckled themselves into ridiculously tiny steel chairs. They wore helmets with earphones and mikes, and quickly passed through an intercom check; Groves had to fiddle with the connecting cord before he could get sound in his earphones, but eventually everything functioned.

Then they waited, as the engines started, one by one. They could feel the vibration of the big power plants, the pulse of the propellers starting to spin, and then they could hear wind blasting against the thin aluminum skin of the aircraft. Groves pressed his face to the compartment's sole window—looking not outside but into the bomb bay, where the bulging device rested in its cradle. To him it would always be the gadget, but others had taken to calling it Fat Man, and the name seemed apt enough.

Then the power of the engines became momentum, slowly but perceptibly pulling them back in their seats as the Mickey Mouse Express started down the runway, rumbling faster and faster, until finally there was a sense of lightness as they took to the air and—not to say that it got quiet—an easing of noise as the landing gear retracted and the outer doors swung shut.

"Okay, fellas. We're at five thousand feet with the English Channel coming up." Tibbets' voice came over the intercom, distant and tinny. "Time to go to work."

Freeman and Parsons squeezed through the narrow hatch, each going onto one of the catwalks above and to either side of the bomb. Groves watched nervously, biting back bits of pointless advice that kept coming to mind. Both were steady men who knew what they were doing. They checked connections and adjusted the instrumentation, for the time being leaving the bomb still plugged in to the bomber's power supply. There were batteries that would power the bomb's sensors and detonators during the drop, but they wouldn't activate those yet.

"What about that target, now?" Groves asked into his microphone, his mind looking forward as they droned through the sky.

The bombardier came on. "It's outside of Berlin, just to the southwest. Lots of water around. Should be easy to pick it out. A place called Potsdam."

HQ, FIRST UKRAINIAN FRONT, POTSDAM, GERMANY, 1200 HOURS GMT

Marshal Zhukov arrived at Marshal Konev's headquarters with a minimum of ceremony, but there wasn't a man present who didn't sense the import in the audacious visit. The front HQ occupied a lakeshore hotel in this pleasant German city, and the two commanders met on the plaza, overlooking the lake and the isthmus connecting the city to Berlin.

"Ah, Georgi Konstantinovich, greetings, and welcome to my humble field station," said Konev. He gestured across the lake. "As you can see; I have placed my headquarters close to the fighting, so you must forgive the noise of the guns."

"Those guns are music to my ears, Ivan Stepanovich. But I have to ask, why have they not moved farther to the north?"

Konev's face was hard as stone. "The American division in our path proved to be remarkably stubborn. They have taken a pounding such as we were rarely able to give even to the Nazis. Finally they fell back, two full kilometers. We have the city. In another few hours we shall push them out of that forest, if we have to fell every tree. You know, Comrade Marshal, what a woodcutter I can be."

"Indeed. And I tell you, too," said Zhukov, as another roar of firing artillery surged from the great lawns around the hotel. "I admire the placement of your guns. Good for maximum concentration of fire."

He turned, gestured to one of the officers who had come in his entourage. "Comrade Colonel Krigoff!"

"Yes, Comrade Marshal!" The colonel rushed forward. Zhukov pointed up the street, beside the column of tanks that rumbled steadily toward the American line.

"The attack is progressing well. We have hope the Americans will break soon. I would like you to ride up to the front, and give me a firsthand report."

The colonel hastened to obey, waving to a tank commander, getting help from the crew to climb aboard. He rolled forward, toward the guns, and Zhukov watched him with a satisfied smile.

HEADQUARTERS COMPANY, CCA OF THE NINETEENTH ARMORED DIVISION, POTSDAM, GERMANY, 1301 HOURS GMT

"You want us to retreat?" Ballard demanded. "Why?"

He wondered how many of his men had died in the last twenty-four hours, just so they could hold this damned woods line. Now he was being ordered to give up that ground! His hand clenched around the handset of the radiophone and he almost swore at his commanding officer.

Wakefield's voice was stern. "Frank, that's an order. I can't go into details over the air. But you need to get your men into the woods, back from the edge—a hundred feet or more. Hunker down—that ravine I saw behind your position is a perfect spot."

"All right, all right." Ballard was impressed by the old man's vehemence as much as the fact of the direct order. "Do you want this to happen right away?"

"Get your boys moving now, Frank. And if nothing changes during the next forty-five minutes, well, this has been a big waste of your time."

"It's not time I'm worried about, General," Ballard retorted. "It's lives."

ADVANCE POSITIONS, SECOND GUARDS TANK ARMY, POTSDAM, GERMANY, 1303 HOURS GMT

"Colonel Krigoff! Alyosha!"

For a second the Soviet colonel was so startled by the female voice that he didn't respond. When he turned and saw the photographer waving to him from the side of the street, next to the rumbling column of T-34s, he could barely believe his eyes.

"Paulina!" he cried, sliding down from his perch on the still-moving tank; he would catch another ride after he had sent her on her way. "You've got to get out of here!" He took her arms in both his hands, holding her in a firm grip.

Angrily she pulled away. "You are not my commanding officer!" she snapped. Then her tone softened. "But why do you talk like this?"

Krigoff looked back up the road, half fearing that the marshal would be bearing down on him in a command car—or a Stalin tank! "I am on a mission for Field Marshal Zhukov himself—I am to observe the front, and report back."

"I know that he is here," Paulina said slyly, winking her one eye. "I learned that he was coming to this front, and would inspect the battle. I came here, hoping to find you."

"But I have to go!" he pleaded.

"Then take me with you. It's not like I haven't seen a battle before."

"No, it's not," sighed Krigoff, defeated. He waved peremptorily to another tank commander and, like a giant taxi, the T-34 rumbled to a stop so that the intelligence officer and the photographer could climb aboard. Then, with a surge on the accelerator, the tank lunged forward, rejoining the file rumbling toward the Americans.

ABOARD MICKEY MOUSE EXPRESS,
GERMANY, 1320 HOURS GMT

"All right. The weather report is encouraging; about ten to twenty percent cloud cover over the target." Tibbets sounded relaxed as he addressed the crew. After dozens of test drops, no doubt this was all routine to him. "I'd like to start climbing to altitude, General Groves, but your boys will need to get out of the bomb bay and into the pressurized compartment before we do. Is that gadget ready to go back there?"

"Well?" Groves demanded, leaning through the hatch and shouting to Parsons and Freeman, who had just secured the outer shell over another set of testing equipment. "Are you guys ready to finish up with that thing?"

Parsons held up two fingers. "Give us a couple more minutes, Paul," Groves passed on. He watched as the weaponeer changed two plugs on the outside of the bomb, substituting green for red. These activated the battery; the bomb was now self-contained, with its own power source ready to trigger the detonators.

One by one, the two weaponeers lifted themselves up and, with Groves' help, crawled back into the waist compartment. When they were both sitting beside him, Groves clicked his mike. "They're inside, and I'm getting the hatch secured. You can take us as high as you need to."

The B-29 began to climb, the angling very gradual to the men in the tiny, dark compartment. They took turns looking through the porthole at the bomb, which sat still and ominous in its cradle. There was no way even to check if it was still daylight outside of the airplane. Groves looked at his watch, couldn't believe they'd only been flying for ninety minutes. He knew they had at least another hour to go.

He spent the time thinking about everything that could go wrong. What if even one of the connections on the shaped charges failed to spark its split-second message of detonation? Or the battery failed? Or the radar, or the fuses, or any of a hundred other things? What if the plutonium itself, product of a massive industrial effort costing hundreds of millions of dollars, wasn't pure enough?

Any one of these problems could turn the Fat Man from a lethal explosive device into a plummeting hunk of expensive metal, about as dangerous as a good-sized boulder dropped out of the sky.

How much work had gone into bringing it here? He thought of the lab at Los Alamos, some four thousand of the country's most brilliant scientists, sequestered for much of the war. And the money! Huge industrial plants in Oak Ridge, Tennessee, and along the Columbia River in the northwest. These were not simply factories. Each was a whole town—hell, a *city*, for Christ's sake!—in its own right. They had been built, funded, and populated by the

U.S. Government, simply for the sake of bringing this gadget into this place at this time.

"We're closing on the target." Tibbets' voice came through the intercom again. "Remember the drill—we'll dive and turn as soon as we drop the thing, try to get as much space between us and the gadget as possible."

Groves was grateful for the prospect of action. He nodded grimly, watching through the porthole as the bomb bay doors slowly swung downward, admitting a wash of daylight into the center of the fuselage. Looking past the bomb he could see the ground, far, far below, dotted with patches of cloud at lower elevations. There was a swath of water there, a heartbreaking shade of blue.

He wondered how many people were about to die.

"I'd like to lead us in a little prayer," Tibbets said. "If you'll recite with me: Our Father, who art in heaven—"

"Paul," Groves snapped, cutting him off over the intercom. "Shut up."

He didn't worry about hurting the man's feelings. He remembered his earlier thought: This wasn't the sort of thing you prayed about.

A minute later they were leveled out and flying straight. There seemed to be no flak, no sign of enemy fighters. The bombardier was counting off the distance to target . . . "Ten thousand yards . . . nine thousand yards . . ." They were down to a thousand yards when Groves heard a squawk of alarm in Tibbets' voice.

"Look at—!"

The headphones went dead.

"What was that? What is it Paul? Talk!" the general demanded, but all he could hear was static. There was no response, no connection in his intercom set. Then he felt the shift in equilibrium. He couldn't believe his eyes as he looked through the porthole, saw the ground through the bomb bay doors canting slowly to the side. Those doors were coming up, closing!

Furiously he pulled at his headphones, worked the switch on his microphone. Nothing, no sound, no explanation.

But the Mickey Mouse Express was sure as hell turning away from the target.

POTSDAM, 1333 HOURS GMT

The columns of tanks were pushing through Potsdam now, lined up front to back with barely a meter's gap between them on the two widest avenues. They streamed past the elegant hotel and broad parks, and despite the smoke from the monstrous barrage Marshal Zhukov could see the columns stretching for kilometers in both directions. The guns continued to roar, and the sound remained as beautiful to the marshal as ever before.

The clouds had thickened, and the summer afternoon seemed to be growing chilly. The great soldier thought, a little wistfully, of summers long past, of fishing and hunting and living the life of a peaceful man. Someday, he would return to that life. For now, there was a war to win.

The sun came out again, and his momentary melancholy vanished. The Second Guards Tank Army was moving forward, at last.

Nearby, men were looking up at the sky, and Zhukov glanced upward, then raised his binoculars. The aircraft up there was unique, strangely beautiful. He studied the silver bomber through his field glasses, certain it was American, but he had never seen one like it before. It was large, and incredibly high in the air. When he scanned the sky, he saw a couple more of them. Strangely, there didn't seem to be any other Allied aircraft nearby.

A new round of explosions erupted from the nearby guns, and the marshal's attention turned back to the important business of war.

ABOARD MICKEY MOUSE EXPRESS, POTSDAM, GERMANY, 1338 HOURS GMT

Groves furiously plugged and unplugged his intercom cable, and finally after one particularly savage thrust the blur of static gave way to normal background noise. He heard Tibbets and the navigator discussing coordinates.

"What the hell happened? Why did we turn away?" Groves demanded.

"Oh, hi, General. Guess we lost you for a moment there. Sorry about—"

"Just tell me why we didn't drop the goddamn bomb!"

"Clouds, sir." The pilot's tone was formal and stiff. "A patch of overcast obscured the target, but there was clear sky beyond, blowing in with the breeze. So we're coming around for another pass."

Groves leaned back against the bulkhead, weak with relief. He waited, heard the countdown start again, and this time he crossed his fingers as it proceeded . . . "Two thousand yards . . . one thousand yards . . . five hundred yards . . ." The bombardier's voice droned flat over the intercom.

"Bombs away!"

The general wasn't even watching as the bomb dropped free, but he felt the airplane lurch suddenly upward, then heard the engines break into a full-throttle roar as Tibbets nosed the Mickey Mouse Express into a dive.

POTSDAM, 1339 HOURS GMT

Fat Man tumbled downward, quickly stabilized by rear fins so that the blunt, round nose pointed toward the ground. It plummeted through the air with increasing speed, following the immutable laws of physics defined by Newton and Galileo several centuries earlier. Gravity carried it toward earth, accelerated falling speed even against the pressure of surrounding air. For ten thousand feet it fell, altimeter ticking away, recording the elevation as it plunged ever faster. Twenty thousand feet of free fall, still straight and true, and nearly thirty thousand feet . . .

At sixteen hundred feet above the ground, the relevant laws of physics took on a new dimension. No longer was it Newton and Galileo who had paved the way for this moment. The workings of the gadget passed now into the realm of the Curies, of Einstein and Rutherford, of Niels Bohr, and Robert Oppenheimer. The greatest scientific experiment in the history of warfare had come to this point, where a century of theory, decades of practical work, and several years of intense and expensive manufacture, converged in the German sky.

The detonators around the outside of the Composition B case fired in a precise blast, thirty-two simultaneous charges igniting the large shell of explosive into an intensely forceful pressure. Because of the design of the charges, the great impetus of this explosion was directed inward, focused to create even compression around the basketball-sized sphere of tamped uranium, the middle layer of this complex bomb. The wave of pressure squeezed the dense metal into a superpressurized ball. Within that ball, a core of plutonium that had been about the size of a softball was instantaneously crushed to something on the order of a hickory nut.

This core was now an impossibly dense substance. Indeed, for an infinitesimal time, the composition of this hickory nut resembled the primordial stuff of the universe in all its seething fury, the eruption of all mass poised to commence.

And then the atoms within that core began to come apart, a few of them at first, then more in the next wave, and more, and more again, and all of these waves and a hundred, a thousand more of them, happening in the space of time it takes a beam of light to travel from a handheld flashlight to the ground. There was unprecedented energy compressed, momentarily coiled here in the air over this German city, and it could not remain thus.

All that energy would have to escape. It escaped first as light, a searing blast of radiation more brilliant, more intense, than any brightness the surface of the planet had ever known. This light blazed with tremendous power, as if a cosmic furnace had split open to reveal the core of the sun.

The searing flash cooked Marshals Zhukov and Konev, who were standing on the open plaza. It penetrated the stone and plaster of the headquarters building of the First Ukrainian Front to cook the bodies of all those within. It washed over the fields, and along the avenues, and it killed tens of thousands of men of the Second Guards Tank Army, in that still-tiny fraction of a second when the chain reaction occurred.

The radiation was intense enough to boil internal organs, to dry and shrivel the bodies of nearly all within a kilometer of the blast. The resort hotels, the slaughterhouse that had housed the CCA headquarters, the open parklands with their hundreds of guns, were seared into ash simply by the radiant wash of that brilliant white light. Images of people and things were seared into concrete walls, permanent shadows painted by the radiation of the initial chain reaction.

More milliseconds passed. By now the material of the core was exploding, expanding, already scattered beyond its impossible density. The chain reaction was over. But the effects of the dispersing energy had barely begun.

The place in the sky where the reaction occurred was a churning ball of fire, air heated to an impossible degree, expanding with convulsive violence, blasting outward at a speed faster than the eye could follow. A shock wave spread, visible as a ripple in the air—had there been any living being close enough to see. The shock wave tore into the charred stone of the buildings and blasted them flat. It picked up tanks and guns and trucks and men, those that had been far enough—a kilometer, say—away to survive the flash, and scattered them like toys, crushing and tangling the columns of the army, and the city itself.

And only after the shock wave passed did the superheated air surge across the ground, and the lethal fires commence. . . .

"What was that?" Alyosha Krigoff was looking toward the north, where the Americans were fighting from the edge of the forest, when the world turned unnaturally bright, as if an impossibly immense photographer's flash had been fired behind him.

He turned to Paulina. She had been looking in the opposite direction, toward the flash of light. Now she groaned and slumped to the ground, clasping her hands to her remaining good eye.

Krigoff knelt at her side, and was shocked to see that her face was bright red, like a monstrously sudden case of sunburn. Even worse was the sound of her voice, croaking with a fear he had never heard there before.

"I'm blind," she said, somewhere between a gasp and a sob.

Groves felt the Mickey Mouse Express lurch underneath him, and he knew they were all about to die. He could *hear* the metal crumpling, certainly identified the lethal sounds of the wings coming off. He gripped the edge of his seat, knowing that they were about to start falling, hoping his fear didn't register on his face.

But somehow the big airplane stayed in the air, lurching on, engines churning at a fever pitch. A second shock wave washed over them, as violent as the first, and still they didn't come apart. He heard sounds of awe from Tibbets and the flight crew, hoped that the cameras—both aboard this plane and in the two trailing B-29s—would function properly.

"God damn," he said under his breath, amazed in spite of himself. "The son of a bitch worked."

Lukas Vogel had been living in a culvert below a road in the west end of Berlin. Hunger had forced him into a rare daylight outing today. He was startled by the flash, and then stood at the side of the road, just above his culvert, watching in awe and horror as a pillar of black smoke billowed into the sky. Within that column of smoke he saw flashes of red and yellow flame, eerily bright.

He could only imagine that these were the fires of Hell.

"Jesus Christ!" Patton cried, as Sergeant Mims struggled to control the car. Braking, the driver pulled over.

"I'm sorry sir—I couldn't see."

"No kidding, son—me either," said the general, blinking against the white spots that still lingered in his eyes. They had been driving in the direction of the blast, and even from fifteen miles away it had been a flash of unbelievable intensity.

"I'm okay now, General. It just took me by surprise."

"Drive on, then." Patton was trying to grasp the significance of what he had just seen. He understood immediately:

This was the kind of power that would change the world. Indeed, it already had.

The forest brightened for a sudden, startling instant. When the flash had passed, it seemed to Ballard that the woods, mostly dense pines, were darker then ever. He strained to see through the branches, but had followed Wakefield's orders so that he was well back from the open parkland. He reminded himself to stay low, hoped that the men would remember the admonition.

"What was that?" asked Smiggs, who had been sitting beside Ballard, both of them leaning against the bank of a dry ravine.

"I don't know," Ballard said. "But I think it might mean that we just won."

They heard a sound like thunder, deep and resonant, and it came on with speed and fury. Trees cracked and toppled, limbs flew through the air, and everyone who had been poking out after the flash immediately dove flat into whatever shelter he could find. The force of the blast passed in a moment, and now they heard a general roar, like a distant storm, coming from the direction of Potsdam.

Ballard and Smiggy climbed out of the ravine and pushed forward through the woods, quickly finding and following a trail leading toward the edge of the forest. More men of CCA crept from their foxholes, falling in behind the two officers, or making their way forward through the woods.

They came to the edge of the trees, but it was like they were looking at a place that was not on the world they had left behind. A churning wall of dust billowed into the sky, drifting closer to them even as they watched. It was a hundred, maybe two hundred feet high, and utterly impenetrable—a murk so thick that it concealed every detail.

Even so, Ballard sensed that in the heart of that storm there was unspeakable heat, unimaginable fire. Overhead, the fire was visible as glowing flashes in the column of smoke that still climbed skyward. It looked over them like a shadow, inspiring a deep and abiding fear.

There was some movement on the open ground, figures emerging from the murk, coughing, staggering, falling down. These were Russian soldiers, men who had been on the point of the attack—and thus well forward of the blast's epicenter.

The first man, moaning in an almost musical fashion, came closer, and Ballard saw that he was missing his skin.

The churning heat of the explosion lingered in the form of fire, natural combustion established in the presence of anything burnable within reach of that fiery force of destruction. The clouds of dust and smoke spread outward, a ring several miles wide, while the column of smoke rose ten miles into the air, and then billowed into the broad shape of a mushroom.

Within that seething hell, more than four kilometers across, nothing lived. The epicenter of the blast was a bare circle of scorched ground. At the fringes of this there were visible ruins—steel frameworks of sturdy buildings, smoldering hulks of tanks strewn haphazardly across the landscape.

Farther outward there were more ruins, the frameworks of wooden buildings, sheds and shops and shacks. All of these were burning, and the few survivors moved like zombies. Horribly burned, very few of them would survive the night.

Still farther away the murk and dust billowed onward, layering flesh, penetrating pores, soaking into noses and mouths and eyes. The radiation within that dust was invisible, and fickle. Some of these victims, poisoned, would be dead within weeks.

Others, the lucky ones, would live for another few years.

Chuck Porter was scanning the skies from the observation deck at Templehof. He had just lowered his binoculars, looking south, when he sensed a bright flash off to his right. By the time he turned, the brilliant light had passed. It left him with an eerie sensation, since it was full daylight with only a few clouds in the sky, and yet for that split second the light had been brighter than the sun.

Lifting the field glasses again, he searched along the western horizon, and immediately saw a seething cloud of black smoke interspersed by clear flashes of flame. He felt a shiver of awe, knew that he was seeing something unprecedented, and terrible. The cloud expanded upward and down, covering an immense area.

He continued to watch, and the pillar of smoke grew higher and higher until it seemed to burst from its own column, spreading out like the cap of some black, unspeakably deadly, nightshade.

*   *   *

Sanger joined the growing crowd on the street outside the Reichstag. He had never been in an earthquake, but the movement and sound from the explosion were what he imagined one would be like. Overhead, the mushroom cloud, emblem of a new age, was dominating the sky.

"*Mein Gott,*" breathed Müller, standing beside him.

"Or the devil," replied Sanger.

"You're right. If it's this big standing here, there must be nothing left where it hit." He shuddered. "I've seen bombs before, and missiles. If a V-2 could carry this . . ."

"It would mean the end of war as we know it."

"Maybe the end of everything." Müller watched the cloud for a moment. "I wish Günter was here."

"We all do."

"Yes—but specifically here. He would make sense of this; he would have the perfect quote. No one else could say it as well."

"You're right about that," Sanger replied. "One of many reasons to miss him."

Standing nearby was an Indian soldier in a British uniform, one of the paratroop divisions that had participated in Operation Eclipse. He was speaking in a musical-sounding language Sanger had never heard. When he finished, Sanger said, "Excuse me."

"Yes, sir?" replied the soldier in accented English.

"May I ask what language that was?"

"It was Hindu, sir. It is from a holy book, the *Bhagavad Gita*. It means, 'Now I am become Death, the destroyer of worlds.' It is the god Krishna speaking. Its theological context is rather complex, I'm afraid, but the words themselves seemed to fit that cloud rather well."

"'Now I am become Death, the destroyer of worlds,'" repeated Sanger. "Yes, I agree. Thank you. I hope I didn't intrude."

"Not at all, sir." The soldier bowed quite precisely. Sanger tried to emulate it and failed.

THE KREMLIN, MOSCOW, USSR, 1701 HOURS GMT

"I want you to keep trying! There must be some line open, somewhere. Find it!"

Chairman Stalin slammed his fist down on the table, and the three colonels—communications specialists, each of them—who had been the target of his diatribe all but fell over each other in their haste to get out the door.

What was happening? He rose to his feet and stomped across the office, punching at the wall, cursing as he cracked a bone in his hand. What did it all mean?

He went back to his desk, to the sheaf of communiqués from all around Berlin.

THIRD SHOCK ARMY, NEAR TEMPELHOF AIRPORT, REPORTS HUGE MUSH-
ROOM CLOUD TO THE WEST. LOST ALL CONTACT WITH FRONT HQ, AND
WITH MARSHAL ZHUKOV AS WELL.

Their attack had come to a halt. From another army:

COMMUNICATIONS OUT; HALTED, AWAITING FURTHER ORDERS.

There were others, similar stories. Many of them made claims about this mushroom cloud. Others—and some of the same ones—reported a brilliant flash of light. But neither of his marshals could be found.

And then there were the reports, just coming in, from the hospitals. . . .

9 JULY 1945

HQ, THIRD ARMY, REICHSTAG BUILDING, BERLIN, GERMANY, 0651 HOURS GMT

"I want to be ready to push the bastards back, all the way to the lines they had five days ago," Patton declared. "That little firecracker yesterday bought us some time, at the very least. But by damn I want to be ready to take advantage of it."

He paused, then looked around frankly. "The one exception to that is Potsdam. Henry, I don't want your boys—or anyone else—going near the place. The whiz kids who built that bomb say that it's radioactive—read: poisonous—around there."

"That brings something up, General." The speaker was Colonel Franzene, a surgeon and the CO of Third Army's hospital units. "We've got a lot of Soviet wounded that came in. Real nasty stuff. Men with half their skin toasted off, flash burns, or tunics melted right into them. A lot of 'em we can only give some morphine, and wait. Others are different—we had fellows come in, didn't even look hurt. But they puked all night, and died."

"Do what you can for them," the general declared. "Without endangering the care you can give to our own men."

Field Marshal Rommel spoke up. "There are many places around the front where the Russians ceased their attacks, shortly after the bomb was dropped. I suggest that in those locales, we do not advance aggressively, but rather stand firm without a resumption of the hostilities."

"Good idea, yes," Patton said. "Where they've stopped shooting, we can stop shooting."

"I have a question. What was that 'firecracker,' anyway, General?" asked Henry Wakefield. "I know they're calling it an atom bomb, but I mean what the hell are we talking about here?"

Patton started to say something, then closed his mouth. "Colonel Sanger, will you field that one?"

Reid Sanger shrugged noncommittally. "It's been a pretty well kept secret, obviously. I just learned about it two days ago, when we had to pick a target. But it seems that some of our scientists took their slide rules off into the desert—New Mexico, somewhere—for most of the war. This was the result of their work: a bomb that causes atoms to split, with the results that we saw yesterday."

"Damn," Wakefield said, shaking his head. "Get a few of those dropped on him, that would make a fella not too willing to fight a war."

"Yep, Hank," said Patton. He knew that he sounded tired, and he felt every one of his years. "That's what we're hoping."

SHAEF, REIMS, FRANCE, 1031 HOURS GMT

"General Eisenhower?" Kay Summersby's eyes were wide as she cupped the receiver of the phone with her long fingers. "This is a Russian translator. He says that Chairman Stalin is calling for you."

"Damn." Ike crushed out his cigarette, drew a breath, and took the phone.

"Mr. Chairman?" He decided to play it with a hearty tone.

"General Eisenhower? Is this you?"

"Yes it is, Chairman. I am glad you called. We had an unfortunate communications breakdown a few days ago—I haven't been able to get through to you, or your marshals."

"Yes. Ah . . . it truly was an unfortunate failure to communicate. In point of fact, there has been a regrettable misunderstanding in our relative positions at the city of Berlin. I am sorry to report that recently one of my colonels acted impetuously, and triggered an accidental outbreak of hostilities. The matter has been addressed. But I do regret any loss of life that has occurred."

"Do I understand you to say that you—I mean, that the error has been corrected, and that the offensive will cease?"

"Offensive? Certainly you did not mistake that for a genuine offensive?" The Soviet dictator chuckled genially. "No, I assure you, General, that was merely a few young officers acting without authority. If it had in fact been an offensive, I trust you would have known."

"Yes, of course. Sorry for the misunderstanding."

"Unfortunate that lives were lost, I agree. But I have given explicit orders that no further hostile action be taken."

"I am relieved to hear that, Mr. Chairman. Know, of course, that our forces in Berlin will be only too willing to go along with this . . . um . . . ceasefire. That is, until we can get something more permanent established."

"Indeed, yes. Permanent. Marshal Rossokovsky is now in charge of Soviet forces along the front. He will contact you directly within a day. In any event, I thank you for your time, General."

"And you too, Mr. Chairman," Ike replied. "I appreciate the call." He set the receiver back in its cradle, and looked up at Summersby.

"It's amazing how much he *didn't* talk about," noted the Supreme Commander.

LONDON, ENGLAND, 1219 HOURS GMT

The world had changed, a new force had been unleashed, and the fires of Hell were in the possession of the Americans. None of that, however, would stop an Englishman from his daily routine. Kim Philby had been invited to lunch at the Metropolitan Club with a friend, a minor official in the Admiralty.

Philby well understood that lunch was an action, and he had a regular schedule of lunches that was all part of keeping himself connected and in the know. It was a particularly charming springtime day, the flowers were in bloom and the air was fresh, the sun shone brightly, and even Kim Philby had to put his cares aside and simply bask in the pleasure of the moment. For the first time in a long while, he felt completely off duty, able to relax, get a little drunk, and not worry.

The Metropolitan Club was redolent of cigar and pipe smoke, some likely centuries old, with accents of old leather and varnished wood. It was an odor that reminded him somewhat of his father, which was odd—he had not thought of his father in ages.

He hadn't waited for more than a few minutes when his luncheon host arrived. "Ah, Kim, old chap. Frightfully good to see you."

"And you, Sir James." Admiral Sir James Parsons was some twenty years Philby's senior, but Philby had great fondness for him nonetheless, fondness that he usually did not grant to members of the British establishment. But Sir James Parsons, though regrettably retrograde in his social outlook in certain respects, had commendable wisdom, a wide and rich view of the world, exceptional gossip, and a taste for young men—of whom Philby had been one, back in his Westminster School days. He had had quite a schoolboy's crush on the once handsome and debonair Naval officer, which had been quite torridly reciprocated, and although both were older now and their mutual passion had long since cooled, their friendship had remained solid for these many years.

They started in the bar with Peter Dawson wetted down with a few cubes of ice, and when their table was ready ordered a mixed broil and a bottle of a rather good Beaujolais, then a second bottle, and Sir James told a perfectly scandalous story about a Lord of the Admiralty who had been caught en fla-grante in the brig of a destroyer with an ordinary seaman, all hushed up, of course, as these things were. They switched to port with the cheese course, a Stilton, and Philby shared a few stories that were not quite as good, but they were all he had.

"And what do you think about the new super bomb?" asked Sir James. His face had gone rather ruddy.

"I-I can't s-say," Philby replied. "It's r-rather large, isn't it?"

Sir James put a finger aside his nose and leaned forward. "I can tell you something, but it's really telling tales out of school. You'll have to keep it under your hat."

Philby leaned forward as well. He was a bit unsteady. "You can trust me. You can always t-trust me."

"Good fellow. Of course I can. Never doubted it. Here it is. They've picked up on a Soviet mole."

Philby blinked. "A Soviet mole? Where?"

"Here."

"In the Metropolitan Club? Pre-preposterous!"

"No, no, no. Not in the Metropolitan Club, in the Government. In the SIS, to be precise. Your outfit."

"Really? Do you know w-who it is?" Everything seemed somewhat distant to Philby. He poured himself another glass of port to steady the room a bit.

"No idea. Perhaps you can finger the chap. Evidently reasonably high up. But the joke is, they haven't arrested him, they fooled him."

"Fooled him? How?"

Sir James smiled. "Made him think there are lots and lots and lots of bombs. Filled a warehouse with them. Fakes. All of them. Well, all but one, anyway. There's just one."

Suddenly everything in the room stopped moving for Philby. "Just one, you say?"

"Just the one. And that was a prototype." Sir James pronounced "pro-to-type" very carefully. "They were crossing their fingers as they flew, putting the thing together with tape and string, you know. Americans! Can't get it right for anything!"

"There aren't any others?" Philby asked. His voice was slow. The room was spinning.

"I gather there are one or two others back in the States, but they aren't finished. They can still make more, you know, but not quickly. Maybe a few months before there are any more. But you know what's so funny?" He snorted with laughter.

"What?"

"Right now, if Stalin only knew, he could just roll right into Berlin with all his armies, and we don't have enough wherewithal to stop him! Isn't that funny? We've bid four no-trump and we don't have a single ace in the hand!"

Philby stood up. He was slightly unsteady on his feet. He picked up the port and finished his drink. "I'm sorry, Sir James, I have to go. I have to go immediately. There is an emergency. I'm very sorry."

"What's the matter, Philby? You don't look well. You don't look well at all."

"I'm sorry. It's an emergency. I've got to go. Good-bye, Sir James."

"Philby, old chap, wait a minute—"

Kim Philby moved as rapidly as he could through the dining room, navigating by holding onto the backs of chairs. He did not notice the gentleman at the next table who stood to follow him as he left, or his companion who also left, heading toward the manager's office to use the telephone.

As Philby hurried down the main staircase to the entrance doors, one man followed him down as a second man waited impatiently for someone to pick up the telephone at the other end. "It's Mowgli, sir," he said when he heard a voice on the other end. "It looks like he's gotten tipped off. Send units to all known drop sites. I think he's planning to go to ground, but he'll try to get a message through first."

There was no line at the taxi queue, so Philby took the first one; the following man took the one behind. Now sensitized, Philby could tell he was being followed. "Where to, guv'nor?" asked the cabbie.

"Not sure of the address," Philby said. "Turn right here, if you don't mind. Then on down a bit—I'll know it when we come to it." He turned to look at his pursuer. Only one. If he'd gotten away cleanly enough, he would only have the single pursuer to shake and that should not prove too difficult. He could retrieve his emergency documents and currency from their hiding place and be gone quickly enough, get a message through to the embassy to notify the Soviets—act now! *Victory could still be ours!*

He shook his head. How wonderfully elaborate the trap had been, and how well they had snared him. Later he would review the operation in detail, find out where he might have slipped up, but he suspected the problem was what he had feared from the outset—this program simply had so much security around it that simply to inquire was to invite investigation. Well, it couldn't be helped, and if this information reached Moscow in time, it would still have been worth it. And if he reached Moscow safely, then he would start his new career as an NKVD officer, open and proud, running agents aggressively against the pathetically incompetent West. It would still be all right.

Traffic up ahead. "Go left, please." Now the crowd was thick enough. "Ah, I see where I want to be. Stop here please, and keep the change." He slipped out of the cab, lost himself in a crowd. He knew his pursuer would follow on foot, but here he had the advantage. There was Harrods, and he was in one exit, and shortly out the other, then down into the Underground. Three transfers later, he felt relatively safe. He would not return to his office nor to his flat, but straight to his emergency drop. He took a pen and a small journalist's notebook from his breast pocket and scrawled a brief note, tore off the note and slipped it in his pants pocket before returning pen and notebook to their home.

He got off not at his stop but one stop later, then backtracked, scanning for anything that looked like stakeout. Nothing set off his internal alarms, but then there had not been time for anyone to do much that was formal. One of his drop-off points was behind a loose brick in a wall surrounding a small park; he looked around and in a clear moment he slipped the note in place. The alert for that drop off was located not too far away, the Underground sign for the station he would normally have used had a metal ring around it. He twisted the ring so that the screw faced the stairs instead of the sidewalk. There. That was done. Now, into the park. It was relatively small, but old enough that the shrubbery was thick and dense. Behind an oak tree, however, he could crouch low and there was a virtual cave within the shrubbery, and in it a large stone. He heaved the stone aside and underneath there was a piece of oilcloth wrapped around a briefcase. He removed the briefcase, as good as new except for a slight earthy smell, and heaved the stone back on top of the oilcloth. Brushing himself off as well as possible, he waited until the path was momentarily clear, then stepped out, briefcase in hand, to saunter casually down the path in the lovely springtime air, for the Underground and freedom.

He looked both ways before crossing the street. As he stepped off the curb, however, a large white delivery van sped around the corner and accelerated. "Look out, man!" a voice cried. Philby looked up at the van and tried to move.

"Here, now; here, now; move along; nothing to see," came the comforting voice of a policeman.

"He's alive, just a few broken bones; he should heal up pretty well." There were hands touching him gently, but they still hurt. All of him hurt. He opened his eyes. The figures wore white. Ambulance workers. They were moving him onto a stretcher. "Be careful with him. Don't want to move his back or neck until after X-rays."

He found himself trembling. "He's going into shock. Get a blanket over him. Keep him warm. You're going to be all right, sir. Don't worry." The accent was thick and somewhat furry.

"Think there's any internal bleeding?" one medical person asked another.

"Can't tell. Possible, but can't be too serious or we'd see summat more going wrong with him here. They'll deal with it over at hospital."

They were lifting the stretcher now, loading him in the ambulance. Every jostle, every slight movement was agony. He was alive, but he would not escape now. At least his message had been sent. He closed his eyes.

"Mr. Philby?" The sound of his name made him open his eyes again.

"Yes, Mr. Philby. We know who you are. Just wanted you to know we took the message out from behind the brick, and turned the little ring back around." A man wearing hospital whites was filling a hypodermic needle. He looked nothing like a nurse or doctor. Philby's eyes grew wide, questioning.

"How did we know about that, you ask? Oh, we've been watching you for a very long time. We would have been happy to keep the game going, but you had to run off all in a hurry. Now, I'm afraid we can't keep playing anymore." He rolled up Philby's sleeve, inserted the needle into the inner arm. "Now it's sleepy sleepy, Mr. Philby. Game's over. Point, set, match: England."

The pain began to ebb as the darkness grew.

THE KREMLIN, MOSCOW, USSR, 1300 HOURS GMT

Hartnell Stone had seen Josef Stalin be the warm and friendly Uncle Joe and an ice-cold Josef Vissarionovich. Now he was seeing a third Stalin—the Man of Steel, an eruption of molten fire. "No matter how many of these devil's weapons you have, we will root you out, we will destroy you, we will bury you and every vestige of your corrupt, treacherous, capitalist system!" His fist pounded on his desk over and over, making papers and pens and baskets jump and scatter. Stalin was a strong man, massively built and physically powerful. When enraged, he was terrifying—Stone had never seen anything in his life that scared him as much as Stalin did at that very moment. He stole a sideways glance at Harriman, standing beside him. The American ambassador seemed unfazed by Stalin's rage. Later, Stone would have to remember to ask if that was an act or if there was some secret he should learn.

The news of the atomic bomb had started to arrive in the embassy late the previous night. The more that came in by teletype, the harder it was to believe the magnitude of the device. A Soviet Front headquarters, an army HQ, hundreds of guns, sizeable chunks of three tank divisions—gone in an instant. This weapon would change warfare as dramatically as the invention of gunpowder.

"What have you got to say for yourselves? What lies do you bring us from the capitalist power brokers today?" There was visible sweat on Stalin's forehead. His veins were showing; his face was red. There was always the suspicion that temper like this was a calculated act, and sometimes it was. This, however, seemed to be the real thing.

"How can we work together to meet the legitimate needs of the Soviet Union along with the legitimate needs of the other parties?" asked the ambassador. "We are willing to help resolve your goals. We are not willing to surrender ours in the process. That is the same thing we have said from the beginning, ever since you withdrew from our alliance against the Nazis."

"We fought the Nazis longer and harder than anyone else! How dare you criticize our commitment to fighting the Nazis? No one has suffered more than the Soviet Union at the hands of the Nazi criminals. No one! It is you, Mr. Ambassador, who is seeking to protect the Jew-murdering Nazi scum from justice."

"The United States of America and its remaining alliance partners have pursued and have received unconditional surrender, not only from the Nazi government; but also from the provisional German Republican government that has temporarily taken charge until elections can be held. There will be demilitarization of Germany, there will be full investigation of all war crimes and crimes against humanity, with trials and punishments for those responsible. It is not too late for the Soviet Union to be a partner in that process, although not on the original terms that applied before your withdrawal."

"Partner? *Partner?* You talk to us of being a *partner?* This, after dropping the atomic bomb on our forces? What kind of capitalist double-talk is this?"

"The siege of Berlin had turned into the battle of Berlin. The United States has made it clear for several months that it would not permit the Soviet Union to take Berlin by military force, and has repeatedly insisted that you withdraw behind the Oder River line. When it became clear that your objective was to take Berlin by force in spite of everything, we had no choice but to use the weapons at our disposal."

"It was the aggressive and provocative actions of your own people that started the battle."

"I do not believe that to be the fact. There is reason to believe that this battle began by a series of tragic accidents. As we both know, this is hardly unknown in wartime. But you had troops massed around a military objective, and once the situation began, your generals decided on the military goal to be pursued. Your artillery bombarded our troops in Potsdam for three days. That wasn't an accident. More to the point, however: How it started is therefore of no ultimate consequence."

Standing next to Stalin, face carefully impassive, was Molotov, the foreign minister. Stalin looked at him, and then Molotov spoke. "Tell us of this Soviet-US partnership you propose."

"Thank you, Foreign Minister. The United States government fully recognizes that the Soviet Union has a vital interest in the process and decisions made regarding the fate of Germany following this war, in making sure that Germany does not further threaten the safety and security of its neighbors, in the economic redevelopment and reconstruction of areas devastated by war, and in general in the construction of international institutions to safeguard the peace and secure the future. Regardless of our differences, we believe it is important to the world that the Soviet Union be an active participant."

Stalin grunted. "Pretty words. Coming on the heels of the atomic bomb, what do they signify?"

"As the Chinese say, 'A journey of a thousand miles begins with a single step.' Chairman Stalin, Foreign Minister Molotov, I offer no miracles and expect none in return. It seems to me that our choices are fairly clear right now. We go to war, or we attempt peace. The second option is not guaranteed to have a satisfactory outcome, but the first option is guaranteed to have an unsatisfactory outcome, is it not? The option of going to war is always with us, so we foreclose nothing. And as you in particular know, Chairman Stalin, President Roosevelt has a number of ideas for how to help the postwar world move beyond war to less violent methods of problem-solving among nations."

"Ah, yes, I remember. 'United Nations.' Bah. It will never work. Harriman, you are a liar and you work for liars. Your nation is embracing Nazis because you fear them less than you do Communists. You have a new superweapon and you plan to use it to expand global hegemony and economic domination. Nothing you say can be trusted. But we of the Soviet Union love peace, and love it with far more reason than you, for we have much more experience with the alternative. We will talk, and we will work alongside you. Although you have the atomic bomb, we have the future, for inevitably that future belongs to communism. Enjoy your little victory today, for it will truly be fleeting."

Then, for the first time, Stalin turned toward Hartnell Stone. His eyes seemed to penetrate him. "Young man, I hope you have listened well. You are learning from a great liar in Ambassador Harriman, and a greater liar in President Roosevelt. You live in the heartland of capitalism itself, and to you it seems indestructible. It may well be that Harriman and Roosevelt and Molotov and I will all pass away before the day of the dictatorship of the proletariat truly dawns. But you, young man, will see the great change come upon the world. You will have a choice, to embrace Communism or end up on the ash heap of history. My advice, young man, is to study and think carefully." He looked sharply at Harriman. "What do you think, Ambassador?"

"I think that 'study and think carefully' is fine advice, Chairman. I concur." Harriman smiled genially.

Stalin's face turned dour again. "Molotov will meet with you to work out details. Good-bye."

10 JULY 1945

FROM THE TIMES OF LONDON, EARLY EDITION

> **DEATH NOTICES**
>
> PHILBY, Harold Adrian Russell. Deputy
> Section Chief, Secret Intelligence
> Service, in an automobile accident in
> London yesterday afternoon. Born
> 1912, Ambala, India. Son of the influ-
> ential British explorer and Arabist Harry
> St. John Philby, adviser to King Ibn
> Sa'ud of Saudi Arabia. Educated at
> Westminster School and at Trinity
> College, Cambridge. Journalist, Spanish
> Civil War, London General Press.
> German correspondent, 1939, BEF war
> Correspondent, 1940, The Times. Joined
> SIS 1940. Survived by his father;
> divorced, no children.

SHAEF, REIMS, FRANCE, 1202 HOURS GMT

"The Soviets are going to back up to the Oder, Georgie. Uncle Joe is giving us everything we're asking for." The Supreme Commander sounded more relieved than triumphant, as he passed the news to the Third Army commander over the telephone.

Patton drew a breath and let out a low whistle. "Damn, Ike. That was closer than I'd like to remember, but it was a gamble that came up all sevens! We kept the bastards out of Germany—most of it, anyway."

"Yeah, it looks like we did that. Of course, we'll have to see if they go through with everything they've promised. I'm not holding my breath on that. But at least they've cleared the roads. Hodges and Simpson both have divisions on the way into Berlin. By tomorrow, you should have land connections with the rest of the expeditionary forces."

"So, General. What about these commie bastards? You know, that bomb really knocked them for a loop. I get the feeling that they're kind of on the ropes. Maybe one or two more of those sonsabitches and we could break through their front line like—"

"George!" snapped Eisenhower. "Stop it! We have an armistice. We have peace. Your army survived one hell of a tight pickle. Can't you just take a deep breath, and enjoy it for a few days?"

"Dammit Ike, you know how important timing is in this business. I tell you—hello? Ike?" General Patton couldn't believe it.

The Supreme Commander had hung up on him.

12 JULY 1945

THE KREMLIN, MOSCOW, USSR, 0600 HOURS GMT

"Good morning, Nikolai Aleksandrovich," Stalin said as his defense minister entered the chairman's private conference room.

"And good morning to you, Josef Vissarionovich," replied Bulganin. "I have the new troop movement and dispersal information from Marshal Rokossovsky, who has taken over for both Zhukov and Konev for the time being. All the armies have begun movement back toward the new positions."

"Ah. Here. Let me clear space on this table. Now. Let us review them." Stalin and Bulganin put down paperweights to keep the corners of the unrolled charts flat. "Exactly as I ordered. Good. Copies were furnished, per our agreement to the Western Allies?"

"Suitably redacted, yes."

"Good. Now we make changes. Here . . . and here." He marked off areas short of the Oder River demarcation. "I want these areas fortified with our troops. We will withdraw no further."

"Of course, Comrade Chairman. I will make the necessary changes. But, may I ask . . ."

"Why? Of course, Nikolai Aleksandrovich. You see, Beria has informed me that our top man in the British intelligence service died in an automobile accident not long ago."

"Really?"

"Yes. A very valuable asset. A man of considerable intelligence and skill. Fortunately, he had recruited colleagues, so we are not left without our sources, but a man like Kim Philby cannot be so easily replaced. Philby, you see, discovered that the Allies had a total of twenty of these atomic bombs."

"Twenty! No wonder we had to withdraw."

"Indeed. We were in the position of savages, facing machine guns with bows and arrows. Of course, that will only be true until we have our own atomic weapons. Fortunately, we have deep cover agents inside the atomic bomb program in the United States, and so within a few years, we should have such weapons in our own arsenals. Those agents, however, had been held in secret cities in the American desert for several years, as were all those working in the American program."

"Very logical of them."

"Yes. Unusually so. Now that the secret is revealed, we have been able to contact some of our agents, but they have told us something strange—that to their knowledge, there cannot possibly be twenty bombs."

"Really."

"Yes, and Philby is mysteriously dead. It seems he left a restaurant hurriedly, and shortly thereafter, met his end."

"Oh. I begin to see."

"Perhaps we are savages with bows and arrows, but maybe all we are facing is an *empty* machine gun, comrade. What do you think?"

"If we had only known for sure a few weeks ago . . ."

"Ah, yes. Now, of course, Berlin has been reinforced, and total war is not necessarily the strategy to pursue right now. After all, even if the capitalists do not have twenty bombs, they might have two or three, and even that would not be so good for us. So that is why I don't wish to withdraw as promised. We will sit on their side of the Oder and wait. If they drop another bomb on us, then we know they have more bombs. If they ignore our presence, or merely huff and puff, then that means they have no more bombs at present. This is worth learning either way, do you not agree, Nikolai Aleksandrovich?"

"And we will eventually have this weapon?"

"Oh, yes, that I can promise you. We will have it before too many years have passed. For now, it is time for peace. The communist movement will prosper in the years ahead, and when we have the bomb ourselves, we can at least show that we can inflict damage equal to what the capitalists threaten to inflict on us. And if necessary, we have demonstrated far greater ability to absorb punishment than they have."

Stalin smiled. It was not a pleasant smile. "When we say that war is the continuation of diplomacy by other means, we normally think those other means are necessarily and always violent ones. That, however, is a narrow way of thinking. Violence has it uses, but it is not the only way to wage war. We Soviets know that fact intimately, because we know the power of our General Winter, who does not have a single soldier in his army.

"We will be the peace-loving Soviet Union as far as unsubtle weapons are concerned, and we will wage war primarily through other means. Propaganda, of course. Economic warfare. Espionage and terrorism. Proxy warfare. Time— the capitalists tend toward impatience, for the stock market never waits. Political warfare. Subversion. Nonviolence—Gandhi in India is a most creative military commander who has developed a new form of warfare. If tanks and bombs and bayonets are necessary, we will use them, but we will not be limited. The struggle will be long and hard, but inevitably, we will win."

Bulganin laughed. "With you on our side, the capitalists don't stand a chance!"

PARIS, FRANCE, 1652 HOURS GMT

Generally, a bureau chief of the Associated Press is not expected to cover the news personally. That is why he has reporters. Reporters get paid less. Unfortunately for Chuck Porter, he preferred the bureau chief's salary but the reporter's job. His excuse during his two prolonged absences from the Paris office was to plead "exigencies of war."

First, a routine visit to the Stavelot fuel depot had ended with his capture and presence at Rommel's surrender—and the story got a Pulitzer. Second, going along on a parachute drop had gotten him trapped in the Siege of Berlin and made him an eyewitness to the dropping of the atomic bomb—and he was hoping for a second Pulitzer for that.

New York was not amused. As penance, he had spent the Siege of Berlin setting up and running the AP Berlin Bureau, serving as acting bureau chief (with no extra pay) and as the entire news staff (with no extra pay). They had allowed him a single secretary, and that was it. More evidence, if any was needed, that you can't spell "cheap" without "AP."

Well, here he was, home at last. Steve Denning, his senior editor, had been running the Paris Bureau in his absence. Now that the war in Europe was over, AP would be setting up shop in all the major capitals. Time to decide where he wanted to be—Paris, Berlin, maybe even Moscow—and probably time to settle back into his management responsibilities. The big stories, after all, were over.

He climbed the steps to the second floor offices and opened the door. He was immediately greeted with a cry of, "Hey, boss, long time no see!" Denning and Troy Winter were both in the office. Everyone else was out—but then it was a pretty small team.

"What's going on?" Porter asked, his eyes immediately going to the Teletype.

"Nothing. It's a dead news day. Hell, boss, what else could it be, with you actually *here*?"

Porter joined in the laughter. In the middle, the Teletype started ringing four bells: a Flash bulletin. Everyone stopped and turned toward the machine, as sensitized to the sound of that bell as a mother to a baby's cry. Porter got there first and started reading.

"Jesus Christ," he whispered.

> FLASH/BULLETIN
> ATLANTA BUREAU, 12 JULY 1652 GMT (1152 EST)
> COPY 01 FDR DIES
> DISTRIBUTION: ALL STATIONS
>
> WARM SPRINGS, GEORGIA, 12 JULY (AP) BY JAY EAKER
> FRANKLIN DELANO ROOSEVELT, 32ND PRESIDENT OF THE UNITED
> STATES OF AMERICA, WAS PRONOUNCED DEAD TODAY AT 11:02 AM

EASTERN STANDARD TIME AT HIS WARM SPRINGS, GEORGIA, RETREAT. THE CAUSE OF DEATH WAS LISTED AS A STROKE. THE PRESIDENT HAD BEEN IN ILL HEALTH FOR SEVERAL WEEKS, AND WAS IN WARM SPRINGS FOR REST AND RELAXATION.

VICE PRESIDENT HARRY S TRUMAN TOOK THE OATH OF OFFICE TO BECOME THE NATION'S 33RD PRESIDENT AT 11:30 AM EASTERN STANDARD TIME IN THE UNITED STATES CAPITOL BUILDING IN WASHINGTON, D.C. HE ORDERED FLAGS TO BE FLOWN AT HALF-MAST FOR A PERIOD OF THIRTY DAYS TO MOURN PRESIDENT ROOSEVELT.

TELEGRAMS FROM WORLD LEADERS HAVE STARTED ARRIVING IN WASHINGTON AND WARM SPRINGS AROUND THE CLOCK. PLANS ARE BEING READIED FOR A STATE FUNERAL IN WASHINGTON, D.C. THE PRESIDENT'S WIDOW, ELEANOR ROOSEVELT, WILL ADDRESS THE NATION BY RADIO THIS EVENING AT 8:00 PM EASTERN STANDARD TIME. . . .

MORE

AP ATL 473965 JE/12 JULY 1945

Denning was already reading over his shoulder. "I don't even *remember* anybody else being president," he said.

Four or five quips came into Porter's mind, but he didn't feel like saying any of them. He didn't feel like saying anything at all.

THIRD ARMY OFFICERS' CLUB, BERLIN, GERMANY, 2352 HOURS GMT

"Who th' hell is Harry Truman, 'nyhow?" mumbled Captain Smiggs, unsteadily examining his nearly empty mug.

"Shut up and have another beer," Sanger said, sliding the pitcher across the wet, sticky table. "We been over that. He's our new C in C."

"Well . . ." Smiggy took a long time to pour, carefully leaning the mug, building a nice head. He raised the glass with great ceremony. "Here's t' the pres'den' who won the war. Franklin . . . Del-a-no . . . ROSE—a—velt."

"Hear, hear." Sanger, Ballard, Diaz, and the rest of the officers at the table—mostly majors and colonels of the Nineteenth Armored, with a smattering of the army HQ staff—joined in the toast. It was far from the first of the evening, and Sanger doubted it was the last.

He turned to Ballard, who had been sitting rather quietly in the boisterous club, nursing his beer and leaning back from the companionable group at the big table. "Cheer up, Frank. We won the war!" Sanger said.

"Yeah. I can't believe it's over," said the CCA colonel. "Mostly over, anyway. Don't you have a loose end stashed away in the basement somewhere?"

Sanger snorted. "Damn that smug bastard. Shitty thing is, y'know they won't give him what he deserves!"

"I'd give it to him!" Smiggy snarled, his eyes and his voice suddenly clear. Then he slumped back over his beer, shaking his head dejectedly. "Wha' could I do 'bout it? Nuthin'!"

Sanger thought about that a moment. It didn't seem right, sending Himmler to some nice clean prison. He was distracted by Ballard asking him a question.

"So, Reid. Are you getting out?"

"Just as fast as I can," Sanger pledged. "You?"

Ballard shrugged his shoulders, looked almost sheepish as he spoke. "I've been wondering if they might need me over in Japan. Reckon I'll try to find out."

"So, you're leaving this man's army, are you?" Sanger recognized Major Keegan's voice, the nasal eastern accent grating on his nerves as usual. "Maybe go into a nice steady teaching job, perhaps? A little red schoolhouse out on the prairie, with you as the headmaster?"

Sanger looked up at the major, who had come up to the table unseen, and bit back the well of dislike rising within him. He turned to his mug, then felt a hand on his shoulder.

"Reid?"

It was General Cook, of Third Army intelligence—Sanger's old, and Keegan's current, boss. "Yes, hi, General. Wanna beer?"

"Hell, I'm going to take care of that for you, Colonel. But come with me, there's some esteemed gentlemen that would like to have a word with you."

Sanger rose, and found that the floor was a little unsteady beneath his feet. He was too surprised by the invitation to relish the look of resentment that flashed across Keegan's features as Sanger followed the general through the crowded club.

The band was playing something jazzy, and the dance floor was alive with American officers and German women—fur-lines, the GIs had taken to calling them. Smoke hung like a stratus cloud under the dark beams of the huge room, a former rathskeller in the cabaret section of the city. General Cook led Sanger through double doors at the back of the room, into a smaller, more plush chamber. There were booths around the walls, and several large tables in the middle of the room. Most significant, the bartenders here wore ties.

Suddenly the night had become very starry, for Reid Sanger—there were generals everywhere. All the sections of the army HQ staff were represented, as were most of the divisions of Third Army by their CO, XO, or both. Sanger saw Bob Jackson and Henry Wakefield leaning back in a booth, sprawling out casually on either side of a table. Each of them was smoking a big cigar, and they waved cheerily as the colonel passed.

"Here we are." Cook was leading him to the table in the center of the room. Patton and Rommel sat at opposite ends, with von Manteuffel and their top aides along the sides. General Cook pulled out his own chair, while Patton stood and extended his hand.

"Ah, Sanger, thanks for coming back. We've been talking about you!"

"Me, sir?" The general's mood was cheerful, but the thought of all this brass attention still made Sanger a little squeamish.

A hearty hand clapped him on the shoulder and he turned to see that Rommel had come around to him. The field marshal gave him a zestful handshake. "Yes!" he said in German. "You know, you had a lot to do with making this whole thing work. Germans, Americans, learning to fight side by side. You deserve a lot of credit."

"He's right," said Patton.

"Well, thank you sir. I'm honored, of course." Sanger shook his head. "But it's men like Ballard and Smiggs, guys who put their lives on the line every day, who won this war for us. Anything I contributed—"

"Don't be modest," countered Rommel, with an easy grin. "I remember the way you tore off after a column of SS panzers in the middle of the night."

"Well, sir, I didn't exactly catch them."

The general and the field marshal both laughed. "It's a good thing, too," Patton said with a slap on the back. "It's like a dog chasing after a car. What the hell would he do if he caught it? Come on, join us for some free booze."

Sanger stayed for a drink—several, actually, since his glass magically stayed full. Finally he weaved back to the main room, only to encounter Keegan near the bar.

"Ah, a little brown-nosing never hurts," suggested the major with an arched eyebrow. "Probably a good career move."

"You shouldn't have said that, Keegan," Sanger said, enunciating carefully.

"And why not?" There was a thin, barely amused grin on the man's lips.

Sanger's right jab was a perfect strike, landing on that sculpted, pedigreed nose and crushing it flat. Keegan screamed and toppled over backward, both hands clutching his bleeding face. No one else paid much attention.

"*That's* why," said Sanger. He ambled back to his table. All in all, he felt pretty damned good.

EXCERPT FROM *WAR'S FINAL FURY,*
BY PROFESSOR JARED GRUENWALD

The Berlin Armistice marked not so much the beginning of peace as the start of a new, colder kind of war. Stalin's deliberate provocations in failing to withdraw to the agreed-upon positions were essentially ignored by the Western Allies, and when the new borders of Europe were drawn, that territory, once the heart of Prussia, was granted to Poland by the unilateral actions of the Soviet chairman.

But there is little doubt that Eisenhower's gamble in ordering Berlin seized was responsible for Germany remaining essentially intact after the war. If the Soviets had advanced to the Elbe, as had been the original plan, it seems certain that Germany would have been divided into two halves, democratic in the west, communist in the east. This, of course, would have been similar to what happened to Czechoslovakia. It was partitioned into two halves and, within a few years, had broken into its two component parts: the Czech Republic, a democracy, and the People's Republic of Slovakia, which was to become one of the staunchest communist regimes in the world.

As it was, the Soviets made significant territorial gains as a result of the war. In addition to the countries of Eastern Europe, already susceptible to Russian dominance, the territories that they had gained from Germany in the armistice of August 1944 fell inexorably under the Soviet shadow. In Greece, democratic movements were ruthlessly crushed, and Athens was transformed into a mighty Soviet naval base. The Russians tried to do the same thing in Norway, but there the factors of geography and perhaps the proximity of Britain served to dampen Stalin's push. Though Norway was forced to accept a communist government, the country retained a level of independence unknown throughout the Soviet bloc—with the exception of the comparable arrangement established in Tito's Yugoslavia.

All of this history, of course, pivoted on the remarkable events of July 1945. If the atomic bomb had not arrived on the scene at the exact moment that it did—or if the first attempted use of the weapon had failed—there is little doubt but that the Soviets would have rolled over the Third Army, and that the map of Europe we know today would have been considerably altered. . . .

EPILOGUE

1 6   J U L Y   1 9 4 5 –
1 7   A P R I L   1 9 4 6

One principle must be absolute for the SS man: we must be honest, decent, loyal, and comradely to members of our own blood and to no one else. What happens to the Russians, what happens to the Czechs, is a matter of utter indifference to me. Such good blood of our own kind as there may be among the nations we shall acquire for ourselves, if necessary by taking away the children and bringing them up among us. . . . We shall never be rough or heartless where it is not necessary; that is clear. We Germans, who are the only people in the world who have a decent attitude to animals, will also adopt a decent attitude to these human animals, but it is a crime against our own blood to worry about them and to bring them ideals.

I shall speak to you here with all frankness of a very grave matter. Among ourselves it should be mentioned quite frankly, and yet we will never speak of it publicly. I mean the evacuation of the Jews, the extermination of the Jewish people. . . . Most of you know what it means to see a hundred corpses lying together, five hundred, or a thousand. To have stuck it out and at the same time—apart from exceptions caused by human weakness—to have remained decent fellows, that is what has made us hard. This is a page of glory in our history which has never been written and shall never be written.

—Heinrich Himmler
Speech to SS group leaders
Poznan, 4 October 1943

16 JULY 1945

REICHSTAG BUILDING, BERLIN, GERMANY,
1400 HOURS GMT

Rommel stuck his head into Müller's office. "Colonel Müller? May I interrupt you for a minute?"

"Of course, sir," the pudgy supply officer replied, standing up and accidentally knocking over a cup of pencils on his desk. Rommel sat down and waited for Müller to pick the pencils up and compose himself.

"I want to thank you again for all your exceptional work during these months. I've had to throw you from one impossible challenge into the next, and you've worked miracles."

"You're too kind, Field Marshal, I-I don't know what to say."

Rommel held up his hand. "You don't have to say anything. That's my job, and I'll say it in proper military form shortly. In the meantime, though, I wanted to ask you for still another favor."

"Of course, sir. Whatever I can do."

"This one's more personal than professional."

"Either way, sir. What can I do?"

"It's about our mutual friend, Günter von Reinhardt."

"Oh."

"I didn't know what he was going to do, you know. It was in the middle of Buchenwald, and I was having some difficulty in making sense out of the situation." Rommel paused for a moment. "I've ordered men to their deaths before, not once but many times. I'm not afraid to do that. But von Reinhardt —"

"It had something to do with Goethe, sir—at least I think it did," said Müller. "We had a long talk earlier the same day he talked with you, all about responsibility and guilt and actions."

"I don't think I quite understood him," said Rommel.

"I'm not sure anyone did—including Günter himself," Müller replied.

"Ah, if he were here, he could add just the quote to make it all clear. But as he is not here, then I will ask you a favor." Rommel put a small box and an envelope on the table. "The box first."

Müller opened it. It was a medal box, lined with white satin. His eyes widened when he saw what was inside—the blue and white ribbons of the Pour le Merite, Germany's highest military decoration.

"I thought about this for a long time," Rommel said. "This one in particular

I don't like to give out lightly. This and the letter are for von Reinhardt's parents. I want you to locate them, give them these, and then arrange for a military funeral. I, of course, will attend, and I will expect attendance at state funeral levels. As you can see, I need a talented logistics officer to handle it."

"Then I must put my very best man on the job," said Müller. He smiled, then turned away so that Rommel could not see the liquid welling in his eyes.

20 JULY 1945

LUBYANKA SQUARE, MOSCOW, USSR, 1223 HOURS GMT
The Lubyanka Prison consists of the lower levels of the NKVD headquarters
building in downtown Moscow. Krigoff knew where he was, although he was
brought into the building in a sealed truck through an underground loading
dock and was placed in a windowless cell. There was only one place, really,
where he could be. What he did not know was when—it could be any time,
day or night, for the cycle of day or night meant nothing here. And although he
heard occasional screams, the tramping of marching boots, a scuffle or clash
from time to time, nothing happened to him. No torture, no interrogation, no
bullet in the head, nothing. He was in a bare cell with a bare bulb behind a
wire cage, a steel bucket for use as a toilet, and a mat on which he could sit
and sleep. At intervals—who could say how long?—a tray of food slid under
the door. It was gray and unappetizing but hardly worse than military fare.

He could only think of people he'd met. Paulina. General Yeremko. General Petrovsky. Lieutenant Kraichin. General Benko. The chairman himself.
His thoughts chased themselves around and around and around.

After some timeless period, marked only by a procession of meal trays and
exchange of waste buckets, there came a rattling of keys at his cell door. He
scrambled to his feet, excited at the thought of human company, terrified at the
thought of human company. It was a guard. He carried in two folding chairs
and set them up. Then he walked back into the hall and brought in a small
folding table and placed it beside the two chairs. He left again without saying
a word.

Krigoff looked at the two chairs for a long time, wondering if he was supposed to sit in one. He walked around them, looked at them from all angles,
then touched one, then the other, then the table. Experimentally, he sat in one,
then the other. They were comfortable. After a while, though, he returned to
sit on his mat.

There was a rattle of keys in the lock again. His heart pounding, Krigoff
stood up once more. The door opened. It was another guard, who held open
the door for a man who walked in.

It was Stalin. Stalin himself had come to see him.

"Comrade Chairman!" Krigoff breathed. He saluted. He had not forgotten
his military discipline.

Stalin looked at Krigoff with an expression of friendly sympathy. "Ah,

Alyosha. It's very good to see you. I'm sorry you've had such a difficult time. Come, sit down. Let me offer you a cigarette. Let's talk."

Krigoff took the proffered cigarette with trembling fingers and allowed Stalin to light it for him. The smoke felt good in his lungs; it calmed him almost at once. "Thank you, Comrade Chairman. It's very good of you to come and visit me like this."

"Oh, it's nothing. For an old friend like you it's the very least I can do." Stalin patted Krigoff on the shoulder as he sat down. Krigoff looked at Stalin and felt himself on the verge of tears at the great man's kindness toward him. "Now, now," Stalin said in a soothing voice. "I want you to tell me everything, Alyosha. Tell me what happened."

Slowly and haltingly at first, Krigoff began to tell Stalin the story of his role with Second Guards Tank Army—his battles with both Yeremko and Petrovsky, including the spitting incident, which made Stalin chuckle, and then the events surrounding the final battle for Berlin. He gave his honest impressions of the chaotic aerial battle, and his real notion that American tanks were attacking. He described Marshal Zhukov's plan, even admitted that it would all be Krigoff's fault if it failed. And then . . . he faltered again . . . he remembered that flash of light, Paulina blinded, leading her through what seemed like Hell until they reached a Soviet aid station. Stalin asked him questions from time to time, which Krigoff answered as completely as he could.

Finally, he was finished. "That's what happened, as best as I can tell you."

Stalin nodded. "Thank you, Alyosha. I believe you. You told me exactly what I wanted to know, and it's all right now. Everything is all right. You don't need to worry. I understand. Get some rest now." Krigoff nodded and stayed sitting in his chair.

As he stood up to leave, Stalin nodded at the guard. When Stalin had pulled the door shut before him, the guard took his pistol from its holster.

Krigoff looked at the guard. He smiled; he understood everything now. As the pistol fired, in the millisecond before the bullet tore through Krigoff's brain, he was at peace.

He loved Josef Stalin.

21 JULY 1945

Heinrich Himmler woke up as the truck lurched to a stop. It took him a moment to recover his bearings, and he was about to order his men to be more gentle. Then he saw the rounded, flat-bottomed helmets, and knew that he was still a prisoner of the Americans. Day after day he had awoken, thinking that his imprisonment was merely a bad dream, that he would find himself once again master of Germany.

For months of interrogations he had strung his captors along, especially the young, guilt-ridden Sanger, with his pitiful sympathy for the Jews. His weakness had been so easy to exploit, so easy to manipulate. The Allies were now willing to settle for "truth," as they termed it, and so his life would be spared. He could plan and wait, and look for an opportunity, a crack in their defenses, the inevitable moment when their attention would be focused on the threat from the East, and then he would be free once again.

Calm, he told himself. They are inferior mongrels, almost as bad as Jews—they must not see his fear. But where had they brought him? Why had they come to a halt?

He was confused. For more than a day he had been driven along by these American captors, and he didn't understand why they had not yet delivered him to some higher headquarters, some special prison. And he was in the hands of relatively low-ranking soldiers with only a few vehicles in his escort—an insult for a man of his stature. If he had only known they would be this stupid, he could already have had his rescue waiting for him.

"Why are we stopping?" he demanded, when he saw Sanger—it was always Sanger—getting down from the truck cab. The sergeant who had been riding with him—a black man, posted, he was certain, as an intentional indignity—took his time releasing the handcuffs, then pushed him none too gently toward the dim light at the back of the truck.

"There's some people here we'd like you to meet," Sanger replied cheerfully. "Why don't you come along this way?"

It was daylight, Himmler saw. Although he wouldn't admit it to Sanger, he was grateful for the chance to get out and stretch. He needed to relieve the pressure on his bladder, perhaps even coax something to eat from his captors.

He stepped awkwardly to the ground and walked around the side of the truck, then froze as he saw the tall gates, the guard towers, the barbed wire fences stretching to the right and left. The fence was lined with gaunt people, unshaven and filthy, staring at him in eerie silence.

"I accompanied Field Marshal Rommel into Buchenwald. I stopped him from shooting a couple of your Totenkopf-SS guards, though I was tempted to shoot them myself. I wanted their testimony. The story of what you and yours did will shame humanity for all time," Sanger said as he walked.

"Yes, yes, yes," said Himmler. "You've told me that story already. You've told me again and again and again. Do you think I'm the Pope and I'm going to canonize you or something?" He laughed at his own wit. "I did what I did because it was right for Germany, and nothing you can do can undo a single act of mine. That's what strength is, by the way. You'll never understand that, Sanger, not if you live to be a hundred. You'll never know what it's like to be a man. You ran out on us Germans like a little crybaby the first time you gave some old Jew *ein awah*—" Himmler's mocking use of the baby term for an injury, a "boo-boo," was the sort of insult he regularly used to belittle Sanger's sentimentality and weakness, as he saw it. "—and you expect *me* to be impressed by that? Or by these rag-tag old Jews you've got locked up over there? I've seen Jews in cages before, Sanger. Remember? I put them there."

"I remember," Sanger said.

"So you've got a few leftovers that didn't make it into the gas chambers in time. The sad thing is that they'll breed like vermin and Germans of the future will just have to finish the job we started. That's the only thing I really regret, Sanger. I didn't get to finish the job."

Sanger looked at the camp inmates. "This is a survivors' camp," Sanger said to Himmler. "Not like your camps, of course—we actually are feeding these people, giving them coal and clothing against the elements, and providing medical treatment. But they know what it was like in your camps. Many of these came from Buchenwald, others from camps in the East. This is one of the areas where we're actually successfully cooperating with the Soviets, you know."

"How wonderful." Himmler laughed. "The Slavs are sending you some leftover Jews. Even they don't want them."

One of the Americans, a short major with murderous eyes, snarled something at the führer.

"Oh—pardon my manners," said Sanger. "This is Major Smiggs of the U.S. Nineteenth Armored Division. He particularly wanted to be introduced. He was one of the officers of the task force that captured you."

"How nice for him. He got a medal, I presume?"

"Oh, yes, and a promotion, though I suspect neither of us will be keeping our military rank much longer."

For the first time, Himmler felt a momentary shiver as he looked up into

Sanger's face. Sanger was calm and smiling as he looked toward the camp. "As you know, the Western Allies have created a new organization called the United Nations, and one of their first official roles will be taking custody of international criminals such as yourself. Transfer arrangements have been made, and you are to be remanded to them."

"Yes, yes, I know all that," Himmler said impatiently.

"They've been notified to pick you up here."

"And where are they?"

"They'll be here first thing tomorrow morning." Sanger's smile widened slightly. "There seems to have been a slight mixup in the paperwork." He nodded toward the major.

Himmler started to fight then, turning to run for the woods until Major Smiggs took his arm in a grip like a vise. Himmler shrieked and squirmed in that grip, but the American—who was not large, but was very determined—simply dragged him over to the camp's main entry. Sanger motioned the MPs out of the way and opened the gates himself so that no one else participated in the act.

Pushing the second and final Führer of the Third Reich forward, Smiggs said something in English, something Himmler couldn't understand.

"Smiggs wants you to know that this is for the children of Buchenwald," Sanger said, as the major pushed Heinrich Himmler through the gates to sprawl on the muddy ground. The gates slammed shut, and the prisoners moved forward.

"Wait!" cried Himmler, scrambling to his knees in the cold mud. "Sanger, be reasonable! You can't do this! You'll be court-martialed! Listen, we can work something out! I have a lot of information—I can tell you things—don't walk away like that—come back! You can't! Sanger, please! Don't do this! I'll make it worth your while! Turn around, Sanger! Talk to me!"

As the prisoners closed in on him, Himmler started to scream.

It was a noise that went on for a very long time.

27 JULY 1945

BRANDENBURG GATE, BERLIN, GERMANY, 1302 HOURS GMT

General Dwight D. Eisenhower would of course be hosted at a formal gala in the Reichstag Building in the evening, a fête suitable for his five-star rank. But first there would be a display of marching and drill that would give Third Army and the German Republican Army each the chance to strut before the Supreme Commander. Patton and Rommel had suggested the Charlottenberger Chaussée as the route of the parade, and had posted themselves and Ike on a reviewing stand in the shadow of the historic gate.

Henry Wakefield was here with them. Though Patton had asked him to have the Nineteenth Armored join the parade, Wakefield had refused outright, declaring that his men had been through too much real war to get spruced up for any damned parade. He had glared at his army CO, ready to make a fight of it, and had been surprised to the point of astonishment when Patton had simply nodded, and moved on to order a different division to take part in the festivities.

Which meant that Hank Wakefield got a front-row seat—actually second-row, since he was behind Patton and Ike, with Rommel just off to the side—and a perfect chance to eavesdrop on the great men.

"What do you make of our new boss?" Patton leaned over to ask the Supreme Commander.

"President Truman? I've talked to him a number of times, of course. We haven't met yet. But he seems like a straight-shooting, no-nonsense type. I think he'll do okay facing off with Uncle Joe. Of course, he's pretty focused on getting ready for the big Japan invasion, now that we've got things settled over here."

"Invasion, eh?" Patton said. "Any chance you could get me a command over there?"

Ike shook his head. "Those jobs are taken. And besides, we need you here, Georgie. Who else has such a great relationship with the man who's going to be the next chancellor of Germany?"

Rommel held up his hand. "None of that has been decided. I am a soldier, not a politician."

"Who knows?" Ike said with a wink. "Soldiers can go on to become great politicians. Why, there are those who say that I should think about politics as a new career."

"And are you?" asked the field marshal.

The Supreme Commander waved away the question. "I have a lot of work to do as it is. I haven't even started to think about that."

Wakefield smiled to himself; Ike was *already* sounding like a politician.

"I should think that this new bomb might go a long way toward convincing the Japanese to lay down their arms," noted the field marshal. "Indeed, it is hard to even imagine waging war against a country that possesses such destructive capabilities."

"I'm sure that's getting consideration," Ike agreed. "I know we've sent pictures right into Tokyo, showing them what happened to Potsdam."

"Let's hope they see reason, then," Rommel declared.

"Say," Eisenhower said, turning back to Patton with a serious expression. "We're getting a lot of flak about this Himmler business. First of all, you're sure he's dead?"

"Beyond a doubt," Patton said. "Colonel Sanger identified the body—at least, what was left of it. Seems to have been a snafu in the orders. Just one of those things."

Eisenhower looked sharply at Patton and then at Rommel. Rommel's face was stoic and calm; Patton's had such an exaggerated innocence that it was clear what had really happened. "Yeah. One of those things. There are reporters clamoring for the story. And I've had two senators call me in the last few days, demanding investigations, explanations, you know."

"Hell, Ike." Patton shrugged. "It's just like the report says: We were transferring him from our control to the control of the Occupation Forces. Only some of his former guests got hold of him as we were making the transfer. They had a grudge against ol' Heinrich, and I can't say I blame them. They roughed him up to the point where he wasn't breathing anymore."

"Nobody can blame them. But rogue soldiers, officers who take the law into their own hands . . . people can blame *them*. And I'm afraid they'll want to string somebody up."

"Well, we're having a little trouble establishing who was careless," the Third Army commander said. "But I will keep you posted on the investigation."

"You do that, Georgie. You do that. But . . . Georgie?"

"Yes, sir?"

"Don't look too hard."

17 APRIL 1946

INTERNATIONAL TRIBUNAL, NUREMBERG, GERMANY,
1500 HOURS GMT
The judge's gavel came down, ending this session of the International Tribunal. Sepp Dietrich got laboriously to his feet, shook the hand of his lawyer, and shuffled through the crowd toward the back of the courtroom. It was, as usual, packed with a wide assortment of international journalists, military officials, lawyers representing other defendants, people with an interest in one or more cases. Rommel, whose trial had ended in acquittal several weeks earlier, was sitting a few rows back. He stood as Dietrich approached.

"How did I do?" Dietrich asked.

"You're telling the truth. That's all that matters," Rommel said.

"Well, I'm an old man. There's not much for me to be afraid of anymore. Though I don't remember everything, you know. I've never been much for the past, and a lot of the older stuff I just never think about—bad and good alike. And it all seemed different then." He shook his head. "Were we really all so evil? It didn't feel like it at the time."

"I suspect that how one feels is not such a reliable guide to whether one is committing evil," Rommel said. "I remember overriding twinges of my own conscience more than once. That's all it takes."

Dietrich blew his nose into a handkerchief. "I never had much of a conscience in the first place. It slowed down my drinking." He laughed. "Speaking of drinking, I need a beer right about now. Let's find a bar and I'll treat. All right?"

Rommel chuckled. "All right. Just one, though. Then I have to go back to work."

"Do you ever stop?" Dietrich asked.

"The work never stops, so I can't either," Rommel replied. He held the outer door for Dietrich as both men went out onto the portico. A long flight of stone steps led down to the street. As usual, there was a crowd. Photographers and reporters crowded around, there were some demonstrators with signs, and some military policemen trying to keep order. Rommel noticed a blond-haired youth coming up the steps.

Lukas Vogel had refused to surrender when the Second SS Panzer Division's remnants pulled back from Küstrin, and he refused to surrender now. He had been walking for so long, living off scraps and seeking shelter where he could, that this seemed like normal life now. He could hardly remember what it was like to live in a house, to stay in the same place and eat regular meals and sleep in a bed. It had all gone wrong, and Lukas had figured out when and how it had all gone wrong. Everything had been all right until Rommel changed sides. It was Rommel's treason that had destroyed Germany. It was Rommel's treason that had destroyed Lukas Vogel's life and mission. It was Rommel's treason that had led to Jochen Peiper's death. Well, Lukas knew what to do about that.

He had been moving south, slowly, day by day. From time to time he got some news, heard a bit of a radio broadcast, saw a newspaper headline. There was an International Tribunal in Nuremberg, and they were putting Nazis on trial.

Rommel would be there.

So would Lukas Vogel.

He saw the first of the crowd exiting the courthouse. Today's session had ended. It was time to get ready. He was wearing a uniform coat several sizes too big for him. There was plenty of room in its pocket for a Luger he'd taken from a dead soldier some time back. He slipped his hand into the pocket and grabbed the pistol, and began moving up the steps. There—he saw Field Marshal Rommel leaving the courthouse, starting down the steps. He maneuvered closer, jockeying through the crowd. As he neared his target, he pulled out his Luger. He was at point-blank range. There would be no way he could miss.

Sepp Dietrich also noticed the blond-haired boy approaching them, and then looked closer. There was something familiar about him. Ah—it was the young man from Saint-Vith, the one he thought had died in Küstrin! He had something in his hand . . . a pistol! "Lukas, don't do it," the old general said, as he moved in front of the boy, his hand grabbing for the boy's wrist, but it was too late. The Luger fired. Dietrich felt the impact like a punch in his stomach, felt himself bending over. His hand gripped Lukas' wrist, pulling the Luger down with him.

There was a scream, and a military policeman began running toward him. Guns were coming out of their holsters. "Don't shoot him!" Dietrich cried, but although he mouthed the words, no sound seemed to issue from his lips. Lukas was pulling on the Luger, trying to get it away from Dietrich, but the old man's grip was too strong.

There were more shots now, and Dietrich saw blood spurting from a hole in the boy's side, then more blood from his chest. "No . . . don't kill him . . ." Dietrich pleaded, but he knew it was too late. He fell onto the steps and the boy fell next to him. He was looking directly into Lukas' eyes, and could see that the boy recognized him. "General Dietrich," he whimpered. "I'm sorry . . . I didn't mean it . . . I wanted Rommel . . . I'm sorry . . ."

A shadow crossed over Dietrich's face and he glanced up. Rommel was bent over him, his face grim. "Sepp—hang on, man. Help is coming."

"Not for me, Rommel. The boy. Save the boy," Dietrich whispered. "We knew better. He didn't."

When it was all over, the one-eyed field marshal stood up. Blood spattered his plain uniform. He watched as the bodies of the dead general and the dead youth were loaded into an ambulance and driven away. In spite of the crowd around him, he felt very much alone, as if he stood at a great distance from everyone else.

There were men arriving now, men who had just heard the news. Speidel and Bayerlein got out of a car and headed up the steps toward him. Carl-Heinz had gone to fetch Müller, and Sanger was coming out of an office nearby, where he had been assisting the prosecutors. And there were many more. Von Manteuffel. Patton. Goerdeler. Eisenhower. His wife, Lucie, and his son, Manfred.

He was not alone. There was an immense amount, possibly even an impossible amount, of work to do. But there were people, good and strong people, to help him do it. Step by step, he walked toward them.

ACKNOWLEDGMENTS

This book began on September 11, 2001. We had arranged a working session at Douglas Niles' Wisconsin country home to map out the detailed plot and prepare a schedule for ourselves. Early that morning, Doug turned on the television set. We watched along with the rest of the nation and talked about war and hatred. Some of that found its way into this story.

September 11 was already significant to this tale, for on 11 September 1944, the real-life *Ford's Folly,* the B-24H Liberator on which SSgt. Odell F. Dobson, Michael Dobson's father (and the real-life model for Digger O'Dell), was shot down over Koblenz, Germany All but two members of the crew perished; they are buried at the American Military Cemetery Margraten, The Netherlands.

We have been extremely fortunate in the wealth of people who have generously provided their time, counsel, support, and expertise in the writing, editing, and production of this book.

First, we would like to thank the team at Forge: Brian M. Thomsen, our tireless editor and champion, who first brought the proposal forward, and without whose gentle (and occasionally not so gentle) prodding the story would be far less than it is. Natasha Panza and her predecessor, Jim Minz, provided in-house coordination and listened with great patience and forgiveness to our various excuses for deadline extensions. The eagle-eyed Terry McGarry, our copy editor, caught every ~~mispeling misspellling~~ typo. Heather Drucker, our publicist, made sure the book received every opportunity for visibility in a crowded marketplace.

Our agents, Elizabeth Pomada and Michael Larsen, not only provide able representation but advice, friendship, and support. We're lucky to have them on our side.

Bill Connors did the maps for this volume.

We're grateful for Parker Hurlburt, who sat in a bar in Mission, Kansas, until 2 A.M. with Michael and unwittingly became the first person to hear the very earliest version of what turned into Operation Wolkenbrand. We're grateful for Edward R. Smith, who created the character of Reid Sanger (though with a different name) for a really cool juvenile novel he never actually got around to writing. We're grateful for the members of the Alliterates Literary Society (www.alliterates.com), of which Doug is, by acclamation, the most handsome member, for managing to keep pace, beer for beer.

The German proofreading was done by Thomas Karman and AnneLee Gilder. AnneLee took the time away from her work as coauthor of an upcoming book on Johannes Kepler and Tycho Brahe with her husband Joshua (*Ghost Image*) Gilder.

Technical comments and corrections were made by (in alphabetical order) Mark Acres, Rosemary Bergman Althoff, Fred Baxter, Mark Biniecki, Robert Dustrude (1st Lt. USAAF Ret), Tony Harrison, Peter Jedicke, E. W. Kelly (LtCol USA Ret), Gerard Marzilli, Jr., Donald E. Niles, Sr., Andy Nunez, Rory Patterson, Dan Rinehart, Professor Jan Robin, Kevin Rose, and Mark Vetter. Any errors remaining, of course, are the sole responsibility and fault of the authors.

Friendship, support, and wise counsel came from many sources, notably (also in alphabetical order) Ralph Benko (who loaned his name for a Soviet tank general), Frank Chadwick (whose tireless friendship and scholarship makes him truly One To Foresee For One), Moshe Feder (who said many nice things without having to do so), Elle Furlong (who unraveled the mysteries of the Russian patronymic and taught us several Russian swear words), S. Keith Keel (designer of the Dobsonbooks Web site), Ted Leemann (for advice on marketing, character, and project management), Humayun Mirza (for insight into the Desert Fox and many other players of the period), and Charlotte Porter (for lending her name and a few inside jokes to our own favorite AP guy, Chuck "No Relation" Porter).

We thank our families, especially our wives, Christine Niles and Deborah Dobson, for their patience, love, and support throughout this project.

The Web site at www.dobsonbooks.com has information, bibliographic citations, comments, and game scenarios for Douglas Niles' SPI/TSR boardgames ONSLAUGHT: D-DAY TO THE RHINE™ and WORLD WAR II: EUROPEAN THEATRE OF OPERATIONS™.

Douglas Niles and Michael Dobson
11 September 2001 to 31 January 2003
Delavan, Wisconsin, and Bethesda, Maryland